P9-CRB-415

*Sir Arthur
Conan Doyle*

TALES OF
TERROR AND
MYSTERY

CLASSICS OF
Mystery & Suspense

CLASSICS OF
Mystery & Suspense

Published by Trident Press International
801 12ᵗʰ Avenue South
Suite 302
Naples Florida 34102 USA
www.trident-international.com
email: tridentpress@worldnet.att.net

Copyright © Trident Press International 2001
Printed in Australia
ISBN: 1582791929

The Horror of the Heights

The idea that the extraordinary narrative which has been called the Joyce-Armstrong Fragment is an elaborate practical joke evolved by some unknown person, cursed by a perverted and sinister sense of humour, has now been abandoned by all who have examined the matter. The most macabre and imaginative of plotters would hesitate before linking his morbid fancies with the unquestioned and tragic facts which reinforce the statement. Though the assertions contained in it are amazing and even monstrous, it is none the less forcing itself upon the general intelligence that they are true, and that we must readjust our ideas to the new situation. This world of ours appears to be separated by a slight and precarious margin of safety from a most singular and unexpected danger. I will endeavour in this narrative, which reproduces the original document in its necessarily somewhat fragmentary form, to lay before the reader the whole of the facts up to date, prefacing my statement by saying that, if there be any who doubt the narrative of Joyce-Armstrong, there can be no question at all as to the facts concerning Lieutenant Myrtle, R. N., and Mr. Hay Connor, who undoubtedly met their end in the manner described.

The Joyce-Armstrong Fragment was found in the field which is called Lower Haycock, lying one mile to the westward of the village of Withyham, upon the Kent and Sussex border. It was on the 15th September last that an agricultural labourer, James Flynn, in the employment of Mathew Dodd, farmer, of the Chauntry Farm, Withyham, perceived a briar pipe lying near the footpath which skirts the hedge in Lower Haycock. A few paces farther on he picked up a pair of broken binocular glasses. Finally, among some nettles in the ditch, he caught sight of a flat, canvas-backed book, which proved to be a note-book with detachable leaves, some of which had come loose and were fluttering along the base of the hedge. These he collected, but some, including the first, were never recovered, and leave a deplorable hiatus in this all-important statement. The note-book was taken by the labourer to his master, who in turn showed it to Dr. J. H. Atherton, of Hartfield. This gentleman at once recognized the need for an expert examination, and the manuscript was forwarded to the Aero Club in London, where it now lies.

The first two pages of the manuscript are missing. There is also one torn away at the end of the narrative, though none of these affect the general coherence of the story. It is conjectured that the missing opening is concerned with the record of Mr. Joyce-Armstrong's qualifications as an aeronaut, which can be gathered from other sources and are admitted to be unsurpassed among the air-pilots of England. For many years he has been looked upon as among the most daring and the most intellectual of flying men, a combination which has enabled him to both invent and test several new devices, including the common gyroscopic attachment which is known by his name. The main body of the manuscript is written neatly in ink, but the last few lines are in pencil and are so ragged as to be hardly legible—exactly, in fact, as they might be expected to appear if they were scribbled off hurriedly from the seat of a moving aeroplane. There are, it may be added, several stains, both on the last page and on the outside cover which have been pronounced by the Home Office experts to be blood—probably human and certainly mammalian. The fact that something closely resembling the organism of malaria was discovered in this blood, and that Joyce-Armstrong is known to have suffered from intermittent fever, is a remarkable example of the new weapons which modern science has placed in the hands of our detectives.

And now a word as to the personality of the author of this epoch-making statement. Joyce-Armstrong, according to the few friends who really knew something of the man, was a poet and a dreamer, as well as a mechanic and an inventor. He was a man of considerable wealth, much of which he had spent in the pursuit of his aeronautical hobby. He had four private aeroplanes in his hangars near Devizes, and is said to have made no fewer than one hundred and seventy ascents in the course of last year. He was a retiring man with dark moods, in which he would avoid the society of his fellows. Captain Dangerfield, who knew him better than anyone, says that there were times when his eccentricity threatened to develop into something more serious. His habit of carrying a shot-gun with him in his aeroplane was one manifestation of it.

Another was the morbid effect which the fall of Lieutenant Myrtle had upon his mind. Myrtle, who was attempting the height record, fell from an altitude of something over thirty thousand feet. Horrible to narrate, his head was entirely obliterated, though his body and limbs preserved their configuration. At every gathering of airmen, Joyce-Armstrong, according to Dangerfield, would ask, with an enigmatic smile: "And where, pray, is Myrtle's head?"

On another occasion after dinner, at the mess of the Flying School on Salisbury Plain, he started a debate as to what will be the most permanent danger which airmen will have to encounter. Having listened to successive opinions as to air-pockets, faulty construction, and over-banking, he ended by shrugging his shoulders and refusing to put forward his own views, though he gave the impression that they differed from any advanced by his companions.

It is worth remarking that after his own complete disappearance it was found that his private affairs were arranged with a precision which may show that he had a strong premonition of disaster. With these essential explanations I will now give the narrative exactly as it stands, beginning at page three of the blood-soaked note-book:

"Nevertheless, when I dined at Rheims with Coselli and Gustav Raymond I found that neither of them was aware of any particular danger in the higher layers of the atmosphere. I did not actually say what was in my thoughts, but I got so near to it that if they had any corresponding idea they could not have failed to express it. But then they are two empty, vainglorious fellows with no thought beyond seeing their silly names in the newspaper. It is interesting to note that neither of them had ever been much beyond the twenty-thousand-foot level. Of course, men have been higher than this both in balloons and in the ascent of mountains. It must be well above that point that the aeroplane enters the danger zone—always presuming that my premonitions are correct.

"Aeroplaning has been with us now for more than twenty years, and one might well ask: Why should this peril be only revealing itself in our day? The answer is obvious. In the old days of weak engines, when a hundred horse-power Gnome or Green was considered ample for every need, the flights were very restricted. Now that three hundred horse-power is the rule rather than the exception, visits to the upper layers have become easier and more common. Some of us can remember how, in our youth, Garros made a world-wide reputation by attaining nineteen thousand feet, and it was considered a remarkable achievement to fly over the Alps. Our standard now has been immeasurably raised, and there are twenty high flights for one in former years. Many of them have been undertaken with impunity. The thirty-thousand-foot level has been reached time after time with no discomfort beyond cold and asthma. What does this prove? A visitor might descend upon this planet a thousand times and never see a tiger. Yet tigers exist, and if he chanced to come down into a jungle he might be devoured. There are jungles of the upper air, and there are worse things than tigers which inhabit them. I believe in time they will map these jungles accurately out. Even at the present moment I could name two of them. One of them lies over the Pau-Biarritz district of France. Another is just over my head as I write here in my house in Wiltshire. I rather think there is a third in the Homburg-Wiesbaden district.

"It was the disappearance of the airmen that first set me thinking. Of course, everyone said that they had fallen into the sea, but that did not satisfy me at all. First, there was Verrier in France; his machine was found near Bayonne, but they never got his body. There was the case of Baxter also, who vanished, though his engine and some of the iron fixings were found in a wood in Leicestershire. In that case, Dr. Middleton, of Amesbury, who was watching the flight with a telescope, declares that just before the clouds obscured the view he saw the machine, which was at an enormous height, suddenly rise perpendicularly upwards in a succession of jerks in a manner that he would have thought to be impossible. That was the last seen of Baxter. There was a correspondence in the papers, but it never led to anything. There were several other similar cases, and then there was the death of Hay

Connor. What a cackle there was about an unsolved mystery of the air, and what columns in the halfpenny papers, and yet how little was ever done to get to the bottom of the business! He came down in a tremendous vol-plane from an unknown height. He never got off his machine and died in his pilot's seat. Died of what? 'Heart disease,' said the doctors. Rubbish! Hay Connor's heart was as sound as mine is. What did Venables say? Venables was the only man who was at his side when he died. He said that he was shivering and looked like a man who had been badly scared. 'Died of fright,' said Venables, but could not imagine what he was frightened about. Only said one word to Venables, which sounded like 'Monstrous.' They could make nothing of that at the inquest. But I could make something of it. Monsters! That was the last word of poor Harry Hay Connor. And he DID die of fright, just as Venables thought.

"And then there was Myrtle's head. Do you really believe—does anybody really believe—that a man's head could be driven clean into his body by the force of a fall? Well, perhaps it may be possible, but I, for one, have never believed that it was so with Myrtle. And the grease upon his clothes—'all slimy with grease,' said somebody at the inquest. Queer that nobody got thinking after that! I did—but, then, I had been thinking for a good long time. I've made three ascents—how Dangerfield used to chaff me about my shot-gun—but I've never been high enough. Now, with this new, light Paul Veroner machine and its one hundred and seventy-five Robur, I should easily touch the thirty thousand tomorrow. I'll have a shot at the record. Maybe I shall have a shot at something else as well. Of course, it's dangerous. If a fellow wants to avoid danger he had best keep out of flying altogether and subside finally into flannel slippers and a dressing-gown. But I'll visit the air-jungle tomorrow—and if there's anything there I shall know it. If I return, I'll find myself a bit of a celebrity. If I don't this note-book may explain what I am trying to do, and how I lost my life in doing it. But no drivel about accidents or mysteries, if YOU please.

"I chose my Paul Veroner monoplane for the job. There's nothing like a monoplane when real work is to be done. Beaumont found that out in very early days. For one thing it doesn't mind damp, and the weather looks as if we should be in the clouds all the time. It's a bonny little model and answers my hand like a tender-mouthed horse. The engine is a ten-cylinder rotary Robur working up to one hundred and seventy-five. It has all the modern improvements—enclosed fuselage, high-curved landing skids, brakes, gyroscopic steadiers, and three speeds, worked by an alteration of the angle of the planes upon the Venetian-blind principle. I took a shot-gun with me and a dozen cartridges filled with buck-shot. You should have seen the face of Perkins, my old mechanic, when I directed him to put them in. I was dressed like an Arctic explorer, with two jerseys under my overalls, thick socks inside my padded boots, a storm-cap with flaps, and my talc goggles. It was stifling outside the hangars, but I was going for the summit of the Himalayas, and had to dress for the part. Perkins knew there was something on and implored me to take him with me. Perhaps I should if I were using the biplane, but a monoplane is a one-man show—if you want to get the last foot of life out of it. Of course, I took an oxygen bag; the man who goes for the altitude record without one will either be frozen or smothered—or both.

"I had a good look at the planes, the rudder-bar, and the elevating lever before I got in. Everything was in order so far as I could see. Then I switched on my engine and found that she was running sweetly. When they let her go she rose almost at once upon the lowest speed. I circled my home field once or twice just to warm her up, and then with a wave to Perkins and the others, I flattened out my planes and put her on her highest. She skimmed like a swallow down wind for eight or ten miles until I turned her nose up a little and she began to climb in a great spiral for the cloud-bank above me. It's all-important to rise slowly and adapt yourself to the pressure as you go.

"It was a close, warm day for an English September, and there was the hush and heaviness of impending rain. Now and then there came sudden puffs of wind from the south-west—one of them so gusty and unexpected that it caught me napping and turned me half-round for an instant. I remember the time when gusts and whirls and air-pockets used to be things of danger—before we learned to put an overmastering power into our engines. Just as I reached the cloud-banks, with the altimeter marking three thousand, down came the rain. My word, how it poured! It drummed upon my wings and lashed against my face, blurring my glasses so that I could hardly see. I got down on to a low speed, for it was painful to travel against it. As I got higher it became hail, and I had to turn tail to it. One of my cylinders was out of action—a dirty plug, I should imagine, but still I was rising steadily with plenty of power. After a bit the trouble passed, whatever it was, and I heard the full, deep-throated purr—the ten singing as one. That's where the beauty of our modern silencers comes in. We can at last control our engines by ear. How they squeal and squeak and sob when they are in trouble! All those cries for help were wasted in the old days, when every sound was swallowed up by the monstrous racket of the machine. If only the early aviators could come back to see the beauty and perfection of the mechanism which have been bought at the cost of their lives!

"About nine-thirty I was nearing the clouds. Down below me, all blurred and shadowed with rain, lay the vast expanse of Salisbury Plain. Half a dozen flying machines were doing hackwork at the thousand-foot level, looking like little black swallows against the green background. I dare say they were wondering what I was doing up in cloud-land. Suddenly a grey curtain drew across beneath me and the wet folds of vapours were swirling round my face. It was clammily cold and miserable. But I was above the hailstorm, and that was something gained. The cloud was as dark and thick as a London fog. In my anxiety to get clear, I cocked her nose up until the automatic alarm-bell rang, and I actually began to slide backwards. My sopped and dripping wings had made me heavier than I thought, but presently I was in lighter cloud, and soon had cleared the first layer. There was a second—opalcoloured and fleecy—at a great height above my head, a white, unbroken ceiling above, and a dark, unbroken floor below, with the monoplane labouring upwards upon a vast spiral between them. It is deadly lonely in these cloud-spaces. Once a great flight of some small water-birds went past me, flying very fast to the westwards. The quick whir of their wings and their musical cry were cheery to my ear. I fancy that they were teal, but I am a wretched zoologist. Now that we humans have become birds we must really learn to know our brethren by sight.

"The wind down beneath me whirled and swayed the broad cloud-pain. Once a great eddy formed in it, a whirlpool of vapour, and through it, as down a funnel, I caught sight of the distant world. A large white biplane was passing at a vast depth beneath me. I fancy it was the morning mail service betwixt Bristol and London. Then the drift swirled inwards again and the great solitude was unbroken.

"Just after ten I touched the lower edge of the upper cloud-stratum. It consisted of fine diaphanous vapour drifting swiftly from the westwards. The wind had been steadily rising all this time and it was now blowing a sharp breeze—twenty-eight an hour by my gauge. Already it was very cold, though my altimeter only marked nine thousand. The engines were working beautifully, and we went droning steadily upwards. The cloud-bank was thicker than I had expected, but at last it thinned out into a golden mist before me, and then in an instant I had shot out from it, and there was an unclouded sky and a brilliant sun above my head—all blue and gold above, all shining silver below, one vast, glimmering plain as far as my eyes could reach. It was a quarter past ten o'clock, and the barograph needle pointed to twelve thousand eight hundred. Up I went and up, my ears concentrated upon the deep purring of my motor, my eyes busy always with the watch, the revolution indicator, the petrol lever, and the oil pump. No wonder aviators are said to be a fearless race. With so many things to think of there is no time to trouble about oneself. About this time I noted how unreliable is the compass when above a certain height from earth. At fifteen thousand feet mine was pointing east and a point south. The sun and the wind gave me my true bearings.

"I had hoped to reach an eternal stillness in these high altitudes, but with every thousand feet of ascent the gale grew stronger. My machine groaned and trembled in every joint and rivet as she faced it, and swept away like a sheet of paper when I banked her on the turn, skimming down wind at a greater pace, perhaps, than ever mortal man has moved. Yet I had always to turn again and tack up in the wind's eye, for it was not merely a height record that I was after. By all my calculations it was above little Wiltshire that my air-jungle lay, and all my labour might be lost if I struck the outer layers at some farther point.

"When I reached the nineteen-thousand-foot level, which was about midday, the wind was so severe that I looked with some anxiety to the stays of my wings, expecting momentarily to see them snap or slacken. I even cast loose the parachute behind me, and fastened its hook into the ring of my leathern belt, so as to be ready for the worst. Now was the time when a bit of scamped work by the mechanic is paid for by the life of the aeronaut. But she held together bravely. Every cord and strut was humming and vibrating like so many harp-strings, but it was glorious to see how, for all the beating and the buffeting, she was still the conqueror of Nature and the mistress of the sky. There is surely something divine in man himself that he should rise so superior to the limitations which Creation seemed to impose—rise, too, by such unselfish, heroic devotion as this air-conquest has shown. Talk of human degeneration! When has such a story as this been written in the annals of our race?

"These were the thoughts in my head as I climbed that monstrous, inclined plane with the wind sometimes beating in my face and sometimes whistling behind my ears, while the cloud-land beneath me fell away to such a distance that the folds and hummocks of silver had all smoothed out into one flat, shining plain. But suddenly I had a horrible and unprecedented experience. I have known before what it is to be in what our neighbours have called a tourbillon, but never on such a scale as this. That huge, sweeping river of wind of which I have spoken had, as it appears, whirlpools within it which were as monstrous as itself. Without a moment's warning I was dragged suddenly into the heart of one. I spun round for a minute or two with such velocity that I almost lost my senses, and then fell suddenly, left wing foremost, down the vacuum funnel in the centre. I dropped like a stone, and lost nearly a thousand feet. It was only my belt that kept me in my seat, and the shock and breathlessness left me hanging half-insensible over the side of the fuselage. But I am always capable of a supreme effort—it is my one great merit as an aviator. I was conscious that the descent was slower. The whirlpool was a cone rather than a funnel, and I had come to the apex. With a terrific wrench, throwing my weight all to one side, I levelled my planes and brought her head away from the wind. In an instant I had shot out of the eddies and was skimming down the sky. Then, shaken but victorious, I turned her nose up and began once more my steady grind on the upward spiral. I took a large sweep to avoid the danger-spot of the whirlpool, and soon I was safely above it. Just after one o'clock I was twenty-one thousand feet above the sea-level. To my great joy I had topped the gale, and with every hundred feet of ascent the air grew stiller. On the other hand, it was very cold, and I was conscious of that peculiar nausea which goes with rarefaction of the air. For the first time I unscrewed the mouth of my oxygen bag and took an occasional whiff of the glorious gas. I could feel it running like a cordial through my veins, and I was exhilarated almost to the point of drunkenness. I shouted and sang as I soared upwards into the cold, still outer world.

"It is very clear to me that the insensibility which came upon Glaisher, and in a lesser degree upon Coxwell, when, in 1862, they ascended in a balloon to the height of thirty thousand feet, was due to the extreme speed with which a perpendicular ascent is made. Doing it at an easy gradient and accustoming oneself to the lessened barometric pressure by slow degrees, there are no such dreadful symptoms. At the same great height I found that even without my oxygen inhaler I could breathe without undue distress. It was bitterly cold, however, and my thermometer was at zero, Fahrenheit. At one-thirty I was nearly seven miles above the surface of the earth, and still ascending steadily. I found, however, that the rarefied air was giving markedly less support to my planes, and that my angle of ascent had to be considerably lowered in consequence. It was already clear that even with my light weight and strong engine-power there was a point in front of me where I should be held. To make matters worse, one of my sparking-plugs was in trouble again and there was intermittent misfiring in the engine. My heart was heavy with the fear of failure.

"It was about that time that I had a most extraordinary experience. Something whizzed past me in a trail of smoke and exploded with a loud, hissing sound, sending forth a cloud of steam. For the instant I could not imagine what had happened. Then I remembered that the earth is for ever being bombarded by meteor stones, and would be hardly inhabitable were they not in nearly every case turned to vapour in the outer layers of the atmosphere. Here is a new danger for the high-altitude man, for two others passed me when I was nearing the forty-thousand-foot mark. I cannot doubt that at the edge of the earth's envelope the risk would be a very real one.

"My barograph needle marked forty-one thousand three hundred when I became aware that I could go no farther. Physically, the strain was not as yet greater than I could bear but my machine had reached its limit. The attenuated air gave no firm support to the wings, and the least tilt developed into side-slip, while she seemed sluggish on her controls. Possibly, had the engine been at its best, another thousand feet might have been within our capacity, but it was still misfiring, and two out of the ten cylinders appeared to be out of action. If I had not already reached the zone for which I was searching then I should never see it upon this journey. But was it not possible that I had attained it? Soaring in circles like a monstrous hawk upon the forty-thousand-foot level I let the monoplane guide herself, and with my Mannheim glass I made a careful observation of my surroundings. The heavens were perfectly clear; there was no indication of those dangers which I had imagined.

"I have said that I was soaring in circles. It struck me suddenly that I would do well to take a wider sweep and open up a new airtract. If the hunter entered an earth-jungle he would drive through it if he wished to find his game. My reasoning had led me to believe that the air-jungle which I had imagined lay somewhere over Wiltshire. This should be to the south and west of me. I took my bearings from the sun, for the compass was hopeless and no trace of earth was to be seen—nothing but the distant, silver cloud-plain. However, I got my direction as best I might and kept her head straight to the mark. I reckoned that my petrol supply would not last for more than another hour or so, but I could afford to use it to the last drop, since a single magnificent volplane could at any time take me to the earth.

"Suddenly I was aware of something new. The air in front of me had lost its crystal clearness. It was full of long, ragged wisps of something which I can only compare to very fine cigarette smoke.

It hung about in wreaths and coils, turning and twisting slowly in the sunlight. As the monoplane shot through it, I was aware of a faint taste of oil upon my lips, and there was a greasy scum upon the woodwork of the machine. Some infinitely fine organic matter appeared to be suspended in the atmosphere. There was no life there. It was inchoate and diffuse, extending for many square acres and then fringing off into the void. No, it was not life. But might it not be the remains of life? Above all, might it not be the food of life, of monstrous life, even as the humble grease of the ocean is the food for the mighty whale? The thought was in my mind when my eyes looked upwards and I saw the most wonderful vision that ever man has seen. Can I hope to convey it to you even as I saw it myself last Thursday?

"Conceive a jelly-fish such as sails in our summer seas, bell-shaped and of enormous size—far larger, I should judge, than the dome of St. Paul's. It was of a light pink colour veined with a delicate green, but the whole huge fabric so tenuous that it was but a fairy outline against the dark blue sky. It pulsated with a delicate and regular rhythm. From it there depended two long, drooping, green tentacles, which swayed slowly backwards and forwards. This gorgeous vision passed gently with noiseless dignity over my head, as light and fragile as a soap-bubble, and drifted upon its stately way.

"I had half-turned my monoplane, that I might look after this beautiful creature, when, in a moment, I found myself amidst a perfect fleet of them, of all sizes, but none so large as the first. Some were quite small, but the majority about as big as an average balloon, and with much the same curvature at the top. There was in them a delicacy of texture and colouring which reminded me of the finest Venetian glass. Pale shades of pink and green were the prevailing tints, but all had a lovely iridescence where the sun shimmered through their dainty forms. Some hundreds of them drifted past me, a wonderful fairy squadron of strange unknown argosies of the sky—creatures whose forms and substance were so attuned to these pure heights that one could not conceive anything so delicate within actual sight or sound of earth.

"But soon my attention was drawn to a new phenomenon— the serpents of the outer air. These were long, thin, fantastic coils of vapour-like material, which turned and twisted with great speed, flying round and round at such a pace that the eyes could hardly follow them. Some of these ghost-like creatures were twenty or thirty feet long, but it was difficult to tell their girth, for their outline was so hazy that it seemed to fade away into the air around them. These air-snakes were of a very light grey or smoke colour, with some darker lines within, which gave the impression of a definite organism. One of them whisked past my very face, and I was conscious of a cold, clammy contact, but their composition was so unsubstantial that I could not connect them with any thought of physical danger, any more than the beautiful bell-like creatures which had preceded them. There was no more solidity in their frames than in the floating spume from a broken wave.

"But a more terrible experience was in store for me. Floating downwards from a great height there came a purplish patch of vapour, small as I saw it first, but rapidly enlarging as it approached me, until it appeared to be hundreds of square feet in size. Though fashioned of some transparent, jelly-like substance, it was none the less of much more definite outline and solid consistence than anything which I had seen before. There were more traces, too, of a physical organization, especially two vast, shadowy, circular plates upon either side, which may have been eyes, and a perfectly solid white projection between them which was as curved and cruel as the beak of a vulture.

"The whole aspect of this monster was formidable and threatening, and it kept changing its colour from a very light mauve to a dark, angry purple so thick that it cast a shadow as it drifted between my monoplane and the sun. On the upper curve of its huge body there were three great projections which I can only describe as enormous bubbles, and I was convinced as I looked at them that they were charged with some extremely light gas which served to buoy up the misshapen and semi-solid mass in the rarefied air. The creature moved swiftly along, keeping pace easily with the monoplane, and for twenty miles or more it formed my horrible escort, hovering over me like a bird of prey which is waiting to pounce. Its method of progression—done so swiftly that it was not easy to follow—was to throw out a long, glutinous streamer in front of it, which in turn seemed to draw forward the rest of the writhing body. So elastic and gelatinous was it that never for two successive minutes was it the same shape and yet each change made it more threatening and loathsome than the last.

"I knew that it meant mischief. Every purple flush of its hideous body told me so. The vague, goggling eyes which were turned always upon me were cold and merciless in their viscid hatred. I dipped the nose of my monoplane downwards to escape it. As I did so, as quick as a flash there shot out a long tentacle from this mass of floating blubber, and it fell as light and sinuous as a whip-lash across the front of my machine. There was a loud hiss as it lay for a moment across the hot engine, and it whisked itself into the air again, while the huge, flat body drew itself together as if in sudden pain. I dipped to a vol-pique, but again a tentacle fell over the monoplane and was shorn off by the propeller as easily as it might have cut through a smoke wreath. A long, gliding, sticky serpent-like coil came from behind and caught me round the waist, dragging me out of the fuselage. I tore at it, my fingers sinking into the smooth, glue-like surface, and for an instant I disengaged myself, but only to be caught round the boot by another coil, which gave me a jerk that tilted me almost on to my back.

"As I fell over I blazed off both barrels of my gun, though indeed, it was like attacking an elephant with a pea-shooter to imagine that any human weapon could cripple that mighty bulk. And yet I aimed better than I knew, for, with a loud report, one of the great blisters upon the creature's back exploded with the puncture of the buck-shot. It was very clear that my conjecture was right, and that these vast, clear bladders were distended with some lifting gas, for in an instant the huge, cloud-like body turned sideways, writhing desperately to find its balance, while the white beak snapped and gaped in horrible fury. But already I had shot away on the steepest glide that I dared to attempt, my engine still full on, the flying propeller and the force of gravity shooting me downwards like an aerolite. Far behind me I saw a dull, purplish smudge growing swiftly smaller and merging into the blue sky behind it. I was safe out of the deadly jungle of the outer air.

"Once out of danger I throttled my engine, for nothing tears a machine to pieces quicker than running on full power from a height. It was a glorious, spiral vol-plane from nearly eight miles of altitude—first, to the level of the silver cloud-bank, then to that of the storm-cloud beneath it, and finally, in beating rain, to the surface of the earth. I saw the Bristol Channel beneath me as I broke from the clouds, but, having still some petrol in my tank, I got twenty miles inland before I found myself stranded in a field half a mile from the village of Ashcombe. There I got three tins of petrol from a passing motor-car, and at ten minutes past six that evening I alighted gently in my own home meadow at Devizes, after such a journey as no mortal upon earth has ever yet taken and lived to tell the tale. I have seen the beauty and I have seen the horror of the heights—and greater beauty or greater horror than that is not within the ken of man.

"And now it is my plan to go once again before I give my results to the world. My reason for this is that I must surely have something to show by way of proof before I lay such a tale before my fellow-men. It is true that others will soon follow and will confirm what I have said, and yet I should wish to carry conviction from the first. Those lovely iridescent bubbles of the air should not be hard to capture. They drift slowly upon their way, and the swift monoplane could intercept their leisurely course. It is likely enough that they would dissolve in the heavier layers of the atmosphere, and that some small heap of amorphous jelly might be all that I should bring to earth with me. And yet something there would surely be by which I could substantiate my story. Yes, I will go, even if I run a risk by doing so. These purple horrors would not seem to be numerous. It is probable that I shall not see one. If I do I shall dive at once. At the worst there is always the shot-gun and my knowledge of . . ."

Here a page of the manuscript is unfortunately missing. On the next page is written, in large, straggling writing:

"Forty-three thousand feet. I shall never see earth again. They are beneath me, three of them. God help me; it is a dreadful death to die!"

Such in its entirety is the Joyce-Armstrong Statement. Of the man nothing has since been seen. Pieces of his shattered monoplane have been picked up in the preserves of Mr. Budd-Lushington upon the borders of Kent and Sussex, within a few miles of the spot where the note-book was discovered. If the unfortunate avia-tor's theory is correct that this air-jungle, as he called it, existed only over the south-west of England, then it would seem that he had fled from it at the full speed of his monoplane, but had been overtaken and devoured by these horrible creatures at some spot in the outer atmosphere above the place where the grim relics were found. The picture of that monoplane skimming down the sky, with the nameless terrors flying as swiftly beneath it and cut-ting it off always from the earth while they gradually closed in upon their victim, is one upon which a man who valued his sanity would prefer not to dwell. There are many, as I am aware, who still jeer at the facts which I have here set down, but even they must admit that Joyce-Armstrong has disappeared, and I would com-mend to them his own words: "This note-book may explain what I am trying to do, and how I lost my life in doing it. But no drivel about accidents or mysteries, if YOU please."

The Leather Funnel

My friend, Lionel Dacre, lived in the Avenue de Wagram, Paris. His house was that small one, with the iron railings and grass plot in front of it, on the left-hand side as you pass down from the Arc de Triomphe. I fancy that it had been there long before the avenue was constructed, for the grey tiles were stained with lichens, and the walls were mildewed and discoloured with age. It looked a small house from the street, five windows in front, if I remember right, but it deepened into a single long chamber at the back. It was here that Dacre had that singular library of occult literature, and the fantastic curiosities which served as a hobby for himself, and an amusement for his friends. A wealthy man of refined and eccentric tastes, he had spent much of his life and fortune in gathering together what was said to be a unique private collection of Talmudic, cabalistic, and magical works, many of them of great rarity and value. His tastes leaned toward the marvellous and the monstrous, and I have heard that his experiments in the direction of the unknown have passed all the bounds of civilization and of decorum. To his English friends he never alluded to such matters, and took the tone of the student and virtuoso; but a Frenchman whose tastes were of the same nature has assured me that the worst excesses of the black mass have been perpetrated in that large and lofty hall, which is lined with the shelves of his books, and the cases of his museum.

Dacre's appearance was enough to show that his deep interest in these psychic matters was intellectual rather than spiritual. There was no trace of asceticism upon his heavy face, but there was much mental force in his huge, dome-like skull, which curved upward from amongst his thinning locks, like a snowpeak above its fringe of fir trees. His knowledge was greater than his wisdom, and his powers were far superior to his character. The small bright eyes, buried deeply in his fleshy face, twinkled with intelligence and an unabated curiosity of life, but they were the eyes of a sensualist and an egotist. Enough of the man, for he is dead now, poor devil, dead at the very time that he had made sure that he had at last discovered the elixir of life. It is not with his complex character that I have to deal, but with the very strange and inexplicable incident which had its rise in my visit to him in the early spring of the year '82.

I had known Dacre in England, for my researches in the Assyrian Room of the British Museum had been conducted at the time when he was endeavouring to establish a mystic and esoteric meaning in the Babylonian tablets, and this community of interests had brought us together. Chance remarks had led to daily conversation, and that to something verging upon friendship. I had promised him that on my next visit to Paris I would call upon him. At the time when I was able to fulfil my compact I was living in a cottage at Fontainebleau, and as the evening trains were inconvenient, he asked me to spend the night in his house.

"I have only that one spare couch," said he, pointing to a broad sofa in his large salon; "I hope that you will manage to be comfortable there."

It was a singular bedroom, with its high walls of brown volumes, but there could be no more agreeable furniture to a bookworm like myself, and there is no scent so pleasant to my nostrils as that faint, subtle reek which comes from an ancient book. I assured him that I could desire no more charming chamber, and no more congenial surroundings.

"If the fittings are neither convenient nor conventional, they are at least costly," said he, looking round at his shelves. "I have expended nearly a quarter of a million of money upon these objects which surround you. Books, weapons, gems, carvings, tapestries, images—there is hardly a thing here which has not its history, and it is generally one worth telling."

He was seated as he spoke at one side of the open fire-place, and I at the other. His reading-table was on his right, and the strong lamp above it ringed it with a very vivid circle of golden light. A half-rolled palimpsest lay in the centre, and around it were many quaint articles of bric-a-brac. One of these was a large funnel, such as is used for filling wine casks. It appeared to be made of black wood, and to be rimmed with discoloured brass.

"That is a curious thing," I remarked. "What is the history of that?"

"Ah!" said he, "it is the very question which I have had occasion to ask myself. I would give a good deal to know. Take it in your hands and examine it."

I did so, and found that what I had imagined to be wood was in reality leather, though age had dried it into an extreme hardness. It was a large funnel, and might hold a quart when full. The brass rim encircled the wide end, but the narrow was also tipped with metal.

"What do you make of it?" asked Dacre.

"I should imagine that it belonged to some vintner or maltster in the Middle Ages," said I. "I have seen in England leathern drinking flagons of the seventeenth century—'black jacks' as they were called—which were of the same colour and hardness as this filler."

"I dare say the date would be about the same," said Dacre, "and, no doubt, also, it was used for filling a vessel with liquid. If my suspicions are correct, however, it was a queer vintner who used it, and a very singular cask which was filled. Do you observe nothing strange at the spout end of the funnel."

As I held it to the light I observed that at a spot some five inches above the brass tip the narrow neck of the leather funnel was all haggled and scored, as if someone had notched it round with a blunt knife. Only at that point was there any roughening of the dead black surface.

"Someone has tried to cut off the neck."

"Would you call it a cut?"

"It is torn and lacerated. It must have taken some strength to leave these marks on such tough material, whatever the instrument may have been. But what do you think of it? I can tell that you know more than you say."

Dacre smiled, and his little eyes twinkled with knowledge.

"Have you included the psychology of dreams among your learned studies?" he asked.

"I did not even know that there was such a psychology."

"My dear sir, that shelf above the gem case is filled with volumes, from Albertus Magnus onward, which deal with no other subject. It is a science in itself."

"A science of charlatans."

"The charlatan is always the pioneer. From the astrologer came the astronomer, from the alchemist the chemist, from the mesmerist the experimental psychologist. The quack of yesterday is the professor of tomorrow. Even such subtle and elusive things as dreams will in time be reduced to system and order. When that time comes the researches of our friends on the bookshelf yonder will no longer be the amusement of the mystic, but the foundations of a science."

"Supposing that is so, what has the science of dreams to do with a large, black, brass-rimmed funnel?"

"I will tell you. You know that I have an agent who is always on the look-out for rarities and curiosities for my collection. Some days ago he heard of a dealer upon one of the Quais who had acquired some old rubbish found in a cupboard in an ancient house at the back of the Rue Mathurin, in the Quartier Latin. The dining-room of this old house is decorated with a coat of arms, chevrons, and bars rouge upon a field argent, which prove, upon inquiry, to be the shield of Nicholas de la Reynie, a high official of King Louis XIV. There can be no doubt that the other articles in the cupboard date back to the early days of that king. The inference is, therefore, that they were all the property of this Nicholas de la Reynie, who was, as I understand, the gentleman specially concerned with the maintenance and execution of the Draconic laws of that epoch."

"What then?"

"I would ask you now to take the funnel into your hands once more and to examine the upper brass rim. Can you make out any lettering upon it?"

There were certainly some scratches upon it, almost obliterated by time. The general effect was of several letters, the last of which bore some resemblance to a B.

"You make it a B?"

"Yes, I do."

"So do I. In fact, I have no doubt whatever that it is a B."

"But the nobleman you mentioned would have had R for his initial."

"Exactly! That's the beauty of it. He owned this curious object, and yet he had someone else's initials upon it. Why did he do this?"

"I can't imagine; can you?"

"Well, I might, perhaps, guess. Do you observe something drawn a little farther along the rim?"

"I should say it was a crown."

"It is undoubtedly a crown; but if you examine it in a good light, you will convince yourself that it is not an ordinary crown. It is a heraldic crown—a badge of rank, and it consists of an alternation of four pearls and strawberry leaves, the proper badge of a marquis. We may infer, therefore, that the person whose initials end in B was entitled to wear that coronet."

"Then this common leather filler belonged to a marquis?"

Dacre gave a peculiar smile.

"Or to some member of the family of a marquis," said he. "So much we have clearly gathered from this engraved rim."

"But what has all this to do with dreams?" I do not know whether it was from a look upon Dacre's face, or from some subtle suggestion in his manner, but a feeling of repulsion, of unreasoning horror, came upon me as I looked at the gnarled old lump of leather.

"I have more than once received important information through my dreams," said my companion in the didactic manner which he loved to affect. "I make it a rule now when I am in doubt upon any material point to place the article in question beside me as I sleep, and to hope for some enlightenment. The process does not appear to me to be very obscure, though it has not yet received the blessing of orthodox science. According to my theory, any object which has been intimately associated with any supreme paroxysm of human emotion, whether it be joy or pain, will retain a certain atmosphere or association which it is capable of communicating to a sensitive mind. By a sensitive mind I do not mean an abnormal one, but such a trained and educated mind as you or I possess."

"You mean, for example, that if I slept beside that old sword upon the wall, I might dream of some bloody incident in which that very sword took part?"

"An excellent example, for, as a matter of fact, that sword was used in that fashion by me, and I saw in my sleep the death of its owner, who perished in a brisk skirmish, which I have been unable to identify, but which occurred at the time of the wars of the Frondists. If you think of it, some of our popular observances show that the fact has already been recognized by our ancestors, although we, in our wisdom, have classed it among superstitions."

"For example?"

"Well, the placing of the bride's cake beneath the pillow in order that the sleeper may have pleasant dreams. That is one of several instances which you will find set forth in a small brochure which I am myself writing upon the subject. But to come back to the point, I slept one night with this funnel beside me, and I had a dream which certainly throws a curious light upon its use and origin."

"What did you dream?"

"I dreamed——" He paused, and an intent look of interest came over his massive face. "By Jove, that's well thought of," said he. "This really will be an exceedingly interesting experiment. You are yourself a psychic subject—with nerves which respond readily to any impression."

"I have never tested myself in that direction."

"Then we shall test you tonight. Might I ask you as a very great favour, when you occupy that couch tonight, to sleep with this old funnel placed by the side of your pillow?"

The request seemed to me a grotesque one; but I have myself, in my complex nature, a hunger after all which is bizarre and fantastic. I had not the faintest belief in Dacre's theory, nor any hopes for success in such an experiment; yet it amused me that the experiment should be made. Dacre, with great gravity, drew a small stand to the head of my settee, and placed the funnel upon it. Then, after a short conversation, he wished me good night and left me.

I sat for some little time smoking by the smouldering fire, and turning over in my mind the curious incident which had occurred, and the strange experience which might lie before me. Sceptical as I was, there was something impressive in the assurance of Dacre's manner, and my extraordinary surroundings, the huge room with the strange and often sinister objects which were hung round it, struck solemnity into my soul. Finally I undressed, and turning out the lamp, I lay down. After long tossing I fell asleep. Let me try to describe as accurately as I can the scene which came to me in my dreams. It stands out now in my memory more clearly than anything which I have seen with my waking eyes. There was a room which bore the appearance of a vault. Four spandrels from the corners ran up to join a sharp, cup-shaped roof. The architecture was rough, but very strong. It was evidently part of a great building.

Three men in black, with curious, top-heavy, black velvet hats, sat in a line upon a red-carpeted dais. Their faces were very solemn and sad. On the left stood two long-gowned men with port-folios in their hands, which seemed to be stuffed with papers. Upon the right, looking toward me, was a small woman with blonde hair and singular, light-blue eyes—the eyes of a child. She was past her first youth, but could not yet be called middle-aged. Her figure was inclined to stoutness and her bearing was proud and confident. Her face was pale, but serene. It was a curious face, comely and yet feline, with a subtle suggestion of cruelty about the straight, strong little mouth and chubby jaw. She was draped in some sort of loose, white gown. Beside her stood a thin, eager priest, who whispered in her ear, and continually raised a crucifix before her eyes. She turned her head and looked fixedly past the crucifix at the three men in black, who were, I felt, her judges.

As I gazed the three men stood up and said something, but I could distinguish no words, though I was aware that it was the central one who was speaking. They then swept out of the room, followed by the two men with the papers. At the same instant several rough-looking fellows in stout jerkins came bustling in and removed first the red carpet, and then the boards which formed the dais, so as to entirely clear the room. When this screen was removed I saw some singular articles of furniture behind it. One looked like a bed with wooden rollers at each end, and a winch handle to regulate its length. Another was a wooden horse. There were several other curious objects, and a number of swinging cords which played over pulleys. It was not unlike a modern gymnasium.

When the room had been cleared there appeared a new figure upon the scene. This was a tall, thin person clad in black, with a gaunt and austere face. The aspect of the man made me shudder. His clothes were all shining with grease and mottled with stains. He bore himself with a slow and impressive dignity, as if he took command of all things from the instant of his entrance. In spite of his rude appearance and sordid dress, it was now his business, his room, his to command. He carried a coil of light ropes over his left forearm. The lady looked him up and down with a searching glance, but her expression was unchanged. It was confident—even defiant. But it was very different with the priest. His face was ghastly white, and I saw the moisture glisten and run on his high, sloping forehead. He threw up his hands in prayer and he stooped continually to mutter frantic words in the lady's ear.

The man in black now advanced, and taking one of the cords from his left arm, he bound the woman's hands together. She held them meekly toward him as he did so. Then he took her arm with a rough grip and led her toward the wooden horse, which was little higher than her waist. On to this she was lifted and laid, with her back upon it, and her face to the ceiling, while the priest, quivering with horror, had rushed out of the room. The woman's lips were moving rapidly, and though I could hear nothing I knew that she was praying. Her feet hung down on either side of the horse, and I saw that the rough varlets in attendance had fastened cords to her ankles and secured the other ends to iron rings in the stone floor.

My heart sank within me as I saw these ominous preparations, and yet I was held by the fascination of horror, and I could not take my eyes from the strange spectacle. A man had entered the room with a bucket of water in either hand. Another followed with a third bucket. They were laid beside the wooden horse. The second man had a wooden dipper—a bowl with a straight handle—in his other hand. This he gave to the man in black. At the same moment one of the varlets approached with a dark object in his hand, which even in my dream filled me with a vague feeling of familiarity. It was a leathern filler. With horrible energy he thrust it—but I could stand no more. My hair stood on end with horror. I writhed, I struggled, I broke through the bonds of sleep, and I burst with a shriek into my own life, and found myself lying shivering with terror in the huge library, with the moonlight flooding through the window and throwing strange silver and black traceries upon the opposite wall. Oh, what a blessed relief to feel that I was back in the nineteenth century—back out of that mediaeval vault into a world where men had human hearts within their bosoms. I sat up on my couch, trembling in every limb, my mind divided between thankfulness and horror. To think that such things were ever done—that they could be done without God striking the villains dead. Was it all a fantasy, or did it really stand for something which had happened in the black, cruel days of the world's history? I sank my throbbing head upon my shaking hands. And then, suddenly, my heart seemed to stand still in my bosom, and I could not even scream, so great was my terror. Something was advancing toward me through the darkness of the room.

It is a horror coming upon a horror which breaks a man's spirit. I could not reason, I could not pray; I could only sit like a frozen image, and glare at the dark figure which was coming down the great room. And then it moved out into the white lane of moonlight, and I breathed once more. It was Dacre, and his face showed that he was as frightened as myself.

"Was that you? For God's sake what's the matter?" he asked in a husky voice.

"Oh, Dacre, I am glad to see you! I have been down into hell. It was dreadful."

"Then it was you who screamed?"

"I dare say it was."

"It rang through the house. The servants are all terrified." He struck a match and lit the lamp. "I think we may get the fire to burn up again," he added, throwing some logs upon the embers. "Good God, my dear chap, how white you are! You look as if you had seen a ghost."

"So I have—several ghosts."

"The leather funnel has acted, then?"

"I wouldn't sleep near the infernal thing again for all the money you could offer me."

Dacre chuckled.

"I expected that you would have a lively night of it," said he. "You took it out of me in return, for that scream of yours wasn't a very pleasant sound at two in the morning. I suppose from what you say that you have seen the whole dreadful business."

"What dreadful business?"

"The torture of the water—the 'Extraordinary Question,' as it was called in the genial days of 'Le Roi Soleil.' Did you stand it out to the end?"

"No, thank God, I awoke before it really began."

"Ah! it is just as well for you. I held out till the third bucket. Well, it is an old story, and they are all in their graves now, anyhow, so what does it matter how they got there? I suppose that you have no idea what it was that you have seen?"

"The torture of some criminal. She must have been a terrible malefactor indeed if her crimes are in proportion to her penalty."

"Well, we have that small consolation," said Dacre, wrapping his dressing-gown round him and crouching closer to the fire. "They WERE in proportion to her penalty. That is to say, if I am correct in the lady's identity."

"How could you possibly know her identity?"

For answer Dacre took down an old vellum-covered volume from the shelf.

"Just listen to this," said he; "it is in the French of the seventeenth century, but I will give a rough translation as I go. You will judge for yourself whether I have solved the riddle or not.

"'The prisoner was brought before the Grand Chambers and Tournelles of Parliament, sitting as a court of justice, charged with the murder of Master Dreux d'Aubray, her father, and of her two brothers, MM. d'Aubray, one being civil lieutenant, and the other a counsellor of Parliament. In person it seemed hard to believe that she had really done such wicked deeds, for she was of a mild appearance, and of short stature, with a fair skin and blue eyes. Yet the Court, having found her guilty, condemned her to the ordinary and to the extraordinary question in order that she might be forced to name her accomplices, after which she should be carried in a cart to the Place de Greve, there to have her head cut off, her body being afterwards burned and her ashes scattered to the winds.'

"The date of this entry is July 16, 1676."

"It is interesting," said I, "but not convincing. How do you prove the two women to be the same?"

"I am coming to that. The narrative goes on to tell of the woman's behaviour when questioned. 'When the executioner approached her she recognized him by the cords which he held in his hands, and she at once held out her own hands to him, looking at him from head to foot without uttering a word.' How's that?"

"Yes, it was so."

"'She gazed without wincing upon the wooden horse and rings which had twisted so many limbs and caused so many shrieks of agony. When her eyes fell upon the three pails of water, which were all ready for her, she said with a smile, "All that water must have been brought here for the purpose of drowning me, Monsieur. You have no idea, I trust, of making a person of my small stature swallow it all."' Shall I read the details of the torture?"

"No, for Heaven's sake, don't."

"Here is a sentence which must surely show you that what is here recorded is the very scene which you have gazed upon tonight: 'The good Abbe Pirot, unable to contemplate the agonies which were suffered by his penitent, had hurried from the room.' Does that convince you?"

"It does entirely. There can be no question that it is indeed the same event. But who, then, is this lady whose appearance was so attractive and whose end was so horrible?"

For answer Dacre came across to me, and placed the small lamp upon the table which stood by my bed. Lifting up the ill-omened filler, he turned the brass rim so that the light fell full upon it. Seen in this way the engraving seemed clearer than on the night before.

"We have already agreed that this is the badge of a marquis or of a marquise," said he. "We have also settled that the last letter is B."

"It is undoubtedly so."

"I now suggest to you that the other letters from left to right are, M, M, a small d, A, a small d, and then the final B."

"Yes, I am sure that you are right. I can make out the two small d's quite plainly."

"What I have read to you tonight," said Dacre, "is the official record of the trial of Marie Madeleine d'Aubray, Marquise de Brinvilliers, one of the most famous poisoners and murderers of all time."

I sat in silence, overwhelmed at the extraordinary nature of the incident, and at the completeness of the proof with which Dacre had exposed its real meaning. In a vague way I remembered some details of the woman's career, her unbridled debauchery, the cold-blooded and protracted torture of her sick father, the murder of her brothers for motives of petty gain. I recollected also that the bravery of her end had done something to atone for the horror of her life, and that all Paris had sympathized with her last moments, and blessed her as a martyr within a few days of the time when they had cursed her as a murderess. One objection, and one only, occurred to my mind.

"How came her initials and her badge of rank upon the filler? Surely they did not carry their mediaeval homage to the nobility to the point of decorating instruments of torture with their titles?"

"I was puzzled with the same point," said Dacre, "but it admits of a simple explanation. The case excited extraordinary interest at the time, and nothing could be more natural than that La Reynie, the head of the police, should retain this filler as a grim souvenir. It was not often that a marchioness of France underwent the extraordinary question. That he should engrave her initials upon it for the information of others was surely a very ordinary proceeding upon his part."

"And this?" I asked, pointing to the marks upon the leathern neck.

"She was a cruel tigress," said Dacre, as he turned away. "I think it is evident that like other tigresses her teeth were both strong and sharp."

The New Catacomb

"Look here, Burger," said Kennedy, "I do wish that you would confide in me."

The two famous students of Roman remains sat together in Kennedy's comfortable room overlooking the Corso. The night was cold, and they had both pulled up their chairs to the unsatisfactory Italian stove which threw out a zone of stuffiness rather than of warmth. Outside under the bright winter stars lay the modern Rome, the long, double chain of the electric lamps, the brilliantly lighted cafes, the rushing carriages, and the dense throng upon the footpaths. But inside, in the sumptuous chamber of the rich young English archaelogist, there was only old Rome to be seen. Cracked and timeworn friezes hung upon the walls, grey old busts of senators and soldiers with their fighting heads and their hard, cruel faces peered out from the corners. On the centre table, amidst a litter of inscriptions, fragments, and ornaments, there stood the famous reconstruction by Kennedy of the Baths of Caracalla, which excited such interest and admiration when it was exhibited in Berlin. Amphorae hung from the ceiling, and a litter of curiosities strewed the rich red Turkey carpet. And of them all there was not one which was not of the most unimpeachable authenticity, and of the utmost rarity and value; for Kennedy, though little more than thirty, had a European reputation in this particular branch of research, and was, moreover, provided with that long purse which either proves to be a fatal handicap to the student's energies, or, if his mind is still true to its purpose, gives him an enormous advantage in the race for fame. Kennedy had often been seduced by whim and pleasure from his studies, but his mind was an incisive one, capable of long and concentrated efforts which ended in sharp reactions of sensuous languor. His handsome face, with its high, white forehead, its aggressive nose, and its somewhat loose and sensual mouth, was a fair index of the compromise between strength and weakness in his nature.

Of a very different type was his companion, Julius Burger. He came of a curious blend, a German father and an Italian mother, with the robust qualities of the North mingling strangely with the softer graces of the South. Blue Teutonic eyes lightened his sun-browned face, and above them rose a square, massive forehead, with a fringe of close yellow curls lying round it. His strong, firm jaw was clean-shaven, and his companion had frequently remarked how much it suggested those old Roman busts which peered out from the shadows in the corners of his chamber. Under its bluff German strength there lay always a suggestion of Italian subtlety, but the smile was so honest, and the eyes so frank, that one understood that this was only an indication of his ancestry, with no actual bearing upon his character. In age and in reputation, he was on the same level as his English companion, but his life and his work had both been far more arduous. Twelve years before, he had come as a poor student to Rome, and had lived ever since upon some small endowment for research which had been awarded to him by the University of Bonn. Painfully, slowly, and doggedly, with extraordinary tenacity and single-mindedness, he had climbed from rung to rung of the ladder of fame, until now he was a member of the Berlin Academy, and there was every reason to believe that he would shortly be promoted to the Chair of the greatest of German Universities. But the singleness of purpose which had brought him to the same high level as the rich and brilliant Englishman, had caused him in everything outside their work to stand infinitely below him. He had never found a pause in his studies in which to cultivate the social graces. It was only when he spoke of his own subject that his face was filled with life and soul. At other times he was silent and embarrassed, too conscious of his own limitations in larger subjects, and impatient of that small talk which is the conventional refuge of those who have no thoughts to express.

And yet for some years there had been an acquaintanceship which appeared to be slowly ripening into a friendship between these two very different rivals. The base and origin of this lay in the fact that in their own studies each was the only one of the younger men who had knowledge and enthusiasm enough to properly appreciate the other. Their common interests and pursuits had brought them together, and each had been attracted by the other's knowledge. And then gradually something had been added to this. Kennedy had been amused by the frankness and simplicity of his rival, while Burger in turn had been fascinated by the brilliancy and vivacity which had made Kennedy such a favourite in Roman society. I say "had," because just at the moment the young Englishman was somewhat under a cloud. A love-affair, the details of which had never quite come out, had indicated a heartlessness and callousness upon his part which shocked many of his friends. But in the bachelor circles of students and artists in which he preferred to move there is no very rigid code of honour in such matters, and though a head might be shaken or a pair of shoulders shrugged over the flight of two and the return of one, the general sentiment was probably one of curiosity and perhaps of envy rather than of reprobation.

"Look here, Burger," said Kennedy, looking hard at the placid face of his companion, "I do wish that you would confide in me."

As he spoke he waved his hand in the direction of a rug which lay upon the floor. On the rug stood a long, shallow fruit-basket of the light wicker-work which is used in the Campagna, and this was heaped with a litter of objects, inscribed tiles, broken inscriptions, cracked mosaics, torn papyri, rusty metal ornaments, which to the uninitiated might have seemed to have come straight from a dustman's bin, but which a specialist would have speedily recognized as unique of their kind. The pile of odds and ends in the flat wicker-work basket supplied exactly one of those missing links of social development which are of such interest to the student. It was the German who had brought them in, and the Englishman's eyes were hungry as he looked at them.

"I won't interfere with your treasure-trove, but I should very much like to hear about it," he continued, while Burger very deliberately lit a cigar. "It is evidently a discovery of the first importance. These inscriptions will make a sensation throughout Europe."

"For every one here there are a million there!" said the German. "There are so many that a dozen savants might spend a lifetime over them, and build up a reputation as solid as the Castle of St. Angelo."

Kennedy sat thinking with his fine forehead wrinkled and his fingers playing with his long, fair moustache.

"You have given yourself away, Burger!" said he at last. "Your words can only apply to one thing. You have discovered a new catacomb."

"I had no doubt that you had already come to that conclusion from an examination of these objects."

"Well, they certainly appeared to indicate it, but your last remarks make it certain. There is no place except a catacomb which could contain so vast a store of relics as you describe."

"Quite so. There is no mystery about that. I HAVE discovered a new catacomb."

"Where?"

"Ah, that is my secret, my dear Kennedy. Suffice it that it is so situated that there is not one chance in a million of anyone else coming upon it. Its date is different from that of any known catacomb, and it has been reserved for the burial of the highest Christians, so that the remains and the relics are quite different from anything which has ever been seen before. If I was not aware of your knowledge and of your energy, my friend, I would not hesitate, under the pledge of secrecy, to tell you everything about it. But as it is I think that I must certainly prepare my own report of the matter before I expose myself to such formidable competition."

Kennedy loved his subject with a love which was almost a mania—a love which held him true to it, amidst all the distractions which come to a wealthy and dissipated young man. He had ambition, but his ambition was secondary to his mere abstract joy and interest in everything which concerned the old life and history of the city. He yearned to see this new underworld which his companion had discovered.

"Look here, Burger," said he, earnestly, "I assure you that you can trust me most implicitly in the matter. Nothing would induce me to put pen to paper about anything which I see until I have your express permission. I quite understand your feeling and I think it is most natural, but you have really nothing whatever to fear from me. On the other hand, if you don't tell me I shall make a systematic search, and I shall most certainly discover it. In that case, of course, I should make what use I liked of it, since I should be under no obligation to you."

Burger smiled thoughtfully over his cigar.

"I have noticed, friend Kennedy," said he, "that when I want information over any point you are not always so ready to supply it."

"When did you ever ask me anything that I did not tell you? You remember, for example, my giving you the material for your paper about the temple of the Vestals."

"Ah, well, that was not a matter of much importance. If I were to question you upon some intimate thing would you give me an answer, I wonder! This new catacomb is a very intimate thing to me, and I should certainly expect some sign of confidence in return."

"What you are driving at I cannot imagine," said the Englishman, "but if you mean that you will answer my question about the catacomb if I answer any question which you may put to me I can assure you that I will certainly do so."

"Well, then," said Burger, leaning luxuriously back in his settee, and puffing a blue tree of cigar-smoke into the air, "tell me all about your relations with Miss Mary Saunderson."

Kennedy sprang up in his chair and glared angrily at his impassive companion.

"What the devil do you mean?" he cried. "What sort of a question is this? You may mean it as a joke, but you never made a worse one."

"No, I don't mean it as a joke," said Burger, simply. "I am really rather interested in the details of the matter. I don't know much about the world and women and social life and that sort of thing, and such an incident has the fascination of the unknown for me. I know you, and I knew her by sight—I had even spoken to her once or twice. I should very much like to hear from your own lips exactly what it was which occurred between you."

"I won't tell you a word."

"That's all right. It was only my whim to see if you would give up a secret as easily as you expected me to give up my secret of the new catacomb. You wouldn't, and I didn't expect you to. But why should you expect otherwise of me? There's Saint John's clock striking ten. It is quite time that I was going home."

"No; wait a bit, Burger," said Kennedy; "this is really a ridiculous caprice of yours to wish to know about an old love-affair which has burned out months ago. You know we look upon a man who kisses and tells as the greatest coward and villain possible."

"Certainly," said the German, gathering up his basket of curiosities, "when he tells anything about a girl which is previously unknown he must be so. But in this case, as you must be aware, it was a public matter which was the common talk of Rome, so that you are not really doing Miss Mary Saunderson any injury by discussing her case with me. But still, I respect your scruples; and so good night!"

"Wait a bit, Burger," said Kennedy, laying his hand upon the other's arm; "I am very keen upon this catacomb business, and I can't let it drop quite so easily. Would you mind asking me something else in return—something not quite so eccentric this time?"

"No, no; you have refused, and there is an end of it," said Burger, with his basket on his arm. "No doubt you are quite right not to answer, and no doubt I am quite right also—and so again, my dear Kennedy, good night!"

The Englishman watched Burger cross the room, and he had his hand on the handle of the door before his host sprang up with the air of a man who is making the best of that which cannot be helped.

"Hold on, old fellow," said he; "I think you are behaving in a most ridiculous fashion; but still; if this is your condition, I suppose that I must submit to it. I hate saying anything about a girl, but, as you say, it is all over Rome, and I don't suppose I can tell you anything which you do not know already. What was it you wanted to know?"

The German came back to the stove, and, laying down his basket, he sank into his chair once more.

"May I have another cigar?" said he. "Thank you very much! I never smoke when I work, but I enjoy a chat much more when I am under the influence of tobacco. Now, as regards this young lady, with whom you had this little adventure. What in the world has become of her?"

"She is at home with her own people."

"Oh, really—in England?"

"Yes."

"What part of England—London?"

"No, Twickenham."

"You must excuse my curiosity, my dear Kennedy, and you must put it down to my ignorance of the world. No doubt it is quite a simple thing to persuade a young lady to go off with you for three weeks or so, and then to hand her over to her own family at—what did you call the place?"

"Twickenham."

"Quite so—at Twickenham. But it is something so entirely outside my own experience that I cannot even imagine how you set about it. For example, if you had loved this girl your love could hardly disappear in three weeks, so I presume that you could not have loved her at all. But if you did not love her why should you make this great scandal which has damaged you and ruined her?"

Kennedy looked moodily into the red eye of the stove.

"That's a logical way of looking at it, certainly," said he. "Love is a big word, and it represents a good many different shades of feeling. I liked her, and—well, you say you've seen her—you know how charming she could look. But still I am willing to admit, looking back, that I could never have really loved her."

"Then, my dear Kennedy, why did you do it?"

"The adventure of the thing had a great deal to do with it."

"What! You are so fond of adventures!"

"Where would the variety of life be without them? It was for an adventure that I first began to pay my attentions to her. I've chased a good deal of game in my time, but there's no chase like that of a pretty woman. There was the piquant difficulty of it also, for, as she was the companion of Lady Emily Rood, it was almost impossible to see her alone. On the top of all the other obstacles which attracted me, I learned from her own lips very early in the proceedings that she was engaged."

"Mein Gott! To whom?"

"She mentioned no names."

"I do not think that anyone knows that. So that made the adventure more alluring, did it?"

"Well, it did certainly give a spice to it. Don't you think so?"

"I tell you that I am very ignorant about these things."

"My dear fellow, you can remember that the apple you stole from your neighbour's tree was always sweeter than that which fell from your own. And then I found that she cared for me."

"What—at once?"

"Oh, no, it took about three months of sapping and mining. But at last I won her over. She understood that my judicial separation from my wife made it impossible for me to do the right thing by her—but she came all the same, and we had a delightful time, as long as it lasted."

"But how about the other man?"

Kennedy shrugged his shoulders.

"I suppose it is the survival of the fittest," said he. "If he had been the better man she would not have deserted him. Let's drop the subject, for I have had enough of it!"

"Only one other thing. How did you get rid of her in three weeks?"

"Well, we had both cooled down a bit, you understand. She absolutely refused, under any circumstances, to come back to face the people she had known in Rome. Now, of course, Rome is necessary to me, and I was already pining to be back at my work—so there was one obvious cause of separation. Then, again, her old father turned up at the hotel in London, and there was a scene, and the whole thing became so unpleasant that really—though I missed her dreadfully at first—I was very glad to slip out of it. Now, I rely upon you not to repeat anything of what I have said."

"My dear Kennedy, I should not dream of repeating it. But all that you say interests me very much, for it gives me an insight into your way of looking at things, which is entirely different from mine, for I have seen so little of life. And now you want to know about my new catacomb. There's no use my trying to describe it, for you would never find it by that. There is only one thing, and that is for me to take you there."

"That would be splendid."

"When would you like to come?"

"The sooner the better. I am all impatience to see it."

"Well, it is a beautiful night—though a trifle cold. Suppose we start in an hour. We must be very careful to keep the matter to ourselves. If anyone saw us hunting in couples they would suspect that there was something going on."

"We can't be too cautious," said Kennedy. "Is it far?"

"Some miles."

"Not too far to walk?"

"Oh, no, we could walk there easily."

"We had better do so, then. A cabman's suspicions would be aroused if he dropped us both at some lonely spot in the dead of the night."

"Quite so. I think it would be best for us to meet at the Gate of the Appian Way at midnight. I must go back to my lodgings for the matches and candles and things."

"All right, Burger! I think it is very kind of you to let me into this secret, and I promise you that I will write nothing about it until you have published your report. Good-bye for the present! You will find me at the Gate at twelve."

The cold, clear air was filled with the musical chimes from that city of clocks as Burger, wrapped in an Italian overcoat, with a lantern hanging from his hand, walked up to the rendezvous. Kennedy stepped out of the shadow to meet him.

"You are ardent in work as well as in love!" said the German, laughing.

"Yes; I have been waiting here for nearly half an hour."

"I hope you left no clue as to where we were going."

"Not such a fool! By Jove, I am chilled to the bone! Come on, Burger, let us warm ourselves by a spurt of hard walking."

Their footsteps sounded loud and crisp upon the rough stone paving of the disappointing road which is all that is left of the most famous highway of the world. A peasant or two going home from the wine-shop, and a few carts of country produce coming up to Rome, were the only things which they met. They swung along, with the huge tombs looming up through the darkness upon each side of them, until they had come as far as the Catacombs of St. Calistus, and saw against a rising moon the great circular bastion of Cecilia Metella in front of them. Then Burger stopped with his hand to his side.

"Your legs are longer than mine, and you are more accustomed to walking," said he, laughing. "I think that the place where we turn off is somewhere here. Yes, this is it, round the corner of the trattoria. Now, it is a very narrow path, so perhaps I had better go in front and you can follow."

He had lit his lantern, and by its light they were enabled to follow a narrow and devious track which wound across the marshes of the Campagna. The great Aqueduct of old Rome lay like a monstrous caterpillar across the moonlit landscape, and their road led them under one of its huge arches, and past the circle of crumbling bricks which marks the old arena. At last Burger stopped at a solitary wooden cow-house, and he drew a key from his pocket. "Surely your catacomb is not inside a house!" cried Kennedy

"The entrance to it is. That is just the safeguard which we have against anyone else discovering it."

"Does the proprietor know of it?"

"Not he. He had found one or two objects which made me almost certain that his house was built on the entrance to such a place. So I rented it from him, and did my excavations for myself. Come in, and shut the door behind you."

It was a long, empty building, with the mangers of the cows along one wall. Burger put his lantern down on the ground, and shaded its light in all directions save one by draping his overcoat round it.

"It might excite remark if anyone saw a light in this lonely place," said he. "Just help me to move this boarding."

The flooring was loose in the corner, and plank by plank the two savants raised it and leaned it against the wall. Below there was a square aperture and a stair of old stone steps which led away down into the bowels of the earth.

"Be careful!" cried Burger, as Kennedy, in his impatience, hurried down them. "It is a perfect rabbits'-warren below, and if you were once to lose your way there the chances would be a hundred to one against your ever coming out again. Wait until I bring the light."

"How do you find your own way if it is so complicated?"

"I had some very narrow escapes at first, but I have gradually learned to go about. There is a certain system to it, but it is one which a lost man, if he were in the dark, could not possibly find out. Even now I always spin out a ball of string behind me when I am going far into the catacomb. You can see for yourself that it is difficult, but every one of these passages divides and subdivides a dozen times before you go a hundred yards."

They had descended some twenty feet from the level of the byre, and they were standing now in a square chamber cut out of the soft tufa. The lantern cast a flickering light, bright below and dim above, over the cracked brown walls. In every direction were the black openings of passages which radiated from this common centre.

"I want you to follow me closely, my friend," said Burger. "Do not loiter to look at anything upon the way, for the place to which I will take you contains all that you can see, and more. It will save time for us to go there direct."

He led the way down one of the corridors, and the Englishman followed closely at his heels. Every now and then the passage bifurcated, but Burger was evidently following some secret marks of his own, for he neither stopped nor hesitated. Everywhere along the walls, packed like the berths upon an emigrant ship, lay the Christians of old Rome. The yellow light flickered over the shrivelled features of the mummies, and gleamed upon rounded skulls and long, white armbones crossed over fleshless chests. And everywhere as he passed Kennedy looked with wistful eyes upon inscriptions, funeral vessels, pictures, vestments, utensils, all lying as pious hands had placed them so many centuries ago. It was apparent to him, even in those hurried, passing glances, that this was the earliest and finest of the catacombs, containing such a storehouse of Roman remains as had never before come at one time under the observation of the student.

"What would happen if the light went out?" he asked, as they hurried onwards.

"I have a spare candle and a box of matches in my pocket. By the way, Kennedy, have you any matches?"

"No; you had better give me some."

"Oh, that is all right. There is no chance of our separating."

"How far are we going? It seems to me that we have walked at least a quarter of a mile."

"More than that, I think. There is really no limit to the tombs—at least, I have never been able to find any. This is a very difficult place, so I think that I will use our ball of string."

He fastened one end of it to a projecting stone and he carried the coil in the breast of his coat, paying it out as he advanced. Kennedy saw that it was no unnecessary precaution, for the passages had become more complex and tortuous than ever, with a perfect network of intersecting corridors. But these all ended in one large circular hall with a square pedestal of tufa topped with a slab of marble at one end of it.

"By Jove!" cried Kennedy in an ecstasy, as Burger swung his lantern over the marble. "It is a Christian altar—probably the first one in existence. Here is the little consecration cross cut upon the corner of it. No doubt this circular space was used as a church."

"Precisely," said Burger. "If I had more time I should like to show you all the bodies which are buried in these niches upon the walls, for they are the early popes and bishops of the Church, with their mitres, their croziers, and full canonicals. Go over to that one and look at it!"

Kennedy went across, and stared at the ghastly head which lay loosely on the shredded and mouldering mitre.

"This is most interesting," said he, and his voice seemed to boom against the concave vault. "As far as my experience goes, it is unique. Bring the lantern over, Burger, for I want to see them all."

But the German had strolled away, and was standing in the middle of a yellow circle of light at the other side of the hall.

"Do you know how many wrong turnings there are between this and the stairs?" he asked. "There are over two thousand. No doubt it was one of the means of protection which the Christians adopted. The odds are two thousand to one against a man getting out, even if he had a light; but if he were in the dark it would, of course, be far more difficult."

"So I should think."

"And the darkness is something dreadful. I tried it once for an experiment. Let us try it again!" He stooped to the lantern, and in an instant it was as if an invisible hand was squeezed tightly over each of Kennedy's eyes. Never had he known what such darkness was. It seemed to press upon him and to smother him. It was a solid obstacle against which the body shrank from advancing. He put his hands out to push it back from him.

"That will do, Burger," said he, "let's have the light again."

But his companion began to laugh, and in that circular room the sound seemed to come from every side at once.

"You seem uneasy, friend Kennedy," said he.

"Go on, man, light the candle!" said Kennedy impatiently.

"It's very strange, Kennedy, but I could not in the least tell by the sound in which direction you stand. Could you tell where I am?"

"No; you seem to be on every side of me."

"If it were not for this string which I hold in my hand I should not have a notion which way to go."

"I dare say not. Strike a light, man, and have an end of this nonsense."

"Well, Kennedy, there are two things which I understand that you are very fond of. The one is an adventure, and the other is an obstacle to surmount. The adventure must be the finding of your way out of this catacomb. The obstacle will be the darkness and the two thousand wrong turns which make the way a little difficult to find. But you need not hurry, for you have plenty of time, and when you halt for a rest now and then, I should like you just to think of Miss Mary Saunderson, and whether you treated her quite fairly."

"You devil, what do you mean?" roared Kennedy. He was running about in little circles and clasping at the solid blackness with both hands.

"Good-bye," said the mocking voice, and it was already at some distance. "I really do not think, Kennedy, even by your own showing that you did the right thing by that girl. There was only one little thing which you appeared not to know, and I can supply it. Miss Saunderson was engaged to a poor ungainly devil of a student, and his name was Julius Burger."

There was a rustle somewhere, the vague sound of a foot striking a stone, and then there fell silence upon that old Christian church—a stagnant, heavy silence which closed round Kennedy and shut him in like water round a drowning man.

Some two months afterwards the following paragraph made the round of the European Press:

"One of the most interesting discoveries of recent years is that of the new catacomb in Rome, which lies some distance to the east of the well-known vaults of St. Calixtus. The finding of this important burial-place, which is exceeding rich in most interesting early Christian remains, is due to the energy and sagacity of Dr. Julius Burger, the young German specialist, who is rapidly taking the first place as an authority upon ancient Rome. Although the first to publish his discovery, it appears that a less fortunate adventurer had anticipated Dr. Burger. Some months ago Mr. Kennedy, the well-known English student, disappeared suddenly from his rooms in the Corso, and it was conjectured that his association with a recent scandal had driven him to leave Rome. It appears now that he had in reality fallen a victim to that fervid love of archaeology which had raised him to a distinguished place among living scholars. His body was discovered in the heart of the new catacomb, and it was evident from the condition of his feet and boots that he had tramped for days through the tortuous corridors which make these subterranean tombs so dangerous to explorers. The deceased gentleman had, with inexplicable rashness, made his way into this labyrinth without, as far as can be discovered, taking with him either candles or matches, so that his sad fate was the natural result of his own temerity. What makes the matter more painful is that Dr. Julius Burger was an intimate friend of the deceased. His joy at the extraordinary find which he has been so fortunate as to make has been greatly marred by the terrible fate of his comrade and fellow-worker."

The Case of Lady Sannox

The relations between Douglas Stone and the notorious Lady Sannox were very well known both among the fashionable circles of which she was a brilliant member, and the scientific bodies which numbered him among their most illustrious confreres. There was naturally, therefore, a very widespread interest when it was announced one morning that the lady had absolutely and for ever taken the veil, and that the world would see her no more. When, at the very tail of this rumour, there came the assurance that the celebrated operating surgeon, the man of steel nerves, had been found in the morning by his valet, seated on one side of his bed, smiling pleasantly upon the universe, with both legs jammed into one side of his breeches and his great brain about as valuable as a cap full of porridge, the matter was strong enough to give quite a little thrill of interest to folk who had never hoped that their jaded nerves were capable of such a sensation.

Douglas Stone in his prime was one of the most remarkable men in England. Indeed, he could hardly be said to have ever reached his prime, for he was but nine-and-thirty at the time of this little incident. Those who knew him best were aware that famous as he was as a surgeon, he might have succeeded with even greater rapidity in any of a dozen lines of life. He could have cut his way to fame as a soldier, struggled to it as an explorer, bullied for it in the courts, or built it out of stone and iron as an engineer. He was born to be great, for he could plan what another man dare not do, and he could do what another man dare not plan. In surgery none could follow him. His nerve, his judgement, his intuition, were things apart. Again and again his knife cut away death, but grazed the very springs of life in doing it, until his assistants were as white as the patient. His energy, his audacity, his full-blooded self-confidence—does not the memory of them still linger to the south of Marylebone Road and the north of Oxford Street?

43

His vices were as magnificent as his virtues, and infinitely more picturesque. Large as was his income, and it was the third largest of all professional men in London, it was far beneath the luxury of his living. Deep in his complex nature lay a rich vein of sensualism, at the sport of which he placed all the prizes of his life. The eye, the ear, the touch, the palate, all were his masters. The bouquet of old vintages, the scent of rare exotics, the curves and tints of the daintiest potteries of Europe, it was to these that the quick-running stream of gold was transformed. And then there came his sudden mad passion for Lady Sannox, when a single interview with two challenging glances and a whispered word set him ablaze. She was the loveliest woman in London and the only one to him. He was one of the handsomest men in London, but not the only one to her. She had a liking for new experiences, and was gracious to most men who wooed her. It may have been cause or it may have been effect that Lord Sannox looked fifty, though he was but six-and-thirty.

He was a quiet, silent, neutral-tinted man, this lord, with thin lips and heavy eyelids, much given to gardening, and full of home-like habits. He had at one time been fond of acting, had even rented a theatre in London, and on its boards had first seen Miss Marion Dawson, to whom he had offered his hand, his title, and the third of a county. Since his marriage his early hobby had become distasteful to him. Even in private theatricals it was no longer possible to persuade him to exercise the talent which he had often showed that he possessed. He was happier with a spud and a watering-can among his orchids and chrysanthemums.

It was quite an interesting problem whether he was absolutely devoid of sense, or miserably wanting in spirit. Did he know his lady's ways and condone them, or was he a mere blind, doting fool? It was a point to be discussed over the teacups in snug little drawing-rooms, or with the aid of a cigar in the bow windows of clubs. Bitter and plain were the comments among men upon his conduct. There was but one who had a good word to say for him, and he was the most silent member in the smoking-room. He had seen him break in a horse at the University, and it seemed to have left an impression upon his mind.

But when Douglas Stone became the favourite all doubts as to Lord Sannox's knowledge or ignorance were set for ever at rest.

There was no subterfuge about Stone. In his high-handed, impetuous fashion, he set all caution and discretion at defiance. The scandal became notorious. A learned body intimated that his name had been struck from the list of its vice-presidents. Two friends implored him to consider his professional credit. He cursed them all three, and spent forty guineas on a bangle to take with him to the lady. He was at her house every evening, and she drove in his carriage in the afternoons. There was not an attempt on either side to conceal their relations; but there came at last a little incident to interrupt them.

It was a dismal winter's night, very cold and gusty, with the wind whooping in the chimneys and blustering against the window-panes. A thin spatter of rain tinkled on the glass with each fresh sough of the gale, drowning for the instant the dull gurgle and drip from the eaves. Douglas Stone had finished his dinner, and sat by his fire in the study, a glass of rich port upon the malachite table at his elbow. As he raised it to his lips, he held it up against the lamplight, and watched with the eye of a connoisseur the tiny scales of beeswing which floated in its rich ruby depths. The fire, as it spurted up, threw fitful lights upon his bald, clear-cut face, with its widely-opened grey eyes, its thick and yet firm lips, and the deep, square jaw, which had something Roman in its strength and its animalism. He smiled from time to time as he nestled back in his luxurious chair. Indeed, he had a right to feel well pleased, for, against the advice of six colleagues, he had performed an operation that day of which only two cases were on record, and the result had been brilliant beyond all expectation. No other man in London would have had the daring to plan, or the skill to execute, such a heroic measure.

But he had promised Lady Sannox to see her that evening and it was already half-past eight. His hand was outstretched to the bell to order the carriage when he heard the dull thud of the knocker. An instant later there was the shuffling of feet in the hall, and the sharp closing of a door.

"A patient to see you, sir, in the consulting room," said the butler.

"About himself?"

"No, sir; I think he wants you to go out."

"It is too late," cried Douglas Stone peevishly. "I won't go."

"This is his card, sir."

The butler presented it upon the gold salver which had been given to his master by the wife of a Prime Minister.

"'Hamil Ali, Smyrna.' Hum! The fellow is a Turk, I suppose."

"Yes, sir. He seems as if he came from abroad, sir. And he's in a terrible way."

"Tut, tut! I have an engagement. I must go somewhere else. But I'll see him. Show him in here, Pim."

A few moments later the butler swung open the door and ushered in a small and decrepit man, who walked with a bent back and with the forward push of the face and blink of the eyes which goes with extreme short sight. His face was swarthy, and his hair and beard of the deepest black. In one hand he held a turban of white muslin striped with red, in the other a small chamois-leather bag.

"Good evening," said Douglas Stone, when the butler had closed the door. "You speak English, I presume?"

"Yes, sir. I am from Asia Minor, but I speak English when I speak slow."

"You wanted me to go out, I understand?"

"Yes, sir. I wanted very much that you should see my wife."

"I could come in the morning, but I have an engagement which prevents me from seeing your wife tonight."

The Turk's answer was a singular one. He pulled the string which closed the mouth of the chamois-leather bag, and poured a flood of gold on to the table.

"There are one hundred pounds there," said he, "and I promise you that it will not take you an hour. I have a cab ready at the door."

Douglas Stone glanced at his watch. An hour would not make it too late to visit Lady Sannox. He had been there later. And the fee was an extraordinarily high one. He had been pressed by his creditors lately, and he could not afford to let such a chance pass. He would go.

"What is the case?" he asked.

"Oh, it is so sad a one! So sad a one! You have not, perhaps heard of the daggers of the Almohades?"

"Never."

"Ah, they are Eastern daggers of a great age and of a singular shape, with the hilt like what you call a stirrup. I am a curiosity dealer, you understand, and that is why I have come to England from Smyrna, but next week I go back once more. Many things I brought with me, and I have a few things left, but among them, to my sorrow, is one of these daggers."

"You will remember that I have an appointment, sir," said the surgeon, with some irritation; "pray confine yourself to the necessary details."

"You will see that it is necessary. Today my wife fell down in a faint in the room in which I keep my wares, and she cut her lower lip upon this cursed dagger of Almohades."

"I see," said Douglas Stone, rising. "And you wish me to dress the wound?"

"No, no, it is worse than that."

"What then?"

"These daggers are poisoned."

"Poisoned!"

"Yes, and there is no man, East or West, who can tell now what is the poison or what the cure. But all that is known I know, for my father was in this trade before me, and we have had much to do with these poisoned weapons."

"What are the symptoms?"

"Deep sleep, and death in thirty hours."

"And you say there is no cure. Why then should you pay me this considerable fee?"

"No drug can cure, but the knife may."

"And how?"

"The poison is slow of absorption. It remains for hours in the wound."

"Washing, then, might cleanse it?"

"No more than in a snake bite. It is too subtle and too deadly."

"Excision of the wound, then?"

"That is it. If it be on the finger, take the finger off. So said my father always. But think of where this wound is, and that it is my wife. It is dreadful!"

But familiarity with such grim matters may take the finer edge from a man's sympathy. To Douglas Stone this was already an interesting case, and he brushed aside as irrelevant the feeble objections of the husband.

"It appears to be that or nothing," said he brusquely. "It is better to loose a lip than a life."

"Ah, yes, I know that you are right. Well, well, it is kismet, and it must be faced. I have the cab, and you will come with me and do this thing."

Douglas Stone took his case of bistouries from a drawer, and placed it with a roll of bandage and a compress of lint in his pocket. He must waste no more time if he were to see Lady Sannox.

"I am ready," said he, pulling on his overcoat. "Will you take a glass of wine before you go out into this cold air?"

His visitor shrank away, with a protesting hand upraised.

"You forget that I am a Mussulman, and a true follower of the Prophet," said he. "But tell me what is the bottle of green glass which you have placed in your pocket?"

"It is chloroform."

"Ah, that also is forbidden to us. It is a spirit, and we make no use of such things."

"What! You would allow your wife to go through an operation without an anaesthetic?"

"Ah! she will feel nothing, poor soul. The deep sleep has already come on, which is the first working of the poison. And then I have given her of our Smyrna opium. Come, sir, for already an hour has passed."

As they stepped out into the darkness, a sheet of rain was driven in upon their faces, and the hall lamp, which dangled from the arm of a marble Caryatid, went out with a fluff. Pim, the butler, pushed the heavy door to, straining hard with his shoulder against the wind, while the two men groped their way towards the yellow glare which showed where the cab was waiting. An instant later they were rattling upon their journey.

"Is it far?" asked Douglas Stone.

"Oh, no. We have a very little quiet place off the Euston Road."

The surgeon pressed the spring of his repeater and listened to the little tings which told him the hour. It was a quarter past nine. He calculated the distances, and the short time which it would take him to perform so trivial an operation. He ought to reach Lady Sannox by ten o'clock. Through the fogged windows he saw the blurred gas lamps dancing past, with occasionally the broader glare of a shop front. The rain was pelting and rattling upon the leathern top of the carriage, and the wheels swashed as they rolled through puddle and mud. Opposite to him the white headgear of his companion gleamed faintly through the obscurity. The surgeon felt in his pockets and arranged his needles, his ligatures and his safety-pins, that no time might be wasted when they arrived. He chafed with impatience and drummed his foot upon the floor.

But the cab slowed down at last and pulled up. In an instant Douglas Stone was out, and the Smyrna merchant's toe was at his very heel.

"You can wait," said he to the driver.

It was a mean-looking house in a narrow and sordid street. The surgeon, who knew his London well, cast a swift glance into the shadows, but there was nothing distinctive—no shop, no movement, nothing but a double line of dull, flat-faced houses, a double stretch of wet flagstones which gleamed in the lamplight, and a double rush of water in the gutters which swirled and gurgled towards the sewer gratings. The door which faced them was blotched and discoloured, and a faint light in the fan pane above, it served to show the dust and the grime which covered it. Above in one of the bedroom windows, there was a dull yellow glimmer. The merchant knocked loudly, and, as he turned his dark face towards the light, Douglas Stone could see that it was contracted with anxiety. A bolt was drawn, and an elderly woman with a taper stood in the doorway, shielding the thin flame with her gnarled hand.

"Is all well?" gasped the merchant.

"She is as you left her, sir."

"She has not spoken?"

"No, she is in a deep sleep."

The merchant closed the door, and Douglas Stone walked down the narrow passage, glancing about him in some surprise as he did so. There was no oil-cloth, no mat, no hat-rack. Deep grey dust and heavy festoons of cobwebs met his eyes everywhere. Following the old woman up the winding stair, his firm footfall echoed harshly through the silent house. There was no carpet.

The bedroom was on the second landing. Douglas Stone followed the old nurse into it, with the merchant at his heels. Here, at least, there was furniture and to spare. The floor was littered and the corners piled with Turkish cabinets, inlaid tables, coats of chain mail, strange pipes, and grotesque weapons. A single small lamp stood upon a bracket on the wall. Douglas Stone took it down, and picking his way among the lumber, walked over to a couch in the corner, on which lay a woman dressed in the Turkish fashion, with yashmak and veil. The lower part of the face was exposed, and the surgeon saw a jagged cut which zigzagged along the border of the under lip.

"You will forgive the yashmak," said the Turk. "You know our views about women in the East."

But the surgeon was not thinking about the yashmak. This was no longer a woman to him. It was a case. He stooped and examined the wound carefully.

"There are no signs of irritation," said he. "We might delay the operation until local symptoms develop."

The husband wrung his hands in uncontrollable agitation.

"Oh! sir, sir," he cried. "Do not trifle. You do not know. It is deadly. I know, and I give you my assurance that an operation is absolutely necessary. Only the knife can save her."

"And yet I am inclined to wait," said Douglas Stone.

"That is enough," the Turk cried, angrily. "Every minute is of importance, and I cannot stand here and see my wife allowed to sink. It only remains for me to give you my thanks for having come, and to call in some other surgeon before it is too late."

Douglas Stone hesitated. To refund that hundred pounds was no pleasant matter. But of course if he left the case he must return the money. And if the Turk were right and the woman died, his position before a coroner might be an embarrassing one.

"You have had personal experience of this poison?" he asked.

"I have."

"And you assure me that an operation is needful."

"I swear it by all that I hold sacred."

"The disfigurement will be frightful."

"I can understand that the mouth will not be a pretty one to kiss."

Douglas Stone turned fiercely upon the man. The speech was a brutal one. But the Turk has his own fashion of talk and of thought, and there was no time for wrangling. Douglas Stone drew a bistoury from his case, opened it and felt the keen straight edge with his forefinger. Then he held the lamp closer to the bed. Two dark eyes were gazing up at him through the slit in the yashmak. They were all iris, and the pupil was hardly to be seen.

"You have given her a very heavy dose of opium."

"Yes, she has had a good dose."

He glanced again at the dark eyes which looked straight at his own. They were dull and lustreless, but, even as he gazed, a little shifting sparkle came into them, and the lips quivered.

"She is not absolutely unconscious," said he.

"Would it not be well to use the knife while it will be painless?"

The same thought had crossed the surgeon's mind. He grasped the wounded lip with his forceps, and with two swift cuts he took out a broad V-shaped piece. The woman sprang up on the couch with a dreadful gurgling scream. Her covering was torn from her face. It was a face that he knew. In spite of that protruding upper lip and that slobber of blood, it was a face that he knew, She kept on putting her hand up to the gap and screaming. Douglas Stone sat down at the foot of the couch with his knife and his forceps. The room was whirling round, and he had felt something go like a ripping seam behind his ear. A bystander would have said that his face was the more ghastly of the two. As in a dream, or as if he had been looking at something at the play, he was conscious that the Turk's hair and beard lay upon the table, and that Lord Sannox was leaning against the wall with his hand to his side, laughing silently. The screams had died away now, and the dreadful head had dropped back again upon the pillow, but Douglas Stone still sat motionless, and Lord Sannox still chuckled quietly to himself.

"It was really very necessary for Marion, this operation," said he, "not physically, but morally, you know, morally."

Douglas Stone stooped for yards and began to play with the fringe of the coverlet. His knife tinkled down upon the ground, but he still held the forceps and something more.

"I had long intended to make a little example," said Lord Sannox, suavely. "Your note of Wednesday miscarried, and I have it here in my pocket-book. I took some pains in carrying out my idea. The wound, by the way, was from nothing more dangerous than my signet ring."

He glanced keenly at his silent companion, and cocked the small revolver which he held in his coat pocket. But Douglas Stone was still picking at the coverlet.

"You see you have kept your appointment after all," said Lord Sannox.

And at that Douglas Stone began to laugh. He laughed long and loudly. But Lord Sannox did not laugh now. Something like fear sharpened and hardened his features. He walked from the room, and he walked on tiptoe. The old woman was waiting outside.

"Attend to your mistress when she awakes," said Lord Sannox.

Then he went down to the street. The cab was at the door, and the driver raised his hand to his hat.

"John," said Lord Sannox, "you will take the doctor home first. He will want leading downstairs, I think. Tell his butler that he has been taken ill at a case."

"Very good, sir."

"Then you can take Lady Sannox home."

"And how about yourself, sir?"

"Oh, my address for the next few months will be Hotel di Roma, Venice. Just see that the letters are sent on. And tell Stevens to exhibit all the purple chrysanthemums next Monday, and to wire me the result."

The Terror of Blue John Gap

The following narrative was found among the papers of Dr. James Hardcastle, who died of phthisis on February 4th, 1908, at 36, Upper Coventry Flats, South Kensington. Those who knew him best, while refusing to express an opinion upon this particular statement, are unanimous in asserting that he was a man of a sober and scientific turn of mind, absolutely devoid of imagination, and most unlikely to invent any abnormal series of events. The paper was contained in an envelope, which was docketed, "A Short Account of the Circumstances which occurred near Miss Allerton's Farm in North-West Derbyshire in the Spring of Last Year." The envelope was sealed, and on the other side was written in pencil—

DEAR SEATON,—

"It may interest, and perhaps pain you, to know that the incredulity with which you met my story has prevented me from ever opening my mouth upon the subject again. I leave this record after my death, and perhaps strangers may be found to have more confidence in me than my friend."

Inquiry has failed to elicit who this Seaton may have been. I may add that the visit of the deceased to Allerton's Farm, and the general nature of the alarm there, apart from his particular explanation, have been absolutely established. With this foreword I append his account exactly as he left it. It is in the form of a diary, some entries in which have been expanded, while a few have been erased.

April 17.—Already I feel the benefit of this wonderful upland air. The farm of the Allertons lies fourteen hundred and twenty feet above sea-level, so it may well be a bracing climate. Beyond the usual morning cough I have very little discomfort, and, what with the fresh milk and the home-grown mutton, I have every chance of putting on weight. I think Saunderson will be pleased.

The two Miss Allertons are charmingly quaint and kind, two dear little hard-working old maids, who are ready to lavish all the heart which might have gone out to husband and to children upon an invalid stranger. Truly, the old maid is a most useful person, one of the reserve forces of the community. They talk of the superfluous woman, but what would the poor superfluous man do without her kindly presence? By the way, in their simplicity they very quickly let out the reason why Saunderson recommended their farm. The Professor rose from the ranks himself, and I believe that in his youth he was not above scaring crows in these very fields.

It is a most lonely spot, and the walks are picturesque in the extreme. The farm consists of grazing land lying at the bottom of an irregular valley. On each side are the fantastic limestone hills, formed of rock so soft that you can break it away with your hands. All this country is hollow. Could you strike it with some gigantic hammer it would boom like a drum, or possibly cave in altogether and expose some huge subterranean sea. A great sea there must surely be, for on all sides the streams run into the mountain itself, never to reappear. There are gaps everywhere amid the rocks, and when you pass through them you find yourself in great caverns, which wind down into the bowels of the earth. I have a small bicycle lamp, and it is a perpetual joy to me to carry it into these weird solitudes, and to see the wonderful silver and black effect when I throw its light upon the stalactites which drape the lofty roofs. Shut off the lamp, and you are in the blackest darkness. Turn it on, and it is a scene from the Arabian Nights.

But there is one of these strange openings in the earth which has a special interest, for it is the handiwork, not of nature, but of man. I had never heard of Blue John when I came to these parts. It is the name given to a peculiar mineral of a beautiful purple shade, which is only found at one or two places in the world. It is so rare that an ordinary vase of Blue John would be valued at a great price. The Romans, with that extraordinary instinct of theirs, discovered that it was to be found in this valley, and sank a horizontal shaft deep into the mountain side. The opening of their mine has been called Blue John Gap, a clean-cut arch in the rock, the mouth all overgrown with bushes. It is a goodly passage which the Roman miners have cut, and it intersects some of the great water-worn caves, so that if you enter Blue John Gap you would do well to mark your steps and to have a good store of candles, or you may never make your way back to the daylight again. I have not yet gone deeply into it, but this very day I stood at the mouth of the arched tunnel, and peering down into the black recesses beyond, I vowed that when my health returned I would devote some holiday to exploring those mysterious depths and finding out for myself how far the Roman had penetrated into the Derbyshire hills.

Strange how superstitious these countrymen are! I should have thought better of young Armitage, for he is a man of some education and character, and a very fine fellow for his station in life. I was standing at the Blue John Gap when he came across the field to me.

"Well, doctor," said he, "you're not afraid, anyhow."

"Afraid!" I answered. "Afraid of what?"

"Of it," said he, with a jerk of his thumb towards the black vault, "of the Terror that lives in the Blue John Cave."

How absurdly easy it is for a legend to arise in a lonely countryside! I examined him as to the reasons for his weird belief. It seems that from time to time sheep have been missing from the fields, carried bodily away, according to Armitage. That they could have wandered away of their own accord and disappeared among the mountains was an explanation to which he would not listen. On one occasion a pool of blood had been found, and some tufts of wool. That also, I pointed out, could be explained in a perfectly natural way. Further, the nights upon which sheep disappeared were invariably very dark, cloudy nights with no moon. This I met with the obvious retort that those were the nights which a commonplace sheep-stealer would naturally choose for his work. On one occasion a gap had been made in a wall, and some of the stones scattered for a considerable distance. Human agency again, in my opinion. Finally, Armitage clinched all his arguments by telling me that he had actually heard the Creature—indeed, that anyone could hear it who remained long enough at the Gap. It was a distant roaring of an immense volume. I could not but smile at this, knowing, as I do, the strange reverberations which come out of an underground water system running amid the chasms of a limestone formation. My incredulity annoyed Armitage so that he turned and left me with some abruptness.

And now comes the queer point about the whole business. I was still standing near the mouth of the cave turning over in my mind the various statements of Armitage, and reflecting how readily they could be explained away, when suddenly, from the depth of the tunnel beside me, there issued a most extraordinary sound. How shall I describe it? First of all, it seemed to be a great distance away, far down in the bowels of the earth. Secondly, in spite of this suggestion of distance, it was very loud. Lastly, it was not a boom, nor a crash, such as one would associate with falling water or tumbling rock, but it was a high whine, tremulous and vibrating, almost like the whinnying of a horse. It was certainly a most remarkable experience, and one which for a moment, I must admit, gave a new significance to Armitage's words. I waited by the Blue John Gap for half an hour or more, but there was no return of the sound, so at last I wandered back to the farmhouse, rather mystified by what had occurred. Decidedly I shall explore that cavern when my strength is restored. Of course, Armitage's explanation is too absurd for discussion, and yet that sound was certainly very strange. It still rings in my ears as I write.

April 20.—In the last three days I have made several expeditions to the Blue John Gap, and have even penetrated some short distance, but my bicycle lantern is so small and weak that I dare not trust myself very far. I shall do the thing more systematically. I have heard no sound at all, and could almost believe that I had been the victim of some hallucination suggested, perhaps, by Armitage's conversation. Of course, the whole idea is absurd, and yet I must confess that those bushes at the entrance of the cave do present an appearance as if some heavy creature had forced its way through them. I begin to be keenly interested. I have said nothing to the Miss Allertons, for they are quite superstitious enough already, but I have bought some candles, and mean to investigate for myself.

I observed this morning that among the numerous tufts of sheep's wool which lay among the bushes near the cavern there was one which was smeared with blood. Of course, my reason tells me that if sheep wander into such rocky places they are likely to injure themselves, and yet somehow that splash of crimson gave me a sudden shock, and for a moment I found myself shrinking back in horror from the old Roman arch. A fetid breath seemed to ooze from the black depths into which I peered. Could it indeed be possible that some nameless thing, some dreadful presence, was lurking down yonder? I should have been incapable of such feelings in the days of my strength, but one grows more nervous and fanciful when one's health is shaken.

For the moment I weakened in my resolution, and was ready to leave the secret of the old mine, if one exists, for ever unsolved. But tonight my interest has returned and my nerves grown more steady. Tomorrow I trust that I shall have gone more deeply into this matter.

April 22.—Let me try and set down as accurately as I can my extraordinary experience of yesterday. I started in the afternoon, and made my way to the Blue John Gap. I confess that my misgivings returned as I gazed into its depths, and I wished that I had brought a companion to share my exploration. Finally, with a return of resolution, I lit my candle, pushed my way through the briars, and descended into the rocky shaft.

It went down at an acute angle for some fifty feet, the floor being covered with broken stone. Thence there extended a long, straight passage cut in the solid rock. I am no geologist, but the lining of this corridor was certainly of some harder material than limestone, for there were points where I could actually see the tool-marks which the old miners had left in their excavation, as fresh as if they had been done yesterday. Down this strange, old-world corridor I stumbled, my feeble flame throwing a dim circle of light around me, which made the shadows beyond the more threatening and obscure. Finally, I came to a spot where the Roman tunnel opened into a water-worn cavern—a huge hall, hung with long white icicles of lime deposit. From this central chamber I could dimly perceive that a number of passages worn by the subterranean streams wound away into the depths of the earth. I was standing there wondering whether I had better return, or whether I dare venture farther into this dangerous labyrinth, when my eyes fell upon something at my feet which strongly arrested my attention.

The greater part of the floor of the cavern was covered with boulders of rock or with hard incrustations of lime, but at this particular point there had been a drip from the distant roof, which had left a patch of soft mud. In the very centre of this there was a huge mark—an ill-defined blotch, deep, broad and irregular, as if a great boulder had fallen upon it. No loose stone lay near, however, nor was there anything to account for the impression. It was far too large to be caused by any possible animal, and besides, there was only the one, and the patch of mud was of such a size that no reasonable stride could have covered it. As I rose from the examination of that singular mark and then looked round into the black shadows which hemmed me in, I must confess that I felt for a moment a most unpleasant sinking of my heart, and that, do what I could, the candle trembled in my outstretched hand.

I soon recovered my nerve, however, when I reflected how absurd it was to associate so huge and shapeless a mark with the track of any known animal. Even an elephant could not have produced it. I determined, therefore, that I would not be scared by vague and senseless fears from carrying out my exploration. Before proceeding, I took good note of a curious rock formation in the wall by which I could recognize the entrance of the Roman tunnel. The precaution was very necessary, for the great cave, so far as I could see it, was intersected by passages. Having made sure of my position, and reassured myself by examining my spare candles and my matches, I advanced slowly over the rocky and uneven surface of the cavern.

And now I come to the point where I met with such sudden and desperate disaster. A stream, some twenty feet broad, ran across my path, and I walked for some little distance along the bank to find a spot where I could cross dry-shod. Finally, I came to a place where a single flat boulder lay near the centre, which I could reach in a stride. As it chanced, however, the rock had been cut away and made top-heavy by the rush of the stream, so that it tilted over as I landed on it and shot me into the ice-cold water. My candle went out, and I found myself floundering about in utter and absolute darkness.

I staggered to my feet again, more amused than alarmed by my adventure. The candle had fallen from my hand, and was lost in the stream, but I had two others in my pocket, so that it was of no importance. I got one of them ready, and drew out my box of matches to light it. Only then did I realize my position. The box had been soaked in my fall into the river. It was impossible to strike the matches.

A cold hand seemed to close round my heart as I realized my position. The darkness was opaque and horrible. It was so utter one put one's hand up to one's face as if to press off something solid. I stood still, and by an effort I steadied myself. I tried to reconstruct in my mind a map of the floor of the cavern as I had last seen it. Alas! the bearings which had impressed themselves upon my mind were high on the wall, and not to be found by touch. Still, I remembered in a general way how the sides were situated, and I hoped that by groping my way along them I should at last come to the opening of the Roman tunnel. Moving very slowly, and continually striking against the rocks, I set out on this desperate quest.

But I very soon realized how impossible it was. In that black, velvety darkness one lost all one's bearings in an instant. Before I had made a dozen paces, I was utterly bewildered as to my whereabouts. The rippling of the stream, which was the one sound audible, showed me where it lay, but the moment that I left its bank I was utterly lost. The idea of finding my way back in absolute darkness through that limestone labyrinth was clearly an impossible one.

I sat down upon a boulder and reflected upon my unfortunate plight. I had not told anyone that I proposed to come to the Blue John mine, and it was unlikely that a search party would come after me. Therefore I must trust to my own resources to get clear of the danger. There was only one hope, and that was that the matches might dry. When I fell into the river, only half of me had got thoroughly wet. My left shoulder had remained above the water. I took the box of matches, therefore, and put it into my left armpit. The moist air of the cavern might possibly be counteracted by the heat of my body, but even so, I knew that I could not hope to get a light for many hours. Meanwhile there was nothing for it but to wait.

By good luck I had slipped several biscuits into my pocket before I left the farm-house. These I now devoured, and washed them down with a draught from that wretched stream which had been the cause of all my misfortunes. Then I felt about for a comfortable seat among the rocks, and, having discovered a place where I could get a support for my back, I stretched out my legs and settled myself down to wait. I was wretchedly damp and cold, but I tried to cheer myself with the reflection that modern science prescribed open windows and walks in all weather for my disease. Gradually, lulled by the monotonous gurgle of the stream, and by the absolute darkness, I sank into an uneasy slumber.

How long this lasted I cannot say. It may have been for an hour, it may have been for several. Suddenly I sat up on my rock couch, with every nerve thrilling and every sense acutely on the alert. Beyond all doubt I had heard a sound—some sound very distinct from the gurgling of the waters. It had passed, but the reverberation of it still lingered in my ear. Was it a search party? They would most certainly have shouted, and vague as this sound was which had wakened me, it was very distinct from the human voice. I sat palpitating and hardly daring to breathe. There it was again! And again! Now it had become continuous. It was a tread—yes, surely it was the tread of some living creature. But what a tread it was! It gave one the impression of enormous weight carried upon sponge-like feet, which gave forth a muffled but ear-filling sound. The darkness was as complete as ever, but the tread was regular and decisive. And it was coming beyond all question in my direction.

My skin grew cold, and my hair stood on end as I listened to that steady and ponderous footfall. There was some creature there, and surely by the speed of its advance, it was one which could see in the dark. I crouched low on my rock and tried to blend myself into it. The steps grew nearer still, then stopped, and presently I was aware of a loud lapping and gurgling. The creature was drinking at the stream. Then again there was silence, broken by a succession of long sniffs and snorts of tremendous volume and energy. Had it caught the scent of me? My own nostrils were filled by a low fetid odour, mephitic and abominable. Then I heard the steps again. They were on my side of the stream now. The stones rattled within a few yards of where I lay. Hardly daring to breathe, I crouched upon my rock. Then the steps drew away. I heard the splash as it returned across the river, and the sound died away into the distance in the direction from which it had come.

For a long time I lay upon the rock, too much horrified to move. I thought of the sound which I had heard coming from the depths of the cave, of Armitage's fears, of the strange impression in the mud, and now came this final and absolute proof that there was indeed some inconceivable monster, something utterly unearthly and dreadful, which lurked in the hollow of the mountain. Of its nature or form I could frame no conception, save that it was both light-footed and gigantic. The combat between my reason, which told me that such things could not be, and my senses, which told me that they were, raged within me as I lay. Finally, I was almost ready to persuade myself that this experience had been part of some evil dream, and that my abnormal condition might have conjured up an hallucination. But there remained one final experience which removed the last possibility of doubt from my mind.

I had taken my matches from my armpit and felt them. They seemed perfectly hard and dry. Stooping down into a crevice of the rocks, I tried one of them. To my delight it took fire at once. I lit the candle, and, with a terrified backward glance into the obscure depths of the cavern, I hurried in the direction of the Roman passage. As I did so I passed the patch of mud on which I had seen the huge imprint. Now I stood astonished before it, for there were three similar imprints upon its surface, enormous in size, irregular in outline, of a depth which indicated the ponderous weight which had left them. Then a great terror surged over me. Stooping and shading my candle with my hand, I ran in a frenzy of fear to the rocky archway, hastened up it, and never stopped until, with weary feet and panting lungs, I rushed up the final slope of stones, broke through the tangle of briars, and flung myself exhausted upon the soft grass under the peaceful light of the stars. It was three in the morning when I reached the farmhouse, and today I am all unstrung and quivering after my terrific adventure. As yet I have told no one. I must move warily in the matter. What would the poor lonely women, or the uneducated yokels here think of it if I were to tell them my experience? Let me go to someone who can understand and advise.

April 25.—I was laid up in bed for two days after my incredible adventure in the cavern. I use the adjective with a very definite meaning, for I have had an experience since which has shocked me almost as much as the other. I have said that I was looking round for someone who could advise me. There is a Dr. Mark Johnson who practices some few miles away, to whom I had a note of recommendation from Professor Saunderson. To him I drove, when I was strong enough to get about, and I recounted to him my whole strange experience. He listened intently, and then carefully examined me, paying special attention to my reflexes and to the pupils of my eyes. When he had finished, he refused to discuss my adventure, saying that it was entirely beyond him, but he gave me the card of a Mr. Picton at Castleton, with the advice that I should instantly go to him and tell him the story exactly as I had done to himself. He was, according to my adviser, the very man who was pre-eminently suited to help me. I went on to the station, therefore, and made my way to the little town, which is some ten miles away. Mr. Picton appeared to be a man of importance, as his brass plate was displayed upon the door of a considerable building on the outskirts of the town. I was about to ring his bell, when some misgiving came into my mind, and, crossing to a neighbouring shop, I asked the man behind the counter if he could tell me anything of Mr. Picton. "Why," said he, "he is the best mad doctor in Derbyshire, and yonder is his asylum." You can imagine that it was not long before I had shaken the dust of Castleton from my feet and returned to the farm, cursing all unimaginative pedants who cannot conceive that there may be things in creation which have never yet chanced to come across their mole's vision. After all, now that I am cooler, I can afford to admit that I have been no more sympathetic to Armitage than Dr. Johnson has been to me.

April 27. When I was a student I had the reputation of being a man of courage and enterprise. I remember that when there was a ghost-hunt at Coltbridge it was I who sat up in the haunted house. Is it advancing years (after all, I am only thirty-five), or is it this physical malady which has caused degeneration? Certainly my heart quails when I think of that horrible cavern in the hill, and the certainty that it has some monstrous occupant. What shall I do? There is not an hour in the day that I do not debate the question. If I say nothing, then the mystery remains unsolved. If I do say anything, then I have the alternative of mad alarm over the whole countryside, or of absolute incredulity which may end in consigning me to an asylum. On the whole, I think that my best course is to wait, and to prepare for some expedition which shall be more deliberate and better thought out than the last. As a first step I have been to Castleton and obtained a few essentials—a large acetylene lantern for one thing, and a good double-barrelled sporting rifle for another. The latter I have hired, but I have bought a dozen heavy game cartridges, which would bring down a rhinoceros. Now I am ready for my troglodyte friend. Give me better health and a little spate of energy, and I shall try conclusions with him yet. But who and what is he? Ah! there is the question which stands between me and my sleep. How many theories do I form, only to discard each in turn! It is all so utterly unthinkable. And yet the cry, the footmark, the tread in the cavern—no reasoning can get past these I think of the old-world legends of dragons and of other monsters. Were they, perhaps, not such fairy-tales as we have thought? Can it be that there is some fact which underlies them, and am I, of all mortals, the one who is chosen to expose it?

May 3.—For several days I have been laid up by the vagaries of an English spring, and during those days there have been developments, the true and sinister meaning of which no one can appreciate save myself. I may say that we have had cloudy and moonless nights of late, which according to my information were

the seasons upon which sheep disappeared. Well, sheep have disappeared. Two of Miss Allerton's, one of old Pearson's of the Cat
Walk, and one of Mrs. Moulton's. Four in all during three nights.
No trace is left of them at all, and the countryside is buzzing with
rumours of gipsies and of sheep-stealers.

But there is something more serious than that. Young Armitage
has disappeared also. He left his moorland cottage early on Wednesday night and has never been heard of since. He was an unattached
man, so there is less sensation than would otherwise be the case.
The popular explanation is that he owes money, and has found a situation in some other part of the country, whence he will presently
write for his belongings. But I have grave misgivings. Is it not much
more likely that the recent tragedy of the sheep has caused him to
take some steps which may have ended in his own destruction? He
may, for example, have lain in wait for the creature and been carried
off by it into the recesses of the mountains. What an inconceivable
fate for a civilized Englishman of the twentieth century! And yet I
feel that it is possible and even probable. But in that case, how far
am I answerable both for his death and for any other mishap which
may occur? Surely with the knowledge I already possess it must be
my duty to see that something is done, or if necessary to do it
myself. It must be the latter, for this morning I went down to the
local police-station and told my story. The inspector entered it all in
a large book and bowed me out with commendable gravity, but I
heard a burst of laughter before I had got down his garden path. No
doubt he was recounting my adventure to his family.

June 10.—I am writing this, propped up in bed, six weeks
after my last entry in this journal. I have gone through a terrible
shock both to mind and body, arising from such an experience as
has seldom befallen a human being before. But I have attained my
end. The danger from the Terror which dwells in the Blue John
Gap has passed never to return. Thus much at least I, a broken
invalid, have done for the common good. Let me now recount
what occurred as clearly as I may.

The night of Friday, May 3rd, was dark and cloudy—the very
night for the monster to walk. About eleven o'clock I went from
the farm-house with my lantern and my rifle, having first left a

note upon the table of my bedroom in which I said that, if I were missing, search should be made for me in the direction of the Gap. I made my way to the mouth of the Roman shaft, and, having perched myself among the rocks close to the opening, I shut off my lantern and waited patiently with my loaded rifle ready to my hand.

It was a melancholy vigil. All down the winding valley I could see the scattered lights of the farm-houses, and the church clock of Chapel-le-Dale tolling the hours came faintly to my ears. These tokens of my fellow-men served only to make my own position seem the more lonely, and to call for a greater effort to overcome the terror which tempted me continually to get back to the farm, and abandon for ever this dangerous quest. And yet there lies deep in every man a rooted self-respect which makes it hard for him to turn back from that which he has once undertaken. This feeling of personal pride was my salvation now, and it was that alone which held me fast when every instinct of my nature was dragging me away. I am glad now that I had the strength. In spite of all that is has cost me, my manhood is at least above reproach.

Twelve o'clock struck in the distant church, then one, then two. It was the darkest hour of the night. The clouds were drifting low, and there was not a star in the sky. An owl was hooting somewhere among the rocks, but no other sound, save the gentle sough of the wind, came to my ears. And then suddenly I heard it! From far away down the tunnel came those muffled steps, so soft and yet so ponderous. I heard also the rattle of stones as they gave way under that giant tread. They drew nearer. They were close upon me. I heard the crashing of the bushes round the entrance, and then dimly through the darkness I was conscious of the loom of some enormous shape, some monstrous inchoate creature, passing swiftly and very silently out from the tunnel. I was paralysed with fear and amazement. Long as I had waited, now that it had actually come I was unprepared for the shock. I lay motionless and breathless, whilst the great dark mass whisked by me and was swallowed up in the night.

But now I nerved myself for its return. No sound came from the sleeping countryside to tell of the horror which was loose. In no way could I judge how far off it was, what it was doing, or when it might be back. But not a second time should my nerve fail me, not a second time should it pass unchallenged. I swore it between my clenched teeth as I laid my cocked rifle across the rock.

And yet it nearly happened. There was no warning of approach now as the creature passed over the grass. Suddenly, like a dark, drifting shadow, the huge bulk loomed up once more before me, making for the entrance of the cave. Again came that paralysis of volition which held my crooked forefinger impotent upon the trigger. But with a desperate effort I shook it off. Even as the brushwood rustled, and the monstrous beast blended with the shadow of the Gap, I fired at the retreating form. In the blaze of the gun I caught a glimpse of a great shaggy mass, something with rough and bristling hair of a withered grey colour, fading away to white in its lower parts, the huge body supported upon short, thick, curving legs. I had just that glance, and then I heard the rattle of the stones as the creature tore down into its burrow. In an instant, with a triumphant revulsion of feeling, I had cast my fears to the wind, and uncovering my powerful lantern, with my rifle in my hand, I sprang down from my rock and rushed after the monster down the old Roman shaft.

My splendid lamp cast a brilliant flood of vivid light in front of me, very different from the yellow glimmer which had aided me down the same passage only twelve days before. As I ran, I saw the great beast lurching along before me, its huge bulk filling up the whole space from wall to wall. Its hair looked like coarse faded oakum, and hung down in long, dense masses which swayed as it moved. It was like an enormous unclipped sheep in its fleece, but in size it was far larger than the largest elephant, and its breadth seemed to be nearly as great as its height. It fills me with amazement now to think that I should have dared to follow such a horror into the bowels of the earth, but when one's blood is up, and when one's quarry seems to be flying, the old primeval hunting-spirit awakes and prudence is cast to the wind. Rifle in hand, I ran at the top of my speed upon the trail of the monster.

I had seen that the creature was swift. Now I was to find out to my cost that it was also very cunning. I had imagined that it was in panic flight, and that I had only to pursue it. The idea that it might turn upon me never entered my excited brain. I have already explained that the passage down which I was racing opened into a great central cave. Into this I rushed, fearful lest I should lose all trace of the beast. But he had turned upon his own traces, and in a moment we were face to face.

That picture, seen in the brilliant white light of the lantern, is etched for ever upon my brain. He had reared up on his hind legs as a bear would do, and stood above me, enormous, menacing—such a creature as no nightmare had ever brought to my imagination. I have said that he reared like a bear, and there was something bear-like—if one could conceive a bear which was ten-fold the bulk of any bear seen upon earth—in his whole pose and attitude, in his great crooked forelegs with their ivory-white claws, in his rugged skin, and in his red, gaping mouth, fringed with monstrous fangs. Only in one point did he differ from the bear, or from any other creature which walks the earth, and even at that supreme moment a shudder of horror passed over me as I observed that the eyes which glistened in the glow of my lantern were huge, projecting bulbs, white and sightless. For a moment his great paws swung over my head. The next he fell forward upon me, I and my broken lantern crashed to the earth, and I remember no more.

When I came to myself I was back in the farm-house of the Allertons. Two days had passed since my terrible adventure in the Blue John Gap. It seems that I had lain all night in the cave insensible from concussion of the brain, with my left arm and two ribs badly fractured. In the morning my note had been found, a search party of a dozen farmers assembled, and I had been tracked down and carried back to my bedroom, where I had lain in high delirium ever since. There was, it seems, no sign of the creature, and no bloodstain which would show that my bullet had found him as he passed. Save for my own plight and the marks upon the mud, there was nothing to prove that what I said was true.

Six weeks have now elapsed, and I am able to sit out once more in the sunshine. Just opposite me is the steep hillside, grey with shaly rock, and yonder on its flank is the dark cleft which marks the opening of the Blue John Gap. But it is no longer a source of terror. Never again through that ill-omened tunnel shall any strange shape flit out into the world of men. The educated and the scientific, the Dr. Johnsons and the like, may smile at my narrative, but the poorer folk of the countryside had never a doubt as to its truth. On the day after my recovering consciousness they assembled in their hundreds round the Blue John Gap. As the Castleton Courier said:

"It was useless for our correspondent, or for any of the adventurous gentlemen who had come from Matlock, Buxton, and other parts, to offer to descend, to explore the cave to the end, and to finally test the extraordinary narrative of Dr. James Hardcastle. The country people had taken the matter into their own hands, and from an early hour of the morning they had worked hard in stopping up the entrance of the tunnel. There is a sharp slope where the shaft begins, and great boulders, rolled along by many willing hands, were thrust down it until the Gap was absolutely sealed. So ends the episode which has caused such excitement throughout the country. Local opinion is fiercely divided upon the subject. On the one hand are those who point to Dr. Hardcastle's impaired health, and to the possibility of cerebral lesions of tubercular origin giving rise to strange hallucinations. Some idee fixe, according to these gentlemen, caused the doctor to wander down the tunnel, and a fall among the rocks was sufficient to account for his injuries. On the other hand, a legend of a strange creature in the Gap has existed for some months back, and the farmers look upon Dr. Hardcastle's narrative and his personal injuries as a final corroboration. So the matter stands, and so the matter will continue to stand, for no definite solution seems to us to be now possible. It transcends human wit to give any scientific explanation which could cover the alleged facts."

Perhaps before the Courier published these words they would have been wise to send their representative to me. I have thought the matter out, as no one else has occasion to do, and it is possible that I might have removed some of the more obvious difficulties of the narrative and brought it one degree nearer to scientific acceptance. Let me then write down the only explanation which seems to me to elucidate what I know to my cost to have been a series of facts. My theory may seem to be wildly improbable, but at least no one can venture to say that it is impossible.

My view is—and it was formed, as is shown by my diary, before my personal adventure—that in this part of England there is a vast subterranean lake or sea, which is fed by the great number of streams which pass down through the limestone. Where there is a large collection of water there must also be some evaporation, mists or rain, and a possibility of vegetation. This in turn suggests that there may be animal life, arising, as the vegetable life would also do, from those seeds and types which had been introduced at an early period of the world's history, when communication with the outer air was more easy. This place had then developed a fauna and flora of its own, including such monsters as the one which I had seen, which may well have been the old cave-bear, enormously enlarged and modified by its new environment. For countless aeons the internal and the external creation had kept apart, growing steadily away from each other. Then there had come some rift in the depths of the mountain which had enabled one creature to wander up and, by means of the Roman tunnel, to reach the open air. Like all subterranean life, it had lost the power of sight, but this had no doubt been compensated for by nature in other directions. Certainly it had some means of finding its way about, and of hunting down the sheep upon the hillside. As to its choice of dark nights, it is part of my theory that light was painful to those great white eyeballs, and that it was only a pitch-black world which it could tolerate. Perhaps, indeed, it was the glare of my lantern which saved my life at that awful moment when we were face to face. So I read the riddle. I leave these facts behind me, and if you can explain them, do so; or if you choose to doubt them, do so. Neither your belief nor your incredulity can alter them, nor affect one whose task is nearly over.

So ended the strange narrative of Dr. James Hardcastle.

The Brazilian Cat

It is hard luck on a young fellow to have expensive tastes, great expectations, aristocratic connections, but no actual money in his pocket, and no profession by which he may earn any. The fact was that my father, a good, sanguine, easy-going man, had such confidence in the wealth and benevolence of his bachelor elder brother, Lord Southerton, that he took it for granted that I, his only son, would never be called upon to earn a living for myself. He imagined that if there were not a vacancy for me on the great Southerton Estates, at least there would be found some post in that diplomatic service which still remains the special preserve of our privileged classes. He died too early to realize how false his calculations had been. Neither my uncle nor the State took the slightest notice of me, or showed any interest in my career. An occasional brace of pheasants, or basket of hares, was all that ever reached me to remind me that I was heir to Otwell House and one of the richest estates in the country. In the meantime, I found myself a bachelor and man about town, living in a suite of apartments in Grosvenor Mansions, with no occupation save that of pigeon-shooting and polo-playing at Hurlingham. Month by month I realized that it was more and more difficult to get the brokers to renew my bills, or to cash any further post-obits upon an unentailed property. Ruin lay right across my path, and every day I saw it clearer, nearer, and more absolutely unavoidable.

What made me feel my own poverty the more was that, apart from the great wealth of Lord Southerton, all my other relations were fairly well-to-do. The nearest of these was Everard King, my father's nephew and my own first cousin, who had spent an adventurous life in Brazil, and had now returned to this country to settle down on his fortune. We never knew how he made his money, but he appeared to have plenty of it, for he bought the estate of Greylands, near Clipton-on-the-Marsh, in Suffolk. For the first year of his residence in England he took no more notice of me than my miserly uncle; but at last one summer morning, to my very great relief and joy, I received a letter asking me to come down that very day and spend a short visit at Greylands Court. I was expecting a rather long visit to Bankruptcy Court at the time, and this interruption seemed almost providential. If I could only get on terms with this unknown relative of mine, I might pull through yet. For the family credit he could not let me go entirely to the wall. I ordered my valet to pack my valise, and I set off the same evening for Clipton-on-the-Marsh.

After changing at Ipswich, a little local train deposited me at a small, deserted station lying amidst a rolling grassy country, with a sluggish and winding river curving in and out amidst the valleys, between high, silted banks, which showed that we were within reach of the tide. No carriage was awaiting me (I found afterwards that my telegram had been delayed), so I hired a dogcart at the local inn. The driver, an excellent fellow, was full of my relative's praises, and I learned from him that Mr. Everard King was already a name to conjure with in that part of the county. He had entertained the school-children, he had thrown his grounds open to visitors, he had subscribed to charities—in short, his benevolence had been so universal that my driver could only account for it on the supposition that he had parliamentary ambitions.

My attention was drawn away from my driver's panegyric by the appearance of a very beautiful bird which settled on a telegraph-post beside the road. At first I thought that it was a jay, but it was larger, with a brighter plumage. The driver accounted for its presence at once by saying that it belonged to the very man whom we were about to visit. It seems that the acclimatization of foreign creatures was one of his hobbies, and that he had brought with him from Brazil a number of birds and beasts which he was endeavouring to rear in England. When once we had passed the gates of Greylands Park we had ample evidence of this taste of his. Some small spotted deer, a curious wild pig known, I believe, as a peccary, a gorgeously feathered oriole, some sort of armadillo, and a singular lumbering in-toed beast like a very fat badger, were among the creatures which I observed as we drove along the winding avenue.

Mr. Everard King, my unknown cousin, was standing in person upon the steps of his house, for he had seen us in the distance, and guessed that it was I. His appearance was very homely and benevolent, short and stout, forty-five years old, perhaps, with a round, good-humoured face, burned brown with the tropical sun, and shot with a thousand wrinkles. He wore white linen clothes, in true planter style, with a cigar between his lips, and a large Panama hat upon the back of his head. It was such a figure as one associates with a verandahed bungalow, and it looked curiously out of place in front of this broad, stone English mansion, with its solid wings and its Palladio pillars before the doorway.

"My dear!" he cried, glancing over his shoulder; "my dear, here is our guest! Welcome, welcome to Greylands! I am delighted to make your acquaintance, Cousin Marshall, and I take it as a great compliment that you should honour this sleepy little country place with your presence."

Nothing could be more hearty than his manner, and he set me at my ease in an instant. But it needed all his cordiality to atone for the frigidity and even rudeness of his wife, a tall, haggard woman, who came forward at his summons. She was, I believe, of Brazilian extraction, though she spoke excellent English, and I excused her manners on the score of her ignorance of our customs. She did not attempt to conceal, however, either then or afterwards, that I was no very welcome visitor at Greylands Court. Her actual words were, as a rule, courteous, but she was the possessor of a pair of particularly expressive dark eyes, and I read in them very clearly from the first that she heartily wished me back in London once more.

However, my debts were too pressing and my designs upon my wealthy relative were too vital for me to allow them to be upset by the ill-temper of his wife, so I disregarded her coldness and reciprocated the extreme cordiality of his welcome. No pains had been spared by him to make me comfortable. My room was a charming one. He implored me to tell him anything which could add to my happiness. It was on the tip of my tongue to inform him that a blank cheque would materially help towards that end, but I felt that it might be premature in the present state of our acquaintance. The dinner was excellent, and as we sat together afterwards over his Havanas and coffee, which later he told me was specially prepared upon his own plantation, it seemed to me that all my driver's eulogies were justified, and that I had never met a more large-hearted and hospitable man.

But, in spite of his cheery good nature, he was a man with a strong will and a fiery temper of his own. Of this I had an example upon the following morning. The curious aversion which Mrs. Everard King had conceived towards me was so strong, that her manner at breakfast was almost offensive. But her meaning became unmistakable when her husband had quitted the room.

"The best train in the day is at twelve-fifteen," said she.

"But I was not thinking of going today," I answered, frankly—perhaps even defiantly, for I was determined not to be driven out by this woman.

"Oh, if it rests with you—" said she, and stopped with a most insolent expression in her eyes.

"I am sure," I answered, "that Mr. Everard King would tell me if I were outstaying my welcome."

"What's this? What's this?" said a voice, and there he was in the room. He had overheard my last words, and a glance at our faces had told him the rest. In an instant his chubby, cheery face set into an expression of absolute ferocity.

"Might I trouble you to walk outside, Marshall?" said he. (I may mention that my own name is Marshall King.)

He closed the door behind me, and then, for an instant, I heard him talking in a low voice of concentrated passion to his wife. This gross breach of hospitality had evidently hit upon his tenderest point. I am no eavesdropper, so I walked out on to the lawn. Presently I heard a hurried step behind me, and there was the lady, her face pale with excitement, and her eyes red with tears.

"My husband has asked me to apologize to you, Mr. Marshall King," said she, standing with downcast eyes before me.

"Please do not say another word, Mrs. King."

Her dark eyes suddenly blazed out at me.

"You fool!" she hissed, with frantic vehemence, and turning on her heel swept back to the house.

The insult was so outrageous, so insufferable, that I could only stand staring after her in bewilderment. I was still there when my host joined me. He was his cheery, chubby self once more.

"I hope that my wife has apologized for her foolish remarks," said he.

"Oh, yes—yes, certainly!"

He put his hand through my arm and walked with me up and down the lawn.

"You must not take it seriously," said he. "It would grieve me inexpressibly if you curtailed your visit by one hour. The fact is—there is no reason why there should be any concealment between relatives—that my poor dear wife is incredibly jealous. She hates that anyone—male or female—should for an instant come between us. Her ideal is a desert island and an eternal tete-a-tete. That gives you the clue to her actions, which are, I confess, upon this particular point, not very far removed from mania. Tell me that you will think no more of it."

"No, no; certainly not."

"Then light this cigar and come round with me and see my little menagerie."

The whole afternoon was occupied by this inspection, which included all the birds, beasts, and even reptiles which he had imported. Some were free, some in cages, a few actually in the house. He spoke with enthusiasm of his successes and his failures, his births and his deaths, and he would cry out in his delight, like a schoolboy, when, as we walked, some gaudy bird would flutter up from the grass, or some curious beast slink into the cover. Finally he led me down a corridor which extended from one wing of the house. At the end of this there was a heavy door with a sliding shutter in it, and beside it there projected from the wall an iron handle attached to a wheel and a drum. A line of stout bars extended across the passage.

"I am about to show you the jewel of my collection," said he. "There is only one other specimen in Europe, now that the Rotterdam cub is dead. It is a Brazilian cat."

"But how does that differ from any other cat?"

"You will soon see that," said he, laughing. "Will you kindly draw that shutter and look through?"

I did so, and found that I was gazing into a large, empty room, with stone flags, and small, barred windows upon the farther wall. In the centre of this room, lying in the middle of a golden patch of sunlight, there was stretched a huge creature, as large as a tiger, but as black and sleek as ebony. It was simply a very enormous and very well-kept black cat, and it cuddled up and basked in that yellow pool of light exactly as a cat would do. It was so graceful, so sinewy, and so gently and smoothly diabolical, that I could not take my eyes from the opening.

"Isn't he splendid?" said my host, enthusiastically.

"Glorious! I never saw such a noble creature."

"Some people call it a black puma, but really it is not a puma at all. That fellow is nearly eleven feet from tail to tip. Four years ago he was a little ball of back fluff, with two yellow eyes staring out of it. He was sold me as a new-born cub up in the wild country at the head-waters of the Rio Negro. They speared his mother to death after she had killed a dozen of them."

"They are ferocious, then?"

"The most absolutely treacherous and bloodthirsty creatures upon earth. You talk about a Brazilian cat to an up-country Indian, and see him get the jumps. They prefer humans to game. This fellow has never tasted living blood yet, but when he does he will be a terror. At present he won't stand anyone but me in his den. Even Baldwin, the groom, dare not go near him. As to me, I am his mother and father in one."

As he spoke he suddenly, to my astonishment, opened the door and slipped in, closing it instantly behind him. At the sound of his voice the huge, lithe creature rose, yawned and rubbed its round, black head affectionately against his side, while he patted and fondled it.

"Now, Tommy, into your cage!" said he.

The monstrous cat walked over to one side of the room and coiled itself up under a grating. Everard King came out, and taking the iron handle which I have mentioned, he began to turn it. As he did so the line of bars in the corridor began to pass through a slot in the wall and closed up the front of this grating, so as to make an effective cage. When it was in position he opened the door once more and invited me into the room, which was heavy with the pungent, musty smell peculiar to the great carnivora.

"That's how we work it," said he. "We give him the run of the room for exercise, and then at night we put him in his cage. You can let him out by turning the handle from the passage, or you can, as you have seen, coop him up in the same way. No, no, you should not do that!"

I had put my hand between the bars to pat the glossy, heaving flank. He pulled it back, with a serious face.

"I assure you that he is not safe. Don't imagine that because I can take liberties with him anyone else can. He is very exclusive in his friends—aren't you, Tommy? Ah, he hears his lunch coming to him! Don't you, boy?"

A step sounded in the stone-flagged passage, and the creature had sprung to his feet, and was pacing up and down the narrow cage, his yellow eyes gleaming, and his scarlet tongue rippling and quivering over the white line of his jagged teeth. A groom entered with a coarse joint upon a tray, and thrust it through the bars to him. He pounced lightly upon it, carried it off to the corner, and there, holding it between his paws, tore and wrenched at it, raising his bloody muzzle every now and then to look at us. It was a malignant and yet fascinating sight.

"You can't wonder that I am fond of him, can you?" said my host, as we left the room, "especially when you consider that I have had the rearing of him. It was no joke bringing him over from the centre of South America; but here he is safe and sound—and, as I have said, far the most perfect specimen in Europe. The people at the Zoo are dying to have him, but I really can't part with him. Now, I think that I have inflicted my hobby upon you long enough, so we cannot do better than follow Tommy's example, and go to our lunch."

My South American relative was so engrossed by his grounds and their curious occupants, that I hardly gave him credit at first for having any interests outside them. That he had some, and pressing ones, was soon borne in upon me by the number of telegrams which he received. They arrived at all hours, and were always opened by him with the utmost eagerness and anxiety upon his face. Sometimes I imagined that it must be the Turf, and sometimes the Stock Exchange, but certainly he had some very urgent business going forwards which was not transacted upon the Downs of Suffolk. During the six days of my visit he had never fewer than three or four telegrams a day, and sometimes as many as seven or eight.

I had occupied these six days so well, that by the end of them I had succeeded in getting upon the most cordial terms with my cousin. Every night we had sat up late in the billiard-room, he telling me the most extraordinary stories of his adventures in America—stories so desperate and reckless, that I could hardly associate them with the brown little, chubby man before me. In return, I ventured upon some of my own reminiscences of London life, which interested him so much, that he vowed he would come up to Grosvenor Mansions and stay with me. He was anxious to see the faster side of city life, and certainly, though I say it, he could not have chosen a more competent guide. It was not until the last day of my visit that I ventured to approach that which was on my mind. I told him frankly about my pecuniary difficulties and my impending ruin, and I asked his advice—though I hoped for something more solid. He listened attentively, puffing hard at his cigar.

"But surely," said he, "you are the heir of our relative, Lord Southerton?"

"I have every reason to believe so, but he would never make me any allowance."

"No, no, I have heard of his miserly ways. My poor Marshall, your position has been a very hard one. By the way, have you heard any news of Lord Southerton's health lately?"

"He has always been in a critical condition ever since my childhood."

"Exactly—a creaking hinge, if ever there was one. Your inheritance may be a long way off. Dear me, how awkwardly situated you are!"

"I had some hopes, sir, that you, knowing all the facts, might be inclined to advance——"

"Don't say another word, my dear boy," he cried, with the utmost cordiality; "we shall talk it over tonight, and I give you my word that whatever is in my power shall be done."

I was not sorry that my visit was drawing to a close, for it is unpleasant to feel that there is one person in the house who eagerly desires your departure. Mrs. King's sallow face and forbidding eyes had become more and more hateful to me. She was no longer actively rude—her fear of her husband prevented her—but she pushed her insane jealousy to the extent of ignoring me, never addressing me, and in every way making my stay at Greylands as uncomfortable as she could. So offensive was her manner during that last day, that I should certainly have left had it not been for that interview with my host in the evening which would, I hoped, retrieve my broken fortunes.

It was very late when it occurred, for my relative, who had been receiving even more telegrams than usual during the day, went off to his study after dinner, and only emerged when the household had retired to bed. I heard him go round locking the doors, as custom was of a night, and finally he joined me in the billiard-room. His stout figure was wrapped in a dressing-gown, and he wore a pair of red Turkish slippers without any heels. Settling down into an arm-chair, he brewed himself a glass of grog, in which I could not help noticing that the whisky considerably predominated over the water.

"My word!" said he, "what a night!"

It was, indeed. The wind was howling and screaming round the house, and the latticed windows rattled and shook as if they were coming in. The glow of the yellow lamps and the flavour of our cigars seemed the brighter and more fragrant for the contrast.

"Now, my boy," said my host, "we have the house and the night to ourselves. Let me have an idea of how your affairs stand, and I will see what can be done to set them in order. I wish to hear every detail."

Thus encouraged, I entered into a long exposition, in which all my tradesmen and creditors from my landlord to my valet, figured in turn. I had notes in my pocket-book, and I marshalled my facts, and gave, I flatter myself, a very businesslike statement of my own unbusinesslike ways and lamentable position. I was depressed, however, to notice that my companion's eyes were vacant and his attention elsewhere. When he did occasionally throw out a remark it was so entirely perfunctory and pointless, that I was sure he had not in the least followed my remarks. Every now and then he roused himself and put on some show of interest, asking me to repeat or to explain more fully, but it was always to sink once more into the same brown study. At last he rose and threw the end of his cigar into the grate.

"I'll tell you what, my boy," said he. "I never had a head for figures, so you will excuse me. You must jot it all down upon paper, and let me have a note of the amount. I'll understand it when I see it in black and white."

The proposal was encouraging. I promised to do so.

"And now it's time we were in bed. By Jove, there's one o'clock striking in the hall."

The tingling of the chiming clock broke through the deep roar of the gale. The wind was sweeping past with the rush of a great river.

"I must see my cat before I go to bed," said my host. "A high wind excites him. Will you come?"

"Certainly," said I.

"Then tread softly and don't speak, for everyone is asleep."

We passed quietly down the lamp-lit Persian-rugged hall, and through the door at the farther end. All was dark in the stone corridor, but a stable lantern hung on a hook, and my host took it down and lit it. There was no grating visible in the passage, so I knew that the beast was in its cage.

"Come in!" said my relative, and opened the door.

A deep growling as we entered showed that the storm had really excited the creature. In the flickering light of the lantern, we saw it, a huge black mass coiled in the corner of its den and throwing a squat, uncouth shadow upon the whitewashed wall. Its tail switched angrily among the straw.

"Poor Tommy is not in the best of tempers," said Everard King, holding up the lantern and looking in at him. "What a black devil he looks, doesn't he? I must give him a little supper to put him in a better humour. Would you mind holding the lantern for a moment?"

I took it from his hand and he stepped to the door.

"His larder is just outside here," said he. "You will excuse me for an instant won't you?" He passed out, and the door shut with a sharp metallic click behind him.

That hard crisp sound made my heart stand still. A sudden wave of terror passed over me. A vague perception of some monstrous treachery turned me cold. I sprang to the door, but there was no handle upon the inner side.

"Here!" I cried. "Let me out!"

"All right! Don't make a row!" said my host from the passage. "You've got the light all right."

"Yes, but I don't care about being locked in alone like this."

"Don't you?" I heard his hearty, chuckling laugh. "You won't be alone long."

"Let me out, sir!" I repeated angrily. "I tell you I don't allow practical jokes of this sort."

"Practical is the word," said he, with another hateful chuckle. And then suddenly I heard, amidst the roar of the storm, the creak and whine of the winch-handle turning and the rattle of the grating as it passed through the slot. Great God, he was letting loose the Brazilian cat!

In the light of the lantern I saw the bars sliding slowly before me. Already there was an opening a foot wide at the farther end. With a scream I seized the last bar with my hands and pulled with the strength of a madman. I WAS a madman with rage and horror. For a minute or more I held the thing motionless. I knew that he was straining with all his force upon the handle, and that the leverage was sure to overcome me. I gave inch by inch, my feet sliding along the stones, and all the time I begged and prayed this inhuman monster to save me from this horrible death. I conjured him by his kinship. I reminded him that I was his guest; I begged to know what harm I had ever done him. His only answers were the tugs and jerks upon the handle, each of which, in spite of all my struggles, pulled another bar through the opening. Clinging and clutching, I was dragged across the whole front of the cage, until at last, with aching wrists and lacerated fingers, I gave up the hopeless struggle. The grating clanged back as I released it, and an instant later I heard the shuffle of the Turkish slippers in the passage, and the slam of the distant door. Then everything was silent.

The creature had never moved during this time. He lay still in the corner, and his tail had ceased switching. This apparition of a man adhering to his bars and dragged screaming across him had apparently filled him with amazement. I saw his great eyes staring steadily at me. I had dropped the lantern when I seized the bars, but it still burned upon the floor, and I made a movement to grasp it, with some idea that its light might protect me. But the instant I moved, the beast gave a deep and menacing growl. I stopped and stood still, quivering with fear in every limb. The cat (if one may call so fearful a creature by so homely a name) was not more than ten feet from me. The eyes glimmered like two disks of phosphorus in the darkness. They appalled and yet fascinated me. I could not take my own eyes from them. Nature plays strange tricks with us at such moments of intensity, and those glimmering lights waxed and waned with a steady rise and fall. Sometimes they seemed to be tiny points of extreme brilliancy—little electric sparks in the black obscurity—then they would widen and widen until all that corner of the room was filled with their shifting and sinister light. And then suddenly they went out altogether.

The beast had closed its eyes. I do not know whether there may be any truth in the old idea of the dominance of the human gaze, or whether the huge cat was simply drowsy, but the fact remains that, far from showing any symptom of attacking me, it simply rested its sleek, black head upon its huge forepaws and seemed to sleep. I stood, fearing to move lest I should rouse it into malignant life once more. But at least I was able to think clearly now that the baleful eyes were off me. Here I was shut up for the night with the ferocious beast. My own instincts, to say nothing of the words of the plausible villain who laid this trap for me, warned me that the animal was as savage as its master. How could I stave it off until morning? The door was hopeless, and so were the narrow, barred windows. There was no shelter anywhere in the bare, stone-flagged room. To cry for assistance was absurd. I knew that this den was an outhouse, and that the corridor which connected it with the house was at least a hundred feet long. Besides, with the gale thundering outside, my cries were not likely to be heard. I had only my own courage and my own wits to trust to.

And then, with a fresh wave of horror, my eyes fell upon the lantern. The candle had burned low, and was already beginning to gutter. In ten minutes it would be out. I had only ten minutes then in which to do something, for I felt that if I were once left in the dark with that fearful beast I should be incapable of action. The very thought of it paralysed me. I cast my despairing eyes round this chamber of death, and they rested upon one spot which seemed to promise I will not say safety, but less immediate and imminent danger than the open floor.

I have said that the cage had a top as well as a front, and this top was left standing when the front was wound through the slot in the wall. It consisted of bars at a few inches' interval, with stout wire netting between, and it rested upon a strong stanchion at each end. It stood now as a great barred canopy over the crouching figure in the corner. The space between this iron shelf and the roof may have been from two or three feet. If I could only get up there, squeezed in between bars and ceiling, I should have only one vulnerable side. I should be safe from below, from behind, and from each side. Only on the open face of it could I be attacked. There, it is true, I had no protection whatever; but at least, I should be out of the brute's path when he began to pace about his den. He would have to come out of his way to reach me. It was now or never, for if once the light were out it would be impossible. With a gulp in my throat I sprang up, seized the iron edge of the top, and swung myself panting on to it. I writhed in face downwards, and found myself looking straight into the terrible eyes and yawning jaws of the cat. Its fetid breath came up into my face like the steam from some foul pot.

It appeared, however, to be rather curious than angry. With a sleek ripple of its long, black back it rose, stretched itself, and then rearing itself on its hind legs, with one forepaw against the wall, it raised the other, and drew its claws across the wire meshes beneath me. One sharp, white hook tore through my trousers—for I may mention that I was still in evening dress—and dug a furrow in my knee. It was not meant as an attack, but rather as an experiment, for upon my giving a sharp cry of pain he dropped down again, and springing lightly into the room, he began walking swiftly round it, looking up every now and again in my direction. For my part I shuffled backwards until I lay with my back against the wall, screwing myself into the smallest space possible. The farther I got the more difficult it was for him to attack me.

He seemed more excited now that he had begun to move about, and he ran swiftly and noiselessly round and round the den, passing continually underneath the iron couch upon which I lay. It was wonderful to see so great a bulk passing like a shadow, with hardly the softest thudding of velvety pads. The candle was burning low—so low that I could hardly see the creature. And then, with a last flare and splutter it went out altogether. I was alone with the cat in the dark!

It helps one to face a danger when one knows that one has done all that possibly can be done. There is nothing for it then but to quietly await the result. In this case, there was no chance of safety anywhere except the precise spot where I was. I stretched myself out, therefore, and lay silently, almost breathlessly, hoping that the beast might forget my presence if I did nothing to remind him. I reckoned that it must already be two o'clock. At four it would be full dawn. I had not more than two hours to wait for daylight.

Outside, the storm was still raging, and the rain lashed continually against the little windows. Inside, the poisonous and fetid air was overpowering. I could neither hear nor see the cat. I tried to think about other things—but only one had power enough to draw my mind from my terrible position. That was the contemplation of my cousin's villainy, his unparalleled hypocrisy, his malignant hatred of me. Beneath that cheerful face there lurked the spirit of a mediaeval assassin. And as I thought of it I saw more clearly how cunningly the thing had been arranged. He had apparently gone to bed with the others. No doubt he had his witness to prove it. Then, unknown to them, he had slipped down, had lured me into his den and abandoned me. His story would be so simple.

He had left me to finish my cigar in the billiard-room. I had gone down on my own account to have a last look at the cat. I had entered the room without observing that the cage was opened, and I had been caught. How could such a crime be brought home to him? Suspicion, perhaps—but proof, never!

How slowly those dreadful two hours went by! Once I heard a low, rasping sound, which I took to be the creature licking its own fur. Several times those greenish eyes gleamed at me through the darkness, but never in a fixed stare, and my hopes grew stronger that my presence had been forgotten or ignored. At last the least faint glimmer of light came through the windows—I first dimly saw them as two grey squares upon the black wall, then grey turned to white, and I could see my terrible companion once more. And he, alas, could see me!

It was evident to me at once that he was in a much more dangerous and aggressive mood than when I had seen him last. The cold of the morning had irritated him, and he was hungry as well. With a continual growl he paced swiftly up and down the side of the room which was farthest from my refuge, his whiskers bristling angrily, and his tail switching and lashing. As he turned at the corners his savage eyes always looked upwards at me with a dreadful menace. I knew then that he meant to kill me. Yet I found myself even at that moment admiring the sinuous grace of the devilish thing, its long, undulating, rippling movements, the gloss of its beautiful flanks, the vivid, palpitating scarlet of the glistening tongue which hung from the jet-black muzzle. And all the time that deep, threatening growl was rising and rising in an unbroken crescendo. I knew that the crisis was at hand.

It was a miserable hour to meet such a death—so cold, so comfortless, shivering in my light dress clothes upon this gridiron of torment upon which I was stretched. I tried to brace myself to it, to raise my soul above it, and at the same time, with the lucidity which comes to a perfectly desperate man, I cast round for some possible means of escape. One thing was clear to me. If that front of the cage was only back in its position once more, I could find a sure refuge behind it. Could I possibly pull it back? I hardly dared to move for fear of bringing the creature upon me. Slowly, very slowly, I put my hand forward until it grasped the edge of the front, the final bar which protruded through the wall. To my surprise it came quite easily to my jerk. Of course the difficulty of drawing it out arose from the fact that I was clinging to it. I pulled again, and three inches of it came through. It ran apparently on wheels. I pulled again . . . and then the cat sprang!

It was so quick, so sudden, that I never saw it happen. I simply heard the savage snarl, and in an instant afterwards the blazing yellow eyes, the flattened black head with its red tongue and flashing teeth, were within reach of me. The impact of the creature shook the bars upon which I lay, until I thought (as far as I could think of anything at such a moment) that they were coming down. The cat swayed there for an instant, the head and front paws quite close to me, the hind paws clawing to find a grip upon the edge of the grating. I heard the claws rasping as they clung to the wire-netting, and the breath of the beast made me sick. But its bound had been miscalculated. It could not retain its position. Slowly, grinning with rage, and scratching madly at the bars, it swung backwards and dropped heavily upon the floor. With a growl it instantly faced round to me and crouched for another spring.

I knew that the next few moments would decide my fate. The creature had learned by experience. It would not miscalculate again. I must act promptly, fearlessly, if I were to have a chance for life. In an instant I had formed my plan. Pulling off my dress-coat, I threw it down over the head of the beast. At the same moment I dropped over the edge, seized the end of the front grating, and pulled it frantically out of the wall.

It came more easily than I could have expected. I rushed across the room, bearing it with me; but, as I rushed, the accident of my position put me upon the outer side. Had it been the other way, I might have come off scathless. As it was, there was a moment's pause as I stopped it and tried to pass in through the opening which I had left. That moment was enough to give time to the creature to toss off the coat with which I had blinded him and to spring upon me. I hurled myself through the gap and pulled the rails to behind me, but he seized my leg before I could entirely withdraw it. One stroke of that huge paw tore off my calf as a shaving of wood curls off before a plane. The next moment, bleeding and fainting, I was lying among the foul straw with a line of friendly bars between me and the creature which ramped so frantically against them.

Too wounded to move, and too faint to be conscious of fear, I could only lie, more dead than alive, and watch it. It pressed its broad, black chest against the bars and angled for me with its crooked paws as I have seen a kitten do before a mouse-trap. It ripped my clothes, but, stretch as it would, it could not quite reach me. I have heard of the curious numbing effect produced by wounds from the great carnivora, and now I was destined to experience it, for I had lost all sense of personality, and was as interested in the cat's failure or success as if it were some game which I was watching. And then gradually my mind drifted away into strange vague dreams, always with that black face and red tongue coming back into them, and so I lost myself in the nirvana of delirium, the blessed relief of those who are too sorely tried.

Tracing the course of events afterwards, I conclude that I must have been insensible for about two hours. What roused me to consciousness once more was that sharp metallic click which had been the precursor of my terrible experience. It was the shooting back of the spring lock. Then, before my senses were clear enough to entirely apprehend what they saw, I was aware of the round, benevolent face of my cousin peering in through the open door. What he saw evidently amazed him. There was the cat crouching on the floor. I was stretched upon my back in my shirt-sleeves within the cage, my trousers torn to ribbons and a great pool of blood all round me. I can see his amazed face now, with the morning sunlight upon it. He peered at me, and peered again. Then he closed the door behind him, and advanced to the cage to see if I were really dead.

I cannot undertake to say what happened. I was not in a fit state to witness or to chronicle such events. I can only say that I was suddenly conscious that his face was away from me—that he was looking towards the animal.

"Good old Tommy!" he cried. "Good old Tommy!"

Then he came near the bars, with his back still towards me.

"Down, you stupid beast!" he roared. "Down, sir! Don't you know your master?"

Suddenly even in my bemuddled brain a remembrance came of those words of his when he had said that the taste of blood would turn the cat into a fiend. My blood had done it, but he was to pay the price.

"Get away!" he screamed. "Get away, you devil! Baldwin! Baldwin! Oh, my God!"

And then I heard him fall, and rise, and fall again, with a sound like the ripping of sacking. His screams grew fainter until they were lost in the worrying snarl. And then, after I thought that he was dead, I saw, as in a nightmare, a blinded, tattered, blood-soaked figure running wildly round the room—and that was the last glimpse which I had of him before I fainted once again.

I was many months in my recovery—in fact, I cannot say that I have ever recovered, for to the end of my days I shall carry a stick as a sign of my night with the Brazilian cat. Baldwin, the groom, and the other servants could not tell what had occurred, when, drawn by the death-cries of their master, they found me behind the bars, and his remains—or what they afterwards discovered to be his remains—in the clutch of the creature which he had reared. They stalled him off with hot irons, and afterwards shot him through the loophole of the door before they could finally extricate me. I was carried to my bedroom, and there, under the roof of my would-be murderer, I remained between life and death for several weeks. They had sent for a surgeon from Clipton and a nurse from London, and in a month I was able to be carried to the station, and so conveyed back once more to Grosvenor Mansions.

I have one remembrance of that illness, which might have been part of the ever-changing panorama conjured up by a delirious brain were it not so definitely fixed in my memory. One night, when the nurse was absent, the door of my chamber opened, and a tall woman in blackest mourning slipped into the room. She came across to me, and as she bent her sallow face I saw by the faint gleam of the night-light that it was the Brazilian woman whom my cousin had married. She stared intently into my face, and her expression was more kindly than I had ever seen it.

"Are you conscious?" she asked.

I feebly nodded—for I was still very weak.

"Well; then, I only wished to say to you that you have yourself to blame. Did I not do all I could for you? From the beginning I tried to drive you from the house. By every means, short of betraying my husband, I tried to save you from him. I knew that he had a reason for bringing you here. I knew that he would never let you get away again. No one knew him as I knew him, who had suffered from him so often. I did not dare to tell you all this. He would have killed me. But I did my best for you. As things have turned out, you have been the best friend that I have ever had. You have set me free, and I fancied that nothing but death would do that. I am sorry if you are hurt, but I cannot reproach myself. I told you that you were a fool—and a fool you have been." She crept out of the room, the bitter, singular woman, and I was never destined to see her again. With what remained from her husband's property she went back to her native land, and I have heard that she afterwards took the veil at Pernambuco.

It was not until I had been back in London for some time that the doctors pronounced me to be well enough to do business. It was not a very welcome permission to me, for I feared that it would be the signal for an inrush of creditors; but it was Summers, my lawyer, who first took advantage of it.

"I am very glad to see that your lordship is so much better," said he. "I have been waiting a long time to offer my congratulations."

"What do you mean, Summers? This is no time for joking."

"I mean what I say," he answered. "You have been Lord Southerton for the last six weeks, but we feared that it would retard your recovery if you were to learn it."

Lord Southerton! One of the richest peers in England! I could not believe my ears. And then suddenly I thought of the time which had elapsed, and how it coincided with my injuries.

"Then Lord Southerton must have died about the same time that I was hurt?"

"His death occurred upon that very day." Summers looked hard at me as I spoke, and I am convinced—for he was a very shrewd fellow—that he had guessed the true state of the case. He paused for a moment as if awaiting a confidence from me, but I could not see what was to be gained by exposing such a family scandal.

"Yes, a very curious coincidence," he continued, with the same knowing look. "Of course, you are aware that your cousin Everard King was the next heir to the estates. Now, if it had been you instead of him who had been torn to pieces by this tiger, or whatever it was, then of course he would have been Lord Southerton at the present moment."

"No doubt," said I.

"And he took such an interest in it," said Summers. "I happen to know that the late Lord Southerton's valet was in his pay, and that he used to have telegrams from him every few hours to tell him how he was getting on. That would be about the time when you were down there. Was it not strange that he should wish to be so well informed, since he knew that he was not the direct heir?"

"Very strange," said I. "And now, Summers, if you will bring me my bills and a new cheque-book, we will begin to get things into order."

The Lost Special

The confession of Herbert de Lernac, now lying under sentence of death at Marseilles, has thrown a light upon one of the most inexplicable crimes of the century—an incident which is, I believe, absolutely unprecedented in the criminal annals of any country: Although there is a reluctance to discuss the matter in official circles, and little information has been given to the Press, there are still indications that the statement of this arch-criminal is corroborated by the facts, and that we have at last found a solution for a most astounding business. As the matter is eight years old, and as its importance was somewhat obscured by a political crisis which was engaging the public attention at the time, it may be as well to state the facts as far as we have been able to ascertain them. They are collated from the Liverpool papers of that date, from the proceedings at the inquest upon John Slater, the engine-driver, and from the records of the London and West Coast Railway Company, which have been courteously put at my disposal. Briefly, they are as follows:

On the 3rd of June, 1890, a gentleman, who gave his name as Monsieur Louis Caratal, desired an interview with Mr. James Bland, the superintendent of the London and West Coast Central Station in Liverpool. He was a small man, middle-aged and dark, with a stoop which was so marked that it suggested some deformity of the spine. He was accompanied by a friend, a man of imposing physique, whose deferential manner and constant attention showed that his position was one of dependence. This friend or companion, whose name did not transpire, was certainly a foreigner, and probably from his swarthy complexion, either a Spaniard or a South American. One peculiarity was observed in him. He carried in his left hand a small black, leather dispatch box, and it was noticed by a sharp-eyed clerk in the Central office that this box was fastened to his wrist by a strap. No importance was attached to the fact at the time, but subsequent events endowed it with some significance. Monsieur Caratal was shown up to Mr. Bland's office, while his companion remained outside.

Monsieur Caratal's business was quickly dispatched. He had arrived that afternoon from Central America. Affairs of the utmost importance demanded that he should be in Paris without the loss of an unnecessary hour. He had missed the London express. A special must be provided. Money was of no importance. Time was everything. If the company would speed him on his way, they might make their own terms.

Mr. Bland struck the electric bell, summoned Mr. Potter Hood, the traffic manager, and had the matter arranged in five minutes. The train would start in three-quarters of an hour. It would take that time to insure that the line should be clear. The powerful engine called Rochdale (No. 247 on the company's register) was attached to two carriages, with a guard's van behind. The first carriage was solely for the purpose of decreasing the inconvenience arising from the oscillation. The second was divided, as usual, into four compartments, a first-class, a first-class smoking, a second-class, and a second-class smoking. The first compartment, which was nearest to the engine, was the one allotted to the travellers. The other three were empty. The guard of the special train was James McPherson, who had been some years in the service of the company. The stoker, William Smith, was a new hand.

Monsieur Caratal, upon leaving the superintendent's office, rejoined his companion, and both of them manifested extreme impatience to be off. Having paid the money asked, which amounted to fifty pounds five shillings, at the usual special rate of five shillings a mile, they demanded to be shown the carriage, and at once took their seats in it, although they were assured that the better part of an hour must elapse before the line could be cleared. In the meantime a singular coincidence had occurred in the office which Monsieur Caratal had just quitted.

A request for a special is not a very uncommon circumstance in a rich commercial centre, but that two should be required upon the same afternoon was most unusual. It so happened, however, that Mr. Bland had hardly dismissed the first traveller before a second entered with a similar request. This was a Mr. Horace Moore, a gentlemanly man of military appearance, who alleged that the sudden serious illness of his wife in London made it absolutely imperative that he should not lose an instant in starting upon the journey. His distress and anxiety were so evident that Mr. Bland did all that was possible to meet his wishes. A second special was out of the question, as the ordinary local service was already somewhat deranged by the first. There was the alternative, however, that Mr. Moore should share the expense of Monsieur Caratal's train, and should travel in the other empty first-class compartment, if Monsieur Caratal objected to having him in the one which he occupied. It was difficult to see any objection to such an arrangement, and yet Monsieur Caratal, upon the suggestion being made to him by Mr. Potter Hood, absolutely refused to consider it for an instant. The train was his, he said, and he would insist upon the exclusive use of it. All argument failed to overcome his ungracious objections, and finally the plan had to be abandoned. Mr. Horace Moore left the station in great distress, after learning that his only course was to take the ordinary slow train which leaves Liverpool at six o'clock. At four thirty-one exactly by the station clock the special train, containing the crippled Monsieur Caratal and his gigantic companion, steamed out of the Liverpool station. The line was at that time clear, and there should have been no stoppage before Manchester.

The trains of the London and West Coast Railway run over the lines of another company as far as this town, which should have been reached by the special rather before six o'clock. At a quarter after six considerable surprise and some consternation were caused amongst the officials at Liverpool by the receipt of a telegram from Manchester to say that it had not yet arrived. An inquiry directed to St. Helens, which is a third of the way between the two cities, elicited the following reply—

"To James Bland, Superintendent, Central L. & W. C., Liverpool.—Special passed here at 4:52, well up to time.—Dowster, St. Helens."

This telegram was received at six-forty. At six-fifty a second message was received from Manchester—

"No sign of special as advised by you."

And then ten minutes later a third, more bewildering—

"Presume some mistake as to proposed running of special. Local train from St. Helens timed to follow it has just arrived and has seen nothing of it. Kindly wire advices.—Manchester."

The matter was assuming a most amazing aspect, although in some respects the last telegram was a relief to the authorities at Liverpool. If an accident had occurred to the special, it seemed hardly possible that the local train could have passed down the same line without observing it. And yet, what was the alternative? Where could the train be? Had it possibly been sidetracked for some reason in order to allow the slower train to go past? Such an explanation was possible if some small repair had to be effected. A telegram was dispatched to each of the stations between St. Helens and Manchester, and the superintendent and traffic manager waited in the utmost suspense at the instrument for the series of replies which would enable them to say for certain what had become of the missing train. The answers came back in the order of questions, which was the order of the stations beginning at the St. Helens end—

"Special passed here five o'clock.—Collins Green."

"Special passed here six past five.—Earlstown."

"Special passed here 5:10.—Newton."

"Special passed here 5:20.—Kenyon Junction."

"No special train has passed here.—Barton Moss."

The two officials stared at each other in amazement.

"This is unique in my thirty years of experience," said Mr. Bland.

"Absolutely unprecedented and inexplicable, sir. The special has gone wrong between Kenyon Junction and Barton Moss."

"And yet there is no siding, so far as my memory serves me, between the two stations. The special must have run off the metals."

"But how could the four-fifty parliamentary pass over the same line without observing it?"

"There's no alternative, Mr. Hood. It must be so. Possibly the local train may have observed something which may throw some light upon the matter. We will wire to Manchester for more information, and to Kenyon Junction with instructions that the line be examined instantly as far as Barton Moss." The answer from Manchester came within a few minutes.

"No news of missing special. Driver and guard of slow train positive no accident between Kenyon Junction and Barton Moss. Line quite clear, and no sign of anything unusual.—Manchester."

"That driver and guard will have to go," said Mr. Bland, grimly. "There has been a wreck and they have missed it. The special has obviously run off the metals without disturbing the line—how it could have done so passes my comprehension—but so it must be, and we shall have a wire from Kenyon or Barton Moss presently to say that they have found her at the bottom of an embankment."

But Mr. Bland's prophecy was not destined to be fulfilled. Half an hour passed, and then there arrived the following message from the station-master of Kenyon Junction—

"There are no traces of the missing special. It is quite certain that she passed here, and that she did not arrive at Barton Moss. We have detached engine from goods train, and I have myself ridden down the line, but all is clear, and there is no sign of any accident."

Mr. Bland tore his hair in his perplexity.

"This is rank lunacy, Hood!" he cried. "Does a train vanish into thin air in England in broad daylight? The thing is preposterous. An engine, a tender, two carriages, a van, five human beings—and all lost on a straight line of railway! Unless we get something positive within the next hour I'll take Inspector Collins, and go down myself."

And then at last something positive did occur. It took the shape of another telegram from Kenyon Junction.

"Regret to report that the dead body of John Slater, driver of the special train, has just been found among the gorse bushes at a point two and a quarter miles from the Junction. Had fallen from his engine, pitched down the embankment, and rolled among the bushes. Injuries to his head, from the fall, appear to be cause of death. Ground has now been carefully examined, and there is no trace of the missing train."

The country was, as has already been stated, in the throes of a political crisis, and the attention of the public was further distracted by the important and sensational developments in Paris, where a huge scandal threatened to destroy the Government and to wreck the reputations of many of the leading men in France. The papers were full of these events, and the singular disappearance of the special train attracted less attention than would have been the case in more peaceful times. The grotesque nature of the event helped to detract from its importance, for the papers were disinclined to believe the facts as reported to them. More than one of the London journals treated the matter as an ingenious hoax, until the coroner's inquest upon the unfortunate driver (an inquest which elicited nothing of importance) convinced them of the tragedy of the incident.

Mr. Bland, accompanied by Inspector Collins, the senior detective officer in the service of the company, went down to Kenyon Junction the same evening, and their research lasted throughout the following day, but was attended with purely negative results. Not only was no trace found of the missing train, but no conjecture could be put forward which could possibly explain the facts. At the same time, Inspector Collins's official report (which lies before me as I write) served to show that the possibilities were more numerous than might have been expected.

"In the stretch of railway between these two points," said he, "the country is dotted with ironworks and collieries. Of these, some are being worked and some have been abandoned. There are no fewer than twelve which have small-gauge lines which run trolly-cars down to the main line. These can, of course, be disregarded. Besides these, however, there are seven which have, or have had, proper lines running down and connecting with points to the main line, so as to convey their produce from the mouth of the mine to the great centres of distribution. In every case these lines are only a few miles in length. Out of the seven, four belong to collieries which are worked out, or at least to shafts which are no longer used. These are the Redgauntlet, Hero, Slough of Despond, and Heartsease mines, the latter having ten years ago been one of the principal mines in Lancashire. These four side lines may be eliminated from our inquiry, for, to prevent possible accidents, the rails nearest to the main line have been taken up, and there is no longer any connection. There remain three other side lines leading—

(a) To the Carnstock Iron Works;

(b) To the Big Ben Colliery;

(c) To the Perseverance Colliery.

"Of these the Big Ben line is not more than a quarter of a mile long, and ends at a dead wall of coal waiting removal from the mouth of the mine. Nothing had been seen or heard there of any special. The Carnstock Iron Works line was blocked all day upon the 3rd of June by sixteen truckloads of hematite. It is a single line, and nothing could have passed. As to the Perseverance line, it is a large double line, which does a considerable traffic, for the output of the mine is very large. On the 3rd of June this traffic proceeded as usual; hundreds of men including a gang of railway platelayers were working along the two miles and a quarter which constitute the total length of the line, and it is inconceivable that an unexpected train could have come down there without attracting universal attention. It may be remarked in conclusion that this branch line is nearer to St. Helens than the point at which the engine-driver was discovered, so that we have every reason to believe that the train was past that point before misfortune overtook her.

"As to John Slater, there is no clue to be gathered from his appearance or injuries. We can only say that, so far as we can see, he met his end by falling off his engine, though why he fell, or what became of the engine after his fall, is a question upon which I do not feel qualified to offer an opinion." In conclusion, the inspector offered his resignation to the Board, being much nettled by an accusation of incompetence in the London papers.

A month elapsed, during which both the police and the company prosecuted their inquiries without the slightest success. A reward was offered and a pardon promised in case of crime, but they were both unclaimed. Every day the public opened their papers with the conviction that so grotesque a mystery would at last be solved, but week after week passed by, and a solution remained as far off as ever. In broad daylight, upon a June afternoon in the most thickly inhabited portion of England, a train with its occupants had disappeared as completely as if some master of subtle chemistry had volatilized it into gas. Indeed, among the various conjectures which were put forward in the public Press, there were some which seriously asserted that supernatural, or, at least, preternatural, agencies had been at work, and that the deformed Monsieur Caratal was probably a person who was better known under a less polite name. Others fixed upon his swarthy companion as being the author of the mischief, but what it was exactly which he had done could never be clearly formulated in words.

Amongst the many suggestions put forward by various newspapers or private individuals, there were one or two which were feasible enough to attract the attention of the public. One which appeared in The Times, over the signature of an amateur reasoner of some celebrity at that date, attempted to deal with the matter in a critical and semi-scientific manner. An extract must suffice, although the curious can see the whole letter in the issue of the 3rd of July.

"It is one of the elementary principles of practical reasoning," he remarked, "that when the impossible has been eliminated the residuum, HOWEVER IMPROBABLE, must contain the truth. It is certain that the train left Kenyon Junction. It is certain that it did not reach Barton Moss. It is in the highest degree unlikely, but still possible, that it may have taken one of the seven available side lines. It is obviously impossible for a train to run where there are no rails, and, therefore, we may reduce our improbables to the three open lines, namely the Carnstock Iron Works, the Big Ben, and the Perseverance. Is there a secret society of colliers, an English Camorra, which is capable of destroying both train and passengers? It is improbable, but it is not impossible. I confess that I am unable to suggest any other solution. I should certainly advise the company to direct all their energies towards the observation of those three lines, and of the workmen at the end of them. A careful supervision of the pawnbrokers' shops of the district might possibly bring some suggestive facts to light."

The suggestion coming from a recognized authority upon such matters created considerable interest, and a fierce opposition from those who considered such a statement to be a preposterous libel upon an honest and deserving set of men. The only answer to this criticism was a challenge to the objectors to lay any more feasible explanations before the public. In reply to this two others were forthcoming (Times, July 7th and 9th). The first suggested

that the train might have run off the metals and be lying submerged in the Lancashire and Staffordshire Canal, which runs
parallel to the railway for some hundred of yards. This suggestion
was thrown out of court by the published depth of the canal,
which was entirely insufficient to conceal so large an object. The
second correspondent wrote calling attention to the bag which
appeared to be the sole luggage which the travellers had brought
with them, and suggesting that some novel explosive of immense
and pulverizing power might have been concealed in it. The obvious absurdity, however, of supposing that the whole train might
be blown to dust while the metals remained uninjured reduced
any such explanation to a farce. The investigation had drifted into
this hopeless position when a new and most unexpected incident
occurred.

This was nothing less than the receipt by Mrs. McPherson of
a letter from her husband, James McPherson, who had been the
guard on the missing train. The letter, which was dated July 5th,
1890, was posted from New York and came to hand upon July
14th. Some doubts were expressed as to its genuine character but
Mrs. McPherson was positive as to the writing, and the fact that it
contained a remittance of a hundred dollars in five-dollar notes
was enough in itself to discount the idea of a hoax. No address was
given in the letter, which ran in this way:

MY DEAR WIFE,—
"I have been thinking a great deal, and I find it very hard to
give you up. The same with Lizzie. I try to fight against it, but it
will always come back to me. I send you some money which will
change into twenty English pounds. This should be enough to
bring both Lizzie and you across the Atlantic, and you will find the
Hamburg boats which stop at Southampton very good boats, and
cheaper than Liverpool. If you could come here and stop at the
Johnston House I would try and send you word how to meet, but
things are very difficult with me at present, and I am not very
happy, finding it hard to give you both up. So no more at present,
from your loving husband,

"James McPherson."

For a time it was confidently anticipated that this letter would lead to the clearing up of the whole matter, the more so as it was ascertained that a passenger who bore a close resemblance to the missing guard had travelled from Southampton under the name of Summers in the Hamburg and New York liner Vistula, which started upon the 7th of June. Mrs. McPherson and her sister Lizzie Dolton went across to New York as directed and stayed for three weeks at the Johnston House, without hearing anything from the missing man. It is probable that some injudicious comments in the Press may have warned him that the police were using them as a bait. However, this may be, it is certain that he neither wrote nor came, and the women were eventually compelled to return to Liverpool.

And so the matter stood, and has continued to stand up to the present year of 1898. Incredible as it may seem, nothing has transpired during these eight years which has shed the least light upon the extraordinary disappearance of the special train which contained Monsieur Caratal and his companion. Careful inquiries into the antecedents of the two travellers have only established the fact that Monsieur Caratal was well known as a financier and political agent in Central America, and that during his voyage to Europe he had betrayed extraordinary anxiety to reach Paris. His companion, whose name was entered upon the passenger lists as Eduardo Gomez, was a man whose record was a violent one, and whose reputation was that of a bravo and a bully. There was evidence to show, however, that he was honestly devoted to the interests of Monsieur Caratal, and that the latter, being a man of puny physique, employed the other as a guard and protector. It may be added that no information came from Paris as to what the objects of Monsieur Caratal's hurried journey may have been. This comprises all the facts of the case up to the publication in the Marseilles papers of the recent confession of Herbert de Lernac, now under sentence of death for the murder of a merchant named Bonvalot. This statement may be literally translated as follows:

"It is not out of mere pride or boasting that I give this information, for, if that were my object, I could tell a dozen actions of mine which are quite as splendid; but I do it in order that certain gentlemen in Paris may understand that I, who am able here to tell about the fate of Monsieur Caratal, can also tell in whose interest and at whose request the deed was done, unless the reprieve which I am awaiting comes to me very quickly. Take warning, messieurs, before it is too late! You know Herbert de Lernac, and you are aware that his deeds are as ready as his words. Hasten then, or you are lost!

"At present I shall mention no names—if you only heard the names, what would you not think!—but I shall merely tell you how cleverly I did it. I was true to my employers then, and no doubt they will be true to me now. I hope so, and until I am convinced that they have betrayed me, these names, which would convulse Europe, shall not be divulged. But on that day . . . well, I say no more!

"In a word, then, there was a famous trial in Paris, in the year 1890, in connection with a monstrous scandal in politics and finance. How monstrous that scandal was can never be known save by such confidential agents as myself. The honour and careers of many of the chief men in France were at stake. You have seen a group of ninepins standing, all so rigid, and prim, and unbending. Then there comes the ball from far away and pop, pop, pop— there are your ninepins on the floor. Well, imagine some of the greatest men in France as these ninepins and then this Monsieur Caratal was the ball which could be seen coming from far away. If he arrived, then it was pop, pop, pop for all of them. It was determined that he should not arrive.

"I do not accuse them all of being conscious of what was to happen. There were, as I have said, great financial as well as political interests at stake, and a syndicate was formed to manage the business. Some subscribed to the syndicate who hardly understood what were its objects. But others understood very well, and they can rely upon it that I have not forgotten their names. They had ample warning that Monsieur Caratal was coming long before he left South America, and they knew that the evidence which he held would certainly mean ruin to all of them. The syndicate had the command of an unlimited amount of money—absolutely unlimited, you understand. They looked round for an agent who was capable of wielding this gigantic power. The man chosen must be inventive, resolute, adaptive—a man in a million. They chose Herbert de Lernac, and I admit that they were right.

"My duties were to choose my subordinates, to use freely the power which money gives, and to make certain that Monsieur Caratal should never arrive in Paris. With characteristic energy I set about my commission within an hour of receiving my instructions, and the steps which I took were the very best for the purpose which could possibly be devised.

"A man whom I could trust was dispatched instantly to South America to travel home with Monsieur Caratal. Had he arrived in time the ship would never have reached Liverpool; but alas! it had already started before my agent could reach it. I fitted out a small armed brig to intercept it, but again I was unfortunate. Like all great organizers I was, however, prepared for failure, and had a series of alternatives prepared, one or the other of which must succeed. You must not underrate the difficulties of my undertaking, or imagine that a mere commonplace assassination would meet the case. We must destroy not only Monsieur Caratal, but Monsieur Caratal's documents, and Monsieur Caratal's companions also, if we had reason to believe that he had communicated his secrets to them. And you must remember that they were on the alert, and keenly suspicious of any such attempt. It was a task which was in every way worthy of me, for I am always most masterful where another would be appalled.

"I was all ready for Monsieur Caratal's reception in Liverpool, and I was the more eager because I had reason to believe that he had made arrangements by which he would have a considerable guard from the moment that he arrived in London. Anything which was to be done must be done between the moment of his setting foot upon the Liverpool quay and that of his arrival at the London and West Coast terminus in London. We prepared six plans, each more elaborate than the last; which plan would be used would depend upon his own movements. Do what he would, we were ready for him. If he had stayed in Liverpool, we were ready. If he took an ordinary train, an express, or a special, all was ready. Everything had been foreseen and provided for.

"You may imagine that I could not do all this myself. What could I know of the English railway lines? But money can procure willing agents all the world over, and I soon had one of the acutest brains in England to assist me. I will mention no names, but it would be unjust to claim all the credit for myself. My English ally was worthy of such an alliance. He knew the London and West Coast line thoroughly, and he had the command of a band of workers who were trustworthy and intelligent. The idea was his, and my own judgement was only required in the details. We bought over several officials, amongst whom the most important was James McPherson, whom we had ascertained to be the guard most likely to be employed upon a special train. Smith, the stoker, was also in our employ. John Slater, the engine-driver, had been approached, but had been found to be obstinate and dangerous, so we desisted. We had no certainty that Monsieur Caratal would take a special, but we thought it very probable, for it was of the utmost importance to him that he should reach Paris without delay. It was for this contingency, therefore, that we made special preparations—preparations which were complete down to the last detail long before his steamer had sighted the shores of England. You will be amused to learn that there was one of my agents in the pilot-boat which brought that steamer to its moorings.

"The moment that Caratal arrived in Liverpool we knew that he suspected danger and was on his guard. He had brought with him as an escort a dangerous fellow, named Gomez, a man who carried weapons, and was prepared to use them. This fellow carried Caratal's confidential papers for him, and was ready to protect either them or his master. The probability was that Caratal had taken him into his counsel, and that to remove Caratal without removing Gomez would be a mere waste of energy. It was necessary that they should be involved in a common fate, and our plans to that end were much facilitated by their request for a special train. On that special train you will understand that two out of the three servants of the company were really in our employ, at a price which would make them independent for a lifetime. I do not go so far as to say that the English are more honest than any other nation, but I have found them more expensive to buy.

"I have already spoken of my English agent—who is a man with a considerable future before him, unless some complaint of the throat carries him off before his time. He had charge of all arrangements at Liverpool, whilst I was stationed at the inn at Kenyon, where I awaited a cipher signal to act. When the special was arranged for, my agent instantly telegraphed to me and warned me how soon I should have everything ready. He himself under the name of Horace Moore applied immediately for a special also, in the hope that he would be sent down with Monsieur Caratal, which might under certain circumstances have been helpful to us. If, for example, our great coup had failed, it would then have become the duty of my agent to have shot them both and destroyed their papers. Caratal was on his guard, however, and refused to admit any other traveller. My agent then left the station, returned by another entrance, entered the guard's van on the side farthest from the platform, and travelled down with McPherson the guard.

"In the meantime you will be interested to know what my movements were. Everything had been prepared for days before, and only the finishing touches were needed. The side line which we had chosen had once joined the main line, but it had been disconnected. We had only to replace a few rails to connect it once more. These rails had been laid down as far as could be done without danger of attracting attention, and now it was merely a case of completing a juncture with the line, and arranging the points as they had been before. The sleepers had never been removed, and the rails, fish-plates and rivets were all ready, for we had taken them from a siding on the abandoned portion of the line. With my small but competent band of workers, we had everything ready long before the special arrived. When it did arrive, it ran off upon the small side line so easily that the jolting of the points appears to have been entirely unnoticed by the two travellers.

"Our plan had been that Smith, the stoker, should chloroform John Slater, the driver, so that he should vanish with the others. In this respect, and in this respect only, our plans miscarried—I except the criminal folly of McPherson in writing home to his wife. Our stoker did his business so clumsily that Slater in his struggles fell off the engine, and though fortune was with us so far that he broke his neck in the fall, still he remained as a blot upon that which would otherwise have been one of those complete masterpieces which are only to be contemplated in silent admiration. The criminal expert will find in John Slater the one flaw in all our admirable combinations. A man who has had as many triumphs as I can afford to be frank, and I therefore lay my finger upon John Slater, and I proclaim him to be a flaw.

"But now I have got our special train upon the small line two kilometres, or rather more than one mile, in length, which leads, or rather used to lead, to the abandoned Heartsease mine, once one of the largest coal mines in England. You will ask how it is that no one saw the train upon this unused line. I answer that along its entire length it runs through a deep cutting, and that, unless someone had been on the edge of that cutting, he could not have seen it. There WAS someone on the edge of that cutting. I was there. And now I will tell you what I saw.

"My assistant had remained at the points in order that he might superintend the switching off of the train. He had four armed men with him, so that if the train ran off the line—we thought it probable, because the points were very rusty—we might still have resources to fall back upon. Having once seen it safely on the side line, he handed over the responsibility to me. I was waiting at a point which overlooks the mouth of the mine, and I was also armed, as were my two companions. Come what might, you see, I was always ready.

"The moment that the train was fairly on the side line, Smith, the stoker, slowed-down the engine, and then, having turned it on to the fullest speed again, he and McPherson, with my English lieutenant, sprang off before it was too late. It may be that it was this slowing-down which first attracted the attention of the travellers, but the train was running at full speed again before their heads appeared at the open window. It makes me smile to think how bewildered they must have been. Picture to yourself your own feelings if, on looking out of your luxurious carriage, you suddenly perceived that the lines upon which you ran were rusted and corroded, red and yellow with disuse and decay! What a catch must have come in their breath as in a second it flashed upon them that it was not Manchester but Death which was waiting for them at the end of that sinister line. But the train was running with frantic speed, rolling and rocking over the rotten line, while the wheels made a frightful screaming sound upon the rusted surface. I was close to them, and could see their faces. Caratal was praying, I think—there was something like a rosary dangling out of his hand. The other roared like a bull who smells the blood of the slaughter-house. He saw us standing on the bank, and he beckoned to us like a madman. Then he tore at his wrist and threw his dispatch-box out of the window in our direction. Of course, his meaning was obvious. Here was the evidence, and they would promise to be silent if their lives were spared. It would have been very agreeable if we could have done so, but business is business. Besides, the train was now as much beyond our controls as theirs.

"He ceased howling when the train rattled round the curve and they saw the black mouth of the mine yawning before them. We had removed the boards which had covered it, and we had cleared the square entrance. The rails had formerly run very close to the shaft for the convenience of loading the coal, and we had only to add two or three lengths of rail in order to lead to the very brink of the shaft. In fact, as the lengths would not quite fit, our line projected about three feet over the edge. We saw the two heads at the window: Caratal below, Gomez above; but they had both been struck silent by what they saw. And yet they could not withdraw their heads. The sight seemed to have paralysed them.

"I had wondered how the train running at a great speed would take the pit into which I had guided it, and I was much interested in watching it. One of my colleagues thought that it would actually jump it, and indeed it was not very far from doing so. Fortunately, however, it fell short, and the buffers of the engine struck the other lip of the shaft with a tremendous crash. The funnel flew off into the air. The tender, carriages, and van were all smashed up into one jumble, which, with the remains of the engine, choked for a minute or so the mouth of the pit. Then something gave way in the middle, and the whole mass of green iron, smoking coals, brass fittings, wheels, wood-work, and cushions all crumbled together and crashed down into the mine. We heard the rattle, rattle, rattle, as the debris struck against the walls, and then, quite a long time afterwards, there came a deep roar as the remains of the train struck the bottom. The boiler may have burst, for a sharp crash came after the roar, and then a dense cloud of steam and smoke swirled up out of the black depths, falling in a spray as thick as rain all round us. Then the vapour shredded off into thin wisps, which floated away in the summer sunshine, and all was quiet again in the Heartsease mine.

"And now, having carried out our plans so successfully, it only remained to leave no trace behind us. Our little band of workers at the other end had already ripped up the rails and disconnected the side line, replacing everything as it had been before. We were equally busy at the mine. The funnel and other fragments were thrown in, the shaft was planked over as it used to be, and the lines which led to it were torn up and taken away. Then, without flurry, but without delay, we all made our way out of the country, most of us to Paris, my English colleague to Manchester, and McPherson to Southampton, whence he emigrated to America. Let the English papers of that date tell how throughly we had done our work, and how completely we had thrown the cleverest of their detectives off our track.

"You will remember that Gomez threw his bag of papers out of the window, and I need not say that I secured that bag and brought them to my employers. It may interest my employers now, however, to learn that out of that bag I took one or two little papers as a souvenir of the occasion. I have no wish to publish these papers; but, still, it is every man for himself in this world, and what else can I do if my friends will not come to my aid when I want them? Messieurs, you may believe that Herbert de Lernac is quite as formidable when he is against you as when he is with you, and that he is not a man to go to the guillotine until he has seen that every one of you is en route for New Caledonia. For your own sake, if not for mine, make haste, Monsieur de——, and General——, and Baron——(you can fill up the blanks for yourselves as you read this). I promise you that in the next edition there will be no blanks to fill.

"P.S.—As I look over my statement there is only one omission which I can see. It concerns the unfortunate man McPherson, who was foolish enough to write to his wife and to make an appointment with her in New York. It can be imagined that when interests like ours were at stake, we could not leave them to the chance of whether a man in that class of life would or would not give away his secrets to a woman. Having once broken his oath by writing to his wife, we could not trust him any more. We took steps therefore to insure that he should not see his wife. I have sometimes thought that it would be a kindness to write to her and to assure her that there is no impediment to her marrying again."

The Beetle-Hunter

A curious experience? said the Doctor. Yes, my friends, I have had one very curious experience. I never expect to have another, for it is against all doctrines of chances that two such events would befall any one man in a single lifetime. You may believe me or not, but the thing happened exactly as I tell it.

I had just become a medical man, but I had not started in practice, and I lived in rooms in Gower Street. The street has been renumbered since then, but it was in the only house which has a bow-window, upon the left-hand side as you go down from the Metropolitan Station. A widow named Murchison kept the house at that time, and she had three medical students and one engineer as lodgers. I occupied the top room, which was the cheapest, but cheap as it was it was more than I could afford. My small resources were dwindling away, and every week it became more necessary that I should find something to do. Yet I was very unwilling to go into general practice, for my tastes were all in the direction of science, and especially of zoology, towards which I had always a strong leaning. I had almost given the fight up and resigned myself to being a medical drudge for life, when the turning-point of my struggles came in a very extraordinary way.

One morning I had picked up the Standard and was glancing over its contents. There was a complete absence of news, and I was about to toss the paper down again, when my eyes were caught by an advertisement at the head of the personal column. It was worded in this way:

"Wanted for one or more days the services of a medical man. It is essential that he should be a man of strong physique, of steady nerves, and of a resolute nature. Must be an entomologist— coleopterist preferred. Apply, in person, at 77B, Brook Street. Application must be made before twelve o'clock today."

Now, I have already said that I was devoted to zoology. Of all branches of zoology, the study of insects was the most attractive to me, and of all insects beetles were the species with which I was most familiar. Butterfly collectors are numerous, but beetles are far more varied, and more accessible in these islands than are butterflies. It was this fact which had attracted my attention to them, and I had myself made a collection which numbered some hundred varieties. As to the other requisites of the advertisement, I knew that my nerves could be depended upon, and I had won the weight-throwing competition at the inter-hospital sports. Clearly, I was the very man for the vacancy. Within five minutes of my having read the advertisement I was in a cab and on my was to Brook Street.

As I drove, I kept turning the matter over in my head and trying to make a guess as to what sort of employment it could be which needed such curious qualifications. A strong physique, a resolute nature, a medical training, and a knowledge of beetles— what connection could there be between these various requisites? And then there was the disheartening fact that the situation was not a permanent one, but terminable from day to day, according to the terms of the advertisement. The more I pondered over it the more unintelligible did it become; but at the end of my meditations I always came back to the ground fact that, come what might, I had nothing to lose, that I was completely at the end of my resources, and that I was ready for any adventure, however desperate, which would put a few honest sovereigns into my pocket. The man fears to fail who has to pay for his failure, but there was no penalty which Fortune could exact from me. I was like the gambler with empty pockets, who is still allowed to try his luck with the others.

No. 77B, Brook Street, was one of those dingy and yet imposing houses, dun-coloured and flat-faced, with the intensely respectable and solid air which marks the Georgian builder. As I alighted from the cab, a young man came out of the door and walked swiftly down the street. In passing me, I noticed that he cast an inquisitive and somewhat malevolent glance at me, and I took the incident as a good omen, for his appearance was that of a rejected candidate, and if he resented my application it meant that the vacancy was not yet filled up. Full of hope, I ascended the broad steps and rapped with the heavy knocker.

A footman in powder and livery opened the door. Clearly I was in touch with the people of wealth and fashion.

"Yes, sir?" said the footman.

"I came in answer to——"

"Quite so, sir," said the footman. "Lord Linchmere will see you at once in the library."

Lord Linchmere! I had vaguely heard the name, but could not for the instant recall anything about him. Following the footman, I was shown into a large, book-lined room in which there was seated behind a writing-desk a small man with a pleasant, clean-shaven, mobile face, and long hair shot with grey, brushed back from his forehead. He looked me up and down with a very shrewd, penetrating glance, holding the card which the footman had given him in his right hand. Then he smiled pleasantly, and I felt that externally at any rate I possessed the qualifications which he desired.

"You have come in answer to my advertisement, Dr. Hamilton?" he asked.

"Yes, sir."

"Do you fulfil the conditions which are there laid down?"

"I believe that I do."

"You are a powerful man, or so I should judge from your appearance.

"I think that I am fairly strong."

"And resolute?"

"I believe so."

"Have you ever known what it was to be exposed to imminent danger?"

"No, I don't know that I ever have."

"But you think you would be prompt and cool at such a time?"

"I hope so."

"Well, I believe that you would. I have the more confidence in you because you do not pretend to be certain as to what you would do in a position that was new to you. My impression is that, so far as personal qualities go, you are the very man of whom I am in search. That being settled, we may pass on to the next point."

"Which is?"

"To talk to me about beetles."

I looked across to see if he was joking, but, on the contrary, he was leaning eagerly forward across his desk, and there was an expression of something like anxiety in his eyes.

"I am afraid that you do not know about beetles," he cried.

"On the contrary, sir, it is the one scientific subject about which I feel that I really do know something."

"I am overjoyed to hear it. Please talk to me about beetles."

I talked. I do not profess to have said anything original upon the subject, but I gave a short sketch of the characteristics of the beetle, and ran over the more common species, with some allusions to the specimens in my own little collection and to the article upon "Burying Beetles" which I had contributed to the Journal of Entomological Science.

"What! not a collector?" cried Lord Linchmere. "You don't mean that you are yourself a collector?" His eyes danced with pleasure at the thought.

"You are certainly the very man in London for my purpose. I thought that among five millions of people there must be such a man, but the difficulty is to lay one's hands upon him. I have been extraordinarily fortunate in finding you."

He rang a gong upon the table, and the footman entered.

"Ask Lady Rossiter to have the goodness to step this way," said his lordship, and a few moments later the lady was ushered into the room. She was a small, middle-aged woman, very like Lord Linchmere in appearance, with the same quick, alert features and grey-black hair. The expression of anxiety, however, which I had observed upon his face was very much more marked upon hers. Some great grief seemed to have cast its shadow over her features. As Lord Linchmere presented me she turned her face full upon me, and I was shocked to observe a half-healed scar extending for two inches over her right eyebrow. It was partly concealed by plaster, but none the less I could see that it had been a serious wound and not long inflicted.

"Dr. Hamilton is the very man for our purpose, Evelyn," said Lord Linchmere. "He is actually a collector of beetles, and he has written articles upon the subject."

"Really!" said Lady Rossiter. "Then you must have heard of my husband. Everyone who knows anything about beetles must have heard of Sir Thomas Rossiter."

For the first time a thin little ray of light began to break into the obscure business. Here, at last, was a connection between these people and beetles. Sir Thomas Rossiter—he was the greatest authority upon the subject in the world. He had made it his life-long study, and had written a most exhaustive work upon it. I hastened to assure her that I had read and appreciated it.

"Have you met my husband?" she asked.

"No, I have not."

"But you shall," said Lord Linchmere, with decision.

The lady was standing beside the desk, and she put her hand upon his shoulder. It was obvious to me as I saw their faces together that they were brother and sister.

"Are you really prepared for this, Charles? It is noble of you, but you fill me with fears." Her voice quavered with apprehension, and he appeared to me to be equally moved, though he was making strong efforts to conceal his agitation.

"Yes, yes, dear; it is all settled, it is all decided; in fact, there is no other possible way, that I can see."

"There is one obvious way."

"No, no, Evelyn, I shall never abandon you—never. It will come right—depend upon it; it will come right, and surely it looks like the interference of Providence that so perfect an instrument should be put into our hands."

My position was embarrassing, for I felt that for the instant they had forgotten my presence. But Lord Linchmere came back suddenly to me and to my engagement.

"The business for which I want you, Dr. Hamilton, is that you should put yourself absolutely at my disposal. I wish you to come for a short journey with me, to remain always at my side, and to promise to do without question whatever I may ask, however unreasonable it may appear to you to be."

"That is a good deal to ask," said I.

"Unfortunately I cannot put it more plainly, for I do not myself know what turn matters may take. You may be sure, however, that you will not be asked to do anything which your conscience does not approve; and I promise you that, when all is over, you will be proud to have been concerned in so good a work."

"If it ends happily," said the lady.

"Exactly; if it ends happily," his lordship repeated.

"And terms?" I asked.

"Twenty pounds a day."

I was amazed at the sum, and must have showed my surprise upon my features.

"It is a rare combination of qualities, as must have struck you when you first read the advertisement," said Lord Linchmere; "such varied gifts may well command a high return, and I do not conceal from you that your duties might be arduous or even dangerous. Besides, it is possible that one or two days may bring the matter to an end."

"Please God!" sighed his sister.

"So now, Dr. Hamilton, may I rely upon your aid?"

"Most undoubtedly," said I. "You have only to tell me what my duties are."

"Your first duty will be to return to your home. You will pack up whatever you may need for a short visit to the country. We start together from Paddington Station at 3:40 this afternoon."

"Do we go far?"

"As far as Pangbourne. Meet me at the bookstall at 3:30. I shall have the tickets. Goodbye, Dr. Hamilton! And, by the way, there are two things which I should be very glad if you would bring with you, in case you have them. One is your case for collecting beetles, and the other is a stick, and the thicker and heavier the better."

You may imagine that I had plenty to think of from the time that I left Brook Street until I set out to meet Lord Linchmere at Paddington. The whole fantastic business kept arranging and rearranging itself in kaleidoscopic forms inside my brain, until I had thought out a dozen explanations, each of them more grotesquely improbable than the last. And yet I felt that the truth must be something grotesquely improbable also. At last I gave up all attempts at finding a solution, and contented myself with exactly carrying out the instructions which I had received. With a hand valise, specimen-case, and a loaded cane, I was waiting at the

Paddington bookstall when Lord Linchmere arrived. He was an even smaller man than I had thought—frail and peaky, with a manner which was more nervous than it had been in the morning. He wore a long, thick travelling ulster, and I observed that he carried a heavy blackthorn cudgel in his hand.

"I have the tickets," said he, leading the way up the platform.

"This is our train. I have engaged a carriage, for I am particularly anxious to impress one or two things upon you while we travel down."

And yet all that he had to impress upon me might have been said in a sentence, for it was that I was to remember that I was there as a protection to himself, and that I was not on any consideration to leave him for an instant. This he repeated again and again as our journey drew to a close, with an insistence which showed that his nerves were thoroughly shaken.

"Yes," he said at last, in answer to my looks rather than to my words, "I AM nervous, Dr. Hamilton. I have always been a timid man, and my timidity depends upon my frail physical health. But my soul is firm, and I can bring myself up to face a danger which a less-nervous man might shrink from. What I am doing now is done from no compulsion, but entirely from a sense of duty, and yet it is, beyond doubt, a desperate risk. If things should go wrong, I will have some claims to the title of martyr."

This eternal reading of riddles was too much for me. I felt that I must put a term to it.

"I think it would very much better, sir, if you were to trust me entirely," said I. "It is impossible for me to act effectively, when I do not know what are the objects which we have in view, or even where we are going."

"Oh, as to where we are going, there need be no mystery about that," said he; "we are going to Delamere Court, the residence of Sir Thomas Rossiter, with whose work you are so conversant. As to the exact object of our visit, I do not know that at this stage of the proceedings anything would be gained, Dr. Hamilton, by taking you into my complete confidence. I may tell you that we are acting—I say 'we,' because my sister, Lady Rossiter, takes the same view as myself—with the one object of preventing anything in the nature of a family scandal. That being so, you can understand that I am loath to give any explanations which are not absolutely necessary. It would be a different matter, Dr. Hamilton, if I were asking your advice. As matters stand, it is only your active help which I need, and I will indicate to you from time to time how you can best give it."

There was nothing more to be said, and a poor man can put up with a good deal for twenty pounds a day, but I felt none the less that Lord Linchmere was acting rather scurvily towards me. He wished to convert me into a passive tool, like the blackthorn in his hand. With his sensitive disposition I could imagine, however, that scandal would be abhorrent to him, and I realized that he would not take me into his confidence until no other course was open to him. I must trust to my own eyes and ears to solve the mystery, but I had every confidence that I should not trust to them in vain.

Delamere Court lies a good five miles from Pangbourne Station, and we drove for that distance in an open fly. Lord Linchmere sat in deep thought during the time, and he never opened his mouth until we were close to our destination. When he did speak it was to give me a piece of information which surprised me.

"Perhaps you are not aware," said he, "that I am a medical man like yourself?"

"No, sir, I did not know it."

"Yes, I qualified in my younger days, when there were several lives between me and the peerage. I have not had occasion to practise, but I have found it a useful education, all the same. I never regretted the years which I devoted to medical study. These are the gates of Delamere Court."

We had come to two high pillars crowned with heraldic monsters which flanked the opening of a winding avenue. Over the laurel bushes and rhododendrons, I could see a long, many-gabled mansion, girdled with ivy, and toned to the warm, cheery, mellow glow of old brick-work. My eyes were still fixed in admiration upon this delightful house when my companion plucked nervously at my sleeve.

"Here's Sir Thomas," he whispered. "Please talk beetle all you can."

A tall, thin figure, curiously angular and bony, had emerged through a gap in the hedge of laurels. In his hand he held a spud, and he wore gauntleted gardener's gloves. A broad-brimmed, grey hat cast his face into shadow, but it struck me as exceedingly austere, with an ill-nourished beard and harsh, irregular features. The fly pulled up and Lord Linchmere sprang out.

"My dear Thomas, how are you?" said he, heartily.

But the heartiness was by no means reciprocal. The owner of the grounds glared at me over his brother-in-law's shoulder, and I caught broken scraps of sentences—"well-known wishes . . . hatred of strangers . . . unjustifiable intrusion . . . perfectly inexcusable." Then there was a muttered explanation, and the two of them came over together to the side of the fly.

"Let me present you to Sir Thomas Rossiter, Dr. Hamilton," said Lord Linchmere. "You will find that you have a strong community of tastes."

I bowed. Sir Thomas stood very stiffly, looking at me severely from under the broad brim of his hat.

"Lord Linchmere tells me that you know something about beetles," said he. "What do you know about beetles?"

"I know what I have learned from your work upon the coleoptera, Sir Thomas," I answered.

"Give me the names of the better-known species of the British scarabaei," said he.

I had not expected an examination, but fortunately I was ready for one. My answers seemed to please him, for his stern features relaxed.

"You appear to have read my book with some profit, sir," said he. "It is a rare thing for me to meet anyone who takes an intelligent interest in such matters. People can find time for such trivialities as sport or society, and yet the beetles are overlooked. I can assure you that the greater part of the idiots in this part of the country are unaware that I have ever written a book at all—I, the first man who ever described the true function of the elytra. I am glad to see you, sir, and I have no doubt that I can show you some specimens which will interest you." He stepped into the fly and drove up with us to the house, expounding to me as we went some recent researches which he had made into the anatomy of the lady-bird.

I have said that Sir Thomas Rossiter wore a large hat drawn down over his brows. As he entered the hall he uncovered himself, and I was at once aware of a singular characteristic which the hat had concealed. His forehead, which was naturally high, and higher still on account of receding hair, was in a continual state of movement. Some nervous weakness kept the muscles in a constant spasm, which sometimes produced a mere twitching and sometimes a curious rotary movement unlike anything which I had ever seen before. It was strikingly visible as he turned towards us after entering the study, and seemed the more singular from the contrast with the hard, steady, grey eyes which looked out from underneath those palpitating brows.

"I am sorry," said he, "that Lady Rossiter is not here to help me to welcome you. By the way, Charles, did Evelyn say anything about the date of her return?"

"She wished to stay in town for a few more days," said Lord Linchmere. "You know how ladies' social duties accumulate if they have been for some time in the country. My sister has many old friends in London at present."

"Well, she is her own mistress, and I should not wish to alter her plans, but I shall be glad when I see her again. It is very lonely here without her company."

"I was afraid that you might find it so, and that was partly why I ran down. My young friend, Dr. Hamilton, is so much interested in the subject which you have made your own, that I thought you would not mind his accompanying me."

"I lead a retired life, Dr. Hamilton, and my aversion to strangers grows upon me," said our host. "I have sometimes thought that my nerves are not so good as they were. My travels in search of beetles in my younger days took me into many malarious and unhealthy places. But a brother coleopterist like yourself is always a welcome guest, and I shall be delighted if you will look over my collection, which I think that I may without exaggeration describe as the best in Europe."

And so no doubt it was. He had a huge, oaken cabinet arranged in shallow drawers, and here, neatly ticketed and classified, were beetles from every corner of the earth, black, brown, blue, green, and mottled. Every now and then as he swept his hand over the lines and lines of impaled insects he would catch up some rare specimen, and, handling it with as much delicacy and reverence as if it were a precious relic, he would hold forth upon its peculiarities and the circumstances under which it came into his possession. It was evidently an unusual thing for him to meet with a sympathetic listener, and he talked and talked until the spring evening had deepened into night, and the gong announced that it was time to dress for dinner. All the time Lord Linchmere said nothing, but he stood at his brother-in-law's elbow, and I caught him continually shooting curious little, questioning glances into his face. And his own features expressed some strong emotion, apprehension, sympathy, expectation: I seemed to read them all. I was sure that Lord Linchmere was fearing something and awaiting something, but what that something might be I could not imagine.

The evening passed quietly but pleasantly, and I should have been entirely at my ease if it had not been for that continual sense of tension upon the part of Lord Linchmere. As to our host, I found that he improved upon acquaintance. He spoke constantly with affection of his absent wife, and also of his little son, who had recently been sent to school. The house, he said, was not the same without them. If it were not for his scientific studies, he did not know how he could get through the days. After dinner we smoked for some time in the billiard-room, and finally went early to bed.

And then it was that, for the first time, the suspicion that Lord Linchmere was a lunatic crossed my mind. He followed me into my bedroom, when our host had retired.

"Doctor," said he, speaking in a low, hurried voice, "you must come with me. You must spend the night in my bedroom."

"What do you mean?"

"I prefer not to explain. But this is part of your duties. My room is close by, and you can return to your own before the servant calls you in the morning."

"But why?" I asked.

"Because I am nervous of being alone," said he. "That's the reason, since you must have a reason."

It seemed rank lunacy, but the argument of those twenty pounds would overcome many objections. I followed him to his room.

"Well," said I, "there's only room for one in that bed."

"Only one shall occupy it," said he.

"And the other?"

"Must remain on watch."

"Why?" said I. "One would think you expected to be attacked."

"Perhaps I do."

"In that case, why not lock your door?"

"Perhaps I WANT to be attacked."

It looked more and more like lunacy. However, there was nothing for it but to submit. I shrugged my shoulders and sat down in the arm-chair beside the empty fireplace.

"I am to remain on watch, then?" said I, ruefully.

"We will divide the night. If you will watch until two, I will watch the remainder."

"Very good."

"Call me at two o'clock, then."

"I will do so."

"Keep your ears open, and if you hear any sounds wake me instantly—instantly, you hear?"

"You can rely upon it." I tried to look as solemn as he did.

"And for God's sake don't go to sleep," said he, and so, taking off only his coat, he threw the coverlet over him and settled down for the night.

It was a melancholy vigil, and made more so by my own sense of its folly. Supposing that by any chance Lord Linchmere had cause to suspect that he was subject to danger in the house of Sir Thomas Rossiter, why on earth could he not lock his door and so protect himself?" His own answer that he might wish to be attacked was absurd. Why should he possibly wish to be attacked? And who would wish to attack him? Clearly, Lord Linchmere was suffering from some singular delusion, and the result was that on an imbecile pretext I was to be deprived of my night's rest. Still, however absurd, I was determined to carry out his injunctions to the letter as long as I was in his employment. I sat, therefore, beside the empty fireplace, and listened to a sonorous chiming clock somewhere down the passage which gurgled and struck every quarter of an hour. It was an endless vigil. Save for that single clock, an absolute silence reigned throughout the great house. A small lamp stood on the table at my elbow, throwing a circle of light round my chair, but leaving the corners of the room draped in shadow. On the bed Lord Linchmere was breathing peacefully. I envied him his quiet sleep, and again and again my own eyelids drooped, but every time my sense of duty came to my help, and I sat up, rubbing my eyes and pinching myself with a determination to see my irrational watch to an end.

And I did so. From down the passage came the chimes of two o'clock, and I laid my hand upon the shoulder of the sleeper. Instantly he was sitting up, with an expression of the keenest interest upon his face.

"You have heard something?"

"No, sir. It is two o'clock."

"Very good. I will watch. You can go to sleep."

I lay down under the coverlet as he had done and was soon unconscious. My last recollection was of that circle of lamplight, and of the small, hunched-up figure and strained, anxious face of Lord Linchmere in the centre of it.

How long I slept I do not know; but I was suddenly aroused by a sharp tug at my sleeve. The room was in darkness, but a hot smell of oil told me that the lamp had only that instant been extinguished.

"Quick! Quick!" said Lord Linchmere's voice in my ear.

I sprang out of bed, he still dragging at my arm.

"Over here!" he whispered, and pulled me into a corner of the room. "Hush! Listen!"

In the silence of the night I could distinctly hear that someone was coming down the corridor. It was a stealthy step, faint and intermittent, as of a man who paused cautiously after every stride. Sometimes for half a minute there was no sound, and then came the shuffle and creak which told of a fresh advance. My companion was trembling with excitement. His hand, which still held my sleeve, twitched like a branch in the wind.

"What is it?" I whispered.

"It's he!"

"Sir Thomas?"

"Yes."

"What does he want?"

"Hush! Do nothing until I tell you."

I was conscious now that someone was trying the door. There was the faintest little rattle from the handle, and then I dimly saw a thin slit of subdued light. There was a lamp burning somewhere far down the passage, and it just sufficed to make the outside visible from the darkness of our room. The greyish slit grew broader and broader, very gradually, very gently, and then outlined against it I saw the dark figure of a man. He was squat and crouching, with the silhouette of a bulky and misshapen dwarf. Slowly the door swung open with this ominous shape framed in the centre of it. And then, in an instant, the crouching figure shot up, there was a tiger spring across the room and thud, thud, thud, came three tremendous blows from some heavy object upon the bed.

I was so paralysed with amazement that I stood motionless and staring until I was aroused by a yell for help from my companion. The open door shed enough light for me to see the outline of things, and there was little Lord Linchmere with his arms round the neck of his brother-in-law, holding bravely on to him like a game bull-terrier with its teeth into a gaunt deerhound. The tall, bony man dashed himself about, writhing round and round to get a grip upon his assailant; but the other, clutching on from behind, still kept his hold, though his shrill, frightened cries showed how unequal he felt the contest to be. I sprang to the rescue, and the two of us managed to throw Sir Thomas to the ground, though he made his teeth meet in my shoulder. With all my youth and weight and strength, it was a desperate struggle before we could master his frenzied struggles; but at last we secured his arms with the waist-cord of the dressing-gown which he was wearing. I was holding his legs while Lord Linchmere was endeavouring to relight the lamp, when there came the pattering of many feet in the passage, and the butler and two footmen, who had been alarmed by the cries, rushed into the room. With their aid we had no further difficulty in securing our prisoner, who lay foaming and glaring upon the ground. One glance at his face was enough to prove that he was a dangerous maniac, while the short, heavy hammer which lay beside the bed showed how murderous had been his intentions.

"Do not use any violence!" said Lord Linchmere, as we raised the struggling man to his feet. "He will have a period of stupor after this excitement. I believe that it is coming on already." As he spoke the convulsions became less violent, and the madman's head fell forward upon his breast, as if he were overcome by sleep. We led him down the passage and stretched him upon his own bed, where he lay unconscious, breathing heavily.

"Two of you will watch him," said Lord Linchmere. "And now, Dr. Hamilton, if you will return with me to my room, I will give you the explanation which my horror of scandal has perhaps caused me to delay too long. Come what may, you will never have cause to regret your share in this night's work.

"The case may be made clear in a very few words," he continued, when we were alone. "My poor brother-in-law is one of the best fellows upon earth, a loving husband and an estimable father, but he comes from a stock which is deeply tainted with insanity. He has more than once had homicidal outbreaks, which are the more painful because his inclination is always to attack the very person to whom he is most attached. His son was sent away to school to avoid this danger, and then came an attempt upon my sister, his wife, from which she escaped with injuries that you may have observed when you met her in London. You understand that he knows nothing of the matter when he is in his sound senses, and would ridicule the suggestion that he could under any circumstances injure those whom he loves so dearly. It is often, as you know, a characteristic of such maladies that it is absolutely impossible to convince the man who suffers from them of their existence.

"Our great object was, of course, to get him under restraint before he could stain his hands with blood, but the matter was full of difficulty. He is a recluse in his habits, and would not see any medical man. Besides, it was necessary for our purpose that the medical man should convince himself of his insanity; and he is sane as you or I, save on these very rare occasions. But, fortunately, before he has these attacks he always shows certain premonitory symptoms, which are providential danger-signals, warning us to be upon our guard. The chief of these is that nervous contortion of the forehead which you must have observed. This is a phenomenon which always appears from three to four days before his attacks of frenzy. The moment it showed itself his wife came into town on some pretext, and took refuge in my house in Brook Street.

"It remained for me to convince a medical man of Sir Thomas's insanity, without which it was impossible to put him where he could do no harm. The first problem was how to get a medical man into his house. I bethought me of his interest in beetles, and his love for anyone who shared his tastes. I advertised, therefore, and was fortunate enough to find in you the very man I wanted. A stout companion was necessary, for I knew that the lunacy could only be proved by a murderous assault, and I had every reason to believe that that assault would be made upon myself, since he had the warmest regard for me in his moments of sanity. I think your intelligence will supply all the rest. I did not know that the attack would come by night, but I thought it very probable, for the crises of such cases usually do occur in the early hours of the morning. I am a very nervous man myself, but I saw no other way in which I could remove this terrible danger from my sister's life. I need not ask you whether you are willing to sign the lunacy papers."

"Undoubtedly. But TWO signatures are necessary."

"You forget that I am myself a holder of a medical degree. I have the papers on a side-table here, so if you will be good enough to sign them now, we can have the patient removed in the morning."

So that was my visit to Sir Thomas Rossiter, the famous beetle-hunter, and that was also my first step upon the ladder of success, for Lady Rossiter and Lord Linchmere have proved to be staunch friends, and they have never forgotten my association with them in the time of their need. Sir Thomas is out and said to be cured, but I still think that if I spent another night at Delamere Court, I should be inclined to lock my door upon the inside.

The Man with the Watches

There are many who will still bear in mind the singular circumstances which, under the heading of the Rugby Mystery, filled many columns of the daily Press in the spring of the year 1892. Coming as it did at a period of exceptional dullness, it attracted perhaps rather more attention than it deserved, but it offered to the public that mixture of the whimsical and the tragic which is most stimulating to the popular imagination. Interest drooped, however, when, after weeks of fruitless investigation, it was found that no final explanation of the facts was forthcoming, and the tragedy seemed from that time to the present to have finally taken its place in the dark catalogue of inexplicable and unexpiated crimes. A recent communication (the authenticity of which appears to be above question) has, however, thrown some new and clear light upon the matter. Before laying it before the public it would be as well, perhaps, that I should refresh their memories as to the singular facts upon which this commentary is founded. These facts were briefly as follows:

At five o'clock on the evening of the 18th of March in the year already mentioned a train left Euston Station for Manchester. It was a rainy, squally day, which grew wilder as it progressed, so it was by no means the weather in which anyone would travel who was not driven to do so by necessity. The train, however, is a favourite one among Manchester business men who are returning from town, for it does the journey in four hours and twenty minutes, with only three stoppages upon the way. In spite of the inclement evening it was, therefore, fairly well filled upon the occasion of which I speak. The guard of the train was a tried servant of the company—a man who had worked for twenty-two years without a blemish or complaint. His name was John Palmer.

The station clock was upon the stroke of five, and the guard was about to give the customary signal to the engine-driver when he observed two belated passengers hurrying down the platform.

The one was an exceptionally tall man, dressed in a long black overcoat with astrakhan collar and cuffs. I have already said that the evening was an inclement one, and the tall traveller had the high, warm collar turned up to protect his throat against the bitter March wind. He appeared, as far as the guard could judge by so hurried an inspection, to be a man between fifty and sixty years of age, who had retained a good deal of the vigour and activity of his youth. In one hand he carried a brown leather Gladstone bag. His companion was a lady, tall and erect, walking with a vigorous step which outpaced the gentleman beside her. She wore a long, fawn-coloured dust-cloak, a black, close-fitting toque, and a dark veil which concealed the greater part of her face. The two might very well have passed as father and daughter. They walked swiftly down the line of carriages, glancing in at the windows, until the guard, John Palmer, overtook them.

"Now then, sir, look sharp, the train is going," said he.

"First-class," the man answered.

The guard turned the handle of the nearest door. In the carriage which he had opened, there sat a small man with a cigar in his mouth. His appearance seems to have impressed itself upon the guard's memory, for he was prepared, afterwards, to describe or to identify him. He was a man of thirty-four or thirty-five years of age, dressed in some grey material, sharp-nosed, alert, with a ruddy, weather-beaten face, and a small, closely cropped, black beard. He glanced up as the door was opened. The tall man paused with his foot upon the step.

"This is a smoking compartment. The lady dislikes smoke," said he, looking round at the guard.

"All right! Here you are, sir!" said John Palmer. He slammed the door of the smoking carriage, opened that of the next one, which was empty, and thrust the two travellers in. At the same moment he sounded his whistle and the wheels of the train began to move. The man with the cigar was at the window of his carriage, and said something to the guard as he rolled past him, but the words were lost in the bustle of the departure. Palmer stepped into the guard's van, as it came up to him, and thought no more of the incident.

Twelve minutes after its departure the train reached Willesden Junction, where it stopped for a very short interval. An examination of the tickets has made it certain that no one either joined or left it at this time, and no passenger was seen to alight upon the platform. At 5:14 the journey to Manchester was resumed, and Rugby was reached at 6:50, the express being five minutes late.

At Rugby the attention of the station officials was drawn to the fact that the door of one of the first-class carriages was open. An examination of that compartment, and of its neighbour, disclosed a remarkable state of affairs.

The smoking carriage in which the short, red-faced man with the black beard had been seen was now empty. Save for a half-smoked cigar, there was no trace whatever of its recent occupant. The door of this carriage was fastened. In the next compartment, to which attention had been originally drawn, there was no sign either of the gentleman with the astrakhan collar or of the young lady who accompanied him. All three passengers had disappeared. On the other hand, there was found upon the floor of this carriage—the one in which the tall traveller and the lady had been—a young man fashionably dressed and of elegant appearance. He lay with his knees drawn up, and his head resting against the farther door, an elbow upon either seat. A bullet had penetrated his heart and his death must have been instantaneous. No one had seen such a man enter the train, and no railway ticket was found in his pocket, neither were there any markings upon his linen, nor papers nor personal property which might help to identify him. Who he was, whence he had come, and how he had met his end were each as great a mystery as what had occurred to the three people who had started an hour and a half before from Willesden in those two compartments.

I have said that there was no personal property which might help to identify him, but it is true that there was one peculiarity about this unknown young man which was much commented upon at the time. In his pockets were found no fewer than six valuable gold watches, three in the various pockets of his waistcoat, one in his ticket-pocket, one in his breast-pocket, and one small one set in a leather strap and fastened round his left wrist. The obvious explanation that the man was a pickpocket, and that this was his plunder, was discounted by the fact that all six were of American make and of a type which is rare in England. Three of them bore the mark of the Rochester Watchmaking Company; one was by Mason, of Elmira; one was unmarked; and the small one, which was highly jewelled and ornamented, was from Tiffany, of New York. The other contents of his pocket consisted of an ivory knife with a corkscrew by Rodgers, of Sheffield; a small, circular mirror, one inch in diameter; a readmission slip to the Lyceum Theatre; a silver box full of vesta matches, and a brown leather cigar-case containing two cheroots—also two pounds fourteen shillings in money. It was clear, then, that whatever motives may have led to his death, robbery was not among them. As already mentioned, there were no markings upon the man's linen, which appeared to be new, and no tailor's name upon his coat. In appearance he was young, short, smooth-cheeked, and delicately featured. One of his front teeth was conspicuously stopped with gold.

On the discovery of the tragedy an examination was instantly made of the tickets of all passengers, and the number of the passengers themselves was counted. It was found that only three tickets were unaccounted for, corresponding to the three travellers who were missing. The express was then allowed to proceed, but a new guard was sent with it, and John Palmer was detained as a witness at Rugby. The carriage which included the two compartments in question was uncoupled and side-tracked. Then, on the arrival of Inspector Vane, of Scotland Yard, and of Mr. Henderson, a detective in the service of the railway company, an exhaustive inquiry was made into all the circumstances.

That crime had been committed was certain. The bullet, which appeared to have come from a small pistol or revolver, had been fired from some little distance, as there was no scorching of the clothes. No weapon was found in the compartment (which finally disposed of the theory of suicide), nor was there any sign of the brown leather bag which the guard had seen in the hand of the tall gentleman. A lady's parasol was found upon the rack, but no other trace was to be seen of the travellers in either of the sections. Apart from the crime, the question of how or why three passengers (one of them a lady) could get out of the train, and one other get in during the unbroken run between Willesden and Rugby, was one which excited the utmost curiosity among the general public, and gave rise to much speculation in the London Press.

John Palmer, the guard was able at the inquest to give some evidence which threw a little light upon the matter. There was a spot between Tring and Cheddington, according to his statement, where, on account of some repairs to the line, the train had for a few minutes slowed down to a pace not exceeding eight or ten miles an hour. At that place it might be possible for a man, or even for an exceptionally active woman, to have left the train without serious injury. It was true that a gang of platelayers was there, and that they had seen nothing, but it was their custom to stand in the middle between the metals, and the open carriage door was upon the far side, so that it was conceivable that someone might have alighted unseen, as the darkness would by that time be drawing in. A steep embankment would instantly screen anyone who sprang out from the observation of the navvies.

The guard also deposed that there was a good deal of movement upon the platform at Willesden Junction, and that though it was certain that no one had either joined or left the train there, it was still quite possible that some of the passengers might have changed unseen from one compartment to another. It was by no means uncommon for a gentleman to finish his cigar in a smoking carriage and then to change to a clearer atmosphere. Supposing that the man with the black beard had done so at Willesden (and the half-smoked cigar upon the floor seemed to favour the supposition), he would naturally go into the nearest section, which would bring him into the company of the two other actors in this drama. Thus the first stage of the affair might be surmised without any great breach of probability. But what the second stage had been, or how the final one had been arrived at, neither the guard nor the experienced detective officers could suggest.

A careful examination of the line between Willesden and Rugby resulted in one discovery which might or might not have a bearing upon the tragedy. Near Tring, at the very place where the train slowed down, there was found at the bottom of the embankment a small pocket Testament, very shabby and worn. It was printed by the Bible Society of London, and bore an inscription:

"From John to Alice. Jan. 13th, 1856," upon the fly-leaf. Underneath was written: "James. July 4th, 1859," and beneath that again: "Edward. Nov. 1st, 1869," all the entries being in the same handwriting. This was the only clue, if it could be called a clue, which the police obtained, and the coroner's verdict of "Murder by a person or persons unknown" was the unsatisfactory ending of a singular case. Advertisement, rewards, and inquiries proved equally fruitless, and nothing could be found which was solid enough to form the basis for a profitable investigation.

It would be a mistake, however, to suppose that no theories were formed to account for the facts. On the contrary, the Press, both in England and in America, teemed with suggestions and suppositions, most of which were obviously absurd. The fact that the watches were of American make, and some peculiarities in connection with the gold stopping of his front tooth, appeared to indicate that the deceased was a citizen of the United States, though his linen, clothes and boots were undoubtedly of British manufacture. It was surmised, by some, that he was concealed under the seat, and that, being discovered, he was for some reason, possibly because he had overheard their guilty secrets, put to death by his fellow-passengers. When coupled with generalities as to the ferocity and cunning of anarchical and other secret societies, this theory sounded as plausible as any.

The fact that he should be without a ticket would be consistent with the idea of concealment, and it was well known that women played a prominent part in the Nihilistic propaganda. On the other hand, it was clear, from the guard's statement, that the man must have been hidden there BEFORE the others arrived, and how unlikely the coincidence that conspirators should stray exactly into the very compartment in which a spy was already concealed! Besides, this explanation ignored the man in the smoking carriage, and gave no reason at all for his simultaneous disappearance. The police had little difficulty in showing that such a theory would not cover the facts, but they were unprepared in the absence of evidence to advance any alternative explanation.

There was a letter in the Daily Gazette, over the signature of a well-known criminal investigator, which gave rise to considerable discussion at the time. He had formed a hypothesis which had at least ingenuity to recommend it, and I cannot do better than append it in his own words.

"Whatever may be the truth," said he, "it must depend upon some bizarre and rare combination of events, so we need have no hesitation in postulating such events in our explanation. In the absence of data we must abandon the analytic or scientific method of investigation, and must approach it in the synthetic fashion. In a word, instead of taking known events and deducing from them what has occurred, we must build up a fanciful explanation if it will only be consistent with known events. We can then test this explanation by any fresh facts which may arise. If they all fit into their places, the probability is that we are upon the right track, and with each fresh fact this probability increases in a geometrical progression until the evidence becomes final and convincing.

"Now, there is one most remarkable and suggestive fact which has not met with the attention which it deserves. There is a local train running through Harrow and King's Langley, which is timed in such a way that the express must have overtaken it at or about the period when it eased down its speed to eight miles an hour on account of the repairs of the line. The two trains would at that time be travelling in the same direction at a similar rate of speed and upon parallel lines. It is within every one's experience how, under such circumstances, the occupant of each carriage can see very plainly the passengers in the other carriages opposite to him. The lamps of the express had been lit at Willesden, so that each compartment was brightly illuminated, and most visible to an observer from outside.

"Now, the sequence of events as I reconstruct them would be after this fashion. This young man with the abnormal number of watches was alone in the carriage of the slow train. His ticket, with his papers and gloves and other things, was, we will suppose, on the seat beside him. He was probably an American, and also probably a man of weak intellect. The excessive wearing of jewellery is an early symptom in some forms of mania.

"As he sat watching the carriages of the express which were (on account of the state of the line) going at the same pace as himself, he suddenly saw some people in it whom he knew. We will suppose for the sake of our theory that these people were a woman whom he loved and a man whom he hated—and who in return hated him. The young man was excitable and impulsive. He opened the door of his carriage, stepped from the footboard of the local train to the footboard of the express, opened the other door, and made his way into the presence of these two people. The feat (on the supposition that the trains were going at the same pace) is by no means so perilous as it might appear.

"Having now got our young man, without his ticket, into the carriage in which the elder man and the young woman are travelling, it is not difficult to imagine that a violent scene ensued. It is possible that the pair were also Americans, which is the more probable as the man carried a weapon—an unusual thing in England. If our supposition of incipient mania is correct, the young man is likely to have assaulted the other. As the upshot of the quarrel the elder man shot the intruder, and then made his escape from the carriage, taking the young lady with him. We will suppose that all this happened very rapidly, and that the train was still going at so slow a pace that it was not difficult for them to leave it. A woman might leave a train going at eight miles an hour. As a matter of fact, we know that this woman DID do so.

"And now we have to fit in the man in the smoking carriage. Presuming that we have, up to this point, reconstructed the tragedy correctly, we shall find nothing in this other man to cause us to reconsider our conclusions. According to my theory, this man saw the young fellow cross from one train to the other, saw him open the door, heard the pistol-shot, saw the two fugitives spring out on to the line, realized that murder had been done, and sprang out himself in pursuit. Why he has never been heard of since—whether he met his own death in the pursuit, or whether, as is more likely, he was made to realize that it was not a case for his interference—is a detail which we have at present no means of explaining. I acknowledge that there are some difficulties in the way. At first sight, it might seem improbable that at such a moment a murderer would burden himself in his flight with a brown leather bag. My answer is that he was well aware that if the bag were found his identity would be established. It was absolutely necessary for him to take it with him. My theory stands or falls upon one point, and I call upon the railway company to make strict inquiry as to whether a ticket was found unclaimed in the local train through Harrow and King's Langley upon the 18th of March. If such a ticket were found my case is proved. If not, my theory may still be the correct one, for it is conceivable either that he travelled without a ticket or that his ticket was lost."

To this elaborate and plausible hypothesis the answer of the police and of the company was, first, that no such ticket was found; secondly, that the slow train would never run parallel to the express; and, thirdly, that the local train had been stationary in King's Langley Station when the express, going at fifty miles an hour, had flashed past it. So perished the only satisfying explanation, and five years have elapsed without supplying a new one. Now, at last, there comes a statement which covers all the facts, and which must be regarded as authentic. It took the shape of a letter dated from New York, and addressed to the same criminal investigator whose theory I have quoted. It is given here in extenso, with the exception of the two opening paragraphs, which are personal in their nature:

"You'll excuse me if I'm not very free with names. There's less reason now than there was five years ago when mother was still living. But for all that, I had rather cover up our tracks all I can. But I owe you an explanation, for if your idea of it was wrong, it was a mighty ingenious one all the same. I'll have to go back a little so as you may understand all about it.

"My people came from Bucks, England, and emigrated to the States in the early fifties. They settled in Rochester, in the State of New York, where my father ran a large dry goods store. There were only two sons: myself, James, and my brother, Edward. I was ten years older than my brother, and after my father died I sort of took the place of a father to him, as an elder brother would. He was a bright, spirited boy, and just one of the most beautiful creatures that ever lived. But there was always a soft spot in him, and it was like mould in cheese, for it spread and spread, and nothing that you could do would stop it. Mother saw it just as clearly as I did, but she went on spoiling him all the same, for he had such a way with him that you could refuse him nothing. I did all I could to hold him in, and he hated me for my pains.

"At last he fairly got his head, and nothing that we could do would stop him. He got off into New York, and went rapidly from bad to worse. At first he was only fast, and then he was criminal; and then, at the end of a year or two, he was one of the most notorious young crooks in the city. He had formed a friendship with Sparrow MacCoy, who was at the head of his profession as a bunco-steerer, green goodsman and general rascal. They took to card-sharping, and frequented some of the best hotels in New York. My brother was an excellent actor (he might have made an honest name for himself if he had chosen), and he would take the parts of a young Englishman of title, of a simple lad from the West, or of a college undergraduate, whichever suited Sparrow MacCoy's purpose. And then one day he dressed himself as a girl, and he carried it off so well, and made himself such a valuable decoy, that it was their favourite game afterwards. They had made it right with Tammany and with the police, so it seemed as if nothing could ever stop them, for those were in the days before the Lexow Commission, and if you only had a pull, you could do pretty nearly everything you wanted.

"And nothing would have stopped them if they had only stuck to cards and New York, but they must needs come up Rochester way, and forge a name upon a cheque. It was my brother that did it, though everyone knew that it was under the influence of Sparrow MacCoy. I bought up that cheque, and a pretty sum it cost me. Then I went to my brother, laid it before him on the table, and swore to him that I would prosecute if he did not clear out of the country. At first he simply laughed. I could not prosecute, he said, without breaking our mother's heart, and he knew that I would not do that. I made him understand, however, that our mother's heart was being broken in any case, and that I had set firm on the point that I would rather see him in Rochester gaol than in a New York hotel. So at last he gave in, and he made me a solemn promise that he would see Sparrow MacCoy no more, that he would go to Europe, and that he would turn his hand to any honest trade that I helped him to get. I took him down right away to an old family friend, Joe Willson, who is an exporter of American watches and clocks, and I got him to give Edward an agency in

London, with a small salary and a 15 per cent commission on all business. His manner and appearance were so good that he won the old man over at once, and within a week he was sent off to London with a case full of samples.

"It seemed to me that this business of the cheque had really given my brother a fright, and that there was some chance of his settling down into an honest line of life. My mother had spoken with him, and what she said had touched him, for she had always been the best of mothers to him and he had been the great sorrow of her life. But I knew that this man Sparrow MacCoy had a great influence over Edward and my chance of keeping the lad straight lay in breaking the connection between them. I had a friend in the New York detective force, and through him I kept a watch upon MacCoy. When, within a fortnight of my brother's sailing, I heard that MacCoy had taken a berth in the Etruria, I was as certain as if he had told me that he was going over to England for the purpose of coaxing Edward back again into the ways that he had left. In an instant I had resolved to go also, and to pit my influence against MacCoy's. I knew it was a losing fight, but I thought, and my mother thought, that it was my duty. We passed the last night together in prayer for my success, and she gave me her own Testament that my father had given her on the day of their marriage in the Old Country, so that I might always wear it next my heart.

"I was a fellow-traveller, on the steamship, with Sparrow MacCoy, and at least I had the satisfaction of spoiling his little game for the voyage. The very first night I went into the smoking-room, and found him at the head of a card-table, with a half a dozen young fellows who were carrying their full purses and their empty skulls over to Europe. He was settling down for his harvest, and a rich one it would have been. But I soon changed all that.

"'Gentlemen,' said I, 'are you aware whom you are playing with?'

"'What's that to you? You mind your own business!' said he, with an oath.

"'Who is it, anyway?' asked one of the dudes.

"'He's Sparrow MacCoy, the most notorious card-sharper in the States.'

"Up he jumped with a bottle in his hand, but he remembered that he was under the flag of the effete Old Country, where law and order run, and Tammany has no pull. Gaol and the gallows wait for violence and murder, and there's no slipping out by the back door on board an ocean liner.

"'Prove your words, you———!' said he.

"'I will!' said I. 'If you will turn up your right shirt-sleeve to the shoulder, I will either prove my words or I will eat them.'

"He turned white and said not a word. You see, I knew something of his ways, and I was aware of that part of the mechanism which he and all such sharpers use consists of an elastic down the arm with a clip just above the wrist. It is by means of this clip that they withdraw from their hands the cards which they do not want, while they substitute other cards from another hiding place. I reckoned on it being there, and it was. He cursed me, slunk out of the saloon, and was hardly seen again during the voyage. For once, at any rate, I got level with Mister Sparrow MacCoy.

"But he soon had his revenge upon me, for when it came to influencing my brother he outweighed me every time. Edward had kept himself straight in London for the first few weeks, and had done some business with his American watches, until this villain came across his path once more. I did my best, but the best was little enough. The next thing I heard there had been a scandal at one of the Northumberland Avenue hotels: a traveller had been fleeced of a large sum by two confederate card-sharpers, and the matter was in the hands of Scotland Yard. The first I learned of it was in the evening paper, and I was at once certain that my brother and MacCoy were back at their old games. I hurried at once to Edward's lodgings. They told me that he and a tall gentleman (whom I recognized as MacCoy) had gone off together, and that he had left the lodgings and taken his things with him. The landlady had heard them give several directions to the cabman, ending with Euston Station, and she had accidentally overheard the tall gentleman saying something about Manchester. She believed that that was their destination.

"A glance at the time-table showed me that the most likely train was at five, though there was another at 4:35 which they might have caught. I had only time to get the later one, but found no sign of them either at the depot or in the train. They must have gone on by the earlier one, so I determined to follow them to Manchester and search for them in the hotels there. One last appeal to my brother by all that he owed to my mother might even now be the salvation of him. My nerves were overstrung, and I lit a cigar to steady them. At that moment, just as the train was moving off, the door of my compartment was flung open, and there were MacCoy and my brother on the platform.

"They were both disguised, and with good reason, for they knew that the London police were after them. MacCoy had a great astrakhan collar drawn up, so that only his eyes and nose were showing. My brother was dressed like a woman, with a black veil half down his face, but of course it did not deceive me for an instant, nor would it have done so even if I had not known that he had often used such a dress before. I started up, and as I did so MacCoy recognized me. He said something, the conductor slammed the door, and they were shown into the next compartment. I tried to stop the train so as to follow them, but the wheels were already moving, and it was too late.

"When we stopped at Willesden, I instantly changed my carriage. It appears that I was not seen to do so, which is not surprising, as the station was crowded with people. MacCoy, of course, was expecting me, and he had spent the time between Euston and Willesden in saying all he could to harden my brother's heart and set him against me. That is what I fancy, for I had never found him so impossible to soften or to move. I tried this way and I tried that; I pictured his future in an English gaol; I described the sorrow of his mother when I came back with the news; I said everything to touch his heart, but all to no purpose. He sat there with a fixed sneer upon his handsome face, while every now and then Sparrow MacCoy would throw in a taunt at me, or some word of encouragement to hold my brother to his resolutions.

"'Why don't you run a Sunday-school?' he would say to me, and then, in the same breath: 'He thinks you have no will of your own. He thinks you are just the baby brother and that he can lead you where he likes. He's only just finding out that you are a man as well as he.'

"It was those words of his which set me talking bitterly. We had left Willesden, you understand, for all this took some time. My temper got the better of me, and for the first time in my life I let my brother see the rough side of me. Perhaps it would have been better had I done so earlier and more often.

"'A man!' said I. 'Well, I'm glad to have your friend's assurance of it, for no one would suspect it to see you like a boarding-school missy. I don't suppose in all this country there is a more contemptible-looking creature than you are as you sit there with that Dolly pinafore upon you.' He coloured up at that, for he was a vain man, and he winced from ridicule.

"'It's only a dust-cloak,' said he, and he slipped it off. 'One has to throw the coppers off one's scent, and I had no other way to do it.' He took his toque off with the veil attached, and he put both it and the cloak into his brown bag. 'Anyway, I don't need to wear it until the conductor comes round,' said he.

"'Nor then, either,' said I, and taking the bag I slung it with all my force out of the window. 'Now,' said I, 'you'll never make a Mary Jane of yourself while I can help it. If nothing but that disguise stands between you and a gaol, then to gaol you shall go.'

"That was the way to manage him. I felt my advantage at once. His supple nature was one which yielded to roughness far more readily than to entreaty. He flushed with shame, and his eyes filled with tears. But MacCoy saw my advantage also, and was determined that I should not pursue it.

"'He's my pard, and you shall not bully him,' he cried.

"'He's my brother, and you shall not ruin him,' said I. 'I believe a spell of prison is the very best way of keeping you apart, and you shall have it, or it will be no fault of mine.'

"'Oh, you would squeal, would you?' he cried, and in an instant he whipped out his revolver. I sprang for his hand, but saw that I was too late, and jumped aside. At the same instant he fired, and the bullet which would have struck me passed through the heart of my unfortunate brother.

"He dropped without a groan upon the floor of the compartment, and MacCoy and I, equally horrified, knelt at each side of him, trying to bring back some signs of life. MacCoy still held the loaded revolver in his hand, but his anger against me and my resentment towards him had both for the moment been swallowed up in this sudden tragedy. It was he who first realized the situation. The train was for some reason going very slowly at the moment, and he saw his opportunity for escape. In an instant he had the door open, but I was as quick as he, and jumping upon him the two of us fell off the footboard and rolled in each other's arms down a steep embankment. At the bottom I struck my head against a stone, and I remembered nothing more. When I came to myself I was lying among some low bushes, not far from the railroad track, and somebody was bathing my head with a wet handkerchief. It was Sparrow MacCoy.

"'I guess I couldn't leave you,' said he. 'I didn't want to have the blood of two of you on my hands in one day. You loved your brother, I've no doubt; but you didn't love him a cent more than I loved him, though you'll say that I took a queer way to show it. Anyhow, it seems a mighty empty world now that he is gone, and I don't care a continental whether you give me over to the hangman or not.'

"He had turned his ankle in the fall, and there we sat, he with his useless foot, and I with my throbbing head, and we talked and talked until gradually my bitterness began to soften and to turn into something like sympathy. What was the use of revenging his death upon a man who was as much stricken by that death as I was? And then, as my wits gradually returned, I began to realize also that I could do nothing against MacCoy which would not recoil upon my mother and myself. How could we convict him without a full account of my brother's career being made public— the very thing which of all others we wished to avoid? It was really as much our interest as his to cover the matter up, and from being an avenger of crime I found myself changed to a conspirator against Justice. The place in which we found ourselves was one of those pheasant preserves which are so common in the Old Country, and as we groped our way through it I found myself consulting the slayer of my brother as to how far it would be possible to hush it up.

"I soon realized from what he said that unless there were some papers of which we knew nothing in my brother's pockets, there was really no possible means by which the police could identify him or learn how he had got there. His ticket was in MacCoy's pocket, and so was the ticket for some baggage which they had left at the depot. Like most Americans, he had found it cheaper and easier to buy an outfit in London than to bring one from New York, so that all his linen and clothes were new and unmarked. The bag, containing the dust-cloak, which I had thrown out of the window, may have fallen among some bramble patch where it is still concealed, or may have been carried off by some tramp, or may have come into the possession of the police, who kept the incident to themselves. Anyhow, I have seen nothing about it in the London papers. As to the watches, they were a selection from those which had been intrusted to him for business purposes. It may have been for the same business purposes that he was taking them to Manchester, but—well, it's too late to enter into that.

"I don't blame the police for being at fault. I don't see how it could have been otherwise. There was just one little clue that they might have followed up, but it was a small one. I mean that small, circular mirror which was found in my brother's pocket. It isn't a very common thing for a young man to carry about with him, is it? But a gambler might have told you what such a mirror may mean to a card-sharper. If you sit back a little from the table, and lay the mirror, face upwards, upon your lap, you can see, as you deal, every card that you give to your adversary. It is not hard to say whether you see a man or raise him when you know his cards as well as your own. It was as much a part of a sharper's outfit as the elastic clip upon Sparrow MacCoy's arm. Taking that, in connection with the recent frauds at the hotels, the police might have got hold of one end of the string.

"I don't think there is much more for me to explain. We got to a village called Amersham that night in the character of two gentlemen upon a walking tour, and afterwards we made our way quietly to London, whence MacCoy went on to Cairo and I returned to New York. My mother died six months afterwards, and I am glad to say that to the day of her death she never knew what happened. She was always under the delusion that Edward was earning an honest living in London, and I never had the heart to tell her the truth. He never wrote; but, then, he never did write at any time, so that made no difference. His name was the last upon her lips.

"There's just one other thing that I have to ask you, sir, and I should take it as a kind return for all this explanation, if you could do it for me. You remember that Testament that was picked up. I always carried it in my inside pocket, and it must have come out in my fall. I value it very highly, for it was the family book with my birth and my brother's marked by my father in the beginning of it. I wish you would apply at the proper place and have it sent to me. It can be of no possible value to anyone else. If you address it to X, Bassano's Library, Broadway, New York, it is sure to come to hand."

The Japanned Box

It WAS a curious thing, said the private tutor; one of those grotesque and whimsical incidents which occur to one as one goes through life. I lost the best situation which I am ever likely to have through it. But I am glad that I went to Thorpe Place, for I gained—well, as I tell you the story you will learn what I gained.

I don't know whether you are familiar with that part of the Midlands which is drained by the Avon. It is the most English part of England. Shakespeare, the flower of the whole race, was born right in the middle of it. It is a land of rolling pastures, rising in higher folds to the westwards, until they swell into the Malvern Hills. There are no towns, but numerous villages, each with its grey Norman church. You have left the brick of the southern and eastern counties behind you, and everything is stone—stone for the walls, and lichened slabs of stone for the roofs. It is all grim and solid and massive, as befits the heart of a great nation.

It was in the middle of this country, not very far from Evesham, that Sir John Bollamore lived in the old ancestral home of Thorpe Place, and thither it was that I came to teach his two little sons. Sir John was a widower—his wife had died three years before—and he had been left with these two lads aged eight and ten, and one dear little girl of seven. Miss Witherton, who is now my wife, was governess to this little girl. I was tutor to the two boys. Could there be a more obvious prelude to an engagement? She governs me now, and I tutor two little boys of our own. But, there—I have already revealed what it was which I gained in Thorpe Place!

It was a very, very old house, incredibly old—pre-Norman, some of it—and the Bollamores claimed to have lived in that situation since long before the Conquest. It struck a chill to my heart when first I came there, those enormously thick grey walls, the rude crumbling stones, the smell as from a sick animal which exhaled from the rotting plaster of the aged building. But the modern wing was bright and the garden was well kept. No house could be dismal which had a pretty girl inside it and such a show of roses in front.

Apart from a very complete staff of servants there were only four of us in the household. These were Miss Witherton, who was at that time four-and-twenty and as pretty—well, as pretty as Mrs. Colmore is now—myself, Frank Colmore, aged thirty, Mrs. Stevens, the housekeeper, a dry, silent woman, and Mr. Richards, a tall military-looking man, who acted as steward to the Bollamore estates. We four always had our meals together, but Sir John had his usually alone in the library. Sometimes he joined us at dinner, but on the whole we were just as glad when he did not.

For he was a very formidable person. Imagine a man six feet three inches in height, majestically built, with a high-nosed, aristocratic face, brindled hair, shaggy eyebrows, a small, pointed Mephistophelian beard, and lines upon his brow and round his eyes as deep as if they had been carved with a penknife. He had grey eyes, weary, hopeless-looking eyes, proud and yet pathetic, eyes which claimed your pity and yet dared you to show it. His back was rounded with study, but otherwise he was as fine a looking man of his age—five-and-fifty perhaps—as any woman would wish to look upon.

But his presence was not a cheerful one. He was always courteous, always refined, but singularly silent and retiring. I have never lived so long with any man and known so little of him. If he were indoors he spent his time either in his own small study in the Eastern Tower, or in the library in the modern wing. So regular was his routine that one could always say at any hour exactly where he would be. Twice in the day he would visit his study, once after breakfast, and once about ten at night. You might set your watch by the slam of the heavy door. For the rest of the day he would be in his library—save that for an hour or two in the afternoon he would take a walk or a ride, which was solitary like the rest of his existence. He loved his children, and was keenly interested in the progress of their studies, but they were a little awed by the silent, shaggy-browed figure, and they avoided him as much as they could. Indeed, we all did that.

It was some time before I came to know anything about the circumstances of Sir John Bollamore's life, for Mrs. Stevens, the housekeeper, and Mr. Richards, the land-steward, were too loyal to talk easily of their employer's affairs. As to the governess, she knew no more than I did, and our common interest was one of the causes which drew us together. At last, however, an incident occurred which led to a closer acquaintance with Mr. Richards and a fuller knowledge of the life of the man whom I served.

The immediate cause of this was no less than the falling of Master Percy, the youngest of my pupils, into the mill-race, with imminent danger both to his life and to mine, since I had to risk myself in order to save him. Dripping and exhausted—for I was far more spent than the child—I was making for my room when Sir John, who had heard the hubbub, opened the door of his little study and asked me what was the matter. I told him of the accident, but assured him that his child was in no danger, while he listened with a rugged, immobile face, which expressed in its intense eyes and tightened lips all the emotion which he tried to conceal.

"One moment! Step in here! Let me have the details!" said he, turning back through the open door.

And so I found myself within that little sanctum, inside which, as I afterwards learned, no other foot had for three years been set save that of the old servant who cleaned it out. It was a round room, conforming to the shape of the tower in which it was situated, with a low ceiling, a single narrow, ivy-wreathed window, and the simplest of furniture. An old carpet, a single chair, a deal table, and a small shelf of books made up the whole contents. On the table stood a full-length photograph of a woman—I took no particular notice of the features, but I remember, that a certain gracious gentleness was the prevailing impression. Beside it were a large black japanned box and one or two bundles of letters or papers fastened together with elastic bands.

Our interview was a short one, for Sir John Bollamore perceived that I was soaked, and that I should change without delay. The incident led, however, to an instructive talk with Richards, the agent, who had never penetrated into the chamber which chance had opened to me. That very afternoon he came to me, all curiosity, and walked up and down the garden path with me, while my two charges played tennis upon the lawn beside us.

"You hardly realize the exception which has been made in your favour," said he. "That room has been kept such a mystery, and Sir John's visits to it have been so regular and consistent, that an almost superstitious feeling has arisen about it in the household. I assure you that if I were to repeat to you the tales which are flying about, tales of mysterious visitors there, and of voices overheard by the servants, you might suspect that Sir John had relapsed into his old ways."

"Why do you say relapsed?" I asked.

He looked at me in surprise.

"Is it possible," said he, "that Sir John Bollamore's previous history is unknown to you?"

"Absolutely."

"You astound me. I thought that every man in England knew something of his antecedents. I should not mention the matter if it were not that you are now one of ourselves, and that the facts might come to your ears in some harsher form if I were silent upon them. I always took it for granted that you knew that you were in the service of 'Devil' Bollamore."

"But why 'Devil'?" I asked.

"Ah, you are young and the world moves fast, but twenty years ago the name of 'Devil' Bollamore was one of the best known in London. He was the leader of the fastest set, bruiser, driver, gambler, drunkard—a survival of the old type, and as bad as the worst of them."

I stared at him in amazement.

"What!" I cried, "that quiet, studious, sad-faced man?"

"The greatest rip and debauchee in England! All between ourselves, Colmore. But you understand now what I mean when I say that a woman's voice in his room might even now give rise to suspicions."

"But what can have changed him so?"

"Little Beryl Clare, when she took the risk of becoming his wife. That was the turning point. He had got so far that his own fast set had thrown him over. There is a world of difference, you know, between a man who drinks and a drunkard. They all drink, but they taboo a drunkard. He had become a slave to it—hopeless and helpless. Then she stepped in, saw the possibilities of a fine man in the wreck, took her chance in marrying him though she might have had the pick of a dozen, and, by devoting her life to it, brought him back to manhood and decency. You have observed that no liquor is ever kept in the house. There never has been any since her foot crossed its threshold. A drop of it would be like blood to a tiger even now."

"Then her influence still holds him?"

"That is the wonder of it. When she died three years ago, we all expected and feared that he would fall back into his old ways. She feared it herself, and the thought gave a terror to death, for she was like a guardian angel to that man, and lived only for the one purpose. By the way, did you see a black japanned box in his room?"

"Yes."

"I fancy it contains her letters. If ever he has occasion to be away, if only for a single night, he invariably takes his black japanned box with him. Well, well, Colmore, perhaps I have told you rather more than I should, but I shall expect you to reciprocate if anything of interest should come to your knowledge."

I could see that the worthy man was consumed with curiosity and just a little piqued that I, the newcomer, should have been the first to penetrate into the untrodden chamber. But the fact raised me in his esteem, and from that time onwards I found myself upon more confidential terms with him.

And now the silent and majestic figure of my employer became an object of greater interest to me. I began to understand that strangely human look in his eyes, those deep lines upon his care-worn face. He was a man who was fighting a ceaseless battle, holding at arm's length, from morning till night, a horrible adversary who was forever trying to close with him—an adversary which would destroy him body and soul could it but fix its claws once more upon him. As I watched the grim, round-backed figure pacing the corridor or walking in the garden, this imminent danger seemed to take bodily shape, and I could almost fancy that I saw this most loathsome and dangerous of all the fiends crouching closely in his very shadow, like a half-cowed beast which slinks beside its keeper, ready at any unguarded moment to spring at his throat. And the dead woman, the woman who had spent her life in warding off this danger, took shape also to my imagination, and I saw her as a shadowy but beautiful presence which intervened for ever with arms uplifted to screen the man whom she loved.

In some subtle way he divined the sympathy which I had for him, and he showed in his own silent fashion that he appreciated it. He even invited me once to share his afternoon walk, and although no word passed between us on this occasion, it was a mark of confidence which he had never shown to anyone before. He asked me also to index his library (it was one of the best private libraries in England), and I spent many hours in the evening in his presence, if not in his society, he reading at his desk and I sitting in a recess by the window reducing to order the chaos which existed among his books. In spite of these close relations I was never again asked to enter the chamber in the turret.

And then came my revulsion of feeling. A single incident changed all my sympathy to loathing, and made me realize that my employer still remained all that he had ever been, with the additional vice of hypocrisy. What happened was as follows.

One evening Miss Witherton had gone down to Broadway, the neighbouring village, to sing at a concert for some charity, and I, according to my promise, had walked over to escort her back. The drive sweeps round under the eastern turret, and I observed as I passed that the light was lit in the circular room. It was a summer evening, and the window, which was a little higher than our heads, was open. We were, as it happened, engrossed in our own conversation at the moment and we had paused upon the lawn which skirts the old turret, when suddenly something broke in upon our talk and turned our thoughts away from our own affairs.

It was a voice—the voice undoubtedly of a woman. It was low—so low that it was only in that still night air that we could have heard it, but, hushed as it was, there was no mistaking its feminine timbre. It spoke hurriedly, gaspingly for a few sentences, and then was silent—a piteous, breathless, imploring sort of voice. Miss Witherton and I stood for an instant staring at each other. Then we walked quickly in the direction of the hall-door.

"It came through the window," I said.

"We must not play the part of eavesdroppers," she answered. "We must forget that we have ever heard it."

There was an absence of surprise in her manner which suggested a new idea to me.

"You have heard it before," I cried.

"I could not help it. My own room is higher up on the same turret. It has happened frequently."

"Who can the woman be?"

"I have no idea. I had rather not discuss it."

Her voice was enough to show me what she thought. But granting that our employer led a double and dubious life, who could she be, this mysterious woman who kept him company in the old tower? I knew from my own inspection how bleak and bare a room it was. She certainly did not live there. But in that case where did she come from? It could not be anyone of the household. They were all under the vigilant eyes of Mrs. Stevens. The visitor must come from without. But how?

And then suddenly I remembered how ancient this building was, and how probable that some mediaeval passage existed in it. There is hardly an old castle without one. The mysterious room was the basement of the turret, so that if there were anything of the sort it would open through the floor. There were numerous cottages in the immediate vicinity. The other end of the secret passage might lie among some tangle of bramble in the neighbouring copse. I said nothing to anyone, but I felt that the secret of my employer lay within my power.

And the more convinced I was of this the more I marvelled at the manner in which he concealed his true nature. Often as I watched his austere figure, I asked myself if it were indeed possible that such a man should be living this double life, and I tried to persuade myself that my suspicions might after all prove to be ill-founded. But there was the female voice, there was the secret nightly rendezvous in the turret-chamber—how could such facts admit of an innocent interpretation. I conceived a horror of the man. I was filled with loathing at his deep, consistent hypocrisy.

Only once during all those months did I ever see him without that sad but impassive mask which he usually presented towards his fellow-man. For an instant I caught a glimpse of those volcanic fires which he had damped down so long. The occasion was an unworthy one, for the object of his wrath was none other than the aged charwoman whom I have already mentioned as being the one person who was allowed within his mysterious chamber. I was passing the corridor which led to the turret—for my own room lay in that direction—when I heard a sudden, startled scream, and merged in it the husky, growling note of a man who is inarticulate with passion. It was the snarl of a furious wild beast. Then I heard his voice thrilling with anger. "You would dare!" he cried. "You would dare to disobey my directions!" An instant later the charwoman passed me, flying down the passage, white-faced and tremulous, while the terrible voice thundered behind her. "Go to Mrs. Stevens for your money! Never set foot in Thorpe Place again!" Consumed with curiosity, I could not help following the woman, and found her round the corner leaning against the wall and palpitating like a frightened rabbit.

"What is the matter, Mrs. Brown?" I asked.

"It's master!" she gasped. "Oh, 'ow 'e frightened me! If you had seen 'is eyes, Mr. Colmore, sir. I thought 'e would 'ave been the death of me."

"But what had you done?"

"Done, sir! Nothing. At least nothing to make so much of. Just laid my 'and on that black box of 'is—'adn't even opened it, when in 'e came and you 'eard the way 'e went on. I've lost my place, and glad I am of it, for I would never trust myself within reach of 'im again."

So it was the japanned box which was the cause of this outburst—the box from which he would never permit himself to be separated. What was the connection, or was there any connection between this and the secret visits of the lady whose voice I had overheard? Sir John Bollamore's wrath was enduring as well as fiery, for from that day Mrs. Brown, the charwoman, vanished from our ken, and Thorpe Place knew her no more.

And now I wish to tell you the singular chance which solved all these strange questions and put my employer's secret in my possession. The story may leave you with some lingering doubts as to whether my curiosity did not get the better of my honour, and whether I did not condescend to play the spy. If you choose to think so I cannot help it, but can only assure you that, improbable as it may appear, the matter came about exactly as I describe it.

The first stage in this denouement was that the small room in the turret became uninhabitable. This occurred through the fall of the worm-eaten oaken beam which supported the ceiling. Rotten with age, it snapped in the middle one morning, and brought down a quantity of plaster with it. Fortunately Sir John was not in the room at the time. His precious box was rescued from amongst the debris and brought into the library, where, henceforward, it was locked within his bureau. Sir John took no steps to repair the damage, and I never had an opportunity of searching for that secret passage, the existence of which I had surmised. As to the lady, I had thought that this would have brought her visits to an end, had I not one evening heard Mr. Richards asking Mrs. Stevens who the woman was whom he had overheard talking to Sir John in the library. I could not catch her reply, but I saw from her manner that it was not the first time that she had had to answer or avoid the same question.

"You've heard the voice, Colmore?" said the agent.

I confessed that I had.

"And what do YOU think of it?"

I shrugged my shoulders, and remarked that it was no business of mine.

"Come, come, you are just as curious as any of us. Is it a woman or not?"

"It is certainly a woman."

"Which room did you hear it from?"

"From the turret-room, before the ceiling fell."

"But I heard it from the library only last night. I passed the doors as I was going to bed, and I heard something wailing and praying just as plainly as I hear you. It may be a woman——"

"Why, what else COULD it be?"

He looked at me hard.

"There are more things in heaven and earth," said he. "If it is a woman, how does she get there?"

"I don't know."

"No, nor I. But if it is the other thing—but there, for a practical business man at the end of the nineteenth century this is rather a ridiculous line of conversation." He turned away, but I saw that he felt even more than he had said. To all the old ghost stories of Thorpe Place a new one was being added before our very eyes. It may by this time have taken its permanent place, for though an explanation came to me, it never reached the others.

And my explanation came in this way. I had suffered a sleepless night from neuralgia, and about midday I had taken a heavy dose of chlorodyne to alleviate the pain. At that time I was finishing the indexing of Sir John Bollamore's library, and it was my custom to work there from five till seven. On this particular day I struggled against the double effect of my bad night and the narcotic. I have already mentioned that there was a recess in the library, and in this it was my habit to work. I settled down steadily to my task, but my weariness overcame me and, falling back upon the settee, I dropped into a heavy sleep.

How long I slept I do not know, but it was quite dark when I awoke. Confused by the chlorodyne which I had taken, I lay motionless in a semi-conscious state. The great room with its high walls covered with books loomed darkly all round me. A dim radiance from the moonlight came through the farther window, and against this lighter background I saw that Sir John Bollamore was sitting at his study table. His well-set head and clearly cut profile were sharply outlined against the glimmering square behind him. He bent as I watched him, and I heard the sharp turning of a key and the rasping of metal upon metal. As if in a dream I was vaguely conscious that this was the japanned box which stood in front of him, and that he had drawn something out of it, something squat and uncouth, which now lay before him upon the table. I never realized—it never occurred to my bemuddled and torpid brain that I was intruding upon his privacy, that he imagined himself to be alone in the room. And then, just as it rushed upon my horrified perceptions, and I had half risen to announce my presence, I heard a strange, crisp, metallic clicking, and then the voice.

Yes, it was a woman's voice; there could not be a doubt of it. But a voice so charged with entreaty and with yearning love, that it will ring for ever in my ears. It came with a curious faraway tinkle, but every word was clear, though faint—very faint, for they were the last words of a dying woman.

"I am not really gone, John," said the thin, gasping voice. "I am here at your very elbow, and shall be until we meet once more. I die happy to think that morning and night you will hear my voice. Oh, John, be strong, be strong, until we meet again."

I say that I had risen in order to announce my presence, but I could not do so while the voice was sounding. I could only remain half lying, half sitting, paralysed, astounded, listening to those yearning distant musical words. And he—he was so absorbed that even if I had spoken he might not have heard me. But with the silence of the voice came my half articulated apologies and explanations. He sprang across the room, switched on the electric light, and in its white glare I saw him, his eyes gleaming with anger, his face twisted with passion, as the hapless charwoman may have seen him weeks before.

"Mr. Colmore!" he cried. "You here! What is the meaning of this, sir?"

With halting words I explained it all, my neuralgia, the narcotic, my luckless sleep and singular awakening. As he listened the glow of anger faded from his face, and the sad, impassive mask closed once more over his features.

"My secret is yours, Mr. Colmore," said he. "I have only myself to blame for relaxing my precautions. Half confidences are worse than no confidences, and so you may know all since you know so much. The story may go where you will when I have passed away, but until then I rely upon your sense of honour that no human soul shall hear it from your lips. I am proud still—God help me!—or, at least, I am proud enough to resent that pity which this story would draw upon me. I have smiled at envy, and disregarded hatred, but pity is more than I can tolerate.

"You have heard the source from which the voice comes—that voice which has, as I understand, excited so much curiosity in my household. I am aware of the rumours to which it has given rise. These speculations, whether scandalous or superstitious, are such as I can disregard and forgive. What I should never forgive would be a disloyal spying and eavesdropping in order to satisfy an illicit curiosity. But of that, Mr. Colmore, I acquit you.

"When I was a young man, sir, many years younger than you are now, I was launched upon town without a friend or adviser, and with a purse which brought only too many false friends and false advisers to my side. I drank deeply of the wine of life—if there is a man living who has drunk more deeply he is not a man whom I envy. My purse suffered, my character suffered, my constitution suffered, stimulants became a necessity to me, I was a creature from whom my memory recoils. And it was at that time, the time of my blackest degradation, that God sent into my life the gentlest, sweetest spirit that ever descended as a ministering angel from above. She loved me, broken as I was, loved me, and spent her life in making a man once more of that which had degraded itself to the level of the beasts.

"But a fell disease struck her, and she withered away before my eyes. In the hour of her agony it was never of herself, of her own sufferings and her own death that she thought. It was all of me. The one pang which her fate brought to her was the fear that when her influence was removed I should revert to that which I had been. It was in vain that I made oath to her that no drop of wine would ever cross my lips. She knew only too well the hold that the devil had upon me—she who had striven so to loosen it—and it haunted her night and day the thought that my soul might again be within his grip.

"It was from some friend's gossip of the sick room that she heard of this invention—this phonograph—and with the quick insight of a loving woman she saw how she might use it for her ends. She sent me to London to procure the best which money could buy. With her dying breath she gasped into it the words which have held me straight ever since. Lonely and broken, what else have I in all the world to uphold me? But it is enough. Please God, I shall face her without shame when He is pleased to reunite us! That is my secret, Mr. Colmore, and whilst I live I leave it in your keeping."

The Black Doctor

Bishop's Crossing is a small village lying ten miles in a south-westerly direction from Liverpool. Here in the early seventies there settled a doctor named Aloysius Lana. Nothing was known locally either of his antecedents or of the reasons which had prompted him to come to this Lancashire hamlet. Two facts only were certain about him; the one that he had gained his medical qualification with some distinction at Glasgow; the other that he came undoubtedly of a tropical race, and was so dark that he might almost have had a strain of the Indian in his composition. His predominant features were, however, European, and he possessed a stately courtesy and carriage which suggested a Spanish extraction. A swarthy skin, raven-black hair, and dark, sparkling eyes under a pair of heavily-tufted brows made a strange contrast to the flaxen or chestnut rustics of England, and the newcomer was soon known as "The Black Doctor of Bishop's Crossing." At first it was a term of ridicule and reproach; as the years went on it became a title of honour which was familiar to the whole countryside, and extended far beyond the narrow confines of the village.

For the newcomer proved himself to be a capable surgeon and an accomplished physician. The practice of that district had been in the hands of Edward Rowe, the son of Sir William Rowe, the Liverpool consultant, but he had not inherited the talents of his father, and Dr. Lana, with his advantages of presence and of manner, soon beat him out of the field. Dr. Lana's social success was as rapid as his professional. A remarkable surgical cure in the case of the Hon. James Lowry, the second son of Lord Belton, was the means of introducing him to county society, where he became a favourite through the charm of his conversation and the elegance of his manners. An absence of antecedents and of relatives is sometimes an aid rather than an impediment to social advancement, and the distinguished individuality of the handsome doctor was its own recommendation.

His patients had one fault—and one fault only—to find with him. He appeared to be a confirmed bachelor. This was the more remarkable since the house which he occupied was a large one, and it was known that his success in practice had enabled him to save considerable sums. At first the local matchmakers were continually coupling his name with one or other of the eligible ladies, but as years passed and Dr. Lana remained unmarried, it came to be generally understood that for some reason he must remain a bachelor. Some even went so far as to assert that he was already married, and that it was in order to escape the consequence of an early misalliance that he had buried himself at Bishop's Crossing. And, then, just as the matchmakers had finally given him up in despair, his engagement was suddenly announced to Miss Frances Morton, of Leigh Hall.

Miss Morton was a young lady who was well known upon the country-side, her father, James Haldane Morton, having been the Squire of Bishop's Crossing. Both her parents were, however, dead, and she lived with her only brother, Arthur Morton, who had inherited the family estate. In person Miss Morton was tall and stately, and she was famous for her quick, impetuous nature and for her strength of character. She met Dr. Lana at a garden-party, and a friendship, which quickly ripened into love, sprang up between them. Nothing could exceed their devotion to each other. There was some discrepancy in age, he being thirty-seven, and she twenty-four; but, save in that one respect, there was no possible objection to be found with the match. The engagement was in February, and it was arranged that the marriage should take place in August.

Upon the 3rd of June Dr. Lana received a letter from abroad. In a small village the postmaster is also in a position to be the gossip-master, and Mr. Bankley, of Bishop's Crossing, had many of the secrets of his neighbours in his possession. Of this particular letter he remarked only that it was in a curious envelope, that it was in a man's handwriting, that the postscript was Buenos Ayres, and the stamp of the Argentine Republic. It was the first letter which he had ever known Dr. Lana to have from abroad and this was the reason why his attention was particularly called to it before he handed it to the local postman. It was delivered by the evening delivery of that date.

Next morning—that is, upon the 4th of June—Dr. Lana called upon Miss Morton, and a long interview followed, from which he was observed to return in a state of great agitation. Miss Morton remained in her room all that day, and her maid found her several times in tears. In the course of a week it was an open secret to the whole village that the engagement was at an end, that Dr. Lana had behaved shamefully to the young lady, and that Arthur Morton, her brother, was talking of horse-whipping him. In what particular respect the doctor had behaved badly was unknown—some surmised one thing and some another; but it was observed, and taken as the obvious sign of a guilty conscience, that he would go for miles round rather than pass the windows of Leigh Hall, and that he gave up attending morning service upon Sundays where he might have met the young lady. There was an advertisement also in the Lancet as to the sale of a practice which mentioned no names, but which was thought by some to refer to Bishop's Crossing, and to mean that Dr. Lana was thinking of abandoning the scene of his success. Such was the position of affairs when, upon the evening of Monday, June 21st, there came a fresh development which changed what had been a mere village scandal into a tragedy which arrested the attention of the whole nation. Some detail is necessary to cause the facts of that evening to present their full significance.

The sole occupants of the doctor's house were his house-keeper, an elderly and most respectable woman, named Martha Woods, and a young servant—Mary Pilling. The coachman and the surgery-boy slept out. It was the custom of the doctor to sit at night in his study, which was next the surgery in the wing of the house which was farthest from the servants' quarters. This side of the house had a door of its own for the convenience of patients, so that it was possible for the doctor to admit and receive a visitor there without the knowledge of anyone. As a matter of fact, when patients came late it was quite usual for him to let them in and out by the surgery entrance, for the maid and the housekeeper were in the habit of retiring early.

On this particular night Martha Woods went into the doctor's study at half-past nine, and found him writing at his desk. She bade him good night, sent the maid to bed, and then occupied herself until a quarter to eleven in household matters. It was striking eleven upon the hall clock when she went to her own room. She had been there about a quarter of an hour or twenty minutes when she heard a cry or call, which appeared to come from within the house. She waited some time, but it was not repeated. Much alarmed, for the sound was loud and urgent, she put on a dressing-gown, and ran at the top of her speed to the doctor's study.

"Who's there?" cried a voice, as she tapped at the door.

"I am here, sir—Mrs. Woods."

"I beg that you will leave me in peace. Go back to your room this instant!" cried the voice, which was, to the best of her belief, that of her master. The tone was so harsh and so unlike her master's usual manner, that she was surprised and hurt.

"I thought I heard you calling, sir," she explained, but no answer was given to her. Mrs. Woods looked at the clock as she returned to her room, and it was then half-past eleven.

At some period between eleven and twelve (she could not be positive as to the exact hour) a patient called upon the doctor and was unable to get any reply from him. This late visitor was Mrs. Madding, the wife of the village grocer, who was dangerously ill of typhoid fever. Dr. Lana had asked her to look in the last thing and let him know how her husband was progressing. She observed that the light was burning in the study, but having knocked several times at the surgery door without response, she concluded that the doctor had been called out, and so returned home.

There is a short, winding drive with a lamp at the end of it leading down from the house to the road. As Mrs. Madding emerged from the gate a man was coming along the footpath. Thinking that it might be Dr. Lana returning from some professional visit, she waited for him, and was surprised to see that it was Mr. Arthur Morton, the young squire. In the light of the lamp she observed that his manner was excited, and that he carried in his hand a heavy hunting-crop. He was turning in at the gate when she addressed him.

"The doctor is not in, sir," said she.

"How do you know that?" he asked harshly.

"I have been to the surgery door, sir."

"I see a light," said the young squire, looking up the drive. "That is in his study, is it not?"

"Yes, sir; but I am sure that he is out."

"Well, he must come in again," said young Morton, and passed through the gate while Mrs. Madding went upon her homeward way.

At three o'clock that morning her husband suffered a sharp relapse, and she was so alarmed by his symptoms that she determined to call the doctor without delay. As she passed through the gate she was surprised to see someone lurking among the laurel bushes. It was certainly a man, and to the best of her belief Mr. Arthur Morton. Preoccupied with her own troubles, she gave no particular attention to the incident, but hurried on upon her errand.

When she reached the house she perceived to her surprise that the light was still burning in the study. She therefore tapped at the surgery door. There was no answer. She repeated the knocking several times without effect. It appeared to her to be unlikely that the doctor would either go to bed or go out leaving so brilliant a light behind him, and it struck Mrs. Madding that it was possible that he might have dropped asleep in his chair. She tapped at the study window, therefore, but without result. Then, finding that there was an opening between the curtain and the woodwork, she looked through.

The small room was brilliantly lighted from a large lamp on the central table, which was littered with the doctor's books and instruments. No one was visible, nor did she see anything unusual, except that in the farther shadow thrown by the table a dingy white glove was lying upon the carpet. And then suddenly, as her eyes became more accustomed to the light, a boot emerged from the other end of the shadow, and she realized, with a thrill of horror, that what she had taken to be a glove was the hand of a man, who was prostrate upon the floor. Understanding that something terrible had occurred, she rang at the front door, roused

Mrs. Woods, the housekeeper, and the two women made their way into the study, having first dispatched the maidservant to the police-station.

At the side of the table, away from the window, Dr. Lana was discovered stretched upon his back and quite dead. It was evident that he had been subjected to violence, for one of his eyes was blackened and there were marks of bruises about his face and neck. A slight thickening and swelling of his features appeared to suggest that the cause of his death had been strangulation. He was dressed in his usual professional clothes, but wore cloth slippers, the soles of which were perfectly clean. The carpet was marked all over, especially on the side of the door, with traces of dirty boots, which were presumably left by the murderer. It was evident that someone had entered by the surgery door, had killed the doctor, and had then made his escape unseen. That the assailant was a man was certain, from the size of the footprints and from the nature of the injuries. But beyond that point the police found it very difficult to go.

There were no signs of robbery, and the doctor's gold watch was safe in his pocket. He kept a heavy cash-box in the room, and this was discovered to be locked but empty. Mrs. Woods had an impression that a large sum was usually kept there, but the doctor had paid a heavy corn bill in cash only that very day, and it was conjectured that it was to this and not to a robber that the emptiness of the box was due. One thing in the room was missing—but that one thing was suggestive. The portrait of Miss Morton, which had always stood upon the side-table, had been taken from its frame, and carried off. Mrs. Woods had observed it there when she waited upon her employer that evening, and now it was gone. On the other hand, there was picked up from the floor a green eye-patch, which the housekeeper could not remember to have seen before. Such a patch might, however, be in the possession of a doctor, and there was nothing to indicate that it was in any way connected with the crime.

Suspicion could only turn in one direction, and Arthur Morton, the young squire, was immediately arrested. The evidence against him was circumstantial, but damning. He was devoted to his sister, and it was shown that since the rupture between her and

Dr. Lana he had been heard again and again to express himself in the most vindictive terms towards her former lover. He had, as stated, been seen somewhere about eleven o'clock entering the doctor's drive with a hunting-crop in his hand. He had then, according to the theory of the police, broken in upon the doctor, whose exclamation of fear or of anger had been loud enough to attract the attention of Mrs. Woods. When Mrs. Woods descended, Dr. Lana had made up his mind to talk it over with his visitor, and had, therefore, sent his housekeeper back to her room. This conversation had lasted a long time, had become more and more fiery, and had ended by a personal struggle, in which the doctor lost his life. The fact, revealed by a post-mortem, that his heart was much diseased—an ailment quite unsuspected during his life—would make it possible that death might in his case ensue from injuries which would not be fatal to a healthy man. Arthur Morton had then removed his sister's photograph, and had made his way homeward, stepping aside into the laurel bushes to avoid Mrs. Madding at the gate. This was the theory of the prosecution, and the case which they presented was a formidable one.

On the other hand, there were some strong points for the defence. Morton was high-spirited and impetuous, like his sister, but he was respected and liked by everyone, and his frank and honest nature seemed to be incapable of such a crime. His own explanation was that he was anxious to have a conversation with Dr. Lana about some urgent family matters (from first to last he refused even to mention the name of his sister). He did not attempt to deny that this conversation would probably have been of an unpleasant nature. He had heard from a patient that the doctor was out, and he therefore waited until about three in the morning for his return, but as he had seen nothing of him up to that hour, he had given it up and had returned home. As to his death, he knew no more about it than the constable who arrested him. He had formerly been an intimate friend of the deceased man; but circumstances, which he would prefer not to mention, had brought about a change in his sentiments.

There were several facts which supported his innocence. It was certain that Dr. Lana was alive and in his study at half-past eleven o'clock. Mrs. Woods was prepared to swear that it was at that hour that she had heard his voice. The friends of the prisoner contended that it was probable that at that time Dr. Lana was not alone. The sound which had originally attracted the attention of the housekeeper, and her master's unusual impatience that she should leave him in peace, seemed to point to that. If this were so then it appeared to be probable that he had met his end between the moment when the housekeeper heard his voice and the time when Mrs. Madding made her first call and found it impossible to attract his attention. But if this were the time of his death, then it was certain that Mr. Arthur Morton could not be guilty, as it was AFTER this that she had met the young squire at the gate.

If this hypothesis were correct, and someone was with Dr. Lana before Mrs. Madding met Mr. Arthur Morton, then who was this someone, and what motives had he for wishing evil to the doctor? It was universally admitted that if the friends of the accused could throw light upon this, they would have gone a long way towards establishing his innocence. But in the meanwhile it was open to the public to say—as they did say—that there was no proof that anyone had been there at all except the young squire; while, on the other hand, there was ample proof that his motives in going were of a sinister kind. When Mrs. Madding called, the doctor might have retired to his room, or he might, as she thought at the time, have gone out and returned afterwards to find Mr. Arthur Morton waiting for him. Some of the supporters of the accused laid stress upon the fact that the photograph of his sister Frances, which had been removed from the doctor's room, had not been found in her brother's possession. This argument, however, did not count for much, as he had ample time before his arrest to burn it or to destroy it. As to the only positive evidence in the case—the muddy footmarks upon the floor—they were so blurred by the softness of the carpet that it was impossible to make any trustworthy deduction from them. The most that could be said was that their appearance was not inconsistent with the theory that they were made by the accused, and it was further shown that his boots were very muddy upon that night. There had been a heavy shower in the afternoon, and all boots were probably in the same condition.

Such is a bald statement of the singular and romantic series of events which centred public attention upon this Lancashire tragedy. The unknown origin of the doctor, his curious and distinguished personality, the position of the man who was accused of the murder, and the love affair which had preceded the crimes all combined to make the affair one of those dramas which absorb the whole interest of a nation. Throughout the three kingdoms men discussed the case of the Black Doctor of Bishop's Crossing, and many were the theories put forward to explain the facts; but it may safely be said that among them all there was not one which prepared the minds of the public for the extraordinary sequel, which caused so much excitement upon the first day of the trial, and came to a climax upon the second. The long files of the Lancaster Weekly with their report of the case lie before me as I write, but I must content myself with a synopsis of the case up to the point when, upon the evening of the first day, the evidence of Miss Frances Morton threw a singular light upon the case.

Mr. Porlock Carr, the counsel for the prosecution, had marshalled his facts with his usual skill, and as the day wore on, it became more and more evident how difficult was the task which Mr. Humphrey, who had been retained for the defence, had before him. Several witnesses were put up to swear to the intemperate expressions which the young squire had been heard to utter about the doctor, and the fiery manner in which he resented the alleged ill-treatment of his sister. Mrs. Madding repeated her evidence as to the visit which had been paid late at night by the prisoner to the deceased, and it was shown by another witness that the prisoner was aware that the doctor was in the habit of sitting up alone in this isolated wing of the house, and that he had chosen this very late hour to call because he knew that his victim would then be at his mercy. A servant at the squire's house was compelled to admit that he had heard his master return about three that morning, which corroborated Mrs. Madding's statement that she had seen him among the laurel bushes near the gate upon the occasion of her second visit. The muddy boots and an alleged similarity in the footprints were duly dwelt upon, and it was felt when the case for the prosecution had been presented that, however circumstantial it might be, it was none the less so complete and so convincing, that the fate of the prisoner was sealed, unless something quite unexpected should be disclosed by the defence. It was three o'clock when the prosecution closed. At half-past four, when the court rose, a new and unlooked-for development had occurred. I extract the incident, or part of it, from the journal which I have already mentioned, omitting the preliminary observations of the counsel.

Considerable sensation was caused in the crowded court when the first witness called for the defence proved to be Miss Frances Morton, the sister of the prisoner. Our readers will remember that the young lady had been engaged to Dr. Lana, and that it was his anger over the sudden termination of this engagement which was thought to have driven her brother to the perpetration of this crime. Miss Morton had not, however, been directly implicated in the case in any way, either at the inquest or at the police-court proceedings, and her appearance as the leading witness for the defence came as a surprise upon the public.

Miss Frances Morton, who was a tall and handsome brunette, gave her evidence in a low but clear voice, though it was evident throughout that she was suffering from extreme emotion. She alluded to her engagement to the doctor, touched briefly upon its termination, which was due, she said, to personal matters connected with his family, and surprised the court by asserting that she had always considered her brother's resentment to be unreasonable and intemperate. In answer to a direct question from her counsel, she replied that she did not feel that she had any grievance whatever against Dr. Lana, and that in her opinion he had acted in a perfectly honourable manner. Her brother, on an insufficient knowledge of the facts, had taken another view, and she was compelled to acknowledge that, in spite of her entreaties, he had uttered threats of personal violence against the doctor, and had, upon the evening of the tragedy, announced his intention of "having it out with him." She had done her best to bring him to a more reasonable frame of mind, but he was very headstrong where his emotions or prejudices were concerned.

Up to this point the young lady's evidence had appeared to make against the prisoner rather than in his favour. The questions of her counsel, however, soon put a very different light upon the matter, and disclosed an unexpected line of defence.

Mr. Humphrey: Do you believe your brother to be guilty of this crime?

The Judge: I cannot permit that question, Mr. Humphrey. We are here to decide upon questions of fact—not of belief.

Mr. Humphrey: Do you know that your brother is not guilty of the death of Doctor Lana?

Miss Morton: Yes.

Mr. Humphrey: How do you know it?

Miss Morton: Because Dr. Lana is not dead.

There followed a prolonged sensation in court, which interrupted the examination of the witness.

Mr. Humphrey: And how do you know, Miss Morton, that Dr. Lana is not dead?

Miss Morton: Because I have received a letter from him since the date of his supposed death.

Mr. Humphrey: Have you this letter?

Miss Morton: Yes, but I should prefer not to show it.

Mr. Humphrey: Have you the envelope?

Miss Morton: Yes, it is here.

Mr. Humphrey: What is the post-mark?

Miss Morton: Liverpool.

Mr. Humphrey: And the date?

Miss Morton: June the 22nd.

Mr. Humphrey: That being the day after his alleged death. Are you prepared to swear to this handwriting, Miss Morton?

Miss Morton: Certainly.

Mr. Humphrey: I am prepared to call six other witnesses, my lord, to testify that this letter is in the writing of Doctor Lana.

The Judge: Then you must call them tomorrow.

Mr. Porlock Carr (counsel for the prosecution): In the meantime, my lord, we claim possession of this document, so that we may obtain expert evidence as to how far it is an imitation of the handwriting of the gentleman whom we still confidently assert to be deceased. I need not point out that the theory so unexpectedly sprung upon us may prove to be a very obvious device adopted by the friends of the prisoner in order to divert this inquiry. I would draw attention to the fact that the young lady must, according to her own account, have possessed this letter during the proceedings at the inquest and at the police-court. She desires us to believe that she permitted these to proceed, although she held in her pocket evidence which would at any moment have brought them to an end.

Mr. Humphrey: Can you explain this, Miss Morton?
Miss Morton: Dr. Lana desired his secret to be preserved.
Mr. Porlock Carr: Then why have you made this public?
Miss Morton: To save my brother.

A murmur of sympathy broke out in court, which was instantly suppressed by the Judge.

The Judge: Admitting this line of defence, it lies with you, Mr. Humphrey, to throw a light upon who this man is whose body has been recognized by so many friends and patients of Dr. Lana as being that of the doctor himself.
A Juryman: Has anyone up to now expressed any doubt about the matter?
Mr. Porlock Carr: Not to my knowledge.
Mr. Humphrey: We hope to make the matter clear.
The Judge: Then the court adjourns until tomorrow.

This new development of the case excited the utmost interest among the general public. Press comment was prevented by the fact that the trial was still undecided, but the question was everywhere argued as to how far there could be truth in Miss Morton's declaration, and how far it might be a daring ruse for the purpose of saving her brother. The obvious dilemma in which the missing doctor stood was that if by any extraordinary chance he was not dead, then he must be held responsible for the death of this unknown man, who resembled him so exactly, and who was found in his study. This letter which Miss Morton refused to produce was possibly a confession of guilt, and she might find herself in the terrible position of only being able to save her brother from the gallows by the sacrifice of her former lover. The court next morning was crammed to overflowing, and a murmur of excitement passed over it when Mr. Humphrey was observed to enter in a state of emotion, which even his trained nerves could not conceal, and to confer with the opposing counsel. A few hurried words—words which left a look of amazement upon Mr. Porlock Carr's face—passed between them, and then the counsel for the defence, addressing the Judge, announced that, with the consent of the prosecution, the young lady who had given evidence upon the sitting before would not be recalled.

> *The Judge:* But you appear, Mr. Humphrey, to have left matters in a very unsatisfactory state.
> *Mr. Humphrey:* Perhaps, my lord, my next witness may help to clear them up.
> *The Judge:* Then call your next witness.
> *Mr. Humphrey:* I call Dr. Aloysius Lana.

The learned counsel has made many telling remarks in his day, but he has certainly never produced such a sensation with so short a sentence. The court was simply stunned with amazement as the very man whose fate had been the subject of so much contention appeared bodily before them in the witness-box. Those among the spectators who had known him at Bishop's Crossing saw him now, gaunt and thin, with deep lines of care upon his face. But in spite of his melancholy bearing and despondent expression, there were few who could say that they had ever seen a man of more distinguished presence. Bowing to the judge, he asked if he might be allowed to make a statement, and having been duly informed that whatever he said might be used against him, he bowed once more, and proceeded:

"My wish," said he, "is to hold nothing back, but to tell with perfect frankness all that occurred upon the night of the 21st of June. Had I known that the innocent had suffered, and that so much trouble had been brought upon those whom I love best in the world, I should have come forward long ago; but there were reasons which prevented these things from coming to my ears. It was my desire that an unhappy man should vanish from the world which had known him, but I had not foreseen that others would be affected by my actions. Let me to the best of my ability repair the evil which I have done.

"To anyone who is acquainted with the history of the Argentine Republic the name of Lana is well known. My father, who came of the best blood of old Spain, filled all the highest offices of the State, and would have been President but for his death in the riots of San Juan. A brilliant career might have been open to my twin brother Ernest and myself had it not been for financial losses which made it necessary that we should earn our own living. I apologize, sir, if these details appear to be irrelevant, but they are a necessary introduction to that which is to follow.

"I had, as I have said, a twin brother named Ernest, whose resemblance to me was so great that even when we were together people could see no difference between us. Down to the smallest detail we were exactly the same. As we grew older this likeness became less marked because our expression was not the same, but with our features in repose the points of difference were very slight.

"It does not become me to say too much of one who is dead, the more so as he is my only brother, but I leave his character to those who knew him best. I will only say—for I HAVE to say it— that in my early manhood I conceived a horror of him, and that I had good reason for the aversion which filled me. My own reputation suffered from his actions, for our close resemblance caused me to be credited with many of them. Eventually, in a peculiarly disgraceful business, he contrived to throw the whole odium upon me in such a way that I was forced to leave the Argentine for ever, and to seek a career in Europe. The freedom from his hated presence more than compensated me for the loss of my native land. I had enough money to defray my medical studies at Glasgow, and I finally settled in practice at Bishop's Crossing, in the firm conviction that in that remote Lancashire hamlet I should never hear of him again.

"For years my hopes were fulfilled, and then at last he discovered me. Some Liverpool man who visited Buenos Ayres put him upon my track. He had lost all his money, and he thought that he would come over and share mine. Knowing my horror of him, he rightly thought that I would be willing to buy him off. I received a letter from him saying that he was coming. It was at a crisis in my own affairs, and his arrival might conceivably bring trouble, and even disgrace, upon some whom I was especially bound to shield from anything of the kind. I took steps to insure that any evil which might come should fall on me only, and that"—here he turned and looked at the prisoner—"was the cause of conduct upon my part which has been too harshly judged. My only motive was to screen those who were dear to me from any possible connection with scandal or disgrace. That scandal and disgrace would come with my brother was only to say that what had been would be again.

"My brother arrived himself one night not very long after my receipt of the letter. I was sitting in my study after the servants had gone to bed, when I heard a footstep upon the gravel outside, and an instant later I saw his face looking in at me through the window. He was a clean-shaven man like myself, and the resemblance between us was still so great that, for an instant, I thought it was my own reflection in the glass. He had a dark patch over his eye, but our features were absolutely the same. Then he smiled in a sardonic way which had been a trick of his from his boyhood, and I knew that he was the same brother who had driven me from my native land, and brought disgrace upon what had been an honourable name. I went to the door and I admitted him. That would be about ten o'clock that night.

"When he came into the glare of the lamp, I saw at once that he had fallen upon very evil days. He had walked from Liverpool, and he was tired and ill. I was quite shocked by the expression upon his face. My medical knowledge told me that there was some serious internal malady. He had been drinking also, and his face was bruised as the result of a scuffle which he had had with some sailors. It was to cover his injured eye that he wore this patch, which he removed when he entered the room. He was himself dressed in a pea-jacket and flannel shirt, and his feet were bursting through his boots. But his poverty had only made him more savagely vindictive towards me. His hatred rose to the height of a mania. I had been rolling in money in England, according to his account, while he had been starving in South America. I cannot describe to you the threats which he uttered or the insults which he poured upon me. My impression is, that hardships and debauchery had unhinged his reason. He paced about the room like a wild beast, demanding drink, demanding money, and all in the foulest language. I am a hot-tempered man, but I thank God that I am able to say that I remained master of myself, and that I never raised a hand against him. My coolness only irritated him the more. He raved, he cursed, he shook his fists in my face, and then suddenly a horrible spasm passed over his features, he clapped his hand to his side, and with a loud cry he fell in a heap at my feet. I raised him up and stretched him upon the sofa, but no answer came to my exclamations, and the hand which I held in mine was cold and clammy. His diseased heart had broken down. His own violence had killed him.

"For a long time I sat as if I were in some dreadful dream, staring at the body of my brother. I was aroused by the knocking of Mrs. Woods, who had been disturbed by that dying cry. I sent her away to bed. Shortly afterwards a patient tapped at the surgery door, but as I took no notice, he or she went off again. Slowly and gradually as I sat there a plan was forming itself in my head in the curious automatic way in which plans do form. When I rose from my chair my future movements were finally decided upon without my having been conscious of any process of thought. It was an instinct which irresistibly inclined me towards one course.

"Ever since that change in my affairs to which I have alluded, Bishop's Crossing had become hateful to me. My plans of life had been ruined, and I had met with hasty judgments and unkind treatment where I had expected sympathy. It is true that any danger of scandal from my brother had passed away with his life; but still, I was sore about the past, and felt that things could never be as they had been. It may be that I was unduly sensitive, and that I had not made sufficient allowance for others, but my feelings were as I describe. Any chance of getting away from Bishop's Crossing and of everyone in it would be most welcome to me. And here was such a chance as I could never have dared to hope for, a chance which would enable me to make a clean break with the past.

"There was this dead man lying upon the sofa, so like me that save for some little thickness and coarseness of the features there was no difference at all. No one had seen him come and no one would miss him. We were both clean-shaven, and his hair was about the same length as my own. If I changed clothes with him, then Dr. Aloysius Lana would be found lying dead in his study, and there would be an end of an unfortunate fellow, and of a blighted career. There was plenty of ready money in the room, and this I could carry away with me to help me to start once more in some other land. In my brother's clothes I could walk by night unobserved as far as Liverpool, and in that great seaport I would soon find some means of leaving the country. After my lost hopes, the humblest existence where I was unknown was far preferable, in my estimation, to a practice, however successful, in Bishop's Crossing, where at any moment I might come face to face with those whom I should wish, if it were possible, to forget. I determined to effect the change.

"And I did so. I will not go into particulars, for the recollection is as painful as the experience; but in an hour my brother lay, dressed down to the smallest detail in my clothes, while I slunk out by the surgery door, and taking the back path which led across some fields, I started off to make the best of my way to Liverpool, where I arrived the same night. My bag of money and a certain portrait were all I carried out of the house, and I left behind me in my hurry the shade which my brother had been wearing over his eye. Everything else of his I took with me.

"I give you my word, sir, that never for one instant did the idea occur to me that people might think that I had been murdered, nor did I imagine that anyone might be caused serious danger through this stratagem by which I endeavoured to gain a fresh start in the world. On the contrary, it was the thought of relieving others from the burden of my presence which was always uppermost in my mind. A sailing vessel was leaving Liverpool that very day for Corunna, and in this I took my passage, thinking that the voyage would give me time to recover my balance, and to consider the future. But before I left my resolution softened. I bethought me that there was one person in the world to whom I would not cause an hour of sadness. She would mourn me in her heart, however harsh and unsympathetic her relatives might be. She understood and appreciated the motives upon which I had acted, and if the rest of her family condemned me, she, at least, would not forget. And so I sent her a note under the seal of secrecy to save her from a baseless grief. If under the pressure of events she broke that seal, she has my entire sympathy and forgiveness.

"It was only last night that I returned to England, and during all this time I have heard nothing of the sensation which my supposed death had caused, nor of the accusation that Mr. Arthur Morton had been concerned in it. It was in a late evening paper that I read an account of the proceedings of yesterday, and I have come this morning as fast as an express train could bring me to testify to the truth."

Such was the remarkable statement of Dr. Aloysius Lana which brought the trial to a sudden termination. A subsequent investigation corroborated it to the extent of finding out the vessel in which his brother Ernest Lana had come over from South America. The ship's doctor was able to testify that he had complained of a weak heart during the voyage, and that his symptoms were consistent with such a death as was described.

As to Dr. Aloysius Lana, he returned to the village from which he had made so dramatic a disappearance, and a complete reconciliation was effected between him and the young squire, the latter having acknowledged that he had entirely misunderstood the other's motives in withdrawing from his engagement. That another reconciliation followed may be judged from a notice extracted from a prominent column in the Morning Post:

"A marriage was solemnized upon September 19th, by the Rev. Stephen Johnson, at the parish church of Bishop's Crossing, between Aloysius Xavier Lana, son of Don Alfredo Lana, formerly Foreign Minister of the Argentine Republic, and Frances Morton, only daughter of the late James Morton, J.P., of Leigh Hall, Bishop's Crossing, Lancashire."

The Jew's Breastplate

My particular friend, Ward Mortimer, was one of the best men of his day at everything connected with Oriental archaeology. He had written largely upon the subject, he had lived two years in a tomb at Thebes, while he excavated in the Valley of the Kings, and finally he had created a considerable sensation by his exhumation of the alleged mummy of Cleopatra in the inner room of the Temple of Horus, at Philae. With such a record at the age of thirty-one, it was felt that a considerable career lay before him, and no one was surprised when he was elected to the curatorship of the Belmore Street Museum, which carries with it the lectureship at the Oriental College, and an income which has sunk with the fall in land, but which still remains at that ideal sum which is large enough to encourage an investigator, but not so large as to enervate him.

There was only one reason which made Ward Mortimer's position a little difficult at the Belmore Street Museum, and that was the extreme eminence of the man whom he had to succeed. Professor Andreas was a profound scholar and a man of European reputation. His lectures were frequented by students from every part of the world, and his admirable management of the collection intrusted to his care was a commonplace in all learned societies. There was, therefore, considerable surprise when, at the age of fifty-five, he suddenly resigned his position and retired from those duties which had been both his livelihood and his pleasure. He and his daughter left the comfortable suite of rooms which had formed his official residence in connection with the museum, and my friend, Mortimer, who was a bachelor, took up his quarters there.

On hearing of Mortimer's appointment Professor Andreas had written him a very kindly and flattering congratulatory letter. I was actually present at their first meeting, and I went with Mortimer round the museum when the Professor showed us the admirable collection which he had cherished so long. The Professor's beautiful daughter and a young man, Captain Wilson, who was, as I understood, soon to be her husband, accompanied us in our inspection. There were fifteen rooms, but the Babylonian, the Syrian, and the central hall, which contained the Jewish and Egyptian collection, were the finest of all. Professor Andreas was a quiet, dry, elderly man, with a clean-shaven face and an impassive manner, but his dark eyes sparkled and his features quickened into enthusiastic life as he pointed out to us the rarity and the beauty of some of his specimens. His hand lingered so fondly over them, that one could read his pride in them and the grief in his heart now that they were passing from his care into that of another.

He had shown us in turn his mummies, his papyri, his rare scarabs, his inscriptions, his Jewish relics, and his duplication of the famous seven-branched candlestick of the Temple, which was brought to Rome by Titus, and which is supposed by some to be lying at this instant in the bed of the Tiber. Then he approached a case which stood in the very centre of the hall, and he looked down through the glass with reverence in his attitude and manner.

"This is no novelty to an expert like yourself, Mr. Mortimer," said he; "but I daresay that your friend, Mr. Jackson, will be interested to see it."

Leaning over the case I saw an object, some five inches square, which consisted of twelve precious stones in a framework of gold, with golden hooks at two of the corners. The stones were all varying in sort and colour, but they were of the same size. Their shapes, arrangement, and gradation of tint made me think of a box of water-colour paints. Each stone had some hieroglyphic scratched upon its surface.

"You have heard, Mr. Jackson, of the urim and thummim?"

I had heard the term, but my idea of its meaning was exceedingly vague.

"The urim and thummim was a name given to the jewelled plate which lay upon the breast of the high priest of the Jews. They had a very special feeling of reverence for it—something of the feeling which an ancient Roman might have for the Sibylline books in the Capitol. There are, as you see, twelve magnificent stones, inscribed with mystical characters. Counting from the left-hand top corner, the stones are carnelian, peridot, emerald, ruby, lapis lazuli, onyx, sapphire, agate, amethyst, topaz, beryl, and jasper."

I was amazed at the variety and beauty of the stones.

"Has the breastplate any particular history?" I asked.

"It is of great age and of immense value," said Professor Andreas. "Without being able to make an absolute assertion, we have many reasons to think that it is possible that it may be the original urim and thummim of Solomon's Temple. There is certainly nothing so fine in any collection in Europe. My friend, Captain Wilson, here, is a practical authority upon precious stones, and he would tell you how pure these are."

Captain Wilson, a man with a dark, hard, incisive face, was standing beside his fiancee at the other side of the case.

"Yes," said he, curtly, "I have never seen finer stones."

"And the gold-work is also worthy of attention. The ancients excelled in———"——he was apparently about to indicate the setting of the stones, when Captain Wilson interrupted him.

"You will see a finer example of their gold-work in this candlestick," said he, turning to another table, and we all joined him in his admiration of its embossed stem and delicately ornamented branches. Altogether it was an interesting and a novel experience to have objects of such rarity explained by so great an expert; and when, finally, Professor Andreas finished our inspection by formally handing over the precious collection to the care of my friend, I could not help pitying him and envying his successor whose life was to pass in so pleasant a duty. Within a week, Ward Mortimer was duly installed in his new set of rooms, and had become the autocrat of the Belmore Street Museum.

About a fortnight afterwards my friend gave a small dinner to half a dozen bachelor friends to celebrate his promotion. When his guests were departing he pulled my sleeve and signalled to me that he wished me to remain.

"You have only a few hundred yards to go," said he—I was living in chambers in the Albany. "You may as well stay and have a quiet cigar with me. I very much want your advice."

I relapsed into an arm-chair and lit one of his excellent Matronas. When he had returned from seeing the last of his guests out, he drew a letter from his dress-jacket and sat down opposite to me.

"This is an anonymous letter which I received this morning," said he. "I want to read it to you and to have your advice."

"You are very welcome to it for what it is worth."

"This is how the note runs: 'Sir,—I should strongly advise you to keep a very careful watch over the many valuable things which are committed to your charge. I do not think that the present system of a single watchman is sufficient. Be upon your guard, or an irreparable misfortune may occur.'"

"Is that all?"

"Yes, that is all."

"Well," said I, "it is at least obvious that it was written by one of the limited number of people who are aware that you have only one watchman at night."

Ward Mortimer handed me the note, with a curious smile. "Have you an eye for handwriting?" said he. "Now, look at this!" He put another letter in front of me. "Look at the c in 'congratulate' and the c in 'committed.' Look at the capital I. Look at the trick of putting in a dash instead of a stop!"

"They are undoubtedly from the same hand—with some attempt at disguise in the case of this first one."

"The second," said Ward Mortimer, "is the letter of congratulation which was written to me by Professor Andreas upon my obtaining my appointment."

I stared at him in amazement. Then I turned over the letter in my hand, and there, sure enough, was "Martin Andreas" signed upon the other side. There could be no doubt, in the mind of anyone who had the slightest knowledge of the science of graphology, that the Professor had written an anonymous letter, warning his successor against thieves. It was inexplicable, but it was certain.

"Why should he do it?" I asked.

"Precisely what I should wish to ask you. If he had any such misgivings, why could he not come and tell me direct?"

"Will you speak to him about it?"

"There again I am in doubt. He might choose to deny that he wrote it."

"At any rate," said I, "this warning is meant in a friendly spirit, and I should certainly act upon it. Are the present precautions enough to insure you against robbery?"

"I should have thought so. The public are only admitted from ten till five, and there is a guardian to every two rooms. He stands at the door between them, and so commands them both."

"But at night?"

"When the public are gone, we at once put up the great iron shutters, which are absolutely burglar-proof. The watchman is a capable fellow. He sits in the lodge, but he walks round every three hours. We keep one electric light burning in each room all night."

"It is difficult to suggest anything more—short of keeping your day watches all night."

"We could not afford that."

"At least, I should communicate with the police, and have a special constable put on outside in Belmore Street," said I. "As to the letter, if the writer wishes to be anonymous, I think he has a right to remain so. We must trust to the future to show some reason for the curious course which he has adopted."

So we dismissed the subject, but all that night after my return to my chambers I was puzzling my brain as to what possible motive Professor Andreas could have for writing an anonymous warning letter to his successor—for that the writing was his was as certain to me as if I had seen him actually doing it. He foresaw some danger to the collection. Was it because he foresaw it that he abandoned his charge of it? But if so, why should he hesitate to warn Mortimer in his own name? I puzzled and puzzled until at last I fell into a troubled sleep, which carried me beyond my usual hour of rising.

I was aroused in a singular and effective method, for about nine o'clock my friend Mortimer rushed into my room with an expression of consternation upon his face. He was usually one of the most tidy men of my acquaintance, but now his collar was undone at one end, his tie was flying, and his hat at the back of his head. I read his whole story in his frantic eyes.

"The museum has been robbed!" I cried, springing up in bed.

"I fear so! Those jewels! The jewels of the urim and thummim!" he gasped, for he was out of breath with running. "I'm going on to the police-station. Come to the museum as soon as you can, Jackson! Good-bye!" He rushed distractedly out of the room, and I heard him clatter down the stairs.

I was not long in following his directions, but I found when I arrived that he had already returned with a police inspector, and another elderly gentleman, who proved to be Mr. Purvis, one of the partners of Morson and Company, the well-known diamond merchants. As an expert in stones he was always prepared to advise the police. They were grouped round the case in which the breastplate of the Jewish priest had been exposed. The plate had been taken out and laid upon the glass top of the case, and the three heads were bent over it.

"It is obvious that it has been tampered with," said Mortimer. "It caught my eye the moment that I passed through the room this morning. I examined it yesterday evening, so that it is certain that this has happened during the night."

It was, as he had said, obvious that someone had been at work upon it. The settings of the uppermost row of four stones—the carnelian, peridot, emerald, and ruby—were rough and jagged as if someone had scraped all round them. The stones were in their places, but the beautiful gold-work which we had admired only a few days before had been very clumsily pulled about.

"It looks to me," said the police inspector, "as if someone had been trying to take out the stones."

"My fear is," said Mortimer, "that he not only tried, but succeeded. I believe these four stones to be skilful imitations which have been put in the place of the originals."

The same suspicion had evidently been in the mind of the expert, for he had been carefully examining the four stones with the aid of a lens. He now submitted them to several tests, and finally turned cheerfully to Mortimer.

"I congratulate you, sir," said he, heartily. "I will pledge my reputation that all four of these stones are genuine, and of a most unusual degree of purity."

The colour began to come back to my poor friend's frightened face, and he drew a long breath of relief.

"Thank God!" he cried. "Then what in the world did the thief want?"

"Probably he meant to take the stones, but was interrupted."

"In that case one would expect him to take them out one at a time, but the setting of each of these has been loosened, and yet the stones are all here."

"It is certainly most extraordinary," said the inspector. "I never remember a case like it. Let us see the watchman."

The commissionaire was called—a soldierly, honest-faced man, who seemed as concerned as Ward Mortimer at the incident.

"No, sir, I never heard a sound," he answered, in reply to the questions of the inspector. "I made my rounds four times, as usual, but I saw nothing suspicious. I've been in my position ten years, but nothing of the kind has ever occurred before."

"No thief could have come through the windows?"

"Impossible, sir."

"Or passed you at the door?"

"No, sir; I never left my post except when I walked my rounds."

"What other openings are there in the museum?"

"There is the door into Mr. Ward Mortimer's private rooms."

"That is locked at night," my friend explained, "and in order to reach it anyone from the street would have to open the outside door as well."

"Your servants?"

"Their quarters are entirely separate."

"Well, well," said the inspector, "this is certainly very obscure. However, there has been no harm done, according to Mr. Purvis."

"I will swear that those stones are genuine."

"So that the case appears to be merely one of malicious damage. But none the less, I should be very glad to go carefully round the premises, and to see if we can find any trace to show us who your visitor may have been."

His investigation, which lasted all the morning, was careful and intelligent, but it led in the end to nothing. He pointed out to us that there were two possible entrances to the museum which we had not considered. The one was from the cellars by a trap-door opening in the passage. The other through a skylight from the lumber-room, overlooking that very chamber to which the intruder had penetrated. As neither the cellar nor the lumber-room could be entered unless the thief was already within the locked doors, the matter was not of any practical importance, and the dust of cellar and attic assured us that no one had used either one or the other. Finally, we ended as we began, without the slightest clue as to how, why, or by whom the setting of these four jewels had been tampered with.

There remained one course for Mortimer to take, and he took it. Leaving the police to continue their fruitless researches, he asked me to accompany him that afternoon in a visit to Professor Andreas. He took with him the two letters, and it was his intention to openly tax his predecessor with having written the anonymous warning, and to ask him to explain the fact that he should have anticipated so exactly that which had actually occurred. The Professor was living in a small villa in Upper Norwood, but we were informed by the servant that he was away from home. Seeing our disappointment, she asked us if we should like to see Miss Andreas, and showed us into the modest drawing-room.

I have mentioned incidentally that the Professor's daughter was a very beautiful girl. She was a blonde, tall and graceful, with a skin of that delicate tint which the French call "mat," the colour of old ivory, or of the lighter petals of the sulphur rose. I was shocked, however, as she entered the room to see how much she had changed in the last fortnight. Her young face was haggard and her bright eyes heavy with trouble.

"Father has gone to Scotland," she said. "He seems to be tired, and has had a good deal to worry him. He only left us yesterday."

"You look a little tired yourself, Miss Andreas," said my friend.

"I have been so anxious about father."

"Can you give me his Scotch address?"

"Yes, he is with his brother, the Rev. David Andreas, 1, Arran Villas, Ardrossan."

Ward Mortimer made a note of the address, and we left without saying anything as to the object of our visit. We found ourselves in Belmore Street in the evening in exactly the same position in which we had been in the morning. Our only clue was the Professor's letter, and my friend had made up his mind to start for Ardrossan next day, and to get to the bottom of the anonymous letter, when a new development came to alter our plans.

Very early on the following morning I was aroused from my sleep by a tap upon my bedroom door. It was a messenger with a note from Mortimer.

"Do come round," it said; "the matter is becoming more and more extraordinary."

When I obeyed his summons I found him pacing excitedly up and down the central room, while the old soldier who guarded the premises stood with military stiffness in a corner.

"My dear Jackson," he cried, "I am so delighted that you have come, for this is a most inexplicable business."

"What has happened, then?"

He waved his hand towards the case which contained the breastplate.

"Look at it," said he.

I did so, and could not restrain a cry of surprise. The setting of the middle row of precious stones had been profaned in the same manner as the upper ones. Of the twelve jewels eight had been now tampered with in this singular fashion. The setting of the lower four was neat and smooth. The others jagged and irregular.

"Have the stones been altered?" I asked.

"No, I am certain that these upper four are the same which the expert pronounced to be genuine, for I observed yesterday that little discoloration on the edge of the emerald. Since they have not extracted the upper stones, there is no reason to think the lower have been transposed. You say that you heard nothing, Simpson?"

"No, sir," the commissionaire answered. "But when I made my round after daylight I had a special look at these stones, and I saw at once that someone had been meddling with them. Then I called you, sir, and told you. I was backwards and forwards all night, and I never saw a soul or heard a sound."

"Come up and have some breakfast with me," said Mortimer, and he took me into his own chambers.—"Now, what DO you think of this, Jackson?" he asked.

"It is the most objectless, futile, idiotic business that ever I heard of. It can only be the work of a monomaniac."

"Can you put forward any theory?"

A curious idea came into my head. "This object is a Jewish relic of great antiquity and sanctity," said I. "How about the anti-Semitic movement? Could one conceive that a fanatic of that way of thinking might desecrate——"

"No, no, no!" cried Mortimer. "That will never do! Such a man might push his lunacy to the length of destroying a Jewish relic, but why on earth should he nibble round every stone so carefully that he can only do four stones in a night? We must have a better solution than that, and we must find it for ourselves, for I do not think that our inspector is likely to help us. First of all, what do you think of Simpson, the porter?"

"Have you any reason to suspect him?"

"Only that he is the one person on the premises."

"But why should he indulge in such wanton destruction? Nothing has been taken away. He has no motive."

"Mania?"

"No, I will swear to his sanity."

"Have you any other theory?"

"Well, yourself, for example. You are not a somnambulist, by any chance?"

"Nothing of the sort, I assure you."

"Then I give it up."

"But I don't—and I have a plan by which we will make it all clear."

"To visit Professor Andreas?"

"No, we shall find our solution nearer than Scotland. I will tell you what we shall do. You know that skylight which overlooks the central hall? We will leave the electric lights in the hall, and we will keep watch in the lumber-room, you and I, and solve the mystery for ourselves. If our mysterious visitor is doing four stones at a time, he has four still to do, and there is every reason to think that he will return tonight and complete the job."

"Excellent!" I cried.

"We will keep our own secret, and say nothing either to the police or to Simpson. Will you join me?"

"With the utmost pleasure," said I; and so it was agreed.

It was ten o'clock that night when I returned to the Belmore Street Museum. Mortimer was, as I could see, in a state of suppressed nervous excitement, but it was still too early to begin our vigil, so we remained for an hour or so in his chambers, discussing all the possibilities of the singular business which we had met to solve. At last the roaring stream of hansom cabs and the rush of hurrying feet became lower and more intermittent as the pleasure-seekers passed on their way to their stations or their homes. It was nearly twelve when Mortimer led the way to the lumber-room which overlooked the central hall of the museum.

He had visited it during the day, and had spread some sacking so that we could lie at our ease, and look straight down into the museum. The skylight was of unfrosted glass, but was so covered with dust that it would be impossible for anyone looking up from below to detect that he was overlooked. We cleared a small piece at each corner, which gave us a complete view of the room beneath us. In the cold white light of the electric lamps everything stood out hard and clear, and I could see the smallest detail of the contents of the various cases.

Such a vigil is an excellent lesson, since one has no choice but to look hard at those objects which we usually pass with such half-hearted interest. Through my little peep hole I employed the hours in studying every specimen, from the huge mummy-case which leaned against the wall to those very jewels which had brought us there, gleaming and sparkling in their glass case immediately beneath us. There was much precious gold-work and many valuable stones scattered through the numerous cases, but those wonderful twelve which made up the urim and thummim glowed and burned with a radiance which far eclipsed the others. I studied in turn the tomb-pictures of Sicara, the friezes from Karnak, the statues of Memphis, and the inscriptions of Thebes, but my eyes would always come back to that wonderful Jewish relic, and my mind to the singular mystery which surrounded it. I was lost in the thought of it when my companion suddenly drew his breath sharply in, and seized my arm in a convulsive grip. At the same instant I saw what it was which had excited him.

I have said that against the wall—on the right-hand side of the doorway (the right-hand side as we looked at it, but the left as one entered)—there stood a large mummy-case. To our unutterable amazement it was slowly opening. Gradually, gradually the lid was swinging back, and the black slit which marked the opening was becoming wider and wider. So gently and carefully was it done that the movement was almost imperceptible. Then, as we breathlessly watched it, a white thin hand appeared at the opening, pushing back the painted lid, then another hand, and finally a face—a face which was familiar to us both, that of Professor Andreas. Stealthily he slunk out of the mummy-case, like a fox stealing from its burrow, his head turning incessantly to left and to right, stepping, then pausing, then stepping again, the very image of craft and of caution. Once some sound in the street struck him motionless, and he stood listening, with his ear turned, ready to dart back to the shelter behind him. Then he crept onwards again upon tiptoe, very, very softly and slowly, until he had reached the case in the centre of the room. There he took a bunch of keys from his pocket, unlocked the case, took out the Jewish breastplate, and, laying it upon the glass in front of him, began to work upon it with some sort of small, glistening tool. He was so directly underneath us that his bent head covered his work, but we could guess from the movement of his hand that he was engaged in finishing the strange disfigurement which he had begun.

I could realize from the heavy breathing of my companion, and the twitchings of the hand which still clutched my wrist, the furious indignation which filled his heart as he saw this vandalism in the quarter of all others where he could least have expected it. He, the very man who a fortnight before had reverently bent over this unique relic, and who had impressed its antiquity and its sanctity upon us, was now engaged in this outrageous profanation. It was impossible, unthinkable—and yet there, in the white glare of the electric light beneath us, was that dark figure with the bent grey head, and the twitching elbow. What inhuman hypocrisy, what hateful depth of malice against his successor must underlie these sinister nocturnal labours. It was painful to think of and dreadful to watch. Even I, who had none of the acute feelings of a virtuoso, could not bear to look on and see this deliberate mutilation of so ancient a relic. It was a relief to me when my companion tugged at my sleeve as a signal that I was to follow him as he softly crept out of the room. It was not until we were within his own quarters that he opened his lips, and then I saw by his agitated face how deep was his consternation.

"The abominable Goth!" he cried. "Could you have believed it?"

"It is amazing."

"He is a villain or a lunatic—one or the other. We shall very soon see which. Come with me, Jackson, and we shall get to the bottom of this black business."

A door opened out of the passage which was the private entrance from his rooms into the museum. This he opened softly with his key, having first kicked off his shoes, an example which I followed. We crept together through room after room, until the large hall lay before us, with that dark figure still stooping and working at the central case. With an advance as cautious as his own we closed in upon him, but softly as we went we could not take him entirely unawares. We were still a dozen yards from him when he looked round with a start, and uttering a husky cry of terror, ran frantically down the museum.

"Simpson! Simpson!" roared Mortimer, and far away down the vista of electric lighted doors we saw the stiff figure of the old soldier suddenly appear. Professor Andreas saw him also, and stopped running, with a gesture of despair. At the same instant we each laid a hand upon his shoulder.

"Yes, yes, gentlemen," he panted, "I will come with you. To your room, Mr Ward Mortimer, if you please! I feel that I owe you an explanation."

My companion's indignation was so great that I could see that he dared not trust himself to reply. We walked on each side of the old Professor, the astonished commissionaire bringing up the rear. When we reached the violated case, Mortimer stopped and examined the breastplate. Already one of the stones of the lower row had had its setting turned back in the same manner as the others. My friend held it up and glanced furiously at his prisoner.

"How could you!" he cried. "How could you!"

"It is horrible—horrible!" said the Professor. "I don't wonder at your feelings. Take me to your room."

"But this shall not be left exposed!" cried Mortimer. He picked the breastplate up and carried it tenderly in his hand, while I walked beside the Professor, like a policeman with a malefactor.

We passed into Mortimer's chambers, leaving the amazed old soldier to understand matters as best he could. The Professor sat down in Mortimer's arm-chair, and turned so ghastly a colour that for the instant all our resentment was changed to concern. A stiff glass of brandy brought the life back to him once more.

"There, I am better now!" said he. "These last few days have been too much for me. I am convinced that I could not stand it any longer. It is a nightmare—a horrible nightmare—that I should be arrested as a burglar in what has been for so long my own museum. And yet I cannot blame you. You could not have done otherwise. My hope always was that I should get it all over before I was detected. This would have been my last night's work."

"How did you get in?" asked Mortimer.

"By taking a very great liberty with your private door. But the object justified it. The object justified everything. You will not be angry when you know everything—at least, you will not be angry with me. I had a key to your side door and also to the museum door. I did not give them up when I left. And so you see it was not difficult for me to let myself into the museum. I used to come in early before the crowd had cleared from the street. Then I hid myself in the mummy-case, and took refuge there whenever Simpson came round. I could always hear him coming. I used to leave in the same way as I came."

"You ran a risk."

"I had to."

"But why? What on earth was your object—YOU to do a thing like that!" Mortimer pointed reproachfully at the plate which lay before him on the table.

"I could devise no other means. I thought and thought, but there was no alternate except a hideous public scandal, and a private sorrow which would have clouded our lives. I acted for the best, incredible as it may seem to you, and I only ask your attention to enable me to prove it."

"I will hear what you have to say before I take any further steps," said Mortimer, grimly.

"I am determined to hold back nothing, and to take you both completely into my confidence. I will leave it to your own generosity how far you will use the facts with which I supply you."

"We have the essential facts already."

"And yet you understand nothing. Let me go back to what passed a few weeks ago, and I will make it all clear to you. Believe me that what I say is the absolute and exact truth.

"You have met the person who calls himself Captain Wilson. I say 'calls himself' because I have reason now to believe that it is not his correct name. It would take me too long if I were to describe all the means by which he obtained an introduction to me and ingratiated himself into my friendship and the affection of my daughter. He brought letters from foreign colleagues which compelled me to show him some attention. And then, by his own attainments, which are considerable, he succeeded in making himself a very welcome visitor at my rooms. When I learned that my daughter's affections had been gained by him, I may have thought it premature, but I certainly was not surprised, for he had a charm of manner and of conversation which would have made him conspicuous in any society.

"He was much interested in Oriental antiquities, and his knowledge of the subject justified his interest. Often when he spent the evening with us he would ask permission to go down into the museum and have an opportunity of privately inspecting the various specimens. You can imagine that I, as an enthusiast, was in sympathy with such a request, and that I felt no surprise at the constancy of his visits. After his actual engagement to Elise, there was hardly an evening which he did not pass with us, and an hour or two were generally devoted to the museum. He had the free run of the place, and when I have been away for the evening I had no objection to his doing whatever he wished here. This state of things was only terminated by the fact of my resignation of my official duties and my retirement to Norwood, where I hoped to have the leisure to write a considerable work which I had planned.

"It was immediately after this—within a week or so—that I first realized the true nature and character of the man whom I had so imprudently introduced into my family. The discovery came to me through letters from my friends abroad, which showed me that his introductions to me had been forgeries. Aghast at the revelation, I asked myself what motive this man could originally have had in practising this elaborate deception upon me. I was too poor a man for any fortune-hunter to have marked me down. Why, then, had he come? I remembered that some of the most precious gems in Europe had been under my charge, and I remembered also the ingenious excuses by which this man had made himself familiar with the cases in which they were kept. He was a rascal who was planning some gigantic robbery. How could I, without striking my own daughter, who was infatuated about him, prevent him from carrying out any plan which he might have formed? My device was a clumsy one, and yet I could think of nothing more effective. If I had written a letter under my own name, you would naturally have turned to me for details which I did not wish to give. I resorted to an anonymous letter, begging you to be upon your guard.

"I may tell you that my change from Belmore Street to Norwood had not affected the visits of this man, who had, I believe, a real and overpowering affection for my daughter. As to her, I could not have believed that any woman could be so completely under the influence of a man as she was. His stronger nature seemed to entirely dominate her. I had not realized how far this was the case, or the extent of the confidence which existed between them, until that very evening when his true character for the first time was made clear to me. I had given orders that when he called he should be shown into my study instead of to the drawing-room. There I told him bluntly that I knew all about him, that I had taken steps to defeat his designs, and that neither I nor my daughter desired ever to see him again. I added that I thanked God that I had found him out before he had time to harm those precious objects which it had been the work of my life-time to protect.

"He was certainly a man of iron nerve. He took my remarks without a sign either of surprise or of defiance, but listened gravely and attentively until I had finished. Then he walked across the room without a word and struck the bell.

"'Ask Miss Andreas to be so kind as to step this way,' said he to the servant.

"My daughter entered, and the man closed the door behind her. Then he took her hand in his.

"'Elise,' said he, 'your father has just discovered that I am a villain. He knows now what you knew before.'

"She stood in silence, listening.

"'He says that we are to part for ever,' said he.

"She did not withdraw her hand.

"'Will you be true to me, or will you remove the last good influence which is ever likely to come into my life?'

"'John,' she cried, passionately. 'I will never abandon you! Never, never, not if the whole world were against you.'

"In vain I argued and pleaded with her. It was absolutely useless. Her whole life was bound up in this man before me. My daughter, gentlemen, is all that I have left to love, and it filled me with agony when I saw how powerless I was to save her from her ruin. My helplessness seemed to touch this man who was the cause of my trouble.

"'It may not be as bad as you think, sir,' said he, in his quiet, inflexible way. 'I love Elise with a love which is strong enough to rescue even one who has such a record as I have. It was but yesterday that I promised her that never again in my whole life would I do a thing of which she should be ashamed. I have made up my mind to it, and never yet did I make up my mind to a thing which I did not do.'

"He spoke with an air which carried conviction with it. As he concluded he put his hand into his pocket and he drew out a small cardboard box.

"'I am about to give you a proof of my determination,' said he. 'This, Elise, shall be the first-fruits of your redeeming influence over me. You are right, sir, in thinking that I had designs upon the jewels in your possession. Such ventures have had a charm for me, which depended as much upon the risk run as upon the value of the prize. Those famous and antique stones of the Jewish priest were a challenge to my daring and my ingenuity. I determined to get them.'

"'I guessed as much.'

"'There was only one thing that you did not guess.'

"'And what is that?'

"'That I got them. They are in this box.'

"He opened the box, and tilted out the contents upon the corner of my desk. My hair rose and my flesh grew cold as I looked. There were twelve magnificent square stones engraved with mystical characters. There could be no doubt that they were the jewels of the urim and thummim.

"'Good God!' I cried. 'How have you escaped discovery?'

"'By the substitution of twelve others, made especially to my order, in which the originals are so carefully imitated that I defy the eye to detect the difference.'

"'Then the present stones are false?' I cried.

"'They have been for some weeks.'

"We all stood in silence, my daughter white with emotion, but still holding this man by the hand.

"'You see what I am capable of, Elise,' said he.

"'I see that you are capable of repentance and restitution,' she answered.

"'Yes, thanks to your influence! I leave the stones in your hands, sir. Do what you like about it. But remember that whatever you do against me, is done against the future husband of your only daughter. You will hear from me soon again, Elise. It is the last time that I will ever cause pain to your tender heart,' and with these words he left both the room and the house.

"My position was a dreadful one. Here I was with these precious relics in my possession, and how could I return them without a scandal and an exposure? I knew the depth of my daughter's nature too well to suppose that I would ever be able to detach her from this man now that she had entirely given him her heart. I was not even sure how far it was right to detach her if she had such an ameliorating influence over him. How could I expose him without injuring her—and how far was I justified in exposing him when he had voluntarily put himself into my power? I thought and thought until at last I formed a resolution which may seem to you to be a foolish one, and yet, if I had to do it again, I believe it would be the best course open to me.

"My idea was to return the stones without anyone being the wiser. With my keys I could get into the museum at any time, and I was confident that I could avoid Simpson, whose hours and methods were familiar to me. I determined to take no one into my confidence—not even my daughter—whom I told that I was about to visit my brother in Scotland. I wanted a free hand for a few nights, without inquiry as to my comings and goings. To this end I took a room in Harding Street that very night, with an intimation that I was a Pressman, and that I should keep very late hours.

"That night I made my way into the museum, and I replaced four of the stones. It was hard work, and took me all night. When Simpson came round I always heard his footsteps, and concealed myself in the mummy-case. I had some knowledge of gold-work, but was far less skilful than the thief had been. He had replaced the setting so exactly that I defy anyone to see the difference. My work was rude and clumsy. However, I hoped that the plate might not be carefully examined, or the roughness of the setting observed, until my task was done. Next night I replaced four more stones. And tonight I should have finished my task had it not been for the unfortunate circumstance which has caused me to reveal so much which I should have wished to keep concealed. I appeal to you, gentlemen, to your sense of honour and of compassion, whether what I have told you should go any farther or not. My own happiness, my daughter's future, the hopes of this man's regeneration, all depend upon your decision.

"Which is," said my friend, "that all is well that ends well and that the whole matter ends here and at once. Tomorrow the loose settings shall be tightened by an expert goldsmith, and so passes the greatest danger to which, since the destruction of the Temple, the urim and thummim has been exposed. Here is my hand, Professor Andreas, and I can only hope that under such difficult circumstances I should have carried myself as unselfishly and as well."

Just one footnote to this narrative. Within a month Elise Andreas was married to a man whose name, had I the indiscretion to mention it, would appeal to my readers as one who is now widely and deservedly honoured. But if the truth were known that honour is due not to him, but to the gentle girl who plucked him back when he had gone so far down that dark road along which few return.

THE LOST WORLD

I have wrought my simple plan
If I give one hour of joy
To the boy who's half a man,
Or the man who's half a boy.

Foreword

Mr. E. D. Malone desires to state that both the injunction for restraint and the libel action have been withdrawn unreservedly by Professor G. E. Challenger, who, being satisfied that no criticism or comment in this book is meant in an offensive spirit, has guaranteed that he will place no impediment to its publication and circulation.

Chapter I "There Are Heroisms All Round Us"

Mr. Hungerton, her father, really was the most tactless person upon earth,—a fluffy, feathery, untidy cockatoo of a man, perfectly good-natured, but absolutely centered upon his own silly self. If anything could have driven me from Gladys, it would have been the thought of such a father-in-law. I am convinced that he really believed in his heart that I came round to the Chestnuts three days a week for the pleasure of his company, and very especially to hear his views upon bimetallism, a subject upon which he was by way of being an authority.

For an hour or more that evening I listened to his monotonous chirrup about bad money driving out good, the token value of silver, the depreciation of the rupee, and the true standards of exchange.

"Suppose," he cried with feeble violence, "that all the debts in the world were called up simultaneously, and immediate payment insisted upon,—what under our present conditions would happen then?"

I gave the self-evident answer that I should be a ruined man, upon which he jumped from his chair, reproved me for my habitual levity, which made it impossible for him to discuss any reasonable subject in my presence, and bounced off out of the room to dress for a Masonic meeting.

At last I was alone with Gladys, and the moment of Fate had come! All that evening I had felt like the soldier who awaits the signal which will send him on a forlorn hope; hope of victory and fear of repulse alternating in his mind.

She sat with that proud, delicate profile of hers outlined against the red curtain. How beautiful she was! And yet how aloof! We had been friends, quite good friends; but never could I get beyond the same comradeship which I might have established with one of my fellow-reporters upon the Gazette,—perfectly frank, perfectly kindly, and perfectly unsexual. My instincts are all against a woman being too frank and at her ease with me. It is no compliment to a man. Where the real sex feeling begins, timidity and distrust are its companions, heritage from old wicked days when love and violence went often hand in hand. The bent head, the averted eye, the faltering voice, the wincing figure—these, and not the unshrinking gaze and frank reply, are the true signals of passion. Even in my short life I had learned as much as that—or had inherited it in that race memory which we call instinct.

Gladys was full of every womanly quality. Some judged her to be cold and hard; but such a thought was treason. That delicately bronzed skin, almost oriental in its coloring, that raven hair, the large liquid eyes, the full but exquisite lips,—all the stigmata of passion were there. But I was sadly conscious that up to now I had never found the secret of drawing it forth. However, come what might, I should have done with suspense and bring matters to a head to-night. She could but refuse me, and better be a repulsed lover than an accepted brother.

So far my thoughts had carried me, and I was about to break the long and uneasy silence, when two critical, dark eyes looked round at me, and the proud head was shaken in smiling reproof. "I have a presentiment that you are going to propose, Ned. I do wish you wouldn't; for things are so much nicer as they are."

I drew my chair a little nearer. "Now, how did you know that I was going to propose?" I asked in genuine wonder.

"Don't women always know? Do you suppose any woman in the world was ever taken unawares? But—oh, Ned, our friendship has been so good and so pleasant! What a pity to spoil it! Don't you feel how splendid it is that a young man and a young woman should be able to talk face to face as we have talked?"

"I don't know, Gladys. You see, I can talk face to face with—with the station-master." I can't imagine how that official came into the matter; but in he trotted, and set us both laughing. "That does not satisfy me in the least. I want my arms round you, and your head on my breast, and—oh, Gladys, I want——"

She had sprung from her chair, as she saw signs that I proposed to demonstrate some of my wants. "You've spoiled everything, Ned," she said. "It's all so beautiful and natural until this kind of thing comes in! It is such a pity! Why can't you control yourself?"

"I didn't invent it," I pleaded. "It's nature. It's love."

"Well, perhaps if both love, it may be different. I have never felt it."

"But you must—you, with your beauty, with your soul! Oh, Gladys, you were made for love! You must love!"

"One must wait till it comes."

"But why can't you love me, Gladys? Is it my appearance, or what?"

She did unbend a little. She put forward a hand—such a gracious, stooping attitude it was—and she pressed back my head. Then she looked into my upturned face with a very wistful smile.

"No it isn't that," she said at last. "You're not a conceited boy by nature, and so I can safely tell you it is not that. It's deeper."

"My character?"

She nodded severely.

"What can I do to mend it? Do sit down and talk it over. No, really, I won't if you'll only sit down!"

She looked at me with a wondering distrust which was much more to my mind than her whole-hearted confidence. How primitive and bestial it looks when you put it down in black and white!—and perhaps after all it is only a feeling peculiar to myself. Anyhow, she sat down.

"Now tell me what's amiss with me?"

"I'm in love with somebody else," said she.

It was my turn to jump out of my chair.

"It's nobody in particular," she explained, laughing at the expression of my face: "only an ideal. I've never met the kind of man I mean."

"Tell me about him. What does he look like?"

"Oh, he might look very much like you."

"How dear of you to say that! Well, what is it that he does that I don't do? Just say the word,—teetotal, vegetarian, aeronaut, theosophist, superman. I'll have a try at it, Gladys, if you will only give me an idea what would please you."

She laughed at the elasticity of my character. "Well, in the first place, I don't think my ideal would speak like that," said she. "He would be a harder, sterner man, not so ready to adapt himself to a silly girl's whim. But, above all, he must be a man who could do, who could act, who could look Death in the face and have no fear of him, a man of great deeds and strange experiences. It is never a man that I should love, but always the glories he had won; for they would be reflected upon me. Think of Richard Burton! When I read his wife's life of him I could so understand her love! And Lady Stanley! Did you ever read the wonderful last chapter of that book about her husband? These are the sort of men that a woman could worship with all her soul, and yet be the greater, not the less, on account of her love, honored by all the world as the inspirer of noble deeds."

She looked so beautiful in her enthusiasm that I nearly brought down the whole level of the interview. I gripped myself hard, and went on with the argument.

"We can't all be Stanleys and Burtons," said I; "besides, we don't get the chance,—at least, I never had the chance. If I did, I should try to take it."

"But chances are all around you. It is the mark of the kind of man I mean that he makes his own chances. You can't hold him back. I've never met him, and yet I seem to know him so well. There are heroisms all round us waiting to be done. It's for men to do them, and for women to reserve their love as a reward for such men. Look at that young Frenchman who went up last week in a balloon. It was blowing a gale of wind; but because he was announced to go he insisted on starting. The wind blew him fifteen hundred miles in twenty-four hours, and he fell in the middle of Russia. That was the kind of man I mean. Think of the woman he loved, and how other women must have envied her! That's what I should like to be,—envied for my man."

"I'd have done it to please you."

"But you shouldn't do it merely to please me. You should do it because you can't help yourself, because it's natural to you, because the man in you is crying out for heroic expression. Now, when you described the Wigan coal explosion last month, could you not have gone down and helped those people, in spite of the choke-damp?"

"I did."

"You never said so."

"There was nothing worth bucking about."

"I didn't know." She looked at me with rather more interest. "That was brave of you."

"I had to. If you want to write good copy, you must be where the things are."

"What a prosaic motive! It seems to take all the romance out of it. But, still, whatever your motive, I am glad that you went down that mine." She gave me her hand; but with such sweetness and dignity that I could only stoop and kiss it. "I dare say I am merely a foolish woman with a young girl's fancies. And yet it is so real with me, so entirely part of my very self, that I cannot help acting upon it. If I marry, I do want to marry a famous man!"

"Why should you not?" I cried. "It is women like you who brace men up. Give me a chance, and see if I will take it! Besides, as you say, men ought to MAKE their own chances, and not wait until they are given. Look at Clive—just a clerk, and he conquered India! By George! I'll do something in the world yet!"

She laughed at my sudden Irish effervescence. "Why not?" she said. "You have everything a man could have,—youth, health, strength, education, energy. I was sorry you spoke. And now I am glad—so glad—if it wakens these thoughts in you!"

"And if I do——"

Her dear hand rested like warm velvet upon my lips. "Not another word, Sir! You should have been at the office for evening duty half an hour ago; only I hadn't the heart to remind you. Some day, perhaps, when you have won your place in the world, we shall talk it over again."

And so it was that I found myself that foggy November evening pursuing the Camberwell tram with my heart glowing within me, and with the eager determination that not another day should elapse before I should find some deed which was worthy of my lady. But who—who in all this wide world could ever have imagined the incredible shape which that deed was to take, or the strange steps by which I was led to the doing of it?

And, after all, this opening chapter will seem to the reader to have nothing to do with my narrative; and yet there would have been no narrative without it, for it is only when a man goes out into the world with the thought that there are heroisms all round him, and with the desire all alive in his heart to follow any which may come within sight of him, that he breaks away as I did from the life he knows, and ventures forth into the wonderful mystic twilight land where lie the great adventures and the great rewards. Behold me, then, at the office of the Daily Gazette, on the staff of which I was a most insignificant unit, with the settled determination that very night, if possible, to find the quest which should be worthy of my Gladys! Was it hardness, was it selfishness, that she should ask me to risk my life for her own glorification? Such thoughts may come to middle age; but never to ardent three-and-twenty in the fever of his first love.

Chapter II   "Try Your Luck with Professor Challenger"

I always liked McArdle, the crabbed, old, round-backed, red-headed news editor, and I rather hoped that he liked me. Of course, Beaumont was the real boss; but he lived in the rarefied atmosphere of some Olympian height from which he could distinguish nothing smaller than an international crisis or a split in the Cabinet. Sometimes we saw him passing in lonely majesty to his inner sanctum, with his eyes staring vaguely and his mind hovering over the Balkans or the Persian Gulf. He was above and beyond us. But McArdle was his first lieutenant, and it was he that we knew. The old man nodded as I entered the room, and he pushed his spectacles far up on his bald forehead.

"Well, Mr. Malone, from all I hear, you seem to be doing very well," said he in his kindly Scotch accent.

I thanked him.

"The colliery explosion was excellent. So was the Southwark fire. You have the true descreeptive touch. What did you want to see me about?"

"To ask a favor."

He looked alarmed, and his eyes shunned mine. "Tut, tut! What is it?"

"Do you think, Sir, that you could possibly send me on some mission for the paper? I would do my best to put it through and get you some good copy."

"What sort of meesion had you in your mind, Mr. Malone?"

"Well, Sir, anything that had adventure and danger in it. I really would do my very best. The more difficult it was, the better it would suit me."

"You seem very anxious to lose your life."

"To justify my life, Sir."

"Dear me, Mr. Malone, this is very—very exalted. I'm afraid the day for this sort of thing is rather past. The expense of the 'special meesion' business hardly justifies the result, and, of course, in any case it would only be an experienced man with a name that would command public confidence who would get such an order. The big blank spaces in the map are all being filled in, and there's no room for romance anywhere. Wait a bit, though!" he added, with a sudden smile upon his face. "Talking of the blank spaces of the map gives me an idea. What about exposing a fraud—a modern Munchausen—and making him rideeculous? You could show him up as the liar that he is! Eh, man, it would be fine. How does it appeal to you?"

"Anything—anywhere—I care nothing."

McArdle was plunged in thought for some minutes.

"I wonder whether you could get on friendly—or at least on talking terms with the fellow," he said, at last. "You seem to have a sort of genius for establishing relations with people—seempathy, I suppose, or animal magnetism, or youthful vitality, or something. I am conscious of it myself."

"You are very good, sir."

"So why should you not try your luck with Professor Challenger, of Enmore Park?"

I dare say I looked a little startled.

"Challenger!" I cried. "Professor Challenger, the famous zoologist! Wasn't he the man who broke the skull of Blundell, of the Telegraph?"

The news editor smiled grimly.

"Do you mind? Didn't you say it was adventures you were after?"

"It is all in the way of business, sir," I answered.

"Exactly. I don't suppose he can always be so violent as that. I'm thinking that Blundell got him at the wrong moment, maybe, or in the wrong fashion. You may have better luck, or more tact in handling him. There's something in your line there, I am sure, and the Gazette should work it."

"I really know nothing about him," said I. I only remember his name in connection with the police-court proceedings, for striking Blundell."

"I have a few notes for your guidance, Mr. Malone. I've had my eye on the Professor for some little time." He took a paper from a drawer. "Here is a summary of his record. I give it you briefly:—

"'Challenger, George Edward. Born: Largs, N. B., 1863. Educ.: Largs Academy; Edinburgh University. British Museum Assistant, 1892. Assistant-Keeper of Comparative Anthropology Department, 1893. Resigned after acrimonious correspondence same year. Winner of Crayston Medal for Zoological Research. Foreign Member of'—well, quite a lot of things, about two inches of small type—'Societe Belge, American Academy of Sciences, La Plata, etc., etc. Ex-President Palaeontological Society. Section H, British Association'—so on, so on!—'Publications: "Some Observations Upon a Series of Kalmuck Skulls"; "Outlines of Vertebrate Evolution"; and numerous papers, including "The underlying fallacy of Weissmannism," which caused heated discussion at the Zoological Congress of Vienna. Recreations: Walking, Alpine climbing. Address: Enmore Park, Kensington, W.'

"There, take it with you. I've nothing more for you to-night."

I pocketed the slip of paper.

"One moment, sir," I said, as I realized that it was a pink bald head, and not a red face, which was fronting me. "I am not very clear yet why I am to interview this gentleman. What has he done?"

The face flashed back again.

"Went to South America on a solitary expedeetion two years ago. Came back last year. Had undoubtedly been to South America, but refused to say exactly where. Began to tell his adventures in a vague way, but somebody started to pick holes, and he just shut up like an oyster. Something wonderful happened—or the man's a champion liar, which is the more probable supposeetion. Had some damaged photographs, said to be fakes. Got so touchy that he assaults anyone who asks questions, and heaves reporters doun the stairs. In my opinion he's just a homicidal megalomaniac with a turn for science. That's your man, Mr. Malone. Now, off you run, and see what you can make of him. You're big enough to look after yourself. Anyway, you are all safe. Employers' Liability Act, you know."

A grinning red face turned once more into a pink oval, fringed with gingery fluff; the interview was at an end.

I walked across to the Savage Club, but instead of turning into it I leaned upon the railings of Adelphi Terrace and gazed thoughtfully for a long time at the brown, oily river. I can always think most sanely and clearly in the open air. I took out the list of Professor Challenger's exploits, and I read it over under the electric lamp. Then I had what I can only regard as an inspiration. As a Pressman, I felt sure from what I had been told that I could never hope to get into touch with this cantankerous Professor. But these recriminations, twice mentioned in his skeleton biography, could only mean that he was a fanatic in science. Was there not an exposed margin there upon which he might be accessible? I would try.

I entered the club. It was just after eleven, and the big room was fairly full, though the rush had not yet set in. I noticed a tall, thin, angular man seated in an arm-chair by the fire. He turned as I drew my chair up to him. It was the man of all others whom I should have chosen—Tarp Henry, of the staff of Nature, a thin, dry, leathery creature, who was full, to those who knew him, of kindly humanity. I plunged instantly into my subject.

"What do you know of Professor Challenger?"

"Challenger?" He gathered his brows in scientific disapproval. "Challenger was the man who came with some cock-and-bull story from South America."

"What story?"

"Oh, it was rank nonsense about some queer animals he had discovered. I believe he has retracted since. Anyhow, he has suppressed it all. He gave an interview to Reuter's, and there was such a howl that he saw it wouldn't do. It was a discreditable business. There were one or two folk who were inclined to take him seriously, but he soon choked them off."

"How?"

"Well, by his insufferable rudeness and impossible behavior. There was poor old Wadley, of the Zoological Institute. Wadley sent a message: 'The President of the Zoological Institute presents his compliments to Professor Challenger, and would take it as a personal favor if he would do them the honor to come to their next meeting.' The answer was unprintable."

"You don't say?"

"Well, a bowdlerized version of it would run: 'Professor Challenger presents his compliments to the President of the Zoological Institute, and would take it as a personal favor if he would go to the devil.'"

"Good Lord!"

"Yes, I expect that's what old Wadley said. I remember his wail at the meeting, which began: 'In fifty years experience of scientific intercourse——' It quite broke the old man up."

"Anything more about Challenger?"

"Well, I'm a bacteriologist, you know. I live in a nine-hundred-diameter microscope. I can hardly claim to take serious notice of anything that I can see with my naked eye. I'm a frontiersman from the extreme edge of the Knowable, and I feel quite out of place when I leave my study and come into touch with all you great, rough, hulking creatures. I'm too detached to talk scandal, and yet at scientific conversaziones I HAVE heard something of Challenger, for he is one of those men whom nobody can ignore. He's as clever as they make 'em—a full-charged battery of force and vitality, but a quarrelsome, ill-conditioned faddist, and unscrupulous at that. He had gone the length of faking some photographs over the South American business."

"You say he is a faddist. What is his particular fad?"

"He has a thousand, but the latest is something about Weissmann and Evolution. He had a fearful row about it in Vienna, I believe."

"Can't you tell me the point?"

"Not at the moment, but a translation of the proceedings exists. We have it filed at the office. Would you care to come?"

"It's just what I want. I have to interview the fellow, and I need some lead up to him. It's really awfully good of you to give me a lift. I'll go with you now, if it is not too late."

Half an hour later I was seated in the newspaper office with a huge tome in front of me, which had been opened at the article "Weissmann versus Darwin," with the sub heading, "Spirited Protest at Vienna. Lively Proceedings." My scientific education having been somewhat neglected, I was unable to follow the whole argument, but it was evident that the English Professor had handled his subject in a very aggressive fashion, and had thoroughly annoyed his Continental colleagues. "Protests," "Uproar," and "General appeal to the Chairman" were three of the first brackets which caught my eye. Most of the matter might have been written in Chinese for any definite meaning that it conveyed to my brain.

"I wish you could translate it into English for me," I said, pathetically, to my help-mate.

"Well, it is a translation."

"Then I'd better try my luck with the original."

"It is certainly rather deep for a layman."

"If I could only get a single good, meaty sentence which seemed to convey some sort of definite human idea, it would serve my turn. Ah, yes, this one will do. I seem in a vague way almost to understand it. I'll copy it out. This shall be my link with the terrible Professor."

"Nothing else I can do?"

"Well, yes; I propose to write to him. If I could frame the letter here, and use your address it would give atmosphere."

"We'll have the fellow round here making a row and breaking the furniture."

"No, no; you'll see the letter—nothing contentious, I assure you."

"Well, that's my chair and desk. You'll find paper there. I'd like to censor it before it goes."

It took some doing, but I flatter myself that it wasn't such a bad job when it was finished. I read it aloud to the critical bacteriologist with some pride in my handiwork.

"DEAR PROFESSOR CHALLENGER," it said, "As a humble student of Nature, I have always taken the most profound interest in your speculations as to the differences between Darwin and Weissmann. I have recently had occasion to refresh my memory by re-reading——"

"You infernal liar!" murmured Tarp Henry.

—"by re-reading your masterly address at Vienna. That lucid and admirable statement seems to be the last word in the matter. There is one sentence in it, however—namely: 'I protest strongly against the insufferable and entirely dogmatic assertion that each separate id is a microcosm possessed of an historical architecture elaborated slowly through the series of generations.' Have you no desire, in view of later research, to modify this statement? Do you not think that it is over-accentuated? With your permission, I would ask the favor of an interview, as I feel strongly upon the subject, and have certain suggestions which I could only elaborate in a personal conversation. With your consent, I trust to have the honor of calling at eleven o'clock the day after to-morrow (Wednesday) morning.

"I remain, Sir, with assurances of profound respect, yours very truly, EDWARD D. MALONE."

"How's that?" I asked, triumphantly.

"Well if your conscience can stand it——"

"It has never failed me yet."

"But what do you mean to do?"

"To get there. Once I am in his room I may see some opening. I may even go the length of open confession. If he is a sportsman he will be tickled."

"Tickled, indeed! He's much more likely to do the tickling. Chain mail, or an American football suit—that's what you'll want.

Well, good-bye. I'll have the answer for you here on Wednesday morning—if he ever deigns to answer you. He is a violent, dangerous, cantankerous character, hated by everyone who comes across him, and the butt of the students, so far as they dare take a liberty with him. Perhaps it would be best for you if you never heard from the fellow at all."

Chapter III   "He is a Perfectly Impossible Person"

My friend's fear or hope was not destined to be realized. When I called on Wednesday there was a letter with the West Kensington postmark upon it, and my name scrawled across the envelope in a handwriting which looked like a barbed-wire railing. The contents were as follows:—

"ENMORE PARK, W.

"SIR,—I have duly received your note, in which you claim to endorse my views, although I am not aware that they are dependent upon endorsement either from you or anyone else. You have ventured to use the word 'speculation' with regard to my statement upon the subject of Darwinism, and I would call your attention to the fact that such a word in such a connection is offensive to a degree. The context convinces me, however, that you have sinned rather through ignorance and tactlessness than through malice, so I am content to pass the matter by. You quote an isolated sentence from my lecture, and appear to have some difficulty in understanding it. I should have thought that only a sub-human intelligence could have failed to grasp the point, but if it really needs amplification I shall consent to see you at the hour named, though visits and visitors of every sort are exceeding distasteful to me. As to your suggestion that I may modify my opinion, I would have you know that it is not my habit to do so after a deliberate expression of my mature views. You will kindly show the envelope of this letter to my man, Austin, when you call, as he has to take every precaution to shield me from the intrusive rascals who call themselves 'journalists.' "Yours faithfully, "GEORGE EDWARD CHALLENGER."

This was the letter that I read aloud to Tarp Henry, who had come down early to hear the result of my venture. His only remark was, "There's some new stuff, cuticura or something, which is better than arnica." Some people have such extraordinary notions of humor.

It was nearly half-past ten before I had received my message, but a taxicab took me round in good time for my appointment. It was an imposing porticoed house at which we stopped, and the heavily-curtained windows gave every indication of wealth upon the part of this formidable Professor. The door was opened by an odd, swarthy, dried-up person of uncertain age, with a dark pilot jacket and brown leather gaiters. I found afterwards that he was the chauffeur, who filled the gaps left by a succession of fugitive butlers. He looked me up and down with a searching light blue eye.

"Expected?" he asked.

"An appointment."

"Got your letter?"

I produced the envelope.

"Right!" He seemed to be a person of few words. Following him down the passage I was suddenly interrupted by a small woman, who stepped out from what proved to be the dining-room door. She was a bright, vivacious, dark-eyed lady, more French than English in her type.

"One moment," she said. "You can wait, Austin. Step in here, sir. May I ask if you have met my husband before?"

"No, madam, I have not had the honor."

"Then I apologize to you in advance. I must tell you that he is a perfectly impossible person—absolutely impossible. If you are forewarned you will be the more ready to make allowances."

"It is most considerate of you, madam."

"Get quickly out of the room if he seems inclined to be violent. Don't wait to argue with him. Several people have been injured through doing that. Afterwards there is a public scandal and it reflects upon me and all of us. I suppose it wasn't about South America you wanted to see him?"

I could not lie to a lady.

"Dear me! That is his most dangerous subject. You won't believe a word he says—I'm sure I don't wonder. But don't tell him so, for it makes him very violent. Pretend to believe him, and you may get through all right. Remember he believes it himself. Of that you may be assured. A more honest man never lived. Don't wait any longer or he may suspect. If you find him dangerous— really dangerous—ring the bell and hold him off until I come. Even at his worst I can usually control him."

With these encouraging words the lady handed me over to the taciturn Austin, who had waited like a bronze statue of discretion during our short interview, and I was conducted to the end of the passage. There was a tap at a door, a bull's bellow from within, and I was face to face with the Professor.

He sat in a rotating chair behind a broad table, which was covered with books, maps, and diagrams. As I entered, his seat spun round to face me. His appearance made me gasp. I was prepared for something strange, but not for so overpowering a personality as this. It was his size which took one's breath away—his size and his imposing presence. His head was enormous, the largest I have ever seen upon a human being. I am sure that his top-hat, had I ever ventured to don it, would have slipped over me entirely and rested on my shoulders. He had the face and beard which I associate with an Assyrian bull; the former florid, the latter so black as almost to have a suspicion of blue, spade-shaped and rippling down over his chest. The hair was peculiar, plastered down in front in a long, curving wisp over his massive forehead. The eyes were blue-gray under great black tufts, very clear, very critical, and very masterful. A huge spread of shoulders and a chest like a barrel were the other parts of him which appeared above the table, save for two enormous hands covered with long black hair. This and a bellowing, roaring, rumbling voice made up my first impression of the notorious Professor Challenger.

"Well?" said he, with a most insolent stare. "What now?"

I must keep up my deception for at least a little time longer, otherwise here was evidently an end of the interview.

"You were good enough to give me an appointment, sir," said I, humbly, producing his envelope.

He took my letter from his desk and laid it out before him.

"Oh, you are the young person who cannot understand plain English, are you? My general conclusions you are good enough to approve, as I understand?"

"Entirely, sir—entirely!" I was very emphatic.

"Dear me! That strengthens my position very much, does it not? Your age and appearance make your support doubly valuable. Well, at least you are better than that herd of swine in Vienna, whose gregarious grunt is, however, not more offensive than the isolated effort of the British hog." He glared at me as the present representative of the beast.

"They seem to have behaved abominably," said I.

"I assure you that I can fight my own battles, and that I have no possible need of your sympathy. Put me alone, sir, and with my back to the wall. G. E. C. is happiest then. Well, sir, let us do what we can to curtail this visit, which can hardly be agreeable to you, and is inexpressibly irksome to me. You had, as I have been led to believe, some comments to make upon the proposition which I advanced in my thesis."

There was a brutal directness about his methods which made evasion difficult. I must still make play and wait for a better opening. It had seemed simple enough at a distance. Oh, my Irish wits, could they not help me now, when I needed help so sorely? He transfixed me with two sharp, steely eyes. "Come, come!" he rumbled.

"I am, of course, a mere student," said I, with a fatuous smile, "hardly more, I might say, than an earnest inquirer. At the same time, it seemed to me that you were a little severe upon Weissmann in this matter. Has not the general evidence since that date tended to—well, to strengthen his position?"

"What evidence?" He spoke with a menacing calm.

"Well, of course, I am aware that there is not any what you might call DEFINITE evidence. I alluded merely to the trend of modern thought and the general scientific point of view, if I might so express it."

He leaned forward with great earnestness.

"I suppose you are aware," said he, checking off points upon his fingers, "that the cranial index is a constant factor?"

"Naturally," said I.

"And that telegony is still sub judice?"

"Undoubtedly."

"And that the germ plasm is different from the partheno-genetic egg?"

"Why, surely!" I cried, and gloried in my own audacity.

"But what does that prove?" he asked, in a gentle, persuasive voice.

"Ah, what indeed?" I murmured. "What does it prove?"

"Shall I tell you?" he cooed.

"Pray do."

"It proves," he roared, with a sudden blast of fury, "that you are the damnedest imposter in London—a vile, crawling journalist, who has no more science than he has decency in his composition!"

He had sprung to his feet with a mad rage in his eyes. Even at that moment of tension I found time for amazement at the discovery that he was quite a short man, his head not higher than my shoulder—a stunted Hercules whose tremendous vitality had all run to depth, breadth, and brain.

"Gibberish!" he cried, leaning forward, with his fingers on the table and his face projecting. "That's what I have been talking to you, sir—scientific gibberish! Did you think you could match cunning with me—you with your walnut of a brain? You think you are omnipotent, you infernal scribblers, don't you? That your praise can make a man and your blame can break him? We must all bow to you, and try to get a favorable word, must we? This man shall have a leg up, and this man shall have a dressing down! Creeping vermin, I know you! You've got out of your station. Time was when your ears were clipped. You've lost your sense of proportion. Swollen gas-bags! I'll keep you in your proper place. Yes, sir, you haven't got over G. E. C. There's one man who is still your master. He warned you off, but if you WILL come, by the Lord you do it at your own risk. Forfeit, my good Mr. Malone, I claim forfeit! You have played a rather dangerous game, and it strikes me that you have lost it."

"Look here, sir," said I, backing to the door and opening it; "you can be as abusive as you like. But there is a limit. You shall not assault me."

"Shall I not?" He was slowly advancing in a peculiarly menacing way, but he stopped now and put his big hands into the side-pockets of a rather boyish short jacket which he wore. "I have thrown several of you out of the house. You will be the fourth or fifth. Three pound fifteen each—that is how it averaged. Expensive, but very necessary. Now, sir, why should you not follow your brethren? I rather think you must." He resumed his unpleasant and stealthy advance, pointing his toes as he walked, like a dancing master.

I could have bolted for the hall door, but it would have been too ignominious. Besides, a little glow of righteous anger was springing up within me. I had been hopelessly in the wrong before, but this man's menaces were putting me in the right.

"I'll trouble you to keep your hands off, sir. I'll not stand it."

"Dear me!" His black moustache lifted and a white fang twinkled in a sneer. "You won't stand it, eh?"

"Don't be such a fool, Professor!" I cried. "What can you hope for? I'm fifteen stone, as hard as nails, and play center three-quarter every Saturday for the London Irish. I'm not the man——"

It was at that moment that he rushed me. It was lucky that I had opened the door, or we should have gone through it. We did a Catharine-wheel together down the passage. Somehow we gathered up a chair upon our way, and bounded on with it towards the street. My mouth was full of his beard, our arms were locked, our bodies intertwined, and that infernal chair radiated its legs all round us. The watchful Austin had thrown open the hall door. We went with a back somersault down the front steps. I have seen the two Macs attempt something of the kind at the halls, but it appears to take some practise to do it without hurting oneself. The chair went to matchwood at the bottom, and we rolled apart into the gutter. He sprang to his feet, waving his fists and wheezing like an asthmatic.

"Had enough?" he panted.

"You infernal bully!" I cried, as I gathered myself together.

Then and there we should have tried the thing out, for he was effervescing with fight, but fortunately I was rescued from an odious situation. A policeman was beside us, his notebook in his hand.

"What's all this? You ought to be ashamed" said the policeman. It was the most rational remark which I had heard in Enmore Park. "Well," he insisted, turning to me, "what is it, then?"

"This man attacked me," said I.

"Did you attack him?" asked the policeman.

The Professor breathed hard and said nothing.

"It's not the first time, either," said the policeman, severely, shaking his head. "You were in trouble last month for the same thing. You've blackened this young man's eye. Do you give him in charge, sir?"

I relented.

"No," said I, "I do not."

"What's that?" said the policeman.

"I was to blame myself. I intruded upon him. He gave me fair warning."

The policeman snapped up his notebook.

"Don't let us have any more such goings-on," said he. "Now, then! Move on, there, move on!" This to a butcher's boy, a maid, and one or two loafers who had collected. He clumped heavily down the street, driving this little flock before him. The Professor looked at me, and there was something humorous at the back of his eyes.

"Come in!" said he. "I've not done with you yet."

The speech had a sinister sound, but I followed him none the less into the house. The man-servant, Austin, like a wooden image, closed the door behind us.

Chapter IV   "It's Just the Very Biggest Thing in the World"

Hardly was it shut when Mrs. Challenger darted out from the dining-room. The small woman was in a furious temper. She barred her husband's way like an enraged chicken in front of a bulldog. It was evident that she had seen my exit, but had not observed my return.

"You brute, George!" she screamed. "You've hurt that nice young man."

He jerked backwards with his thumb.

"Here he is, safe and sound behind me."

She was confused, but not unduly so.

"I am so sorry, I didn't see you."

"I assure you, madam, that it is all right."

"He has marked your poor face! Oh, George, what a brute you are! Nothing but scandals from one end of the week to the other. Everyone hating and making fun of you. You've finished my patience. This ends it."

"Dirty linen," he rumbled.

"It's not a secret," she cried. "Do you suppose that the whole street—the whole of London, for that matter—Get away, Austin, we don't want you here. Do you suppose they don't all talk about you? Where is your dignity? You, a man who should have been Regius Professor at a great University with a thousand students all revering you. Where is your dignity, George?"

"How about yours, my dear?"

"You try me too much. A ruffian—a common brawling ruffian—that's what you have become."

"Be good, Jessie."

"A roaring, raging bully!"

"That's done it! Stool of penance!" said he.

To my amazement he stooped, picked her up, and placed her sitting upon a high pedestal of black marble in the angle of the hall. It was at least seven feet high, and so thin that she could hardly balance upon it. A more absurd object than she presented cocked up there with her face convulsed with anger, her feet dangling, and her body rigid for fear of an upset, I could not imagine.

"Let me down!" she wailed.

"Say 'please.'"

"You brute, George! Let me down this instant!"

"Come into the study, Mr. Malone."

"Really, sir——!" said I, looking at the lady.

"Here's Mr. Malone pleading for you, Jessie. Say 'please,' and down you come."

"Oh, you brute! Please! please!"

"You must behave yourself, dear. Mr. Malone is a Pressman. He will have it all in his rag to-morrow, and sell an extra dozen among our neighbors. 'Strange story of high life'—you felt fairly high on that pedestal, did you not? Then a sub-title, 'Glimpse of a singular menage.' He's a foul feeder, is Mr. Malone, a carrion eater, like all of his kind—porcus ex grege diaboli—a swine from the devil's herd. That's it, Malone—what?"

"You are really intolerable!" said I, hotly.

He bellowed with laughter.

"We shall have a coalition presently," he boomed, looking from his wife to me and puffing out his enormous chest. Then, suddenly altering his tone, "Excuse this frivolous family badinage, Mr. Malone. I called you back for some more serious purpose than to mix you up with our little domestic pleasantries. Run away, little woman, and don't fret." He placed a huge hand upon each of her shoulders. "All that you say is perfectly true. I should be a better man if I did what you advise, but I shouldn't be quite George Edward Challenger. There are plenty of better men, my dear, but only one G. E. C. So make the best of him." He suddenly gave her a resounding kiss, which embarrassed me even more than his violence had done. "Now, Mr. Malone," he continued, with a great accession of dignity, "this way, if YOU please."

We re-entered the room which we had left so tumultuously ten minutes before. The Professor closed the door carefully behind us, motioned me into an arm-chair, and pushed a cigar-box under my nose.

"Real San Juan Colorado," he said. "Excitable people like you are the better for narcotics. Heavens! don't bite it! Cut—and cut with reverence! Now lean back, and listen attentively to whatever I may care to say to you. If any remark should occur to you, you can reserve it for some more opportune time.

"First of all, as to your return to my house after your most justifiable expulsion"—he protruded his beard, and stared at me as one who challenges and invites contradiction—"after, as I say, your well-merited expulsion. The reason lay in your answer to that most officious policeman, in which I seemed to discern some glimmering of good feeling upon your part—more, at any rate, than I am accustomed to associate with your profession. In admitting that the fault of the incident lay with you, you gave some evidence of a certain mental detachment and breadth of view which attracted my favorable notice. The sub-species of the human race to which you unfortunately belong has always been below my mental horizon. Your words brought you suddenly above it. You swam up into my serious notice. For this reason I asked you to return with me, as I was minded to make your further acquaintance. You will kindly deposit your ash in the small Japanese tray on the bamboo table which stands at your left elbow."

All this he boomed forth like a professor addressing his class. He had swung round his revolving chair so as to face me, and he sat all puffed out like an enormous bull-frog, his head laid back and his eyes half-covered by supercilious lids. Now he suddenly turned himself sideways, and all I could see of him was tangled hair with a red, protruding ear. He was scratching about among the litter of papers upon his desk. He faced me presently with what looked like a very tattered sketch-book in his hand.

"I am going to talk to you about South America," said he. "No comments if you please. First of all, I wish you to understand that nothing I tell you now is to be repeated in any public way unless you have my express permission. That permission will, in all human probability, never be given. Is that clear?"

"It is very hard," said I. "Surely a judicious account——"

He replaced the notebook upon the table.

"That ends it," said he. "I wish you a very good morning."

"No, no!" I cried. "I submit to any conditions. So far as I can see, I have no choice."

"None in the world," said he.

"Well, then, I promise."

"Word of honor?"

"Word of honor."

He looked at me with doubt in his insolent eyes.

"After all, what do I know about your honor?" said he.

"Upon my word, sir," I cried, angrily, "you take very great liberties! I have never been so insulted in my life."

He seemed more interested than annoyed at my outbreak.

"Round-headed," he muttered. "Brachycephalic, gray-eyed, black-haired, with suggestion of the negroid. Celtic, I presume?"

"I am an Irishman, sir."

"Irish Irish?"

"Yes, sir."

"That, of course, explains it. Let me see; you have given me your promise that my confidence will be respected? That confidence, I may say, will be far from complete. But I am prepared to give you a few indications which will be of interest. In the first place, you are probably aware that two years ago I made a journey to South America—one which will be classical in the scientific history of the world? The object of my journey was to verify some conclusions of Wallace and of Bates, which could only be done by observing their reported facts under the same conditions in which they had themselves noted them. If my expedition had no other results it would still have been noteworthy, but a curious incident occurred to me while there which opened up an entirely fresh line of inquiry.

"You are aware—or probably, in this half-educated age, you are not aware—that the country round some parts of the Amazon is still only partially explored, and that a great number of tributaries, some of them entirely uncharted, run into the main river. It was my business to visit this little-known back-country and to examine its fauna, which furnished me with the materials for several chapters for that great and monumental work upon zoology which will be my life's justification. I was returning, my work accomplished, when I had occasion to spend a night at a small Indian village at a point where a certain tributary—the name and position of which I withhold—opens into the main river. The natives were Cucama Indians, an amiable but degraded race, with mental powers hardly superior to the average Londoner. I had effected some cures among them upon my way up the river, and had impressed them considerably with my personality, so that I was not surprised to find myself eagerly awaited upon my return. I gathered from their signs that someone had urgent need of my medical services, and I followed the chief to one of his huts. When I entered I found that the sufferer to whose aid I had been summoned had that instant expired. He was, to my surprise, no Indian, but a white man; indeed, I may say a very white man, for he was flaxen-haired and had some characteristics of an albino. He was clad in rags, was very emaciated, and bore every trace of prolonged hardship. So far as I could understand the account of the natives, he was a complete stranger to them, and had come upon their village through the woods alone and in the last stage of exhaustion.

"The man's knapsack lay beside the couch, and I examined the contents. His name was written upon a tab within it—Maple White, Lake Avenue, Detroit, Michigan. It is a name to which I am prepared always to lift my hat. It is not too much to say that it will rank level with my own when the final credit of this business comes to be apportioned.

"From the contents of the knapsack it was evident that this man had been an artist and poet in search of effects. There were scraps of verse. I do not profess to be a judge of such things, but they appeared to me to be singularly wanting in merit. There were also some rather commonplace pictures of river scenery, a paint-box, a box of colored chalks, some brushes, that curved bone which lies upon my inkstand, a volume of Baxter's 'Moths and Butterflies,' a cheap revolver, and a few cartridges. Of personal equipment he either had none or he had lost it in his journey. Such were the total effects of this strange American Bohemian.

"I was turning away from him when I observed that something projected from the front of his ragged jacket. It was this sketch-book, which was as dilapidated then as you see it now. Indeed, I can assure you that a first folio of Shakespeare could not be treated with greater reverence than this relic has been since it came into my possession. I hand it to you now, and I ask you to take it page by page and to examine the contents."

He helped himself to a cigar and leaned back with a fiercely critical pair of eyes, taking note of the effect which this document would produce.

I had opened the volume with some expectation of a revelation, though of what nature I could not imagine. The first page was disappointing, however, as it contained nothing but the picture of a very fat man in a pea-jacket, with the legend, "Jimmy Colver on the Mail-boat," written beneath it. There followed several pages which were filled with small sketches of Indians and their ways. Then came a picture of a cheerful and corpulent ecclesiastic in a shovel hat, sitting opposite a very thin European, and the inscription: "Lunch with Fra Cristofero at Rosario." Studies of women and babies accounted for several more pages, and then there was an unbroken series of animal drawings with such explanations as "Manatee upon Sandbank," "Turtles and Their Eggs," "Black Ajouti under a Miriti Palm"—the matter disclosing some sort of pig-like animal; and finally came a double page of studies of long-snouted and very unpleasant saurians. I could make nothing of it, and said so to the Professor.

"Surely these are only crocodiles?"

"Alligators! Alligators! There is hardly such a thing as a true crocodile in South America. The distinction between them——"

"I meant that I could see nothing unusual—nothing to justify what you have said."

He smiled serenely.

"Try the next page," said he.

I was still unable to sympathize. It was a full-page sketch of a landscape roughly tinted in color—the kind of painting which an open-air artist takes as a guide to a future more elaborate effort. There was a pale-green foreground of feathery vegetation, which sloped upwards and ended in a line of cliffs dark red in color, and curiously ribbed like some basaltic formations which I have seen. They extended in an unbroken wall right across the background. At one point was an isolated pyramidal rock, crowned by a great tree, which appeared to be separated by a cleft from the main crag. Behind it all, a blue tropical sky. A thin green line of vegetation fringed the summit of the ruddy cliff.

"Well?" he asked.

"It is no doubt a curious formation," said I "but I am not geologist enough to say that it is wonderful."

"Wonderful!" he repeated. "It is unique. It is incredible. No one on earth has ever dreamed of such a possibility. Now the next."

I turned it over, and gave an exclamation of surprise. There was a full-page picture of the most extraordinary creature that I had ever seen. It was the wild dream of an opium smoker, a vision of delirium. The head was like that of a fowl, the body that of a bloated lizard, the trailing tail was furnished with upward-turned spikes, and the curved back was edged with a high serrated fringe, which looked like a dozen cocks' wattles placed behind each other. In front of this creature was an absurd mannikin, or dwarf, in human form, who stood staring at it.

"Well, what do you think of that?" cried the Professor, rubbing his hands with an air of triumph.

"It is monstrous—grotesque."

"But what made him draw such an animal?"

"Trade gin, I should think."

"Oh, that's the best explanation you can give, is it?"

"Well, sir, what is yours?"

"The obvious one that the creature exists. That is actually sketched from the life."

I should have laughed only that I had a vision of our doing another Catharine-wheel down the passage.

"No doubt," said I, "no doubt," as one humors an imbecile. "I confess, however," I added, "that this tiny human figure puzzles me. If it were an Indian we could set it down as evidence of some pigmy race in America, but it appears to be a European in a sun-hat."

The Professor snorted like an angry buffalo. "You really touch the limit," said he. "You enlarge my view of the possible. Cerebral paresis! Mental inertia! Wonderful!"

He was too absurd to make me angry. Indeed, it was a waste of energy, for if you were going to be angry with this man you would be angry all the time. I contented myself with smiling wearily. "It struck me that the man was small," said I.

"Look here!" he cried, leaning forward and dabbing a great hairy sausage of a finger on to the picture. "You see that plant behind the animal; I suppose you thought it was a dandelion or a Brussels sprout—what? Well, it is a vegetable ivory palm, and they run to about fifty or sixty feet. Don't you see that the man is put in for a purpose? He couldn't really have stood in front of that brute and lived to draw it. He sketched himself in to give a scale of heights. He was, we will say, over five feet high. The tree is ten times bigger, which is what one would expect."

"Good heavens!" I cried. "Then you think the beast was— Why, Charing Cross station would hardly make a kennel for such a brute!"

"Apart from exaggeration, he is certainly a well-grown specimen," said the Professor, complacently.

"But," I cried, "surely the whole experience of the human race is not to be set aside on account of a single sketch"—I had turned over the leaves and ascertained that there was nothing more in the book—"a single sketch by a wandering American artist who may have done it under hashish, or in the delirium of fever, or simply in order to gratify a freakish imagination. You can't, as a man of science, defend such a position as that."

For answer the Professor took a book down from a shelf.

"This is an excellent monograph by my gifted friend, Ray Lankester!" said he. "There is an illustration here which would interest you. Ah, yes, here it is! The inscription beneath it runs: 'Probable appearance in life of the Jurassic Dinosaur Stegosaurus. The hind leg alone is twice as tall as a full-grown man.' Well, what do you make of that?"

He handed me the open book. I started as I looked at the picture. In this reconstructed animal of a dead world there was certainly a very great resemblance to the sketch of the unknown artist.

"That is certainly remarkable," said I.

"But you won't admit that it is final?"

"Surely it might be a coincidence, or this American may have seen a picture of the kind and carried it in his memory. It would be likely to recur to a man in a delirium."

"Very good," said the Professor, indulgently; "we leave it at that. I will now ask you to look at this bone." He handed over the one which he had already described as part of the dead man's possessions. It was about six inches long, and thicker than my thumb, with some indications of dried cartilage at one end of it.

"To what known creature does that bone belong?" asked the Professor.

I examined it with care and tried to recall some half-forgotten knowledge.

"It might be a very thick human collar-bone," I said.

My companion waved his hand in contemptuous deprecation.

"The human collar-bone is curved. This is straight. There is a groove upon its surface showing that a great tendon played across it, which could not be the case with a clavicle."

"Then I must confess that I don't know what it is."

"You need not be ashamed to expose your ignorance, for I don't suppose the whole South Kensington staff could give a name to it." He took a little bone the size of a bean out of a pill-box. "So far as I am a judge this human bone is the analogue of the one which you hold in your hand. That will give you some idea of the size of the creature. You will observe from the cartilage that this is no fossil specimen, but recent. What do you say to that?"

"Surely in an elephant——"

He winced as if in pain.

"Don't! Don't talk of elephants in South America. Even in these days of Board schools——"

"Well, I interrupted, "any large South American animal—a tapir, for example."

"You may take it, young man, that I am versed in the elements of my business. This is not a conceivable bone either of a tapir or of any other creature known to zoology. It belongs to a very large, a very strong, and, by all analogy, a very fierce animal which exists upon the face of the earth, but has not yet come under the notice of science. You are still unconvinced?"

"I am at least deeply interested."

"Then your case is not hopeless. I feel that there is reason lurking in you somewhere, so we will patiently grope round for it. We will now leave the dead American and proceed with my narrative. You can imagine that I could hardly come away from the Amazon without probing deeper into the matter. There were indications as to the direction from which the dead traveler had come. Indian legends would alone have been my guide, for I found that rumors of a strange land were common among all the riverine tribes. You have heard, no doubt, of Curupuri?"

"Never."

"Curupuri is the spirit of the woods, something terrible, something malevolent, something to be avoided. None can describe its shape or nature, but it is a word of terror along the Amazon. Now all tribes agree as to the direction in which Curupuri lives. It was the same direction from which the American had come. Something terrible lay that way. It was my business to find out what it was."

"What did you do?" My flippancy was all gone. This massive man compelled one's attention and respect.

"I overcame the extreme reluctance of the natives—a reluctance which extends even to talk upon the subject—and by judicious persuasion and gifts, aided, I will admit, by some threats of coercion, I got two of them to act as guides. After many adventures which I need not describe, and after traveling a distance which I will not mention, in a direction which I withhold, we came at last to a tract of country which has never been described, nor, indeed, visited save by my unfortunate predecessor. Would you kindly look at this?"

He handed me a photograph—half-plate size.

"The unsatisfactory appearance of it is due to the fact," said he, "that on descending the river the boat was upset and the case which contained the undeveloped films was broken, with disastrous results. Nearly all of them were totally ruined—an irreparable loss. This is one of the few which partially escaped. This explanation of deficiencies or abnormalities you will kindly accept. There was talk of faking. I am not in a mood to argue such a point."

The photograph was certainly very off-colored. An unkind critic might easily have misinterpreted that dim surface. It was a dull gray landscape, and as I gradually deciphered the details of it I realized that it represented a long and enormously high line of cliffs exactly like an immense cataract seen in the distance, with a sloping, tree-clad plain in the foreground.

"I believe it is the same place as the painted picture," said I.

"It is the same place," the Professor answered. "I found traces of the fellow's camp. Now look at this."

It was a nearer view of the same scene, though the photograph was extremely defective. I could distinctly see the isolated, tree-crowned pinnacle of rock which was detached from the crag.

"I have no doubt of it at all," said I.

"Well, that is something gained," said he. "We progress, do we not? Now, will you please look at the top of that rocky pinnacle? Do you observe something there?"

"An enormous tree."

"But on the tree?"

"A large bird," said I.

He handed me a lens.

"Yes," I said, peering through it, "a large bird stands on the tree. It appears to have a considerable beak. I should say it was a pelican."

"I cannot congratulate you upon your eyesight," said the Professor. "It is not a pelican, nor, indeed, is it a bird. It may interest you to know that I succeeded in shooting that particular specimen. It was the only absolute proof of my experiences which I was able to bring away with me."

"You have it, then?" Here at last was tangible corroboration.

"I had it. It was unfortunately lost with so much else in the same boat accident which ruined my photographs. I clutched at it as it disappeared in the swirl of the rapids, and part of its wing was left in my hand. I was insensible when washed ashore, but the miserable remnant of my superb specimen was still intact; I now lay it before you."

From a drawer he produced what seemed to me to be the upper portion of the wing of a large bat. It was at least two feet in length, a curved bone, with a membranous veil beneath it.

"A monstrous bat!" I suggested.

"Nothing of the sort," said the Professor, severely. "Living, as I do, in an educated and scientific atmosphere, I could not have conceived that the first principles of zoology were so little known. Is it possible that you do not know the elementary fact in comparative anatomy, that the wing of a bird is really the forearm, while the wing of a bat consists of three elongated fingers with membranes between? Now, in this case, the bone is certainly not the forearm, and you can see for yourself that this is a single membrane hanging upon a single bone, and therefore that it cannot belong to a bat. But if it is neither bird nor bat, what is it?"

My small stock of knowledge was exhausted.

"I really do not know," said I.

He opened the standard work to which he had already referred me.

"Here," said he, pointing to the picture of an extraordinary flying monster, "is an excellent reproduction of the dimorphodon, or pterodactyl, a flying reptile of the Jurassic period. On the next page is a diagram of the mechanism of its wing. Kindly compare it with the specimen in your hand."

A wave of amazement passed over me as I looked. I was convinced. There could be no getting away from it. The cumulative proof was overwhelming. The sketch, the photographs, the narrative, and now the actual specimen—the evidence was complete. I said so—I said so warmly, for I felt that the Professor was an ill-used man. He leaned back in his chair with drooping eyelids and a tolerant smile, basking in this sudden gleam of sunshine.

"It's just the very biggest thing that I ever heard of!" said I, though it was my journalistic rather than my scientific enthusiasm that was roused. "It is colossal. You are a Columbus of science who has discovered a lost world. I'm awfully sorry if I seemed to doubt you. It was all so unthinkable. But I understand evidence when I see it, and this should be good enough for anyone."

The Professor purred with satisfaction.

"And then, sir, what did you do next?"

"It was the wet season, Mr. Malone, and my stores were exhausted. I explored some portion of this huge cliff, but I was unable to find any way to scale it. The pyramidal rock upon which I saw and shot the pterodactyl was more accessible. Being something of a cragsman, I did manage to get half way to the top of that. From that height I had a better idea of the plateau upon the top of the crags. It appeared to be very large; neither to east nor to west could I see any end to the vista of green-capped cliffs. Below, it is a swampy, jungly region, full of snakes, insects, and fever. It is a natural protection to this singular country."

"Did you see any other trace of life?"

"No, sir, I did not; but during the week that we lay encamped at the base of the cliff we heard some very strange noises from above."

"But the creature that the American drew? How do you account for that?"

"We can only suppose that he must have made his way to the summit and seen it there. We know, therefore, that there is a way up. We know equally that it must be a very difficult one, otherwise the creatures would have come down and overrun the surrounding country. Surely that is clear?"

"But how did they come to be there?"

"I do not think that the problem is a very obscure one," said the Professor; "there can only be one explanation. South America is, as you may have heard, a granite continent. At this single point in the interior there has been, in some far distant age, a great, sudden volcanic upheaval. These cliffs, I may remark, are basaltic, and therefore plutonic. An area, as large perhaps as Sussex, has been lifted up en bloc with all its living contents, and cut off by perpendicular precipices of a hardness which defies erosion from all the rest of the continent. What is the result? Why, the ordinary laws of Nature are suspended. The various checks which influence the struggle for existence in the world at large are all neutralized or altered. Creatures survive which would otherwise disappear. You will observe that both the pterodactyl and the stegosaurus are Jurassic, and therefore of a great age in the order of life. They have been artificially conserved by those strange accidental conditions."

"But surely your evidence is conclusive. You have only to lay it before the proper authorities."

"So in my simplicity, I had imagined," said the Professor, bitterly. "I can only tell you that it was not so, that I was met at every turn by incredulity, born partly of stupidity and partly of jealousy. It is not my nature, sir, to cringe to any man, or to seek to prove a fact if my word has been doubted. After the first I have not condescended to show such corroborative proofs as I possess. The subject became hateful to me—I would not speak of it. When men like yourself, who represent the foolish curiosity of the public, came to disturb my privacy I was unable to meet them with dignified reserve. By nature I am, I admit, somewhat fiery, and under provocation I am inclined to be violent. I fear you may have remarked it."

I nursed my eye and was silent.

"My wife has frequently remonstrated with me upon the subject, and yet I fancy that any man of honor would feel the same. To-night, however, I propose to give an extreme example of the control of the will over the emotions. I invite you to be present at the exhibition." He handed me a card from his desk. "You will perceive that Mr. Percival Waldron, a naturalist of some popular repute, is announced to lecture at eight-thirty at the Zoological Institute's Hall upon 'The Record of the Ages.' I have been specially invited to be present upon the platform, and to move a vote of thanks to the lecturer. While doing so, I shall make it my business, with infinite tact and delicacy, to throw out a few remarks which may arouse the interest of the audience and cause some of them to desire to go more deeply into the matter. Nothing contentious, you understand, but only an indication that there are greater deeps beyond. I shall hold myself strongly in leash, and see whether by this self-restraint I attain a more favorable result."

"And I may come?" I asked eagerly.

"Why, surely," he answered, cordially. He had an enormously massive genial manner, which was almost as overpowering as his violence. His smile of benevolence was a wonderful thing, when his cheeks would suddenly bunch into two red apples, between his half-closed eyes and his great black beard. "By all means, come. It will be a comfort to me to know that I have one ally in the hall, however inefficient and ignorant of the subject he may be. I fancy there will be a large audience, for Waldron, though an absolute charlatan, has a considerable popular following. Now, Mr. Malone, I have given you rather more of my time than I had intended. The individual must not monopolize what is meant for the world. I shall be pleased to see you at the lecture to-night. In the meantime, you will understand that no public use is to be made of any of the material that I have given you."

"But Mr. McArdle—my news editor, you know—will want to know what I have done."

"Tell him what you like. You can say, among other things, that if he sends anyone else to intrude upon me I shall call upon him with a riding-whip. But I leave it to you that nothing of all this appears in print. Very good. Then the Zoological Institute's Hall at eight-thirty to-night." I had a last impression of red cheeks, blue rippling beard, and intolerant eyes, as he waved me out of the room.

Chapter V   "Question!"

What with the physical shocks incidental to my first interview with Professor Challenger and the mental ones which accompanied the second, I was a somewhat demoralized journalist by the time I found myself in Enmore Park once more. In my aching head the one thought was throbbing that there really was truth in this man's story, that it was of tremendous consequence, and that it would work up into inconceivable copy for the Gazette when I could obtain permission to use it. A taxicab was waiting at the end of the road, so I sprang into it and drove down to the office. McArdle was at his post as usual.

"Well," he cried, expectantly, "what may it run to? I'm thinking, young man, you have been in the wars. Don't tell me that he assaulted you."

"We had a little difference at first."

"What a man it is! What did you do?"

"Well, he became more reasonable and we had a chat. But I got nothing out of him—nothing for publication."

"I'm not so sure about that. You got a black eye out of him, and that's for publication. We can't have this reign of terror, Mr. Malone. We must bring the man to his bearings. I'll have a leaderette on him to-morrow that will raise a blister. Just give me the material and I will engage to brand the fellow for ever. Professor Munchausen—how's that for an inset headline? Sir John Mandeville redivivus—Cagliostro—all the imposters and bullies in history. I'll show him up for the fraud he is."

"I wouldn't do that, sir."

"Why not?"

"Because he is not a fraud at all."

"What!" roared McArdle. "You don't mean to say you really believe this stuff of his about mammoths and mastodons and great sea sairpents?"

"Well, I don't know about that. I don't think he makes any claims of that kind. But I do believe he has got something new."

"Then for Heaven's sake, man, write it up!"

"I'm longing to, but all I know he gave me in confidence and on condition that I didn't." I condensed into a few sentences the Professor's narrative. "That's how it stands."

McArdle looked deeply incredulous.

"Well, Mr. Malone," he said at last, "about this scientific meeting to-night; there can be no privacy about that, anyhow. I don't suppose any paper will want to report it, for Waldron has been reported already a dozen times, and no one is aware that Challenger will speak. We may get a scoop, if we are lucky. You'll be there in any case, so you'll just give us a pretty full report. I'll keep space up to midnight."

My day was a busy one, and I had an early dinner at the Savage Club with Tarp Henry, to whom I gave some account of my adventures. He listened with a sceptical smile on his gaunt face, and roared with laughter on hearing that the Professor had convinced me.

"My dear chap, things don't happen like that in real life. People don't stumble upon enormous discoveries and then lose their evidence. Leave that to the novelists. The fellow is as full of tricks as the monkey-house at the Zoo. It's all bosh."

"But the American poet?"

"He never existed."

"I saw his sketch-book."

"Challenger's sketch-book."

"You think he drew that animal?"

"Of course he did. Who else?"

"Well, then, the photographs?"

"There was nothing in the photographs. By your own admission you only saw a bird."

"A pterodactyl."

"That's what HE says. He put the pterodactyl into your head."

"Well, then, the bones?"

"First one out of an Irish stew. Second one vamped up for the occasion. If you are clever and know your business you can fake a bone as easily as you can a photograph."

I began to feel uneasy. Perhaps, after all, I had been premature in my acquiescence. Then I had a sudden happy thought.

"Will you come to the meeting?" I asked.

Tarp Henry looked thoughtful.

"He is not a popular person, the genial Challenger," said he. "A lot of people have accounts to settle with him. I should say he is about the best-hated man in London. If the medical students turn out there will be no end of a rag. I don't want to get into a bear-garden."

"You might at least do him the justice to hear him state his own case."

"Well, perhaps it's only fair. All right. I'm your man for the evening."

When we arrived at the hall we found a much greater concourse than I had expected. A line of electric broughams discharged their little cargoes of white-bearded professors, while the dark stream of humbler pedestrians, who crowded through the arched door-way, showed that the audience would be popular as well as scientific. Indeed, it became evident to us as soon as we had taken our seats that a youthful and even boyish spirit was abroad in the gallery and the back portions of the hall. Looking behind me, I could see rows of faces of the familiar medical student type. Apparently the great hospitals had each sent down their contingent. The behavior of the audience at present was good-humored, but mischievous. Scraps of popular songs were chorused with an enthusiasm which was a strange prelude to a scientific lecture, and there was already a tendency to personal chaff which promised a jovial evening to others, however embarrassing it might be to the recipients of these dubious honors.

Thus, when old Doctor Meldrum, with his well-known curly-brimmed opera-hat, appeared upon the platform, there was such a universal query of "Where DID you get that tile?" that he hurriedly removed it, and concealed it furtively under his chair. When gouty Professor Wadley limped down to his seat there were general affectionate inquiries from all parts of the hall as to the exact state of his poor toe, which caused him obvious embarrassment. The greatest demonstration of all, however, was at the entrance of my new acquaintance, Professor Challenger, when he passed down to take his place at the extreme end of the front row of the platform. Such a yell of welcome broke forth when his black beard first protruded round the corner that I began to suspect Tarp Henry was right in his surmise, and that this assemblage was there not merely for the sake of the lecture, but because it had got rumored abroad that the famous Professor would take part in the proceedings.

There was some sympathetic laughter on his entrance among the front benches of well-dressed spectators, as though the demonstration of the students in this instance was not unwelcome to them. That greeting was, indeed, a frightful outburst of sound, the uproar of the carnivora cage when the step of the bucket-bearing keeper is heard in the distance. There was an offensive tone in it, perhaps, and yet in the main it struck me as mere riotous outcry, the noisy reception of one who amused and interested them, rather than of one they disliked or despised. Challenger smiled with weary and tolerant contempt, as a kindly man would meet the yapping of a litter of puppies. He sat slowly down, blew out his chest, passed his hand caressingly down his beard, and looked with drooping eyelids and supercilious eyes at the crowded hall before him. The uproar of his advent had not yet died away when Professor Ronald Murray, the chairman, and Mr. Waldron, the lecturer, threaded their way to the front, and the proceedings began.

Professor Murray will, I am sure, excuse me if I say that he has the common fault of most Englishmen of being inaudible. Why on earth people who have something to say which is worth hearing should not take the slight trouble to learn how to make it heard is one of the strange mysteries of modern life. Their methods are as reasonable as to try to pour some precious stuff from the spring to the reservoir through a non-conducting pipe, which could by the least effort be opened. Professor Murray made several profound remarks to his white tie and to the water-carafe upon the table, with a humorous, twinkling aside to the silver candlestick upon his right. Then he sat down, and Mr. Waldron, the famous popular lecturer, rose amid a general murmur of applause. He was a stern, gaunt man, with a harsh voice, and an aggressive manner, but he had the merit of knowing how to assimilate the ideas of other men, and to pass them on in a way which was intelligible and even interesting to the lay public, with a happy knack of being funny about the most unlikely objects, so that the precession of the Equinox or the formation of a vertebrate became a highly humorous process as treated by him.

It was a bird's-eye view of creation, as interpreted by science, which, in language always clear and sometimes picturesque, he unfolded before us. He told us of the globe, a huge mass of flaming gas, flaring through the heavens. Then he pictured the solidification, the cooling, the wrinkling which formed the mountains, the steam which turned to water, the slow preparation of the stage upon which was to be played the inexplicable drama of life. On the origin of life itself he was discreetly vague. That the germs of it could hardly have survived the original roasting was, he declared, fairly certain. Therefore it had come later. Had it built itself out of the cooling, inorganic elements of the globe? Very likely. Had the germs of it arrived from outside upon a meteor? It was hardly conceivable. On the whole, the wisest man was the least dogmatic upon the point. We could not—or at least we had not succeeded up to date in making organic life in our laboratories out of inorganic materials. The gulf between the dead and the living was something which our chemistry could not as yet bridge. But there was a higher and subtler chemistry of Nature, which, working with great forces over long epochs, might well produce results which were impossible for us. There the matter must be left.

This brought the lecturer to the great ladder of animal life, beginning low down in molluscs and feeble sea creatures, then up rung by rung through reptiles and fishes, till at last we came to a kangaroo-rat, a creature which brought forth its young alive, the direct ancestor of all mammals, and presumably, therefore, of everyone in the audience. ("No, no," from a sceptical student in the back row.) If the young gentleman in the red tie who cried "No, no," and who presumably claimed to have been hatched out of an egg, would wait upon him after the lecture, he would be glad to see such a curiosity. (Laughter.) It was strange to think that the climax of all the age-long process of Nature had been the creation of that gentleman in the red tie. But had the process stopped? Was this gentleman to be taken as the final type—the be-all and end-all of development? He hoped that he would not hurt the feelings of the gentleman in the red tie if he maintained that, whatever virtues that gentleman might possess in private life, still the vast processes of the universe were not fully justified if they were to end entirely in his production. Evolution was not a spent force, but one still working, and even greater achievements were in store.

Having thus, amid a general titter, played very prettily with his interrupter, the lecturer went back to his picture of the past, the drying of the seas, the emergence of the sand-bank, the sluggish, viscous life which lay upon their margins, the overcrowded lagoons, the tendency of the sea creatures to take refuge upon the mud-flats, the abundance of food awaiting them, their consequent enormous growth. "Hence, ladies and gentlemen," he added, "that frightful brood of saurians which still affright our eyes when seen in the Wealden or in the Solenhofen slates, but which were fortunately extinct long before the first appearance of mankind upon this planet."

"Question!" boomed a voice from the platform.

Mr. Waldron was a strict disciplinarian with a gift of acid humor, as exemplified upon the gentleman with the red tie, which made it perilous to interrupt him. But this interjection appeared to him so absurd that he was at a loss how to deal with it. So looks the Shakespearean who is confronted by a rancid Baconian, or the astronomer who is assailed by a flat-earth fanatic. He paused for a moment, and then, raising his voice, repeated slowly the words: "Which were extinct before the coming of man."

"Question!" boomed the voice once more.

Waldron looked with amazement along the line of professors upon the platform until his eyes fell upon the figure of Challenger, who leaned back in his chair with closed eyes and an amused expression, as if he were smiling in his sleep.

"I see!" said Waldron, with a shrug. "It is my friend Professor Challenger," and amid laughter he renewed his lecture as if this was a final explanation and no more need be said.

But the incident was far from being closed. Whatever path the lecturer took amid the wilds of the past seemed invariably to lead him to some assertion as to extinct or prehistoric life which instantly brought the same bulls' bellow from the Professor. The audience began to anticipate it and to roar with delight when it came. The packed benches of students joined in, and every time Challenger's beard opened, before any sound could come forth, there was a yell of "Question!" from a hundred voices, and an answering counter cry of "Order!" and "Shame!" from as many more. Waldron, though a hardened lecturer and a strong man, became rattled. He hesitated, stammered, repeated himself, got snarled in a long sentence, and finally turned furiously upon the cause of his troubles.

"This is really intolerable!" he cried, glaring across the platform. "I must ask you, Professor Challenger, to cease these ignorant and unmannerly interruptions."

There was a hush over the hall, the students rigid with delight at seeing the high gods on Olympus quarrelling among themselves. Challenger levered his bulky figure slowly out of his chair.

"I must in turn ask you, Mr. Waldron," he said, "to cease to make assertions which are not in strict accordance with scientific fact."

The words unloosed a tempest. "Shame! Shame!" "Give him a hearing!" "Put him out!" "Shove him off the platform!" "Fair play!" emerged from a general roar of amusement or execration. The chairman was on his feet flapping both his hands and bleating excitedly. "Professor Challenger—personal—views—later," were the solid peaks above his clouds of inaudible mutter. The interrupter bowed, smiled, stroked his beard, and relapsed into his chair. Waldron, very flushed and warlike, continued his observations. Now and then, as he made an assertion, he shot a venomous glance at his opponent, who seemed to be slumbering deeply, with the same broad, happy smile upon his face.

At last the lecture came to an end—I am inclined to think that it was a premature one, as the peroration was hurried and disconnected. The thread of the argument had been rudely broken, and the audience was restless and expectant. Waldron sat down, and, after a chirrup from the chairman, Professor Challenger rose and advanced to the edge of the platform. In the interests of my paper I took down his speech verbatim.

"Ladies and Gentlemen," he began, amid a sustained interruption from the back. "I beg pardon—Ladies, Gentlemen, and
Children—I must apologize, I had inadvertently omitted a considerable section of this audience" (tumult, during which the
Professor stood with one hand raised and his enormous head
nodding sympathetically, as if he were bestowing a pontifical
blessing upon the crowd), "I have been selected to move a vote of
thanks to Mr. Waldron for the very picturesque and imaginative
address to which we have just listened. There are points in it with
which I disagree, and it has been my duty to indicate them as they
arose, but, none the less, Mr. Waldron has accomplished his
object well, that object being to give a simple and interesting
account of what he conceives to have been the history of our
planet. Popular lectures are the easiest to listen to, but Mr. Waldron" (here he beamed and blinked at the lecturer) "will excuse
me when I say that they are necessarily both superficial and mis-
leading, since they have to be graded to the comprehension of an
ignorant audience." (Ironical cheering.) "Popular lecturers are in
their nature parasitic." (Angry gesture of protest from Mr. Waldron.) "They exploit for fame or cash the work which has been
done by their indigent and unknown brethren. One smallest new
fact obtained in the laboratory, one brick built into the temple of
science, far outweighs any second-hand exposition which passes
an idle hour, but can leave no useful result behind it. I put forward this obvious reflection, not out of any desire to disparage
Mr. Waldron in particular, but that you may not lose your sense
of proportion and mistake the acolyte for the high priest." (At
this point Mr. Waldron whispered to the chairman, who half rose
and said something severely to his water-carafe.) "But enough of
this!" (Loud and prolonged cheers.) "Let me pass to some subject
of wider interest. What is the particular point upon which I, as an
original investigator, have challenged our lecturer's accuracy? It is
upon the permanence of certain types of animal life upon the
earth. I do not speak upon this subject as an amateur, nor, I may
add, as a popular lecturer, but I speak as one whose scientific conscience compels him to adhere closely to facts, when I say that
Mr. Waldron is very wrong in supposing that because he has

never himself seen a so-called prehistoric animal, therefore these creatures no longer exist. They are indeed, as he has said, our ancestors, but they are, if I may use the expression, our contemporary ancestors, who can still be found with all their hideous and formidable characteristics if one has but the energy and hardihood to seek their haunts. Creatures which were supposed to be Jurassic, monsters who would hunt down and devour our largest and fiercest mammals, still exist." (Cries of "Bosh!" "Prove it!" "How do YOU know?" "Question!") "How do I know, you ask me? I know because I have visited their secret haunts. I know because I have seen some of them." (Applause, uproar, and a voice, "Liar!") "Am I a liar?" (General hearty and noisy assent.) "Did I hear someone say that I was a liar? Will the person who called me a liar kindly stand up that I may know him?" (A voice, "Here he is, sir!" and an inoffensive little person in spectacles, struggling violently, was held up among a group of students.) "Did you venture to call me a liar?" ("No, sir, no!" shouted the accused, and disappeared like a jack-in-the-box.) "If any person in this hall dares to doubt my veracity, I shall be glad to have a few words with him after the lecture." ("Liar!") "Who said that?" (Again the inoffensive one plunging desperately, was elevated high into the air.) "If I come down among you——" (General chorus of "Come, love, come!" which interrupted the proceedings for some moments, while the chairman, standing up and waving both his arms, seemed to be conducting the music. The Professor, with his face flushed, his nostrils dilated, and his beard bristling, was now in a proper Berserk mood.) "Every great discoverer has been met with the same incredulity—the sure brand of a generation of fools. When great facts are laid before you, you have not the intuition, the imagination which would help you to understand them. You can only throw mud at the men who have risked their lives to open new fields to science. You persecute the prophets! Galileo! Darwin, and I——" (Prolonged cheering and complete interruption.)

All this is from my hurried notes taken at the time, which give little notion of the absolute chaos to which the assembly had by this time been reduced. So terrific was the uproar that several ladies had already beaten a hurried retreat. Grave and reverend seniors seemed to have caught the prevailing spirit as badly as the students, and I saw white-bearded men rising and shaking their fists at the obdurate Professor. The whole great audience seethed and simmered like a boiling pot. The Professor took a step forward and raised both his hands. There was something so big and arresting and virile in the man that the clatter and shouting died gradually away before his commanding gesture and his masterful eyes. He seemed to have a definite message. They hushed to hear it.

"I will not detain you," he said. "It is not worth it. Truth is truth, and the noise of a number of foolish young men—and, I fear I must add, of their equally foolish seniors—cannot affect the matter. I claim that I have opened a new field of science. You dispute it." (Cheers.) "Then I put you to the test. Will you accredit one or more of your own number to go out as your representatives and test my statement in your name?"

Mr. Summerlee, the veteran Professor of Comparative Anatomy, rose among the audience, a tall, thin, bitter man, with the withered aspect of a theologian. He wished, he said, to ask Professor Challenger whether the results to which he had alluded in his remarks had been obtained during a journey to the headwaters of the Amazon made by him two years before.

Professor Challenger answered that they had.

Mr. Summerlee desired to know how it was that Professor Challenger claimed to have made discoveries in those regions which had been overlooked by Wallace, Bates, and other previous explorers of established scientific repute.

Professor Challenger answered that Mr. Summerlee appeared to be confusing the Amazon with the Thames; that it was in reality a somewhat larger river; that Mr. Summerlee might be interested to know that with the Orinoco, which communicated with it, some fifty thousand miles of country were opened up, and that in so vast a space it was not impossible for one person to find what another had missed.

Mr. Summerlee declared, with an acid smile, that he fully appreciated the difference between the Thames and the Amazon, which lay in the fact that any assertion about the former could be tested, while about the latter it could not. He would be obliged if Professor Challenger would give the latitude and the longitude of the country in which prehistoric animals were to be found.

Professor Challenger replied that he reserved such information for good reasons of his own, but would be prepared to give it with proper precautions to a committee chosen from the audience. Would Mr. Summerlee serve on such a committee and test his story in person?

Mr. Summerlee: "Yes, I will." (Great cheering.)

Professor Challenger: "Then I guarantee that I will place in your hands such material as will enable you to find your way. It is only right, however, since Mr. Summerlee goes to check my state-ment that I should have one or more with him who may check his. I will not disguise from you that there are difficulties and dangers. Mr. Summerlee will need a younger colleague. May I ask for volunteers?"

It is thus that the great crisis of a man's life springs out at him. Could I have imagined when I entered that hall that I was about to pledge myself to a wilder adventure than had ever come to me in my dreams? But Gladys—was it not the very opportunity of which she spoke? Gladys would have told me to go. I had sprung to my feet. I was speaking, and yet I had prepared no words. Tarp Henry, my companion, was plucking at my skirts and I heard him whispering, "Sit down, Malone! Don't make a public ass of yourself." At the same time I was aware that a tall, thin man, with dark gingery hair, a few seats in front of me, was also upon his feet. He glared back at me with hard angry eyes, but I refused to give way.

"I will go, Mr. Chairman," I kept repeating over and over again.

"Name! Name!" cried the audience.

"My name is Edward Dunn Malone. I am the reporter of the Daily Gazette. I claim to be an absolutely unprejudiced witness."

"What is YOUR name, sir?" the chairman asked of my tall rival.

"I am Lord John Roxton. I have already been up the Amazon, I know all the ground, and have special qualifications for this investigation."

"Lord John Roxton's reputation as a sportsman and a traveler is, of course, world-famous," said the chairman; "at the same time it would certainly be as well to have a member of the Press upon such an expedition."

"Then I move," said Professor Challenger, "that both these gentlemen be elected, as representatives of this meeting, to accompany Professor Summerlee upon his journey to investigate and to report upon the truth of my statements."

And so, amid shouting and cheering, our fate was decided, and I found myself borne away in the human current which swirled towards the door, with my mind half stunned by the vast new project which had risen so suddenly before it. As I emerged from the hall I was conscious for a moment of a rush of laughing students—down the pavement, and of an arm wielding a heavy umbrella, which rose and fell in the midst of them. Then, amid a mixture of groans and cheers, Professor Challenger's electric brougham slid from the curb, and I found myself walking under the silvery lights of Regent Street, full of thoughts of Gladys and of wonder as to my future.

Suddenly there was a touch at my elbow. I turned, and found myself looking into the humorous, masterful eyes of the tall, thin man who had volunteered to be my companion on this strange quest.

"Mr. Malone, I understand," said he. "We are to be companions—what? My rooms are just over the road, in the Albany. Perhaps you would have the kindness to spare me half an hour, for there are one or two things that I badly want to say to you."

Chapter VI "I Was the Flail of the Lord"

Lord John Roxton and I turned down Vigo Street together and through the dingy portals of the famous aristocratic rookery. At the end of a long drab passage my new acquaintance pushed open a door and turned on an electric switch. A number of lamps shining through tinted shades bathed the whole great room before us in a ruddy radiance. Standing in the doorway and glancing round me, I had a general impression of extraordinary comfort and elegance combined with an atmosphere of masculine virility. Everywhere there were mingled the luxury of the wealthy man of taste and the careless untidiness of the bachelor. Rich furs and strange iridescent mats from some Oriental bazaar were scattered upon the floor. Pictures and prints which even my unpractised eyes could recognize as being of great price and rarity hung thick upon the walls. Sketches of boxers, of ballet-girls, and of racehorses alternated with a sensuous Fragonard, a martial Girardet, and a dreamy Turner. But amid these varied ornaments there were scattered the trophies which brought back strongly to my recollection the fact that Lord John Roxton was one of the great all-round sportsmen and athletes of his day. A dark-blue oar crossed with a cherry-pink one above his mantel-piece spoke of the old Oxonian and Leander man, while the foils and boxing-gloves above and below them were the tools of a man who had won supremacy with each. Like a dado round the room was the jutting line of splendid heavy game-heads, the best of their sort from every quarter of the world, with the rare white rhinoceros of the Lado Enclave drooping its supercilious lip above them all.

In the center of the rich red carpet was a black and gold Louis Quinze table, a lovely antique, now sacrilegiously desecrated with marks of glasses and the scars of cigar-stumps. On it stood a silver tray of smokables and a burnished spirit-stand, from which and an adjacent siphon my silent host proceeded to charge two high glasses. Having indicated an arm-chair to me and placed my refreshment near it, he handed me a long, smooth Havana. Then, seating himself opposite to me, he looked at me long and fixedly with his strange, twinkling, reckless eyes—eyes of a cold light blue, the color of a glacier lake.

Through the thin haze of my cigar-smoke I noted the details of a face which was already familiar to me from many photographs—the strongly-curved nose, the hollow, worn cheeks, the dark, ruddy hair, thin at the top, the crisp, virile moustaches, the small, aggressive tuft upon his projecting chin. Something there was of Napoleon III., something of Don Quixote, and yet again something which was the essence of the English country gentleman, the keen, alert, open-air lover of dogs and of horses. His skin was of a rich flower-pot red from sun and wind. His eyebrows were tufted and overhanging, which gave those naturally cold eyes an almost ferocious aspect, an impression which was increased by his strong and furrowed brow. In figure he was spare, but very strongly built—indeed, he had often proved that there were few men in England capable of such sustained exertions. His height was a little over six feet, but he seemed shorter on account of a peculiar rounding of the shoulders. Such was the famous Lord John Roxton as he sat opposite to me, biting hard upon his cigar and watching me steadily in a long and embarrassing silence.

"Well," said he, at last, "we've gone and done it, young fellah my lad." (This curious phrase he pronounced as if it were all one word—"young-fellah-me-lad.") "Yes, we've taken a jump, you an' me. I suppose, now, when you went into that room there was no such notion in your head—what?"

"No thought of it."

"The same here. No thought of it. And here we are, up to our necks in the tureen. Why, I've only been back three weeks from Uganda, and taken a place in Scotland, and signed the lease and all. Pretty goin's on—what? How does it hit you?"

"Well, it is all in the main line of my business. I am a journalist on the Gazette."

"Of course—you said so when you took it on. By the way, I've got a small job for you, if you'll help me."

"With pleasure."

"Don't mind takin' a risk, do you?"

"What is the risk?"

"Well, it's Ballinger—he's the risk. You've heard of him?"

"No."

"Why, young fellah, where HAVE you lived? Sir John Ballinger is the best gentleman jock in the north country. I could hold him on the flat at my best, but over jumps he's my master. Well, it's an open secret that when he's out of trainin' he drinks hard—strikin' an average, he calls it. He got delirium on Toosday, and has been ragin' like a devil ever since. His room is above this. The doctors say that it is all up with the old dear unless some food is got into him, but as he lies in bed with a revolver on his coverlet, and swears he will put six of the best through anyone that comes near him, there's been a bit of a strike among the serving-men. He's a hard nail, is Jack, and a dead shot, too, but you can't leave a Grand National winner to die like that—what?"

"What do you mean to do, then?" I asked.

"Well, my idea was that you and I could rush him. He may be dozin', and at the worst he can only wing one of us, and the other should have him. If we can get his bolster-cover round his arms and then 'phone up a stomach-pump, we'll give the old dear the supper of his life."

It was a rather desperate business to come suddenly into one's day's work. I don't think that I am a particularly brave man. I have an Irish imagination which makes the unknown and the untried more terrible than they are. On the other hand, I was brought up with a horror of cowardice and with a terror of such a stigma. I dare say that I could throw myself over a precipice, like the Hun in the history books, if my courage to do it were questioned, and yet it would surely be pride and fear, rather than courage, which would be my inspiration. Therefore, although every nerve in my body shrank from the whisky-maddened figure which I pictured in the room above, I still answered, in as careless a voice as I could command, that I was ready to go. Some further remark of Lord Roxton's about the danger only made me irritable.

"Talking won't make it any better," said I. "Come on."

I rose from my chair and he from his. Then with a little confidential chuckle of laughter, he patted me two or three times on the chest, finally pushing me back into my chair.

"All right, sonny my lad—you'll do," said he. I looked up in surprise.

"I saw after Jack Ballinger myself this mornin'. He blew a hole in the skirt of my kimono, bless his shaky old hand, but we got a jacket on him, and he's to be all right in a week. I say, young fellah, I hope you don't mind—what? You see, between you an' me close-tiled, I look on this South American business as a mighty serious thing, and if I have a pal with me I want a man I can bank on. So I sized you down, and I'm bound to say that you came well out of it. You see, it's all up to you and me, for this old Summerlee man will want dry-nursin' from the first. By the way, are you by any chance the Malone who is expected to get his Rugby cap for Ireland?"

"A reserve, perhaps."

"I thought I remembered your face. Why, I was there when you got that try against Richmond—as fine a swervin' run as I saw the whole season. I never miss a Rugby match if I can help it, for it is the manliest game we have left. Well, I didn't ask you in here just to talk sport. We've got to fix our business. Here are the sailin's, on the first page of the Times. There's a Booth boat for Para next Wednesday week, and if the Professor and you can work it, I think we should take it—what? Very good, I'll fix it with him. What about your outfit?"

"My paper will see to that."

"Can you shoot?"

"About average Territorial standard."

"Good Lord! as bad as that? It's the last thing you young fellahs think of learnin'. You're all bees without stings, so far as lookin' after the hive goes. You'll look silly, some o' these days, when someone comes along an' sneaks the honey. But you'll need to hold your gun straight in South America, for, unless our friend the Professor is a madman or a liar, we may see some queer things before we get back. What gun have you?"

He crossed to an oaken cupboard, and as he threw it open I caught a glimpse of glistening rows of parallel barrels, like the pipes of an organ.

"I'll see what I can spare you out of my own battery," said he.

One by one he took out a succession of beautiful rifles, opening and shutting them with a snap and a clang, and then patting them as he put them back into the rack as tenderly as a mother would fondle her children.

"This is a Bland's .577 axite express," said he. "I got that big fellow with it." He glanced up at the white rhinoceros. "Ten more yards, and he'd would have added me to HIS collection.

'On that conical bullet his one chance hangs, 'Tis the weak one's advantage fair.'

Hope you know your Gordon, for he's the poet of the horse and the gun and the man that handles both. Now, here's a useful tool—.470, telescopic sight, double ejector, point-blank up to three-fifty. That's the rifle I used against the Peruvian slave-drivers three years ago. I was the flail of the Lord up in those parts, I may tell you, though you won't find it in any Blue-book. There are times, young fellah, when every one of us must make a stand for human right and justice, or you never feel clean again. That's why I made a little war on my own. Declared it myself, waged it myself, ended it myself. Each of those nicks is for a slave murderer—a good row of them—what? That big one is for Pedro Lopez, the king of them all, that I killed in a backwater of the Putomayo River. Now, here's something that would do for you." He took out a beautiful brown-and-silver rifle. "Well rubbered at the stock, sharply sighted, five cartridges to the clip. You can trust your life to that." He handed it to me and closed the door of his oak cabinet.

"By the way," he continued, coming back to his chair, "what do you know of this Professor Challenger?"

"I never saw him till to-day."

"Well, neither did I. It's funny we should both sail under sealed orders from a man we don't know. He seemed an uppish old bird. His brothers of science don't seem too fond of him, either. How came you to take an interest in the affair?"

I told him shortly my experiences of the morning, and he listened intently. Then he drew out a map of South America and laid it on the table.

"I believe every single word he said to you was the truth," said he, earnestly, "and, mind you, I have something to go on when I speak like that. South America is a place I love, and I think, if you take it right through from Darien to Fuego, it's the grandest, richest, most wonderful bit of earth upon this planet. People don't know it yet, and don't realize what it may become. I've been up an' down it from end to end, and had two dry seasons in those very parts, as I told you when I spoke of the war I made on the slave-dealers. Well, when I was up there I heard some yarns of the same kind—traditions of Indians and the like, but with somethin' behind them, no doubt. The more you knew of that country, young fellah, the more you would understand that anythin' was possible—ANYTHIN'. There are just some narrow water-lanes along which folk travel, and outside that it is all darkness. Now, down here in the Matto Grande"—he swept his cigar over a part of the map—"or up in this corner where three countries meet, nothin' would surprise me. As that chap said to-night, there are fifty-thousand miles of water-way runnin' through a forest that is very near the size of Europe. You and I could be as far away from each other as Scotland is from Constantinople, and yet each of us be in the same great Brazilian forest. Man has just made a track here and a scrape there in the maze. Why, the river rises and falls the best part of forty feet, and half the country is a morass that you can't pass over. Why shouldn't somethin' new and wonderful lie in such a country? And why shouldn't we be the men to find it out? Besides," he added, his queer, gaunt face shining with delight, "there's a sportin' risk in every mile of it. I'm like an old golf-ball—I've had all the white paint knocked off me long ago. Life can whack me about now, and it can't leave a mark. But a sportin' risk, young fellah, that's the salt of existence. Then it's worth livin' again. We're all gettin' a deal too soft and dull and comfy. Give me the great waste lands and the wide spaces, with a gun in my fist and somethin' to look for that's worth findin'. I've tried war and steeplechasin' and aeroplanes, but this huntin' of beasts that look like a lobster-supper dream is a brand-new sensation." He chuckled with glee at the prospect.

Perhaps I have dwelt too long upon this new acquaintance, but he is to be my comrade for many a day, and so I have tried to set him down as I first saw him, with his quaint personality and his queer little tricks of speech and of thought. It was only the need of getting in the account of my meeting which drew me at last from his company. I left him seated amid his pink radiance, oiling the lock of his favorite rifle, while he still chuckled to himself at the thought of the adventures which awaited us. It was very clear to me that if dangers lay before us I could not in all England have found a cooler head or a braver spirit with which to share them.

That night, wearied as I was after the wonderful happenings of the day, I sat late with McArdle, the news editor, explaining to him the whole situation, which he thought important enough to bring next morning before the notice of Sir George Beaumont, the chief. It was agreed that I should write home full accounts of my adventures in the shape of successive letters to McArdle, and that these should either be edited for the Gazette as they arrived, or held back to be published later, according to the wishes of Professor Challenger, since we could not yet know what conditions he might attach to those directions which should guide us to the unknown land. In response to a telephone inquiry, we received nothing more definite than a fulmination against the Press, ending up with the remark that if we would notify our boat he would hand us any directions which he might think it proper to give us at the moment of starting. A second question from us failed to elicit any answer at all, save a plaintive bleat from his wife to the effect that her husband was in a very violent temper already, and that she hoped we would do nothing to make it worse. A third attempt, later in the day, provoked a terrific crash, and a subsequent message from the Central Exchange that Professor Challenger's receiver had been shattered. After that we abandoned all attempt at communication.

And now my patient readers, I can address you directly no longer. From now onwards (if, indeed, any continuation of this narrative should ever reach you) it can only be through the paper which I represent. In the hands of the editor I leave this account of the events which have led up to one of the most remarkable expeditions of all time, so that if I never return to England there shall be some record as to how the affair came about. I am writing these last lines in the saloon of the Booth liner Francisca, and they will go back by the pilot to the keeping of Mr. McArdle. Let me draw one last picture before I close the notebook—a picture which is the last memory of the old country which I bear away with me. It is a wet, foggy morning in the late spring; a thin, cold rain is falling. Three shining mackintoshed figures are walking down the quay, making for the gang-plank of the great liner from which the blue-peter is flying. In front of them a porter pushes a trolley piled high with trunks, wraps, and gun-cases. Professor Summerlee, a long, melancholy figure, walks with dragging steps and drooping head, as one who is already profoundly sorry for himself. Lord John Roxton steps briskly, and his thin, eager face beams forth between his hunting-cap and his muffler. As for myself, I am glad to have got the bustling days of preparation and the pangs of leave-taking behind me, and I have no doubt that I show it in my bearing. Suddenly, just as we reach the vessel, there is a shout behind us. It is Professor Challenger, who had promised to see us off. He runs after us, a puffing, red-faced, irascible figure.

"No thank you," says he; "I should much prefer not to go aboard. I have only a few words to say to you, and they can very well be said where we are. I beg you not to imagine that I am in any way indebted to you for making this journey. I would have you to understand that it is a matter of perfect indifference to me, and I refuse to entertain the most remote sense of personal obligation. Truth is truth, and nothing which you can report can affect it in any way, though it may excite the emotions and allay the curiosity of a number of very ineffectual people. My directions for your instruction and guidance are in this sealed envelope. You will open it when you reach a town upon the Amazon which is called Manaos, but not until the date and hour which is marked upon the outside. Have I made myself clear? I leave the strict observance of my conditions entirely to your honor. No, Mr. Malone, I will place no restriction upon your correspondence, since the ventilation of the facts is the object of your journey; but I demand that you shall give no particulars as to your exact destination, and that nothing be actually published until your return. Good-bye, sir. You have done something to mitigate my feelings for the loathsome profession to which you unhappily belong. Good-bye, Lord John. Science is, as I understand, a sealed book to you; but you may congratulate yourself upon the hunting-field which awaits you. You will, no doubt, have the opportunity of describing in the Field how you brought down the rocketing dimorphodon. And good-bye to you also, Professor Summerlee. If you are still capable of self-improvement, of which I am frankly unconvinced, you will surely return to London a wiser man."

So he turned upon his heel, and a minute later from the deck I could see his short, squat figure bobbing about in the distance as he made his way back to his train. Well, we are well down Channel now. There's the last bell for letters, and it's good-bye to the pilot. We'll be "down, hull-down, on the old trail" from now on. God bless all we leave behind us, and send us safely back.

Chapter VII   "To-morrow We Disappear into the Unknown"

I will not bore those whom this narrative may reach by an account of our luxurious voyage upon the Booth liner, nor will I tell of our week's stay at Para (save that I should wish to acknowledge the great kindness of the Pereira da Pinta Company in helping us to get together our equipment). I will also allude very briefly to our river journey, up a wide, slow-moving, clay-tinted stream, in a steamer which was little smaller than that which had carried us across the Atlantic. Eventually we found ourselves through the narrows of Obidos and reached the town of Manaos. Here we were rescued from the limited attractions of the local inn by Mr. Shortman, the representative of the British and Brazilian Trading Company. In his hospital Fazenda we spent our time until the day when we were empowered to open the letter of instructions given to us by Professor Challenger. Before I reach the surprising events of that date I would desire to give a clearer sketch of my comrades in this enterprise, and of the associates whom we had already gathered together in South America. I speak freely, and I leave the use of my material to your own discretion, Mr. McArdle, since it is through your hands that this report must pass before it reaches the world.

The scientific attainments of Professor Summerlee are too well known for me to trouble to recapitulate them. He is better equipped for a rough expedition of this sort than one would imagine at first sight. His tall, gaunt, stringy figure is insensible to fatigue, and his dry, half-sarcastic, and often wholly unsympathetic manner is uninfluenced by any change in his surroundings. Though in his sixty-sixth year, I have never heard him express any dissatisfaction at the occasional hardships which we have had to encounter. I had regarded his presence as an encumbrance to the expedition, but, as a matter of fact, I am now well convinced that his power of endurance is as great as my own. In temper he is naturally acid and sceptical. From the beginning he has never concealed his belief that Professor Challenger is an absolute fraud, that we are all embarked upon an absurd wild-goose chase and that we are likely to reap nothing but disappointment and danger in South America, and corresponding ridicule in England. Such are the views which, with much passionate distortion of his thin features and wagging of his thin, goat-like beard, he poured into our ears all the way from Southampton to Manaos. Since landing from the boat he has obtained some consolation from the beauty and variety of the insect and bird life around him, for he is absolutely whole-hearted in his devotion to science. He spends his days flitting through the woods with his shot-gun and his butterfly-net, and his evenings in mounting the many specimens he has acquired. Among his minor peculiarities are that he is careless as to his attire, unclean in his person, exceedingly absent-minded in his habits, and addicted to smoking a short briar pipe, which is seldom out of his mouth. He has been upon several scientific expeditions in his youth (he was with Robertson in Papua), and the life of the camp and the canoe is nothing fresh to him.

Lord John Roxton has some points in common with Professor Summerlee, and others in which they are the very antithesis to each other. He is twenty years younger, but has something of the same spare, scraggy physique. As to his appearance, I have, as I recollect, described it in that portion of my narrative which I have left behind me in London. He is exceedingly neat and prim in his ways, dresses always with great care in white drill suits and high brown mosquito-boots, and shaves at least once a day. Like most men of action, he is laconic in speech, and sinks readily into his own thoughts, but he is always quick to answer a question or join in a conversation, talking in a queer, jerky, half-humorous fashion. His knowledge of the world, and very especially of South America, is surprising, and he has a whole-hearted belief in the possibilities of our journey which is not to be dashed by the sneers of Professor Summerlee. He has a gentle voice and a quiet manner, but behind his twinkling blue eyes there lurks a capacity for furious wrath and implacable resolution, the more dangerous because they are held in leash. He spoke little of his own exploits in Brazil and Peru, but it was a revelation to me to find the excitement which was caused by his presence among the riverine natives, who looked upon him as their champion and protector. The exploits of the Red Chief, as they called him, had become legends among them, but the real facts, as far as I could learn them, were amazing enough.

These were that Lord John had found himself some years before in that no-man's-land which is formed by the half-defined frontiers between Peru, Brazil, and Columbia. In this great district the wild rubber tree flourishes, and has become, as in the Congo, a curse to the natives which can only be compared to their forced labor under the Spaniards upon the old silver mines of Darien. A handful of villainous half-breeds dominated the country, armed such Indians as would support them, and turned the rest into slaves, terrorizing them with the most inhuman tortures in order to force them to gather the india-rubber, which was then floated down the river to Para. Lord John Roxton expostulated on behalf of the wretched victims, and received nothing but threats and insults for his pains. He then formally declared war against Pedro Lopez, the leader of the slave-drivers, enrolled a band of runaway slaves in his service, armed them, and conducted a campaign, which ended by his killing with his own hands the notorious half-breed and breaking down the system which he represented.

No wonder that the ginger-headed man with the silky voice and the free and easy manners was now looked upon with deep interest upon the banks of the great South American river, though the feelings he inspired were naturally mixed, since the gratitude of the natives was equaled by the resentment of those who desired to exploit them. One useful result of his former experiences was that he could talk fluently in the Lingoa Geral, which is the peculiar talk, one-third Portuguese and two-thirds Indian, which is current all over Brazil.

I have said before that Lord John Roxton was a South Americomaniac. He could not speak of that great country without ardor, and this ardor was infectious, for, ignorant as I was, he fixed my attention and stimulated my curiosity. How I wish I could reproduce the glamour of his discourses, the peculiar mixture of accurate knowledge and of racy imagination which gave them their fascination, until even the Professor's cynical and sceptical smile would gradually vanish from his thin face as he listened. He would tell the history of the mighty river so rapidly explored (for some of the first conquerors of Peru actually crossed the entire continent upon its waters), and yet so unknown in regard to all that lay behind its ever-changing banks.

"What is there?" he would cry, pointing to the north. "Wood and marsh and unpenetrated jungle. Who knows what it may shelter? And there to the south? A wilderness of swampy forest, where no white man has ever been. The unknown is up against us on every side. Outside the narrow lines of the rivers what does anyone know? Who will say what is possible in such a country? Why should old man Challenger not be right?" At which direct defiance the stubborn sneer would reappear upon Professor Summerlee's face, and he would sit, shaking his sardonic head in unsympathetic silence, behind the cloud of his briar-root pipe.

So much, for the moment, for my two white companions, whose characters and limitations will be further exposed, as surely as my own, as this narrative proceeds. But already we have enrolled certain retainers who may play no small part in what is to come. The first is a gigantic negro named Zambo, who is a black Hercules, as willing as any horse, and about as intelligent. Him we enlisted at Para, on the recommendation of the steamship company, on whose vessels he had learned to speak a halting English.

It was at Para also that we engaged Gomez and Manuel, two half-breeds from up the river, just come down with a cargo of redwood. They were swarthy fellows, bearded and fierce, as active and wiry as panthers. Both of them had spent their lives in those upper waters of the Amazon which we were about to explore, and it was this recommendation which had caused Lord John to engage them. One of them, Gomez, had the further advantage that he could speak excellent English. These men were willing to act as our personal servants, to cook, to row, or to make themselves useful in any way at a payment of fifteen dollars a month. Besides these, we had engaged three Mojo Indians from Bolivia, who are the most skilful at fishing and boat work of all the river tribes. The chief of these we called Mojo, after his tribe, and the others are known as Jose and Fernando. Three white men, then, two half-breeds, one negro, and three Indians made up the personnel of the little expedition which lay waiting for its instructions at Manaos before starting upon its singular quest.

At last, after a weary week, the day had come and the hour. I ask you to picture the shaded sitting-room of the Fazenda St. Ignatio, two miles inland from the town of Manaos. Outside lay the yellow, brassy glare of the sunshine, with the shadows of the palm trees as black and definite as the trees themselves. The air was calm, full of the eternal hum of insects, a tropical chorus of many octaves, from the deep drone of the bee to the high, keen pipe of the mosquito. Beyond the veranda was a small cleared garden, bounded with cactus hedges and adorned with clumps of flowering shrubs, round which the great blue butterflies and the tiny humming-birds fluttered and darted in crescents of sparkling light. Within we were seated round the cane table, on which lay a sealed envelope. Inscribed upon it, in the jagged handwriting of Professor Challenger, were the words:—

"Instructions to Lord John Roxton and party. To be opened at Manaos upon July 15th, at 12 o'clock precisely."

Lord John had placed his watch upon the table beside him.

"We have seven more minutes," said he. "The old dear is very precise."

Professor Summerlee gave an acid smile as he picked up the envelope in his gaunt hand.

"What can it possibly matter whether we open it now or in seven minutes?" said he. "It is all part and parcel of the same system of quackery and nonsense, for which I regret to say that the writer is notorious."

"Oh, come, we must play the game accordin' to rules," said Lord John. "It's old man Challenger's show and we are here by his good will, so it would be rotten bad form if we didn't follow his instructions to the letter."

"A pretty business it is!" cried the Professor, bitterly. "It struck me as preposterous in London, but I'm bound to say that it seems even more so upon closer acquaintance. I don't know what is inside this envelope, but, unless it is something pretty definite, I shall be much tempted to take the next down-river boat and catch the Bolivia at Para. After all, I have some more responsible work in the world than to run about disproving the assertions of a lunatic. Now, Roxton, surely it is time."

"Time it is," said Lord John. "You can blow the whistle." He took up the envelope and cut it with his penknife. From it he drew a folded sheet of paper. This he carefully opened out and flattened on the table. It was a blank sheet. He turned it over. Again it was blank. We looked at each other in a bewildered silence, which was broken by a discordant burst of derisive laughter from Professor Summerlee.

"It is an open admission," he cried. "What more do you want? The fellow is a self-confessed humbug. We have only to return home and report him as the brazen imposter that he is."

"Invisible ink!" I suggested.

"I don't think!" said Lord Roxton, holding the paper to the light. "No, young fellah my lad, there is no use deceiving yourself. I'll go bail for it that nothing has ever been written upon this paper."

"May I come in?" boomed a voice from the veranda.

The shadow of a squat figure had stolen across the patch of sunlight. That voice! That monstrous breadth of shoulder! We sprang to our feet with a gasp of astonishment as Challenger, in a round, boyish straw-hat with a colored ribbon—Challenger, with his hands in his jacket-pockets and his canvas shoes daintily pointing as he walked—appeared in the open space before us. He threw back his head, and there he stood in the golden glow with all his old Assyrian luxuriance of beard, all his native insolence of drooping eyelids and intolerant eyes.

"I fear," said he, taking out his watch, "that I am a few minutes too late. When I gave you this envelope I must confess that I had never intended that you should open it, for it had been my fixed intention to be with you before the hour. The unfortunate delay can be apportioned between a blundering pilot and an intrusive sandbank. I fear that it has given my colleague, Professor Summerlee, occasion to blaspheme."

"I am bound to say, sir," said Lord John, with some sternness of voice, "that your turning up is a considerable relief to us, for our mission seemed to have come to a premature end. Even now I can't for the life of me understand why you should have worked it in so extraordinary a manner."

Instead of answering, Professor Challenger entered, shook hands with myself and Lord John, bowed with ponderous insolence to Professor Summerlee, and sank back into a basket-chair, which creaked and swayed beneath his weight.

"Is all ready for your journey?" he asked.

"We can start to-morrow."

"Then so you shall. You need no chart of directions now, since you will have the inestimable advantage of my own guidance. From the first I had determined that I would myself preside over your investigation. The most elaborate charts would, as you will readily admit, be a poor substitute for my own intelligence and advice. As to the small ruse which I played upon you in the matter of the envelope, it is clear that, had I told you all my intentions, I should have been forced to resist unwelcome pressure to travel out with you."

"Not from me, sir!" exclaimed Professor Summerlee, heartily. "So long as there was another ship upon the Atlantic."

Challenger waved him away with his great hairy hand.

"Your common sense will, I am sure, sustain my objection and realize that it was better that I should direct my own movements and appear only at the exact moment when my presence was needed. That moment has now arrived. You are in safe hands. You will not now fail to reach your destination. From henceforth I take command of this expedition, and I must ask you to complete your preparations to-night, so that we may be able to make an early start in the morning. My time is of value, and the same thing may be said, no doubt, in a lesser degree of your own. I propose, therefore, that we push on as rapidly as possible, until I have demonstrated what you have come to see."

Lord John Roxton has chartered a large steam launch, the Esmeralda, which was to carry us up the river. So far as climate goes, it was immaterial what time we chose for our expedition, as the temperature ranges from seventy-five to ninety degrees both summer and winter, with no appreciable difference in heat. In moisture, however, it is otherwise; from December to May is the period of the rains, and during this time the river slowly rises until it attains a height of nearly forty feet above its low-water mark. It floods the banks, extends in great lagoons over a monstrous waste of country, and forms a huge district, called locally the Gapo, which is for the most part too marshy for foot-travel and too shallow for boating. About June the waters begin to fall, and are at their lowest at October or November. Thus our expedition was at the time of the dry season, when the great river and its tributaries were more or less in a normal condition.

The current of the river is a slight one, the drop being not greater than eight inches in a mile. No stream could be more convenient for navigation, since the prevailing wind is south-east, and sailing boats may make a continuous progress to the Peruvian frontier, dropping down again with the current. In our own case the excellent engines of the Esmeralda could disregard the sluggish flow of the stream, and we made as rapid progress as if we were navigating a stagnant lake. For three days we steamed north-westwards up a stream which even here, a thousand miles from its mouth, was still so enormous that from its center the two banks were mere shadows upon the distant skyline. On the fourth day after leaving Manaos we turned into a tributary which at its mouth was little smaller than the main stream. It narrowed rapidly, however, and after two more days' steaming we reached an Indian village, where the Professor insisted that we should land, and that the Esmeralda should be sent back to Manaos. We should soon come upon rapids, he explained, which would make its further use impossible. He added privately that we were now approaching the door of the unknown country, and that the fewer whom we took into our confidence the better it would be. To this end also he made each of us give our word of honor that we would publish or say nothing which would give any exact clue as to the whereabouts of our travels, while the servants were all solemnly sworn to the same effect. It is for this reason that I am compelled to be vague in my narrative, and I would warn my readers that in any map or diagram which I may give the relation of places to each other may be correct, but the points of the compass are carefully confused, so that in no way can it be taken as an actual guide to the country. Professor Challenger's reasons for secrecy may be valid or not, but we had no choice but to adopt them, for he was prepared to abandon the whole expedition rather than modify the conditions upon which he would guide us.

It was August 2nd when we snapped our last link with the outer world by bidding farewell to the Esmeralda. Since then four days have passed, during which we have engaged two large canoes from the Indians, made of so light a material (skins over a bamboo framework) that we should be able to carry them round any obstacle. These we have loaded with all our effects, and have engaged two additional Indians to help us in the navigation. I understand that they are the very two—Ataca and Ipetu by name—who accompanied Professor Challenger upon his previous journey. They appeared to be terrified at the prospect of repeating it, but the chief has patriarchal powers in these countries, and if the bargain is good in his eyes the clansman has little choice in the matter.

So to-morrow we disappear into the unknown. This account I am transmitting down the river by canoe, and it may be our last word to those who are interested in our fate. I have, according to our arrangement, addressed it to you, my dear Mr. McArdle, and I leave it to your discretion to delete, alter, or do what you like with it. From the assurance of Professor Challenger's manner—and in spite of the continued scepticism of Professor Summerlee—I have no doubt that our leader will make good his statement, and that we are really on the eve of some most remarkable experiences.

Chapter VIII   "The Outlying Pickets of the New World"

Our friends at home may well rejoice with us, for we are at our goal, and up to a point, at least, we have shown that the statement of Professor Challenger can be verified. We have not, it is true, ascended the plateau, but it lies before us, and even Professor Summerlee is in a more chastened mood. Not that he will for an instant admit that his rival could be right, but he is less persistent in his incessant objections, and has sunk for the most part into an observant silence. I must hark back, however, and continue my narrative from where I dropped it. We are sending home one of our local Indians who is injured, and I am committing this letter to his charge, with considerable doubts in my mind as to whether it will ever come to hand.

When I wrote last we were about to leave the Indian village where we had been deposited by the Esmeralda. I have to begin my report by bad news, for the first serious personal trouble (I pass over the incessant bickerings between the Professors) occurred this evening, and might have had a tragic ending. I have spoken of our English-speaking half-breed, Gomez—a fine worker and a willing fellow, but afflicted, I fancy, with the vice of curiosity, which is common enough among such men. On the last evening he seems to have hid himself near the hut in which we were discussing our plans, and, being observed by our huge negro Zambo, who is as faithful as a dog and has the hatred which all his race bear to the half-breeds, he was dragged out and carried into our presence. Gomez whipped out his knife, however, and but for the huge strength of his captor, which enabled him to disarm him with one hand, he would certainly have stabbed him. The matter has ended in reprimands, the opponents have been compelled to shake hands, and there is every hope that all will be well. As to the feuds of the two learned men, they are continuous and bitter. It must be admitted that Challenger is provocative in the last degree, but Summerlee has an acid tongue, which makes matters worse. Last night Challenger said that he never cared to walk on the Thames Embankment and look up the river, as it was always sad to see one's own eventual goal. He is convinced, of course, that he is destined for Westminster Abbey. Summerlee rejoined, however, with a sour smile, by saying that he understood that Millbank Prison had been pulled down. Challenger's conceit is too colossal to allow him to be really annoyed. He only smiled in his beard and repeated "Really! Really!" in the pitying tone one would use to a child. Indeed, they are children both—the one wizened and cantankerous, the other formidable and overbearing, yet each with a brain which has put him in the front rank of his scientific age. Brain, character, soul—only as one sees more of life does one understand how distinct is each.

The very next day we did actually make our start upon this remarkable expedition. We found that all our possessions fitted very easily into the two canoes, and we divided our personnel, six in each, taking the obvious precaution in the interests of peace of putting one Professor into each canoe. Personally, I was with Challenger, who was in a beatific humor, moving about as one in a

silent ecstasy and beaming benevolence from every feature. I have
had some experience of him in other moods, however, and shall
be the less surprised when the thunderstorms suddenly come up
amidst the sunshine. If it is impossible to be at your ease, it is
equally impossible to be dull in his company, for one is always in a
state of half-tremulous doubt as to what sudden turn his
formidable temper may take.

For two days we made our way up a good-sized river some
hundreds of yards broad, and dark in color, but transparent, so that
one could usually see the bottom. The affluents of the Amazon are,
half of them, of this nature, while the other half are whitish and
opaque, the difference depending upon the class of country
through which they have flowed. The dark indicate vegetable
decay, while the others point to clayey soil. Twice we came across
rapids, and in each case made a portage of half a mile or so to avoid
them. The woods on either side were primeval, which are more
easily penetrated than woods of the second growth, and we had no
great difficulty in carrying our canoes through them. How shall I
ever forget the solemn mystery of it? The height of the trees and the
thickness of the boles exceeded anything which I in my town-bred
life could have imagined, shooting upwards in magnificent
columns until, at an enormous distance above our heads, we could
dimly discern the spot where they threw out their side-branches
into Gothic upward curves which coalesced to form one great matted roof of verdure, through which only an occasional golden ray
of sunshine shot downwards to trace a thin dazzling line of light
amidst the majestic obscurity. As we walked noiselessly amid the
thick, soft carpet of decaying vegetation the hush fell upon our
souls which comes upon us in the twilight of the Abbey, and even
Professor Challenger's full-chested notes sank into a whisper.
Alone, I should have been ignorant of the names of these giant
growths, but our men of science pointed out the cedars, the great
silk cotton trees, and the redwood trees, with all that profusion of
various plants which has made this continent the chief supplier to
the human race of those gifts of Nature which depend upon the
vegetable world, while it is the most backward in those products
which come from animal life. Vivid orchids and wonderful colored

lichens smoldered upon the swarthy tree-trunks and where a wandering shaft of light fell full upon the golden allamanda, the scarlet star-clusters of the tacsonia, or the rich deep blue of ipomaea, the effect was as a dream of fairyland. In these great wastes of forest, life, which abhors darkness, struggles ever upwards to the light. Every plant, even the smaller ones, curls and writhes to the green surface, twining itself round its stronger and taller brethren in the effort. Climbing plants are monstrous and luxuriant, but others which have never been known to climb elsewhere learn the art as an escape from that somber shadow, so that the common nettle, the jasmine, and even the jacitara palm tree can be seen circling the stems of the cedars and striving to reach their crowns. Of animal life there was no movement amid the majestic vaulted aisles which stretched from us as we walked, but a constant movement far above our heads told of that multitudinous world of snake and monkey, bird and sloth, which lived in the sunshine, and looked down in wonder at our tiny, dark, stumbling figures in the obscure depths immeasurably below them. At dawn and at sunset the howler monkeys screamed together and the parrakeets broke into shrill chatter, but during the hot hours of the day only the full drone of insects, like the beat of a distant surf, filled the ear, while nothing moved amid the solemn vistas of stupendous trunks, fading away into the darkness which held us in. Once some bandy-legged, lurching creature, an ant-eater or a bear, scuttled clumsily amid the shadows. It was the only sign of earth life which I saw in this great Amazonian forest.

And yet there were indications that even human life itself was not far from us in those mysterious recesses. On the third day out we were aware of a singular deep throbbing in the air, rhythmic and solemn, coming and going fitfully throughout the morning. The two boats were paddling within a few yards of each other when first we heard it, and our Indians remained motionless, as if they had been turned to bronze, listening intently with expressions of terror upon their faces.

"What is it, then?" I asked.

"Drums," said Lord John, carelessly; "war drums. I have heard them before."

"Yes, sir, war drums," said Gomez, the half-breed. "Wild Indians, bravos, not mansos; they watch us every mile of the way; kill us if they can."

"How can they watch us?" I asked, gazing into the dark, motionless void.

The half-breed shrugged his broad shoulders.

"The Indians know. They have their own way. They watch us. They talk the drum talk to each other. Kill us if they can."

By the afternoon of that day—my pocket diary shows me that it was Tuesday, August 18th—at least six or seven drums were throbbing from various points. Sometimes they beat quickly, sometimes slowly, sometimes in obvious question and answer, one far to the east breaking out in a high staccato rattle, and being followed after a pause by a deep roll from the north. There was something indescribably nerve-shaking and menacing in that constant mutter, which seemed to shape itself into the very syllables of the half-breed, endlessly repeated, "We will kill you if we can. We will kill you if we can." No one ever moved in the silent woods. All the peace and soothing of quiet Nature lay in that dark curtain of vegetation, but away from behind there came ever the one message from our fellow-man. "We will kill you if we can," said the men in the east. "We will kill you if we can," said the men in the north.

All day the drums rumbled and whispered, while their menace reflected itself in the faces of our colored companions. Even the hardy, swaggering half-breed seemed cowed. I learned, however, that day once for all that both Summerlee and Challenger possessed that highest type of bravery, the bravery of the scientific mind. Theirs was the spirit which upheld Darwin among the gauchos of the Argentine or Wallace among the head-hunters of Malaya. It is decreed by a merciful Nature that the human brain cannot think of two things simultaneously, so that if it be steeped in curiosity as to science it has no room for merely personal considerations. All day amid that incessant and mysterious menace our two Professors watched every bird upon the wing, and every shrub upon the bank, with many a sharp wordy contention, when the snarl of Summerlee came quick upon the deep growl of Challenger, but with no more sense of danger and no more reference to drum-beating Indians than if they were seated together in the smoking-room of the Royal Society's Club in St. James's Street. Once only did they condescend to discuss them.

"Miranha or Amajuaca cannibals," said Challenger, jerking his thumb towards the reverberating wood.

"No doubt, sir," Summerlee answered. "Like all such tribes, I shall expect to find them of poly-synthetic speech and of Mongolian type."

"Polysynthetic certainly," said Challenger, indulgently. "I am not aware that any other type of language exists in this continent, and I have notes of more than a hundred. The Mongolian theory I regard with deep suspicion."

"I should have thought that even a limited knowledge of comparative anatomy would have helped to verify it," said Summerlee, bitterly.

Challenger thrust out his aggressive chin until he was all beard and hat-rim. "No doubt, sir, a limited knowledge would have that effect. When one's knowledge is exhaustive, one comes to other conclusions." They glared at each other in mutual defiance, while all round rose the distant whisper, "We will kill you—we will kill you if we can."

That night we moored our canoes with heavy stones for anchors in the center of the stream, and made every preparation for a possible attack. Nothing came, however, and with the dawn we pushed upon our way, the drum-beating dying out behind us. About three o'clock in the afternoon we came to a very steep rapid, more than a mile long—the very one in which Professor Challenger had suffered disaster upon his first journey. I confess that the sight of it consoled me, for it was really the first direct corroboration, slight as it was, of the truth of his story. The Indians carried first our canoes and then our stores through the brushwood, which is very thick at this point, while we four whites, our rifles on our shoulders, walked between them and any danger coming from the woods. Before evening we had successfully passed the rapids, and made our way some ten miles above them, where we anchored for the night. At this point I reckoned that we had come not less than a hundred miles up the tributary from the main stream.

It was in the early forenoon of the next day that we made the great departure. Since dawn Professor Challenger had been acutely uneasy, continually scanning each bank of the river. Suddenly he gave an exclamation of satisfaction and pointed to a single tree, which projected at a peculiar angle over the side of the stream.

"What do you make of that?" he asked.

"It is surely an Assai palm," said Summerlee.

"Exactly. It was an Assai palm which I took for my landmark. The secret opening is half a mile onwards upon the other side of the river. There is no break in the trees. That is the wonder and the mystery of it. There where you see light-green rushes instead of dark-green undergrowth, there between the great cotton woods, that is my private gate into the unknown. Push through, and you will understand."

It was indeed a wonderful place. Having reached the spot marked by a line of light-green rushes, we poled out two canoes through them for some hundreds of yards, and eventually emerged into a placid and shallow stream, running clear and transparent over a sandy bottom. It may have been twenty yards across, and was banked in on each side by most luxuriant vegetation. No one who had not observed that for a short distance reeds had taken the place of shrubs, could possibly have guessed the existence of such a stream or dreamed of the fairyland beyond.

For a fairyland it was—the most wonderful that the imagination of man could conceive. The thick vegetation met overhead, interlacing into a natural pergola, and through this tunnel of verdure in a golden twilight flowed the green, pellucid river, beautiful in itself, but marvelous from the strange tints thrown by the vivid light from above filtered and tempered in its fall. Clear as crystal, motionless as a sheet of glass, green as the edge of an iceberg, it stretched in front of us under its leafy archway, every stroke of our paddles sending a thousand ripples across its shining surface. It was a fitting avenue to a land of wonders. All sign of the Indians had passed away, but animal life was more frequent, and the tameness of the creatures showed that they knew nothing of the hunter. Fuzzy little black-velvet monkeys, with snow-white teeth and gleaming, mocking eyes, chattered at us as we passed. With a dull, heavy splash an occasional cayman plunged in from the bank. Once a dark, clumsy tapir stared at us from a gap in the bushes, and then lumbered away through the forest; once, too, the yellow, sinuous form of a great puma whisked amid the brushwood, and its green, baleful eyes glared hatred at us over its tawny shoulder. Bird life was abundant, especially the wading birds, stork, heron, and ibis gathering in little groups, blue, scarlet, and white, upon every log which jutted from the bank, while beneath us the crystal water was alive with fish of every shape and color.

For three days we made our way up this tunnel of hazy green sunshine. On the longer stretches one could hardly tell as one looked ahead where the distant green water ended and the distant green archway began. The deep peace of this strange waterway was unbroken by any sign of man.

"No Indian here. Too much afraid. Curupuri," said Gomez.

"Curupuri is the spirit of the woods," Lord John explained. "It's a name for any kind of devil. The poor beggars think that there is something fearsome in this direction, and therefore they avoid it."

On the third day it became evident that our journey in the canoes could not last much longer, for the stream was rapidly growing more shallow. Twice in as many hours we stuck upon the bottom. Finally we pulled the boats up among the brushwood and spent the night on the bank of the river. In the morning Lord John and I made our way for a couple of miles through the forest, keeping parallel with the stream; but as it grew ever shallower we returned and reported, what Professor Challenger had already suspected, that we had reached the highest point to which the canoes could be brought. We drew them up, therefore, and concealed them among the bushes, blazing a tree with our axes, so that we should find them again. Then we distributed the various burdens among us—guns, ammunition, food, a tent, blankets, and the rest—and, shouldering our packages, we set forth upon the more laborious stage of our journey.

An unfortunate quarrel between our pepper-pots marked the outset of our new stage. Challenger had from the moment of joining us issued directions to the whole party, much to the evident discontent of Summerlee. Now, upon his assigning some duty to his fellow-Professor (it was only the carrying of an aneroid barometer), the matter suddenly came to a head.

"May I ask, sir," said Summerlee, with vicious calm, "in what capacity you take it upon yourself to issue these orders?"

Challenger glared and bristled.

"I do it, Professor Summerlee, as leader of this expedition."

"I am compelled to tell you, sir, that I do not recognize you in that capacity."

"Indeed!" Challenger bowed with unwieldy sarcasm. "Perhaps you would define my exact position."

"Yes, sir. You are a man whose veracity is upon trial, and this committee is here to try it. You walk, sir, with your judges."

"Dear me!" said Challenger, seating himself on the side of one of the canoes. "In that case you will, of course, go on your way, and I will follow at my leisure. If I am not the leader you cannot expect me to lead."

Thank heaven that there were two sane men—Lord John Roxton and myself—to prevent the petulance and folly of our learned Professors from sending us back empty-handed to London. Such arguing and pleading and explaining before we could get them mollified! Then at last Summerlee, with his sneer and his pipe, would move forwards, and Challenger would come rolling and grumbling after. By some good fortune we discovered about this time that both our savants had the very poorest opinion of Dr. Illingworth of Edinburgh. Thenceforward that was our one safety, and every strained situation was relieved by our introducing the name of the Scotch zoologist, when both our Professors would form a temporary alliance and friendship in their detestation and abuse of this common rival.

Advancing in single file along the bank of the stream, we soon found that it narrowed down to a mere brook, and finally that it lost itself in a great green morass of sponge-like mosses, into which we sank up to our knees. The place was horribly haunted by clouds of mosquitoes and every form of flying pest, so we were glad to find solid ground again and to make a circuit among the trees, which enabled us to outflank this pestilent morass, which droned like an organ in the distance, so loud was it with insect life.

On the second day after leaving our canoes we found that the whole character of the country changed. Our road was persistently upwards, and as we ascended the woods became thinner and lost their tropical luxuriance. The huge trees of the alluvial Amazonian plain gave place to the Phoenix and coco palms, growing in scattered clumps, with thick brushwood between. In the damper hollows the Mauritia palms threw out their graceful drooping fronds. We traveled entirely by compass, and once or twice there were differences of opinion between Challenger and the two Indians, when, to quote the Professor's indignant words, the whole party agreed to "trust the fallacious instincts of undeveloped savages rather than the highest product of modern European culture." That we were justified in doing so was shown upon the third day, when Challenger admitted that he recognized several landmarks of his former journey, and in one spot we actually came upon four fire-blackened stones, which must have marked a camping-place.

The road still ascended, and we crossed a rock-studded slope which took two days to traverse. The vegetation had again changed, and only the vegetable ivory tree remained, with a great profusion of wonderful orchids, among which I learned to recognize the rare Nuttonia Vexillaria and the glorious pink and scarlet blossoms of Cattleya and odontoglossum. Occasional brooks with pebbly bottoms and fern-draped banks gurgled down the shallow gorges in the hill, and offered good camping-grounds every evening on the banks of some rock-studded pool, where swarms of little blue-backed fish, about the size and shape of English trout, gave us a delicious supper.

On the ninth day after leaving the canoes, having done, as I reckon, about a hundred and twenty miles, we began to emerge from the trees, which had grown smaller until they were mere shrubs. Their place was taken by an immense wilderness of bamboo, which grew so thickly that we could only penetrate it by cutting a pathway with the machetes and billhooks of the Indians. It took us a long day, traveling from seven in the morning till eight at night, with only two breaks of one hour each, to get through this obstacle. Anything more monotonous and wearying could not be imagined, for, even at the most open places, I could not see more

than ten or twelve yards, while usually my vision was limited to
the back of Lord John's cotton jacket in front of me, and to the yellow wall within a foot of me on either side. From above came one
thin knife-edge of sunshine, and fifteen feet over our heads one
saw the tops of the reeds swaying against the deep blue sky. I do
not know what kind of creatures inhabit such a thicket, but several
times we heard the plunging of large, heavy animals quite close to
us. From their sounds Lord John judged them to be some form of
wild cattle. Just as night fell we cleared the belt of bamboos, and at
once formed our camp, exhausted by the interminable day.

Early next morning we were again afoot, and found that the
character of the country had changed once again. Behind us was
the wall of bamboo, as definite as if it marked the course of a river.
In front was an open plain, sloping slightly upwards and dotted
with clumps of tree-ferns, the whole curving before us until it
ended in a long, whale-backed ridge. This we reached about midday, only to find a shallow valley beyond, rising once again into a
gentle incline which led to a low, rounded sky-line. It was here,
while we crossed the first of these hills, that an incident occurred
which may or may not have been important.

Professor Challenger, who with the two local Indians was in
the van of the party, stopped suddenly and pointed excitedly to
the right. As he did so we saw, at the distance of a mile or so, something which appeared to be a huge gray bird flap slowly up from
the ground and skim smoothly off, flying very low and straight,
until it was lost among the tree-ferns.

"Did you see it?" cried Challenger, in exultation. "Summerlee,
did you see it?"

His colleague was staring at the spot where the creature had
disappeared.

"What do you claim that it was?" he asked.

"To the best of my belief, a pterodactyl."

Summerlee burst into derisive laughter "A pter-fiddlestick!"
said he. "It was a stork, if ever I saw one."

Challenger was too furious to speak. He simply swung his
pack upon his back and continued upon his march. Lord John
came abreast of me, however, and his face was more grave than
was his wont. He had his Zeiss glasses in his hand.

"I focused it before it got over the trees," said he. "I won't undertake to say what it was, but I'll risk my reputation as a sportsman that it wasn't any bird that ever I clapped eyes on in my life."

So there the matter stands. Are we really just at the edge of the unknown, encountering the outlying pickets of this lost world of which our leader speaks? I give you the incident as it occurred and you will know as much as I do. It stands alone, for we saw nothing more which could be called remarkable.

And now, my readers, if ever I have any, I have brought you up the broad river, and through the screen of rushes, and down the green tunnel, and up the long slope of palm trees, and through the bamboo brake, and across the plain of tree-ferns. At last our destination lay in full sight of us. When we had crossed the second ridge we saw before us an irregular, palm-studded plain, and then the line of high red cliffs which I have seen in the picture. There it lies, even as I write, and there can be no question that it is the same. At the nearest point it is about seven miles from our present camp, and it curves away, stretching as far as I can see. Challenger struts about like a prize peacock, and Summerlee is silent, but still sceptical. Another day should bring some of our doubts to an end. Meanwhile, as Jose, whose arm was pierced by a broken bamboo, insists upon returning, I send this letter back in his charge, and only hope that it may eventually come to hand. I will write again as the occasion serves. I have enclosed with this a rough chart of our journey, which may have the effect of making the account rather easier to understand.

Chapter IX   "Who Could Have Foreseen It?"

A dreadful thing has happened to us. Who could have foreseen it? I cannot foresee any end to our troubles. It may be that we are condemned to spend our whole lives in this strange, inaccessible place. I am still so confused that I can hardly think clearly of the facts of the present or of the chances of the future. To my astounded senses the one seems most terrible and the other as black as night.

No men have ever found themselves in a worse position; nor is there any use in disclosing to you our exact geographical situation and asking our friends for a relief party. Even if they could send one, our fate will in all human probability be decided long before it could arrive in South America.

We are, in truth, as far from any human aid as if we were in the moon. If we are to win through, it is only our own qualities which can save us. I have as companions three remarkable men, men of great brain-power and of unshaken courage. There lies our one and only hope. It is only when I look upon the untroubled faces of my comrades that I see some glimmer through the darkness. Outwardly I trust that I appear as unconcerned as they. Inwardly I am filled with apprehension.

Let me give you, with as much detail as I can, the sequence of events which have led us to this catastrophe.

When I finished my last letter I stated that we were within seven miles from an enormous line of ruddy cliffs, which encircled, beyond all doubt, the plateau of which Professor Challenger spoke. Their height, as we approached them, seemed to me in some places to be greater than he had stated—running up in parts to at least a thousand feet—and they were curiously striated, in a manner which is, I believe, characteristic of basaltic upheavals. Something of the sort is to be seen in Salisbury Crags at Edinburgh. The summit showed every sign of a luxuriant vegetation, with bushes near the edge, and farther back many high trees. There was no indication of any life that we could see.

That night we pitched our camp immediately under the cliff—a most wild and desolate spot. The crags above us were not merely perpendicular, but curved outwards at the top, so that ascent was out of the question. Close to us was the high thin pinnacle of rock which I believe I mentioned earlier in this narrative. It is like a broad red church spire, the top of it being level with the plateau, but a great chasm gaping between. On the summit of it there grew one high tree. Both pinnacle and cliff were comparatively low—some five or six hundred feet, I should think.

"It was on that," said Professor Challenger, pointing to this tree, "that the pterodactyl was perched. I climbed half-way up the rock before I shot him. I am inclined to think that a good mountaineer like myself could ascend the rock to the top, though he would, of course, be no nearer to the plateau when he had done so."

As Challenger spoke of his pterodactyl I glanced at Professor Summerlee, and for the first time I seemed to see some signs of a dawning credulity and repentance. There was no sneer upon his thin lips, but, on the contrary, a gray, drawn look of excitement and amazement. Challenger saw it, too, and reveled in the first taste of victory.

"Of course," said he, with his clumsy and ponderous sarcasm, "Professor Summerlee will understand that when I speak of a pterodactyl I mean a stork—only it is the kind of stork which has no feathers, a leathery skin, membranous wings, and teeth in its jaws." He grinned and blinked and bowed until his colleague turned and walked away.

In the morning, after a frugal breakfast of coffee and manioc—we had to be economical of our stores—we held a council of war as to the best method of ascending to the plateau above us.

Challenger presided with a solemnity as if he were the Lord Chief Justice on the Bench. Picture him seated upon a rock, his absurd boyish straw hat tilted on the back of his head, his supercilious eyes dominating us from under his drooping lids, his great black beard wagging as he slowly defined our present situation and our future movements.

Beneath him you might have seen the three of us—myself, sunburnt, young, and vigorous after our open-air tramp; Summerlee, solemn but still critical, behind his eternal pipe; Lord John, as keen as a razor-edge, with his supple, alert figure leaning upon his rifle, and his eager eyes fixed eagerly upon the speaker. Behind us were grouped the two swarthy half-breeds and the little knot of Indians, while in front and above us towered those huge, ruddy ribs of rocks which kept us from our goal.

"I need not say," said our leader, "that on the occasion of my last visit I exhausted every means of climbing the cliff, and where I failed I do not think that anyone else is likely to succeed, for I am something of a mountaineer. I had none of the appliances of a rock-climber with me, but I have taken the precaution to bring them now. With their aid I am positive I could climb that detached pinnacle to the summit; but so long as the main cliff overhangs, it is vain to attempt ascending that. I was hurried upon my last visit by the approach of the rainy season and by the exhaustion of my supplies. These considerations limited my time, and I can only claim that I have surveyed about six miles of the cliff to the east of us, finding no possible way up. What, then, shall we now do?"

"There seems to be only one reasonable course," said Professor Summerlee. "If you have explored the east, we should travel along the base of the cliff to the west, and seek for a practicable point for our ascent."

"That's it," said Lord John. "The odds are that this plateau is of no great size, and we shall travel round it until we either find an easy way up it, or come back to the point from which we started."

"I have already explained to our young friend here," said Challenger (he has a way of alluding to me as if I were a school child ten years old), "that it is quite impossible that there should be an easy way up anywhere, for the simple reason that if there were the summit would not be isolated, and those conditions would not obtain which have effected so singular an interference with the general laws of survival. Yet I admit that there may very well be places where an expert human climber may reach the summit, and yet a cumbrous and heavy animal be unable to descend. It is certain that there is a point where an ascent is possible."

"How do you know that, sir?" asked Summerlee, sharply.

"Because my predecessor, the American Maple White, actually made such an ascent. How otherwise could he have seen the monster which he sketched in his notebook?"

"There you reason somewhat ahead of the proved facts," said the stubborn Summerlee. "I admit your plateau, because I have seen it; but I have not as yet satisfied myself that it contains any form of life whatever."

"What you admit, sir, or what you do not admit, is really of inconceivably small importance. I am glad to perceive that the plateau itself has actually obtruded itself upon your intelligence." He glanced up at it, and then, to our amazement, he sprang from his rock, and, seizing Summerlee by the neck, he tilted his face into the air. "Now sir!" he shouted, hoarse with excitement. "Do I help you to realize that the plateau contains some animal life?"

I have said that a thick fringe of green overhung the edge of the cliff. Out of this there had emerged a black, glistening object. As it came slowly forth and overhung the chasm, we saw that it was a very large snake with a peculiar flat, spade-like head. It wavered and quivered above us for a minute, the morning sun gleaming upon its sleek, sinuous coils. Then it slowly drew inwards and disappeared.

Summerlee had been so interested that he had stood unresisting while Challenger tilted his head into the air. Now he shook his colleague off and came back to his dignity.

"I should be glad, Professor Challenger," said he, "if you could see your way to make any remarks which may occur to you without seizing me by the chin. Even the appearance of a very ordinary rock python does not appear to justify such a liberty."

"But there is life upon the plateau all the same," his colleague replied in triumph. "And now, having demonstrated this important conclusion so that it is clear to anyone, however prejudiced or obtuse, I am of opinion that we cannot do better than break up our camp and travel to westward until we find some means of ascent."

The ground at the foot of the cliff was rocky and broken so that the going was slow and difficult. Suddenly we came, however, upon something which cheered our hearts. It was the site of an old encampment, with several empty Chicago meat tins, a bottle labeled "Brandy," a broken tin-opener, and a quantity of other travelers' debris. A crumpled, disintegrated newspaper revealed itself as the Chicago Democrat, though the date had been obliterated.

"Not mine," said Challenger. "It must be Maple White's."

Lord John had been gazing curiously at a great tree-fern which overshadowed the encampment. "I say, look at this," said he. "I believe it is meant for a sign-post."

A slip of hard wood had been nailed to the tree in such a way as to point to the westward.

"Most certainly a sign-post," said Challenger. "What else? Finding himself upon a dangerous errand, our pioneer has left this sign so that any party which follows him may know the way he has taken. Perhaps we shall come upon some other indications as we proceed."

We did indeed, but they were of a terrible and most unexpected nature. Immediately beneath the cliff there grew a considerable patch of high bamboo, like that which we had traversed in our journey. Many of these stems were twenty feet high, with sharp, strong tops, so that even as they stood they made formidable spears. We were passing along the edge of this cover when my eye was caught by the gleam of something white within it. Thrusting in my head between the stems, I found myself gazing at a fleshless skull. The whole skeleton was there, but the skull had detached itself and lay some feet nearer to the open.

With a few blows from the machetes of our Indians we cleared the spot and were able to study the details of this old tragedy. Only a few shreds of clothes could still be distinguished, but there were the remains of boots upon the bony feet, and it was very clear that the dead man was a European. A gold watch by Hudson, of New York, and a chain which held a stylographic pen, lay among the bones. There was also a silver cigarette-case, with "J. C., from A. E. S.," upon the lid. The state of the metal seemed to show that the catastrophe had occurred no great time before.

"Who can he be?" asked Lord John. "Poor devil! every bone in his body seems to be broken."

"And the bamboo grows through his smashed ribs," said Summerlee. "It is a fast-growing plant, but it is surely inconceivable that this body could have been here while the canes grew to be twenty feet in length."

"As to the man's identity," said Professor Challenger, "I have no doubt whatever upon that point. As I made my way up the river before I reached you at the fazenda I instituted very particular inquiries about Maple White. At Para they knew nothing. Fortunately, I had a definite clew, for there was a particular picture in his sketch-book which showed him taking lunch with a certain ecclesiastic at Rosario. This priest I was able to find, and though he proved a very argumentative fellow, who took it absurdly amiss that I should point out to him the corrosive effect which modern science must have upon his beliefs, he none the less gave me some positive information. Maple White passed Rosario four years ago, or two years before I saw his dead body. He was not alone at the time, but there was a friend, an American named James Colver, who remained in the boat and did not meet this ecclesiastic. I think, therefore, that there can be no doubt that we are now looking upon the remains of this James Colver."

"Nor," said Lord John, "is there much doubt as to how he met his death. He has fallen or been chucked from the top, and so been impaled. How else could he come by his broken bones, and how could he have been stuck through by these canes with their points so high above our heads?"

A hush came over us as we stood round these shattered remains and realized the truth of Lord John Roxton's words. The beetling head of the cliff projected over the cane-brake. Undoubtedly he had fallen from above. But had he fallen? Had it been an accident? Or—already ominous and terrible possibilities began to form round that unknown land.

We moved off in silence, and continued to coast round the line of cliffs, which were as even and unbroken as some of those monstrous Antarctic ice-fields which I have seen depicted as stretching from horizon to horizon and towering high above the mast-heads of the exploring vessel.

In five miles we saw no rift or break. And then suddenly we perceived something which filled us with new hope. In a hollow of the rock, protected from rain, there was drawn a rough arrow in chalk, pointing still to the westwards.

"Maple White again," said Professor Challenger. "He had some presentiment that worthy footsteps would follow close behind him."

"He had chalk, then?"

"A box of colored chalks was among the effects I found in his knapsack. I remember that the white one was worn to a stump."

"That is certainly good evidence," said Summerlee. "We can only accept his guidance and follow on to the westward."

We had proceeded some five more miles when again we saw a white arrow upon the rocks. It was at a point where the face of the cliff was for the first time split into a narrow cleft. Inside the cleft

was a second guidance mark, which pointed right up it with the
tip somewhat elevated, as if the spot indicated were above the level
of the ground.

It was a solemn place, for the walls were so gigantic and the
slit of blue sky so narrow and so obscured by a double fringe of
verdure, that only a dim and shadowy light penetrated to the bottom. We had had no food for many hours, and were very weary
with the stony and irregular journey, but our nerves were too
strung to allow us to halt. We ordered the camp to be pitched,
however, and, leaving the Indians to arrange it, we four, with the
two half-breeds, proceeded up the narrow gorge.

It was not more than forty feet across at the mouth, but it
rapidly closed until it ended in an acute angle, too straight and
smooth for an ascent. Certainly it was not this which our pioneer
had attempted to indicate. We made our way back—the whole
gorge was not more than a quarter of a mile deep—and then suddenly the quick eyes of Lord John fell upon what we were seeking.
High up above our heads, amid the dark shadows, there was one
circle of deeper gloom. Surely it could only be the opening of a
cave.

The base of the cliff was heaped with loose stones at the spot,
and it was not difficult to clamber up. When we reached it, all
doubt was removed. Not only was it an opening into the rock, but
on the side of it there was marked once again the sign of the arrow.
Here was the point, and this the means by which Maple White and
his ill-fated comrade had made their ascent.

We were too excited to return to the camp, but must make
our first exploration at once. Lord John had an electric torch in his
knapsack, and this had to serve us as light. He advanced, throwing
his little clear circlet of yellow radiance before him, while in single
file we followed at his heels.

The cave had evidently been water-worn, the sides being
smooth and the floor covered with rounded stones. It was of such
a size that a single man could just fit through by stooping. For fifty
yards it ran almost straight into the rock, and then it ascended at
an angle of forty-five. Presently this incline became even steeper,
and we found ourselves climbing upon hands and knees among

loose rubble which slid from beneath us. Suddenly an exclamation broke from Lord Roxton.

"It's blocked!" said he.

Clustering behind him we saw in the yellow field of light a wall of broken basalt which extended to the ceiling.

"The roof has fallen in!"

In vain we dragged out some of the pieces. The only effect was that the larger ones became detached and threatened to roll down the gradient and crush us. It was evident that the obstacle was far beyond any efforts which we could make to remove it. The road by which Maple White had ascended was no longer available.

Too much cast down to speak, we stumbled down the dark tunnel and made our way back to the camp.

One incident occurred, however, before we left the gorge, which is of importance in view of what came afterwards.

We had gathered in a little group at the bottom of the chasm, some forty feet beneath the mouth of the cave, when a huge rock rolled suddenly downwards—and shot past us with tremendous force. It was the narrowest escape for one or all of us. We could not ourselves see whence the rock had come, but our half-breed servants, who were still at the opening of the cave, said that it had flown past them, and must therefore have fallen from the summit. Looking upwards, we could see no sign of movement above us amidst the green jungle which topped the cliff. There could be little doubt, however, that the stone was aimed at us, so the incident surely pointed to humanity—and malevolent humanity—upon the plateau.

We withdrew hurriedly from the chasm, our minds full of this new development and its bearing upon our plans. The situation was difficult enough before, but if the obstructions of Nature were increased by the deliberate opposition of man, then our case was indeed a hopeless one. And yet, as we looked up at that beautiful fringe of verdure only a few hundreds of feet above our heads, there was not one of us who could conceive the idea of returning to London until we had explored it to its depths.

On discussing the situation, we determined that our best course was to continue to coast round the plateau in the hope of finding some other means of reaching the top. The line of cliffs, which had decreased considerably in height, had already begun to trend from west to north, and if we could take this as representing the arc of a circle, the whole circumference could not be very great. At the worst, then, we should be back in a few days at our starting-point.

We made a march that day which totaled some two-and-twenty miles, without any change in our prospects. I may mention that our aneroid shows us that in the continual incline which we have ascended since we abandoned our canoes we have risen to no less than three thousand feet above sea-level. Hence there is a considerable change both in the temperature and in the vegetation. We have shaken off some of that horrible insect life which is the bane of tropical travel. A few palms still survive, and many tree-ferns, but the Amazonian trees have been all left behind. It was pleasant to see the convolvulus, the passion-flower, and the begonia, all reminding me of home, here among these inhospitable rocks. There was a red begonia just the same color as one that is kept in a pot in the window of a certain villa in Streatham—but I am drifting into private reminiscence.

That night—I am still speaking of the first day of our circumnavigation of the plateau—a great experience awaited us, and one which for ever set at rest any doubt which we could have had as to the wonders so near us.

You will realize as you read it, my dear Mr. McArdle, and possibly for the first time that the paper has not sent me on a wild-goose chase, and that there is inconceivably fine copy waiting for the world whenever we have the Professor's leave to make use of it. I shall not dare to publish these articles unless I can bring back my proofs to England, or I shall be hailed as the journalistic Munchausen of all time. I have no doubt that you feel the same way yourself, and that you would not care to stake the whole credit of the *Gazette* upon this adventure until we can meet the chorus of criticism and scepticism which such articles must of necessity elicit. So this wonderful incident, which would make such a headline for the old paper, must still wait its turn in the editorial drawer.

And yet it was all over in a flash, and there was no sequel to it, save in our own convictions.

What occurred was this. Lord John had shot an ajouti—which is a small, pig-like animal—and, half of it having been given to the Indians, we were cooking the other half upon our fire. There is a chill in the air after dark, and we had all drawn close to the blaze. The night was moonless, but there were some stars, and one could see for a little distance across the plain. Well, suddenly out of the darkness, out of the night, there swooped something with a swish like an aeroplane. The whole group of us were covered for an instant by a canopy of leathery wings, and I had a momentary vision of a long, snake-like neck, a fierce, red, greedy eye, and a great snapping beak, filled, to my amazement, with little, gleaming teeth. The next instant it was gone—and so was our dinner. A huge black shadow, twenty feet across, skimmed up into the air; for an instant the monster wings blotted out the stars, and then it vanished over the brow of the cliff above us. We all sat in amazed silence round the fire, like the heroes of Virgil when the Harpies came down upon them. It was Summerlee who was the first to speak.

"Professor Challenger," said he, in a solemn voice, which quavered with emotion, "I owe you an apology. Sir, I am very much in the wrong, and I beg that you will forget what is past."

It was handsomely said, and the two men for the first time shook hands. So much we have gained by this clear vision of our first pterodactyl. It was worth a stolen supper to bring two such men together.

But if prehistoric life existed upon the plateau it was not superabundant, for we had no further glimpse of it during the next three days. During this time we traversed a barren and forbidding country, which alternated between stony desert and desolate marshes full of many wild-fowl, upon the north and east of the cliffs. From that direction the place is really inaccessible, and, were it not for a hardish ledge which runs at the very base of the precipice, we should have had to turn back. Many times we were up to our waists in the slime and blubber of an old, semi-tropical swamp. To make matters worse, the place seemed to be a favorite breeding-place of the Jaracaca snake, the most venomous and aggressive in South America. Again and again these horrible creatures came writhing and springing towards us across the surface of this putrid bog, and it was only by keeping our shot-guns for ever ready that we could feel safe from them. One funnel-shaped depression in the morass, of a livid green in color from some lichen which festered in it, will always remain as a nightmare memory in my mind. It seems to have been a special nest of these vermins, and the slopes were alive with them, all writhing in our direction, for it is a peculiarity of the Jaracaca that he will always attack man at first sight. There were too many for us to shoot, so we fairly took to our heels and ran until we were exhausted. I shall always remember as we looked back how far behind we could see the heads and necks of our horrible pursuers rising and falling amid the reeds. Jaracaca Swamp we named it in the map which we are constructing.

The cliffs upon the farther side had lost their ruddy tint, being chocolate-brown in color; the vegetation was more scattered along the top of them, and they had sunk to three or four hundred feet in height, but in no place did we find any point where they could be ascended. If anything, they were more impossible than at the first point where we had met them. Their absolute steepness is indicated in the photograph which I took over the stony desert.

"Surely," said I, as we discussed the situation, "the rain must find its way down somehow. There are bound to be water-channels in the rocks."

"Our young friend has glimpses of lucidity," said Professor Challenger, patting me upon the shoulder.

"The rain must go somewhere," I repeated.

"He keeps a firm grip upon actuality. The only drawback is that we have conclusively proved by ocular demonstration that there are no water channels down the rocks."

"Where, then, does it go?" I persisted.

"I think it may be fairly assumed that if it does not come outwards it must run inwards."

"Then there is a lake in the center."

"So I should suppose."

"It is more than likely that the lake may be an old crater," said Summerlee. "The whole formation is, of course, highly volcanic. But, however that may be, I should expect to find the surface of the plateau slope inwards with a considerable sheet of water in the center, which may drain off, by some subterranean channel, into the marshes of the Jaracaca Swamp."

"Or evaporation might preserve an equilibrium," remarked Challenger, and the two learned men wandered off into one of their usual scientific arguments, which were as comprehensible as Chinese to the layman.

On the sixth day we completed our first circuit of the cliffs, and found ourselves back at the first camp, beside the isolated pinnacle of rock. We were a disconsolate party, for nothing could have been more minute than our investigation, and it was absolutely certain that there was no single point where the most active human being could possibly hope to scale the cliff. The place which Maple White's chalk-marks had indicated as his own means of access was now entirely impassable.

What were we to do now? Our stores of provisions, supplemented by our guns, were holding out well, but the day must come when they would need replenishment. In a couple of months the rains might be expected, and we should be washed out of our camp. The rock was harder than marble, and any attempt at cutting a path for so great a height was more than our time or resources would admit. No wonder that we looked gloomily at each other that night, and sought our blankets with hardly a word exchanged. I remember that as I dropped off to sleep my last recollection was that Challenger was squatting, like a monstrous bull-frog, by the fire, his huge head in his hands, sunk apparently in the deepest thought, and entirely oblivious to the good-night which I wished him.

But it was a very different Challenger who greeted us in the morning—a Challenger with contentment and self-congratulation shining from his whole person. He faced us as we assembled for breakfast with a deprecating false modesty in his eyes, as who should say, "I know that I deserve all that you can say, but I pray you to spare my blushes by not saying it." His beard bristled exultantly, his chest was thrown out, and his hand was thrust into the front of his jacket. So, in his fancy, may he see himself sometimes, gracing the vacant pedestal in Trafalgar Square, and adding one more to the horrors of the London streets.

"Eureka!" he cried, his teeth shining through his beard. "Gentlemen, you may congratulate me and we may congratulate each other. The problem is solved."

"You have found a way up?"

"I venture to think so."

"And where?"

For answer he pointed to the spire-like pinnacle upon our right.

Our faces—or mine, at least—fell as we surveyed it. That it could be climbed we had our companion's assurance. But a horrible abyss lay between it and the plateau.

"We can never get across," I gasped.

"We can at least all reach the summit," said he. "When we are up I may be able to show you that the resources of an inventive mind are not yet exhausted."

After breakfast we unpacked the bundle in which our leader had brought his climbing accessories. From it he took a coil of the strongest and lightest rope, a hundred and fifty feet in length, with climbing irons, clamps, and other devices. Lord John was an experienced mountaineer, and Summerlee had done some rough climbing at various times, so that I was really the novice at rockwork of the party; but my strength and activity may have made up for my want of experience.

It was not in reality a very stiff task, though there were moments which made my hair bristle upon my head. The first half was perfectly easy, but from there upwards it became continually steeper until, for the last fifty feet, we were literally clinging with our fingers and toes to tiny ledges and crevices in the rock. I could not have accomplished it, nor could Summerlee, if Challenger had not gained the summit (it was extraordinary to see such activity in so unwieldy a creature) and there fixed the rope round the trunk of the considerable tree which grew there. With this as our support, we were soon able to scramble up the jagged wall until we found ourselves upon the small grassy platform, some twenty-five feet each way, which formed the summit.

The first impression which I received when I had recovered my breath was of the extraordinary view over the country which we had traversed. The whole Brazilian plain seemed to lie beneath us, extending away and away until it ended in dim blue mists upon the farthest sky-line. In the foreground was the long slope, strewn with rocks and dotted with tree-ferns; farther off in the middle distance, looking over the saddle-back hill, I could just see the yellow and green mass of bamboos through which we had passed; and then, gradually, the vegetation increased until it formed the huge forest which extended as far as the eyes could reach, and for a good two thousand miles beyond.

I was still drinking in this wonderful panorama when the heavy hand of the Professor fell upon my shoulder.

"This way, my young friend," said he; "vestigia nulla retrorsum. Never look rearwards, but always to our glorious goal."

The level of the plateau, when I turned, was exactly that on which we stood, and the green bank of bushes, with occasional trees, was so near that it was difficult to realize how inaccessible it remained. At a rough guess the gulf was forty feet across, but, so far as I could see, it might as well have been forty miles. I placed one arm round the trunk of the tree and leaned over the abyss. Far down were the small dark figures of our servants, looking up at us. The wall was absolutely precipitous, as was that which faced me.

"This is indeed curious," said the creaking voice of Professor Summerlee.

I turned, and found that he was examining with great interest the tree to which I clung. That smooth bark and those small, ribbed leaves seemed familiar to my eyes. "Why," I cried, "it's a beech!"

"Exactly," said Summerlee. "A fellow-countryman in a far land."

"Not only a fellow-countryman, my good sir," said Challenger, "but also, if I may be allowed to enlarge your simile, an ally of the first value. This beech tree will be our saviour."

"By George!" cried Lord John, "a bridge!"

"Exactly, my friends, a bridge! It is not for nothing that I expended an hour last night in focusing my mind upon the situation. I have some recollection of once remarking to our young friend here that G. E. C. is at his best when his back is to the wall.

Last night you will admit that all our backs were to the wall. But where will-power and intellect go together, there is always a way out. A drawbridge had to be found which could be dropped across the abyss. Behold it!"

It was certainly a brilliant idea. The tree was a good sixty feet in height, and if it only fell the right way it would easily cross the chasm. Challenger had slung the camp axe over his shoulder when he ascended. Now he handed it to me.

"Our young friend has the thews and sinews," said he. "I think he will be the most useful at this task. I must beg, however, that you will kindly refrain from thinking for yourself, and that you will do exactly what you are told."

Under his direction I cut such gashes in the sides of the trees as would ensure that it should fall as we desired. It had already a strong, natural tilt in the direction of the plateau, so that the matter was not difficult. Finally I set to work in earnest upon the trunk, taking turn and turn with Lord John. In a little over an hour there was a loud crack, the tree swayed forward, and then crashed over, burying its branches among the bushes on the farther side. The severed trunk rolled to the very edge of our platform, and for one terrible second we all thought it was over. It balanced itself, however, a few inches from the edge, and there was our bridge to the unknown.

All of us, without a word, shook hands with Professor Challenger, who raised his straw hat and bowed deeply to each in turn.

"I claim the honor," said he, "to be the first to cross to the unknown land—a fitting subject, no doubt, for some future historical painting."

He had approached the bridge when Lord John laid his hand upon his coat.

"My dear chap," said he, "I really cannot allow it."

"Cannot allow it, sir!" The head went back and the beard forward.

"When it is a matter of science, don't you know, I follow your lead because you are by way of bein' a man of science. But it's up to you to follow me when you come into my department."

"Your department, sir?"

"We all have our professions, and soldierin' is mine. We are, accordin' to my ideas, invadin' a new country, which may or may not be chock-full of enemies of sorts. To barge blindly into it for want of a little common sense and patience isn't my notion of management."

The remonstrance was too reasonable to be disregarded. Challenger tossed his head and shrugged his heavy shoulders.

"Well, sir, what do you propose?"

"For all I know there may be a tribe of cannibals waitin' for lunch-time among those very bushes," said Lord John, looking across the bridge. "It's better to learn wisdom before you get into a cookin'-pot; so we will content ourselves with hopin' that there is no trouble waitin' for us, and at the same time we will act as if there were. Malone and I will go down again, therefore, and we will fetch up the four rifles, together with Gomez and the other. One man can then go across and the rest will cover him with guns, until he sees that it is safe for the whole crowd to come along."

Challenger sat down upon the cut stump and groaned his impatience; but Summerlee and I were of one mind that Lord John was our leader when such practical details were in question. The climb was a more simple now that the rope dangled down the face of the worst part of the ascent. Within an hour we had brought up the rifles and a shot-gun. The half-breeds had ascended also, and under Lord John's orders they had carried up a bale of provisions in case our first exploration should be a long one. We had each bandoliers of cartridges.

"Now, Challenger, if you really insist upon being the first man in," said Lord John, when every preparation was complete.

"I am much indebted to you for your gracious permission," said the angry Professor; for never was a man so intolerant of every form of authority. "Since you are good enough to allow it, I shall most certainly take it upon myself to act as pioneer upon this occasion."

Seating himself with a leg overhanging the abyss on each side, and his hatchet slung upon his back, Challenger hopped his way across the trunk and was soon at the other side. He clambered up and waved his arms in the air.

"At last!" he cried; "at last!"

I gazed anxiously at him, with a vague expectation that some terrible fate would dart at him from the curtain of green behind him. But all was quiet, save that a strange, many-colored bird flew up from under his feet and vanished among the trees.

Summerlee was the second. His wiry energy is wonderful in so frail a frame. He insisted upon having two rifles slung upon his back, so that both Professors were armed when he had made his transit. I came next, and tried hard not to look down into the horrible gulf over which I was passing. Summerlee held out the butt-end of his rifle, and an instant later I was able to grasp his hand. As to Lord John, he walked across—actually walked without support! He must have nerves of iron.

And there we were, the four of us, upon the dreamland, the lost world, of Maple White. To all of us it seemed the moment of our supreme triumph. Who could have guessed that it was the prelude to our supreme disaster? Let me say in a few words how the crushing blow fell upon us.

We had turned away from the edge, and had penetrated about fifty yards of close brushwood, when there came a frightful rending crash from behind us. With one impulse we rushed back the way that we had come. The bridge was gone!

Far down at the base of the cliff I saw, as I looked over, a tangled mass of branches and splintered trunk. It was our beech tree. Had the edge of the platform crumbled and let it through? For a moment this explanation was in all our minds. The next, from the farther side of the rocky pinnacle before us a swarthy face, the face of Gomez the half-breed, was slowly protruded. Yes, it was Gomez, but no longer the Gomez of the demure smile and the mask-like expression. Here was a face with flashing eyes and distorted features, a face convulsed with hatred and with the mad joy of gratified revenge.

"Lord Roxton!" he shouted. "Lord John Roxton!"

"Well," said our companion, "here I am."

A shriek of laughter came across the abyss.

"Yes, there you are, you English dog, and there you will remain! I have waited and waited, and now has come my chance.

You found it hard to get up; you will find it harder to get down. You cursed fools, you are trapped, every one of you!"

We were too astounded to speak. We could only stand there staring in amazement. A great broken bough upon the grass showed whence he had gained his leverage to tilt over our bridge. The face had vanished, but presently it was up again, more frantic than before.

"We nearly killed you with a stone at the cave," he cried; "but this is better. It is slower and more terrible. Your bones will whiten up there, and none will know where you lie or come to cover them. As you lie dying, think of Lopez, whom you shot five years ago on the Putomayo River. I am his brother, and, come what will I will die happy now, for his memory has been avenged." A furious hand was shaken at us, and then all was quiet.

Had the half-breed simply wrought his vengeance and then escaped, all might have been well with him. It was that foolish, irresistible Latin impulse to be dramatic which brought his own downfall. Roxton, the man who had earned himself the name of the Flail of the Lord through three countries, was not one who could be safely taunted. The half-breed was descending on the farther side of the pinnacle; but before he could reach the ground Lord John had run along the edge of the plateau and gained a point from which he could see his man. There was a single crack of his rifle, and, though we saw nothing, we heard the scream and then the distant thud of the falling body. Roxton came back to us with a face of granite.

"I have been a blind simpleton," said he, bitterly, "It's my folly that has brought you all into this trouble. I should have remembered that these people have long memories for blood-feuds, and have been more upon my guard."

"What about the other one? It took two of them to lever that tree over the edge."

"I could have shot him, but I let him go. He may have had no part in it. Perhaps it would have been better if I had killed him, for he must, as you say, have lent a hand."

Now that we had the clue to his action, each of us could cast back and remember some sinister act upon the part of the half-breed—his constant desire to know our plans, his arrest outside our tent when he was over-hearing them, the furtive looks of hatred which from time to time one or other of us had surprised. We were still discussing it, endeavoring to adjust our minds to these new conditions, when a singular scene in the plain below arrested our attention.

A man in white clothes, who could only be the surviving half-breed, was running as one does run when Death is the pacemaker. Behind him, only a few yards in his rear, bounded the huge ebony figure of Zambo, our devoted negro. Even as we looked, he sprang upon the back of the fugitive and flung his arms round his neck. They rolled on the ground together. An instant afterwards Zambo rose, looked at the prostrate man, and then, waving his hand joyously to us, came running in our direction. The white figure lay motionless in the middle of the great plain.

Our two traitors had been destroyed, but the mischief that they had done lived after them. By no possible means could we get back to the pinnacle. We had been natives of the world; now we were natives of the plateau. The two things were separate and apart. There was the plain which led to the canoes. Yonder, beyond the violet, hazy horizon, was the stream which led back to civilization. But the link between was missing. No human ingenuity could suggest a means of bridging the chasm which yawned between ourselves and our past lives. One instant had altered the whole conditions of our existence.

It was at such a moment that I learned the stuff of which my three comrades were composed. They were grave, it is true, and thoughtful, but of an invincible serenity. For the moment we could only sit among the bushes in patience and wait the coming of Zambo. Presently his honest black face topped the rocks and his Herculean figure emerged upon the top of the pinnacle.

"What I do now?" he cried. "You tell me and I do it."

It was a question which it was easier to ask than to answer. One thing only was clear. He was our one trusty link with the outside world. On no account must he leave us.

"No no!" he cried. "I not leave you. Whatever come, you always find me here. But no able to keep Indians. Already they say too much Curupuri live on this place, and they go home. Now you leave them me no able to keep them."

It was a fact that our Indians had shown in many ways of late that they were weary of their journey and anxious to return. We realized that Zambo spoke the truth, and that it would be impossible for him to keep them.

"Make them wait till to-morrow, Zambo," I shouted; "then I can send letter back by them."

"Very good, sarr! I promise they wait till to-morrow, said the negro. "But what I do for you now?"

There was plenty for him to do, and admirably the faithful fellow did it. First of all, under our directions, he undid the rope from the tree-stump and threw one end of it across to us. It was not thicker than a clothes-line, but it was of great strength, and though we could not make a bridge of it, we might well find it invaluable if we had any climbing to do. He then fastened his end of the rope to the package of supplies which had been carried up, and we were able to drag it across. This gave us the means of life for at least a week, even if we found nothing else. Finally he descended and carried up two other packets of mixed goods—a box of ammunition and a number of other things, all of which we got across by throwing our rope to him and hauling it back. It was evening when he at last climbed down, with a final assurance that he would keep the Indians till next morning.

And so it is that I have spent nearly the whole of this our first night upon the plateau writing up our experiences by the light of a single candle-lantern.

We supped and camped at the very edge of the cliff, quenching our thirst with two bottles of Apollinaris which were in one of the cases. It is vital to us to find water, but I think even Lord John himself had had adventures enough for one day, and none of us felt inclined to make the first push into the unknown. We forbore to light a fire or to make any unnecessary sound.

To-morrow (or to-day, rather, for it is already dawn as I write) we shall make our first venture into this strange land. When I shall be able to write again—or if I ever shall write again—I know not. Meanwhile, I can see that the Indians are still in their place, and I am sure that the faithful Zambo will be here presently to get my letter. I only trust that it will come to hand.

P.S.—The more I think the more desperate does our position seem. I see no possible hope of our return. If there were a high tree near the edge of the plateau we might drop a return bridge across, but there is none within fifty yards. Our united strength could not carry a trunk which would serve our purpose. The rope, of course, is far too short that we could descend by it. No, our position is hopeless—hopeless!

Chapter X   "The Most Wonderful Things Have Happened"

The most wonderful things have happened and are continually happening to us. All the paper that I possess consists of five old note-books and a lot of scraps, and I have only the one stylographic pencil; but so long as I can move my hand I will continue to set down our experiences and impressions, for, since we are the only men of the whole human race to see such things, it is of enormous importance that I should record them whilst they are fresh in my memory and before that fate which seems to be constantly impending does actually overtake us. Whether Zambo can at last take these letters to the river, or whether I shall myself in some miraculous way carry them back with me, or, finally, whether some daring explorer, coming upon our tracks with the advantage, perhaps, of a perfected monoplane, should find this bundle of manuscript, in any case I can see that what I am writing is destined to immortality as a classic of true adventure.

On the morning after our being trapped upon the plateau by the villainous Gomez we began a new stage in our experiences. The first incident in it was not such as to give me a very favorable opinion of the place to which we had wandered. As I roused myself from a short nap after day had dawned, my eyes fell upon a most singular appearance upon my own leg. My trouser had slipped up, exposing a few inches of my skin above my sock. On this there rested a large, purplish grape. Astonished at the sight, I leaned forward to pick it off, when, to my horror, it burst between my finger and thumb, squirting blood in every direction. My cry of disgust had brought the two professors to my side.

"Most interesting," said Summerlee, bending over my shin. "An enormous blood-tick, as yet, I believe, unclassified."

"The first-fruits of our labors," said Challenger in his booming, pedantic fashion. "We cannot do less than call it Ixodes Maloni. The very small inconvenience of being bitten, my young friend, cannot, I am sure, weigh with you as against the glorious privilege of having your name inscribed in the deathless roll of zoology. Unhappily you have crushed this fine specimen at the moment of satiation."

"Filthy vermin!" I cried.

Professor Challenger raised his great eyebrows in protest, and placed a soothing paw upon my shoulder.

"You should cultivate the scientific eye and the detached scientific mind," said he. "To a man of philosophic temperament like myself the blood-tick, with its lancet-like proboscis and its distending stomach, is as beautiful a work of Nature as the peacock or, for that matter, the aurora borealis. It pains me to hear you speak of it in so unappreciative a fashion. No doubt, with due diligence, we can secure some other specimen."

"There can be no doubt of that," said Summerlee, grimly, "for one has just disappeared behind your shirt-collar."

Challenger sprang into the air bellowing like a bull, and tore frantically at his coat and shirt to get them off. Summerlee and I laughed so that we could hardly help him. At last we exposed that monstrous torso (fifty-four inches, by the tailor's tape). His body was all matted with black hair, out of which jungle we picked the wandering tick before it had bitten him. But the bushes round were full of the horrible pests, and it was clear that we must shift our camp.

But first of all it was necessary to make our arrangements with the faithful negro, who appeared presently on the pinnacle with a number of tins of cocoa and biscuits, which he tossed over to us. Of the stores which remained below he was ordered to retain as much as would keep him for two months. The Indians were to have the remainder as a reward for their services and as payment for taking our letters back to the Amazon. Some hours later we saw them in single file far out upon the plain, each with a bundle on his head, making their way back along the path we had come. Zambo occupied our little tent at the base of the pinnacle, and there he remained, our one link with the world below.

And now we had to decide upon our immediate movements. We shifted our position from among the tick-laden bushes until we came to a small clearing thickly surrounded by trees upon all sides. There were some flat slabs of rock in the center, with an excellent well close by, and there we sat in cleanly comfort while we made our first plans for the invasion of this new country. Birds were calling among the foliage—especially one with a peculiar whooping cry which was new to us—but beyond these sounds there were no signs of life.

Our first care was to make some sort of list of our own stores, so that we might know what we had to rely upon. What with the things we had ourselves brought up and those which Zambo had sent across on the rope, we were fairly well supplied. Most important of all, in view of the dangers which might surround us, we had our four rifles and one thousand three hundred rounds, also a shot-gun, but not more than a hundred and fifty medium pellet cartridges. In the matter of provisions we had enough to last for several weeks, with a sufficiency of tobacco and a few scientific implements, including a large telescope and a good field-glass. All these things we collected together in the clearing, and as a first precaution, we cut down with our hatchet and knives a number of thorny bushes, which we piled round in a circle some fifteen yards in diameter. This was to be our headquarters for the time—our place of refuge against sudden danger and the guard-house for our stores. Fort Challenger, we called it.

IT was midday before we had made ourselves secure, but the heat was not oppressive, and the general character of the plateau, both in its temperature and in its vegetation, was almost temperate. The beech, the oak, and even the birch were to be found among the tangle of trees which girt us in. One huge gingko tree, topping all the others, shot its great limbs and maidenhair foliage over the fort which we had constructed. In its shade we continued our discussion, while Lord John, who had quickly taken command in the hour of action, gave us his views.

"So long as neither man nor beast has seen or heard us, we are safe," said he. "From the time they know we are here our troubles begin. There are no signs that they have found us out as yet. So our game surely is to lie low for a time and spy out the land. We want to have a good look at our neighbors before we get on visitin' terms."

"But we must advance," I ventured to remark.

"By all means, sonny my boy! We will advance. But with common sense. We must never go so far that we can't get back to our base. Above all, we must never, unless it is life or death, fire off our guns."

"But YOU fired yesterday," said Summerlee.

"Well, it couldn't be helped. However, the wind was strong and blew outwards. It is not likely that the sound could have traveled far into the plateau. By the way, what shall we call this place? I suppose it is up to us to give it a name?"

There were several suggestions, more or less happy, but Challenger's was final.

"It can only have one name," said he. "It is called after the pioneer who discovered it. It is Maple White Land."

Maple White Land it became, and so it is named in that chart which has become my special task. So it will, I trust, appear in the atlas of the future.

The peaceful penetration of Maple White Land was the pressing subject before us. We had the evidence of our own eyes that the place was inhabited by some unknown creatures, and there was that of Maple White's sketch-book to show that more dreadful and more dangerous monsters might still appear. That there might also prove to be human occupants and that they were of a malevolent character was suggested by the skeleton impaled upon the bamboos, which could not have got there had it not been dropped from above. Our situation, stranded without possibility of escape in such a land, was clearly full of danger, and our reasons endorsed every measure of caution which Lord John's experience could suggest. Yet it was surely impossible that we should halt on the edge of this world of mystery when our very souls were tingling with impatience to push forward and to pluck the heart from it.

We therefore blocked the entrance to our zareba by filling it up with several thorny bushes, and left our camp with the stores entirely surrounded by this protecting hedge. We then slowly and cautiously set forth into the unknown, following the course of the little stream which flowed from our spring, as it should always serve us as a guide on our return.

Hardly had we started when we came across signs that there were indeed wonders awaiting us. After a few hundred yards of thick forest, containing many trees which were quite unknown to me, but which Summerlee, who was the botanist of the party, recognized as forms of conifera and of cycadaceous plants which have long passed away in the world below, we entered a region where the stream widened out and formed a considerable bog. High reeds of a peculiar type grew thickly before us, which were pronounced to be equisetacea, or mare's-tails, with tree-ferns scattered amongst them, all of them swaying in a brisk wind. Suddenly Lord John, who was walking first, halted with uplifted hand.

"Look at this!" said he. "By George, this must be the trail of the father of all birds!"

An enormous three-toed track was imprinted in the soft mud before us. The creature, whatever it was, had crossed the swamp and had passed on into the forest. We all stopped to examine that monstrous spoor. If it were indeed a bird—and what animal could leave such a mark?—its foot was so much larger than an ostrich's that its height upon the same scale must be enormous. Lord John looked eagerly round him and slipped two cartridges into his elephant-gun.

"I'll stake my good name as a shikarree," said he, "that the track is a fresh one. The creature has not passed ten minutes. Look how the water is still oozing into that deeper print! By Jove! See, here is the mark of a little one!"

Sure enough, smaller tracks of the same general form were running parallel to the large ones.

"But what do you make of this?" cried Professor Summerlee, triumphantly, pointing to what looked like the huge print of a five-fingered human hand appearing among the three-toed marks.

"Wealden!" cried Challenger, in an ecstasy. "I've seen them in the Wealden clay. It is a creature walking erect upon three-toed feet, and occasionally putting one of its five-fingered forepaws upon the ground. Not a bird, my dear Roxton—not a bird."

"A beast?"

"No; a reptile—a dinosaur. Nothing else could have left such a track. They puzzled a worthy Sussex doctor some ninety years ago; but who in the world could have hoped—hoped—to have seen a sight like that?"

His words died away into a whisper, and we all stood in motionless amazement. Following the tracks, we had left the morass and passed through a screen of brushwood and trees. Beyond was an open glade, and in this were five of the most extraordinary creatures that I have ever seen. Crouching down among the bushes, we observed them at our leisure.

There were, as I say, five of them, two being adults and three young ones. In size they were enormous. Even the babies were as big as elephants, while the two large ones were far beyond all creatures I have ever seen. They had slate-colored skin, which was scaled like a lizard's and shimmered where the sun shone upon it. All five were sitting up, balancing themselves upon their broad, powerful tails and their huge three-toed hind-feet, while with their small five-fingered front-feet they pulled down the branches upon which they browsed. I do not know that I can bring their appearance home to you better than by saying that they looked like monstrous kangaroos, twenty feet in length, and with skins like black crocodiles.

I do not know how long we stayed motionless gazing at this marvelous spectacle. A strong wind blew towards us and we were well concealed, so there was no chance of discovery. From time to time the little ones played round their parents in unwieldy gambols, the great beasts bounding into the air and falling with dull thuds upon the earth. The strength of the parents seemed to be limitless, for one of them, having some difficulty in reaching a bunch of foliage which grew upon a considerable-sized tree, put his fore-legs round the trunk and tore it down as if it had been a sapling. The action seemed, as I thought, to show not only the great development of its muscles, but also the small one of its brain, for the whole weight came crashing down upon the top of it, and it uttered a series of shrill yelps to show that, big as it was, there was a limit to what it could endure. The incident made it think, apparently, that the neighborhood was dangerous, for it slowly lurched off through the wood, followed by its mate and its three enormous infants. We saw the shimmering slaty gleam of their skins between the tree-trunks, and their heads undulating high above the brush-wood. Then they vanished from our sight.

I looked at my comrades. Lord John was standing at gaze with his finger on the trigger of his elephant-gun, his eager hunter's soul shining from his fierce eyes. What would he not give for one such head to place between the two crossed oars above the mantelpiece in his snuggery at the Albany! And yet his reason held him in, for all our exploration of the wonders of this unknown land depended upon our presence being concealed from its inhabitants. The two professors were in silent ecstasy. In their excitement they had unconsciously seized each other by the hand, and stood like two little children in the presence of a marvel, Challenger's cheeks bunched up into a seraphic smile, and Summerlee's sardonic face softening for the moment into wonder and reverence.

"Nunc dimittis!" he cried at last. "What will they say in England of this?"

"My dear Summerlee, I will tell you with great confidence exactly what they will say in England," said Challenger. "They will say that you are an infernal liar and a scientific charlatan, exactly as you and others said of me."

"In the face of photographs?"

"Faked, Summerlee! Clumsily faked!"

"In the face of specimens?"

"Ah, there we may have them! Malone and his filthy Fleet Street crew may be all yelping our praises yet. August the twenty-eighth—the day we saw five live iguanodons in a glade of Maple White Land. Put it down in your diary, my young friend, and send it to your rag."

"And be ready to get the toe-end of the editorial boot in return," said Lord John. "Things look a bit different from the latitude of London, young fellah my lad. There's many a man who never tells his adventures, for he can't hope to be believed. Who's to blame them? For this will seem a bit of a dream to ourselves in a month or two. WHAT did you say they were?"

"Iguanodons," said Summerlee. "You'll find their footmarks all over the Hastings sands, in Kent, and in Sussex. The South of

England was alive with them when there was plenty of good lush green-stuff to keep them going. Conditions have changed, and the beasts died. Here it seems that the conditions have not changed, and the beasts have lived."

"If ever we get out of this alive, I must have a head with me," said Lord John. "Lord, how some of that Somaliland-Uganda crowd would turn a beautiful pea-green if they saw it! I don't know what you chaps think, but it strikes me that we are on mighty thin ice all this time."

I had the same feeling of mystery and danger around us. In the gloom of the trees there seemed a constant menace and as we looked up into their shadowy foliage vague terrors crept into one's heart. It is true that these monstrous creatures which we had seen were lumbering, inoffensive brutes which were unlikely to hurt anyone, but in this world of wonders what other survivals might there not be—what fierce, active horrors ready to pounce upon us from their lair among the rocks or brushwood? I knew little of prehistoric life, but I had a clear remembrance of one book which I had read in which it spoke of creatures who would live upon our lions and tigers as a cat lives upon mice. What if these also were to be found in the woods of Maple White Land!

It was destined that on this very morning—our first in the new country—we were to find out what strange hazards lay around us. It was a loathsome adventure, and one of which I hate to think. If, as Lord John said, the glade of the iguanodons will remain with us as a dream, then surely the swamp of the ptero-dactyls will forever be our nightmare. Let me set down exactly what occurred.

We passed very slowly through the woods, partly because Lord Roxton acted as scout before he would let us advance, and partly because at every second step one or other of our professors would fall, with a cry of wonder, before some flower or insect which presented him with a new type. We may have traveled two or three miles in all, keeping to the right of the line of the stream, when we came upon a considerable opening in the trees. A belt of brushwood led up to a tangle of rocks—the whole plateau was strewn with boulders. We were walking slowly towards these rocks, among bushes which reached over our waists, when we became aware of a strange low gabbling and whistling sound, which filled the air with a constant clamor and appeared to come from some spot immediately before us. Lord John held up his hand as a signal for us to stop, and he made his way swiftly, stooping and running, to the line of rocks. We saw him peep over them and give a gesture of amazement. Then he stood staring as if forgetting us, so utterly entranced was he by what he saw. Finally he waved us to come on, holding up his hand as a signal for caution. His whole bearing made me feel that something wonderful but dangerous lay before us.

Creeping to his side, we looked over the rocks. The place into which we gazed was a pit, and may, in the early days, have been one of the smaller volcanic blow-holes of the plateau. It was bowl-shaped and at the bottom, some hundreds of yards from where we lay, were pools of green-scummed, stagnant water, fringed with bullrushes. It was a weird place in itself, but its occupants made it seem like a scene from the Seven Circles of Dante. The place was a rookery of pterodactyls. There were hundreds of them congregated within view. All the bottom area round the water-edge was alive with their young ones, and with hideous mothers brooding upon their leathery, yellowish eggs. From this crawling flapping mass of obscene reptilian life came the shocking clamor which filled the air and the mephitic, horrible, musty odor which turned us sick. But above, perched each upon its own stone, tall, gray, and withered, more like dead and dried specimens than actual living creatures, sat the horrible males, absolutely motionless save for the rolling of their red eyes or an occasional snap of their rat-trap beaks as a dragon-fly went past them. Their huge, membranous wings were closed by folding their fore-arms, so that they sat like gigantic old women, wrapped in hideous web-colored shawls, and with their ferocious heads protruding above them. Large and small, not less than a thousand of these filthy creatures lay in the hollow before us.

Our professors would gladly have stayed there all day, so entranced were they by this opportunity of studying the life of a prehistoric age. They pointed out the fish and dead birds lying about among the rocks as proving the nature of the food of these creatures, and I heard them congratulating each other on having cleared up the point why the bones of this flying dragon are found in such great numbers in certain well-defined areas, as in the Cambridge Green-sand, since it was now seen that, like penguins, they lived in gregarious fashion.

Finally, however, Challenger, bent upon proving some point which Summerlee had contested, thrust his head over the rock and nearly brought destruction upon us all. In an instant the nearest male gave a shrill, whistling cry, and flapped its twenty-foot span of leathery wings as it soared up into the air. The females and young ones huddled together beside the water, while the whole circle of sentinels rose one after the other and sailed off into the sky. It was a wonderful sight to see at least a hundred creatures of such enormous size and hideous appearance all swooping like swallows with swift, shearing wing-strokes above us; but soon we realized that it was not one on which we could afford to linger. At first the great brutes flew round in a huge ring, as if to make sure what the exact extent of the danger might be. Then, the flight grew lower and the circle narrower, until they were whizzing round and round us, the dry, rustling flap of their huge slate-colored wings filling the air with a volume of sound that made me think of Hendon aerodrome upon a race day.

"Make for the wood and keep together," cried Lord John, clubbing his rifle. "The brutes mean mischief."

The moment we attempted to retreat the circle closed in upon us, until the tips of the wings of those nearest to us nearly touched our faces. We beat at them with the stocks of our guns, but there was nothing solid or vulnerable to strike. Then suddenly out of the whizzing, slate-colored circle a long neck shot out, and a fierce beak made a thrust at us. Another and another followed. Summerlee gave a cry and put his hand to his face, from which the blood was streaming. I felt a prod at the back of my neck, and turned dizzy with the shock. Challenger fell, and as I stooped to pick him up I was again struck from behind and dropped on the top of him. At the same instant I heard the crash of Lord John's elephant-gun, and, looking up, saw one of the creatures with a broken wing struggling upon the ground, spitting and gurgling at us with a wide-opened beak and blood-shot, goggled eyes, like some devil in a medieval picture. Its comrades had flown higher at the sudden sound, and were circling above our heads.

"Now," cried Lord John, "now for our lives!"

We staggered through the brushwood, and even as we reached the trees the harpies were on us again. Summerlee was knocked down, but we tore him up and rushed among the trunks. Once there we were safe, for those huge wings had no space for their sweep beneath the branches. As we limped homewards, sadly mauled and discomfited, we saw them for a long time flying at a great height against the deep blue sky above our heads, soaring round and round, no bigger than wood-pigeons, with their eyes no doubt still following our progress. At last, however, as we reached the thicker woods they gave up the chase, and we saw them no more.

A most interesting and convincing experience," said Challenger, as we halted beside the brook and he bathed a swollen knee. "We are exceptionally well informed, Summerlee, as to the habits of the enraged pterodactyl."

Summerlee was wiping the blood from a cut in his forehead, while I was tying up a nasty stab in the muscle of the neck. Lord John had the shoulder of his coat torn away, but the creature's teeth had only grazed the flesh.

"It is worth noting," Challenger continued, "that our young friend has received an undoubted stab, while Lord John's coat could only have been torn by a bite. In my own case, I was beaten about the head by their wings, so we have had a remarkable exhibition of their various methods of offence."

"It has been touch and go for our lives," said Lord John, gravely, "and I could not think of a more rotten sort of death than to be outed by such filthy vermin. I was sorry to fire my rifle, but, by Jove! there was no great choice."

"We should not be here if you hadn't," said I, with conviction.

"It may do no harm," said he. "Among these woods there must be many loud cracks from splitting or falling trees which would be just like the sound of a gun. But now, if you are of my opinion, we have had thrills enough for one day, and had best get back to the surgical box at the camp for some carbolic. Who knows what venom these beasts may have in their hideous jaws?"

But surely no men ever had just such a day since the world began. Some fresh surprise was ever in store for us. When, following the course of our brook, we at last reached our glade and saw the thorny barricade of our camp, we thought that our adventures were at an end. But we had something more to think of before we could rest. The gate of Fort Challenger had been untouched, the walls were unbroken, and yet it had been visited by some strange and powerful creature in our absence. No foot-mark showed a trace of its nature, and only the overhanging branch of the enormous ginko tree suggested how it might have come and gone; but of its malevolent strength there was ample evidence in the condition of our stores. They were strewn at random all over the ground, and one tin of meat had been crushed into pieces so as to extract the contents. A case of cartridges had been shattered into matchwood, and one of the brass shells lay shredded into pieces beside it. Again the feeling of vague horror came upon our souls, and we gazed round with frightened eyes at the dark shadows which lay around us, in all of which some fearsome shape might be lurking. How good it was when we were hailed by the voice of Zambo, and, going to the edge of the plateau, saw him sitting grinning at us upon the top of the opposite pinnacle.

"All well, Massa Challenger, all well!" he cried. "Me stay here. No fear. You always find me when you want."

His honest black face, and the immense view before us, which carried us half-way back to the affluent of the Amazon, helped us to remember that we really were upon this earth in the twentieth century, and had not by some magic been conveyed to some raw planet in its earliest and wildest state. How difficult it was to realize that the violet line upon the far horizon was well advanced to that great river upon which huge steamers ran, and folk talked of the small affairs of life, while we, marooned among the creatures of a bygone age, could but gaze towards it and yearn for all that it meant!

One other memory remains with me of this wonderful day, and with it I will close this letter. The two professors, their tempers aggravated no doubt by their injuries, had fallen out as to whether our assailants were of the genus pterodactylus or dimorphodon, and high words had ensued. To avoid their wrangling I moved some little way apart, and was seated smoking upon the trunk of a fallen tree, when Lord John strolled over in my direction.

"I say, Malone," said he, "do you remember that place where those beasts were?"

"Very clearly."

"A sort of volcanic pit, was it not?"

"Exactly," said I.

"Did you notice the soil?"

"Rocks."

"But round the water—where the reeds were?"

"It was a bluish soil. It looked like clay."

"Exactly. A volcanic tube full of blue clay."

"What of that?" I asked.

"Oh, nothing, nothing," said he, and strolled back to where the voices of the contending men of science rose in a prolonged duet, the high, strident note of Summerlee rising and falling to the sonorous bass of Challenger. I should have thought no more of Lord John's remark were it not that once again that night I heard him mutter to himself: "Blue clay—clay in a volcanic tube!" They were the last words I heard before I dropped into an exhausted sleep.

Chapter XI   "For once I was the Hero"

Lord John Roxton was right when he thought that some specially toxic quality might lie in the bite of the horrible creatures which had attacked us. On the morning after our first adventure upon the plateau, both Summerlee and I were in great pain and fever, while Challenger's knee was so bruised that he could hardly limp. We kept to our camp all day, therefore, Lord John busying himself, with such help as we could give him, in raising the height and thickness of the thorny walls which were our only defense. I remember that during the whole long day I was haunted by the feeling that we were closely observed, though by whom or whence I could give no guess.

So strong was the impression that I told Professor Challenger of it, who put it down to the cerebral excitement caused by my fever. Again and again I glanced round swiftly, with the conviction that I was about to see something, but only to meet the dark tangle of our hedge or the solemn and cavernous gloom of the great trees which arched above our heads. And yet the feeling grew ever stronger in my own mind that something observant and something malevolent was at our very elbow. I thought of the Indian superstition of the Curupuri—the dreadful, lurking spirit of the woods—and I could have imagined that his terrible presence haunted those who had invaded his most remote and sacred retreat.

That night (our third in Maple White Land) we had an experience which left a fearful impression upon our minds, and made us thankful that Lord John had worked so hard in making our retreat impregnable. We were all sleeping round our dying fire when we were aroused—or, rather, I should say, shot out of our slumbers—by a succession of the most frightful cries and screams to which I have ever listened. I know no sound to which I could compare this amazing tumult, which seemed to come from some spot within a few hundred yards of our camp. It was as ear-splitting as any whistle of a railway-engine; but whereas the whistle is a clear, mechanical, sharp-edged sound, this was far deeper in volume and vibrant with the uttermost strain of agony and horror. We clapped our hands to our ears to shut out that nerve-shaking appeal. A cold sweat broke out over my body, and my heart turned sick at the misery of it. All the woes of tortured life, all its stupendous indictment of high heaven, its innumerable sorrows, seemed to be centered and condensed into that one dreadful, agonized cry. And then, under this high-pitched, ringing sound there was another, more intermittent, a low, deep-chested laugh, a growling, throaty gurgle of merriment which formed a grotesque accompaniment to the shriek with which it was blended. For three or four minutes on end the fearsome duet continued, while all the foliage rustled with the rising of startled birds. Then it shut off as suddenly as it began. For a long time we sat in horrified silence. Then Lord John threw a bundle of twigs upon the fire, and their red glare lit up the intent faces of my companions and flickered over the great boughs above our heads.

"What was it?" I whispered.

"We shall know in the morning," said Lord John. "It was close to us—not farther than the glade."

"We have been privileged to overhear a prehistoric tragedy, the sort of drama which occurred among the reeds upon the border of some Jurassic lagoon, when the greater dragon pinned the lesser among the slime," said Challenger, with more solemnity than I had ever heard in his voice. "It was surely well for man that he came late in the order of creation. There were powers abroad in earlier days which no courage and no mechanism of his could have met. What could his sling, his throwing-stick, or his arrow avail him against such forces as have been loose to-night? Even with a modern rifle it would be all odds on the monster."

"I think I should back my little friend," said Lord John, caressing his Express. "But the beast would certainly have a good sporting chance."

Summerlee raised his hand.

"Hush!" he cried. "Surely I hear something?"

From the utter silence there emerged a deep, regular pat-pat. It was the tread of some animal——the rhythm of soft but heavy pads placed cautiously upon the ground. It stole slowly round the camp, and then halted near our gateway. There was a low, sibilant rise and fall——the breathing of the creature. Only our feeble hedge separated us from this horror of the night. Each of us had seized his rifle, and Lord John had pulled out a small bush to make an embrasure in the hedge.

"By George!" he whispered. "I think I can see it!"

I stooped and peered over his shoulder through the gap. Yes, I could see it, too. In the deep shadow of the tree there was a deeper shadow yet, black, inchoate, vague——a crouching form full of savage vigor and menace. It was no higher than a horse, but the dim outline suggested vast bulk and strength. That hissing pant, as regular and full-volumed as the exhaust of an engine, spoke of a monstrous organism. Once, as it moved, I thought I saw the glint of two terrible, greenish eyes. There was an uneasy rustling, as if it were crawling slowly forward.

"I believe it is going to spring!" said I, cocking my rifle.

"Don't fire! Don't fire!" whispered Lord John. "The crash of a gun in this silent night would be heard for miles. Keep it as a last card."

"If it gets over the hedge we're done," said Summerlee, and his voice crackled into a nervous laugh as he spoke.

"No, it must not get over," cried Lord John; "but hold your fire to the last. Perhaps I can make something of the fellow. I'll chance it, anyhow."

It was as brave an act as ever I saw a man do. He stooped to the fire, picked up a blazing branch, and slipped in an instant through a sallyport which he had made in our gateway. The thing moved forward with a dreadful snarl. Lord John never hesitated, but, running towards it with a quick, light step, he dashed the flaming wood into the brute's face. For one moment I had a vision of a horrible mask like a giant toad's, of a warty, leprous skin, and of a loose mouth all beslobbered with fresh blood. The next, there was a crash in the underwood and our dreadful visitor was gone.

"I thought he wouldn't face the fire," said Lord John, laughing, as he came back and threw his branch among the faggots.

"You should not have taken such a risk!" we all cried.

"There was nothin' else to be done. If he had got among us we should have shot each other in tryin' to down him. On the other hand, if we had fired through the hedge and wounded him he would soon have been on the top of us—to say nothin' of giving ourselves away. On the whole, I think that we are jolly well out of it. What was he, then?"

Our learned men looked at each other with some hesitation.

"Personally, I am unable to classify the creature with any certainty," said Summerlee, lighting his pipe from the fire.

"In refusing to commit yourself you are but showing a proper scientific reserve," said Challenger, with massive condescension. "I am not myself prepared to go farther than to say in general terms that we have almost certainly been in contact tonight with some form of carnivorous dinosaur. I have already expressed my anticipation that something of the sort might exist upon this plateau."

"We have to bear in mind," remarked Summerlee, that there are many prehistoric forms which have never come down to us. It would be rash to suppose that we can give a name to all that we are likely to meet."

"Exactly. A rough classification may be the best that we can attempt. To-morrow some further evidence may help us to an identification. Meantime we can only renew our interrupted slumbers."

"But not without a sentinel," said Lord John, with decision. "We can't afford to take chances in a country like this. Two-hour spells in the future, for each of us."

"Then I'll just finish my pipe in starting the first one," said Professor Summerlee; and from that time onwards we never trusted ourselves again without a watchman.

In the morning it was not long before we discovered the source of the hideous uproar which had aroused us in the night. The iguanodon glade was the scene of a horrible butchery. From the pools of blood and the enormous lumps of flesh scattered in every direction over the green sward we imagined at first that a number of animals had been killed, but on examining the remains more closely we discovered that all this carnage came from one of these unwieldy monsters, which had been literally torn to pieces by some creature not larger, perhaps, but far more ferocious, than itself.

Our two professors sat in absorbed argument, examining piece after piece, which showed the marks of savage teeth and of enormous claws.

"Our judgment must still be in abeyance," said Professor Challenger, with a huge slab of whitish-colored flesh across his knee. "The indications would be consistent with the presence of a saber-toothed tiger, such as are still found among the breccia of our caverns; but the creature actually seen was undoubtedly of a larger and more reptilian character. Personally, I should pronounce for allosaurus."

"Or megalosaurus," said Summerlee.

"Exactly. Any one of the larger carnivorous dinosaurs would meet the case. Among them are to be found all the most terrible types of animal life that have ever cursed the earth or blessed a museum." He laughed sonorously at his own conceit, for, though he had little sense of humor, the crudest pleasantry from his own lips moved him always to roars of appreciation.

"The less noise the better," said Lord Roxton, curtly. "We don't know who or what may be near us. If this fellah comes back for his breakfast and catches us here we won't have so much to laugh at. By the way, what is this mark upon the iguanodon's hide?"

On the dull, scaly, slate-colored skin somewhere above the shoulder, there was a singular black circle of some substance which looked like asphalt. None of us could suggest what it meant, though Summerlee was of opinion that he had seen something similar upon one of the young ones two days before. Challenger said nothing, but looked pompous and puffy, as if he could if he would, so that finally Lord John asked his opinion direct.

"If your lordship will graciously permit me to open my mouth, I shall be happy to express my sentiments," said he, with elaborate sarcasm. I am not in the habit of being taken to task in the fashion which seems to be customary with your lordship. I was not aware that it was necessary to ask your permission before smiling at a harmless pleasantry."

It was not until he had received his apology that our touchy friend would suffer himself to be appeased. When at last his ruffled feelings were at ease, he addressed us at some length from his seat upon a fallen tree, speaking, as his habit was, as if he were imparting most precious information to a class of a thousand.

"With regard to the marking," said he, "I am inclined to agree with my friend and colleague, Professor Summerlee, that the stains are from asphalt. As this plateau is, in its very nature, highly volcanic, and as asphalt is a substance which one associates with Plutonic forces, I cannot doubt that it exists in the free liquid state, and that the creatures may have come in contact with it. A much more important problem is the question as to the existence of the carnivorous monster which has left its traces in this glade. We know roughly that this plateau is not larger than an average English county. Within this confined space a certain number of creatures, mostly types which have passed away in the world below, have lived together for innumerable years. Now, it is very clear to me that in so long a period one would have expected that the carnivorous creatures, multiplying unchecked, would have exhausted their food supply and have been compelled to either modify their flesh-eating habits or die of hunger. This we see has not been so. We can only imagine, therefore, that the balance of Nature is preserved by some check which limits the numbers of these ferocious creatures. One of the many interesting problems, therefore, which await our solution is to discover what that check may be and how it operates. I venture to trust that we may have some future opportunity for the closer study of the carnivorous dinosaurs."

"And I venture to trust we may not," I observed.

The Professor only raised his great eyebrows, as the school-master meets the irrelevant observation of the naughty boy.

"Perhaps Professor Summerlee may have an observation to make," he said, and the two savants ascended together into some rarefied scientific atmosphere, where the possibilities of a modification of the birth-rate were weighed against the decline of the food supply as a check in the struggle for existence.

That morning we mapped out a small portion of the plateau, avoiding the swamp of the pterodactyls, and keeping to the east of our brook instead of to the west. In that direction the country was still thickly wooded, with so much undergrowth that our progress was very slow.

I have dwelt up to now upon the terrors of Maple White Land; but there was another side to the subject, for all that morning we wandered among lovely flowers—mostly, as I observed, white or yellow in color, these being, as our professors explained, the primitive flower-shades. In many places the ground was absolutely covered with them, and as we walked ankle-deep on that wonderful yielding carpet, the scent was almost intoxicating in its sweetness and intensity. The homely English bee buzzed everywhere around us. Many of the trees under which we passed had their branches bowed down with fruit, some of which were of familiar sorts, while other varieties were new. By observing which of them were pecked by the birds we avoided all danger of poison and added a delicious variety to our food reserve. In the jungle which we traversed were numerous hard-trodden paths made by the wild beasts, and in the more marshy places we saw a profusion of strange footmarks, including many of the iguanodon. Once in a grove we observed several of these great creatures grazing, and Lord John, with his glass, was able to report that they also were spotted with asphalt, though in a different place to the one which we had examined in the morning. What this phenomenon meant we could not imagine.

We saw many small animals, such as porcupines, a scaly anteater, and a wild pig, piebald in color and with long curved tusks. Once, through a break in the trees, we saw a clear shoulder of green hill some distance away, and across this a large dun-colored animal was traveling at a considerable pace. It passed so swiftly that we were unable to say what it was; but if it were a deer, as was claimed by Lord John, it must have been as large as those monstrous Irish elk which are still dug up from time to time in the bogs of my native land.

Ever since the mysterious visit which had been paid to our camp we always returned to it with some misgivings. However, on this occasion we found everything in order.

That evening we had a grand discussion upon our present situation and future plans, which I must describe at some length, as it led to a new departure by which we were enabled to gain a more complete knowledge of Maple White Land than might have come in many weeks of exploring. It was Summerlee who opened the debate. All day he had been querulous in manner, and now some remark of Lord John's as to what we should do on the morrow brought all his bitterness to a head.

"What we ought to be doing to-day, to-morrow, and all the time," said he, "is finding some way out of the trap into which we have fallen. You are all turning your brains towards getting into this country. I say that we should be scheming how to get out of it."

"I am surprised, sir," boomed Challenger, stroking his majestic beard, "that any man of science should commit himself to so ignoble a sentiment. You are in a land which offers such an inducement to the ambitious naturalist as none ever has since the world began, and you suggest leaving it before we have acquired more than the most superficial knowledge of it or of its contents. I expected better things of you, Professor Summerlee."

"You must remember," said Summerlee, sourly, "that I have a large class in London who are at present at the mercy of an extremely inefficient locum tenens. This makes my situation different from yours, Professor Challenger, since, so far as I know, you have never been entrusted with any responsible educational work."

"Quite so," said Challenger. "I have felt it to be a sacrilege to divert a brain which is capable of the highest original research to any lesser object. That is why I have sternly set my face against any proffered scholastic appointment."

"For example?" asked Summerlee, with a sneer; but Lord John hastened to change the conversation.

"I must say," said he, "that I think it would be a mighty poor thing to go back to London before I know a great deal more of this place than I do at present."

"I could never dare to walk into the back office of my paper and face old McArdle," said I. (You will excuse the frankness of this report, will you not, sir?) "He'd never forgive me for leaving such unexhausted copy behind me. Besides, so far as I can see it is not worth discussing, since we can't get down, even if we wanted."

"Our young friend makes up for many obvious mental lacunae by some measure of primitive common sense, remarked Challenger. "The interests of his deplorable profession are immaterial to us; but, as he observes, we cannot get down in any case, so it is a waste of energy to discuss it."

"It is a waste of energy to do anything else," growled Summerlee from behind his pipe. "Let me remind you that we came here upon a perfectly definite mission, entrusted to us at the meeting of the Zoological Institute in London. That mission was to test the truth of Professor Challenger's statements. Those statements, as I am bound to admit, we are now in a position to endorse. Our ostensible work is therefore done. As to the detail which remains to be worked out upon this plateau, it is so enormous that only a large expedition, with a very special equipment, could hope to cope with it. Should we attempt to do so ourselves, the only possible result must be that we shall never return with the important contribution to science which we have already gained. Professor Challenger has devised means for getting us on to this plateau when it appeared to be inaccessible; I think that we should now call upon him to use the same ingenuity in getting us back to the world from which we came."

I confess that as Summerlee stated his view it struck me as altogether reasonable. Even Challenger was affected by the consideration that his enemies would never stand confuted if the confirmation of his statements should never reach those who had doubted them.

"The problem of the descent is at first sight a formidable one," said he, "and yet I cannot doubt that the intellect can solve it. I am prepared to agree with our colleague that a protracted stay in Maple White Land is at present inadvisable, and that the question of our return will soon have to be faced. I absolutely refuse to leave, however, until we have made at least a superficial examination of this country, and are able to take back with us something in the nature of a chart."

Professor Summerlee gave a snort of impatience.

"We have spent two long days in exploration," said he, "and we are no wiser as to the actual geography of the place than when we started. It is clear that it is all thickly wooded, and it would take months to penetrate it and to learn the relations of one part to another. If there were some central peak it would be different, but it all slopes downwards, so far as we can see. The farther we go the less likely it is that we will get any general view."

It was at that moment that I had my inspiration. My eyes chanced to light upon the enormous gnarled trunk of the gingko tree which cast its huge branches over us. Surely, if its bole exceeded that of all others, its height must do the same. If the rim of the plateau was indeed the highest point, then why should this mighty tree not prove to be a watchtower which commanded the whole country? Now, ever since I ran wild as a lad in Ireland I have been a bold and skilled tree-climber. My comrades might be my masters on the rocks, but I knew that I would be supreme among those branches. Could I only get my legs on to the lowest of the giant off-shoots, then it would be strange indeed if I could not make my way to the top. My comrades were delighted at my idea.

"Our young friend," said Challenger, bunching up the red apples of his cheeks, "is capable of acrobatic exertions which would be impossible to a man of a more solid, though possibly of a more commanding, appearance. I applaud his resolution."

"By George, young fellah, you've put your hand on it!" said Lord John, clapping me on the back. "How we never came to think of it before I can't imagine! There's not more than an hour of daylight left, but if you take your notebook you may be able to get some rough sketch of the place. If we put these three ammunition cases under the branch, I will soon hoist you on to it."

He stood on the boxes while I faced the trunk, and was gently raising me when Challenger sprang forward and gave me such a thrust with his huge hand that he fairly shot me into the tree. With both arms clasping the branch, I scrambled hard with my feet until I had worked, first my body, and then my knees, onto it. There were three excellent off-shoots, like huge rungs of a ladder, above my head, and a tangle of convenient branches beyond, so that I clambered onwards with such speed that I soon lost sight of the ground and had nothing but foliage beneath me. Now and then I encountered a check, and once I had to shin up a creeper for eight or ten feet, but I made excellent progress, and the booming of Challenger's voice seemed to be a great distance beneath me. The tree was, however, enormous, and, looking upwards, I could see no thinning of the leaves above my head. There was some thick, bush-like clump which seemed to be a parasite upon a branch up which I was swarming. I leaned my head round it in order to see what was beyond, and I nearly fell out of the tree in my surprise and horror at what I saw.

A face was gazing into mine—at the distance of only a foot or two. The creature that owned it had been crouching behind the parasite, and had looked round it at the same instant that I did. It was a human face—or at least it was far more human than any monkey's that I have ever seen. It was long, whitish, and blotched with pimples, the nose flattened, and the lower jaw projecting, with a bristle of coarse whiskers round the chin. The eyes, which were under thick and heavy brows, were bestial and ferocious, and as it opened its mouth to snarl what sounded like a curse at me I observed that it had curved, sharp canine teeth. For an instant I read hatred and menace in the evil eyes. Then, as quick as a flash, came an expression of overpowering fear. There was a crash of broken boughs as it dived wildly down into the tangle of green. I caught a glimpse of a hairy body like that of a reddish pig, and then it was gone amid a swirl of leaves and branches.

"What's the matter?" shouted Roxton from below. "Anything wrong with you?"

"Did you see it?" I cried, with my arms round the branch and all my nerves tingling.

"We heard a row, as if your foot had slipped. What was it?"

I was so shocked at the sudden and strange appearance of this ape-man that I hesitated whether I should not climb down again and tell my experience to my companions. But I was already so far up the great tree that it seemed a humiliation to return without having carried out my mission.

After a long pause, therefore, to recover my breath and my courage, I continued my ascent. Once I put my weight upon a rotten branch and swung for a few seconds by my hands, but in the main it was all easy climbing. Gradually the leaves thinned around me, and I was aware, from the wind upon my face, that I had topped all the trees of the forest. I was determined, however, not to look about me before I had reached the very highest point, so I scrambled on until I had got so far that the topmost branch was bending beneath my weight. There I settled into a convenient fork, and, balancing myself securely, I found myself looking down at a most wonderful panorama of this strange country in which we found ourselves.

The sun was just above the western sky-line, and the evening was a particularly bright and clear one, so that the whole extent of the plateau was visible beneath me. It was, as seen from this height, of an oval contour, with a breadth of about thirty miles and a width of twenty. Its general shape was that of a shallow funnel, all the sides sloping down to a considerable lake in the center. This lake may have been ten miles in circumference, and lay very green and beautiful in the evening light, with a thick fringe of reeds at its edges, and with its surface broken by several yellow sandbanks, which gleamed golden in the mellow sunshine. A number of long dark objects, which were too large for alligators and too long for canoes, lay upon the edges of these patches of sand. With my glass I could clearly see that they were alive, but what their nature might be I could not imagine.

From the side of the plateau on which we were, slopes of woodland, with occasional glades, stretched down for five or six miles to the central lake. I could see at my very feet the glade of the iguanodons, and farther off was a round opening in the trees which marked the swamp of the pterodactyls. On the side facing me, however, the plateau presented a very different aspect. There the basalt cliffs of the outside were reproduced upon the inside, forming an escarpment about two hundred feet high, with a woody slope beneath it. Along the base of these red cliffs, some distance above the ground, I could see a number of dark holes through the glass, which I conjectured to be the mouths of caves. At the opening of one of these something white was shimmering, but I was unable to make out what it was. I sat charting the country until the sun had set and it was so dark that I could no longer distinguish details. Then I climbed down to my companions waiting for me so eagerly at the bottom of the great tree. For once I was the hero of the expedition. Alone I had thought of it, and alone I had done it; and here was the chart which would save us a month's blind groping among unknown dangers. Each of them shook me solemnly by the hand.

But before they discussed the details of my map I had to tell them of my encounter with the ape-man among the branches.

"He has been there all the time," said I.

"How do you know that?" asked Lord John.

"Because I have never been without that feeling that something malevolent was watching us. I mentioned it to you, Professor Challenger."

"Our young friend certainly said something of the kind. He is also the one among us who is endowed with that Celtic temperament which would make him sensitive to such impressions."

"The whole theory of telepathy——" began Summerlee, filling his pipe.

"Is too vast to be now discussed," said Challenger, with decision. "Tell me, now," he added, with the air of a bishop addressing a Sunday-school, "did you happen to observe whether the creature could cross its thumb over its palm?"

"No, indeed."

"Had it a tail?"

"No."

"Was the foot prehensile?"

"I do not think it could have made off so fast among the branches if it could not get a grip with its feet."

"In South America there are, if my memory serves me—you will check the observation, Professor Summerlee—some thirty-six species of monkeys, but the anthropoid ape is unknown. It is clear, however, that he exists in this country, and that he is not the hairy, gorilla-like variety, which is never seen out of Africa or the East." (I was inclined to interpolate, as I looked at him, that I had seen his first cousin in Kensington.) "This is a whiskered and colorless type, the latter characteristic pointing to the fact that he spends his days in arboreal seclusion. The question which we have to face is whether he approaches more closely to the ape or the man. In the latter case, he may well approximate to what the vulgar have called the 'missing link.' The solution of this problem is our immediate duty."

"It is nothing of the sort," said Summerlee, abruptly. "Now that, through the intelligence and activity of Mr. Malone" (I cannot help quoting the words), "we have got our chart, our one and only immediate duty is to get ourselves safe and sound out of this awful place."

"The flesh-pots of civilization," groaned Challenger.

"The ink-pots of civilization, sir. It is our task to put on record what we have seen, and to leave the further exploration to others. You all agreed as much before Mr. Malone got us the chart."

"Well," said Challenger, "I admit that my mind will be more at ease when I am assured that the result of our expedition has been conveyed to our friends. How we are to get down from this place I have not as yet an idea. I have never yet encountered any problem, however, which my inventive brain was unable to solve, and I promise you that to-morrow I will turn my attention to the question of our descent." And so the matter was allowed to rest.

But that evening, by the light of the fire and of a single candle, the first map of the lost world was elaborated. Every detail which I had roughly noted from my watch-tower was drawn out in its relative place. Challenger's pencil hovered over the great blank which marked the lake.

"What shall we call it?" he asked.

"Why should you not take the chance of perpetuating your own name?" said Summerlee, with his usual touch of acidity.

"I trust, sir, that my name will have other and more personal claims upon posterity," said Challenger, severely. "Any ignoramus can hand down his worthless memory by imposing it upon a mountain or a river. I need no such monument."

Summerlee, with a twisted smile, was about to make some fresh assault when Lord John hastened to intervene.

"It's up to you, young fellah, to name the lake," said he. "You saw it first, and, by George, if you choose to put 'Lake Malone' on it, no one has a better right."

"By all means. Let our young friend give it a name," said Challenger.

"Then, said I, blushing, I dare say, as I said it, "let it be named Lake Gladys."

"Don't you think the Central Lake would be more descriptive?" remarked Summerlee.

"I should prefer Lake Gladys."

Challenger looked at me sympathetically, and shook his great head in mock disapproval. "Boys will be boys," said he. "Lake Gladys let it be."

Chapter XII   "It Was Dreadful in the Forest"

I have said—or perhaps I have not said, for my memory plays me sad tricks these days—that I glowed with pride when three such men as my comrades thanked me for having saved, or at least greatly helped, the situation. As the youngster of the party, not merely in years, but in experience, character, knowledge, and all that goes to make a man, I had been overshadowed from the first. And now I was coming into my own. I warmed at the thought. Alas! for the pride which goes before a fall! That little glow of self-satisfaction, that added measure of self-confidence, were to lead me on that very night to the most dreadful experience of my life, ending with a shock which turns my heart sick when I think of it.

It came about in this way. I had been unduly excited by the adventure of the tree, and sleep seemed to be impossible. Summerlee was on guard, sitting hunched over our small fire, a quaint, angular figure, his rifle across his knees and his pointed, goat-like beard wagging with each weary nod of his head. Lord John lay silent, wrapped in the South American poncho which he wore, while Challenger snored with a roll and rattle which reverberated through the woods. The full moon was shining brightly, and the air was crisply cold. What a night for a walk! And then suddenly came the thought, "Why not?" Suppose I stole softly away, suppose I made my way down to the central lake, suppose I was back at breakfast with some record of the place—would I not in that case be thought an even more worthy associate? Then, if Summerlee carried the day and some means of escape were found, we should return to London with first-hand knowledge of the central mystery of the plateau, to which I alone, of all men, would have penetrated. I thought of Gladys, with her "There are heroisms all round us." I seemed to hear her voice as she said it. I thought also of McArdle. What a three column article for the paper! What a foundation for a career! A correspondentship in the next great war might be within my reach. I clutched at a gun—my pockets were full of cartridges—and, parting the thorn bushes at the gate of our zareba, quickly slipped out. My last glance showed me the unconscious Summerlee, most futile of sentinels, still nodding away like a queer mechanical toy in front of the smouldering fire.

I had not gone a hundred yards before I deeply repented my rashness. I may have said somewhere in this chronicle that I am too imaginative to be a really courageous man, but that I have an overpowering fear of seeming afraid. This was the power which now carried me onwards. I simply could not slink back with nothing done. Even if my comrades should not have missed me, and should never know of my weakness, there would still remain some intolerable self-shame in my own soul. And yet I shuddered at the position in which I found myself, and would have given all I possessed at that moment to have been honorably free of the whole business.

It was dreadful in the forest. The trees grew so thickly and their foliage spread so widely that I could see nothing of the moon-light save that here and there the high branches made a tangled filigree against the starry sky. As the eyes became more used to the obscurity one learned that there were different degrees of darkness among the trees—that some were dimly visible, while between and among them there were coal-black shadowed patches, like the mouths of caves, from which I shrank in horror as I passed. I thought of the despairing yell of the tortured iguanodon—that dreadful cry which had echoed through the woods. I thought, too, of the glimpse I had in the light of Lord John's torch of that bloated, warty, blood-slavering muzzle. Even now I was on its hunting-ground. At any instant it might spring upon me from the shadows—this nameless and horrible monster. I stopped, and, picking a cartridge from my pocket, I opened the breech of my gun. As I touched the lever my heart leaped within me. It was the shot-gun, not the rifle, which I had taken!

Again the impulse to return swept over me. Here, surely, was a most excellent reason for my failure—one for which no one would think the less of me. But again the foolish pride fought against that very word. I could not—must not—fail. After all, my rifle would probably have been as useless as a shot-gun against such dangers as I might meet. If I were to go back to camp to change my weapon I could hardly expect to enter and to leave again without being seen. In that case there would be explanations, and my attempt would no longer be all my own. After a little hesitation, then, I screwed up my courage and continued upon my way, my useless gun under my arm.

The darkness of the forest had been alarming, but even worse was the white, still flood of moonlight in the open glade of the iguanodons. Hid among the bushes, I looked out at it. None of the great brutes were in sight. Perhaps the tragedy which had befallen one of them had driven them from their feeding-ground. In the misty, silvery night I could see no sign of any living thing. Taking courage, therefore, I slipped rapidly across it, and among the jungle on the farther side I picked up once again the brook which was my guide. It was a cheery companion, gurgling and chuckling as it ran, like the dear old trout-stream in the West Country where I have fished at night in my boyhood. So long as I followed it down I must come to the lake, and so long as I followed it back I must come to the camp. Often I had to lose sight of it on account of the tangled brush-wood, but I was always within earshot of its tinkle and splash.

As one descended the slope the woods became thinner, and bushes, with occasional high trees, took the place of the forest. I could make good progress, therefore, and I could see without being seen. I passed close to the pterodactyl swamp, and as I did so, with a dry, crisp, leathery rattle of wings, one of these great creatures—it was twenty feet at least from tip to tip—rose up from somewhere near me and soared into the air. As it passed across the face of the moon the light shone clearly through the membranous wings, and it looked like a flying skeleton against the white, tropical radiance. I crouched low among the bushes, for I knew from past experience that with a single cry the creature could bring a hundred of its loathsome mates about my ears. It was not until it had settled again that I dared to steal onwards upon my journey.

The night had been exceedingly still, but as I advanced I became conscious of a low, rumbling sound, a continuous murmur, somewhere in front of me. This grew louder as I proceeded, until at last it was clearly quite close to me. When I stood still the sound was constant, so that it seemed to come from some stationary cause. It was like a boiling kettle or the bubbling of some great pot. Soon I came upon the source of it, for in the center of a small clearing I found a lake—or a pool, rather, for it was not larger than the basin of the Trafalgar Square fountain—of some black, pitch-like stuff, the surface of which rose and fell in great blisters of bursting gas. The air above it was shimmering with heat, and the ground round was so hot that I could hardly bear to lay my hand on it. It was clear that the great volcanic outburst which had raised this strange plateau so many years ago had not yet entirely spent its forces. Blackened rocks and mounds of lava I had already seen everywhere peeping out from amid the luxuriant vegetation which draped them, but this asphalt pool in the jungle was the first sign that we had of actual existing activity on the slopes of the ancient crater. I had no time to examine it further for I had need to hurry if I were to be back in camp in the morning.

It was a fearsome walk, and one which will be with me so long as memory holds. In the great moonlight clearings I slunk along among the shadows on the margin. In the jungle I crept forward, stopping with a beating heart whenever I heard, as I often did, the crash of breaking branches as some wild beast went past. Now and then great shadows loomed up for an instant and were gone— great, silent shadows which seemed to prowl upon padded feet. How often I stopped with the intention of returning, and yet every time my pride conquered my fear, and sent me on again until my object should be attained.

At last (my watch showed that it was one in the morning) I saw the gleam of water amid the openings of the jungle, and ten minutes later I was among the reeds upon the borders of the central lake. I was exceedingly dry, so I lay down and took a long draught of its waters, which were fresh and cold. There was a broad pathway with many tracks upon it at the spot which I had found, so that it was clearly one of the drinking-places of the animals. Close to the water's edge there was a huge isolated block of lava. Up this I climbed, and, lying on the top, I had an excellent view in every direction.

The first thing which I saw filled me with amazement. When I described the view from the summit of the great tree, I said that on the farther cliff I could see a number of dark spots, which appeared to be the mouths of caves. Now, as I looked up at the same cliffs, I saw discs of light in every direction, ruddy, clearly-defined patches, like the port-holes of a liner in the darkness. For a moment I thought it was the lava-glow from some volcanic action; but this could not be so. Any volcanic action would surely be down in the hollow and not high among the rocks. What, then, was the alternative? It was wonderful, and yet it must surely be. These ruddy spots must be the reflection of fires within the caves—fires which could only be lit by the hand of man. There were human beings, then, upon the plateau. How gloriously my expedition was justified! Here was news indeed for us to bear back with us to London!

For a long time I lay and watched these red, quivering blotches of light. I suppose they were ten miles off from me, yet even at that distance one could observe how, from time to time, they twinkled or were obscured as someone passed before them. What would I not have given to be able to crawl up to them, to peep in, and to take back some word to my comrades as to the appearance and character of the race who lived in so strange a place! It was out of the question for the moment, and yet surely we could not leave the plateau until we had some definite knowledge upon the point.

Lake Gladys—my own lake—lay like a sheet of quicksilver before me, with a reflected moon shining brightly in the center of it. It was shallow, for in many places I saw low sandbanks protruding above the water. Everywhere upon the still surface I could see signs of life, sometimes mere rings and ripples in the water, sometimes the gleam of a great silver-sided fish in the air, sometimes the arched, slate-colored back of some passing monster. Once upon a yellow sandbank I saw a creature like a huge swan, with a clumsy body and a high, flexible neck, shuffling about upon the margin. Presently it plunged in, and for some time I could see the arched neck and darting head undulating over the water. Then it dived, and I saw it no more.

My attention was soon drawn away from these distant sights and brought back to what was going on at my very feet. Two creatures like large armadillos had come down to the drinking-place, and were squatting at the edge of the water, their long, flexible tongues like red ribbons shooting in and out as they lapped. A huge deer, with branching horns, a magnificent creature which carried itself like a king, came down with its doe and two fawns and drank beside the armadillos. No such deer exist anywhere else upon earth, for the moose or elks which I have seen would hardly have reached its shoulders. Presently it gave a warning snort, and was off with its family among the reeds, while the armadillos also scuttled for shelter. A new-comer, a most monstrous animal, was coming down the path.

For a moment I wondered where I could have seen that ungainly shape, that arched back with triangular fringes along it, that strange bird-like head held close to the ground. Then it came back, to me. It was the stegosaurus—the very creature which Maple White had preserved in his sketch-book, and which had been the first object which arrested the attention of Challenger!

There he was—perhaps the very specimen which the American artist had encountered. The ground shook beneath his tremendous weight, and his gulpings of water resounded through the still night. For five minutes he was so close to my rock that by stretching out my hand I could have touched the hideous waving hackles upon his back. Then he lumbered away and was lost among the boulders.

Looking at my watch, I saw that it was half-past two o'clock, and high time, therefore, that I started upon my homeward journey. There was no difficulty about the direction in which I should return for all along I had kept the little brook upon my left, and it opened into the central lake within a stone's-throw of the boulder upon which I had been lying. I set off, therefore, in high spirits, for I felt that I had done good work and was bringing back a fine budget of news for my companions. Foremost of all, of course, were the sight of the fiery caves and the certainty that some troglodytic race inhabited them. But besides that I could speak from experience of the central lake. I could testify that it was full of strange creatures, and I had seen several land forms of primeval life which we had not before encountered. I reflected as I walked that few men in the world could have spent a stranger night or added more to human knowledge in the course of it.

I was plodding up the slope, turning these thoughts over in my mind, and had reached a point which may have been half-way to home, when my mind was brought back to my own position by a strange noise behind me. It was something between a snore and a growl, low, deep, and exceedingly menacing. Some strange creature was evidently near me, but nothing could be seen, so I hastened more rapidly upon my way. I had traversed half a mile or so when suddenly the sound was repeated, still behind me, but louder and more menacing than before. My heart stood still within me as it flashed across me that the beast, whatever it was, must surely be after ME. My skin grew cold and my hair rose at the thought. That these monsters should tear each other to pieces was a part of the strange struggle for existence, but that they should turn upon modern man, that they should deliberately track and hunt down the predominant human, was a staggering and fearsome thought. I remembered again the blood-beslobbered face which we had seen in the glare of Lord John's torch, like some horrible vision from the deepest circle of Dante's hell. With my knees shaking beneath me, I stood and glared with starting eyes down the moonlit path which lay behind me. All was quiet as in a dream landscape. Silver clearings and the black patches of the bushes—nothing else could I see. Then from out of the silence, imminent and threatening, there came once more that low, throaty croaking, far louder and closer than before. There could no longer be a doubt. Something was on my trail, and was closing in upon me every minute.

I stood like a man paralyzed, still staring at the ground which I had traversed. Then suddenly I saw it. There was movement among the bushes at the far end of the clearing which I had just traversed. A great dark shadow disengaged itself and hopped out into the clear moonlight. I say "hopped" advisedly, for the beast moved like a kangaroo, springing along in an erect position upon its powerful hind legs, while its front ones were held bent in front of it. It was of enormous size and power, like an erect elephant, but its movements, in spite of its bulk, were exceedingly alert. For a moment, as I saw its shape, I hoped that it was an iguanodon, which I knew to be harmless, but, ignorant as I was, I soon saw that this was a very different creature. Instead of the gentle, deer-shaped head of the great three-toed leaf-eater, this beast had a broad, squat, toad-like face like that which had alarmed us in our camp. His ferocious cry and the horrible energy of his pursuit both assured me that this was surely one of the great flesh-eating dinosaurs, the most terrible beasts which have ever walked this earth. As the huge brute loped along it dropped forward upon its fore-paws and brought its nose to the ground every twenty yards or so. It was smelling out my trail. Sometimes, for an instant, it was at fault. Then it would catch it up again and come bounding swiftly along the path I had taken.

Even now when I think of that nightmare the sweat breaks out upon my brow. What could I do? My useless fowling-piece was in my hand. What help could I get from that? I looked desperately round for some rock or tree, but I was in a bushy jungle with nothing higher than a sapling within sight, while I knew that the creature behind me could tear down an ordinary tree as though it were a reed. My only possible chance lay in flight. I could not move swiftly over the rough, broken ground, but as I looked round me in despair I saw a well-marked, hard-beaten path which ran across in front of me. We had seen several of the sort, the runs of various wild beasts, during our expeditions. Along this I could perhaps hold my own, for I was a fast runner, and in excellent condition. Flinging away my useless gun, I set myself to do such a half-mile as I have never done before or since. My limbs ached, my chest heaved, I felt that my throat would burst for want of air, and yet with that horror behind me I ran and I ran and ran. At last I paused, hardly able to move. For a moment I thought that I had thrown him off. The path lay still behind me. And then suddenly, with a crashing and a rending, a thudding of giant feet and a panting of monster lungs the beast was upon me once more. He was at my very heels. I was lost.

Madman that I was to linger so long before I fled! Up to then he had hunted by scent, and his movement was slow. But he had actually seen me as I started to run. From then onwards he had hunted by sight, for the path showed him where I had gone. Now, as he came round the curve, he was springing in great bounds. The moonlight shone upon his huge projecting eyes, the row of enormous teeth in his open mouth, and the gleaming fringe of claws upon his short, powerful forearms. With a scream of terror I turned and rushed wildly down the path. Behind me the thick, gasping breathing of the creature sounded louder and louder. His heavy footfall was beside me. Every instant I expected to feel his grip upon my back. And then suddenly there came a crash—I was falling through space, and everything beyond was darkness and rest.

As I emerged from my unconsciousness—which could not, I think, have lasted more than a few minutes—I was aware of a most dreadful and penetrating smell. Putting out my hand in the darkness I came upon something which felt like a huge lump of meat, while my other hand closed upon a large bone. Up above me there was a circle of starlit sky, which showed me that I was lying at the bottom of a deep pit. Slowly I staggered to my feet and felt myself all over. I was stiff and sore from head to foot, but there was no limb which would not move, no joint which would not bend.

As the circumstances of my fall came back into my confused brain, I looked up in terror, expecting to see that dreadful head silhouetted against the paling sky. There was no sign of the monster, however, nor could I hear any sound from above. I began to walk slowly round, therefore, feeling in every direction to find out what this strange place could be into which I had been so opportunely precipitated.

It was, as I have said, a pit, with sharply-sloping walls and a level bottom about twenty feet across. This bottom was littered with great gobbets of flesh, most of which was in the last state of putridity. The atmosphere was poisonous and horrible. After tripping and stumbling over these lumps of decay, I came suddenly against something hard, and I found that an upright post was firmly fixed in the center of the hollow. It was so high that I could not reach the top of it with my hand, and it appeared to be covered with grease.

Suddenly I remembered that I had a tin box of wax-vestas in my pocket. Striking one of them, I was able at last to form some opinion of this place into which I had fallen. There could be no question as to its nature. It was a trap—made by the hand of man. The post in the center, some nine feet long, was sharpened at the upper end, and was black with the stale blood of the creatures who had been impaled upon it. The remains scattered about were fragments of the victims, which had been cut away in order to clear the stake for the next who might blunder in. I remembered that Challenger had declared that man could not exist upon the plateau, since with his feeble weapons he could not hold his own against the monsters who roamed over it. But now it was clear enough how it could be done. In their narrow-mouthed caves the natives, whoever they might be, had refuges into which the huge saurians could not penetrate, while with their developed brains they were capable of setting such traps, covered with branches, across the paths which marked the run of the animals as would destroy them in spite of all their strength and activity. Man was always the master.

The sloping wall of the pit was not difficult for an active man to climb, but I hesitated long before I trusted myself within reach of the dreadful creature which had so nearly destroyed me. How did I know that he was not lurking in the nearest clump of bushes, waiting for my reappearance? I took heart, however, as I recalled a conversation between Challenger and Summerlee upon the habits of the great saurians. Both were agreed that the monsters were practically brainless, that there was no room for reason in their tiny cranial cavities, and that if they have disappeared from the rest of the world it was assuredly on account of their own stupidity, which made it impossible for them to adapt themselves to changing conditions.

To lie in wait for me now would mean that the creature had appreciated what had happened to me, and this in turn would argue some power connecting cause and effect. Surely it was more likely that a brainless creature, acting solely by vague predatory instinct, would give up the chase when I disappeared, and, after a pause of astonishment, would wander away in search of some other prey? I clambered to the edge of the pit and looked over. The stars were fading, the sky was whitening, and the cold wind of morning blew pleasantly upon my face. I could see or hear nothing of my enemy. Slowly I climbed out and sat for a while upon the ground, ready to spring back into my refuge if any danger should appear. Then, reassured by the absolute stillness and by the growing light, I took my courage in both hands and stole back along the path which I had come. Some distance down it I picked up my gun, and shortly afterwards struck the brook which was my guide. So, with many a frightened backward glance, I made for home.

And suddenly there came something to remind me of my absent companions. In the clear, still morning air there sounded far away the sharp, hard note of a single rifle-shot. I paused and listened, but there was nothing more. For a moment I was shocked at the thought that some sudden danger might have befallen them. But then a simpler and more natural explanation came to my mind. It was now broad daylight. No doubt my absence had been noticed. They had imagined, that I was lost in the woods, and had fired this shot to guide me home. It is true that we had made a strict resolution against firing, but if it seemed to them that I might be in danger they would not hesitate. It was for me now to hurry on as fast as possible, and so to reassure them.

I was weary and spent, so my progress was not so fast as I wished; but at last I came into regions which I knew. There was the swamp of the pterodactyls upon my left; there in front of me was the glade of the iguanodons. Now I was in the last belt of trees which separated me from Fort Challenger. I raised my voice in a cheery shout to allay their fears. No answering greeting came back to me. My heart sank at that ominous stillness. I quickened my pace into a run. The zareba rose before me, even as I had left it, but the gate was open. I rushed in. In the cold, morning light it was a fearful sight which met my eyes. Our effects were scattered in wild confusion over the ground; my comrades had disappeared, and close to the smouldering ashes of our fire the grass was stained crimson with a hideous pool of blood.

I was so stunned by this sudden shock that for a time I must have nearly lost my reason. I have a vague recollection, as one remembers a bad dream, of rushing about through the woods all round the empty camp, calling wildly for my companions. No answer came back from the silent shadows. The horrible thought that I might never see them again, that I might find myself abandoned all alone in that dreadful place, with no possible way of descending into the world below, that I might live and die in that nightmare country, drove me to desperation. I could have torn my hair and beaten my head in my despair. Only now did I realize how I had learned to lean upon my companions, upon the serene self-confidence of Challenger, and upon the masterful, humorous coolness of Lord John Roxton. Without them I was like a child in the dark, helpless and powerless. I did not know which way to turn or what I should do first.

After a period, during which I sat in bewilderment, I set myself to try and discover what sudden misfortune could have befallen my companions. The whole disordered appearance of the camp showed that there had been some sort of attack, and the rifle-shot no doubt marked the time when it had occurred. That there should have been only one shot showed that it had been all over in an instant. The rifles still lay upon the ground, and one of them—Lord John's—had the empty cartridge in the breech. The blankets of Challenger and of Summerlee beside the fire suggested that they had been asleep at the time. The cases of ammunition and of food were scattered about in a wild litter, together with our unfortunate cameras and plate-carriers, but none of them were missing. On the other hand, all the exposed provisions—and I remembered that there were a considerable quantity of them— were gone. They were animals, then, and not natives, who had made the inroad, for surely the latter would have left nothing behind.

But if animals, or some single terrible animal, then what had become of my comrades? A ferocious beast would surely have destroyed them and left their remains. It is true that there was that one hideous pool of blood, which told of violence. Such a monster as had pursued me during the night could have carried away a victim as easily as a cat would a mouse. In that case the others would have followed in pursuit. But then they would assuredly have taken their rifles with them. The more I tried to think it out with my confused and weary brain the less could I find any plausible explanation. I searched round in the forest, but could see no tracks which could help me to a conclusion. Once I lost myself, and it was only by good luck, and after an hour of wandering, that I found the camp once more.

Suddenly a thought came to me and brought some little comfort to my heart. I was not absolutely alone in the world. Down at the bottom of the cliff, and within call of me, was waiting the faithful Zambo. I went to the edge of the plateau and looked over. Sure enough, he was squatting among his blankets beside his fire in his little camp. But, to my amazement, a second man was seated in front of him. For an instant my heart leaped for joy, as I thought that one of my comrades had made his way safely down. But a second glance dispelled the hope. The rising sun shone red upon the man's skin. He was an Indian. I shouted loudly and waved my handkerchief. Presently Zambo looked up, waved his hand, and turned to ascend the pinnacle. In a short time he was standing close to me and listening with deep distress to the story which I told him.

"Devil got them for sure, Massa Malone," said he. "You got into the devil's country, sah, and he take you all to himself. You take advice, Massa Malone, and come down quick, else he get you as well."

"How can I come down, Zambo?"

"You get creepers from trees, Massa Malone. Throw them over here. I make fast to this stump, and so you have bridge."

"We have thought of that. There are no creepers here which could bear us."

"Send for ropes, Massa Malone."

"Who can I send, and where?"

"Send to Indian villages, sah. Plenty hide rope in Indian village. Indian down below; send him."

"Who is he?

"One of our Indians. Other ones beat him and take away his pay. He come back to us. Ready now to take letter, bring rope,—anything."

To take a letter! Why not? Perhaps he might bring help; but in any case he would ensure that our lives were not spent for nothing, and that news of all that we had won for Science should reach our friends at home. I had two completed letters already waiting. I would spend the day in writing a third, which would bring my experiences absolutely up to date. The Indian could bear this back to the world. I ordered Zambo, therefore, to come again in the evening, and I spent my miserable and lonely day in recording my own adventures of the night before. I also drew up a note, to be given to any white merchant or captain of a steam-boat whom the Indian could find, imploring them to see that ropes were sent to us, since our lives must depend upon it. These documents I threw to Zambo in the evening, and also my purse, which contained three English sovereigns. These were to be given to the Indian, and he was promised twice as much if he returned with the ropes.

So now you will understand, my dear Mr. McArdle, how this communication reaches you, and you will also know the truth, in case you never hear again from your unfortunate correspondent. To-night I am too weary and too depressed to make my plans. To-morrow I must think out some way by which I shall keep in touch with this camp, and yet search round for any traces of my unhappy friends.

Chapter XIII   "A Sight Which I Shall Never Forget"

Just as the sun was setting upon that melancholy night I saw the lonely figure of the Indian upon the vast plain beneath me, and I watched him, our one faint hope of salvation, until he disappeared in the rising mists of evening which lay, rose-tinted from the setting sun, between the far-off river and me.

It was quite dark when I at last turned back to our stricken camp, and my last vision as I went was the red gleam of Zambo's fire, the one point of light in the wide world below, as was his faithful presence in my own shadowed soul. And yet I felt happier than I had done since this crushing blow had fallen upon me, for it was good to think that the world should know what we had done, so that at the worst our names should not perish with our bodies, but should go down to posterity associated with the result of our labors.

It was an awesome thing to sleep in that ill-fated camp; and yet it was even more unnerving to do so in the jungle. One or the other it must be. Prudence, on the one hand, warned me that I should remain on guard, but exhausted Nature, on the other, declared that I should do nothing of the kind. I climbed up on to a limb of the great gingko tree, but there was no secure perch on its rounded surface, and I should certainly have fallen off and broken my neck the moment I began to doze. I got down, therefore, and pondered over what I should do. Finally, I closed the door of the zareba, lit three separate fires in a triangle, and having eaten a hearty supper dropped off into a profound sleep, from which I had a strange and most welcome awakening. In the early morning, just as day was breaking, a hand was laid upon my arm, and starting up, with all my nerves in a tingle and my hand feeling for a rifle, I gave a cry of joy as in the cold gray light I saw Lord John Roxton kneeling beside me.

It was he—and yet it was not he. I had left him calm in his bearing, correct in his person, prim in his dress. Now he was pale and wild-eyed, gasping as he breathed like one who has run far and fast. His gaunt face was scratched and bloody, his clothes were hanging in rags, and his hat was gone. I stared in amazement, but he gave me no chance for questions. He was grabbing at our stores all the time he spoke.

"Quick, young fellah! Quick!" he cried. "Every moment counts. Get the rifles, both of them. I have the other two. Now, all the cartridges you can gather. Fill up your pockets. Now, some food. Half a dozen tins will do. That's all right! Don't wait to talk or think. Get a move on, or we are done!"

Still half-awake, and unable to imagine what it all might mean, I found myself hurrying madly after him through the wood, a rifle under each arm and a pile of various stores in my hands. He dodged in and out through the thickest of the scrub until he came to a dense clump of brush-wood. Into this he rushed, regardless of thorns, and threw himself into the heart of it, pulling me down by his side.

"There!" he panted. "I think we are safe here. They'll make for the camp as sure as fate. It will be their first idea. But this should puzzle 'em."

"What is it all?" I asked, when I had got my breath. "Where are the professors? And who is it that is after us?"

"The ape-men," he cried. "My God, what brutes! Don't raise your voice, for they have long ears—sharp eyes, too, but no power of scent, so far as I could judge, so I don't think they can sniff us out. Where have you been, young fellah? You were well out of it."

In a few sentences I whispered what I had done.

"Pretty bad," said he, when he had heard of the dinosaur and the pit. "It isn't quite the place for a rest cure. What? But I had no idea what its possibilities were until those devils got hold of us. The man-eatin' Papuans had me once, but they are Chesterfields compared to this crowd."

"How did it happen?" I asked.

"It was in the early mornin'. Our learned friends were just stirrin'. Hadn't even begun to argue yet. Suddenly it rained apes. They came down as thick as apples out of a tree. They had been assemblin' in the dark, I suppose, until that great tree over our heads was heavy with them. I shot one of them through the belly, but before we knew where we were they had us spread-eagled on our backs. I call them apes, but they carried sticks and stones in their hands and jabbered talk to each other, and ended up by tyin' our hands with creepers, so they are ahead of any beast that I have seen in my wanderin's. Ape-men—that's what they are—Missin'

Links, and I wish they had stayed missin'. They carried off their wounded comrade—he was bleedin' like a pig—and then they sat around us, and if ever I saw frozen murder it was in their faces. They were big fellows, as big as a man and a deal stronger. Curious glassy gray eyes they have, under red tufts, and they just sat and gloated and gloated. Challenger is no chicken, but even he was cowed. He managed to struggle to his feet, and yelled out at them to have done with it and get it over. I think he had gone a bit off his head at the suddenness of it, for he raged and cursed at them like a lunatic. If they had been a row of his favorite Pressmen he could not have slanged them worse."

"Well, what did they do?" I was enthralled by the strange story which my companion was whispering into my ear, while all the time his keen eyes were shooting in every direction and his hand grasping his cocked rifle.

"I thought it was the end of us, but instead of that it started them on a new line. They all jabbered and chattered together. Then one of them stood out beside Challenger. You'll smile, young fellah, but 'pon my word they might have been kinsmen. I couldn't have believed it if I hadn't seen it with my own eyes. This old ape-man—he was their chief—was a sort of red Challenger, with every one of our friend's beauty points, only just a trifle more so. He had the short body, the big shoulders, the round chest, no neck, a great ruddy frill of a beard, the tufted eyebrows, the 'What do you want, damn you!' look about the eyes, and the whole catalogue. When the ape-man stood by Challenger and put his paw on his shoulder, the thing was complete. Summerlee was a bit hysterical, and he laughed till he cried. The ape-men laughed too—or at least they put up the devil of a cacklin'—and they set to work to drag us off through the forest. They wouldn't touch the guns and things—thought them dangerous, I expect—but they carried away all our loose food. Summerlee and I got some rough handlin' on the way—there's my skin and my clothes to prove it—for they took us a bee-line through the brambles, and their own hides are like leather. But Challenger was all right. Four of them carried him shoulder high, and he went like a Roman emperor. What's that?"

It was a strange clicking noise in the distance not unlike castanets.

"There they go!" said my companion, slipping cartridges into the second double barrelled "Express." "Load them all up, young fellah my lad, for we're not going to be taken alive, and don't you think it! That's the row they make when they are excited. By George! they'll have something to excite them if they put us up. The 'Last Stand of the Grays' won't be in it. 'With their rifles grasped in their stiffened hands, mid a ring of the dead and dyin', as some fathead sings. Can you hear them now?"

"Very far away."

"That little lot will do no good, but I expect their search parties are all over the wood. Well, I was telling you my tale of woe. They got us soon to this town of theirs—about a thousand huts of branches and leaves in a great grove of trees near the edge of the cliff. It's three or four miles from here. The filthy beasts fingered me all over, and I feel as if I should never be clean again. They tied us up—the fellow who handled me could tie like a bosun—and there we lay with our toes up, beneath a tree, while a great brute stood guard over us with a club in his hand. When I say 'we' I mean Summerlee and myself. Old Challenger was up a tree, eatin' pines and havin' the time of his life. I'm bound to say that he managed to get some fruit to us, and with his own hands he loosened our bonds. If you'd seen him sitting up in that tree hob-nobbin' with his twin brother—and singin' in that rollin' bass of his, 'Ring out, wild bells,' 'cause music of any kind seemed to put 'em in a good humor, you'd have smiled; but we weren't in much mood for laughin', as you can guess. They were inclined, within limits, to let him do what he liked, but they drew the line pretty sharply at us. It was a mighty consolation to us all to know that you were runnin' loose and had the archives in your keepin'.

"Well, now, young fellah, I'll tell you what will surprise you. You say you saw signs of men, and fires, traps, and the like. Well, we have seen the natives themselves. Poor devils they were, down-faced little chaps, and had enough to make them so. It seems that the humans hold one side of this plateau—over yonder, where you saw the caves—and the ape-men hold this side, and there is bloody war between them all the time. That's the situation, so far as I could follow it. Well, yesterday the ape-men got hold of a dozen of the humans and brought them in as prisoners. You never heard such a jabberin' and shriekin' in your life. The men were little red fellows, and had been bitten and clawed so that they could hardly walk. The ape-men put two of them to death there and then—fairly pulled the arm off one of them—it was perfectly beastly. Plucky little chaps they are, and hardly gave a squeak. But it turned us absolutely sick. Summerlee fainted, and even Challenger had as much as he could stand. I think they have cleared, don't you?"

We listened intently, but nothing save the calling of the birds broke the deep peace of the forest. Lord Roxton went on with his story.

"I Think you have had the escape of your life, young fellah my lad. It was catchin' those Indians that put you clean out of their heads, else they would have been back to the camp for you as sure as fate and gathered you in. Of course, as you said, they have been watchin' us from the beginnin' out of that tree, and they knew perfectly well that we were one short. However, they could think only of this new haul; so it was I, and not a bunch of apes, that dropped in on you in the morning. Well, we had a horrid business afterwards. My God! what a nightmare the whole thing is! You remember the great bristle of sharp canes down below where we found the skeleton of the American? Well, that is just under ape-town, and that's the jumpin'-off place of their prisoners. I expect there's heaps of skeletons there, if we looked for 'em. They have a sort of clear parade-ground on the top, and they make a proper ceremony about it. One by one the poor devils have to jump, and the game is to see whether they are merely dashed to pieces or whether they get skewered on the canes. They took us out to see it, and the whole tribe lined up on the edge. Four of the Indians jumped, and the canes went through 'em like knittin' needles through a pat of butter. No wonder we found that poor Yankee's skeleton with the canes growin' between his ribs. It was horrible—but it was doocedly interestin' too. We were all fascinated to see them take the dive, even when we thought it would be our turn next on the spring-board.

"Well, it wasn't. They kept six of the Indians up for to-day—that's how I understood it—but I fancy we were to be the star performers in the show. Challenger might get off, but Summerlee and

I were in the bill. Their language is more than half signs, and it was not hard to follow them. So I thought it was time we made a break for it. I had been plottin' it out a bit, and had one or two things clear in my mind. It was all on me, for Summerlee was useless and Challenger not much better. The only time they got together they got slangin' because they couldn't agree upon the scientific classification of these red-headed devils that had got hold of us. One said it was the dryopithecus of Java, the other said it was pithecanthropus. Madness, I call it—Loonies, both. But, as I say, I had thought out one or two points that were helpful. One was that these brutes could not run as fast as a man in the open. They have short, bandy legs, you see, and heavy bodies. Even Challenger could give a few yards in a hundred to the best of them, and you or I would be a perfect Shrubb. Another point was that they knew nothin' about guns. I don't believe they ever understood how the fellow I shot came by his hurt. If we could get at our guns there was no sayin' what we could do.

"So I broke away early this mornin', gave my guard a kick in the tummy that laid him out, and sprinted for the camp. There I got you and the guns, and here we are."

"But the professors!" I cried, in consternation.

"Well, we must just go back and fetch 'em. I couldn't bring 'em with me. Challenger was up the tree, and Summerlee was not fit for the effort. The only chance was to get the guns and try a rescue. Of course they may scupper them at once in revenge. I don't think they would touch Challenger, but I wouldn't answer for Summerlee. But they would have had him in any case. Of that I am certain. So I haven't made matters any worse by boltin'. But we are honor bound to go back and have them out or see it through with them. So you can make up your soul, young fellah my lad, for it will be one way or the other before evenin'."

I have tried to imitate here Lord Roxton's jerky talk, his short, strong sentences, the half-humorous, half-reckless tone that ran through it all. But he was a born leader. As danger thickened his jaunty manner would increase, his speech become more racy, his cold eyes glitter into ardent life, and his Don Quixote moustache bristle with joyous excitement. His love of danger, his intense appreciation of the drama of an adventure—all the more intense for being held tightly in—his consistent view that every peril in life is a form of sport, a fierce game betwixt you and Fate, with Death as a forfeit, made him a wonderful companion at such hours. If it were not for our fears as to the fate of our companions, it would have been a positive joy to throw myself with such a man into such an affair. We were rising from our brushwood hiding-place when suddenly I felt his grip upon my arm.

"By George!" he whispered, "here they come!"

From where we lay we could look down a brown aisle, arched with green, formed by the trunks and branches. Along this a party of the ape-men were passing. They went in single file, with bent legs and rounded backs, their hands occasionally touching the ground, their heads turning to left and right as they trotted along. Their crouching gait took away from their height, but I should put them at five feet or so, with long arms and enormous chests. Many of them carried sticks, and at the distance they looked like a line of very hairy and deformed human beings. For a moment I caught this clear glimpse of them. Then they were lost among the bushes.

"Not this time," said Lord John, who had caught up his rifle. "Our best chance is to lie quiet until they have given up the search. Then we shall see whether we can't get back to their town and hit 'em where it hurts most. Give 'em an hour and we'll march."

We filled in the time by opening one of our food tins and making sure of our breakfast. Lord Roxton had had nothing but some fruit since the morning before and ate like a starving man. Then, at last, our pockets bulging with cartridges and a rifle in each hand, we started off upon our mission of rescue. Before leaving it we carefully marked our little hiding-place among the brush-wood and its bearing to Fort Challenger, that we might find it again if we needed it. We slunk through the bushes in silence until we came to the very edge of the cliff, close to the old camp. There we halted, and Lord John gave me some idea of his plans.

"So long as we are among the thick trees these swine are our masters," said he. "They can see us and we cannot see them. But in the open it is different. There we can move faster than they. So we must stick to the open all we can. The edge of the plateau has fewer large trees than further inland. So that's our line of advance. Go slowly, keep your eyes open and your rifle ready. Above all, never let them get you prisoner while there is a cartridge left—that's my last word to you, young fellah."

When we reached the edge of the cliff I looked over and saw our good old black Zambo sitting smoking on a rock below us. I would have given a great deal to have hailed him and told him how we were placed, but it was too dangerous, lest we should be heard. The woods seemed to be full of the ape-men; again and again we heard their curious clicking chatter. At such times we plunged into the nearest clump of bushes and lay still until the sound had passed away. Our advance, therefore, was very slow, and two hours at least must have passed before I saw by Lord John's cautious movements that we must be close to our destination. He motioned to me to lie still, and he crawled forward himself. In a minute he was back again, his face quivering with eagerness.

"Come!" said he. "Come quick! I hope to the Lord we are not too late already!

I found myself shaking with nervous excitement as I scrambled forward and lay down beside him, looking out through the bushes at a clearing which stretched before us.

It was a sight which I shall never forget until my dying day—so weird, so impossible, that I do not know how I am to make you realize it, or how in a few years I shall bring myself to believe in it if I live to sit once more on a lounge in the Savage Club and look out on the drab solidity of the Embankment. I know that it will seem then to be some wild nightmare, some delirium of fever. Yet I will set it down now, while it is still fresh in my memory, and one at least, the man who lay in the damp grasses by my side, will know if I have lied.

A wide, open space lay before us—some hundreds of yards across—all green turf and low bracken growing to the very edge of the cliff. Round this clearing there was a semi-circle of trees with curious huts built of foliage piled one above the other among the branches. A rookery, with every nest a little house, would best convey the idea. The openings of these huts and the branches of the trees were thronged with a dense mob of ape-people, whom from their size I took to be the females and infants of the tribe. They formed the background of the picture, and were all looking out with eager interest at the same scene which fascinated and bewildered us.

In the open, and near the edge of the cliff, there had assembled a crowd of some hundred of these shaggy, red-haired creatures, many of them of immense size, and all of them horrible to look upon. There was a certain discipline among them, for none of them attempted to break the line which had been formed. In front there stood a small group of Indians—little, clean-limbed, red fellows, whose skins glowed like polished bronze in the strong sunlight. A tall, thin white man was standing beside them, his head bowed, his arms folded, his whole attitude expressive of his horror and dejection. There was no mistaking the angular form of Professor Summerlee.

In front of and around this dejected group of prisoners were several ape-men, who watched them closely and made all escape impossible. Then, right out from all the others and close to the edge of the cliff, were two figures, so strange, and under other circumstances so ludicrous, that they absorbed my attention. The one was our comrade, Professor Challenger. The remains of his coat still hung in strips from his shoulders, but his shirt had been all torn out, and his great beard merged itself in the black tangle which covered his mighty chest. He had lost his hat, and his hair, which had grown long in our wanderings, was flying in wild disorder. A single day seemed to have changed him from the highest product of modern civilization to the most desperate savage in South America. Beside him stood his master, the king of the ape-men. In all things he was, as Lord John had said, the very image of our Professor, save that his coloring was red instead of black. The same short, broad figure, the same heavy shoulders, the same forward hang of the arms, the same bristling beard merging itself in the hairy chest. Only above the eyebrows, where the sloping forehead and low, curved skull of the ape-man were in sharp contrast to the broad brow and magnificent cranium of the European, could one see any marked difference. At every other point the king was an absurd parody of the Professor.

All this, which takes me so long to describe, impressed itself upon me in a few seconds. Then we had very different things to think of, for an active drama was in progress. Two of the ape-men had seized one of the Indians out of the group and dragged him forward to the edge of the cliff. The king raised his hand as a signal.

They caught the man by his leg and arm, and swung him three times backwards and forwards with tremendous violence. Then, with a frightful heave they shot the poor wretch over the precipice. With such force did they throw him that he curved high in the air before beginning to drop. As he vanished from sight, the whole assembly, except the guards, rushed forward to the edge of the precipice, and there was a long pause of absolute silence, broken by a mad yell of delight. They sprang about, tossing their long, hairy arms in the air and howling with exultation. Then they fell back from the edge, formed themselves again into line, and waited for the next victim.

This time it was Summerlee. Two of his guards caught him by the wrists and pulled him brutally to the front. His thin figure and long limbs struggled and fluttered like a chicken being dragged from a coop. Challenger had turned to the king and waved his hands frantically before him. He was begging, pleading, imploring for his comrade's life. The ape-man pushed him roughly aside and shook his head. It was the last conscious movement he was to make upon earth. Lord John's rifle cracked, and the king sank down, a tangled red sprawling thing, upon the ground.

"Shoot into the thick of them! Shoot! sonny, shoot!" cried my companion.

There are strange red depths in the soul of the most commonplace man. I am tenderhearted by nature, and have found my eyes moist many a time over the scream of a wounded hare. Yet the blood lust was on me now. I found myself on my feet emptying one magazine, then the other, clicking open the breech to re-load, snapping it to again, while cheering and yelling with pure ferocity and joy of slaughter as I did so. With our four guns the two of us made a horrible havoc. Both the guards who held Summerlee were down, and he was staggering about like a drunken man in his amazement, unable to realize that he was a free man. The dense mob of ape-men ran about in bewilderment, marveling whence this storm of death was coming or what it might mean. They waved, gesticulated, screamed, and tripped up over those who had fallen. Then, with a sudden impulse, they all rushed in a howling crowd to the trees for shelter, leaving the ground behind them spotted with their stricken comrades. The prisoners were left for the moment standing alone in the middle of the clearing.

Challenger's quick brain had grasped the situation. He seized the bewildered Summerlee by the arm, and they both ran towards us. Two of their guards bounded after them and fell to two bullets from Lord John. We ran forward into the open to meet our friends, and pressed a loaded rifle into the hands of each. But Summerlee was at the end of his strength. He could hardly totter. Already the ape-men were recovering from their panic. They were coming through the brushwood and threatening to cut us off. Challenger and I ran Summerlee along, one at each of his elbows, while Lord John covered our retreat, firing again and again as savage heads snarled at us out of the bushes. For a mile or more the chattering brutes were at our very heels. Then the pursuit slackened, for they learned our power and would no longer face that unerring rifle. When we had at last reached the camp, we looked back and found ourselves alone.

So it seemed to us; and yet we were mistaken. We had hardly closed the thornbush door of our zareba, clasped each other's hands, and thrown ourselves panting upon the ground beside our spring, when we heard a patter of feet and then a gentle, plaintive crying from outside our entrance. Lord Roxton rushed forward, rifle in hand, and threw it open. There, prostrate upon their faces, lay the little red figures of the four surviving Indians, trembling with fear of us and yet imploring our protection. With an expressive sweep of his hands one of them pointed to the woods around them, and indicated that they were full of danger. Then, darting forward, he threw his arms round Lord John's legs, and rested his face upon them.

"By George!" cried our peer, pulling at his moustache in great perplexity, "I say—what the deuce are we to do with these people? Get up, little chappie, and take your face off my boots."

Summerlee was sitting up and stuffing some tobacco into his old briar.

"We've got to see them safe," said he. "You've pulled us all out of the jaws of death. My word! it was a good bit of work!"

"Admirable!" cried Challenger. "Admirable! Not only we as individuals, but European science collectively, owe you a deep debt of gratitude for what you have done. I do not hesitate to say that the disappearance of Professor Summerlee and myself would have left an appreciable gap in modern zoological history. Our young friend here and you have done most excellently well."

He beamed at us with the old paternal smile, but European science would have been somewhat amazed could they have seen their chosen child, the hope of the future, with his tangled, unkempt head, his bare chest, and his tattered clothes. He had one of the meat-tins between his knees, and sat with a large piece of cold Australian mutton between his fingers. The Indian looked up at him, and then, with a little yelp, cringed to the ground and clung to Lord John's leg.

"Don't you be scared, my bonnie boy," said Lord John, patting the matted head in front of him. "He can't stick your appearance, Challenger; and, by George! I don't wonder. All right, little chap, he's only a human, just the same as the rest of us."

"Really, sir!" cried the Professor.

"Well, it's lucky for you, Challenger, that you ARE a little out of the ordinary. If you hadn't been so like the king——"

"Upon my word, Lord John, you allow yourself great latitude."

"Well, it's a fact."

"I beg, sir, that you will change the subject. Your remarks are irrelevant and unintelligible. The question before us is what are we to do with these Indians? The obvious thing is to escort them home, if we knew where their home was."

"There is no difficulty about that," said I. "They live in the caves on the other side of the central lake."

"Our young friend here knows where they live. I gather that it is some distance."

"A good twenty miles," said I.

Summerlee gave a groan.

"I, for one, could never get there. Surely I hear those brutes still howling upon our track."

As he spoke, from the dark recesses of the woods we heard far away the jabbering cry of the ape-men. The Indians once more set up a feeble wail of fear.

"We must move, and move quick!" said Lord John. "You help Summerlee, young fellah. These Indians will carry stores. Now, then, come along before they can see us."

In less than half-an-hour we had reached our brushwood retreat and concealed ourselves. All day we heard the excited calling of the ape-men in the direction of our old camp, but none of them came our way, and the tired fugitives, red and white, had a long, deep sleep. I was dozing myself in the evening when someone plucked my sleeve, and I found Challenger kneeling beside me.

"You keep a diary of these events, and you expect eventually to publish it, Mr. Malone," said he, with solemnity.

"I am only here as a Press reporter," I answered.

"Exactly. You may have heard some rather fatuous remarks of Lord John Roxton's which seemed to imply that there was some—some resemblance——"

"Yes, I heard them."

"I need not say that any publicity given to such an idea—any levity in your narrative of what occurred—would be exceedingly offensive to me."

"I will keep well within the truth."

"Lord John's observations are frequently exceedingly fanciful, and he is capable of attributing the most absurd reasons to the respect which is always shown by the most undeveloped races to dignity and character. You follow my meaning?"

"Entirely."

"I leave the matter to your discretion." Then, after a long pause, he added: "The king of the ape-men was really a creature of great distinction—a most remarkably handsome and intelligent personality. Did it not strike you?"

"A most remarkable creature," said I.

And the Professor, much eased in his mind, settled down to his slumber once more.

Chapter XIV   "Those Were the Real Conquests"

We had imagined that our pursuers, the ape-men, knew nothing of our brush-wood hiding-place, but we were soon to find out our mistake. There was no sound in the woods—not a leaf moved upon the trees, and all was peace around us—but we should have been warned by our first experience how cunningly and how patiently these creatures can watch and wait until their chance comes. Whatever fate may be mine through life, I am very sure that I shall never be nearer death than I was that morning. But I will tell you the thing in its due order.

We all awoke exhausted after the terrific emotions and scanty food of yesterday. Summerlee was still so weak that it was an effort for him to stand; but the old man was full of a sort of surly courage which would never admit defeat. A council was held, and it was agreed that we should wait quietly for an hour or two where we were, have our much-needed breakfast, and then make our way across the plateau and round the central lake to the caves where my observations had shown that the Indians lived. We relied upon the fact that we could count upon the good word of those whom we had rescued to ensure a warm welcome from their fellows. Then, with our mission accomplished and possessing a fuller knowledge of the secrets of Maple White Land, we should turn our whole thoughts to the vital problem of our escape and return. Even Challenger was ready to admit that we should then have done all for which we had come, and that our first duty from that time onwards was to carry back to civilization the amazing discoveries we had made.

We were able now to take a more leisurely view of the Indians whom we had rescued. They were small men, wiry, active, and well-built, with lank black hair tied up in a bunch behind their heads with a leathern thong, and leathern also were their loin-clothes. Their faces were hairless, well formed, and good-humored. The lobes of their ears, hanging ragged and bloody, showed that they had been pierced for some ornaments which their captors had torn out. Their speech, though unintelligible to us, was fluent among themselves, and as they pointed to each other and uttered the word "Accala" many times over, we gathered that this was the name of the nation. Occasionally, with faces which were convulsed with fear and hatred, they shook their clenched hands at the woods round and cried: "Doda! Doda!" which was surely their term for their enemies.

What do you make of them, Challenger?" asked Lord John. "One thing is very clear to me, and that is that the little chap with the front of his head shaved is a chief among them."

It was indeed evident that this man stood apart from the others, and that they never ventured to address him without every sign of deep respect. He seemed to be the youngest of them all, and yet, so proud and high was his spirit that, upon Challenger laying his great hand upon his head, he started like a spurred horse and, with a quick flash of his dark eyes, moved further away from the Professor. Then, placing his hand upon his breast and holding himself with great dignity, he uttered the word "Maretas" several times. The Professor, unabashed, seized the nearest Indian by the shoulder and proceeded to lecture upon him as if he were a potted specimen in a class-room.

"The type of these people," said he in his sonorous fashion, "whether judged by cranial capacity, facial angle, or any other test, cannot be regarded as a low one; on the contrary, we must place it as considerably higher in the scale than many South American tribes which I can mention. On no possible supposition can we explain the evolution of such a race in this place. For that matter, so great a gap separates these ape-men from the primitive animals which have survived upon this plateau, that it is inadmissible to think that they could have developed where we find them."

"Then where the dooce did they drop from?" asked Lord John.

"A question which will, no doubt, be eagerly discussed in every scientific society in Europe and America," the Professor answered. "My own reading of the situation for what it is worth—" he inflated his chest enormously and looked insolently around him at the words—"is that evolution has advanced under the peculiar conditions of this country up to the vertebrate stage, the old types surviving and living on in company with the newer ones. Thus we find such modern creatures as the tapir—an animal with quite a respectable length of pedigree—the great deer, and the ant-eater in the companionship of reptilian forms of jurassic type. So much is clear. And now come the ape-men and the Indian. What is the scientific mind to think of their presence? I can only account for it by an invasion from outside. It is probable that there existed an anthropoid ape in South America, who in past ages found his way to this place, and that he developed into the creatures we have seen, some of which"—here he looked hard at me—

"were of an appearance and shape which, if it had been accompanied by corresponding intelligence, would, I do not hesitate to say, have reflected credit upon any living race. As to the Indians I cannot doubt that they are more recent immigrants from below. Under the stress of famine or of conquest they have made their way up here. Faced by ferocious creatures which they had never before seen, they took refuge in the caves which our young friend has described, but they have no doubt had a bitter fight to hold their own against wild beasts, and especially against the ape-men who would regard them as intruders, and wage a merciless war upon them with a cunning which the larger beasts would lack. Hence the fact that their numbers appear to be limited. Well, gentlemen, have I read you the riddle aright, or is there any point which you would query?"

Professor Summerlee for once was too depressed to argue, though he shook his head violently as a token of general disagreement. Lord John merely scratched his scanty locks with the remark that he couldn't put up a fight as he wasn't in the same weight or class. For my own part I performed my usual role of bringing things down to a strictly prosaic and practical level by the remark that one of the Indians was missing.

"He has gone to fetch some water," said Lord Roxton. "We fitted him up with an empty beef tin and he is off."

"To the old camp?" I asked.

"No, to the brook. It's among the trees there. It can't be more than a couple of hundred yards. But the beggar is certainly taking his time."

"I'll go and look after him," said I. I picked up my rifle and strolled in the direction of the brook, leaving my friends to lay out the scanty breakfast. It may seem to you rash that even for so short a distance I should quit the shelter of our friendly thicket, but you will remember that we were many miles from Ape-town, that so far as we knew the creatures had not discovered our retreat, and that in any case with a rifle in my hands I had no fear of them. I had not yet learned their cunning or their strength.

I could hear the murmur of our brook somewhere ahead of me, but there was a tangle of trees and brushwood between me and it. I was making my way through this at a point which was just out of sight of my companions, when, under one of the trees, I noticed something red huddled among the bushes. As I approached it, I was shocked to see that it was the dead body of the missing Indian. He lay upon his side, his limbs drawn up, and his head screwed round at a most unnatural angle, so that he seemed to be looking straight over his own shoulder. I gave a cry to warn my friends that something was amiss, and running forwards I stooped over the body. Surely my guardian angel was very near me then, for some instinct of fear, or it may have been some faint rustle of leaves, made me glance upwards. Out of the thick green foliage which hung low over my head, two long muscular arms covered with reddish hair were slowly descending. Another instant and the great stealthy hands would have been round my throat. I sprang backwards, but quick as I was, those hands were quicker still. Through my sudden spring they missed a fatal grip, but one of them caught the back of my neck and the other one my face. I threw my hands up to protect my throat, and the next moment the huge paw had slid down my face and closed over them. I was lifted lightly from the ground, and I felt an intolerable pressure forcing my head back and back until the strain upon the cervical spine was more than I could bear. My senses swam, but I still tore at the hand and forced it out from my chin. Looking up I saw a frightful face with cold inexorable light blue eyes looking down into mine. There was something hypnotic in those terrible eyes. I could struggle no longer. As the creature felt me grow limp in his grasp, two white canines gleamed for a moment at each side of the vile mouth, and the grip tightened still more upon my chin, forcing it always upwards and back. A thin, oval-tinted mist formed before my eyes and little silvery bells tinkled in my ears. Dully and far off I heard the crack of a rifle and was feebly aware of the shock as I was dropped to the earth, where I lay without sense or motion.

I awoke to find myself on my back upon the grass in our lair within the thicket. Someone had brought the water from the brook, and Lord John was sprinkling my head with it, while Challenger and Summerlee were propping me up, with concern in their faces. For a moment I had a glimpse of the human spirits behind their scientific masks. It was really shock, rather than any injury, which had prostrated me, and in half-an-hour, in spite of aching head and stiff neck, I was sitting up and ready for anything.

"But you've had the escape of your life, young fellah my lad," said Lord Roxton. "When I heard your cry and ran forward, and saw your head twisted half-off and your stohwassers kickin' in the air, I thought we were one short. I missed the beast in my flurry, but he dropped you all right and was off like a streak. By George! I wish I had fifty men with rifles. I'd clear out the whole infernal gang of them and leave this country a bit cleaner than we found it."

It was clear now that the ape-men had in some way marked us down, and that we were watched on every side. We had not so much to fear from them during the day, but they would be very likely to rush us by night; so the sooner we got away from their neighborhood the better. On three sides of us was absolute forest, and there we might find ourselves in an ambush. But on the fourth side—that which sloped down in the direction of the lake—there was only low scrub, with scattered trees and occasional open glades. It was, in fact, the route which I had myself taken in my solitary journey, and it led us straight for the Indian caves. This then must for every reason be our road.

One great regret we had, and that was to leave our old camp behind us, not only for the sake of the stores which remained there, but even more because we were losing touch with Zambo, our link with the outside world. However, we had a fair supply of cartridges and all our guns, so, for a time at least, we could look after ourselves, and we hoped soon to have a chance of returning and restoring our communications with our negro. He had faithfully promised to stay where he was, and we had not a doubt that he would be as good as his word.

It was in the early afternoon that we started upon our journey. The young chief walked at our head as our guide, but refused indignantly to carry any burden. Behind him came the two surviving Indians with our scanty possessions upon their backs. We four white men walked in the rear with rifles loaded and ready. As we started there broke from the thick silent woods behind us a sudden great ululation of the ape-men, which may have been a cheer of triumph at our departure or a jeer of contempt at our flight.

Looking back we saw only the dense screen of trees, but that long-drawn yell told us how many of our enemies lurked among them. We saw no sign of pursuit, however, and soon we had got into more open country and beyond their power.

As I tramped along, the rearmost of the four, I could not help smiling at the appearance of my three companions in front. Was this the luxurious Lord John Roxton who had sat that evening in the Albany amidst his Persian rugs and his pictures in the pink radiance of the tinted lights? And was this the imposing Professor who had swelled behind the great desk in his massive study at Enmore Park? And, finally, could this be the austere and prim figure which had risen before the meeting at the Zoological Institute? No three tramps that one could have met in a Surrey lane could have looked more hopeless and bedraggled. We had, it is true, been only a week or so upon the top of the plateau, but all our spare clothing was in our camp below, and the one week had been a severe one upon us all, though least to me who had not to endure the handling of the ape-men. My three friends had all lost their hats, and had now bound handkerchiefs round their heads, their clothes hung in ribbons about them, and their unshaven grimy faces were hardly to be recognized. Both Summerlee and Challenger were limping heavily, while I still dragged my feet from weakness after the shock of the morning, and my neck was as stiff as a board from the murderous grip that held it. We were indeed a sorry crew, and I did not wonder to see our Indian companions glance back at us occasionally with horror and amazement on their faces.

In the late afternoon we reached the margin of the lake, and as we emerged from the bush and saw the sheet of water stretching before us our native friends set up a shrill cry of joy and pointed eagerly in front of them. It was indeed a wonderful sight which lay before us. Sweeping over the glassy surface was a great flotilla of canoes coming straight for the shore upon which we stood. They were some miles out when we first saw them, but they shot forward with great swiftness, and were soon so near that the rowers could distinguish our persons. Instantly a thunderous shout of delight burst from them, and we saw them rise from their seats, waving their paddles and spears madly in the air. Then bending to their work once more, they flew across the intervening water, beached their boats upon the sloping sand, and rushed up to us, prostrating themselves with loud cries of greeting before the young chief. Finally one of them, an elderly man, with a necklace and bracelet of great lustrous glass beads and the skin of some beautiful mottled amber-colored animal slung over his shoulders, ran forward and embraced most tenderly the youth whom we had saved. He then looked at us and asked some questions, after which he stepped up with much dignity and embraced us also each in turn. Then, at his order, the whole tribe lay down upon the ground before us in homage. Personally I felt shy and uncomfortable at this obsequious adoration, and I read the same feeling in the faces of Roxton and Summerlee, but Challenger expanded like a flower in the sun.

"They may be undeveloped types," said he, stroking his beard and looking round at them, "but their deportment in the presence of their superiors might be a lesson to some of our more advanced Europeans. Strange how correct are the instincts of the natural man!"

It was clear that the natives had come out upon the war-path, for every man carried his spear—a long bamboo tipped with bone—his bow and arrows, and some sort of club or stone battle-axe slung at his side. Their dark, angry glances at the woods from which we had come, and the frequent repetition of the word "Doda," made it clear enough that this was a rescue party who had set forth to save or revenge the old chief's son, for such we gathered that the youth must be. A council was now held by the whole tribe squatting in a circle, whilst we sat near on a slab of basalt and watched their proceedings. Two or three warriors spoke, and finally our young friend made a spirited harangue with such eloquent features and gestures that we could understand it all as clearly as if we had known his language.

"What is the use of returning?" he said. "Sooner or later the thing must be done. Your comrades have been murdered. What if I have returned safe? These others have been done to death. There is no safety for any of us. We are assembled now and ready." Then he pointed to us. "These strange men are our friends. They are great fighters, and they hate the ape-men even as we do. They command," here he pointed up to heaven, "the thunder and the lightning. When shall we have such a chance again? Let us go forward, and either die now or live for the future in safety. How else shall we go back unashamed to our women?"

The little red warriors hung upon the words of the speaker, and when he had finished they burst into a roar of applause, waving their rude weapons in the air. The old chief stepped forward to us, and asked us some questions, pointing at the same time to the woods. Lord John made a sign to him that he should wait for an answer and then he turned to us.

"Well, it's up to you to say what you will do," said he; "for my part I have a score to settle with these monkey-folk, and if it ends by wiping them off the face of the earth I don't see that the earth need fret about it. I'm goin' with our little red pals and I mean to see them through the scrap. What do you say, young fellah?"

"Of course I will come."

"And you, Challenger?"

"I will assuredly co-operate."

"And you, Summerlee?"

"We seem to be drifting very far from the object of this expedition, Lord John. I assure you that I little thought when I left my professional chair in London that it was for the purpose of heading a raid of savages upon a colony of anthropoid apes."

"To such base uses do we come," said Lord John, smiling. "But we are up against it, so what's the decision?"

"It seems a most questionable step," said Summerlee, argumentative to the last, "but if you are all going, I hardly see how I can remain behind."

"Then it is settled," said Lord John, and turning to the chief he nodded and slapped his rifle.

The old fellow clasped our hands, each in turn, while his men cheered louder than ever. It was too late to advance that night, so the Indians settled down into a rude bivouac. On all sides their fires began to glimmer and smoke. Some of them who had disappeared into the jungle came back presently driving a young iguanodon before them. Like the others, it had a daub of asphalt upon its shoulder, and it was only when we saw one of the natives step forward with the air of an owner and give his consent to the beast's slaughter that we understood at last that these great creatures were as much private property as a herd of cattle, and that these symbols which had so perplexed us were nothing more than the marks of the owner. Helpless, torpid, and vegetarian, with great limbs but a minute brain, they could be rounded up and driven by a child. In a few minutes the huge beast had been cut up and slabs of him were hanging over a dozen camp fires, together with great scaly ganoid fish which had been speared in the lake.

Summerlee had lain down and slept upon the sand, but we others roamed round the edge of the water, seeking to learn something more of this strange country. Twice we found pits of blue clay, such as we had already seen in the swamp of the pterodactyls. These were old volcanic vents, and for some reason excited the greatest interest in Lord John. What attracted Challenger, on the other hand, was a bubbling, gurgling mud geyser, where some strange gas formed great bursting bubbles upon the surface. He thrust a hollow reed into it and cried out with delight like a schoolboy then he was able, on touching it with a lighted match, to cause a sharp explosion and a blue flame at the far end of the tube. Still more pleased was he when, inverting a leathern pouch over the end of the reed, and so filling it with the gas, he was able to send it soaring up into the air.

"An inflammable gas, and one markedly lighter than the atmosphere. I should say beyond doubt that it contained a considerable proportion of free hydrogen. The resources of G. E. C. are not yet exhausted, my young friend. I may yet show you how a great mind molds all Nature to its use." He swelled with some secret purpose, but would say no more.

There was nothing which we could see upon the shore which seemed to me so wonderful as the great sheet of water before us. Our numbers and our noise had frightened all living creatures away, and save for a few pterodactyls, which soared round high above our heads while they waited for the carrion, all was still around the camp. But it was different out upon the rose-tinted waters of the central lake. It boiled and heaved with strange life. Great slate-colored backs and high serrated dorsal fins shot up with a fringe of silver, and then rolled down into the depths again. The sand-banks far out were spotted with uncouth crawling forms, huge turtles, strange saurians, and one great flat creature like a writhing, palpitating mat of black greasy leather, which flopped its way slowly to the lake. Here and there high serpent heads projected out of the water, cutting swiftly through it with a little collar of foam in front, and a long swirling wake behind, rising and falling in graceful, swan-like undulations as they went. It was not until one of these creatures wriggled on to a sand-bank within a few hundred yards of us, and exposed a barrel-shaped body and huge flippers behind the long serpent neck, that Challenger, and Summerlee, who had joined us, broke out into their duet of wonder and admiration.

"Plesiosaurus! A fresh-water plesiosaurus!" cried Summerlee. "That I should have lived to see such a sight! We are blessed, my dear Challenger, above all zoologists since the world began!"

It was not until the night had fallen, and the fires of our savage allies glowed red in the shadows, that our two men of science could be dragged away from the fascinations of that primeval lake. Even in the darkness as we lay upon the strand, we heard from time to time the snort and plunge of the huge creatures who lived therein.

At earliest dawn our camp was astir and an hour later we had started upon our memorable expedition. Often in my dreams have I thought that I might live to be a war correspondent. In what wildest one could I have conceived the nature of the campaign which it should be my lot to report! Here then is my first despatch from a field of battle:

Our numbers had been reinforced during the night by a fresh batch of natives from the caves, and we may have been four or five hundred strong when we made our advance. A fringe of scouts was thrown out in front, and behind them the whole force in a solid column made their way up the long slope of the bush country until we were near the edge of the forest. Here they spread out into a long straggling line of spearmen and bowmen. Roxton and Summerlee took their position upon the right flank, while Challenger and I were on the left. It was a host of the stone age that we were accompanying to battle—we with the last word of the gunsmith's art from St. James' Street and the Strand.

We had not long to wait for our enemy. A wild shrill clamor rose from the edge of the wood and suddenly a body of ape-men rushed out with clubs and stones, and made for the center of the Indian line. It was a valiant move but a foolish one, for the great bandy-legged creatures were slow of foot, while their opponents were as active as cats. It was horrible to see the fierce brutes with foaming mouths and glaring eyes, rushing and grasping, but forever missing their elusive enemies, while arrow after arrow buried itself in their hides. One great fellow ran past me roaring with pain, with a dozen darts sticking from his chest and ribs. In mercy I put a bullet through his skull, and he fell sprawling among the aloes. But this was the only shot fired, for the attack had been on the center of the line, and the Indians there had needed no help of ours in repulsing it. Of all the ape-men who had rushed out into the open, I do not think that one got back to cover.

But the matter was more deadly when we came among the trees. For an hour or more after we entered the wood, there was a desperate struggle in which for a time we hardly held our own. Springing out from among the scrub the ape-men with huge clubs broke in upon the Indians and often felled three or four of them before they could be speared. Their frightful blows shattered everything upon which they fell. One of them knocked Summerlee's rifle to matchwood and the next would have crushed his skull had an Indian not stabbed the beast to the heart. Other ape-men in the trees above us hurled down stones and logs of wood, occasionally dropping bodily on to our ranks and fighting furiously until they were felled. Once our allies broke under the pressure, and had it not been for the execution done by our rifles they would certainly have taken to their heels. But they were gallantly rallied by their old chief and came on with such a rush that the ape-men began in turn to give way. Summerlee was weaponless, but I was emptying my magazine as quick as I could fire, and on the further flank we heard the continuous cracking of our companion's rifles.

Then in a moment came the panic and the collapse. Screaming and howling, the great creatures rushed away in all directions through the brushwood, while our allies yelled in their savage delight, following swiftly after their flying enemies. All the feuds of countless generations, all the hatreds and cruelties of their narrow history, all the memories of ill-usage and persecution were to be purged that day. At last man was to be supreme and the man-beast to find forever his allotted place. Fly as they would the fugitives were too slow to escape from the active savages, and from every side in the tangled woods we heard the exultant yells, the twanging of bows, and the crash and thud as ape-men were brought down from their hiding-places in the trees.

I was following the others, when I found that Lord John and Challenger had come across to join us.

"It's over," said Lord John. "I think we can leave the tidying up to them. Perhaps the less we see of it the better we shall sleep."

Challenger's eyes were shining with the lust of slaughter.

"We have been privileged," he cried, strutting about like a gamecock, "to be present at one of the typical decisive battles of history—the battles which have determined the fate of the world. What, my friends, is the conquest of one nation by another? It is meaningless. Each produces the same result. But those fierce fights, when in the dawn of the ages the cave-dwellers held their own against the tiger folk, or the elephants first found that they had a master, those were the real conquests—the victories that count. By this strange turn of fate we have seen and helped to decide even such a contest. Now upon this plateau the future must ever be for man."

It needed a robust faith in the end to justify such tragic means. As we advanced together through the woods we found the ape-men lying thick, transfixed with spears or arrows. Here and there a little group of shattered Indians marked where one of the anthropoids had turned to bay, and sold his life dearly. Always in front of us we heard the yelling and roaring which showed the direction of the pursuit. The ape-men had been driven back to their city, they had made a last stand there, once again they had been broken, and now we were in time to see the final fearful scene of all. Some eighty or a hundred males, the last survivors, had been driven across that same little clearing which led to the edge of the cliff, the scene of our own exploit two days before. As we arrived the Indians, a semicircle of spearmen, had closed in on them, and in a minute it was over, Thirty or forty died where they stood. The others, screaming and clawing, were thrust over the precipice, and went hurtling down, as their prisoners had of old, on to the sharp bamboos six hundred feet below. It was as Challenger had said, and the reign of man was assured forever in Maple White Land. The males were exterminated, Ape Town was destroyed, the females and young were driven away to live in bondage, and the long rivalry of untold centuries had reached its bloody end.

For us the victory brought much advantage. Once again we were able to visit our camp and get at our stores. Once more also we were able to communicate with Zambo, who had been terrified by the spectacle from afar of an avalanche of apes falling from the edge of the cliff.

"Come away, Massas, come away!" he cried, his eyes starting from his head. "The debbil get you sure if you stay up there."

"It is the voice of sanity!" said Summerlee with conviction. "We have had adventures enough and they are neither suitable to our character or our position. I hold you to your word, Challenger. From now onwards you devote your energies to getting us out of this horrible country and back once more to civilization."

Chapter XV   "Our Eyes have seen Great Wonders"

I write this from day to day, but I trust that before I come to the end of it, I may be able to say that the light shines, at last, through our clouds. We are held here with no clear means of making our escape, and bitterly we chafe against it. Yet, I can well imagine that the day may come when we may be glad that we were kept, against our will, to see something more of the wonders of this singular place, and of the creatures who inhabit it.

The victory of the Indians and the annihilation of the ape-men, marked the turning point of our fortunes. From then onwards, we were in truth masters of the plateau, for the natives looked upon us with a mixture of fear and gratitude, since by our strange powers we had aided them to destroy their hereditary foe. For their own sakes they would, perhaps, be glad to see the departure of such formidable and incalculable people, but they have not themselves suggested any way by which we may reach the plains below. There had been, so far as we could follow their signs, a tunnel by which the place could be approached, the lower exit of which we had seen from below. By this, no doubt, both ape-men and Indians had at different epochs reached the top, and Maple White with his companion had taken the same way. Only the year before, however, there had been a terrific earthquake, and the upper end of the tunnel had fallen in and completely disappeared. The Indians now could only shake their heads and shrug their shoulders when we expressed by signs our desire to descend. It may be that they cannot, but it may also be that they will not, help us to get away.

At the end of the victorious campaign the surviving ape-folk were driven across the plateau (their wailings were horrible) and established in the neighborhood of the Indian caves, where they would, from now onwards, be a servile race under the eyes of their masters. It was a rude, raw, primeval version of the Jews in Babylon or the Israelites in Egypt. At night we could hear from amid the trees the long-drawn cry, as some primitive Ezekiel mourned for fallen greatness and recalled the departed glories of Ape Town. Hewers of wood and drawers of water, such were they from now onwards.

We had returned across the plateau with our allies two days after the battle, and made our camp at the foot of their cliffs. They would have had us share their caves with them, but Lord John would by no means consent to it considering that to do so would put us in their power if they were treacherously disposed. We kept our independence, therefore, and had our weapons ready for any emergency, while preserving the most friendly relations. We also continually visited their caves, which were most remarkable places, though whether made by man or by Nature we have never been able to determine. They were all on the one stratum, hollowed out of some soft rock which lay between the volcanic basalt forming the ruddy cliffs above them, and the hard granite which formed their base.

The openings were about eighty feet above the ground, and were led up to by long stone stairs, so narrow and steep that no large animal could mount them. Inside they were warm and dry, running in straight passages of varying length into the side of the hill, with smooth gray walls decorated with many excellent pictures done with charred sticks and representing the various animals of the plateau. If every living thing were swept from the country the future explorer would find upon the walls of these caves ample evidence of the strange fauna—the dinosaurs, iguanodons, and fish lizards—which had lived so recently upon earth.

Since we had learned that the huge iguanodons were kept as tame herds by their owners, and were simply walking meat-stores, we had conceived that man, even with his primitive weapons, had established his ascendancy upon the plateau. We were soon to discover that it was not so, and that he was still there upon tolerance.

It was on the third day after our forming our camp near the Indian caves that the tragedy occurred. Challenger and Summerlee had gone off together that day to the lake where some of the natives, under their direction, were engaged in harpooning specimens of the great lizards. Lord John and I had remained in our camp, while a number of the Indians were scattered about upon the grassy slope in front of the caves engaged in different ways. Suddenly there was a shrill cry of alarm, with the word "Stoa" resounding from a hundred tongues. From every side men, women, and children were rushing wildly for shelter, swarming up the staircases and into the caves in a mad stampede.

Looking up, we could see them waving their arms from the rocks above and beckoning to us to join them in their refuge. We had both seized our magazine rifles and ran out to see what the danger could be. Suddenly from the near belt of trees there broke forth a group of twelve or fifteen Indians, running for their lives, and at their very heels two of those frightful monsters which had disturbed our camp and pursued me upon my solitary journey. In shape they were like horrible toads, and moved in a succession of springs, but in size they were of an incredible bulk, larger than the largest elephant. We had never before seen them save at night, and indeed they are nocturnal animals save when disturbed in their lairs, as these had been. We now stood amazed at the sight, for their blotched and warty skins were of a curious fish-like iridescence, and the sunlight struck them with an ever-varying rainbow bloom as they moved.

We had little time to watch them, however, for in an instant they had overtaken the fugitives and were making a dire slaughter among them. Their method was to fall forward with their full weight upon each in turn, leaving him crushed and mangled, to bound on after the others. The wretched Indians screamed with terror, but were helpless, run as they would, before the relentless purpose and horrible activity of these monstrous creatures. One after another they went down, and there were not half-a-dozen surviving by the time my companion and I could come to their help. But our aid was of little avail and only involved us in the same peril. At the range of a couple of hundred yards we emptied our magazines, firing bullet after bullet into the beasts, but with no more effect than if we were pelting them with pellets of paper. Their slow reptilian natures cared nothing for wounds, and the springs of their lives, with no special brain center but scattered throughout their spinal cords, could not be tapped by any modern weapons. The most that we could do was to check their progress by distracting their attention with the flash and roar of our guns, and so to give both the natives and ourselves time to reach the steps which led to safety. But where the conical explosive bullets of the twentieth century were of no avail, the poisoned arrows of the natives, dipped in the juice of strophanthus and steeped afterwards in decayed carrion, could succeed. Such arrows were of little avail to the hunter who attacked the beast, because their action in that torpid circulation was slow, and before its powers failed it could certainly overtake and slay its assailant. But now, as the two monsters hounded us to the very foot of the stairs, a drift of darts came whistling from every chink in the cliff above them. In a minute they were feathered with them, and yet with no sign of pain they clawed and slobbered with impotent rage at the steps which would lead them to their victims, mounting clumsily up for a few yards and then sliding down again to the ground. But at last the poison worked. One of them gave a deep rumbling groan and dropped his huge squat head on to the earth. The other bounded round in an eccentric circle with shrill, wailing cries, and then lying down writhed in agony for some minutes before it also stiffened and lay still. With yells of triumph the Indians came flocking down from their caves and danced a frenzied dance of victory round the dead bodies, in mad joy that two more of the most dangerous of all their enemies had been slain. That night they cut up and removed the bodies, not to eat—for the poison was still active—but lest they should breed a pestilence. The great reptilian hearts, however, each as large as a cushion, still lay there, beating slowly and steadily, with a gentle rise and fall, in horrible independent life. It was only upon the third day that the ganglia ran down and the dreadful things were still.

Some day, when I have a better desk than a meat-tin and more helpful tools than a worn stub of pencil and a last, tattered note-book, I will write some fuller account of the Accala Indians—of our life amongst them, and of the glimpses which we had of the strange conditions of wondrous Maple White Land. Memory, at least, will never fail me, for so long as the breath of life is in me, every hour and every action of that period will stand out as hard and clear as do the first strange happenings of our childhood. No new impressions could efface those which are so deeply cut. When the time comes I will describe that wondrous moonlit night upon the great lake when a young ichthyosaurus—a strange creature, half seal, half fish, to look at, with bone-covered eyes on each side of his snout, and a third eye fixed upon the top of his head—was entangled in an Indian net, and nearly upset our canoe before we towed it ashore; the same night that a green water-snake shot out from the rushes and carried off in its coils the steersman of Challenger's canoe. I will tell, too, of the great nocturnal white thing—to this day we do not know whether it was beast or reptile—which lived in a vile swamp to the east of the lake, and flitted about with a faint phosphorescent glimmer in the darkness. The Indians were so terrified at it that they would not go near the place, and, though we twice made expeditions and saw it each time, we could not make our way through the deep marsh in which it lived. I can only say that it seemed to be larger than a cow and had the strangest musky odor. I will tell also of the huge bird which chased Challenger to the shelter of the rocks one day—a great running bird, far taller than an ostrich, with a vulture-like neck and cruel head which made it a walking death. As Challenger climbed to safety one dart of that savage curving beak shore off the heel of his boot as if it had been cut with a chisel. This time at least modern weapons prevailed and the great creature, twelve feet from head to foot—phororachus its name, according to our panting but exultant Professor—went down before Lord Roxton's rifle in a flurry of waving feathers and kicking limbs, with two remorseless yellow eyes glaring up from the midst of it. May I live to see that flattened vicious skull in its own niche amid the trophies of the Albany. Finally, I will assuredly give some account of the toxodon, the giant ten-foot guinea pig, with projecting chisel teeth, which we killed as it drank in the gray of the morning by the side of the lake.

All this I shall some day write at fuller length, and amidst these more stirring days I would tenderly sketch in these lovely summer evenings, when with the deep blue sky above us we lay in good comradeship among the long grasses by the wood and marveled at the strange fowl that swept over us and the quaint new creatures which crept from their burrows to watch us, while above us the boughs of the bushes were heavy with luscious fruit, and below us strange and lovely flowers peeped at us from among the herbage; or those long moonlit nights when we lay out upon the shimmering surface of the great lake and watched with wonder and awe the huge circles rippling out from the sudden splash of some fantastic monster; or the greenish gleam, far down in the deep water, of some strange creature upon the confines of darkness. These are the scenes which my mind and my pen will dwell upon in every detail at some future day.

But, you will ask, why these experiences and why this delay, when you and your comrades should have been occupied day and night in the devising of some means by which you could return to the outer world? My answer is, that there was not one of us who was not working for this end, but that our work had been in vain. One fact we had very speedily discovered: The Indians would do nothing to help us. In every other way they were our friends—one might almost say our devoted slaves—but when it was suggested that they should help us to make and carry a plank which would bridge the chasm, or when we wished to get from them thongs of leather or liana to weave ropes which might help us, we were met by a good-humored, but an invincible, refusal. They would smile, twinkle their eyes, shake their heads, and there was the end of it. Even the old chief met us with the same obstinate denial, and it was only Maretas, the youngster whom we had saved, who looked wistfully at us and told us by his gestures that he was grieved for our thwarted wishes. Ever since their crowning triumph with the ape-men they looked upon us as supermen, who bore victory in the tubes of strange weapons, and they believed that so long as we remained with them good fortune would be theirs. A little red-skinned wife and a cave of our own were freely offered to each of us if we would but forget our own people and dwell forever upon the plateau. So far all had been kindly, however far apart our desires might be; but we felt well assured that our actual plans of a descent must be kept secret, for we had reason to fear that at the last they might try to hold us by force.

In spite of the danger from dinosaurs (which is not great save at night, for, as I may have said before, they are mostly nocturnal in their habits) I have twice in the last three weeks been over to our old camp in order to see our negro who still kept watch and ward below the cliff. My eyes strained eagerly across the great plain in the hope of seeing afar off the help for which we had prayed. But the long cactus-strewn levels still stretched away, empty and bare, to the distant line of the cane-brake.

"They will soon come now, Massa Malone. Before another week pass Indian come back and bring rope and fetch you down." Such was the cheery cry of our excellent Zambo.

I had one strange experience as I came from this second visit which had involved my being away for a night from my companions. I was returning along the well-remembered route, and had reached a spot within a mile or so of the marsh of the pterodactyls, when I saw an extraordinary object approaching me. It was a man who walked inside a framework made of bent canes so that he was enclosed on all sides in a bell-shaped cage. As I drew nearer I was more amazed still to see that it was Lord John Roxton. When he saw me he slipped from under his curious protection and came towards me laughing, and yet, as I thought, with some confusion in his manner.

"Well, young fellah," said he, "who would have thought of meetin' you up here?"

"What in the world are you doing?" I asked.

"Visitin' my friends, the pterodactyls," said he.

"But why?"

"Interestin' beasts, don't you think? But unsociable! Nasty rude ways with strangers, as you may remember. So I rigged this framework which keeps them from bein' too pressin' in their attentions."

"But what do you want in the swamp?"

He looked at me with a very questioning eye, and I read hesitation in his face.

"Don't you think other people besides Professors can want to know things?" he said at last. "I'm studyin' the pretty dears. That's enough for you."

"No offense," said I.

His good-humor returned and he laughed.

"No offense, young fellah. I'm goin' to get a young devil chick for Challenger. That's one of my jobs. No, I don't want your company. I'm safe in this cage, and you are not. So long, and I'll be back in camp by night-fall."

He turned away and I left him wandering on through the wood with his extraordinary cage around him.

If Lord John's behavior at this time was strange, that of Challenger was more so. I may say that he seemed to possess an extraordinary fascination for the Indian women, and that he always carried a large spreading palm branch with which he beat them off as if they were flies, when their attentions became too pressing. To see him walking like a comic opera Sultan, with this badge of authority in his hand, his black beard bristling in front of him, his toes pointing at each step, and a train of wide-eyed Indian girls behind him, clad in their slender drapery of bark cloth, is one of the most grotesque of all the pictures which I will carry back with me. As to Summerlee, he was absorbed in the insect and bird life of the plateau, and spent his whole time (save that considerable portion which was devoted to abusing Challenger for not getting us out of our difficulties) in cleaning and mounting his specimens.

Challenger had been in the habit of walking off by himself every morning and returning from time to time with looks of portentous solemnity, as one who bears the full weight of a great enterprise upon his shoulders. One day, palm branch in hand, and his crowd of adoring devotees behind him, he led us down to his hidden work-shop and took us into the secret of his plans.

The place was a small clearing in the center of a palm grove. In this was one of those boiling mud geysers which I have already described. Around its edge were scattered a number of leathern thongs cut from iguanodon hide, and a large collapsed membrane which proved to be the dried and scraped stomach of one of the great fish lizards from the lake. This huge sack had been sewn up at one end and only a small orifice left at the other. Into this opening several bamboo canes had been inserted and the other ends of these canes were in contact with conical clay funnels which collected the gas bubbling up through the mud of the geyser. Soon the flaccid organ began to slowly expand and show such a tendency to upward movements that Challenger fastened the cords which held it to the trunks of the surrounding trees. In half an hour a good-sized gas-bag had been formed, and the jerking and straining upon the thongs showed that it was capable of considerable lift. Challenger, like a glad father in the presence of his first-born, stood smiling and stroking his beard, in silent, self-satisfied content as he gazed at the creation of his brain. It was Summerlee who first broke the silence.

"You don't mean us to go up in that thing, Challenger?" said he, in an acid voice.

"I mean, my dear Summerlee, to give you such a demonstration of its powers that after seeing it you will, I am sure, have no hesitation in trusting yourself to it."

"You can put it right out of your head now, at once," said Summerlee with decision, "nothing on earth would induce me to commit such a folly. Lord John, I trust that you will not countenance such madness?"

"Dooced ingenious, I call it," said our peer. "I'd like to see how it works."

"So you shall," said Challenger. "For some days I have exerted my whole brain force upon the problem of how we shall descend from these cliffs. We have satisfied ourselves that we cannot climb down and that there is no tunnel. We are also unable to construct any kind of bridge which may take us back to the pinnacle from which we came. How then shall I find a means to convey us? Some little time ago I had remarked to our young friend here that free hydrogen was evolved from the geyser. The idea of a balloon naturally followed. I was, I will admit, somewhat baffled by the difficulty of discovering an envelope to contain the gas, but the contemplation of the immense entrails of these reptiles supplied me with a solution to the problem. Behold the result!"

He put one hand in the front of his ragged jacket and pointed proudly with the other.

By this time the gas-bag had swollen to a goodly rotundity and was jerking strongly upon its lashings.

"Midsummer madness!" snorted Summerlee.

Lord John was delighted with the whole idea. "Clever old dear, ain't he?" he whispered to me, and then louder to Challenger. "What about a car?"

"The car will be my next care. I have already planned how it is to be made and attached. Meanwhile I will simply show you how capable my apparatus is of supporting the weight of each of us."

"All of us, surely?"

"No, it is part of my plan that each in turn shall descend as in a parachute, and the balloon be drawn back by means which I shall have no difficulty in perfecting. If it will support the weight of one and let him gently down, it will have done all that is required of it. I will now show you its capacity in that direction."

He brought out a lump of basalt of a considerable size, constructed in the middle so that a cord could be easily attached to it. This cord was the one which we had brought with us on to the plateau after we had used it for climbing the pinnacle. It was over a hundred feet long, and though it was thin it was very strong. He had prepared a sort of collar of leather with many straps depending from it. This collar was placed over the dome of the balloon, and the hanging thongs were gathered together below, so that the pressure of any weight would be diffused over a considerable surface. Then the lump of basalt was fastened to the thongs, and the rope was allowed to hang from the end of it, being passed three times round the Professor's arm.

"I will now," said Challenger, with a smile of pleased anticipation, "demonstrate the carrying power of my balloon." As he said so he cut with a knife the various lashings that held it.

Never was our expedition in more imminent danger of complete annihilation. The inflated membrane shot up with frightful velocity into the air. In an instant Challenger was pulled off his feet and dragged after it. I had just time to throw my arms round his ascending waist when I was myself whipped up into the air. Lord John had me with a rat-trap grip round the legs, but I felt that he also was coming off the ground. For a moment I had a vision of four adventurers floating like a string of sausages over the land that they had explored. But, happily, there were limits to the strain which the rope would stand, though none apparently to the lifting powers of this infernal machine. There was a sharp crack, and we were in a heap upon the ground with coils of rope all over us. When we were able to stagger to our feet we saw far off in the deep blue sky one dark spot where the lump of basalt was speeding upon its way.

"Splendid!" cried the undaunted Challenger, rubbing his injured arm. "A most thorough and satisfactory demonstration! I could not have anticipated such a success. Within a week, gentlemen, I promise that a second balloon will be prepared, and that you can count upon taking in safety and comfort the first stage of our homeward journey." So far I have written each of the foregoing events as it occurred. Now I am rounding off my narrative from the old camp, where Zambo has waited so long, with all our difficulties and dangers left like a dream behind us upon the summit of those vast ruddy crags which tower above our heads. We have descended in safety, though in a most unexpected fashion, and all is well with us. In six weeks or two months we shall be in London, and it is possible that this letter may not reach you much earlier than we do ourselves. Already our hearts yearn and our spirits fly towards the great mother city which holds so much that is dear to us.

It was on the very evening of our perilous adventure with Challenger's home-made balloon that the change came in our fortunes. I have said that the one person from whom we had had some sign of sympathy in our attempts to get away was the young chief whom we had rescued. He alone had no desire to hold us against our will in a strange land. He had told us as much by his expressive language of signs. That evening, after dusk, he came down to our little camp, handed me (for some reason he had always shown his attentions to me, perhaps because I was the one who was nearest his age) a small roll of the bark of a tree, and then pointing solemnly up at the row of caves above him, he had put his finger to his lips as a sign of secrecy and had stolen back again to his people.

I took the slip of bark to the firelight and we examined it together. It was about a foot square, and on the inner side there was a singular arrangement of lines, which I here reproduce:

They were neatly done in charcoal upon the white surface, and looked to me at first sight like some sort of rough musical score.

"Whatever it is, I can swear that it is of importance to us," said I. "I could read that on his face as he gave it."

"Unless we have come upon a primitive practical joker," Summerlee suggested, "which I should think would be one of the most elementary developments of man."

"It is clearly some sort of script," said Challenger.

"Looks like a guinea puzzle competition," remarked Lord John, craning his neck to have a look at it. Then suddenly he stretched out his hand and seized the puzzle.

"By George!" he cried, "I believe I've got it. The boy guessed right the very first time. See here! How many marks are on that paper? Eighteen. Well, if you come to think of it there are eighteen cave openings on the hill-side above us."

"He pointed up to the caves when he gave it to me," said I.

"Well, that settles it. This is a chart of the caves. What! Eighteen of them all in a row, some short, some deep, some branching, same as we saw them. It's a map, and here's a cross on it. What's the cross for? It is placed to mark one that is much deeper than the others."

"One that goes through," I cried.

"I believe our young friend has read the riddle," said Challenger. "If the cave does not go through I do not understand why this person, who has every reason to mean us well, should have drawn our attention to it. But if it does go through and comes out at the corresponding point on the other side, we should not have more than a hundred feet to descend."

"A hundred feet!" grumbled Summerlee.

"Well, our rope is still more than a hundred feet long," I cried. "Surely we could get down."

"How about the Indians in the cave?" Summerlee objected.

"There are no Indians in any of the caves above our heads," said I. "They are all used as barns and store-houses. Why should we not go up now at once and spy out the land?"

There is a dry bituminous wood upon the plateau—a species of araucaria, according to our botanist—which is always used by the Indians for torches. Each of us picked up a faggot of this, and we made our way up weed-covered steps to the particular cave which was marked in the drawing. It was, as I had said, empty, save for a great number of enormous bats, which flapped round our heads as we advanced into it. As we had no desire to draw the attention of the Indians to our proceedings, we stumbled along in the dark until we had gone round several curves and penetrated a considerable distance into the cavern. Then, at last, we lit our torches. It was a beautiful dry tunnel with smooth gray walls covered with native symbols, a curved roof which arched over our heads, and white glistening sand beneath our feet. We hurried eagerly along it until, with a deep groan of bitter disappointment, we were brought to a halt. A sheer wall of rock had appeared before us, with no chink through which a mouse could have slipped. There was no escape for us there.

We stood with bitter hearts staring at this unexpected obstacle. It was not the result of any convulsion, as in the case of the ascending tunnel. The end wall was exactly like the side ones. It was, and had always been, a cul-de-sac.

"Never mind, my friends," said the indomitable Challenger. "You have still my firm promise of a balloon."

Summerlee groaned.

"Can we be in the wrong cave?" I suggested.

"No use, young fellah," said Lord John, with his finger on the chart. "Seventeen from the right and second from the left. This is the cave sure enough."

I looked at the mark to which his finger pointed, and I gave a sudden cry of joy.

"I believe I have it! Follow me! Follow me!"

I hurried back along the way we had come, my torch in my hand. "Here," said I, pointing to some matches upon the ground, "is where we lit up."

"Exactly."

"Well, it is marked as a forked cave, and in the darkness we passed the fork before the torches were lit. On the right side as we go out we should find the longer arm."

It was as I had said. We had not gone thirty yards before a great black opening loomed in the wall. We turned into it to find that we were in a much larger passage than before. Along it we hurried in breathless impatience for many hundreds of yards. Then, suddenly, in the black darkness of the arch in front of us we saw a gleam of dark red light. We stared in amazement. A sheet of steady flame seemed to cross the passage and to bar our way. We hastened towards it. No sound, no heat, no movement came from it, but still the great luminous curtain glowed before us, silvering all the cave and turning the sand to powdered jewels, until as we drew closer it discovered a circular edge.

"The moon, by George!" cried Lord John. "We are through, boys! We are through!"

It was indeed the full moon which shone straight down the aperture which opened upon the cliffs. It was a small rift, not larger than a window, but it was enough for all our purposes. As we craned our necks through it we could see that the descent was not a very difficult one, and that the level ground was no very great way below us. It was no wonder that from below we had not observed the place, as the cliffs curved overhead and an ascent at the spot would have seemed so impossible as to discourage close inspection. We satisfied ourselves that with the help of our rope we could find our way down, and then returned, rejoicing, to our camp to make our preparations for the next evening.

What we did we had to do quickly and secretly, since even at this last hour the Indians might hold us back. Our stores we would leave behind us, save only our guns and cartridges. But Challenger had some unwieldy stuff which he ardently desired to take with him, and one particular package, of which I may not speak, which gave us more labor than any. Slowly the day passed, but when the darkness fell we were ready for our departure. With much labor we got our things up the steps, and then, looking back, took one last long survey of that strange land, soon I fear to be vulgarized, the prey of hunter and prospector, but to each of us a dreamland of glamour and romance, a land where we had dared much, suffered much, and learned much—OUR land, as we shall ever fondly call it. Along upon our left the neighboring caves each threw out its ruddy cheery firelight into the gloom. From the slope below us rose the voices of the Indians as they laughed and sang. Beyond was the long sweep of the woods, and in the center, shimmering vaguely through the gloom, was the great lake, the mother of strange monsters. Even as we looked a high whickering cry, the call of some weird animal, rang clear out of the darkness. It was the very voice of Maple White Land bidding us good-bye. We turned and plunged into the cave which led to home.

Two hours later, we, our packages, and all we owned, were at the foot of the cliff. Save for Challenger's luggage we had never a difficulty. Leaving it all where we descended, we started at once for Zambo's camp. In the early morning we approached it, but only to find, to our amazement, not one fire but a dozen upon the plain. The rescue party had arrived. There were twenty Indians from the river, with stakes, ropes, and all that could be useful for bridging the chasm. At least we shall have no difficulty now in carrying our packages, when to-morrow we begin to make our way back to the Amazon.

And so, in humble and thankful mood, I close this account. Our eyes have seen great wonders and our souls are chastened by what we have endured. Each is in his own way a better and deeper man. It may be that when we reach Para we shall stop to refit. If we do, this letter will be a mail ahead. If not, it will reach London on the very day that I do. In either case, my dear Mr. McArdle, I hope very soon to shake you by the hand.

Chapter XVI   "A Procession! A Procession!"

I should wish to place upon record here our gratitude to all our friends upon the Amazon for the very great kindness and hospitality which was shown to us upon our return journey. Very particularly would I thank Senhor Penalosa and other officials of the

Brazilian Government for the special arrangements by which we were helped upon our way, and Senhor Pereira of Para, to whose forethought we owe the complete outfit for a decent appearance in the civilized world which we found ready for us at that town. It seemed a poor return for all the courtesy which we encountered that we should deceive our hosts and benefactors, but under the circumstances we had really no alternative, and I hereby tell them that they will only waste their time and their money if they attempt to follow upon our traces. Even the names have been altered in our accounts, and I am very sure that no one, from the most careful study of them, could come within a thousand miles of our unknown land.

The excitement which had been caused through those parts of South America which we had to traverse was imagined by us to be purely local, and I can assure our friends in England that we had no notion of the uproar which the mere rumor of our experiences had caused through Europe. It was not until the Ivernia was within five hundred miles of Southampton that the wireless messages from paper after paper and agency after agency, offering huge prices for a short return message as to our actual results, showed us how strained was the attention not only of the scientific world but of the general public. It was agreed among us, however, that no definite statement should be given to the Press until we had met the members of the Zoological Institute, since as delegates it was our clear duty to give our first report to the body from which we had received our commission of investigation. Thus, although we found Southampton full of Pressmen, we absolutely refused to give any information, which had the natural effect of focussing public attention upon the meeting which was advertised for the evening of November 7th. For this gathering, the Zoological Hall which had been the scene of the inception of our task was found to be far too small, and it was only in the Queen's Hall in Regent Street that accommodation could be found. It is now common knowledge the promoters might have ventured upon the Albert Hall and still found their space too scanty.

It was for the second evening after our arrival that the great meeting had been fixed. For the first, we had each, no doubt, our own pressing personal affairs to absorb us. Of mine I cannot yet speak. It may be that as it stands further from me I may think of it, and even speak of it, with less emotion. I have shown the reader in the beginning of this narrative where lay the springs of my action. It is but right, perhaps, that I should carry on the tale and show also the results. And yet the day may come when I would not have it otherwise. At least I have been driven forth to take part in a wondrous adventure, and I cannot but be thankful to the force that drove me.

And now I turn to the last supreme eventful moment of our adventure. As I was racking my brain as to how I should best describe it, my eyes fell upon the issue of my own Journal for the morning of the 8th of November with the full and excellent account of my friend and fellow-reporter Macdona. What can I do better than transcribe his narrative—head-lines and all? I admit that the paper was exuberant in the matter, out of compliment to its own enterprise in sending a correspondent, but the other great dailies were hardly less full in their account. Thus, then, friend Mac in his report:

THE NEW WORLD GREAT MEETING
AT THE QUEEN'S HALL
SCENES OF UPROAR
EXTRAORDINARY INCIDENT WHAT WAS IT?
NOCTURNAL RIOT IN REGENT STREET
(Special)

"The much-discussed meeting of the Zoological Institute, convened to hear the report of the Committee of Investigation sent out last year to South America to test the assertions made by Professor Challenger as to the continued existence of prehistoric life upon that Continent, was held last night in the greater Queen's Hall, and it is safe to say that it is likely to be a red letter date in the history of Science, for the proceedings were of so remarkable and sensational a character that no one present is ever likely to forget them." (Oh, brother scribe Macdona, what a monstrous opening sentence!) "The tickets were theoretically confined to members and their friends, but the latter is an elastic term, and long before eight o'clock, the hour fixed for the commencement of the proceedings, all parts of the Great Hall were tightly packed. The general public, however, which most unreasonably entertained a grievance at having been excluded, stormed the doors at a quarter to eight, after a prolonged melee in which several people were injured, including Inspector Scoble of H. Division, whose leg was unfortunately broken. After this unwarrantable invasion, which not only filled every passage, but even intruded upon the space set apart for the Press, it is estimated that nearly five thousand people awaited the arrival of the travelers. When they eventually appeared, they took their places in the front of a platform which already contained all the leading scientific men, not only of this country, but of France and of Germany. Sweden was also represented, in the person of Professor Sergius, the famous Zoologist of the University of Upsala. The entrance of the four heroes of the occasion was the signal for a remarkable demonstration of welcome, the whole audience rising and cheering for some minutes. An acute observer might, however, have detected some signs of dissent amid the applause, and gathered that the proceedings were likely to become more lively than harmonious. It may safely be prophesied, however, that no one could have foreseen the extraordinary turn which they were actually to take.

"Of the appearance of the four wanderers little need be said, since their photographs have for some time been appearing in all the papers. They bear few traces of the hardships which they are said to have undergone. Professor Challenger's beard may be more shaggy, Professor Summerlee's features more ascetic, Lord John Roxton's figure more gaunt, and all three may be burned to a darker tint than when they left our shores, but each appeared to be in most excellent health. As to our own representative, the well-known athlete and international Rugby football player, E. D. Malone, he looks trained to a hair, and as he surveyed the crowd a smile of good-humored contentment pervaded his honest but homely face." (All right, Mac, wait till I get you alone!)

"When quiet had been restored and the audience resumed their seats after the ovation which they had given to the travelers, the chairman, the Duke of Durham, addressed the meeting. 'He would not,' he said, 'stand for more than a moment between that vast assembly and the treat which lay before them. It was not for him to anticipate what Professor Summerlee, who was the spokesman of the committee, had to say to them, but it was common rumor that their expedition had been crowned by extraordinary success.' (Applause.) 'Apparently the age of romance was not dead, and there was common ground upon which the wildest imaginings of the novelist could meet the actual scientific investigations of the searcher for truth. He would only add, before he sat down, that he rejoiced—and all of them would rejoice—that these gentlemen had returned safe and sound from their difficult and dangerous task, for it cannot be denied that any disaster to such an expedition would have inflicted a well-nigh irreparable loss to the cause of Zoological science.' (Great applause, in which Professor Challenger was observed to join.)

"Professor Summerlee's rising was the signal for another extraordinary outbreak of enthusiasm, which broke out again at intervals throughout his address. That address will not be given in extenso in these columns, for the reason that a full account of the whole adventures of the expedition is being published as a supplement from the pen of our own special correspondent. Some general indications will therefore suffice. Having described the genesis of their journey, and paid a handsome tribute to his friend Professor Challenger, coupled with an apology for the incredulity with which his assertions, now fully vindicated, had been received, he gave the actual course of their journey, carefully withholding such information as would aid the public in any attempt to locate this remarkable plateau. Having described, in general terms, their course from the main river up to the time that they actually reached the base of the cliffs, he enthralled his hearers by his account of the difficulties encountered by the expedition in their repeated attempts to mount them, and finally described how they succeeded in their desperate endeavors, which cost the lives of their two devoted half-breed servants." (This amazing reading of the affair was the result of Summerlee's endeavors to avoid raising any questionable matter at the meeting.)

"Having conducted his audience in fancy to the summit, and marooned them there by reason of the fall of their bridge, the Professor proceeded to describe both the horrors and the attractions of that remarkable land. Of personal adventures he said little, but

laid stress upon the rich harvest reaped by Science in the observations of the wonderful beast, bird, insect, and plant life of the
plateau. Peculiarly rich in the coleoptera and in the lepidoptera,
forty-six new species of the one and ninety-four of the other had
been secured in the course of a few weeks. It was, however, in the
larger animals, and especially in the larger animals supposed to
have been long extinct, that the interest of the public was naturally
centered. Of these he was able to give a goodly list, but had little
doubt that it would be largely extended when the place had been
more thoroughly investigated. He and his companions had seen at
least a dozen creatures, most of them at a distance, which corresponded with nothing at present known to Science. These would
in time be duly classified and examined. He instanced a snake, the
cast skin of which, deep purple in color, was fifty-one feet in
length, and mentioned a white creature, supposed to be mammalian, which gave forth well-marked phosphorescence in the
darkness; also a large black moth, the bite of which was supposed
by the Indians to be highly poisonous. Setting aside these entirely
new forms of life, the plateau was very rich in known prehistoric
forms, dating back in some cases to early Jurassic times. Among
these he mentioned the gigantic and grotesque stegosaurus, seen
once by Mr. Malone at a drinking-place by the lake, and drawn in
the sketch-book of that adventurous American who had first penetrated this unknown world. He described also the iguanodon and
the pterodactyl—two of the first of the wonders which they had
encountered. He then thrilled the assembly by some account of
the terrible carnivorous dinosaurs, which had on more than one
occasion pursued members of the party, and which were the most
formidable of all the creatures which they had encountered.
Thence he passed to the huge and ferocious bird, the phororachus,
and to the great elk which still roams upon this upland. It was not,
however, until he sketched the mysteries of the central lake that
the full interest and enthusiasm of the audience were aroused.
One had to pinch oneself to be sure that one was awake as one
heard this sane and practical Professor in cold measured tones
describing the monstrous three-eyed fish-lizards and the huge
water-snakes which inhabit this enchanted sheet of water. Next he
touched upon the Indians, and upon the extraordinary colony of

anthropoid apes, which might be looked upon as an advance upon the pithecanthropus of Java, and as coming therefore nearer than any known form to that hypothetical creation, the missing link. Finally he described, amongst some merriment, the ingenious but highly dangerous aeronautic invention of Professor Challenger, and wound up a most memorable address by an account of the methods by which the committee did at last find their way back to civilization.

"It had been hoped that the proceedings would end there, and that a vote of thanks and congratulation, moved by Professor Sergius, of Upsala University, would be duly seconded and carried; but it was soon evident that the course of events was not destined to flow so smoothly. Symptoms of opposition had been evident from time to time during the evening, and now Dr. James Illingworth, of Edinburgh, rose in the center of the hall. Dr. Illingworth asked whether an amendment should not be taken before a resolution.

"THE CHAIRMAN: 'Yes, sir, if there must be an amendment.'

"DR. ILLINGWORTH: 'Your Grace, there must be an amendment.'

"THE CHAIRMAN: 'Then let us take it at once.'

"PROFESSOR SUMMERLEE (springing to his feet): 'Might I explain, your Grace, that this man is my personal enemy ever since our controversy in the Quarterly Journal of Science as to the true nature of Bathybius?'

"THE CHAIRMAN: 'I fear I cannot go into personal matters. Proceed.'

"Dr. Illingworth was imperfectly heard in part of his remarks on account of the strenuous opposition of the friends of the explorers. Some attempts were also made to pull him down. Being a man of enormous physique, however, and possessed of a very powerful voice, he dominated the tumult and succeeded in finishing his speech. It was clear, from the moment of his rising, that he had a number of friends and sympathizers in the hall, though they formed a minority in the audience. The attitude of the greater part of the public might be described as one of attentive neutrality.

"Dr. Illingworth began his remarks by expressing his high appreciation of the scientific work both of Professor Challenger and of Professor Summerlee. He much regretted that any personal bias should have been read into his remarks, which were entirely dictated by his desire for scientific truth. His position, in fact, was substantially the same as that taken up by Professor Summerlee at the last meeting. At that last meeting Professor Challenger had made certain assertions which had been queried by his colleague. Now this colleague came forward himself with the same assertions and expected them to remain unquestioned. Was this reasonable? ('Yes,' 'No,' and prolonged interruption, during which Professor Challenger was heard from the Press box to ask leave from the chairman to put Dr. Illingworth into the street.) A year ago one man said certain things. Now four men said other and more startling ones. Was this to constitute a final proof where the matters in question were of the most revolutionary and incredible character? There had been recent examples of travelers arriving from the unknown with certain tales which had been too readily accepted. Was the London Zoological Institute to place itself in this position? He admitted that the members of the committee were men of character. But human nature was very complex. Even Professors might be misled by the desire for notoriety. Like moths, we all love best to flutter in the light. Heavy-game shots liked to be in a position to cap the tales of their rivals, and journalists were not averse from sensational coups, even when imagination had to aid fact in the process. Each member of the committee had his own motive for making the most of his results. ('Shame! shame!') He had no desire to be offensive. ('You are!' and interruption.) The corroboration of these wondrous tales was really of the most slender description. What did it amount to? Some photographs. {Was it possible that in this age of ingenious manipulation photographs could be accepted as evidence?} What more? We have a story of a flight and a descent by ropes which precluded the production of larger specimens. It was ingenious, but not convincing. It was understood that Lord John Roxton claimed to have the skull of a phororachus. He could only say that he would like to see that skull.

     "LORD JOHN ROXTON: 'Is this fellow calling me a liar?' (Uproar.)

"THE CHAIRMAN: 'Order! order! Dr. Illingworth, I must direct you to bring your remarks to a conclusion and to move your amendment.'

"DR. ILLINGWORTH: 'Your Grace, I have more to say, but I bow to your ruling. I move, then, that, while Professor Summerlee be thanked for his interesting address, the whole matter shall be regarded as 'non-proven,' and shall be referred back to a larger, and possibly more reliable Committee of Investigation.'

"It is difficult to describe the confusion caused by this amendment. A large section of the audience expressed their indignation at such a slur upon the travelers by noisy shouts of dissent and cries of, 'Don't put it!' 'Withdraw!' 'Turn him out!' On the other hand, the malcontents—and it cannot be denied that they were fairly numerous—cheered for the amendment, with cries of 'Order!' 'Chair!' and 'Fair play!' A scuffle broke out in the back benches, and blows were freely exchanged among the medical students who crowded that part of the hall. It was only the moderating influence of the presence of large numbers of ladies which prevented an absolute riot. Suddenly, however, there was a pause, a hush, and then complete silence. Professor Challenger was on his feet. His appearance and manner are peculiarly arresting, and as he raised his hand for order the whole audience settled down expectantly to give him a hearing.

"'It will be within the recollection of many present,' said Professor Challenger, 'that similar foolish and unmannerly scenes marked the last meeting at which I have been able to address them. On that occasion Professor Summerlee was the chief offender, and though he is now chastened and contrite, the matter could not be entirely forgotten. I have heard to-night similar, but even more offensive, sentiments from the person who has just sat down, and though it is a conscious effort of self-effacement to come down to that person's mental level, I will endeavor to do so, in order to allay any reasonable doubt which could possibly exist in the minds of anyone.' (Laughter and interruption.) 'I need not remind this audience that, though Professor Summerlee, as the head of the Committee of Investigation, has been put up to speak to-night, still it is I who am the real prime mover in this business, and that it is mainly to me that any successful result must be ascribed. I have safely conducted these three gentlemen to the spot mentioned, and I have, as you have heard, convinced them of the accuracy of my previous account. We had hoped that we should find upon our return that no one was so dense as to dispute our joint conclusions. Warned, however, by my previous experience, I have not come without such proofs as may convince a reasonable man. As explained by Professor Summerlee, our cameras have been tampered with by the ape-men when they ransacked our camp, and most of our negatives ruined.' (Jeers, laughter, and 'Tell us another!' from the back.) 'I have mentioned the ape-men, and I cannot forbear from saying that some of the sounds which now meet my ears bring back most vividly to my recollection my experiences with those interesting creatures.' (Laughter.) 'In spite of the destruction of so many invaluable negatives, there still remains in our collection a certain number of corroborative photographs showing the conditions of life upon the plateau. Did they accuse them of having forged these photographs?' (A voice, 'Yes,' and considerable interruption which ended in several men being put out of the hall.) 'The negatives were open to the inspection of experts. But what other evidence had they? Under the conditions of their escape it was naturally impossible to bring a large amount of baggage, but they had rescued Professor Summerlee's collections of butterflies and beetles, containing many new species. Was this not evidence?' (Several voices, 'No.') 'Who said no?'

"DR. ILLINGWORTH (rising): 'Our point is that such a collection might have been made in other places than a prehistoric plateau.' (Applause.)

"PROFESSOR CHALLENGER: 'No doubt, sir, we have to bow to your scientific authority, although I must admit that the name is unfamiliar. Passing, then, both the photographs and the entomological collection, I come to the varied and accurate information which we bring with us upon points which have never before been elucidated. For example, upon the domestic habits of the pterodactyl—'(A voice: 'Bosh,' and uproar)—'I say, that upon the domestic habits of the pterodactyl we can throw a flood of light. I can exhibit to you from my portfolio a picture of that creature taken from life which would convince you——'

"DR. ILLINGWORTH: 'No picture could convince us of anything.'

"PROFESSOR CHALLENGER: 'You would require to see the thing itself?'

"DR. ILLINGWORTH: 'Undoubtedly.'

"PROFESSOR CHALLENGER: 'And you would accept that?'

"DR. ILLINGWORTH (laughing): 'Beyond a doubt.'

"It was at this point that the sensation of the evening arose—a sensation so dramatic that it can never have been paralleled in the history of scientific gatherings. Professor Challenger raised his hand in the air as a signal, and at once our colleague, Mr. E. D. Malone, was observed to rise and to make his way to the back of the platform. An instant later he re-appeared in company of a gigantic negro, the two of them bearing between them a large square packing-case. It was evidently of great weight, and was slowly carried forward and placed in front of the Professor's chair. All sound had hushed in the audience and everyone was absorbed in the spectacle before them. Professor Challenger drew off the top of the case, which formed a sliding lid. Peering down into the box he snapped his fingers several times and was heard from the Press seat to say, 'Come, then, pretty, pretty!' in a coaxing voice. An instant later, with a scratching, rattling sound, a most horrible and loathsome creature appeared from below and perched itself upon the side of the case. Even the unexpected fall of the Duke of Durham into the orchestra, which occurred at this moment, could not distract the petrified attention of the vast audience. The face of the creature was like the wildest gargoyle that the imagination of a mad medieval builder could have conceived. It was malicious, horrible, with two small red eyes as bright as points of burning coal. Its long, savage mouth, which was held half-open, was full of a double row of shark-like teeth. Its shoulders were humped, and round them were draped what appeared to be a faded gray shawl. It was the devil of our childhood in person. There was a turmoil in the audience—someone screamed, two ladies in the front row fell senseless from their chairs, and there was a general movement upon the platform to follow their chairman into the orchestra. For a moment there was danger of a general panic. Professor Challenger threw up his hands to still the commotion, but the movement alarmed the creature beside him. Its strange shawl suddenly unfurled, spread, and fluttered as a pair of leathery wings. Its owner grabbed at its legs, but too late to hold it. It had sprung from the perch and was circling slowly round the Queen's Hall with a dry, leathery flapping of its ten-foot wings, while a putrid and insidious odor pervaded the room. The cries of the people in the galleries, who were alarmed at the near approach of those glowing eyes and that murderous beak, excited the creature to a frenzy. Faster and faster it flew, beating against walls and chandeliers in a blind frenzy of alarm. 'The window! For heaven's sake shut that window!' roared the Professor from the platform, dancing and wringing his hands in an agony of apprehension. Alas, his warning was too late! In a moment the creature, beating and bumping along the wall like a huge moth within a gas-shade, came upon the opening, squeezed its hideous bulk through it, and was gone. Professor Challenger fell back into his chair with his face buried in his hands, while the audience gave one long, deep sigh of relief as they realized that the incident was over.

"Then—oh! how shall one describe what took place then— when the full exuberance of the majority and the full reaction of the minority united to make one great wave of enthusiasm, which rolled from the back of the hall, gathering volume as it came, swept over the orchestra, submerged the platform, and carried the four heroes away upon its crest?" (Good for you, Mac!) "If the audience had done less than justice, surely it made ample amends. Every one was on his feet. Every one was moving, shouting, gesticulating. A dense crowd of cheering men were round the four travelers. 'Up with them! up with them!' cried a hundred voices. In a moment four figures shot up above the crowd. In vain they strove to break loose. They were held in their lofty places of honor. It would have been hard to let them down if it had been wished, so dense was the crowd around them. 'Regent Street! Regent Street!' sounded the voices. There was a swirl in the packed multitude, and a slow current, bearing the four upon their shoulders, made for the door. Out in the street the scene was extraordinary. An assemblage of not less than a hundred thousand people was waiting. The close-packed throng extended from the other side of the Langham Hotel to Oxford Circus. A roar of acclamation greeted the four adventurers as they appeared, high above the heads of the people, under the vivid electric lamps outside the hall. 'A procession! A procession!' was the cry. In a dense phalanx, blocking the streets from side to side, the crowd set forth, taking the route of Regent Street, Pall Mall, St. James's Street, and Piccadilly. The whole central traffic of London was held up, and many collisions were reported between the demonstrators upon the one side and the police and taxi-cabmen upon the other. Finally, it was not until after midnight that the four travelers were released at the entrance to Lord John Roxton's chambers in the Albany, and that the exuberant crowd, having sung 'They are Jolly Good Fellows' in chorus, concluded their program with 'God Save the King.' So ended one of the most remarkable evenings that London has seen for a considerable time."

So far my friend Macdona; and it may be taken as a fairly accurate, if florid, account of the proceedings. As to the main incident, it was a bewildering surprise to the audience, but not, I need hardly say, to us. The reader will remember how I met Lord John Roxton upon the very occasion when, in his protective crinoline, he had gone to bring the "Devil's chick" as he called it, for Professor Challenger. I have hinted also at the trouble which the Professor's baggage gave us when we left the plateau, and had I described our voyage I might have said a good deal of the worry we had to coax with putrid fish the appetite of our filthy companion. If I have not said much about it before, it was, of course, that the Professor's earnest desire was that no possible rumor of the unanswerable argument which we carried should be allowed to leak out until the moment came when his enemies were to be confuted.

One word as to the fate of the London pterodactyl. Nothing can be said to be certain upon this point. There is the evidence of two frightened women that it perched upon the roof of the Queen's Hall and remained there like a diabolical statue for some hours. The next day it came out in the evening papers that Private Miles, of the Coldstream Guards, on duty outside Marlborough House, had deserted his post without leave, and was therefore courtmartialed. Private Miles' account, that he dropped his rifle and took to his heels down the Mall because on looking up he had suddenly seen the devil between him and the moon, was not accepted by the Court, and yet it may have a direct bearing upon the point at issue. The only other evidence which I can adduce is from the log of the SS. Friesland, a Dutch-American liner, which asserts that at nine next morning, Start Point being at the time ten miles upon their starboard quarter, they were passed by something between a flying goat and a monstrous bat, which was heading at a prodigious pace south and west. If its homing instinct led it upon the right line, there can be no doubt that somewhere out in the wastes of the Atlantic the last European pterodactyl found its end.

And Gladys—oh, my Gladys!—Gladys of the mystic lake, now to be re-named the Central, for never shall she have immortality through me. Did I not always see some hard fiber in her nature? Did I not, even at the time when I was proud to obey her behest, feel that it was surely a poor love which could drive a lover to his death or the danger of it? Did I not, in my truest thoughts, always recurring and always dismissed, see past the beauty of the face, and, peering into the soul, discern the twin shadows of selfishness and of fickleness glooming at the back of it? Did she love the heroic and the spectacular for its own noble sake, or was it for the glory which might, without effort or sacrifice, be reflected upon herself? Or are these thoughts the vain wisdom which comes after the event? It was the shock of my life. For a moment it had turned me to a cynic. But already, as I write, a week has passed, and we have had our momentous interview with Lord John Roxton and—well, perhaps things might be worse.

Let me tell it in a few words. No letter or telegram had come to me at Southampton, and I reached the little villa at Streatham about ten o'clock that night in a fever of alarm. Was she dead or alive? Where were all my nightly dreams of the open arms, the smiling face, the words of praise for her man who had risked his life to humor her whim? Already I was down from the high peaks and standing flat-footed upon earth. Yet some good reasons given might still lift me to the clouds once more. I rushed down the garden path, hammered at the door, heard the voice of Gladys within, pushed past the staring maid, and strode into the sitting-room. She was seated in a low settee under the shaded standard lamp by the piano. In three steps I was across the room and had both her hands in mine.

"Gladys!" I cried, "Gladys!"

She looked up with amazement in her face. She was altered in some subtle way. The expression of her eyes, the hard upward stare, the set of the lips, was new to me. She drew back her hands.

"What do you mean?" she said.

"Gladys!" I cried. "What is the matter? You are my Gladys, are you not—little Gladys Hungerton?"

"No," said she, "I am Gladys Potts. Let me introduce you to my husband."

How absurd life is! I found myself mechanically bowing and shaking hands with a little ginger-haired man who was coiled up in the deep arm-chair which had once been sacred to my own use. We bobbed and grinned in front of each other.

"Father lets us stay here. We are getting our house ready," said Gladys.

"Oh, yes," said I.

"You didn't get my letter at Para, then?"

"No, I got no letter."

"Oh, what a pity! It would have made all clear."

"It is quite clear," said I.

"I've told William all about you," said she. "We have no secrets. I am so sorry about it. But it couldn't have been so very deep, could it, if you could go off to the other end of the world and leave me here alone. You're not crabby, are you?"

"No, no, not at all. I think I'll go."

"Have some refreshment," said the little man, and he added, in a confidential way, "It's always like this, ain't it? And must be unless you had polygamy, only the other way round; you understand." He laughed like an idiot, while I made for the door.

I was through it, when a sudden fantastic impulse came upon me, and I went back to my successful rival, who looked nervously at the electric push.

"Will you answer a question?" I asked.

"Well, within reason," said he.

"How did you do it? Have you searched for hidden treasure, or discovered a pole, or done time on a pirate, or flown the Channel, or what? Where is the glamour of romance? How did you get it?"

He stared at me with a hopeless expression upon his vacuous, good-natured, scrubby little face.

"Don't you think all this is a little too personal?" he said.

"Well, just one question," I cried. "What are you? What is your profession?"

"I am a solicitor's clerk," said he. "Second man at Johnson and Merivale's, 41 Chancery Lane."

"Good-night!" said I, and vanished, like all disconsolate and broken-hearted heroes, into the darkness, with grief and rage and laughter all simmering within me like a boiling pot.

One more little scene, and I have done. Last night we all supped at Lord John Roxton's rooms, and sitting together afterwards we smoked in good comradeship and talked our adventures over. It was strange under these altered surroundings to see the old, well-known faces and figures. There was Challenger, with his smile of condescension, his drooping eyelids, his intolerant eyes, his aggressive beard, his huge chest, swelling and puffing as he laid down the law to Summerlee. And Summerlee, too, there he was with his short briar between his thin moustache and his gray goat's-beard, his worn face protruded in eager debate as he queried all Challenger's propositions. Finally, there was our host, with his rugged, eagle face, and his cold, blue, glacier eyes with always a shimmer of devilment and of humor down in the depths of them. Such is the last picture of them that I have carried away.

It was after supper, in his own sanctum—the room of the pink radiance and the innumerable trophies—that Lord John Roxton had something to say to us. From a cupboard he had brought an old cigar-box, and this he laid before him on the table.

"There's one thing," said he, "that maybe I should have spoken about before this, but I wanted to know a little more clearly where I was. No use to raise hopes and let them down again. But it's facts, not hopes, with us now. You may remember that day we found the pterodactyl rookery in the swamp—what? Well, somethin' in the lie of the land took my notice. Perhaps it has escaped you, so I will tell you. It was a volcanic vent full of blue clay." The Professors nodded.

"Well, now, in the whole world I've only had to do with one place that was a volcanic vent of blue clay. That was the great De Beers Diamond Mine of Kimberley—what? So you see I got diamonds into my head. I rigged up a contraption to hold off those stinking beasts, and I spent a happy day there with a spud. This is what I got."

He opened his cigar-box, and tilting it over he poured about twenty or thirty rough stones, varying from the size of beans to that of chestnuts, on the table.

"Perhaps you think I should have told you then. Well, so I should, only I know there are a lot of traps for the unwary, and that stones may be of any size and yet of little value where color and consistency are clean off. Therefore, I brought them back, and on the first day at home I took one round to Spink's, and asked him to have it roughly cut and valued."

He took a pill-box from his pocket, and spilled out of it a beautiful glittering diamond, one of the finest stones that I have ever seen.

"There's the result," said he. "He prices the lot at a minimum of two hundred thousand pounds. Of course it is fair shares between us. I won't hear of anythin' else. Well, Challenger, what will you do with your fifty thousand?"

"If you really persist in your generous view," said the Professor, "I should found a private museum, which has long been one of my dreams."

"And you, Summerlee?"

"I would retire from teaching, and so find time for my final classification of the chalk fossils."

"I'll use my own," said Lord John Roxton, "in fitting a well-formed expedition and having another look at the dear old plateau. As to you, young fellah, you, of course, will spend yours in gettin' married."

"Not just yet," said I, with a rueful smile. "I think, if you will have me, that I would rather go with you."

Lord Roxton said nothing, but a brown hand was stretched out to me across the table.

THE
POISON
BELT

Being an account of another adventure
of Prof. George E. Challenger, Lord John Roxton,
Prof. Summerlee, and Mr. E. D. Malone,
the discoverers of "The Lost World"

Chapter I The Blurring of Lines

It is imperative that now at once, while these stupendous events are still clear in my mind, I should set them down with that exactness of detail which time may blur. But even as I do so, I am overwhelmed by the wonder of the fact that it should be our little group of the "Lost World"—Professor Challenger, Professor Summerlee, Lord John Roxton, and myself—who have passed through this amazing experience.

When, some years ago, I chronicled in the Daily Gazette our epoch-making journey in South America, I little thought that it should ever fall to my lot to tell an even stranger personal experience, one which is unique in all human annals and must stand out in the records of history as a great peak among the humble foothills which surround it. The event itself will always be marvellous, but the circumstances that we four were together at the time of this extraordinary episode came about in a most natural and, indeed, inevitable fashion. I will explain the events which led up to it as shortly and as clearly as I can, though I am well aware that the fuller the detail upon such a subject the more welcome it will be to the reader, for the public curiosity has been and still is insatiable.

It was upon Friday, the twenty-seventh of August—a date forever memorable in the history of the world—that I went down to the office of my paper and asked for three days' leave of absence from Mr. McArdle, who still presided over our news department. The good old Scotchman shook his head, scratched his dwindling fringe of ruddy fluff, and finally put his reluctance into words.

"I was thinking, Mr. Malone, that we could employ you to advantage these days. I was thinking there was a story that you are the only man that could handle as it should be handled."

"I am sorry for that," said I, trying to hide my disappointment. "Of course if I am needed, there is an end of the matter. But the engagement was important and intimate. If I could be spared——"

"Well, I don't see that you can."

It was bitter, but I had to put the best face I could upon it. After all, it was my own fault, for I should have known by this time that a journalist has no right to make plans of his own.

"Then I'll think no more of it," said I with as much cheerfulness as I could assume at so short a notice. "What was it that you wanted me to do?"

"Well, it was just to interview that deevil of a man down at Rotherfield."

"You don't mean Professor Challenger?" I cried.

"Aye, it's just him that I do mean. He ran young Alec Simpson of the Courier a mile down the high road last week by the collar of his coat and the slack of his breeches. You'll have read of it, likely, in the police report. Our boys would as soon interview a loose alligator in the zoo. But you could do it, I'm thinking—an old friend like you."

"Why," said I, greatly relieved, "this makes it all easy. It so happens that it was to visit Professor Challenger at Rotherfield that I was asking for leave of absence. The fact is, that it is the anniversary of our main adventure on the plateau three years ago, and he has asked our whole party down to his house to see him and celebrate the occasion."

"Capital!" cried McArdle, rubbing his hands and beaming through his glasses. "Then you will be able to get his opeenions out of him. In any other man I would say it was all moonshine, but the fellow has made good once, and who knows but he may again!"

"Get what out of him?" I asked. "What has he been doing?"

"Haven't you seen his letter on 'Scientific Possibeelities' in to-day's Times?"

"No."

McArdle dived down and picked a copy from the floor.

"Read it aloud," said he, indicating a column with his finger. "I'd be glad to hear it again, for I am not sure now that I have the man's meaning clear in my head."

This was the letter which I read to the news editor of the Gazette:—

"SCIENTIFIC POSSIBILITIES"

"Sir,—I have read with amusement, not wholly unmixed with some less complimentary emotion, the complacent and wholly fatuous letter of James Wilson MacPhail which has lately appeared in your columns upon the subject of the blurring of Fraunhofer's lines in the spectra both of the planets and of the fixed stars. He dismisses the matter as of no significance. To a wider intelligence it may well seem of very great possible importance—so great as to involve the ultimate welfare of every man, woman, and child upon this planet. I can hardly hope, by the use of scientific language, to convey any sense of my meaning to those ineffectual people who gather their ideas from the columns of a daily newspaper. I will endeavour, therefore, to condescend to their limitation and to indicate the situation by the use of a homely analogy which will be within the limits of the intelligence of your readers."

"Man, he's a wonder—a living wonder!" said McArdle, shaking his head reflectively. "He'd put up the feathers of a suckingdove and set up a riot in a Quakers' meeting. No wonder he has made London too hot for him. It's a peety, Mr. Malone, for it's a grand brain! We'll let's have the analogy."

"We will suppose," I read, "that a small bundle of connected corks was launched in a sluggish current upon a voyage across the Atlantic. The corks drift slowly on from day to day with the same conditions all round them. If the corks were sentient we could imagine that they would consider these conditions to be permanent and assured. But we, with our superior knowledge, know that many things might happen to surprise the corks. They might possibly float up against a ship, or a sleeping whale, or become entangled in seaweed. In any case, their voyage would probably end by their being thrown up on the rocky coast of Labrador. But what could they know of all this while they drifted so gently day by day in what they thought was a limitless and homogeneous ocean?

Your readers will possibly comprehend that the Atlantic, in this parable, stands for the mighty ocean of ether through which we drift and that the bunch of corks represents the little and obscure planetary system to which we belong. A third-rate sun, with its rag tag and bobtail of insignificant satellites, we float under the same daily conditions towards some unknown end, some squalid catastrophe which will overwhelm us at the ultimate confines of space, where we are swept over an etheric Niagara or dashed upon some unthinkable Labrador. I see no room here for the shallow and ignorant optimism of your correspondent, Mr. James Wilson MacPhail, but many reasons why we should watch with a very close and interested attention every indication of change in those cosmic surroundings upon which our own ultimate fate may depend."

"Man, he'd have made a grand meenister," said McArdle. "It just booms like an organ. Let's get doun to what it is that's troubling him."

The general blurring and shifting of Fraunhofer's lines of the spectrum point, in my opinion, to a widespread cosmic change of a subtle and singular character. Light from a planet is the reflected light of the sun. Light from a star is a self-produced light. But the spectra both from planets and stars have, in this instance, all undergone the same change. Is it, then, a change in those planets and stars? To me such an idea is inconceivable. What common change could simultaneously come upon them all? Is it a change in our own atmosphere? It is possible, but in the highest degree improbable, since we see no signs of it around us, and chemical analysis has failed to reveal it. What, then, is the third possibility? That it may be a change in the conducting medium, in that infinitely fine ether which extends from star to star and pervades the whole universe. Deep in that ocean we are floating upon a slow current. Might that current not drift us into belts of ether which are novel and have properties of which we have never conceived? There is a change somewhere. This cosmic disturbance of the spectrum proves it. It may be a good change. It may be an evil one. It may be a neutral one. We do not know. Shallow observers may treat the matter as one which can be disregarded, but one who like myself is possessed of the deeper intelligence of the true philosopher will understand that the possibilities of the universe are incalculable and that the wisest man is he who holds himself ready for the unexpected. To take an obvious example, who would undertake to say that the mysterious and universal outbreak of illness, recorded in your columns this very morning as having broken out among the indigenous races of Sumatra, has no connection with some cosmic change to which they may respond more quickly than the more complex peoples of Europe? I throw out the idea for what it is worth. To assert it is, in the present stage, as unprofitable as to deny it, but it is an unimaginative numskull who is too dense to perceive that it is well within the bounds of scientific possibility.

"Yours faithfully
"GEORGE EDWARD CHALLENGER.
"THE BRIARS, ROTHERFIELD."

"It's a fine, steemulating letter," said McArdle thoughtfully, fitting a cigarette into the long glass tube which he used as a holder. "What's your opeenion of it, Mr. Malone?"

I had to confess my total and humiliating ignorance of the subject at issue. What, for example, were Fraunhofer's lines? McArdle had just been studying the matter with the aid of our tame scientist at the office, and he picked from his desk two of those many-coloured spectral bands which bear a general resemblance to the hat-ribbons of some young and ambitious cricket club. He pointed out to me that there were certain black lines which formed crossbars upon the series of brilliant colours extending from the red at one end through gradations of orange, yellow, green, blue, and indigo to the violet at the other.

"Those dark bands are Fraunhofer's lines," said he. "The colours are just light itself. Every light, if you can split it up with a prism, gives the same colours. They tell us nothing. It is the lines that count, because they vary according to what it may be that produces the light. It is these lines that have been blurred instead of clear this last week, and all the astronomers have been quarreling over the reason. Here's a photograph of the blurred lines for our issue to-morrow. The public have taken no interest in the matter up to now, but this letter of Challenger's in the Times will make them wake up, I'm thinking."

"And this about Sumatra?"

"Well, it's a long cry from a blurred line in a spectrum to a sick nigger in Sumatra. And yet the chiel has shown us once before that he knows what he's talking about. There is some queer illness down yonder, that's beyond all doubt, and to-day there's a cable just come in from Singapore that the lighthouses are out of action in the Straits of Sundan, and two ships on the beach in consequence. Anyhow, it's good enough for you to interview Challenger upon. If you get anything definite, let us have a column by Monday."

I was coming out from the news editor's room, turning over my new mission in my mind, when I heard my name called from the waiting-room below. It was a telegraph-boy with a wire which had been forwarded from my lodgings at Streatham. The message was from the very man we had been discussing, and ran thus:—

Malone, 17, Hill Street, Streatham.
—Bring oxygen.—Challenger.

"Bring oxygen!" The Professor, as I remembered him, had an elephantine sense of humour capable of the most clumsy and unwieldly gambollings. Was this one of those jokes which used to reduce him to uproarious laughter, when his eyes would disappear and he was all gaping mouth and wagging beard, supremely indifferent to the gravity of all around him? I turned the words over, but could make nothing even remotely jocose out of them. Then surely it was a concise order—though a very strange one. He was the last man in the world whose deliberate command I should care to disobey. Possibly some chemical experiment was afoot; possibly——Well, it was no business of mine to speculate upon why he wanted it. I must get it. There was nearly an hour before I should catch the train at Victoria. I took a taxi, and having ascertained the address from the telephone book, I made for the Oxygen Tube Supply Company in Oxford Street.

As I alighted on the pavement at my destination, two youths emerged from the door of the establishment carrying an iron cylinder, which, with some trouble, they hoisted into a waiting motor-car. An elderly man was at their heels scolding and directing in a creaky, sardonic voice. He turned towards me. There was no mistaking those austere features and that goatee beard. It was my old cross-grained companion, Professor Summerlee.

"What!" he cried. "Don't tell me that YOU have had one of these preposterous telegrams for oxygen?"

I exhibited it.

"Well, well! I have had one too, and, as you see, very much against the grain, I have acted upon it. Our good friend is as impossible as ever. The need for oxygen could not have been so urgent that he must desert the usual means of supply and encroach upon the time of those who are really busier than himself. Why could he not order it direct?"

I could only suggest that he probably wanted it at once.

"Or thought he did, which is quite another matter. But it is superfluous now for you to purchase any, since I have this considerable supply."

"Still, for some reason he seems to wish that I should bring oxygen too. It will be safer to do exactly what he tells me."

Accordingly, in spite of many grumbles and remonstrances from Summerlee, I ordered an additional tube, which was placed with the other in his motor-car, for he had offered me a lift to Victoria.

I turned away to pay off my taxi, the driver of which was very cantankerous and abusive over his fare. As I came back to Professor Summerlee, he was having a furious altercation with the men who had carried down the oxygen, his little white goat's beard jerking with indignation. One of the fellows called him, I remember, "a silly old bleached cockatoo," which so enraged his chauffeur that he bounded out of his seat to take the part of his insulted master, and it was all we could do to prevent a riot in the street.

These little things may seem trivial to relate, and passed as mere incidents at the time. It is only now, as I look back, that I see their relation to the whole story which I have to unfold.

The chauffeur must, as it seemed to me, have been a novice or else have lost his nerve in this disturbance, for he drove vilely on the way to the station. Twice we nearly had collisions with other equally erratic vehicles, and I remember remarking to Summerlee that the standard of driving in London had very much declined. Once we brushed the very edge of a great crowd which was watching a fight at the corner of the Mall. The people, who were much excited, raised cries of anger at the clumsy driving, and one fellow sprang upon the step and waved a stick above our heads. I pushed him off, but we were glad when we had got clear of them and safe out of the park. These little events, coming one after the other, left me very jangled in my nerves, and I could see from my companion's petulant manner that his own patience had got to a low ebb.

But our good humour was restored when we saw Lord John Roxton waiting for us upon the platform, his tall, thin figure clad in a yellow tweed shooting-suit. His keen face, with those unforgettable eyes, so fierce and yet so humorous, flushed with pleasure at the sight of us. His ruddy hair was shot with grey, and the furrows upon his brow had been cut a little deeper by Time's chisel, but in all else he was the Lord John who had been our good comrade in the past.

"Hullo, Herr Professor! Hullo, young fella!" he shouted as he came toward us.

He roared with amusement when he saw the oxygen cylinders upon the porter's trolly behind us. "So you've got them too!" he cried. "Mine is in the van. Whatever can the old dear be after?"

"Have you seen his letter in the Times?" I asked.

"What was it?"

"Stuff and nonsense!" said Summerlee Harshly.

"Well, it's at the bottom of this oxygen business, or I am mistaken," said I.

"Stuff and nonsense!" cried Summerlee again with quite unnecessary violence. We had all got into a first-class smoker, and he had already lit the short and charred old briar pipe which seemed to singe the end of his long, aggressive nose.

"Friend Challenger is a clever man," said he with great vehemence. "No one can deny it. It's a fool that denies it. Look at his hat. There's a sixty-ounce brain inside it—a big engine, running smooth, and turning out clean work. Show me the engine-house and I'll tell you the size of the engine. But he is a born charlatan— you've heard me tell him so to his face—a born charlatan, with a kind of dramatic trick of jumping into the limelight. Things are quiet, so friend Challenger sees a chance to set the public talking about him. You don't imagine that he seriously believes all this nonsense about a change in the ether and a danger to the human race? Was ever such a cock-and-bull story in this life?"

He sat like an old white raven, croaking and shaking with sardonic laughter.

A wave of anger passed through me as I listened to Summerlee. It was disgraceful that he should speak thus of the leader who had been the source of all our fame and given us such an experience as no men have ever enjoyed. I had opened my mouth to utter some hot retort, when Lord John got before me.

"You had a scrap once before with old man Challenger," said he sternly, "and you were down and out inside ten seconds. It seems to me, Professor Summerlee, he's beyond your class, and the best you can do with him is to walk wide and leave him alone."

"Besides," said I, "he has been a good friend to every one of us. Whatever his faults may be, he is as straight as a line, and I don't believe he ever speaks evil of his comrades behind their backs."

"Well said, young fellah-my-lad," said Lord John Roxton. Then, with a kindly smile, he slapped Professor Summerlee upon his shoulder. "Come, Herr Professor, we're not going to quarrel at this time of day. We've seen too much together. But keep off the grass when you get near Challenger, for this young fellah and I have a bit of a weakness for the old dear."

But Summerlee was in no humour for compromise. His face was screwed up in rigid disapproval, and thick curls of angry smoke rolled up from his pipe.

"As to you, Lord John Roxton," he creaked, "your opinion upon a matter of science is of as much value in my eyes as my views upon a new type of shot-gun would be in yours. I have my own judgment, sir, and I use it in my own way. Because it has misled me once, is that any reason why I should accept without criticism anything, however far-fetched, which this man may care to put forward? Are we to have a Pope of science, with infallible decrees laid down EX CATHEDRA, and accepted without question by the poor humble public? I tell you, sir, that I have a brain of my own and that I should feel myself to be a snob and a slave if I did not use it. If it pleases you to believe this rigmarole about ether and Fraunhofer's lines upon the spectrum, do so by all means, but do not ask one who is older and wiser than yourself to share in your folly. Is it not evident that if the ether were affected to the degree which he maintains, and if it were obnoxious to human health, the result of it would already be apparent upon ourselves?" Here he laughed with uproarious triumph over his own argument. "Yes, sir, we should already be very far from our normal selves, and instead of sitting quietly discussing scientific problems in a railway train we should be showing actual symptoms of the poison which was working within us. Where do we see any signs of this poisonous cosmic disturbance? Answer me that, sir! Answer me that! Come, come, no evasion! I pin you to an answer!"

I felt more and more angry. There was something very irritating and aggressive in Summerlee's demeanour.

"I think that if you knew more about the facts you might be less positive in your opinion," said I.

Summerlee took his pipe from his mouth and fixed me with a stony stare.

"Pray what do you mean, sir, by that somewhat impertinent observation?"

"I mean that when I was leaving the office the news editor told me that a telegram had come in confirming the general illness of the Sumatra natives, and adding that the lights had not been lit in the Straits of Sunda."

"Really, there should be some limits to human folly!" cried Summerlee in a positive fury. "Is it possible that you do not realize that ether, if for a moment we adopt Challenger's preposterous supposition, is a universal substance which is the same here as at the other side of the world? Do you for an instant suppose that there is an English ether and a Sumatran ether? Perhaps you imagine that the ether of Kent is in some way superior to the ether of Surrey, through which this train is now bearing us. There really are no bounds to the credulity and ignorance of the average layman. Is it conceivable that the ether in Sumatra should be so deadly as to cause total insensibility at the very time when the ether here has had no appreciable effect upon us whatever? Personally, I can truly say that I never felt stronger in body or better balanced in mind in my life."

"That may be. I don't profess to be a scientific man," said I, "though I have heard somewhere that the science of one generation is usually the fallacy of the next. But it does not take much common sense to see that, as we seem to know so little about ether, it might be affected by some local conditions in various parts of the world and might show an effect over there which would only develop later with us."

"With 'might' and 'may' you can prove anything," cried Summerlee furiously. "Pigs may fly. Yes, sir, pigs MAY fly—but they don't. It is not worth arguing with you. Challenger has filled you with his nonsense and you are both incapable of reason. I had as soon lay arguments before those railway cushions."

"I must say, Professor Summerlee, that your manners do not seem to have improved since I last had the pleasure of meeting you," said Lord John severely.

"You lordlings are not accustomed to hear the truth," Summerlee answered with a bitter smile. "It comes as a bit of a shock, does it not, when someone makes you realize that your title leaves you none the less a very ignorant man?"

"Upon my word, sir," said Lord John, very stern and rigid, "if you were a younger man you would not dare to speak to me in so offensive a fashion."

Summerlee thrust out his chin, with its little wagging tuft of goatee beard.

"I would have you know, sir, that, young or old, there has never been a time in my life when I was afraid to speak my mind to an ignorant coxcomb—yes, sir, an ignorant coxcomb, if you had as many titles as slaves could invent and fools could adopt."

For a moment Lord John's eyes blazed, and then, with a tremendous effort, he mastered his anger and leaned back in his seat with arms folded and a bitter smile upon his face. To me all this was dreadful and deplorable. Like a wave, the memory of the past swept over me, the good comradeship, the happy, adventurous days—all that we had suffered and worked for and won. That it should have come to this—to insults and abuse! Suddenly I was sobbing—sobbing in loud, gulping, uncontrollable sobs which refused to be concealed. My companions looked at me in surprise. I covered my face with my hands.

"It's all right," said I. "Only—only it IS such a pity!"

"You're ill, young fellah, that's what's amiss with you," said Lord John. "I thought you were queer from the first."

"Your habits, sir, have not mended in these three years," said Summerlee, shaking his head. "I also did not fail to observe your strange manner the moment we met. You need not waste your sympathy, Lord John. These tears are purely alcoholic. The man has been drinking. By the way, Lord John, I called you a coxcomb just now, which was perhaps unduly severe. But the word reminds me of a small accomplishment, trivial but amusing, which I used to possess. You know me as the austere man of science. Can you believe that I once had a well-deserved reputation in several nurseries as a farmyard imitator? Perhaps I can help you to pass the time in a pleasant way. Would it amuse you to hear me crow like a cock?"

"No, sir," said Lord John, who was still greatly offended, "it would NOT amuse me."

"My imitation of the clucking hen who had just laid an egg was also considered rather above the average. Might I venture?"

"No, sir, no—certainly not."

But in spite of this earnest prohibition, Professor Summerlee laid down his pipe and for the rest of our journey he entertained—or failed to entertain—us by a succession of bird and animal cries which seemed so absurd that my tears were suddenly changed into boisterous laughter, which must have become quite hysterical as I sat opposite this grave Professor and saw him—or rather heard him—in the character of the uproarious rooster or the puppy whose tail had been trodden upon. Once Lord John passed across his newspaper, upon the margin of which he had written in pencil, "Poor devil! Mad as a hatter." No doubt it was very eccentric, and yet the performance struck me as extraordinarily clever and amusing.

Whilst this was going on, Lord John leaned forward and told me some interminable story about a buffalo and an Indian rajah which seemed to me to have neither beginning nor end. Professor Summerlee had just begun to chirrup like a canary, and Lord John to get to the climax of his story, when the train drew up at Jarvis Brook, which had been given us as the station for Rotherfield.

And there was Challenger to meet us. His appearance was glorious. Not all the turkey-cocks in creation could match the slow, high-stepping dignity with which he paraded his own railway station and the benignant smile of condescending encouragement with which he regarded everybody around him. If he had changed in anything since the days of old, it was that his points had become accentuated. The huge head and broad sweep of forehead, with its plastered lock of black hair, seemed even greater than before. His black beard poured forward in a more impressive cascade, and his clear grey eyes, with their insolent and sardonic eyelids, were even more masterful than of yore.

He gave me the amused hand-shake and encouraging smile which the head master bestows upon the small boy, and, having greeted the others and helped to collect their bags and their cylinders of oxygen, he stowed us and them away in a large motor-car which was driven by the same impassive Austin, the man of few words, whom I had seen in the character of butler upon the occasion of my first eventful visit to the Professor. Our journey led us up a winding hill through beautiful country. I sat in front with the chauffeur, but behind me my three comrades seemed to me to be all talking together. Lord John was still struggling with his buffalo story, so far as I could make out, while once again I heard, as of old, the deep rumble of Challenger and the insistent accents of Summerlee as their brains locked in high and fierce scientific debate. Suddenly Austin slanted his mahogany face toward me without taking his eyes from his steering-wheel.

"I'm under notice," said he.

"Dear me!" said I.

Everything seemed strange to-day. Everyone said queer, unexpected things. It was like a dream.

"It's forty-seven times," said Austin reflectively.

"When do you go?" I asked, for want of some better observation. "I don't go," said Austin.

The conversation seemed to have ended there, but presently he came back to it.

"If I was to go, who would look after 'im?" He jerked his head toward his master. "Who would 'e get to serve 'im?"

"Someone else," I suggested lamely.

"Not 'e. No one would stay a week. If I was to go, that 'ouse would run down like a watch with the mainspring out. I'm telling you because you're 'is friend, and you ought to know. If I was to take 'im at 'is word—but there, I wouldn't have the 'eart. 'E and the missus would be like two babes left out in a bundle. I'm just everything. And then 'e goes and gives me notice."

"Why would no one stay?" I asked.

"Well, they wouldn't make allowances, same as I do. 'E's a very clever man, the master—so clever that 'e's clean balmy sometimes. I've seen 'im right off 'is onion, and no error. Well, look what 'e did this morning."

"What did he do?"

Austin bent over to me.

"'E bit the 'ousekeeper," said he in a hoarse whisper.

"Bit her?"

"Yes, sir. Bit 'er on the leg. I saw 'er with my own eyes startin' a marathon from the 'all-door."

"Good gracious!" "So you'd say, sir, if you could see some of the goings on. 'E don't make friends with the neighbors. There's some of them thinks that when 'e was up among those monsters you wrote about, it was just ''Ome, Sweet 'Ome' for the master, and 'e was never in fitter company. That's what THEY say. But I've served 'im ten years, and I'm fond of 'im, and, mind you, 'e's a great man, when all's said an' done, and it's an honor to serve 'im. But 'e does try one cruel at times. Now look at that, sir. That ain't what you might call old-fashioned 'ospitality, is it now? Just you read it for yourself."

The car on its lowest speed had ground its way up a steep, curving ascent. At the corner a notice-board peered over a well-clipped hedge. As Austin said, it was not difficult to read, for the words were few and arresting:—

WARNING.
Visitors, Pressmen, and Mendicants
are not encouraged.
G. E. CHALLENGER.

"No, it's not what you might call 'earty," said Austin, shaking his head and glancing up at the deplorable placard. "It wouldn't look well in a Christmas card. I beg your pardon, sir, for I haven't spoke as much as this for many a long year, but to-day my feelings seem to 'ave got the better of me. 'E can sack me till 'e's blue in the face, but I ain't going, and that's flat. I'm 'is man and 'e's my master, and so it will be, I expect, to the end of the chapter."

We had passed between the white posts of a gate and up a curving drive, lined with rhododendron bushes. Beyond stood a low brick house, picked out with white woodwork, very comfortable and pretty. Mrs. Challenger, a small, dainty, smiling figure, stood in the open doorway to welcome us.

"Well, my dear," said Challenger, bustling out of the car, "here are our visitors. It is something new for us to have visitors, is it not? No love lost between us and our neighbors, is there? If they could get rat poison into our baker's cart, I expect it would be there."

"It's dreadful—dreadful!" cried the lady, between laughter and tears. "George is always quarreling with everyone. We haven't a friend on the countryside."

"It enables me to concentrate my attention upon my incomparable wife," said Challenger, passing his short, thick arm round her waist. Picture a gorilla and a gazelle, and you have the pair of them. "Come, come, these gentlemen are tired from the journey, and luncheon should be ready. Has Sarah returned?"

The lady shook her head ruefully, and the Professor laughed loudly and stroked his beard in his masterful fashion.

"Austin," he cried, "when you have put up the car you will kindly help your mistress to lay the lunch. Now, gentlemen, will you please step into my study, for there are one or two very urgent things which I am anxious to say to you."

Chapter II   The Tide of Death

As we crossed the hall the telephone-bell rang, and we were the involuntary auditors of Professor Challenger's end of the ensuing dialogue. I say "we," but no one within a hundred yards could have failed to hear the booming of that monstrous voice, which reverberated through the house. His answers lingered in my mind.

"Yes, yes, of course, it is I.... Yes, certainly, THE Professor Challenger, the famous Professor, who else? ... Of course, every word of it, otherwise I should not have written it. ... I shouldn't be surprised. ... There is every indication of it. ... Within a day or so at the furthest.... Well, I can't help that, can I? ... Very unpleasant, no doubt, but I rather fancy it will affect more important people than you. There is no use whining about it. . . . No, I couldn't possibly. You must take your chance. . . . That's enough, sir. Nonsense! I have something more important to do than to listen to such twaddle."

He shut off with a crash and led us upstairs into a large airy apartment which formed his study. On the great mahogany desk seven or eight unopened telegrams were lying.

"Really," he said as he gathered them up, "I begin to think that it would save my correspondents' money if I were to adopt a telegraphic address. Possibly 'Noah, Rotherfield,' would be the most appropriate."

As usual when he made an obscure joke, he leaned against the desk and bellowed in a paroxysm of laughter, his hands shaking so that he could hardly open the envelopes.

"Noah! Noah!" he gasped, with a face of beetroot, while Lord John and I smiled in sympathy and Summerlee, like a dyspeptic goat, wagged his head in sardonic disagreement. Finally Challenger, still rumbling and exploding, began to open his telegrams. The three of us stood in the bow window and occupied ourselves in admiring the magnificent view.

It was certainly worth looking at. The road in its gentle curves had really brought us to a considerable elevation—seven hundred feet, as we afterwards discovered. Challenger's house was on the very edge of the hill, and from its southern face, in which was the study window, one looked across the vast stretch of the weald to where the gentle curves of the South Downs formed an undulating horizon. In a cleft of the hills a haze of smoke marked the position of Lewes. Immediately at our feet there lay a rolling plain of heather, with the long, vivid green stretches of the Crowborough golf course, all dotted with the players. A little to the south, through an opening in the woods, we could see a section of the main line from London to Brighton. In the immediate foreground, under our very noses, was a small enclosed yard, in which stood the car which had brought us from the station.

An ejaculation from Challenger caused us to turn. He had read his telegrams and had arranged them in a little methodical pile upon his desk. His broad, rugged face, or as much of it as was visible over the matted beard, was still deeply flushed, and he seemed to be under the influence of some strong excitement.

"Well, gentlemen," he said, in a voice as if he was addressing a public meeting, "this is indeed an interesting reunion, and it takes place under extraordinary—I may say unprecedented—circumstances. May I ask if you have observed anything upon your journey from town?"

"The only thing which I observed," said Summerlee with a sour smile, "was that our young friend here has not improved in his manners during the years that have passed. I am sorry to state that I have had to seriously complain of his conduct in the train, and I should be wanting in frankness if I did not say that it has left a most unpleasant impression in my mind."

"Well, well, we all get a bit prosy sometimes," said Lord John. "The young fellah meant no real harm. After all, he's an International, so if he takes half an hour to describe a game of football he has more right to do it than most folk."

"Half an hour to describe a game!" I cried indignantly. "Why, it was you that took half an hour with some long-winded story about a buffalo. Professor Summerlee will be my witness."

"I can hardly judge which of you was the most utterly wearisome," said Summerlee. "I declare to you, Challenger, that I never wish to hear of football or of buffaloes so long as I live."

"I have never said one word to-day about football," I protested.

Lord John gave a shrill whistle, and Summerlee shook his head sadly.

"So early in the day too," said he. "It is indeed deplorable. As I sat there in sad but thoughtful silence——"

"In silence!" cried Lord John. "Why, you were doin' a music-hall turn of imitations all the way—more like a runaway gramophone than a man."

Summerlee drew himself up in bitter protest.

"You are pleased to be facetious, Lord John," said he with a face of vinegar.

"Why, dash it all, this is clear madness," cried Lord John. "Each of us seems to know what the others did and none of us knows what he did himself. Let's put it all together from the first. We got into a first-class smoker, that's clear, ain't it? Then we began to quarrel over friend Challenger's letter in the Times."

"Oh, you did, did you?" rumbled our host, his eyelids beginning to droop.

"You said, Summerlee, that there was no possible truth in his contention."

"Dear me!" said Challenger, puffing out his chest and stroking his beard. "No possible truth! I seem to have heard the words before. And may I ask with what arguments the great and famous Professor Summerlee proceeded to demolish the humble individual who had ventured to express an opinion upon a matter of scientific possibility? Perhaps before he exterminates that unfortunate nonentity he will condescend to give some reasons for the adverse views which he has formed."

He bowed and shrugged and spread open his hands as he spoke with his elaborate and elephantine sarcasm.

"The reason was simple enough," said the dogged Summerlee. "I contended that if the ether surrounding the earth was so toxic in one quarter that it produced dangerous symptoms, it was hardly likely that we three in the railway carriage should be entirely unaffected."

The explanation only brought uproarious merriment from Challenger. He laughed until everything in the room seemed to rattle and quiver.

"Our worthy Summerlee is, not for the first time, somewhat out of touch with the facts of the situation," said he at last, mopping his heated brow. "Now, gentlemen, I cannot make my point better than by detailing to you what I have myself done this morning. You will the more easily condone any mental abberation upon your own part when you realize that even I have had moments when my balance has been disturbed. We have had for some years in this household a housekeeper—one Sarah, with whose second name I have never attempted to burden my memory. She is a woman of a severe and forbidding aspect, prim and demure in her bearing, very impassive in her nature, and never known within our experience to show signs of any emotion. As I sat alone at my breakfast—Mrs. Challenger is in the habit of keeping her room of a morning—it suddenly entered my head that it would be entertaining and instructive to see whether I could find any limits to this woman's inperturbability. I devised a simple but effective experiment. Having upset a small vase of flowers which stood in the centre of the cloth, I rang the bell and slipped under the table. She entered and, seeing the room empty, imagined that I had withdrawn to the study. As I had expected, she approached and leaned over the table to replace the vase. I had a vision of a cotton stocking and an elastic-sided boot. Protruding my head, I sank my teeth into the calf of her leg. The experiment was successful beyond belief. For some moments she stood paralyzed, staring down at my head. Then with a shriek she tore herself free and rushed from the room. I pursued her with some thoughts of an explanation, but she flew down the drive, and some minutes afterwards I was able to pick her out with my field-glasses traveling very rapidly in a south-westerly direction. I tell you the anecdote for what it is worth. I drop it into your brains and await its germination. Is it illuminative? Has it conveyed anything to your minds? What do YOU think of it, Lord John?"

Lord John shook his head gravely.

"You'll be gettin' into serious trouble some of these days if you don't put a brake on," said he.

"Perhaps you have some observation to make, Summerlee?"

"You should drop all work instantly, Challenger, and take three months in a German watering-place," said he.

"Profound! Profound!" cried Challenger. "Now, my young friend, is it possible that wisdom may come from you where your seniors have so signally failed?"

And it did. I say it with all modesty, but it did. Of course, it all seems obvious enough to you who know what occurred, but it was not so very clear when everything was new. But it came on me suddenly with the full force of absolute conviction.

"Poison!" I cried.

Then, even as I said the word, my mind flashed back over the whole morning's experiences, past Lord John with his buffalo, past my own hysterical tears, past the outrageous conduct of Professor Summerlee, to the queer happenings in London, the row in the park, the driving of the chauffeur, the quarrel at the oxygen ware-house. Everything fitted suddenly into its place.

"Of course," I cried again. "It is poison. We are all poisoned."

"Exactly," said Challenger, rubbing his hands, "we are all poisoned. Our planet has swum into the poison belt of ether, and is now flying deeper into it at the rate of some millions of miles a minute. Our young friend has expressed the cause of all our troubles and perplexities in a single word, 'poison.'"

We looked at each other in amazed silence. No comment seemed to meet the situation.

"There is a mental inhibition by which such symptoms can be checked and controlled," said Challenger. "I cannot expect to find it developed in all of you to the same point which it has reached in me, for I suppose that the strength of our different mental processes bears some proportion to each other. But no doubt it is appreciable even in our young friend here. After the little outburst of high spirits which so alarmed my domestic I sat down and reasoned with myself. I put it to myself that I had never before felt impelled to bite any of my household. The impulse had then been an abnormal one. In an instant I perceived the truth. My pulse upon examination was ten beats above the usual, and my reflexes were increased. I called upon my higher and saner self, the real G. E. C., seated serene and impregnable behind all mere molecular disturbance. I summoned him, I say, to watch the foolish mental tricks which the poison would play. I found that I was indeed the master. I could recognize and control a disordered mind. It was a remarkable exhibition of the victory of mind over matter, for it was a victory over that particular form of matter which is most intimately connected with mind. I might almost say that mind was at fault and that personality controlled it. Thus, when my wife came downstairs and I was impelled to slip behind the door and alarm her by some wild cry as she entered, I was able to stifle the impulse and to greet her with dignity and restraint. An overpowering desire to quack like a duck was met and mastered in the same fashion.

Later, when I descended to order the car and found Austin bending over it absorbed in repairs, I controlled my open hand even after I had lifted it and refrained from giving him an experience which would possibly have caused him to follow in the steps of the housekeeper. On the contrary, I touched him on the shoulder and ordered the car to be at the door in time to meet your train. At the present instant I am most forcibly tempted to take Professor Summerlee by that silly old beard of his and to shake his head violently backwards and forwards. And yet, as you see, I am perfectly restrained. Let me commend my example to you."

"I'll look out for that buffalo," said Lord John.

"And I for the football match." "It may be that you are right, Challenger," said Summerlee in a chastened voice. "I am willing to admit that my turn of mind is critical rather than constructive and that I am not a ready convert to any new theory, especially when it happens to be so unusual and fantastic as this one. However, as I cast my mind back over the events of the morning, and as I reconsider the fatuous conduct of my companions, I find it easy to believe that some poison of an exciting kind was responsible for their symptoms."

Challenger slapped his colleague good-humouredly upon the shoulder. "We progress," said he. "Decidedly we progress."

"And pray, sir," asked Summerlee humbly, "what is your opinion as to the present outlook?"

"With your permission I will say a few words upon that subject." He seated himself upon his desk, his short, stumpy legs swinging in front of him. "We are assisting at a tremendous and awful function. It is, in my opinion, the end of the world."

The end of the world! Our eyes turned to the great bow-window and we looked out at the summer beauty of the country-side, the long slopes of heather, the great country-houses, the cozy farms, the pleasure-seekers upon the links.

The end of the world! One had often heard the words, but the idea that they could ever have an immediate practical significance, that it should not be at some vague date, but now, to-day, that was a tremendous, a staggering thought. We were all struck solemn and waited in silence for Challenger to continue. His overpowering presence and appearance lent such force to the solemnity of his words that for a moment all the crudities and absurdities of the man vanished, and he loomed before us as something majestic and beyond the range of ordinary humanity. Then to me, at least, there came back the cheering recollection of how twice since we had entered the room he had roared with laughter. Surely, I thought, there are limits to mental detachment. The crisis cannot be so great or so pressing after all.

'You will conceive a bunch of grapes," said he, "which are covered by some infinitesimal but noxious bacillus. The gardener passes it through a disinfecting medium. It may be that he desires his grapes to be cleaner. It may be that he needs space to breed some fresh bacillus less noxious than the last. He dips it into the poison and they are gone. Our Gardener is, in my opinion, about to dip the solar system, and the human bacillus, the little mortal vibrio which twisted and wriggled upon the outer rind of the earth, will in an instant be sterilized out of existence."

Again there was silence. It was broken by the high trill of the telephone-bell.

"There is one of our bacilli squeaking for help," said he with a grim smile. "They are beginning to realize that their continued existence is not really one of the necessities of the universe."

He was gone from the room for a minute or two. I remember that none of us spoke in his absence. The situation seemed beyond all words or comments.

"The medical officer of health for Brighton," said he when he returned. "The symptoms are for some reason developing more rapidly upon the sea level. Our seven hundred feet of elevation give us an advantage. Folk seem to have learned that I am the first authority upon the question. No doubt it comes from my letter in the Times. That was the mayor of a provincial town with whom I talked when we first arrived. You may have heard me upon the telephone. He seemed to put an entirely inflated value upon his own life. I helped him to readjust his ideas."

Summerlee had risen and was standing by the window. His thin, bony hands were trembling with his emotion.

"Challenger," said he earnestly, "this thing is too serious for mere futile argument. Do not suppose that I desire to irritate you by any question I may ask. But I put it to you whether there may not be some fallacy in your information or in your reasoning. There is the sun shining as brightly as ever in the blue sky. There are the heather and the flowers and the birds. There are the folk enjoying themselves upon the golf-links and the laborers yonder cutting the corn. You tell us that they and we may be upon the very brink of destruction—that this sunlit day may be that day of doom which the human race has so long awaited. So far as we know, you found this tremendous judgment upon what? Upon some abnormal lines in a spectrum—upon rumours from Sumatra—upon some curious personal excitement which we have discerned in each other. This latter symptom is not so marked but that you and we could, by a deliberate effort, control it. You need not stand on ceremony with us, Challenger. We have all faced death together before now. Speak out, and let us know exactly where we stand, and what, in your opinion, are our prospects for our future."

It was a brave, good speech, a speech from that stanch and strong spirit which lay behind all the acidities and angularities of the old zoologist. Lord John rose and shook him by the hand.

"My sentiment to a tick," said he. "Now, Challenger, it's up to you to tell us where we are. We ain't nervous folk, as you know well; but when it comes to makin' a week-end visit and finding you've run full butt into the Day of Judgment, it wants a bit of explainin'. What's the danger, and how much of it is there, and what are we goin' to do to meet it?"

He stood, tall and strong, in the sunshine at the window, with his brown hand upon the shoulder of Summerlee. I was lying back in an armchair, an extinguished cigarette between my lips, in that sort of half-dazed state in which impressions become exceedingly distinct. It may have been a new phase of the poisoning, but the delirious promptings had all passed away and were succeeded by an exceedingly languid and, at the same time, perceptive state of mind. I was a spectator. It did not seem to be any personal concern of mine. But here were three strong men at a great crisis, and it was fascinating to observe them. Challenger bent his heavy brows and stroked his beard before he answered. One could see that he was very carefully weighing his words.

"What was the last news when you left London?" he asked.

"I was at the Gazette office about ten," said I. "There was a Reuter just come in from Singapore to the effect that the sickness seemed to be universal in Sumatra and that the lighthouses had not been lit in consequence."

"Events have been moving somewhat rapidly since then," said Challenger, picking up his pile of telegrams. "I am in close touch both with the authorities and with the press, so that news is converging upon me from all parts. There is, in fact, a general and very insistent demand that I should come to London; but I see no good end to be served. From the accounts the poisonous effect begins with mental excitement; the rioting in Paris this morning is said to have been very violent, and the Welsh colliers are in a state of uproar. So far as the evidence to hand can be trusted, this stimulative stage, which varies much in races and in individuals, is succeeded by a certain exaltation and mental lucidity—I seem to discern some signs of it in our young friend here—which, after an appreciable interval, turns to coma, deepening rapidly into death. I fancy, so far as my toxicology carries me, that there are some vegetable nerve poisons——"

"Datura," suggested Summerlee. "Excellent!" cried Challenger. "It would make for scientific precision if we named our toxic agent. Let it be daturon. To you, my dear Summerlee, belongs the honour—posthumous, alas, but none the less unique—of having given a name to the universal destroyer, the Great Gardener's disinfectant. The symptoms of daturon, then, may be taken to be such as I indicate. That it will involve the whole world and that no life can possibly remain behind seems to me to be certain, since ether is a universal medium. Up to now it has been capricious in the places which it has attacked, but the difference is only a matter of a few hours, and it is like an advancing tide which covers one strip of sand and then another, running hither and thither in irregular streams, until at last it has submerged it all. There are laws at work in connection with the action and distribution of daturon which would have been of deep interest had the time at our disposal permitted us to study them. So far as I can trace them"—here he glanced over his telegrams—"the less developed races have been the first to respond to its influence. There are deplorable accounts from Africa, and the Australian aborigines appear to have been already exterminated. The Northern races have as yet shown greater resisting power than the Southern. This, you see, is dated from Marseilles at nine-forty-five this morning. I give it to you verbatim:—

"'All night delirious excitement throughout Provence. Tumult of vine growers at Nimes. Socialistic upheaval at Toulon. Sudden illness attended by coma attacked population this morning. PESTE FOUDROYANTE. Great numbers of dead in the streets. Paralysis of business and universal chaos.'

"An hour later came the following, from the same source:—

"'We are threatened with utter extermination. Cathedrals and churches full to overflowing. The dead outnumber the living. It is inconceivable and horrible. Decease seems to be painless, but swift and inevitable.' "There is a similar telegram from Paris, where the development is not yet as acute. India and Persia appear to be utterly wiped out. The Slavonic population of Austria is down, while the Teutonic has hardly been affected. Speaking generally, the dwellers upon the plains and upon the seashore seem, so far as my limited information goes, to have felt the effects more rapidly than those inland or on the heights. Even a little elevation makes a considerable difference, and perhaps if there be a survivor of the human race, he will again be found upon the summit of some Ararat. Even our own little hill may presently prove to be a temporary island amid a sea of disaster. But at the present rate of advance a few short hours will submerge us all."

Lord John Roxton wiped his brow.

"What beats me," said he, "is how you could sit there laughin' with that stack of telegrams under your hand. I've seen death as often as most folk, but universal death—it's awful!"

"As to the laughter," said Challenger, "you will bear in mind that, like yourselves, I have not been exempt from the stimulating cerebral effects of the etheric poison. But as to the horror with which universal death appears to inspire you, I would put it to you that it is somewhat exaggerated. If you were sent to sea alone in an open boat to some unknown destination, your heart might well sink within you. The isolation, the uncertainty, would oppress you. But if your voyage were made in a goodly ship, which bore within it all your relations and your friends, you would feel that, however uncertain your destination might still remain, you would at least have one common and simultaneous experience which would hold you to the end in the same close communion. A lonely death may be terrible, but a universal one, as painless as this would appear to be, is not, in my judgment, a matter for apprehension. Indeed, I could sympathize with the person who took the view that the horror lay in the idea of surviving when all that is learned, famous, and exalted had passed away."

"What, then, do you propose to do?" asked Summerlee, who had for once nodded his assent to the reasoning of his brother scientist.

"To take our lunch," said Challenger as the boom of a gong sounded through the house. "We have a cook whose omelettes are only excelled by her cutlets. We can but trust that no cosmic disturbance has dulled her excellent abilities. My Scharzberger of '96 must also be rescued, so far as our earnest and united efforts can do it, from what would be a deplorable waste of a great vintage." He levered his great bulk off the desk, upon which he had sat while he announced the doom of the planet. "Come," said he. "If there is little time left, there is the more need that we should spend it in sober and reasonable enjoyment."

And, indeed, it proved to be a very merry meal. It is true that we could not forget our awful situation. The full solemnity of the event loomed ever at the back of our minds and tempered our thoughts. But surely it is the soul which has never faced death which shies strongly from it at the end. To each of us men it had, for one great epoch in our lives, been a familiar presence. As to the lady, she leaned upon the strong guidance of her mighty husband and was well content to go whither his path might lead. The future was our fate. The present was our own. We passed it in goodly comradeship and gentle merriment. Our minds were, as I have said, singularly lucid. Even I struck sparks at times. As to Challenger, he was wonderful! Never have I so realized the elemental greatness of the man, the sweep and power of his understanding. Summerlee drew him on with his chorus of subacid criticism, while Lord John and I laughed at the contest and the lady, her hand upon his sleeve, controlled the bellowings of the philosopher. Life, death, fate, the destiny of man—these were the stupendous subjects of that memorable hour, made vital by the fact that as the meal progressed strange, sudden exaltations in my mind and tinglings in my limbs proclaimed that the invisible tide of death was slowly and gently rising around us. Once I saw Lord John put his hand suddenly to his eyes, and once Summerlee dropped back for an instant in his chair. Each breath we breathed was charged with strange forces. And yet our minds were happy and at ease. Presently Austin laid the cigarettes upon the table and was about to withdraw.

"Austin!" said his master.

"Yes, sir?"

"I thank you for your faithful service." A smile stole over the servant's gnarled face.

"I've done my duty, sir."

"I'm expecting the end of the world to-day, Austin."

"Yes, sir. What time, sir?"

"I can't say, Austin. Before evening."

"Very good, sir."

The taciturn Austin saluted and withdrew. Challenger lit a cigarette, and, drawing his chair closer to his wife's, he took her hand in his.

"You know how matters stand, dear," said he. "I have explained it also to our friends here. You're not afraid are you?"

"It won't be painful, George?"

"No more than laughing-gas at the dentist's. Every time you have had it you have practically died."

"But that is a pleasant sensation."

"So may death be. The worn-out bodily machine can't record its impression, but we know the mental pleasure which lies in a dream or a trance. Nature may build a beautiful door and hang it with many a gauzy and shimmering curtain to make an entrance to the new life for our wondering souls. In all my probings of the actual, I have always found wisdom and kindness at the core; and if ever the frightened mortal needs tenderness, it is surely as he makes the passage perilous from life to life. No, Summerlee, I will have none of your materialism, for I, at least, am too great a thing to end in mere physical constituents, a packet of salts and three bucketfuls of water. Here—here"—and he beat his great head with his huge, hairy fist—"there is something which uses matter, but is not of it—something which might destroy death, but which death can never destroy."

"Talkin' of death," said Lord John. "I'm a Christian of sorts, but it seems to me there was somethin' mighty natural in those ancestors of ours who were buried with their axes and bows and arrows and the like, same as if they were livin' on just the same as they used to. I don't know," he added, looking round the table in a shamefaced way, "that I wouldn't feel more homely myself if I was put away with my old .450 Express and the fowlin'-piece, the shorter one with the rubbered stock, and a clip or two of cartridges—just a fool's fancy, of course, but there it is. How does it strike you, Herr Professor?"

"Well," said Summerlee, "since you ask my opinion, it strikes me as an indefensible throwback to the Stone Age or before it. I'm of the twentieth century myself, and would wish to die like a reasonable civilized man. I don't know that I am more afraid of death than the rest of you, for I am an oldish man, and, come what may, I can't have very much longer to live; but it is all against my nature to sit waiting without a struggle like a sheep for the butcher. Is it quite certain, Challenger, that there is nothing we can do?"

"To save us—nothing," said Challenger. "To prolong our lives a few hours and thus to see the evolution of this mighty tragedy before we are actually involved in it—that may prove to be within my powers. I have taken certain steps——"

"The oxygen?"

"Exactly. The oxygen."

"But what can oxygen effect in the face of a poisoning of the ether? There is not a greater difference in quality between a brick-bat and a gas than there is between oxygen and ether. They are different planes of matter. They cannot impinge upon one another. Come, Challenger, you could not defend such a proposition."

"My good Summerlee, this etheric poison is most certainly influenced by material agents. We see it in the methods and distribution of the outbreak. We should not A PRIORI have expected it, but it is undoubtedly a fact. Hence I am strongly of opinion that a gas like oxygen, which increases the vitality and the resisting power of the body, would be extremely likely to delay the action of what you have so happily named the daturon. It may be that I am mistaken, but I have every confidence in the correctness of my reasoning."

"Well," said Lord John, "if we've got to sit suckin' at those tubes like so many babies with their bottles, I'm not takin' any."

"There will be no need for that," Challenger answered. "We have made arrangements—it is to my wife that you chiefly owe it—that her boudoir shall be made as airtight as is practicable. With matting and varnished paper." "Good heavens, Challenger, you don't suppose you can keep out ether with varnished paper?"

"Really, my worthy friend, you are a trifle perverse in missing the point. It is not to keep out the ether that we have gone to such trouble. It is to keep in the oxygen. I trust that if we can ensure an atmosphere hyper-oxygenated to a certain point, we may be able to retain our senses. I had two tubes of the gas and you have brought me three more. It is not much, but it is something."

"How long will they last?"

"I have not an idea. We will not turn them on until our symptoms become unbearable. Then we shall dole the gas out as it is urgently needed. It may give us some hours, possibly even some days, on which we may look out upon a blasted world. Our own fate is delayed to that extent, and we will have the very singular experience, we five, of being, in all probability, the absolute rear guard of the human race upon its march into the unknown. Perhaps you will be kind enough now to give me a hand with the cylinders. It seems to me that the atmosphere already grows somewhat more oppressive."

Chapter III   Submerged

The chamber which was destined to be the scene of our unforgettable experience was a charmingly feminine sitting-room, some fourteen or sixteen feet square. At the end of it, divided by a curtain of red velvet, was a small apartment which formed the Professor's dressing-room. This in turn opened into a large bedroom. The curtain was still hanging, but the boudoir and dressing-room could be taken as one chamber for the purposes of our experiment. One door and the window frame had been plastered round with varnished paper so as to be practically sealed. Above the other door, which opened on to the landing, there hung a fanlight which could be drawn by a cord when some ventilation became absolutely necessary. A large shrub in a tub stood in each corner.

"How to get rid of our excessive carbon dioxide without unduly wasting our oxygen is a delicate and vital question," said

Challenger, looking round him after the five iron tubes had been laid side by side against the wall. "With longer time for preparation I could have brought the whole concentrated force of my intelligence to bear more fully upon the problem, but as it is we must do what we can. The shrubs will be of some small service. Two of the oxygen tubes are ready to be turned on at an instant's notice, so that we cannot be taken unawares. At the same time, it would be well not to go far from the room, as the crisis may be a sudden and urgent one."

There was a broad, low window opening out upon a balcony. The view beyond was the same as that which we had already admired from the study. Looking out, I could see no sign of disorder anywhere. There was a road curving down the side of the hill, under my very eyes. A cab from the station, one of those prehistoric survivals which are only to be found in our country villages, was toiling slowly up the hill. Lower down was a nurse girl wheeling a perambulator and leading a second child by the hand. The blue reeks of smoke from the cottages gave the whole widespread landscape an air of settled order and homely comfort. Nowhere in the blue heaven or on the sunlit earth was there any foreshadowing of a catastrophe. The harvesters were back in the fields once more and the golfers, in pairs and fours, were still streaming round the links. There was so strange a turmoil within my own head, and such a jangling of my overstrung nerves, that the indifference of those people was amazing.

"Those fellows don't seem to feel any ill effects," said I, pointing down at the links.

"Have you played golf?" asked Lord John.

"No, I have not."

"Well, young fellah, when you do you'll learn that once fairly out on a round, it would take the crack of doom to stop a true golfer. Halloa! There's that telephone-bell again."

From time to time during and after lunch the high, insistent ring had summoned the Professor. He gave us the news as it came through to him in a few curt sentences. Such terrific items had never been registered in the world's history before. The great shadow was creeping up from the south like a rising tide of death. Egypt had gone through its delirium and was now comatose. Spain and Portugal, after a wild frenzy in which the Clericals and the Anarchists had fought most desperately, were now fallen silent. No cable messages were received any longer from South America. In North America the southern states, after some terrible racial rioting, had succumbed to the poison. North of Maryland the effect was not yet marked, and in Canada it was hardly perceptible. Belgium, Holland, and Denmark had each in turn been affected. Despairing messages were flashing from every quarter to the great centres of learning, to the chemists and the doctors of world-wide repute, imploring their advice. The astronomers too were deluged with inquiries. Nothing could be done. The thing was universal and beyond our human knowledge or control. It was death—painless but inevitable—death for young and old, for weak and strong, for rich and poor, without hope or possibility of escape. Such was the news which, in scattered, distracted messages, the telephone had brought us. The great cities already knew their fate and so far as we could gather were preparing to meet it with dignity and resignation. Yet here were our golfers and laborers like the lambs who gambol under the shadow of the knife. It seemed amazing. And yet how could they know? It had all come upon us in one giant stride. What was there in the morning paper to alarm them? And now it was but three in the afternoon. Even as we looked some rumour seemed to have spread, for we saw the reapers hurrying from the fields. Some of the golfers were returning to the club-house. They were running as if taking refuge from a shower. Their little caddies trailed behind them. Others were continuing their game. The nurse had turned and was pushing her perambulator hurriedly up the hill again. I noticed that she had her hand to her brow. The cab had stopped and the tired horse, with his head sunk to his knees, was resting. Above there was a perfect summer sky—one huge vault of unbroken blue, save for a few fleecy white clouds over the distant downs. If the human race must die to-day, it was at least upon a glorious death-bed. And yet all that gentle loveliness of nature made this terrific and wholesale destruction the more pitiable and awful. Surely it was too goodly a residence that we should be so swiftly, so ruthlessly, evicted from it!

But I have said that the telephone-bell had rung once more. Suddenly I heard Challenger's tremendous voice from the hall.

"Malone!" he cried. "You are wanted." I rushed down to the instrument. It was McArdle speaking from London.

"That you, Mr. Malone?" cried his familiar voice. "Mr. Malone, there are terrible goings-on in London. For God's sake, see if Professor Challenger can suggest anything that can be done."

"He can suggest nothing, sir," I answered. "He regards the crisis as universal and inevitable. We have some oxygen here, but it can only defer our fate for a few hours."

"Oxygen!" cried the agonized voice. "There is no time to get any. The office has been a perfect pandemonium ever since you left in the morning. Now half of the staff are insensible. I am weighed down with heaviness myself. From my window I can see the people lying thick in Fleet Street. The traffic is all held up. Judging by the last telegrams, the whole world——"

His voice had been sinking, and suddenly stopped. An instant later I heard through the telephone a muffled thud, as if his head had fallen forward on the desk.

"Mr. McArdle!" I cried. "Mr. McArdle!"

There was no answer. I knew as I replaced the receiver that I should never hear his voice again.

At that instant, just as I took a step backwards from the telephone, the thing was on us. It was as if we were bathers, up to our shoulders in water, who suddenly are submerged by a rolling wave. An invisible hand seemed to have quietly closed round my throat and to be gently pressing the life from me. I was conscious of immense oppression upon my chest, great tightness within my head, a loud singing in my ears, and bright flashes before my eyes. I staggered to the balustrades of the stair. At the same moment, rushing and snorting like a wounded buffalo, Challenger dashed past me, a terrible vision, with red-purple face, engorged eyes, and bristling hair. His little wife, insensible to all appearance, was slung over his great shoulder, and he blundered and thundered up the stair, scrambling and tripping, but carrying himself and her through sheer will-force through that mephitic atmosphere to the haven of temporary safety. At the sight of his effort I too rushed up the steps, clambering, falling, clutching at the rail, until I tumbled half senseless upon by face on the upper landing. Lord John's fingers of steel were in the collar of my coat, and a moment later I was stretched upon my back, unable to speak or move, on the boudoir carpet. The woman lay beside me, and Summerlee was bunched in a chair by the window, his head nearly touching his knees. As in a dream I saw Challenger, like a monstrous beetle, crawling slowly across the floor, and a moment later I heard the gentle hissing of the escaping oxygen. Challenger breathed two or three times with enormous gulps, his lungs roaring as he drew in the vital gas.

"It works!" he cried exultantly. "My reasoning has been justified!" He was up on his feet again, alert and strong. With a tube in his hand he rushed over to his wife and held it to her face. In a few seconds she moaned, stirred, and sat up. He turned to me, and I felt the tide of life stealing warmly through my arteries. My reason told me that it was but a little respite, and yet, carelessly as we talk of its value, every hour of existence now seemed an inestimable thing. Never have I known such a thrill of sensuous joy as came with that freshet of life. The weight fell away from my lungs, the band loosened from my brow, a sweet feeling of peace and gentle, languid comfort stole over me. I lay watching Summerlee revive under the same remedy, and finally Lord John took his turn. He sprang to his feet and gave me a hand to rise, while Challenger picked up his wife and laid her on the settee.

"Oh, George, I am so sorry you brought me back," she said, holding him by the hand. "The door of death is indeed, as you said, hung with beautiful, shimmering curtains; for, once the choking feeling had passed, it was all unspeakably soothing and beautiful. Why have you dragged me back?"

"Because I wish that we make the passage together. We have been together so many years. It would be sad to fall apart at the supreme moment."

For a moment in his tender voice I caught a glimpse of a new Challenger, something very far from the bullying, ranting, arrogant man who had alternately amazed and offended his generation. Here in the shadow of death was the innermost Challenger, the man who had won and held a woman's love. Suddenly his mood changed and he was our strong captain once again.

"Alone of all mankind I saw and foretold this catastrophe," said he with a ring of exultation and scientific triumph in his voice. "As to you, my good Summerlee, I trust your last doubts have been resolved as to the meaning of the blurring of the lines in the spectrum and that you will no longer contend that my letter in the Times was based upon a delusion."

For once our pugnacious colleague was deaf to a challenge. He could but sit gasping and stretching his long, thin limbs, as if to assure himself that he was still really upon this planet. Challenger walked across to the oxygen tube, and the sound of the loud hissing fell away till it was the most gentle sibilation.

"We must husband our supply of the gas," said he. "The atmosphere of the room is now strongly hyperoxygenated, and I take it that none of us feel any distressing symptoms. We can only determine by actual experiments what amount added to the air will serve to neutralize the poison. Let us see how that will do."

We sat in silent nervous tension for five minutes or more, observing our own sensations. I had just begun to fancy that I felt the constriction round my temples again when Mrs. Challenger called out from the sofa that she was fainting. Her husband turned on more gas.

"In pre-scientific days," said he, "they used to keep a white mouse in every submarine, as its more delicate organization gave signs of a vicious atmosphere before it was perceived by the sailors. You, my dear, will be our white mouse. I have now increased the supply and you are better."

"Yes, I am better."

"Possibly we have hit upon the correct mixture. When we have ascertained exactly how little will serve we shall be able to compute how long we shall be able to exist. Unfortunately, in resuscitating ourselves we have already consumed a considerable proportion of this first tube."

"Does it matter?" asked Lord John, who was standing with his hands in his pockets close to the window. "If we have to go, what is the use of holdin' on? You don't suppose there's any chance for us?"

Challenger smiled and shook his head.

"Well, then, don't you think there is more dignity in takin' the jump and not waitin' to he pushed in? If it must be so, I'm for sayin' our prayers, turnin' off the gas, and openin' the window."

"Why not?" said the lady bravely. "Surely, George, Lord John is right and it is better so."

"I most strongly object," cried Summerlee in a querulous voice. "When we must die let us by all means die, but to deliberately anticipate death seems to me to be a foolish and unjustifiable action."

"What does our young friend say to it?" asked Challenger.

"I think we should see it to the end."

"And I am strongly of the same opinion," said he.

"Then, George, if you say so, I think so too," cried the lady.

"Well, well, I'm only puttin' it as an argument," said Lord John. "If you all want to see it through I am with you. It's dooced interestin', and no mistake about that. I've had my share of adventures in my life, and as many thrills as most folk, but I'm endin' on my top note."

"Granting the continuity of life," said Challenger.

"A large assumption!" cried Summerlee. Challenger stared at him in silent reproof.

"Granting the continuity of life," said he, in his most didactic manner, "none of us can predicate what opportunities of observation one may have from what we may call the spirit plane to the plane of matter. It surely must be evident to the most obtuse person" (here he glared a Summerlee) "that it is while we are ourselves material that we are most fitted to watch and form a judgment upon material phenomena. Therefore it is only by keeping alive for these few extra hours that we can hope to carry on with us to some future existence a clear conception of the most stupendous event that the world, or the universe so far as we know it, has ever encountered. To me it would seem a deplorable thing that we should in any way curtail by so much as a minute so wonderful an experience."

"I am strongly of the same opinion," cried Summerlee.

"Carried without a division," said Lord John. "By George, that poor devil of a chauffeur of yours down in the yard has made his last journey. No use makin' a sally and bringin' him in?"

"It would be absolute madness," cried Summerlee.

"Well, I suppose it would," said Lord John. "It couldn't help him and would scatter our gas all over the house, even if we ever got back alive. My word, look at the little birds under the trees!"

We drew four chairs up to the long, low window, the lady still resting with closed eyes upon the settee. I remember that the monstrous and grotesque idea crossed my mind—the illusion may have been heightened by the heavy stuffiness of the air which we were breathing—that we were in four front seats of the stalls at the last act of the drama of the world.

In the immediate foreground, beneath our very eyes, was the small yard with the half-cleaned motor-car standing in it. Austin, the chauffeur, had received his final notice at last, for he was sprawling beside the wheel, with a great black bruise upon his forehead where it had struck the step or mud-guard in falling. He still held in his hand the nozzle of the hose with which he had been washing down his machine. A couple of small plane trees stood in the corner of the yard, and underneath them lay several pathetic little balls of fluffy feathers, with tiny feet uplifted. The sweep of death's scythe had included everything, great and small, within its swath.

Over the wall of the yard we looked down upon the winding road, which led to the station. A group of the reapers whom we had seen running from the fields were lying all pell-mell, their bodies crossing each other, at the bottom of it. Farther up, the nurse-girl lay with her head and shoulders propped against the slope of the grassy bank. She had taken the baby from the perambulator, and it was a motionless bundle of wraps in her arms. Close behind her a tiny patch upon the roadside showed where the little boy was stretched. Still nearer to us was the dead cab-horse, kneeling between the shafts. The old driver was hanging over the splash-board like some grotesque scarecrow, his arms dangling absurdly in front of him. Through the window we could dimly discern that a young man was seated inside. The door was swinging open and his hand was grasping the handle, as if he had attempted to leap forth at the last instant. In the middle distance lay the golf links, dotted as they had been in the morning with the dark figures of the golfers, lying motionless upon the grass of the course or among the heather which skirted it. On one particular green there were eight bodies stretched where a foursome with its caddies had held to their game to the last. No bird flew in the blue vault of heaven, no man or beast moved upon the vast countryside which lay before us.

The evening sun shone its peaceful radiance across it, but there brooded over it all the stillness and the silence of universal death— a death in which we were so soon to join. At the present instant that one frail sheet of glass, by holding in the extra oxygen which counteracted the poisoned ether, shut us off from the fate of all our kind. For a few short hours the knowledge and foresight of one man could preserve our little oasis of life in the vast desert of death and save us from participation in the common catastrophe. Then the gas would run low, we too should lie gasping upon that cherry-coloured boudoir carpet, and the fate of the human race and of all earthly life would be complete. For a long time, in a mood which was too solemn for speech, we looked out at the tragic world.

"There is a house on fire," said Challenger at last, pointing to a column of smoke which rose above the trees. "There will, I expect, be many such—possibly whole cities in flames—when we consider how many folk may have dropped with lights in their hands. The fact of combustion is in itself enough to show that the proportion of oxygen in the atmosphere is normal and that it is the ether which is at fault. Ah, there you see another blaze on the top of Crowborough Hill. It is the golf clubhouse, or I am mistaken. There is the church clock chiming the hour. It would interest our philosophers to know that man-made mechanisms has survived the race who made it."

"By George!" cried Lord John, rising excitedly from his chair. "What's that puff of smoke? It's a train."

We heard the roar of it, and presently it came flying into sight, going at what seemed to me to be a prodigious speed. Whence it had come, or how far, we had no means of knowing. Only by some miracle of luck could it have gone any distance. But now we were to see the terrific end of its career. A train of coal trucks stood motionless upon the line. We held our breath as the express roared along the same track. The crash was horrible. Engine and carriages piled themselves into a hill of splintered wood and twisted iron. Red spurts of flame flickered up from the wreckage until it was all ablaze. For half an hour we sat with hardly a word, stunned by the stupendous sight.

"Poor, poor people!" cried Mrs. Challenger at last, clinging with a whimper to her husband's arm.

"My dear, the passengers on that train were no more animate than the coals into which they crashed or the carbon which they have now become," said Challenger, stroking her hand soothingly. "It was a train of the living when it left Victoria, but it was driven and freighted by the dead long before it reached its fate."

"All over the world the same thing must be going on," said I as a vision of strange happenings rose before me. "Think of the ships at sea—how they will steam on and on, until the furnaces die down or until they run full tilt upon some beach. The sailing ships too—how they will back and fill with their cargoes of dead sailors, while their timbers rot and their joints leak, till one by one they sink below the surface. Perhaps a century hence the Atlantic may still be dotted with the old drifting derelicts."

"And the folk in the coal-mines," said Summerlee with a dismal chuckle. "If ever geologists should by any chance live upon earth again they will have some strange theories of the existence of man in carboniferous strata."

"I don't profess to know about such things," remarked Lord John, "but it seems to me the earth will be 'To let, empty,' after this. When once our human crowd is wiped off it, how will it ever get on again?"

"The world was empty before," Challenger answered gravely. "Under laws which in their inception are beyond and above us, it became peopled. Why may the same process not happen again?"

"My dear Challenger, you can't mean that?"

"I am not in the habit, Professor Summerlee, of saying things which I do not mean. The observation is trivial." Out went the beard and down came the eyelids.

"Well, you lived an obstinate dogmatist, and you mean to die one," said Summerlee sourly.

"And you, sir, have lived an unimaginative obstructionist and never can hope now to emerge from it."

"Your worst critics will never accuse you of lacking imagination," Summerlee retorted.

"Upon my word!" said Lord John. "It would be like you if you used up our last gasp of oxygen in abusing each other. What can it matter whether folk come back or not? It surely won't be in our time." "In that remark, sir, you betray your own very pronounced limitations," said Challenger severely. "The true scientific mind is not to be tied down by its own conditions of time and space. It builds itself an observatory erected upon the border line of present, which separates the infinite past from the infinite future. From this sure post it makes its sallies even to the beginning and to the end of all things. As to death, the scientific mind dies at its post working in normal and methodic fashion to the end. It disregards so petty a thing as its own physical dissolution as completely as it does all other limitations upon the plane of matter. Am I right, Professor Summerlee?"

Summerlee grumbled an ungracious assent.

"With certain reservations, I agree," said he.

"The ideal scientific mind," continued Challenger—"I put it in the third person rather than appear to be too self-complacent—the ideal scientific mind should be capable of thinking out a point of abstract knowledge in the interval between its owner falling from a balloon and reaching the earth. Men of this strong fibre are needed to form the conquerors of nature and the bodyguard of truth."

"It strikes me nature's on top this time," said Lord John, looking out of the window. "I've read some leadin' articles about you gentlemen controllin' her, but she's gettin' a bit of her own back."

"It is but a temporary setback," said Challenger with conviction. "A few million years, what are they in the great cycle of time? The vegetable world has, as you can see, survived. Look at the leaves of that plane tree. The birds are dead, but the plant flourishes. From this vegetable life in pond and in marsh will come, in time, the tiny crawling microscopic slugs which are the pioneers of that great army of life in which for the instant we five have the extraordinary duty of serving as rear guard. Once the lowest form of life has established itself, the final advent of man is as certain as the growth of the oak from the acorn. The old circle will swing round once more."

"But the poison?" I asked. "Will that not nip life in the bud?"

"The poison may be a mere stratum or layer in the ether—a mephitic Gulf Stream across that mighty ocean in which we float. Or tolerance may be established and life accommodate itself to a new condition. The mere fact that with a comparatively small hyperoxygenation of our blood we can hold out against it is surely a proof in itself that no very great change would be needed to enable animal life to endure it."

The smoking house beyond the trees had burst into flames. We could see the high tongues of fire shooting up into the air.

"It's pretty awful," muttered Lord John, more impressed than I had ever seen him.

"Well, after all, what does it matter?" I remarked. "The world is dead. Cremation is surely the best burial."

"It would shorten us up if this house went ablaze."

"I foresaw the danger," said Challenger, "and asked my wife to guard against it."

"Everything is quite safe, dear. But my head begins to throb again. What a dreadful atmosphere!"

"We must change it," said Challenger. He bent over his cylinder of oxygen.

"It's nearly empty," said he. "It has lasted us some three and a half hours. It is now close on eight o'clock. We shall get through the night comfortably. I should expect the end about nine o'clock to-morrow morning. We shall see one sunrise, which shall be all our own."

He turned on his second tube and opened for half a minute the fanlight over the door. Then as the air became perceptibly better, but our own symptoms more acute, he closed it once again.

"By the way," said he, "man does not live upon oxygen alone. It's dinner time and over. I assure you, gentlemen, that when I invited you to my home and to what I had hoped would be an interesting reunion, I had intended that my kitchen should justify itself. However, we must do what we can. I am sure that you will agree with me that it would be folly to consume our air too rapidly by lighting an oil-stove. I have some small provision of cold meats, bread, and pickles which, with a couple of bottles of claret, may serve our turn. Thank you, my dear—now as ever you are the queen of managers."

It was indeed wonderful how, with the self-respect and sense of propriety of the British housekeeper, the lady had within a few minutes adorned the central table with a snow-white cloth, laid the napkins upon it, and set forth the simple meal with all the elegance of civilization, including an electric torch lamp in the centre. Wonderful also was it to find that our appetites were ravenous.

"It is the measure of our emotion," said Challenger with that air of condescension with which he brought his scientific mind to the explanation of humble facts. "We have gone through a great crisis. That means molecular disturbance. That in turn means the need for repair. Great sorrow or great joy should bring intense hunger—not abstinence from food, as our novelists will have it."

"That's why the country folk have great feasts at funerals," I hazarded.

"Exactly. Our young friend has hit upon an excellent illustration. Let me give you another slice of tongue."

"The same with savages," said Lord John, cutting away at the beef. "I've seen them buryin' a chief up the Aruwimi River, and they ate a hippo that must have weighed as much as a tribe. There are some of them down New Guinea way that eat the late-lamented himself, just by way of a last tidy up. Well, of all the funeral feasts on this earth, I suppose the one we are takin' is the queerest."

"The strange thing is," said Mrs. Challenger, "that I find it impossible to feel grief for those who are gone. There are my father and mother at Bedford. I know that they are dead, and yet in this tremendous universal tragedy I can feel no sharp sorrow for any individuals, even for them."

"And my old mother in her cottage in Ireland," said I. "I can see her in my mind's eye, with her shawl and her lace cap, lying back with closed eyes in the old high-backed chair near the window, her glasses and her book beside her. Why should I mourn her? She has passed and I am passing, and I may be nearer her in some other life than England is to Ireland. Yet I grieve to think that that dear body is no more."

"As to the body," remarked Challenger, "we do not mourn over the parings of our nails nor the cut locks of our hair, though they were once part of ourselves. Neither does a one-legged man yearn sentimentally over his missing member. The physical body has rather been a source of pain and fatigue to us. It is the constant index of our limitations. Why then should we worry about its detachment from our psychical selves?"

"If they can indeed be detached," Summerlee grumbled. "But, anyhow, universal death is dreadful."

"As I have already explained," said Challenger, "a universal death must in its nature be far less terrible than a isolated one."

"Same in a battle," remarked Lord John. "If you saw a single man lying on that floor with his chest knocked in and a hole in his face it would turn you sick. But I've seen ten thousand on their backs in the Soudan, and it gave me no such feelin', for when you are makin' history the life of any man is too small a thing to worry over. When a thousand million pass over together, same as happened to-day, you can't pick your own partic'lar out of the crowd."

"I wish it were well over with us," said the lady wistfully. "Oh, George, I am so frightened."

"You'll be the bravest of us all, little lady, when the time comes. I've been a blusterous old husband to you, dear, but you'll just bear in mind that G. E. C. is as he was made and couldn't help himself. After all, you wouldn't have had anyone else?"

"No one in the whole wide world, dear," said she, and put her arms round his bull neck. We three walked to the window and stood amazed at the sight which met our eyes.

Darkness had fallen and the dead world was shrouded in gloom. But right across the southern horizon was one long vivid scarlet streak, waxing and waning in vivid pulses of life, leaping suddenly to a crimson zenith and then dying down to a glowing line of fire.

"Lewes is ablaze!"

"No, it is Brighton which is burning," said Challenger, stepping across to join us. "You can see the curved back of the downs against the glow. That fire is miles on the farther side of it. The whole town must be alight."

There were several red glares at different points, and the pile of DEBRIS upon the railway line was still smoldering darkly, but they all seemed mere pin-points of light compared to that monstrous conflagration throbbing beyond the hills. What copy it would have made for the Gazette! Had ever a journalist such an opening and so little chance of using it—the scoop of scoops, and no one to appreciate it? And then, suddenly, the old instinct of recording came over me. If these men of science could be so true to their life's work to the very end, why should not I, in my humble way, be as constant? No human eye might ever rest upon what I had done. But the long night had to be passed somehow, and for me at least, sleep seemed to be out of the question. My notes would help to pass the weary hours and to occupy my thoughts. Thus it is that now I have before me the notebook with its scribbled pages, written confusedly upon my knee in the dim, waning light of our one electric torch. Had I the literary touch, they might have been worthy of the occasion, As it is, they may still serve to bring to other minds the long-drawn emotions and tremors of that awful night.

Chapter IV   A Diary of the Dying

How strange the words look scribbled at the top of the empty page of my book! How stranger still that it is I, Edward Malone, who have written them—I who started only some twelve hours ago from my rooms in Streatham without one thought of the marvels which the day was to bring forth! I look back at the chain of incidents, my interview with McArdle, Challenger's first note of alarm in the Times, the absurd journey in the train, the pleasant luncheon, the catastrophe, and now it has come to this—that we linger alone upon an empty planet, and so sure is our fate that I can regard these lines, written from mechanical professional habit and never to be seen by human eyes, as the words of one who is already dead, so closely does he stand to the shadowed borderland over which all outside this one little circle of friends have already gone. I feel how wise and true were the words of Challenger when he said that the real tragedy would be if we were left behind when all that is noble and good and beautiful had passed. But of that there can surely be no danger. Already our second tube of oxygen is drawing to an end. We can count the poor dregs of our lives almost to a minute.

We have just been treated to a lecture, a good quarter of an hour long, from Challenger, who was so excited that he roared and bellowed as if he were addressing his old rows of scientific sceptics in the Queen's Hall. He had certainly a strange audience to harangue: his wife perfectly acquiescent and absolutely ignorant of his meaning, Summerlee seated in the shadow, querulous and critical but interested, Lord John lounging in a corner somewhat bored by the whole proceeding, and myself beside the window watching the scene with a kind of detached attention, as if it were all a dream or something in which I had no personal interest whatever. Challenger sat at the centre table with the electric light illuminating the slide under the microscope which he had brought from his dressing room. The small vivid circle of white light from the mirror left half of his rugged, bearded face in brilliant radiance and half in deepest shadow. He had, it seems, been working of late upon the lowest forms of life, and what excited him at the present moment was that in the microscopic slide made up the day before he found the amoeba to he still alive.

"You can see it for yourselves," he kept repeating in great excitement. "Summerlee, will you step across and satisfy yourself upon the point? Malone, will you kindly verify what I say? The little spindle-shaped things in the centre are diatoms and may be disregarded since they are probably vegetable rather than animal. But the right-hand side you will see an undoubted amoeba, moving sluggishly across the field. The upper screw is the fine adjustment. Look at it for yourselves."

Summerlee did so and acquiesced. So did I and perceived a little creature which looked as if it were made of ground glass flowing in a sticky way across the lighted circle. Lord John was prepared to take him on trust.

"I'm not troublin' my head whether he's alive or dead," said he. "We don't so much as know each other by sight, so why should I take it to heart? I don't suppose he's worryin' himself over the state of OUR health."

I laughed at this, and Challenger looked in my direction with his coldest and most supercilious stare. It was a most petrifying experience.

"The flippancy of the half-educated is more obstructive to science than the obtuseness of the ignorant," said he. "If Lord John Roxton would condescend——"

"My dear George, don't be so peppery," said his wife, with her hand on the black mane that drooped over the microscope. "What can it matter whether the amoeba is alive or not?"

"It matters a great deal," said Challenger gruffly.

"Well, let's hear about it," said Lord John with a good-humoured smile. "We may as well talk about that as anything else. If you think I've been too off-hand with the thing, or hurt its feelin's in any way, I'll apologize."

"For my part," remarked Summerlee in his creaky, argumentative voice, "I can't see why you should attach such importance to the creature being alive. It is in the same atmosphere as ourselves, so naturally the poison does not act upon it. If it were outside of this room it would be dead, like all other animal life."

"Your remarks, my good Summerlee," said Challenger with enormous condescension (oh, if I could paint that over-bearing, arrogant face in the vivid circle of reflection from the microscope mirror!)—"your remarks show that you imperfectly appreciate the situation. This specimen was mounted yesterday and is hermetically sealed. None of our oxygen can reach it. But the ether, of course, has penetrated to it, as to every other point upon the universe. Therefore, it has survived the poison. Hence, we may argue that every amoeba outside this room, instead of being dead, as you have erroneously stated, has really survived the catastrophe."

"Well, even now I don't feel inclined to hip-hurrah about it," said Lord John. "What does it matter?"

"It just matters this, that the world is a living instead of a dead one. If you had the scientific imagination, you would cast your mind forward from this one fact, and you would see some few millions of years hence—a mere passing moment in the enormous flux of the ages—the whole world teeming once more with the animal and human life which will spring from this tiny root. You have seen a prairie fire where the flames have swept every trace of grass or plant from the surface of the earth and left only a blackened waste. You would think that it must be forever desert. Yet the roots of growth have been left behind, and when you pass the place a few years hence you can no longer tell where the black scars used to be. Here in this tiny creature are the roots of growth of the animal world, and by its inherent development, and evolution, it will surely in time remove every trace of this incomparable crisis in which we are now involved."

"Dooced interestin'!" said Lord John, lounging across and looking through the microscope. "Funny little chap to hang number one among the family portraits. Got a fine big shirt-stud on him!"

"The dark object is his nucleus," said Challenger with the air of a nurse teaching letters to a baby.

"Well, we needn't feel lonely," said Lord John laughing. "There's somebody livin' besides us on the earth."

"You seem to take it for granted, Challenger," said Summerlee, "that the object for which this world was created was that it should produce and sustain human life."

"Well, sir, and what object do you suggest?" asked Challenger, bristling at the least hint of contradiction.

"Sometimes I think that it is only the monstrous conceit of mankind which makes him think that all this stage was erected for him to strut upon."

"We cannot be dogmatic about it, but at least without what you have ventured to call monstrous conceit we can surely say that we are the highest thing in nature."

"The highest of which we have cognizance."

"That, sir, goes without saying."

"Think of all the millions and possibly billions of years that the earth swung empty through space—or, if not empty, at least without a sign or thought of the human race. Think of it, washed by the rain and scorched by the sun and swept by the wind for those unnumbered ages. Man only came into being yesterday so far as geological times goes. Why, then, should it be taken for granted that all this stupendous preparation was for his benefit?"

"For whose then—or for what?"

Summerlee shrugged his shoulders.

"How can we tell? For some reason altogether beyond our conception—and man may have been a mere accident, a by-product evolved in the process. It is as if the scum upon the surface of the ocean imagined that the ocean was created in order to produce and sustain it or a mouse in a cathedral thought that the building was its own proper ordained residence."

I have jotted down the very words of their argument, but now it degenerates into a mere noisy wrangle with much polysyllabic scientific jargon upon each side. It is no doubt a privilege to hear two such brains discuss the highest questions; but as they are in perpetual disagreement, plain folk like Lord John and I get little that is positive from the exhibition. They neutralize each other and we are left as they found us. Now the hubbub has ceased, and Summerlee is coiled up in his chair, while Challenger, still fingering the screws of his microscope, is keeping up a continual low, deep, inarticulate growl like the sea after a storm. Lord John comes over to me, and we look out together into the night.

There is a pale new moon—the last moon that human eyes will ever rest upon—and the stars are most brilliant. Even in the clear plateau air of South America I have never seen them brighter. Possibly this etheric change has some effect upon light. The funeral pyre of Brighton is still blazing, and there is a very distant patch of scarlet in the western sky, which may mean trouble at Arundel or Chichester, possibly even at Portsmouth. I sit and muse and make an occasional note. There is a sweet melancholy in the air. Youth and beauty and chivalry and love—is this to be the end of it all? The starlit earth looks a dreamland of gentle peace. Who would imagine it as the terrible Golgotha strewn with the bodies of the human race? Suddenly, I find myself laughing.

"Halloa, young fellah!" says Lord John, staring at me in surprise. "We could do with a joke in these hard times. What was it, then?"

"I was thinking of all the great unsolved questions," I answer, "the questions that we spent so much labor and thought over. Think of Anglo-German competition, for example—or the Persian Gulf that my old chief was so keen about. Whoever would have guessed, when we fumed and fretted so, how they were to be eventually solved?"

We fall into silence again. I fancy that each of us is thinking of friends that have gone before. Mrs. Challenger is sobbing quietly, and her husband is whispering to her. My mind turns to all the most unlikely people, and I see each of them lying white and rigid as poor Austin does in the yard. There is McArdle, for example, I know exactly where he is, with his face upon his writing desk and his hand on his own telephone, just as I heard him fall. Beaumont, the editor, too—I suppose he is lying upon the blue-and-red Turkey carpet which adorned his sanctum. And the fellows in the reporters' room—Macdona and Murray and Bond. They had certainly died hard at work on their job, with note-books full of vivid impressions and strange happenings in their hands. I could just imagine how this one would have been packed off to the doctors, and that other to Westminster, and yet a third to St. Paul's. What glorious rows of head-lines they must have seen as a last vision beautiful, never destined to materialize in printer's ink! I could see Macdona among the doctors—"Hope in Harley Street"—Mac had always a weakness for alliteration. "Interview with Mr. Soley Wilson." "Famous Specialist says 'Never despair!'" "Our Special Correspondent found the eminent scientist seated upon the roof, whither he had retreated to avoid the crowd of terrified patients who had stormed his dwelling. With a manner which plainly showed his appreciation of the immense gravity of the occasion, the celebrated physician refused to admit that every avenue of hope had been closed." That's how Mac would start. Then there was Bond; he would probably do St. Paul's. He fancied his own literary touch. My word, what a theme for him! "Standing in the little gallery under the dome and looking down upon that packed mass of despairing humanity, groveling at this last instant before a Power which they had so persistently ignored, there rose to my ears from the swaying crowd such a low moan of entreaty and terror, such a shuddering cry for help to the Unknown, that——" and so forth.

Yes, it would be a great end for a reporter, though, like myself, he would die with the treasures still unused. What would Bond not give, poor chap, to see "J. H. B." at the foot of a column like that?

But what drivel I am writing! It is just an attempt to pass the weary time. Mrs. Challenger has gone to the inner dressing-room, and the Professor says that she is asleep. He is making notes and consulting books at the central table, as calmly as if years of placid work lay before him. He writes with a very noisy quill pen which seems to be screeching scorn at all who disagree with him.

Summerlee has dropped off in his chair and gives from time to time a peculiarly exasperating snore. Lord John lies back with his hands in his pockets and his eyes closed. How people can sleep under such conditions is more than I can imagine.

Three-thirty a.m. I have just wakened with a start. It was five minutes past eleven when I made my last entry. I remember winding up my watch and noting the time. So I have wasted some five hours of the little span still left to us. Who would have believed it possible? But I feel very much fresher, and ready for my fate—or try to persuade myself that I am. And yet, the fitter a man is, and the higher his tide of life, the more must he shrink from death. How wise and how merciful is that provision of nature by which his earthly anchor is usually loosened by many little imperceptible tugs, until his consciousness has drifted out of its untenable earthly harbor into the great sea beyond!

Mrs. Challenger is still in the dressing room. Challenger has fallen asleep in his chair. What a picture! His enormous frame leans back, his huge, hairy hands are clasped across his waistcoat, and his head is so tilted that I can see nothing above his collar save a tangled bristle of luxuriant beard. He shakes with the vibration of his own snoring. Summerlee adds his occasional high tenor to Challenger's sonorous bass. Lord John is sleeping also, his long body doubled up sideways in a basket-chair. The first cold light of dawn is just stealing into the room, and everything is grey and mournful.

I look out at the sunrise—that fateful sunrise which will shine upon an unpeopled world. The human race is gone, extinguished in a day, but the planets swing round and the tides rise or fall, and the wind whispers, and all nature goes her way, down, as it would seem, to the very amoeba, with never a sign that he who styled himself the lord of creation had ever blessed or cursed the universe with his presence. Down in the yard lies Austin with sprawling limbs, his face glimmering white in the dawn, and the hose nozzle still projecting from his dead hand. The whole of human kind is typified in that one half-ludicrous and half-pathetic figure, lying so helpless beside the machine which it used to control.

Here end the notes which I made at the time. Henceforward events were too swift and too poignant to allow me to write, but they are too clearly outlined in my memory that any detail could escape me.

Some chokiness in my throat made me look at the oxygen cylinders, and I was startled at what I saw. The sands of our lives were running very low. At some period in the night Challenger had switched the tube from the third to the fourth cylinder. Now it was clear that this also was nearly exhausted. That horrible feeling of constriction was closing in upon me. I ran across and, unscrewing the nozzle, I changed it to our last supply. Even as I did so my conscience pricked me, for I felt that perhaps if I had held my hand all of them might have passed in their sleep. The thought was banished, however, by the voice of the lady from the inner room crying:—

"George, George, I am stifling!"

"It is all right, Mrs. Challenger," I answered as the others started to their feet. "I have just turned on a fresh supply."

Even at such a moment I could not help smiling at Challenger, who with a great hairy fist in each eye was like a huge, bearded baby, new wakened out of sleep. Summerlee was shivering like a man with the ague, human fears, as he realized his position, rising for an instant above the stoicism of the man of science. Lord John, however, was as cool and alert as if he had just been roused on a hunting morning.

"Fifthly and lastly," said he, glancing at the tube. "Say, young fellah, don't tell me you've been writin' up your impressions in that paper on your knee."

"Just a few notes to pass the time."

"Well, I don't believe anyone but an Irishman would have done that. I expect you'll have to wait till little brother amoeba gets grown up before you'll find a reader. He don't seem to take much stock of things just at present. Well, Herr Professor, what are the prospects?"

Challenger was looking out at the great drifts of morning mist which lay over the landscape. Here and there the wooded hills rose like conical islands out of this woolly sea.

"It might be a winding sheet," said Mrs. Challenger, who had entered in her dressing-gown. "There's that song of yours, George, 'Ring out the old, ring in the new.' It was prophetic. But you are shivering, my poor dear friends. I have been warm under a coverlet all night, and you cold in your chairs. But I'll soon set you right."

The brave little creature hurried away, and presently we heard the sizzling of a kettle. She was back soon with five steaming cups of cocoa upon a tray.

"Drink these," said she. "You will feel so much better."

And we did. Summerlee asked if he might light his pipe, and we all had cigarettes. It steadied our nerves, I think, but it was a mistake, for it made a dreadful atmosphere in that stuffy room. Challenger had to open the ventilator.

"How long, Challenger?" asked Lord John.

"Possibly three hours," he answered with a shrug.

"I used to be frightened," said his wife. "But the nearer I get to it, the easier it seems. Don't you think we ought to pray, George?"

"You will pray, dear, if you wish," the big man answered, very gently. "We all have our own ways of praying. Mine is a complete acquiescence in whatever fate may send me—a cheerful acquiescence. The highest religion and the highest science seem to unite on that."

"I cannot truthfully describe my mental attitude as acquiescence and far less cheerful acquiescence," grumbled Summerlee over his pipe. "I submit because I have to. I confess that I should have liked another year of life to finish my classification of the chalk fossils."

"Your unfinished work is a small thing," said Challenger pompously, "when weighed against the fact that my own MAGNUM OPUS, 'The Ladder of Life,' is still in the first stages. My brain, my reading, my experience—in fact, my whole unique equipment—were to be condensed into that epoch-making volume. And yet, as I say, I acquiesce."

"I expect we've all left some loose ends stickin' out," said Lord John. "What are yours, young fellah?"

"I was working at a book of verses," I answered.

"Well, the world has escaped that, anyhow," said Lord John. "There's always compensation somewhere if you grope around."

"What about you?" I asked.

"Well, it just so happens that I was tidied up and ready. I'd promised Merivale to go to Tibet for a snow leopard in the spring. But it's hard on you, Mrs. Challenger, when you have just built up this pretty home."

"Where George is, there is my home. But, oh, what would I not give for one last walk together in the fresh morning air upon those beautiful downs!"

Our hearts re-echoed her words. The sun had burst through the gauzy mists which veiled it, and the whole broad Weald was washed in golden light. Sitting in our dark and poisonous atmosphere that glorious, clean, wind-swept countryside seemed a very dream of beauty. Mrs. Challenger held her hand stretched out to it in her longing. We drew up chairs and sat in a semicircle in the window. The atmosphere was already very close. It seemed to me that the shadows of death were drawing in upon us—the last of our race. It was like an invisible curtain closing down upon every side.

"That cylinder is not lastin' too well," said Lord John with a long gasp for breath.

"The amount contained is variable," said Challenger, "depending upon the pressure and care with which it has been bottled. I am inclined to agree with you, Roxton, that this one is defective."

"So we are to be cheated out of the last hour of our lives," Summerlee remarked bitterly. "An excellent final illustration of the sordid age in which we have lived. Well, Challenger, now is your time if you wish to study the subjective phenomena of physical dissolution."

"Sit on the stool at my knee and give me your hand," said Challenger to his wife. "I think, my friends, that a further delay in this insufferable atmosphere is hardly advisable. You would not desire it, dear, would you?"

His wife gave a little groan and sank her face against his leg.

"I've seen the folk bathin' in the Serpentine in winter," said Lord John. "When the rest are in, you see one or two shiverin' on the bank, envyin' the others that have taken the plunge. It's the last that have the worst of it. I'm all for a header and have done with it."

"You would open the window and face the ether?"

"Better be poisoned than stifled."

Summerlee nodded his reluctant acquiescence and held out his thin hand to Challenger.

"We've had our quarrels in our time, but that's all over," said he. "We were good friends and had a respect for each other under the surface. Good-by!"

"Good-by, young fellah!" said Lord John. "The window's plastered up. You can't open it."

Challenger stooped and raised his wife, pressing her to his breast, while she threw her arms round his neck.

"Give me that field-glass, Malone," said he gravely.

I handed it to him.

"Into the hands of the Power that made us we render ourselves again!" he shouted in his voice of thunder, and at the words he hurled the field-glass through the window.

Full in our flushed faces, before the last tinkle of falling fragments had died away, there came the wholesome breath of the wind, blowing strong and sweet.

I don't know how long we sat in amazed silence. Then as in a dream, I heard Challenger's voice once more.

"We are back in normal conditions," he cried. "The world has cleared the poison belt, but we alone of all mankind are saved."

Chapter V The Dead World

I remember that we all sat gasping in our chairs, with that sweet, wet south-western breeze, fresh from the sea, flapping the muslin curtains and cooling our flushed faces. I wonder how long we sat! None of us afterwards could agree at all on that point. We were bewildered, stunned, semi-conscious. We had all braced our courage for death, but this fearful and sudden new fact—that we must continue to live after we had survived the race to which we belonged—struck us with the shock of a physical blow and left us prostrate. Then gradually the suspended mechanism began to move once more; the shuttles of memory worked; ideas weaved themselves together in our minds. We saw, with vivid, merciless clearness, the relations between the past, the present, and the future—the lives that we had led and the lives which we would have to live. Our eyes turned in silent horror upon those of our companions and found the same answering look in theirs. Instead of the joy which men might have been expected to feel who had so narrowly escaped an imminent death, a terrible wave of darkest depression submerged us. Everything on earth that we loved had been washed away into the great, infinite, unknown ocean, and here were we marooned upon this desert island of a world, without companions, hopes, or aspirations. A few years' skulking like jackals among the graves of the human race and then our belated and lonely end would come.

"It's dreadful, George, dreadful!" the lady cried in an agony of sobs. "If we had only passed with the others! Oh, why did you save us? I feel as if it is we that are dead and everyone else alive."

Challenger's great eyebrows were drawn down in concentrated thought, while his huge, hairy paw closed upon the outstretched hand of his wife. I had observed that she always held out her arms to him in trouble as a child would to its mother.

"Without being a fatalist to the point of nonresistance," said he, "I have always found that the highest wisdom lies in an acquiescence with the actual." He spoke slowly, and there was a vibration of feeling in his sonorous voice.

"I do NOT acquiesce," said Summerlee firmly.

"I don't see that it matters a row of pins whether you acquiesce or whether you don't," remarked Lord John. "You've got to take it, whether you take it fightin' or take it lyin' down, so what's the odds whether you acquiesce or not?

I can't remember that anyone asked our permission before the thing began, and nobody's likely to ask it now. So what difference can it make what we may think of it?"

"It is just all the difference between happiness and misery," said Challenger with an abstracted face, still patting his wife's hand. "You can swim with the tide and have peace in mind and soul, or you can thrust against it and be bruised and weary. This business is beyond us, so let us accept it as it stands and say no more."

"But what in the world are we to do with our lives?" I asked, appealing in desperation to the blue, empty heaven.

"What am I to do, for example? There are no newspapers, so there's an end of my vocation."

"And there's nothin' left to shoot, and no more soldierin', so there's an end of mine," said Lord John.

"And there are no students, so there's an end of mine," cried Summerlee.

"But I have my husband and my house, so I can thank heaven that there is no end of mine," said the lady.

"Nor is there an end of mine," remarked Challenger, "for science is not dead, and this catastrophe in itself will offer us many most absorbing problems for investigation."

He had now flung open the windows and we were gazing out upon the silent and motionless landscape.

"Let me consider," he continued. "It was about three, or a little after, yesterday afternoon that the world finally entered the poison belt to the extent of being completely submerged. It is now nine o'clock. The question is, at what hour did we pass out from it?"

"The air was very bad at daybreak," said I.

"Later than that," said Mrs. Challenger. "As late as eight o'clock I distinctly felt the same choking at my throat which came at the outset."

"Then we shall say that it passed just after eight o'clock. For seventeen hours the world has been soaked in the poisonous ether. For that length of time the Great Gardener has sterilized the human mold which had grown over the surface of His fruit. Is it possible that the work is incompletely done—that others may have survived besides ourselves?"

"That's what I was wonderin'" said Lord John. "Why should we be the only pebbles on the beach?"

"It is absurd to suppose that anyone besides ourselves can possibly have survived," said Summerlee with conviction. "Consider that the poison was so virulent that even a man who is as strong as an ox and has not a nerve in his body, like Malone here, could hardly get up the stairs before he fell unconscious. Is it likely that anyone could stand seventeen minutes of it, far less hours?"

"Unless someone saw it coming and made preparation, same as old friend Challenger did."

"That, I think, is hardly probable," said Challenger, projecting his beard and sinking his eyelids. "The combination of observation, inference, and anticipatory imagination which enabled me to foresee the danger is what one can hardly expect twice in the same generation."

"Then your conclusion is that everyone is certainly dead?"

"There can be little doubt of that. We have to remember, however, that the poison worked from below upwards and would possibly be less virulent in the higher strata of the atmosphere. It is strange, indeed, that it should be so; but it presents one of those features which will afford us in the future a fascinating field for study. One could imagine, therefore, that if one had to search for survivors one would turn one's eyes with best hopes of success to some Tibetan village or some Alpine farm, many thousands of feet above the sea level."

"Well, considerin' that there are no railroads and no steamers you might as well talk about survivors in the moon," said Lord John. "But what I'm askin' myself is whether it's really over or whether it's only half-time."

Summerlee craned his neck to look round the horizon. "It seems clear and fine," said he in a very dubious voice; "but so it did yesterday. I am by no means assured that it is all over."

Challenger shrugged his shoulders.

"We must come back once more to our fatalism," said he. "If the world has undergone this experience before, which is not outside the range of possibility; it was certainly a very long time ago. Therefore, we may reasonably hope that it will be very long before it occurs again. "

"That's all very well," said Lord John, "but if you get an earthquake shock you are mighty likely to have a second one right on the top of it. I think we'd be wise to stretch our legs and have a breath of air while we have the chance. Since our oxygen is exhausted we may just as well be caught outside as in."

It was strange the absolute lethargy which had come upon us as a reaction after our tremendous emotions of the last twenty-four hours. It was both mental and physical, a deep-lying feeling that nothing mattered and that everything was a weariness and a profitless exertion. Even Challenger had succumbed to it, and sat in his chair, with his great head leaning upon his hands and his thoughts far away, until Lord John and I, catching him by each arm, fairly lifted him on to his feet, receiving only the glare and growl of an angry mastiff for our trouble. However, once we had got out of our narrow haven of refuge into the wider atmosphere of everyday life, our normal energy came gradually back to us once more.

But what were we to begin to do in that graveyard of a world? Could ever men have been faced with such a question since the dawn of time? It is true that our own physical needs, and even our luxuries, were assured for the future. All the stores of food, all the vintages of wine, all the treasures of art were ours for the taking. But what were we to DO? Some few tasks appealed to us at once, since they lay ready to our hands. We descended into the kitchen and laid the two domestics upon their respective beds. They seemed to have died without suffering, one in the chair by the fire, the other upon the scullery floor. Then we carried in poor Austin from the yard. His muscles were set as hard as a board in the most exaggerated rigor mortis, while the contraction of the fibres had drawn his mouth into a hard sardonic grin. This symptom was prevalent among all who had died from the poison. Wherever we went we were confronted by those grinning faces, which seemed to mock at our dreadful position, smiling silently and grimly at the ill-fated survivors of their race.

"Look here," said Lord John, who had paced restlessly about the dining-room whilst we partook of some food, "I don't know how you fellows feel about it, but for my part, I simply CAN'T sit here and do nothin'."

"Perhaps," Challenger answered, "you would have the kindness to suggest what you think we ought to do."

"Get a move on us and see all that has happened."

"That is what I should myself propose."

"But not in this little country village. We can see from the window all that this place can teach us."

"Where should we go, then?"

"To London!"

"That's all very well," grumbled Summerlee. "You may be equal to a forty-mile walk, but I'm not so sure about Challenger, with his stumpy legs, and I am perfectly sure about myself." Challenger was very much annoyed.

"If you could see your way, sir, to confining your remarks to your own physical peculiarities, you would find that you had an ample field for comment," he cried.

"I had no intention to offend you, my dear Challenger," cried our tactless friend, "You can't be held responsible for your own physique. If nature has given you a short, heavy body you cannot possibly help having stumpy legs."

Challenger was too furious to answer. He could only growl and blink and bristle. Lord John hastened to intervene before the dispute became more violent.

"You talk of walking. Why should we walk?" said he.

"Do you suggest taking a train?" asked Challenger, still simmering.

"What's the matter with the motor-car? Why should we not go in that?"

"I am not an expert," said Challenger, pulling at his beard reflectively. "At the same time, you are right in supposing that the human intellect in its higher manifestations should be sufficiently flexible to turn itself to anything. Your idea is an excellent one, Lord John. I myself will drive you all to London."

"You will do nothing of the kind," said Summerlee with decision.

"No, indeed, George!" cried his wife. "You only tried once, and you remember how you crashed through the gate of the garage."

"It was a momentary want of concentration," said Challenger complacently. "You can consider the matter settled. I will certainly drive you all to London."

The situation was relieved by Lord John.

"What's the car?" he asked.

"A twenty-horsepower Humber."

"Why, I've driven one for years," said he. "By George!" he added. "I never thought I'd live to take the whole human race in one load. There's just room for five, as I remember it. Get your things on, and I'll be ready at the door by ten o'clock."

Sure enough, at the hour named, the car came purring and crackling from the yard with Lord John at the wheel. I took my seat beside him, while the lady, a useful little buffer state, was squeezed in between the two men of wrath at the back. Then Lord John released his brakes, slid his lever rapidly from first to third, and we sped off upon the strangest drive that ever human beings have taken since man first came upon the earth.

You are to picture the loveliness of nature upon that August day, the freshness of the morning air, the golden glare of the summer sunshine, the cloudless sky, the luxuriant green of the Sussex woods, and the deep purple of heather-clad downs. As you looked round upon the many-coloured beauty of the scene all thought of a vast catastrophe would have passed from your mind had it not been for one sinister sign—the solemn, all-embracing silence. There is a gentle hum of life which pervades a closely-settled country, so deep and constant that one ceases to observe it, as the dweller by the sea loses all sense of the constant murmur of the waves. The twitter of birds, the buzz of insects, the far-off echo of voices, the lowing of cattle, the distant barking of dogs, roar of trains, and rattle of carts—all these form one low, unremitting note, striking unheeded upon the ear. We missed it now. This deadly silence was appalling. So solemn was it, so impressive, that the buzz and rattle of our motor-car seemed an unwarrantable intrusion, an indecent disregard of this reverent stillness which lay like a pall over and round the ruins of humanity. It was this grim hush, and the tall clouds of smoke which rose here and there over the country-side from smoldering buildings, which cast a chill into our hearts as we gazed round at the glorious panorama of the Weald.

And then there were the dead! At first those endless groups of drawn and grinning faces filled us with a shuddering horror. So vivid and mordant was the impression that I can live over again that slow descent of the station hill, the passing by the nurse-girl with the two babes, the sight of the old horse on his knees between the shafts, the cabman twisted across his seat, and the young man inside with his hand upon the open door in the very act of springing out. Lower down were six reapers all in a litter, their limbs crossing, their dead, unwinking eyes gazing upwards at the glare of heaven. These things I see as in a photograph. But soon, by the merciful provision of nature, the over-excited nerve ceased to respond. The very vastness of the horror took away from its personal appeal. Individuals merged into groups, groups into crowds, crowds into a universal phenomenon which one soon accepted as the inevitable detail of every scene. Only here and there, where some particularly brutal or grotesque incident caught the attention, did the mind come back with a sudden shock to the personal and human meaning of it all.

Above all, there was the fate of the children. That, I remember, filled us with the strongest sense of intolerable injustice. We could have wept—Mrs. Challenger did weep—when we passed a great council school and saw the long trail of tiny figures scattered down the road which led from it. They had been dismissed by their terrified teachers and were speeding for their homes when the poison caught them in its net. Great numbers of people were at the open windows of the houses. In Tunbridge Wells there was hardly one which had not its staring, smiling face. At the last instant the need of air, that very craving for oxygen which we alone had been able to satisfy, had sent them flying to the window. The sidewalks too were littered with men and women, hatless and bonnetless, who had rushed out of the houses. Many of them had fallen in the roadway. It was a lucky thing that in Lord John we had found an expert driver, for it was no easy matter to pick one's way. Passing through the villages or towns we could only go at a walking pace, and once, I remember, opposite the school at Tonbridge, we had to halt some time while we carried aside the bodies which blocked our path.

A few small, definite pictures stand out in my memory from amid that long panorama of death upon the Sussex and Kentish high roads. One was that of a great, glittering motor-car standing outside the inn at the village of Southborough. It bore, as I should guess, some pleasure party upon their return from Brighton or from Eastbourne. There were three gaily dressed women, all young and beautiful, one of them with a Peking spaniel upon her lap. With them were a rakish-looking elderly man and a young aristocrat, his eyeglass still in his eye, his cigarette burned down to the stub between the fingers of his begloved hand. Death must have come on them in an instant and fixed them as they sat. Save that the elderly man had at the last moment torn out his collar in an effort to breathe, they might all have been asleep. On one side of the car a waiter with some broken glasses beside a tray was huddled near the step. On the other, two very ragged tramps, a man and a woman, lay where they had fallen, the man with his long, thin arm still outstretched, even as he had asked for alms in his lifetime. One instant of time had put aristocrat, waiter, tramp, and dog upon one common footing of inert and dissolving protoplasm.

I remember another singular picture, some miles on the London side of Sevenoaks. There is a large convent upon the left, with a long, green slope in front of it. Upon this slope were assembled a great number of school children, all kneeling at prayer. In front of them was a fringe of nuns, and higher up the slope, facing towards them, a single figure whom we took to be the Mother Superior. Unlike the pleasure-seekers in the motor-car, these people seemed to have had warning of their danger and to have died beautifully together, the teachers and the taught, assembled for their last common lesson.

My mind is still stunned by that terrific experience, and I grope vainly for means of expression by which I can reproduce the emotions which we felt. Perhaps it is best and wisest not to try, but merely to indicate the facts. Even Summerlee and Challenger were crushed, and we heard nothing of our companions behind us save an occasional whimper from the lady. As to Lord John, he was too intent upon his wheel and the difficult task of threading his way along such roads to have time or inclination for conversation. One phrase he used with such wearisome iteration that it stuck in my memory and at last almost made me laugh as a comment upon the day of doom.

"Pretty doin's! What!"

That was his ejaculation as each fresh tremendous combination of death and disaster displayed itself before us. "Pretty doin's! What!" he cried, as we descended the station hill at Rotherfield, and it was still "Pretty doin's! What!" as we picked our way through a wilderness of death in the High Street of Lewisham and the Old Kent Road.

It was here that we received a sudden and amazing shock. Out of the window of a humble corner house there appeared a fluttering handkerchief waving at the end of a long, thin human arm. Never had the sight of unexpected death caused our hearts to stop and then throb so wildly as did this amazing indication of life. Lord John ran the motor to the curb, and in an instant we had rushed through the open door of the house and up the staircase to the second-floor front room from which the signal proceeded.

A very old lady sat in a chair by the open window, and close to her, laid across a second chair, was a cylinder of oxygen, smaller but of the same shape as those which had saved our own lives. She turned her thin, drawn, bespectacled face toward us as we crowded in at the doorway.

"I feared that I was abandoned here forever," said she, "for I am an invalid and cannot stir."

"Well, madam," Challenger answered, "it is a lucky chance that we happened to pass."

"I have one all-important question to ask you," said she. "Gentlemen, I beg that you will be frank with me. What effect will these events have upon London and North-Western Railway shares?"

We should have laughed had it not been for the tragic eagerness with which she listened for our answer. Mrs. Burston, for that was her name, was an aged widow, whose whole income depended upon a small holding of this stock. Her life had been regulated by the rise and fall of the dividend, and she could form no conception of existence save as it was affected by the quotation of her shares. In vain we pointed out to her that all the money in the world was hers for the taking and was useless when taken. Her old mind would not adapt itself to the new idea, and she wept loudly over her vanished stock. "It was all I had," she wailed. "If that is gone I may as well go too."

Amid her lamentations we found out how this frail old plant had lived where the whole great forest had fallen. She was a confirmed invalid and an asthmatic. Oxygen had been prescribed for her malady, and a tube was in her room at the moment of the crisis. She had naturally inhaled some as had been her habit when there was a difficulty with her breathing. It had given her relief, and by doling out her supply she had managed to survive the night. Finally she had fallen asleep and been awakened by the buzz of our motor-car. As it was impossible to take her on with us, we saw that she had all necessaries of life and promised to communicate with her in a couple of days at the latest. So we left her, still weeping bitterly over her vanished stock.

As we approached the Thames the block in the streets became thicker and the obstacles more bewildering. It was with difficulty that we made our way across London Bridge. The approaches to it upon the Middlesex side were choked from end to end with frozen traffic which made all further advance in that direction impossible. A ship was blazing brightly alongside one of the wharves near the bridge, and the air was full of drifting smuts and of a heavy acrid smell of burning. There was a cloud of dense smoke somewhere near the Houses of Parliament, but it was impossible from where we were to see what was on fire.

"I don't know how it strikes you," Lord John remarked as he brought his engine to a standstill, "but it seems to me the country is more cheerful than the town. Dead London is gettin' on my nerves. I'm for a cast round and then gettin' back to Rotherfield."

"I confess that I do not see what we can hope for here," said Professor Summerlee.

"At the same time," said Challenger, his great voice booming strangely amid the silence, "it is difficult for us to conceive that out of seven millions of people there is only this one old woman who by some peculiarity of constitution or some accident of occupation has managed to survive this catastrophe."

"If there should be others, how can we hope to find them, George?" asked the lady. "And yet I agree with you that we cannot go back until we have tried."

Getting out of the car and leaving it by the curb, we walked with some difficulty along the crowded pavement of King William Street and entered the open door of a large insurance office. It was a corner house, and we chose it as commanding a view in every direction. Ascending the stair, we passed through what I suppose to have been the board-room, for eight elderly men were seated round a long table in the centre of it. The high window was open and we all stepped out upon the balcony. From it we could see the crowded city streets radiating in every direction, while below us the road was black from side to side with the tops of the motionless taxis. All, or nearly all, had their heads pointed outwards, showing how the terrified men of the city had at the last moment made a vain endeavor to rejoin their families in the suburbs or the country. Here and there amid the humbler cabs towered the great brass-spangled motor-car of some wealthy magnate, wedged hopelessly among the dammed stream of arrested traffic. Just beneath us there was such a one of great size and luxurious appearance, with its owner, a fat old man, leaning out, half his gross body through the window, and his podgy hand, gleaming with diamonds, outstretched as he urged his chauffeur to make a last effort to break through the press.

A dozen motor-buses towered up like islands in this flood, the passengers who crowded the roofs lying all huddled together and

across eash others' laps like a child's toys in a nursery. On a broad
lamp pedestal in the centre of the roadway, a burly policeman was
standing, leaning his back against the post in so natural an attitude that it was hard to realize that he was not alive, while at his
feet there lay a ragged newsboy with his bundle of papers on the
ground beside him. A paper-cart had got blocked in the crowd,
and we could read in large letters, black upon yellow, "Scene at
Lord's. County Match Interrupted." This must have been the earliest edition, for there were other placards bearing the legend, "Is It
the End? Great Scientist's Warning." And another, "Is Challenger
Justified? Ominous Rumours."

Challenger pointed the latter placard out to his wife, as it
thrust itself like a banner above the throng. I could see him throw
out his chest and stroke his beard as he looked at it. It pleased and
flattered that complex mind to think that London had died with
his name and his words still present in their thoughts. His feelings
were so evident that they aroused the sardonic comment of his
colleague.

"In the limelight to the last, Challenger," he remarked.

"So it would appear," he answered complacently. "Well," he
added as he looked down the long vista of the radiating streets, all
silent and all choked up with death, "I really see no purpose to be
served by our staying any longer in London. I suggest that we
return at once to Rotherfield and then take counsel as to how we
shall most profitably employ the years which lie before us."

Only one other picture shall I give of the scenes which we carried back in our memories from the dead city. It is a glimpse
which we had of the interior of the old church of St. Mary's, which
is at the very point where our car was awaiting us. Picking our way
among the prostrate figures upon the steps, we pushed open the
swing door and entered. It was a wonderful sight. The church was
crammed from end to end with kneeling figures in every posture
of supplication and abasement. At the last dreadful moment,
brought suddenly face to face with the realities of life, those terrific realities which hang over us even while we follow the shadows, the terrified people had rushed into those old city churches
which for generations had hardly ever held a congregation. There
they huddled as close as they could kneel, many of them in their

agitation still wearing their hats, while above them in the pulpit a young man in lay dress had apparently been addressing them when he and they had been overwhelmed by the same fate. He lay now, like Punch in his booth, with his head and two limp arms hanging over the ledge of the pulpit. It was a nightmare, the grey, dusty church, the rows of agonized figures, the dimness and silence of it all. We moved about with hushed whispers, walking upon our tip-toes.

And then suddenly I had an idea. At one corner of the church, near the door, stood the ancient font, and behind it a deep recess in which there hung the ropes for the bell-ringers. Why should we not send a message out over London which would attract to us anyone who might still be alive? I ran across, and pulling at the list-covered rope, I was surprised to find how difficult it was to swing the bell. Lord John had followed me.

"By George, young fellah!" said he, pulling off his coat. "You've hit on a dooced good notion. Give me a grip and we'll soon have a move on it."

But, even then, so heavy was the bell that it was not until Challenger and Summerlee had added their weight to ours that we heard the roaring and clanging above our heads which told us that the great clapper was ringing out its music. Far over dead London resounded our message of comradeship and hope to any fellow-man surviving. It cheered our own hearts, that strong, metallic call, and we turned the more earnestly to our work, dragged two feet off the earth with each upward jerk of the rope, but all straining together on the downward heave, Challenger the lowest of all, bending all his great strength to the task and flopping up and down like a monstrous bull-frog, croaking with every pull. It was at that moment that an artist might have taken a picture of the four adventurers, the comrades of many strange perils in the past, whom fate had now chosen for so supreme an experience. For half an hour we worked, the sweat dropping from our faces, our arms and backs aching with the exertion. Then we went out into the portico of the church and looked eagerly up and down the silent, crowded streets. Not a sound, not a motion, in answer to our summons.

"It's no use. No one is left," I cried.

"We can do nothing more," said Mrs. Challenger. "For God's sake, George, let us get back to Rotherfield. Another hour of this dreadful, silent city would drive me mad."

We got into the car without another word. Lord John backed her round and turned her to the south. To us the chapter seemed closed. Little did we foresee the strange new chapter which was to open.

Chapter VI   The Great Awakening

And now I come to the end of this extraordinary incident, so over-shadowing in its importance, not only in our own small, individual lives, but in the general history of the human race. As I said when I began my narrative, when that history comes to be written, this occurrence will surely stand out among all other events like a mountain towering among its foothills. Our generation has been reserved for a very special fate since it has been chosen to experience so wonderful a thing. How long its effect may last—how long mankind may preserve the humility and reverence which this great shock has taught it—can only be shown by the future. I think it is safe to say that things can never be quite the same again. Never can one realize how powerless and ignorant one is, and how one is upheld by an unseen hand, until for an instant that hand has seemed to close and to crush. Death has been imminent upon us. We know that at any moment it may be again. That grim presence shadows our lives, but who can deny that in that shadow the sense of duty, the feeling of sobriety and responsibility, the appreciation of the gravity and of the objects of life, the earnest desire to develop and improve, have grown and become real with us to a degree that has leavened our whole society from end to end? It is something beyond sects and beyond dogmas. It is rather an alteration of perspective, a shifting of our sense of proportion, a vivid realization that we are insignificant and evanescent creatures, existing on sufferance and at the mercy of the first chill wind from the unknown. But if the world has grown graver with this knowledge it is not, I think, a sadder place in consequence. Surely we are agreed that the more sober and restrained pleasures of the present are deeper as well as wiser than the noisy, foolish hustle which passed so often for enjoyment in the days of old—days so recent and yet already so inconceivable. Those empty lives which were wasted in aimless visiting and being visited, in the worry of great and unnecessary households, in the arranging and eating of elaborate and tedious meals, have now found rest and health in the reading, the music, the gentle family communion which comes from a simpler and saner division of their time. With greater health and greater pleasure they are richer than before, even after they have paid those increased contributions to the common fund which have so raised the standard of life in these islands.

There is some clash of opinion as to the exact hour of the great awakening. It is generally agreed that, apart from the difference of clocks, there may have been local causes which influenced the action of the poison. Certainly, in each separate district the resurrection was practically simultaneous. There are numerous witnesses that Big Ben pointed to ten minutes past six at the moment. The Astronomer Royal has fixed the Greenwich time at twelve past six. On the other hand, Laird Johnson, a very capable East Anglia observer, has recorded six-twenty as the hour. In the Hebrides it was as late as seven. In our own case there can be no doubt whatever, for I was seated in Challenger's study with his carefully tested chronometer in front of me at the moment. The hour was a quarter-past six.

An enormous depression was weighing upon my spirits. The cumulative effect of all the dreadful sights which we had seen upon our journey was heavy upon my soul. With my abounding animal health and great physical energy any kind of mental clouding was a rare event. I had the Irish faculty of seeing some gleam of humor in every darkness. But now the obscurity was appalling and unrelieved. The others were downstairs making their plans for the future. I sat by the open window, my chin resting upon my hand and my mind absorbed in the misery of our situation. Could we continue to live? That was the question which I had begun to ask myself. Was it possible to exist upon a dead world? Just as in physics the greater body draws to itself the lesser, would we not feel an overpowering attraction from that vast body of humanity which had passed into the unknown? How would the end come?

Would it be from a return of the poison? Or would the earth be uninhabitable from the mephitic products of universal decay? Or, finally, might our awful situation prey upon and unbalance our minds? A group of insane folk upon a dead world! My mind was brooding upon this last dreadful idea when some slight noise caused me to look down upon the road beneath me. The old cab horse was coming up the hill!

I was conscious at the same instant of the twittering of birds, of someone coughing in the yard below, and of a background of movement in the landscape. And yet I remember that it was that absurd, emaciated, superannuated cab-horse which held my gaze. Slowly and wheezily it was climbing the slope. Then my eye traveled to the driver sitting hunched up upon the box and finally to the young man who was leaning out of the window in some excitement and shouting a direction. They were all indubitably, aggressively alive!

Everybody was alive once more! Had it all been a delusion? Was it conceivable that this whole poison belt incident had been an elaborate dream? For an instant my startled brain was really ready to believe it. Then I looked down, and there was the rising blister on my hand where it was frayed by the rope of the city bell. It had really been so, then. And yet here was the world resuscitated—here was life come back in an instant full tide to the planet. Now, as my eyes wandered all over the great landscape, I saw it in every direction—and moving, to my amazement, in the very same groove in which it had halted. There were the golfers. Was it possible that they were going on with their game? Yes, there was a fellow driving off from a tee, and that other group upon the green were surely putting for the hole. The reapers were slowly trooping back to their work. The nurse-girl slapped one of her charges and then began to push the perambulator up the hill. Everyone had unconcernedly taken up the thread at the very point where they had dropped it.

I rushed downstairs, but the hall door was open, and I heard the voices of my companions, loud in astonishment and congratulation, in the yard. How we all shook hands and laughed as we came together, and how Mrs. Challenger kissed us all in her emotion, before she finally threw herself into the bear-hug of her husband.

"But they could not have been asleep!" cried Lord John. "Dash it all, Challenger, you don't mean to believe that those folk were asleep with their staring eyes and stiff limbs and that awful death grin on their faces!"

"It can only have been the condition that is called catalepsy," said Challenger. "It has been a rare phenomenon in the past and has constantly been mistaken for death. While it endures, the temperature falls, the respiration disappears, the heartbeat is indistinguishable—in fact, it IS death, save that it is evanescent. Even the most comprehensive mind"—here he closed his eyes and simpered—"could hardly conceive a universal outbreak of it in this fashion."

"You may label it catalepsy," remarked Summerlee, "but, after all, that is only a name, and we know as little of the result as we do of the poison which has caused it. The most we can say is that the vitiated ether has produced a temporary death."

Austin was seated all in a heap on the step of the car. It was his coughing which I had heard from above. He had been holding his head in silence, but now he was muttering to himself and running his eyes over the car.

"Young fat-head!" he grumbled. "Can't leave things alone!"

"What's the matter, Austin?"

"Lubricators left running, sir. Someone has been fooling with the car. I expect it's that young garden boy, sir."

Lord John looked guilty.

"I don't know what's amiss with me," continued Austin, staggering to his feet. "I expect I came over queer when I was hosing her down. I seem to remember flopping over by the step. But I'll swear I never left those lubricator taps on."

In a condensed narrative the astonished Austin was told what had happened to himself and the world. The mystery of the dripping lubricators was also explained to him. He listened with an air of deep distrust when told how an amateur had driven his car and with absorbed interest to the few sentences in which our experiences of the sleeping city were recorded. I can remember his comment when the story was concluded.

"Was you outside the Bank of England, sir?"

"Yes, Austin."

"With all them millions inside and everybody asleep?"

"That was so."

"And I not there!" he groaned, and turned dismally once more to the hosing of his car.

There was a sudden grinding of wheels upon gravel. The old cab had actually pulled up at Challenger's door. I saw the young occupant step out from it. An instant later the maid, who looked as tousled and bewildered as if she had that instant been aroused from the deepest sleep, appeared with a card upon a tray. Challenger snorted ferociously as he looked at it, and his thick black hair seemed to bristle up in his wrath.

"A pressman!" he growled. Then with a deprecating smile: "After all, it is natural that the whole world should hasten to know what I think of such an episode."

"That can hardly be his errand," said Summerlee, "for he was on the road in his cab before ever the crisis came."

I looked at the card: "James Baxter, London Correspondent, New York Monitor."

"You'll see him?" said I.

"Not I."

"Oh, George! You should be kinder and more considerate to others. Surely you have learned something from what we have undergone."

He tut-tutted and shook his big, obstinate head.

"A poisonous breed! Eh, Malone? The worst weed in modern civilization, the ready tool of the quack and the hindrance of the self-respecting man! When did they ever say a good word for me?"

"When did you ever say a good word to them?" I answered. "Come, sir, this is a stranger who has made a journey to see you. I am sure that you won't be rude to him."

"Well, well," he grumbled, "you come with me and do the talking. I protest in advance against any such outrageous invasion of my private life." Muttering and mumbling, he came rolling after me like an angry and rather ill-conditioned mastiff.

The dapper young American pulled out his notebook and plunged instantly into his subject.

"I came down, sir," said he, "because our people in America would very much like to hear more about this danger which is, in your opinion, pressing upon the world."

"I know of no danger which is now pressing upon the world," Challenger answered gruffly.

The pressman looked at him in mild surprise.

"I meant, sir, the chances that the world might run into a belt of poisonous ether."

"I do not now apprehend any such danger," said Challenger.

The pressman looked even more perplexed.

"You are Professor Challenger, are you not?" he asked.

"Yes, sir; that is my name."

"I cannot understand, then, how you can say that there is no such danger. I am alluding to your own letter, published above your name in the London Times of this morning."

It was Challenger's turn to look surprised.

"This morning?" said he. "No London Times was published this morning."

"Surely, sir," said the American in mild remonstrance, "you must admit that the London Times is a daily paper." He drew out a copy from his inside pocket. "Here is the letter to which I refer."

Challenger chuckled and rubbed his hands.

"I begin to understand," said he. "So you read this letter this morning?"

"Yes, sir."

"And came at once to interview me?"

"Yes, sir."

"Did you observe anything unusual upon the journey down?"

"Well, to tell the truth, your people seemed more lively and generally human than I have ever seen them. The baggage man set out to tell me a funny story, and that's a new experience for me in this country."

"Nothing else?"

"Why, no, sir, not that I can recall."

"Well, now, what hour did you leave Victoria?"

The American smiled.

"I came here to interview you, Professor, but it seems to be a case of 'Is this nigger fishing, or is this fish niggering?' You're doing most of the work."

"It happens to interest me. Do you recall the hour?"

"Sure. It was half-past twelve."

"And you arrived?"

"At a quarter-past two."

"And you hired a cab?"

"That was so."

"How far do you suppose it is to the station?"

"Well, I should reckon the best part of two miles."

"So how long do you think it took you?"

"Well, half an hour, maybe, with that asthmatic in front."

"So it should be three o'clock?"

"Yes, or a trifle after it."

"Look at your watch."

The American did so and then stared at us in astonishment.

"Say!" he cried. "It's run down. That horse has broken every record, sure. The sun is pretty low, now that I come to look at it. Well, there's something here I don't understand."

"Have you no remembrance of anything remarkable as you came up the hill?"

"Well, I seem to recollect that I was mighty sleepy once. It comes back to me that I wanted to say something to the driver and that I couldn't make him heed me. I guess it was the heat, but I felt swimmy for a moment. That's all."

"So it is with the whole human race," said Challenger to me. "They have all felt swimmy for a moment. None of them have as yet any comprehension of what has occurred. Each will go on with his interrupted job as Austin has snatched up his hose-pipe or the golfer continued his game. Your editor, Malone, will continue the issue of his papers, and very much amazed he will be at finding that an issue is missing. Yes, my young friend," he added to the American reporter, with a sudden mood of amused geniality, "it may interest you to know that the world has swum through the poisonous current which swirls like the Gulf Stream through the ocean of ether. You will also kindly note for your own future convenience that to-day is not Friday, August the twenty-seventh, but

Saturday, August the twenty-eighth, and that you sat senseless in your cab for twenty-eight hours upon the Rotherfield hill."

And "right here," as my American colleague would say, I may bring this narrative to an end. It is, as you are probably aware, only a fuller and more detailed version of the account which appeared in the Monday edition of the Daily Gazette—an account which has been universally admitted to be the greatest journalistic scoop of all time, which sold no fewer than three-and-a-half million copies of the paper. Framed upon the wall of my sanctum I retain those magnificent headlines:—

TWENTY-EIGHT HOURS' WORLD COMA
UNPRECEDENTED EXPERIENCE
CHALLENGER JUSTIFIED
OUR CORRESPONDENT ESCAPES
ENTHRALLING NARRATIVE
THE OXYGEN ROOM
WEIRD MOTOR DRIVE
DEAD LONDON
REPLACING THE MISSING PAGE
GREAT FIRES AND LOSS OF LIFE
WILL IT RECUR?

Underneath this glorious scroll came nine and a half columns of narrative, in which appeared the first, last, and only account of the history of the planet, so far as one observer could draw it, during one long day of its existence. Challenger and Summerlee have treated the matter in a joint scientific paper, but to me alone was left the popular account. Surely I can sing "Nunc dimittis." What is left but anti-climax in the life of a journalist after that!

But let me not end on sensational headlines and a merely personal triumph. Rather let me quote the sonorous passages in which the greatest of daily papers ended its admirable leader upon the subject—a leader which might well be filed for reference by every thoughtful man.

"It has been a well-worn truism," said the Times, "that our human race are a feeble folk before the infinite latent forces which surround us. From the prophets of old and from the philosophers of our own time the same message and warning have reached us. But, like all oft-repeated truths, it has in time lost something of its actuality and cogency. A lesson, an actual experience, was needed to bring it home. It is from that salutory but terrible ordeal that we have just emerged, with minds which are still stunned by the suddenness of the blow and with spirits which are chastened by the realization of our own limitations and impotence. The world has paid a fearful price for its schooling. Hardly yet have we learned the full tale of disaster, but the destruction by fire of New York, of Orleans, and of Brighton constitutes in itself one of the greatest tragedies in the history of our race. When the account of the railway and shipping accidents has been completed, it will furnish grim reading, although there is evidence to show that in the vast majority of cases the drivers of trains and engineers of steamers succeeded in shutting off their motive power before succumbing to the poison. But the material damage, enormous as it is both in life and in property, is not the consideration which will be uppermost in our minds to-day. All this may in time be forgotten. But what will not be forgotten, and what will and should continue to obsess our imaginations, is this revelation of the possibilities of the universe, this destruction of our ignorant self-complacency, and this demonstration of how narrow is the path of our material existence and what abysses may lie upon either side of it. Solemnity and humility are at the base of all our emotions to-day. May they be the foundations upon which a more earnest and reverent race may build a more worthy temple."

ROUND THE RED LAMP

Being Facts and Fancies of Medical Life

The Preface

*Being an extract from a long and animated correspondence
with a friend in America.*

I quite recognise the force of your objection that an invalid or a
woman in weak health would get no good from stories which
attempt to treat some features of medical life with a certain
amount of realism. If you deal with this life at all, however, and if
you are anxious to make your doctors something more than mar-
ionettes, it is quite essential that you should paint the darker side,
since it is that which is principally presented to the surgeon or
physician. He sees many beautiful things, it is true, fortitude and
heroism, love and self-sacrifice; but they are all called forth (as our
nobler qualities are always called forth) by bitter sorrow and trial.
One cannot write of medical life and be merry over it.

Then why write of it, you may ask? If a subject is painful why
treat it at all? I answer that it is the province of fiction to treat
painful things as well as cheerful ones. The story which wiles away
a weary hour fulfils an obviously good purpose, but not more so, I
hold, than that which helps to emphasise the graver side of life. A
tale which may startle the reader out of his usual grooves of
thought, and shocks him into seriousness, plays the part of the
alterative and tonic in medicine, bitter to the taste but bracing in
the result. There are a few stories in this little collection which
might have such an effect, and I have so far shared in your feeling
that I have reserved them from serial publication. In book-form
the reader can see that they are medical stories, and can, if he or
she be so minded, avoid them.

Yours very truly,
A. CONAN DOYLE.

P. S.—You ask about the Red Lamp. It is the usual sign of the
general practitioner in England.

Behind the Times

My first interview with Dr. James Winter was under dramatic circumstances. It occurred at two in the morning in the bedroom of an old country house. I kicked him twice on the white waistcoat and knocked off his gold spectacles, while he with the aid of a female accomplice stifled my angry cries in a flannel petticoat and thrust me into a warm bath. I am told that one of my parents, who happened to be present, remarked in a whisper that there was nothing the matter with my lungs. I cannot recall how Dr. Winter looked at the time, for I had other things to think of, but his description of my own appearance is far from flattering. A fluffy head, a body like a trussed goose, very bandy legs, and feet with the soles turned inwards—those are the main items which he can remember.

From this time onwards the epochs of my life were the periodical assaults which Dr. Winter made upon me. He vaccinated me; he cut me for an abscess; he blistered me for mumps. It was a world of peace and he the one dark cloud that threatened. But at last there came a time of real illness—a time when I lay for months together inside my wickerwork-basket bed, and then it was that I learned that that hard face could relax, that those country-made creaking boots could steal very gently to a bedside, and that that rough voice could thin into a whisper when it spoke to a sick child.

And now the child is himself a medical man, and yet Dr. Winter is the same as ever. I can see no change since first I can remember him, save that perhaps the brindled hair is a trifle whiter, and the huge shoulders a little more bowed. He is a very tall man, though he loses a couple of inches from his stoop. That big back of his has curved itself over sick beds until it has set in that shape. His face is of a walnut brown, and tells of long winter drives over bleak country roads, with the wind and the rain in his teeth. It looks smooth at a little distance, but as you approach him you see that it is shot with innumerable fine wrinkles like a last year's apple. They are hardly to be seen when he is in repose; but when he laughs his face breaks like a starred glass, and you realise then that though he looks old, he must be older than he looks.

How old that is I could never discover. I have often tried to find out, and have struck his stream as high up as George IV and even the Regency, but without ever getting quite to the source. His mind must have been open to impressions very early, but it must also have closed early, for the politics of the day have little interest for him, while he is fiercely excited about questions which are entirely prehistoric. He shakes his head when he speaks of the first Reform Bill and expresses grave doubts as to its wisdom, and I have heard him, when he was warmed by a glass of wine, say bitter things about Robert Peel and his abandoning of the Corn Laws. The death of that statesman brought the history of England to a definite close, and Dr. Winter refers to everything which had happened since then as to an insignificant anticlimax.

But it was only when I had myself become a medical man that I was able to appreciate how entirely he is a survival of a past generation. He had learned his medicine under that obsolete and forgotten system by which a youth was apprenticed to a surgeon, in the days when the study of anatomy was often approached through a violated grave. His views upon his own profession are even more reactionary than in politics. Fifty years have brought him little and deprived him of less. Vaccination was well within the teaching of his youth, though I think he has a secret preference for inoculation. Bleeding he would practise freely but for public opinion. Chloroform he regards as a dangerous innovation, and he always clicks with his tongue when it is mentioned. He has even been known to say vain things about Laennec, and to refer to the stethoscope as "a new-fangled French toy." He carries one in his hat out of deference to the expectations of his patients, but he is very hard of hearing, so that it makes little difference whether he uses it or not.

He reads, as a duty, his weekly medical paper, so that he has a general idea as to the advance of modern science. He always persists in looking upon it as a huge and rather ludicrous experiment. The germ theory of disease set him chuckling for a long time, and his favourite joke in the sick room was to say, "Shut the door or the germs will be getting in." As to the Darwinian theory, it struck him as being the crowning joke of the century. "The children in the nursery and the ancestors in the stable," he would cry, and laugh the tears out of his eyes.

He is so very much behind the day that occasionally, as things move round in their usual circle, he finds himself, to his bewilderment, in the front of the fashion. Dietetic treatment, for example, had been much in vogue in his youth, and he has more practical knowledge of it than any one whom I have met. Massage, too, was familiar to him when it was new to our generation. He had been trained also at a time when instruments were in a rudimentary state, and when men learned to trust more to their own fingers. He has a model surgical hand, muscular in the palm, tapering in the fingers, "with an eye at the end of each." I shall not easily forget how Dr. Patterson and I cut Sir John Sirwell, the County Member, and were unable to find the stone. It was a horrible moment. Both our careers were at stake. And then it was that Dr. Winter, whom we had asked out of courtesy to be present, introduced into the wound a finger which seemed to our excited senses to be about nine inches long, and hooked out the stone at the end of it. "It's always well to bring one in your waistcoat-pocket," said he with a chuckle, "but I suppose you youngsters are above all that."

We made him president of our branch of the British Medical Association, but he resigned after the first meeting. "The young men are too much for me," he said. "I don't understand what they are talking about." Yet his patients do very well. He has the healing touch—that magnetic thing which defies explanation or analysis, but which is a very evident fact none the less. His mere presence leaves the patient with more hopefulness and vitality. The sight of disease affects him as dust does a careful housewife. It makes him angry and impatient. "Tut, tut, this will never do!" he cries, as he takes over a new case. He would shoo Death out of the room as though he were an intrusive hen. But when the intruder refuses to be dislodged, when the blood moves more slowly and the eyes grow dimmer, then it is that Dr. Winter is of more avail than all the drugs in his surgery. Dying folk cling to his hand as if the presence of his bulk and vigour gives them more courage to face the change; and that kindly, windbeaten face has been the last earthly impression which many a sufferer has carried into the unknown.

When Dr. Patterson and I—both of us young, energetic, and up-to-date—settled in the district, we were most cordially received by the old doctor, who would have been only too happy to be relieved of some of his patients. The patients themselves, however, followed their own inclinations—which is a reprehensible way that patients have—so that we remained neglected, with our modern instruments and our latest alkaloids, while he was serving out senna and calomel to all the countryside. We both of us loved the old fellow, but at the same time, in the privacy of our own intimate conversations, we could not help commenting upon this deplorable lack of judgment. "It's all very well for the poorer people," said Patterson. "But after all the educated classes have a right to expect that their medical man will know the difference between a mitral murmur and a bronchitic rale. It's the judicial frame of mind, not the sympathetic, which is the essential one."

I thoroughly agreed with Patterson in what he said. It happened, however, that very shortly afterwards the epidemic of influenza broke out, and we were all worked to death. One morning I met Patterson on my round, and found him looking rather pale and fagged out. He made the same remark about me. I was, in fact, feeling far from well, and I lay upon the sofa all the afternoon with a splitting headache and pains in every joint. As evening closed in, I could no longer disguise the fact that the scourge was upon me, and I felt that I should have medical advice without delay. It was of Patterson, naturally, that I thought, but somehow the idea of him had suddenly become repugnant to me. I thought of his cold, critical attitude, of his endless questions, of his tests and his tappings. I wanted something more soothing—something more genial.

"Mrs. Hudson," said I to my housekeeper, would you kindly run along to old Dr. Winter and tell him that I should be obliged to him if he would step round?"

She was back with an answer presently. "Dr. Winter will come round in an hour or so, sir; but he has just been called in to attend Dr. Patterson."

His First Operation

It was the first day of the winter session, and the third year's man was walking with the first year's man. Twelve o'clock was just booming out from the Tron Church.

"Let me see," said the third year's man. "You have never seen an operation?"

"Never."

"Then this way, please. This is Rutherford's historic bar. A glass of sherry, please, for this gentleman. You are rather sensitive, are you not?"

"My nerves are not very strong, I am afraid."

"Hum! Another glass of sherry for this gentleman. We are going to an operation now, you know."

The novice squared his shoulders and made a gallant attempt to look unconcerned.

"Nothing very bad—eh?"

"Well, yes—pretty bad."

"An—an amputation?"

"No; it's a bigger affair than that."

"I think—I think they must be expecting me at home."

"There's no sense in funking. If you don't go to-day, you must to-morrow. Better get it over at once. Feel pretty fit?"

"Oh, yes; all right!" The smile was not a success.

"One more glass of sherry, then. Now come on or we shall be late. I want you to be well in front."

"Surely that is not necessary."

"Oh, it is far better! What a drove of students! There are plenty of new men among them. You can tell them easily enough, can't you? If they were going down to be operated upon them-selves, they could not look whiter."

"I don't think I should look as white."

"Well, I was just the same myself. But the feeling soon wears off. You see a fellow with a face like plaster, and before the week is out he is eating his lunch in the dissecting rooms. I'll tell you all about the case when we get to the theatre."

The students were pouring down the sloping street which led to the infirmary—each with his little sheaf of note-books in his hand. There were pale, frightened lads, fresh from the high schools, and callous old chronics, whose generation had passed on and left them. They swept in an unbroken, tumultuous stream from the university gate to the hospital. The figures and gait of the men were young, but there was little youth in most of their faces. Some looked as if they ate too little—a few as if they drank too much. Tall and short, tweed-coated and black, round-shouldered, bespectacled, and slim, they crowded with clatter of feet and rattle of sticks through the hospital gate. Now and again they thickened into two lines, as the carriage of a surgeon of the staff rolled over the cobblestones between.

"There's going to be a crowd at Archer's," whispered the senior man with suppressed excitement. "It is grand to see him at work. I've seen him jab all round the aorta until it made me jumpy to watch him. This way, and mind the whitewash."

They passed under an archway and down a long, stone-flagged corridor, with drab-coloured doors on either side, each marked with a number. Some of them were ajar, and the novice glanced into them with tingling nerves. He was reassured to catch a glimpse of cheery fires, lines of white-counterpaned beds, and a profusion of coloured texts upon the wall. The corridor opened upon a small hall, with a fringe of poorly clad people seated all round upon benches. A young man, with a pair of scissors stuck like a flower in his buttonhole and a note-book in his hand, was passing from one to the other, whispering and writing.

"Anything good?" asked the third year's man.

"You should have been here yesterday," said the out-patient clerk, glancing up. "We had a regular field day. A popliteal aneurism, a Colles' fracture, a spina bifida, a tropical abscess, and an elephantiasis. How's that for a single haul?"

"I'm sorry I missed it. But they'll come again, I suppose. What's up with the old gentleman?"

A broken workman was sitting in the shadow, rocking himself slowly to and fro, and groaning. A woman beside him was trying to console him, patting his shoulder with a hand which was spotted over with curious little white blisters.

"It's a fine carbuncle," said the clerk, with the air of a connoisseur who describes his orchids to one who can appreciate them. "It's on his back and the passage is draughty, so we must not look at it, must we, daddy? Pemphigus," he added carelessly, pointing to the woman's disfigured hands. "Would you care to stop and take out a metacarpal?"

"No, thank you. We are due at Archer's. Come on!" and they rejoined the throng which was hurrying to the theatre of the famous surgeon.

The tiers of horseshoe benches rising from the floor to the ceiling were already packed, and the novice as he entered saw vague curving lines of faces in front of him, and heard the deep buzz of a hundred voices, and sounds of laughter from somewhere up above him. His companion spied an opening on the second bench, and they both squeezed into it.

"This is grand!" the senior man whispered. "You'll have a rare view of it all."

Only a single row of heads intervened between them and the operating table. It was of unpainted deal, plain, strong, and scrupulously clean. A sheet of brown water-proofing covered half of it, and beneath stood a large tin tray full of sawdust. On the further side, in front of the window, there was a board which was strewed with glittering instruments—forceps, tenacula, saws, canulas, and trocars. A line of knives, with long, thin, delicate blades, lay at one side. Two young men lounged in front of this, one threading needles, the other doing something to a brass coffee-pot-like thing which hissed out puffs of steam.

"That's Peterson," whispered the senior, "the big, bald man in the front row. He's the skin-grafting man, you know. And that's Anthony Browne, who took a larynx out successfully last winter. And there's Murphy, the pathologist, and Stoddart, the eye-man. You'll come to know them all soon."

"Who are the two men at the table?"

"Nobody—dressers. One has charge of the instruments and the other of the puffing Billy. It's Lister's antiseptic spray, you know, and Archer's one of the carbolic-acid men. Hayes is the leader of the cleanliness-and-cold-water school, and they all hate each other like poison."

A flutter of interest passed through the closely packed benches as a woman in petticoat and bodice was led in by two nurses. A red woolen shawl was draped over her head and round her neck. The face which looked out from it was that of a woman in the prime of her years, but drawn with suffering, and of a peculiar beeswax tint. Her head drooped as she walked, and one of the nurses, with her arm round her waist, was whispering consolation in her ear. She gave a quick side-glance at the instrument table as she passed, but the nurses turned her away from it.

"What ails her?" asked the novice.

"Cancer of the parotid. It's the devil of a case; extends right away back behind the carotids. There's hardly a man but Archer would dare to follow it. Ah, here he is himself!"

As he spoke, a small, brisk, iron-grey man came striding into the room, rubbing his hands together as he walked. He had a clean-shaven face, of the naval officer type, with large, bright eyes, and a firm, straight mouth. Behind him came his big house-surgeon, with his gleaming pince-nez, and a trail of dressers, who grouped themselves into the corners of the room.

"Gentlemen," cried the surgeon in a voice as hard and brisk as his manner, "we have here an interesting case of tumour of the parotid, originally cartilaginous but now assuming malignant characteristics, and therefore requiring excision. On to the table, nurse! Thank you! Chloroform, clerk! Thank you! You can take the shawl off, nurse."

The woman lay back upon the water-proofed pillow, and her murderous tumour lay revealed. In itself it was a pretty thing— ivory white, with a mesh of blue veins, and curving gently from jaw to chest. But the lean, yellow face and the stringy throat were in horrible contrast with the plumpness and sleekness of this monstrous growth. The surgeon placed a hand on each side of it and pressed it slowly backwards and forwards.

"Adherent at one place, gentlemen," he cried. "The growth involves the carotids and jugulars, and passes behind the ramus of the jaw, whither we must be prepared to follow it. It is impossible to say how deep our dissection may carry us. Carbolic tray. Thank you! Dressings of carbolic gauze, if you please! Push the chloroform, Mr. Johnson. Have the small saw ready in case it is necessary to remove the jaw."

The patient was moaning gently under the towel which had been placed over her face. She tried to raise her arms and to draw up her knees, but two dressers restrained her. The heavy air was full of the penetrating smells of carbolic acid and of chloroform. A muffled cry came from under the towel, and then a snatch of a song, sung in a high, quavering, monotonous voice:

"He says, says he,
If you fly with me
You'll be mistress of the ice-cream van.
You'll be mistress of the——"

It mumbled off into a drone and stopped. The surgeon came across, still rubbing his hands, and spoke to an elderly man in front of the novice.

"Narrow squeak for the Government," he said.

"Oh, ten is enough."

"They won't have ten long. They'd do better to resign before they are driven to it."

"Oh, I should fight it out."

"What's the use. They can't get past the committee even if they got a vote in the House. I was talking to——"

"Patient's ready, sir," said the dresser.

"Talking to McDonald—but I'll tell you about it presently." He walked back to the patient, who was breathing in long, heavy gasps. "I propose," said he, passing his hand over the tumour in an almost caressing fashion, "to make a free incision over the posterior border, and to take another forward at right angles to the lower end of it. Might I trouble you for a medium knife, Mr. Johnson?"

The novice, with eyes which were dilating with horror, saw the surgeon pick up the long, gleaming knife, dip it into a tin basin, and balance it in his fingers as an artist might his brush. Then he saw him pinch up the skin above the tumour with his left hand. At the sight his nerves, which had already been tried once or twice that day, gave way utterly. His head swain round, and he felt that in another instant he might faint. He dared not look at the patient. He dug his thumbs into his ears lest some scream should come to haunt him, and he fixed his eyes rigidly upon the wooden ledge in front of him. One glance, one cry, would, he knew, break down the shred of self-possession which he still retained. He tried to think of cricket, of green fields and rippling water, of his sisters at home—of anything rather than of what was going on so near him.

And yet somehow, even with his ears stopped up, sounds seemed to penetrate to him and to carry their own tale. He heard, or thought that he heard, the long hissing of the carbolic engine. Then he was conscious of some movement among the dressers. Were there groans, too, breaking in upon him, and some other sound, some fluid sound, which was more dreadfully suggestive still? His mind would keep building up every step of the operation, and fancy made it more ghastly than fact could have been. His nerves tingled and quivered. Minute by minute the giddiness grew more marked, the numb, sickly feeling at his heart more distressing. And then suddenly, with a groan, his head pitching forward, and his brow cracking sharply upon the narrow wooden shelf in front of him, he lay in a dead faint.

When he came to himself, he was lying in the empty theatre, with his collar and shirt undone. The third year's man was dabbing a wet sponge over his face, and a couple of grinning dressers were looking on.

"All right," cried the novice, sitting up and rubbing his eyes. "I'm sorry to have made an ass of myself."

"Well, so I should think," said his companion.

"What on earth did you faint about?"

"I couldn't help it. It was that operation."

"What operation?"

"Why, that cancer."

There was a pause, and then the three students burst out laughing. "Why, you juggins!" cried the senior man, "there never was an operation at all! They found the patient didn't stand the chloroform well, and so the whole thing was off. Archer has been giving us one of his racy lectures, and you fainted just in the middle of his favourite story."

A Straggler of '15

It was a dull October morning, and heavy, rolling fog-wreaths lay low over the wet grey roofs of the Woolwich houses. Down in the long, brick-lined streets all was sodden and greasy and cheerless.

From the high dark buildings of the arsenal came the whirr of many wheels, the thudding of weights, and the buzz and babel of human toil. Beyond, the dwellings of the workingmen, smoke-stained and unlovely, radiated away in a lessening perspective of narrowing road and dwindling wall.

There were few folk in the streets, for the toilers had all been absorbed since break of day by the huge smoke-spouting monster, which sucked in the manhood of the town, to belch it forth weary and work-stained every night. Little groups of children straggled to school, or loitered to peep through the single, front windows at the big, gilt-edged Bibles, balanced upon small, three-legged tables, which were their usual adornment. Stout women, with thick, red arms and dirty aprons, stood upon the whitened doorsteps, leaning upon their brooms, and shrieking their morning greetings across the road. One stouter, redder, and dirtier than the rest, had gathered a small knot of cronies around her and was talking energetically, with little shrill titters from her audience to punctuate her remarks.

"Old enough to know better!" she cried, in answer to an exclamation from one of the listeners. "If he hain't no sense now, I 'specs he won't learn much on this side o'Jordan. Why, 'ow old is he at all? Blessed if I could ever make out."

"Well, it ain't so hard to reckon," said a sharp-featured pale-faced woman with watery blue eyes. "He's been at the battle o' Waterloo, and has the pension and medal to prove it."

"That were a ter'ble long time agone," remarked a third. "It were afore I were born."

"It were fifteen year after the beginnin' of the century," cried a younger woman, who had stood leaning against the wall, with a smile of superior knowledge upon her face. "My Bill was a-saying so last Sabbath, when I spoke to him o' old Daddy Brewster, here."

"And suppose he spoke truth, Missus Simpson, 'ow long agone do that make it?"

"It's eighty-one now," said the original speaker, checking off the years upon her coarse red fingers, "and that were fifteen. Ten and ten, and ten, and ten, and ten—why, it's only sixty-and-six year, so he ain't so old after all."

"But he weren't a newborn babe at the battle, silly!" cried the young woman with a chuckle. "S'pose he were only twenty, then he couldn't be less than six-and-eighty now, at the lowest."

"Aye, he's that—every day of it," cried several.

"I've had 'bout enough of it," remarked the large woman gloomily. "Unless his young niece, or grandniece, or whatever she is, come to-day, I'm off, and he can find some one else to do his work. Your own 'ome first, says I."

"Ain't he quiet, then, Missus Simpson?" asked the youngest of the group.

"Listen to him now," she answered, with her hand half raised and her head turned slantwise towards the open door. From the upper floor there came a shuffling, sliding sound with a sharp tapping of a stick. "There he go back and forrards, doing what he call his sentry go. 'Arf the night through he's at that game, the silly old juggins. At six o'clock this very mornin there he was beatin' with a stick at my door. 'Turn out, guard!' he cried, and a lot more jargon that I could make nothing of. Then what with his coughin' and 'awkin' and spittin', there ain't no gettin' a wink o' sleep. Hark to him now!"

"Missus Simpson, Missus Simpson!" cried a cracked and querulous voice from above.

"That's him!" she cried, nodding her head with an air of triumph. "He do go on somethin' scandalous. Yes, Mr. Brewster, sir."

"I want my morning ration, Missus Simpson."

"It's just ready, Mr. Brewster, sir."

"Blessed if he ain't like a baby cryin' for its pap," said the young woman.

"I feel as if I could shake his old bones up sometimes!" cried Mrs. Simpson viciously. "But who's for a 'arf of fourpenny?"

The whole company were about to shuffle off to the public house, when a young girl stepped across the road and touched the housekeeper timidly upon the arm. "I think that is No. 56 Arsenal View," she said. "Can you tell me if Mr. Brewster lives here?"

The housekeeper looked critically at the newcomer. She was a girl of about twenty, broad-faced and comely, with a turned-up nose and large, honest grey eyes. Her print dress, her straw hat, with its bunch of glaring poppies, and the bundle she carried, had all a smack of the country.

"You're Norah Brewster, I s'pose," said Mrs. Simpson, eyeing her up and down with no friendly gaze.

"Yes, I've come to look after my Granduncle Gregory."

"And a good job too," cried the housekeeper, with a toss of her head. "It's about time that some of his own folk took a turn at it, for I've had enough of it. There you are, young woman! In you go and make yourself at home. There's tea in the caddy and bacon on the dresser, and the old man will be about you if you don't fetch him his breakfast. I'll send for my things in the evenin'." With a nod she strolled off with her attendant gossips in the direction of the public house.

Thus left to her own devices, the country girl walked into the front room and took off her hat and jacket. It was a low-roofed apartment with a sputtering fire upon which a small brass kettle was singing cheerily. A stained cloth lay over half the table, with an empty brown teapot, a loaf of bread, and some coarse crockery. Norah Brewster looked rapidly about her, and in an instant took over her new duties. Ere five minutes had passed the tea was made, two slices of bacon were frizzling on the pan, the table was rearranged, the antimacassars straightened over the sombre brown furniture, and the whole room had taken a new air of comfort and neatness. This done she looked round curiously at the prints upon the walls. Over the fireplace, in a small, square case, a brown medal caught her eye, hanging from a strip of purple ribbon. Beneath was a slip of newspaper cutting. She stood on her tiptoes, with her fingers on the edge of the mantelpiece, and craned her neck up to see it, glancing down from time to time at the bacon which simmered and hissed beneath her. The cutting was yellow with age, and ran in this way:

"On Tuesday an interesting ceremony was performed at the barracks of the Third Regiment of Guards, when, in the presence of the Prince Regent, Lord Hill, Lord Saltoun, and an assemblage which comprised beauty as well as valour, a special medal was presented to Corporal Gregory Brewster, of Captain Haldane's flank company, in recognition of his gallantry in the recent great battle in the Lowlands. It appears that on the ever-memorable 18th of

June four companies of the Third Guards and of the Coldstreams, under the command of Colonels Maitland and Byng, held the important farmhouse of Hougoumont at the right of the British position. At a critical point of the action these troops found themselves short of powder. Seeing that Generals Foy and Jerome Buonaparte were again massing their infantry for an attack on the position, Colonel Byng dispatched Corporal Brewster to the rear to hasten up the reserve ammunition. Brewster came upon two powder tumbrils of the Nassau division, and succeeded, after menacing the drivers with his musket, in inducing them to convey their powder to Hougoumont. In his absence, however, the hedges surrounding the position had been set on fire by a howitzer battery of the French, and the passage of the carts full of powder became a most hazardous matter. The first tumbril exploded, blowing the driver to fragments. Daunted by the fate of his comrade, the second driver turned his horses, but Corporal Brewster, springing upon his seat, hurled the man down, and urging the powder cart through the flames, succeeded in forcing his way to his companions. To this gallant deed may be directly attributed the success of the British arms, for without powder it would have been impossible to have held Hougoumont, and the Duke of Wellington had repeatedly declared that had Hougoumont fallen, as well as La Haye Sainte, he would have found it impossible to have held his ground. Long may the heroic Brewster live to treasure the medal which he has so bravely won, and to look back with pride to the day when, in the presence of his comrades, he received this tribute to his valour from the august hands of the first gentleman of the realm."

The reading of this old cutting increased in the girl's mind the veneration which she had always had for her warrior kinsman. From her infancy he had been her hero, and she remembered how her father used to speak of his courage and his strength, how he could strike down a bullock with a blow of his fist and carry a fat sheep under either arm. True, she had never seen him, but a rude painting at home which depicted a square-faced, clean shaven, stalwart man with a great bearskin cap, rose ever before her memory when she thought of him.

She was still gazing at the brown medal and wondering what the "Dulce et decorum est" might mean, which was inscribed upon the edge, when there came a sudden tapping and shuffling upon the stair, and there at the door was standing the very man who had been so often in her thoughts.

But could this indeed be he? Where was the martial air, the flashing eye, the warrior face which she had pictured? There, framed in the doorway, was a huge twisted old man, gaunt and puckered, with twitching hands and shuffling, purposeless feet. A cloud of fluffy white hair, a red-veined nose, two thick tufts of eyebrow and a pair of dimly questioning, watery blue eyes—these were what met her gaze. He leaned forward upon a stick, while his shoulders rose and fell with his crackling, rasping breathing.

"I want my morning rations," he crooned, as he stumped forward to his chair. "The cold nips me without 'em. See to my fingers!" He held out his distorted hands, all blue at the tips, wrinkled and gnarled, with huge, projecting knuckles.

"It's nigh ready," answered the girl, gazing at him with wonder in her eyes. "Don't you know who I am, granduncle? I am Norah Brewster from Witham."

"Rum is warm," mumbled the old man, rocking to and fro in his chair, "and schnapps is warm, and there's 'eat in soup, but it's a dish o' tea for me. What did you say your name was?"

"Norah Brewster."

"You can speak out, lass. Seems to me folk's voices isn't as loud as they used."

"I'm Norah Brewster, uncle. I'm your grandniece come down from Essex way to live with you."

"You'll be brother Jarge's girl! Lor, to think o' little Jarge having a girl!" He chuckled hoarsely to himself, and the long, stringy sinews of his throat jerked and quivered.

"I am the daughter of your brother George's son," said she, as she turned the bacon.

"Lor, but little Jarge was a rare un!" he continued. "Eh, by Jimini, there was no chousing Jarge. He's got a bull pup o' mine that I gave him when I took the bounty. You've heard him speak of it, likely?"

"Why, grandpa George has been dead this twenty year," said she, pouring out the tea.

"Well, it was a bootiful pup—aye, a well-bred un, by Jimini! I'm cold for lack o' my rations. Rum is good, and so is schnapps, but I'd as lief have tea as either."

He breathed heavily while he devoured his food. "It's a middlin' goodish way you've come," said he at last. "Likely the stage left yesternight."

"The what, uncle?"

"The coach that brought you."

"Nay, I came by the mornin' train."

"Lor, now, think o' that! You ain't afeard o' those newfangled things! By Jimini, to think of you comin' by railroad like that! What's the world a-comin' to!"

There was silence for some minutes while Norah sat stirring her tea and glancing sideways at the bluish lips and champing jaws of her companion.

"You must have seen a deal o' life, uncle," said she. "It must seem a long, long time to you!"

"Not so very long neither. I'm ninety, come Candlemas; but it don't seem long since I took the bounty. And that battle, it might have been yesterday. Eh, but I get a power o' good from my rations!" He did indeed look less worn and colourless than when she first saw him. His face was flushed and his back more erect.

"Have you read that?" he asked, jerking his head towards the cutting.

"Yes, uncle, and I'm sure you must be proud of it."

"Ah, it was a great day for me! A great day! The Regent was there, and a fine body of a man too! 'The ridgment is proud of you,' says he. 'And I'm proud of the ridgment,' say I. 'A damned good answer too!' says he to Lord Hill, and they both bu'st out a-laughin'. But what be you a-peepin' out o' the window for?"

"Oh, uncle, here's a regiment of soldiers coming down the street with the band playing in front of them."

"A ridgment, eh? Where be my glasses? Lor, but I can hear the band, as plain as plain! Here's the pioneers an' the drum-major! What be their number, lass?" His eyes were shining and his bony yellow fingers, like the claws of some fierce old bird, dug into her shoulder.

"They don't seem to have no number, uncle. They've something wrote on their shoulders. Oxfordshire, I think it be."

"Ah, yes!" he growled. "I heard as they'd dropped the numbers and given them newfangled names. There they go, by Jimini! They're young mostly, but they hain't forgot how to march. They have the swing-aye, I'll say that for them. They've got the swing." He gazed after them until the last files had turned the corner and the measured tramp of their marching had died away in the distance.

He had just regained his chair when the door opened and a gentleman stepped in.

"Ah, Mr. Brewster! Better to-day?" he asked.

"Come in, doctor! Yes, I'm better. But there's a deal o' bubbling in my chest. It's all them toobes. If I could but cut the phlegm, I'd be right. Can't you give me something to cut the phlegm?"

The doctor, a grave-faced young man, put his fingers to the furrowed, blue-corded wrist.

"You must be careful," he said. "You must take no liberties." The thin tide of life seemed to thrill rather than to throb under his finger.

The old man chuckled.

"I've got brother Jarge's girl to look after me now. She'll see I don't break barracks or do what I hadn't ought to. Why, darn my skin, I knew something was amiss!

"With what?"

"Why, with them soldiers. You saw them pass, doctor—eh? They'd forgot their stocks. Not one on 'em had his stock on." He croaked and chuckled for a long time over his discovery. "It wouldn't ha' done for the Dook!" he muttered. "No, by Jimini! the Dook would ha' had a word there."

The doctor smiled. "Well, you are doing very well," said he. "I'll look in once a week or so, and see how you are." As Norah followed him to the door, he beckoned her outside.

"He is very weak," he whispered. "If you find him failing you must send for me."

"What ails him, doctor?"

"Ninety years ails him. His arteries are pipes of lime. His heart is shrunken and flabby. The man is worn out."

Norah stood watching the brisk figure of the young doctor, and pondering over these new responsibilities which had come upon her. When she turned a tall, brown-faced artilleryman, with the three gold chevrons of sergeant upon his arm, was standing, carbine in hand, at her elbow.

"Good-morning, miss," said he, raising one thick finger to his jaunty, yellow-banded cap. "I b'lieve there's an old gentleman lives here of the name of Brewster, who was engaged in the battle o' Waterloo?"

"It's my granduncle, sir," said Norah, casting down her eyes before the keen, critical gaze of the young soldier. "He is in the front parlour."

"Could I have a word with him, miss? I'll call again if it don't chance to be convenient."

"I am sure that he would be very glad to see you, sir. He's in here, if you'll step in. Uncle, here's a gentleman who wants to speak with you."

"Proud to see you, sir—proud and glad, sir," cried the sergeant, taking three steps forward into the room, and grounding his carbine while he raised his hand, palm forwards, in a salute. Norah stood by the door, with her mouth and eyes open, wondering if her granduncle had ever, in his prime, looked like this magnificent creature, and whether he, in his turn, would ever come to resemble her granduncle.

The old man blinked up at his visitor, and shook his head slowly. "Sit ye down, sergeant," said he, pointing with his stick to a chair. "You're full young for the stripes. Lordy, it's easier to get three now than one in my day. Gunners were old soldiers then and the grey hairs came quicker than the three stripes."

"I am eight years' service, sir," cried the sergeant. "Macdonald is my name—Sergeant Macdonald, of H Battery, Southern Artillery Division. I have called as the spokesman of my mates at the gunner's barracks to say that we are proud to have you in the town, sir."

Old Brewster chuckled and rubbed his bony hands. "That were what the Regent said," he cried. "'The ridgment is proud of ye,' says he. 'And I am proud of the ridgment,' says I. 'And a damned good answer too,' says he, and he and Lord Hill bu'st out a-laughin.'"

"The non-commissioned mess would be proud and honoured to see you, sir," said Sergeant Macdonald; "and if you could step as far you'll always find a pipe o' baccy and a glass o' grog a-waitin' you."

The old man laughed until he coughed. "Like to see me, would they? The dogs!" said he. "Well, well, when the warm weather comes again I'll maybe drop in. Too grand for a canteen, eh? Got your mess just the same as the orficers. What's the world a-comin' to at all!"

"You was in the line, sir, was you not?" asked the sergeant respectfully.

"The line?" cried the old man, with shrill scorn. "Never wore a shako in my life. I am a guardsman, I am. Served in the Third Guards—the same they call now the Scots Guards. Lordy, but they have all marched away—every man of them—from old Colonel Byng down to the drummer boys, and here am I a straggler—that's what I am, sergeant, a straggler! I'm here when I ought to be there. But it ain't my fault neither, for I'm ready to fall in when the word comes."

"We've all got to muster there," answered the sergeant. "Won't you try my baccy, sir?" handing over a sealskin pouch.

Old Brewster drew a blackened clay pipe from his pocket, and began to stuff the tobacco into the bowl. In an instant it slipped through his fingers, and was broken to pieces on the floor. His lip quivered, his nose puckered up, and he began crying with the long, helpless sobs of a child. "I've broke my pipe," he cried.

"Don't, uncle; oh, don't!" cried Norah, bending over him, and patting his white head as one soothes a baby. "It don't matter. We can easy get another."

"Don't you fret yourself, sir," said the sergeant. "'Ere's a wooden pipe with an amber mouth, if you'll do me the honour to accept it from me. I'd be real glad if you will take it."

"Jimini!" cried he, his smiles breaking in an instant through his tears. "It's a fine pipe. See to my new pipe, Norah. I lay that Jarge never had a pipe like that. You've got your firelock there, sergeant?"

"Yes, sir. I was on my way back from the butts when I looked in."

"Let me have the feel of it. Lordy, but it seems like old times to have one's hand on a musket. What's the manual, sergeant, eh? Cock your firelock—look to your priming—present your fire-lock—eh, sergeant? Oh, Jimini, I've broke your musket in halves!"

"That's all right, sir," cried the gunner laughing. "You pressed on the lever and opened the breech-piece. That's where we load 'em, you know."

"Load 'em at the wrong end! Well, well, to think o' that! And no ramrod neither! I've heard tell of it, but I never believed it afore. Ah! it won't come up to brown Bess. When there's work to be done, you mark my word and see if they don't come back to brown Bess."

"By the Lord, sir!" cried the sergeant hotly, "they need some change out in South Africa now. I see by this mornin's paper that the Government has knuckled under to these Boers. They're hot about it at the non-com. mess, I can tell you, sir."

"Eh—eh," croaked old Brewster. "By Jimini! it wouldn't ha' done for the Dook; the Dook would ha' had a word to say over that."

"Ah, that he would, sir!" cried the sergeant; and God send us another like him. But I've wearied you enough for one sitting. I'll look in again, and I'll bring a comrade or two with me, if I may, for there isn't one but would be proud to have speech with you."

So, with another salute to the veteran and a gleam of white teeth at Norah, the big gunner withdrew, leaving a memory of blue cloth and of gold braid behind him. Many days had not passed, however, before he was back again, and during all the long winter he was a frequent visitor at Arsenal View. There came a time, at last, when it might be doubted to which of the two occu-pants his visits were directed, nor was it hard to say by which he was most anxiously awaited. He brought others with him; and soon, through all the lines, a pilgrimage to Daddy Brewster's came to be looked upon as the proper thing to do. Gunners and sappers, linesmen and dragoons, came bowing and bobbing into the little parlour, with clatter of side arms and clink of spurs, stretching their long legs across the patchwork rug, and hunting in the front of their tunics for the screw of tobacco or paper of snuff which they had brought as a sign of their esteem.

It was a deadly cold winter, with six weeks on end of snow on the ground, and Norah had a hard task to keep the life in that time-worn body. There were times when his mind would leave him, and when, save an animal outcry when the hour of his meals came round, no word would fall from him. He was a white-haired child, with all a child's troubles and emotions. As the warm weather came once more, however, and the green buds peeped forth again upon the trees, the blood thawed in his veins, and he would even drag himself as far as the door to bask in the life-giving sunshine.

"It do hearten me up so," he said one morning, as he glowed in the hot May sun. "It's a job to keep back the flies, though. They get owdacious in this weather, and they do plague me cruel."

"I'll keep them off you, uncle," said Norah.

"Eh, but it's fine! This sunshine makes me think o' the glory to come. You might read me a bit o' the Bible, lass. I find it wonderful soothing."

"What part would you like, uncle?"

"Oh, them wars."

"The wars?"

"Aye, keep to the wars! Give me the Old Testament for choice. There's more taste to it, to my mind. When parson comes he wants to get off to something else; but it's Joshua or nothing with me. Them Israelites was good soldiers—good growed soldiers, all of 'em."

"But, uncle," pleaded Norah, "it's all peace in the next world."

"No, it ain't, gal."

"Oh, yes, uncle, surely!"

The old corporal knocked his stick irritably upon the ground. "I tell ye it ain't, gal. I asked parson."

"Well, what did he say?"

"He said there was to be a last fight. He even gave it a name, he did. The battle of Arm—Arm——"

"Armageddon."

"Aye, that's the name parson said. I 'specs the Third Guards'll be there. And the Dook—the Dook'll have a word to say."

An elderly, grey-whiskered gentleman had been walking down the street, glancing up at the numbers of the houses. Now as his eyes fell upon the old man, he came straight for him.

"Hullo!" said he; "perhaps you are Gregory Brewster?"

"My name, sir," answered the veteran.

"You are the same Brewster, as I understand, who is on the roll of the Scots Guards as having been present at the battle of Waterloo?"

"I am that man, sir, though we called it the Third Guards in those days. It was a fine ridgment, and they only need me to make up a full muster."

"Tut, tut! they'll have to wait years for that," said the gentleman heartily. "But I am the colonel of the Scots Guards, and I thought I would like to have a word with you."

Old Gregory Brewster was up in an instant, with his hand to his rabbit-skin cap. "God bless me!" he cried, "to think of it! to think of it!"

"Hadn't the gentleman better come in?" suggested the practical Norah from behind the door.

"Surely, sir, surely; walk in, sir, if I may be so bold." In his excitement he had forgotten his stick, and as he led the way into the parlour his knees tottered, and he threw out his hands. In an instant the colonel had caught him on one side and Norah on the other.

"Easy and steady," said the colonel, as he led him to his armchair.

"Thank ye, sir; I was near gone that time. But, Lordy I why, I can scarce believe it. To think of me the corporal of the flank company and you the colonel of the battalion! How things come round, to be sure!"

"Why, we are very proud of you in London," said the colonel. "And so you are actually one of the men who held Hougoumont." He looked at the bony, trembling hands, with their huge, knotted knuckles, the stringy throat, and the heaving, rounded shoulders. Could this, indeed, be the last of that band of heroes? Then he glanced at the half-filled phials, the blue liniment bottles, the long-spouted kettle, and the sordid details of the sick room. "Better, surely, had he died under the blazing rafters of the Belgian farm-house," thought the colonel.

"I hope that you are pretty comfortable and happy," he remarked after a pause.

"Thank ye, sir. I have a good deal o' trouble with my toobes— a deal o' trouble. You wouldn't think the job it is to cut the phlegm. And I need my rations. I gets cold without 'em. And the flies! I ain't strong enough to fight against them."

"How's the memory?" asked the colonel.

"Oh, there ain't nothing amiss there. Why, sir, I could give you the name of every man in Captain Haldane's flank company."

"And the battle—you remember it?"

"Why, I sees it all afore me every time I shuts my eyes. Lordy, sir, you wouldn't hardly believe how clear it is to me. There's our line from the paregoric bottle right along to the snuff box. D'ye see? Well, then, the pill box is for Hougoumont on the right— where we was—and Norah's thimble for La Haye Sainte. There it is, all right, sir; and here were our guns, and here behind the reserves and the Belgians. Ach, them Belgians!" He spat furiously into the fire. "Then here's the French, where my pipe lies; and over here, where I put my baccy pouch, was the Proosians a-comin' up on our left flank. Jimini, but it was a glad sight to see the smoke of their guns!"

"And what was it that struck you most now in connection with the whole affair?" asked the colonel.

"I lost three half-crowns over it, I did," crooned old Brewster. "I shouldn't wonder if I was never to get that money now. I lent 'em to Jabez Smith, my rear rank man, in Brussels. 'Only till pay-day, Grig,' says he. By Gosh! he was stuck by a lancer at Quatre Bras, and me with not so much as a slip o' paper to prove the debt! Them three half-crowns is as good as lost to me."

The colonel rose from his chair laughing. "The officers of the Guards want you to buy yourself some little trifle which may add to your comfort," he said. "It is not from me, so you need not thank me." He took up the old man's tobacco pouch and slipped a crisp banknote inside it.

"Thank ye kindly, sir. But there's one favour that I would like to ask you, colonel."

"Yes, my man."

"If I'm called, colonel, you won't grudge me a flag and a firing party? I'm not a civilian; I'm a guardsman—I'm the last of the old Third Guards."

"All right, my man, I'll see to it," said the colonel. "Good-bye; I hope to have nothing but good news from you."

"A kind gentleman, Norah," croaked old Brewster, as they saw him walk past the window; "but, Lordy, he ain't fit to hold the stirrup o' my Colonel Byng!"

It was on the very next day that the old corporal took a sudden change for the worse. Even the golden sunlight streaming through the window seemed unable to warm that withered frame. The doctor came and shook his head in silence. All day the man lay with only his puffing blue lips and the twitching of his scraggy neck to show that he still held the breath of life. Norah and Sergeant Macdonald had sat by him in the afternoon, but he had shown no consciousness of their presence. He lay peacefully, his eyes half closed, his hands under his cheek, as one who is very weary.

They had left him for an instant and were sitting in the front room, where Norah was preparing tea, when of a sudden they heard a shout that rang through the house. Loud and clear and swelling, it pealed in their ears—a voice full of strength and energy and fiery passion. "The Guards need powder!" it cried; and yet again, "The Guards need powder!"

The sergeant sprang from his chair and rushed in, followed by the trembling Norah. There was the old man standing up, his blue eyes sparkling, his white hair bristling, his whole figure towering and expanding, with eagle head and glance of fire. "The Guards need powder!" he thundered once again, "and, by God, they shall have it!" He threw up his long arms, and sank back with a groan into his chair. The sergeant stooped over him, and his face darkened.

"Oh, Archie, Archie," sobbed the frightened girl, "what do you think of him?"

The sergeant turned away. "I think," said he, "that the Third Guards have a full muster now."

The Third Generation

Scudamore Lane, sloping down riverwards from just behind the
Monument, lies at night in the shadow of two black and monstrous walls which loom high above the glimmer of the scattered
gas lamps. The footpaths are narrow, and the causeway is paved
with rounded cobblestones, so that the endless drays roar along it
like breaking waves. A few old-fashioned houses lie scattered
among the business premises, and in one of these, half-way down
on the left-hand side, Dr. Horace Selby conducts his large practice.
It is a singular street for so big a man; but a specialist who has an
European reputation can afford to live where he likes. In his particular branch, too, patients do not always regard seclusion as a
disadvantage.

It was only ten o'clock. The dull roar of the traffic which con-
verged all day upon London Bridge had died away now to a mere
confused murmur. It was raining heavily, and the gas shone dimly
through the streaked and dripping glass, throwing little circles
upon the glistening cobblestones. The air was full of the sounds of
the rain, the thin swish of its fall, the heavier drip from the eaves,
and the swirl and gurgle down the two steep gutters and through
the sewer grating. There was only one figure in the whole length of
Scudamore Lane. It was that of a man, and it stood outside the
door of Dr. Horace Selby.

He had just rung and was waiting for an answer. The fanlight
beat full upon the gleaming shoulders of his waterproof and upon
his upturned features. It was a wan, sensitive, clear-cut face, with
some subtle, nameless peculiarity in its expression, something of
the startled horse in the white-rimmed eye, something too of the
helpless child in the drawn cheek and the weakening of the lower
lip. The man-servant knew the stranger as a patient at a bare
glance at those frightened eyes. Such a look had been seen at that
door many times before.

"Is the doctor in?"

The man hesitated.

"He has had a few friends to dinner, sir. He does not like to be
disturbed outside his usual hours, sir."

"Tell him that I MUST see him. Tell him that it is of the very first importance. Here is my card." He fumbled with his trembling fingers in trying to draw one from his case. "Sir Francis Norton is the name. Tell him that Sir Francis Norton, of Deane Park, must see him without delay."

"Yes, sir." The butler closed his fingers upon the card and the half-sovereign which accompanied it. "Better hang your coat up here in the hall. It is very wet. Now if you will wait here in the consulting-room, I have no doubt that I shall be able to send the doctor in to you."

It was a large and lofty room in which the young baronet found himself. The carpet was so soft and thick that his feet made no sound as he walked across it. The two gas jets were turned only half-way up, and the dim light with the faint aromatic smell which filled the air had a vaguely religious suggestion. He sat down in a shining leather armchair by the smouldering fire and looked gloomily about him. Two sides of the room were taken up with books, fat and sombre, with broad gold lettering upon their backs. Beside him was the high, old-fashioned mantelpiece of white marble—the top of it strewed with cotton wadding and bandages, graduated measures, and little bottles. There was one with a broad neck just above him containing bluestone, and another narrower one with what looked like the ruins of a broken pipestem and "Caustic" outside upon a red label. Thermometers, hypodermic syringes bistouries and spatulas were scattered about both on the mantelpiece and on the central table on either side of the sloping desk. On the same table, to the right, stood copies of the five books which Dr. Horace Selby had written upon the subject with which his name is peculiarly associated, while on the left, on the top of a red medical directory, lay a huge glass model of a human eye the size of a turnip, which opened down the centre to expose the lens and double chamber within.

Sir Francis Norton had never been remarkable for his powers of observation, and yet he found himself watching these trifles with the keenest attention. Even the corrosion of the cork of an acid bottle caught his eye, and he wondered that the doctor did not use glass stoppers. Tiny scratches where the light glinted off from the table, little stains upon the leather of the desk, chemical formulae scribbled upon the labels of the phials—nothing was too slight to arrest his attention. And his sense of hearing was equally alert. The heavy ticking of the solemn black clock above the mantelpiece struck quite painfully upon his ears. Yet in spite of it, and in spite also of the thick, old-fashioned wooden partition, he could hear voices of men talking in the next room, and could even catch scraps of their conversation. "Second hand was bound to take it." "Why, you drew the last of them yourself!"

"How could I play the queen when I knew that the ace was against me?" The phrases came in little spurts falling back into the dull murmur of conversation. And then suddenly he heard the creaking of a door and a step in the hall, and knew with a tingling mixture of impatience and horror that the crisis of his life was at hand.

Dr. Horace Selby was a large, portly man with an imposing presence. His nose and chin were bold and pronounced, yet his features were puffy, a combination which would blend more freely with the wig and cravat of the early Georges than with the close-cropped hair and black frock-coat of the end of the nineteenth century. He was clean shaven, for his mouth was too good to cover—large, flexible, and sensitive, with a kindly human softening at either corner which with his brown sympathetic eyes had drawn out many a shame-struck sinner's secret. Two masterful little bushy side-whiskers bristled out from under his ears spindling away upwards to merge in the thick curves of his brindled hair. To his patients there was something reassuring in the mere bulk and dignity of the man. A high and easy bearing in medicine as in war bears with it a hint of victories in the past, and a promise of others to come. Dr. Horace Selby's face was a consolation, and so too were the large, white, soothing hands, one of which he held out to his visitor.

"I am sorry to have kept you waiting. It is a conflict of duties, you perceive—a host's to his guests and an adviser's to his patient. But now I am entirely at your disposal, Sir Francis. But dear me, you are very cold."

"Yes, I am cold."

"And you are trembling all over. Tut, tut, this will never do! This miserable night has chilled you. Perhaps some little stimulant——"

"No, thank you. I would really rather not. And it is not the night which has chilled me. I am frightened, doctor."

The doctor half-turned in his chair, and he patted the arch of the young man's knee, as he might the neck of a restless horse.

"What then?" he asked, looking over his shoulder at the pale face with the startled eyes.

Twice the young man parted his lips. Then he stooped with a sudden gesture, and turning up the right leg of his trousers he pulled down his sock and thrust forward his shin. The doctor made a clicking noise with his tongue as he glanced at it.

"Both legs?"

"No, only one."

"Suddenly?"

"This morning."

"Hum."

The doctor pouted his lips, and drew his finger and thumb down the line of his chin. "Can you account for it?" he asked briskly.

"No."

A trace of sternness came into the large brown eyes.

"I need not point out to you that unless the most absolute frankness——"

The patient sprang from his chair. "So help me God!" he cried, "I have nothing in my life with which to reproach myself. Do you think that I would be such a fool as to come here and tell you lies. Once for all, I have nothing to regret." He was a pitiful, half-tragic and half-grotesque figure, as he stood with one trouser leg rolled to the knee, and that ever present horror still lurking in his eyes. A burst of merriment came from the card-players in the next room, and the two looked at each other in silence.

"Sit down," said the doctor abruptly, "your assurance is quite sufficient." He stooped and ran his finger down the line of the young man's shin, raising it at one point. "Hum, serpiginous," he murmured, shaking his head. "Any other symptoms?"

"My eyes have been a little weak."

"Let me see your teeth." He glanced at them, and again made the gentle, clicking sound of sympathy and disapprobation.

"Now your eye." He lit a lamp at the patient's elbow, and holding a small crystal lens to concentrate the light, he threw it obliquely upon the patient's eye. As he did so a glow of pleasure came over his large expressive face, a flush of such enthusiasm as the botanist feels when he packs the rare plant into his tin knapsack, or the astronomer when the long-sought comet first swims into the field of his telescope.

"This is very typical—very typical indeed," he murmured, turning to his desk and jotting down a few memoranda upon a sheet of paper. "Curiously enough, I am writing a monograph upon the subject. It is singular that you should have been able to furnish so well-marked a case." He had so forgotten the patient in his symptom, that he had assumed an almost congratulatory air towards its possessor. He reverted to human sympathy again, as his patient asked for particulars.

"My dear sir, there is no occasion for us to go into strictly professional details together," said he soothingly. "If, for example, I were to say that you have interstitial keratitis, how would you be the wiser? There are indications of a strumous diathesis. In broad terms, I may say that you have a constitutional and hereditary taint."

The young baronet sank back in his chair, and his chin fell forwards upon his chest. The doctor sprang to a side-table and poured out half a glass of liqueur brandy which he held to his patient's lips. A little fleck of colour came into his cheeks as he drank it down.

"Perhaps I spoke a little abruptly," said the doctor, "but you must have known the nature of your complaint. Why, otherwise, should you have come to me?"

"God help me, I suspected it; but only today when my leg grew bad. My father had a leg like this."

"It was from him, then——?"

"No, from my grandfather. You have heard of Sir Rupert Norton, the great Corinthian?"

The doctor was a man of wide reading with a retentive, memory. The name brought back instantly to him the remembrance of the sinister reputation of its owner—a notorious buck of the thirties—who had gambled and duelled and steeped himself in drink and debauchery, until even the vile set with whom he consorted had shrunk away from him in horror, and left him to a sinister old age with the barmaid wife whom he had married in some drunken frolic. As he looked at the young man still leaning back in the leather chair, there seemed for the instant to flicker up behind him some vague presentiment of that foul old dandy with his dangling seals, many-wreathed scarf, and dark satyric face. What was he now? An armful of bones in a mouldy box. But his deeds—they were living and rotting the blood in the veins of an innocent man.

"I see that you have heard of him," said the young baronet. "He died horribly, I have been told; but not more horribly than he had lived. My father was his only son. He was a studious man, fond of books and canaries and the country; but his innocent life did not save him."

"His symptoms were cutaneous, I understand."

"He wore gloves in the house. That was the first thing I can remember. And then it was his throat. And then his legs. He used to ask me so often about my own health, and I thought him so fussy, for how could I tell what the meaning of it was. He was always watching me—always with a sidelong eye fixed upon me. Now, at last, I know what he was watching for."

"Had you brothers or sisters?"

"None, thank God."

"Well, well, it is a sad case, and very typical of many which come in my way. You are no lonely sufferer, Sir Francis. There are many thousands who bear the same cross as you do."

"But where is the justice of it, doctor?" cried the young man, springing from his chair and pacing up and down the consulting-room. "If I were heir to my grandfather's sins as well as to their results, I could understand it, but I am of my father's type. I love all that is gentle and beautiful—music and poetry and art. The coarse and animal is abhorrent to me. Ask any of my friends and they would tell you that. And now that this vile, loathsome thing—ach, I am polluted to the marrow, soaked in abomination! And why? Haven't I a right to ask why? Did I do it? Was it my fault? Could I help being born? And look at me now, blighted and blasted, just as life was at its sweetest. Talk about the sins of the father—how about the sins of the Creator?" He shook his two clinched hands in the air—the poor impotent atom with his pin-point of brain caught in the whirl of the infinite.

The doctor rose and placing his hands upon his shoulders he pressed him back into his chair once more. "There, there, my dear lad," said he; "you must not excite yourself. You are trembling all over. Your nerves cannot stand it. We must take these great questions upon trust. What are we, after all? Half-evolved creatures in a transition stage, nearer perhaps to the Medusa on the one side than to perfected humanity on the other. With half a complete brain we can't expect to understand the whole of a complete fact, can we, now? It is all very dim and dark, no doubt; but I think that Pope's famous couplet sums up the whole matter, and from my heart, after fifty years of varied experience, I can say——"

But the young baronet gave a cry of impatience and disgust. "Words, words, words! You can sit comfortably there in your chair and say them—and think them too, no doubt. You've had your life, but I've never had mine. You've healthy blood in your veins; mine is putrid. And yet I am as innocent as you. What would words do for you if you were in this chair and I in that? Ah, it's such a mockery and a make-believe! Don't think me rude, though, doctor. I don't mean to be that. I only say that it is impossible for you or any other man to realise it. But I've a question to ask you, doctor. It's one on which my whole life must depend." He writhed his fingers together in an agony of apprehension.

"Speak out, my dear sir. I have every sympathy with you."

"Do you think—do you think the poison has spent itself on me? Do you think that if I had children they would suffer?"

"I can only give one answer to that. 'The third and fourth generation,' says the trite old text. You may in time eliminate it from your system, but many years must pass before you can think of marriage."

"I am to be married on Tuesday," whispered the patient.

It was the doctor's turn to be thrilled with horror. There were not many situations which would yield such a sensation to his seasoned nerves. He sat in silence while the babble of the card-table broke in upon them again. "We had a double ruff if you had returned a heart." "I was bound to clear the trumps." They were hot and angry about it.

"How could you?" cried the doctor severely. "It was criminal."

"You forget that I have only learned how I stand to-day." He put his two hands to his temples and pressed them convulsively. "You are a man of the world, Dr. Selby. You have seen or heard of such things before. Give me some advice. I'm in your hands. It is all very sudden and horrible, and I don't think I am strong enough to bear it."

The doctor's heavy brows thickened into two straight lines, and he bit his nails in perplexity.

"The marriage must not take place."

"Then what am I to do?"

"At all costs it must not take place."

"And I must give her up?"

"There can be no question about that."

The young man took out a pocketbook and drew from it a small photograph, holding it out towards the doctor. The firm face softened as he looked at it.

"It is very hard on you, no doubt. I can appreciate it more now that I have seen that. But there is no alternative at all. You must give up all thought of it."

"But this is madness, doctor—madness, I tell you. No, I won't raise my voice. I forgot myself. But realise it, man. I am to be married on Tuesday. This coming Tuesday, you understand. And all the world knows it. How can I put such a public affront upon her. It would be monstrous."

"None the less it must be done. My dear lad, there is no way out of it."

"You would have me simply write brutally and break the engagement at the last moment without a reason. I tell you I couldn't do it."

"I had a patient once who found himself in a somewhat similar situation some years ago," said the doctor thoughtfully. "His device was a singular one. He deliberately committed a penal offence, and so compelled the young lady's people to withdraw their consent to the marriage."

The young baronet shook his head. "My personal honour is as yet unstained," said he. "I have little else left, but that, at least, I will preserve."

"Well, well, it is a nice dilemma, and the choice lies with you."

"Have you no other suggestion?"

"You don't happen to have property in Australia?"

"None."

"But you have capital?"

"Yes."

"Then you could buy some. To-morrow morning would do. A thousand mining shares would be enough. Then you might write to say that urgent business affairs have compelled you to start at an hour's notice to inspect your property. That would give you six months, at any rate."

"Well, that would be possible. Yes, certainly, it would be possible. But think of her position. The house full of wedding presents—guests coming from a distance. It is awful. And you say that there is no alternative."

The doctor shrugged his shoulders.

"Well, then, I might write it now, and start to-morrow—eh? Perhaps you would let me use your desk. Thank you. I am so sorry to keep you from your guests so long. But I won't be a moment now."

He wrote an abrupt note of a few lines. Then with a sudden impulse he tore it to shreds and flung it into the fireplace.

"No, I can't sit down and tell her a lie, doctor," he said rising. "We must find some other way out of this. I will think it over and let you know my decision. You must allow me to double your fee as I have taken such an unconscionable time. Now good-bye, and thank you a thousand times for your sympathy and advice."

"Why, dear me, you haven't even got your prescription yet. This is the mixture, and I should recommend one of these powders every morning, and the chemist will put all directions upon the ointment box. You are placed in a cruel situation, but I trust that these may be but passing clouds. When may I hope to hear from you again?"

"To-morrow morning."

"Very good. How the rain is splashing in the street! You have your waterproof there. You will need it. Good-bye, then, until to-morrow."

He opened the door. A gust of cold, damp air swept into the hall. And yet the doctor stood for a minute or more watching the lonely figure which passed slowly through the yellow splotches of the gas lamps, and into the broad bars of darkness between. It was but his own shadow which trailed up the wall as he passed the lights, and yet it looked to the doctor's eye as though some huge and sombre figure walked by a manikin's side and led him silently up the lonely street.

Dr. Horace Selby heard again of his patient next morning, and rather earlier than he had expected. A paragraph in the Daily News caused him to push away his breakfast untasted, and turned him sick and faint while he read it. "A Deplorable Accident," it was headed, and it ran in this way:

"A fatal accident of a peculiarly painful character is reported from King William Street. About eleven o'clock last night a young man was observed while endeavouring to get out of the way of a hansom to slip and fall under the wheels of a heavy, two-horse dray. On being picked up his injuries were found to be of the most shocking character, and he expired while being conveyed to the hospital. An examination of his pocketbook and cardcase shows beyond any question that the deceased is none other than Sir Francis Norton, of Deane Park, who has only within the last year come into the baronetcy. The accident is made the more deplorable as the deceased, who was only just of age, was on the eve of being married to a young lady belonging to one of the oldest families in the South. With his wealth and his talents the ball of fortune was at his feet, and his many friends will be deeply grieved to know that his promising career has been cut short in so sudden and tragic a fashion."

A False Start

"Is Dr. Horace Wilkinson at home?"

"I am he. Pray step in."

The visitor looked somewhat astonished at having the door opened to him by the master of the house.

"I wanted to have a few words."

The doctor, a pale, nervous young man, dressed in an ultra-professional, long black frock-coat, with a high, white collar cutting off his dapper side-whiskers in the centre, rubbed his hands together and smiled. In the thick, burly man in front of him he scented a patient, and it would be his first. His scanty resources had begun to run somewhat low, and, although he had his first quarter's rent safely locked away in the right-hand drawer of his desk, it was becoming a question with him how he should meet the current expenses of his very simple housekeeping. He bowed, therefore, waved his visitor in, closed the hall door in a careless fashion, as though his own presence thereat had been a purely accidental circumstance, and finally led the burly stranger into his scantily furnished front room, where he motioned him to a seat. Dr. Wilkinson planted himself behind his desk, and, placing his finger-tips together, he gazed with some apprehension at his companion. What was the matter with the man? He seemed very red in the face. Some of his old professors would have diagnosed his case by now, and would have electrified the patient by describing his own symptoms before he had said a word about them. Dr. Horace Wilkinson racked his brains for some clue, but Nature had fashioned him as a plodder—a very reliable plodder and nothing more. He could think of nothing save that the visitor's watch-chain had a very brassy appearance, with a corollary to the effect that he would be lucky if he got half-a-crown out of him. Still, even half-a-crown was something in those early days of struggle.

Whilst the doctor had been running his eyes over the stranger, the latter had been plunging his hands into pocket after pocket of his heavy coat. The heat of the weather, his dress, and this exercise of pocket-rummaging had all combined to still further redden his face, which had changed from brick to beet, with a gloss of moisture on his brow. This extreme ruddiness brought a clue at last to the observant doctor. Surely it was not to be attained without alcohol. In alcohol lay the secret of this man's trouble. Some little delicacy was needed, however, in showing him that he had read his case aright—that at a glance he had penetrated to the inmost sources of his ailments.

"It's very hot," observed the stranger, mopping his forehead.

"Yes, it is weather which tempts one to drink rather more beer than is good for one," answered Dr. Horace Wilkinson, looking very knowingly at his companion from over his finger-tips.

"Dear, dear, you shouldn't do that."

"I! I never touch beer."

"Neither do I. I've been an abstainer for twenty years."

This was depressing. Dr. Wilkinson blushed until he was nearly as red as the other. "May I ask what I can do for you?" he asked, picking up his stethoscope and tapping it gently against his thumb-nail.

"Yes, I was just going to tell you. I heard of your coming, but I couldn't get round before——" He broke into a nervous little cough.

"Yes?" said the doctor encouragingly.

"I should have been here three weeks ago, but you know how these things get put off." He coughed again behind his large red hand.

"I do not think that you need say anything more," said the doctor, taking over the case with an easy air of command. "Your cough is quite sufficient. It is entirely bronchial by the sound. No doubt the mischief is circumscribed at present, but there is always the danger that it may spread, so you have done wisely to come to me. A little judicious treatment will soon set you right. Your waistcoat, please, but not your shirt. Puff out your chest and say ninety-nine in a deep voice."

The red-faced man began to laugh. "It's all right, doctor," said he. "That cough comes from chewing tobacco, and I know it's a very bad habit. Nine-and-ninepence is what I have to say to you, for I'm the officer of the gas company, and they have a claim against you for that on the metre."

Dr. Horace Wilkinson collapsed into his chair. "Then you're not a patient?" he gasped.

"Never needed a doctor in my life, sir."

"Oh, that's all right." The doctor concealed his disappointment under an affectation of facetiousness. "You don't look as if you troubled them much. I don't know what we should do if every one were as robust. I shall call at the company's offices and pay this small amount."

"If you could make it convenient, sir, now that I am here, it would save trouble——"

"Oh, certainly!" These eternal little sordid money troubles were more trying to the doctor than plain living or scanty food. He took out his purse and slid the contents on to the table. There were two half-crowns and some pennies. In his drawer he had ten golden sovereigns. But those were his rent. If he once broke in upon them he was lost. He would starve first.

"Dear me! " said he, with a smile, as at some strange, unheard-of incident. "I have run short of small change. I am afraid I shall have to call upon the company, after all."

"Very well, sir." The inspector rose, and with a practised glance around, which valued every article in the room, from the two-guinea carpet to the eight-shilling muslin curtains, he took his departure.

When he had gone Dr. Wilkinson rearranged his room, as was his habit a dozen times in the day. He laid out his large Quain's Dictionary of Medicine in the forefront of the table so as to impress the casual patient that he had ever the best authorities at his elbow. Then he cleared all the little instruments out of his pocket-case—the scissors, the forceps, the bistouries, the lancets—and he laid them all out beside the stethoscope, to make as good a show as possible. His ledger, day-book, and visiting-book were spread in front of him. There was no entry in any of them yet, but it would not look well to have the covers too glossy and new, so he rubbed them together and daubed ink over them. Neither would it be well that any patient should observe that his name was the first in the book, so he filled up the first page of each with notes of imaginary visits paid to nameless patients during the last three weeks. Having done all this, he rested his head upon his hands and relapsed into the terrible occupation of waiting.

Terrible enough at any time to the young professional man, but most of all to one who knows that the weeks, and even the days during which he can hold out are numbered. Economise as he would, the money would still slip away in the countless little claims which a man never understands until he lives under a rooftree of his own. Dr. Wilkinson could not deny, as he sat at his desk and looked at the little heap of silver and coppers, that his chances of being a successful practitioner in Sutton were rapidly vanishing away.

And yet it was a bustling, prosperous town, with so much money in it that it seemed strange that a man with a trained brain and dexterous fingers should be starved out of it for want of employment. At his desk, Dr. Horace Wilkinson could see the never-ending double current of people which ebbed and flowed in front of his window. It was a busy street, and the air was forever filled with the dull roar of life, the grinding of the wheels, and the patter of countless feet. Men, women, and children, thousands and thousands of them passed in the day, and yet each was hurrying on upon his own business, scarce glancing at the small brass plate, or wasting a thought upon the man who waited in the front room. And yet how many of them would obviously, glaringly have been the better for his professional assistance. Dyspeptic men, anemic women, blotched faces, bilious complexions—they flowed past him, they needing him, he needing them, and yet the remorseless bar of professional etiquette kept them forever apart. What could he do? Could he stand at his own front door, pluck the casual stranger by the sleeve, and whisper in his ear, "Sir, you will forgive me for remarking that you are suffering from a severe attack of acne rosacea, which makes you a peculiarly unpleasant object. Allow me to suggest that a small prescription containing arsenic, which will not cost you more than you often spend upon a single meal, will be very much to your advantage." Such an address would be a degradation to the high and lofty profession of Medicine, and there are no such sticklers for the ethics of that profession as some to whom she has been but a bitter and a grudging mother.

Dr. Horace Wilkinson was still looking moodily out of the window, when there came a sharp clang at the bell. Often it had rung, and with every ring his hopes had sprung up, only to dwindle away again, and change to leaden disappointment, as he faced some beggar or touting tradesman. But the doctor's spirit was young and elastic, and again, in spite of all experience, it responded to that exhilarating summons. He sprang to his feet, cast his eyes over the table, thrust out his medical books a little more prominently, and hurried to the door. A groan escaped him as he entered the hall. He could see through the half-glazed upper panels that a gypsy van, hung round with wicker tables and chairs, had halted before his door, and that a couple of the vagrants, with a baby, were waiting outside. He had learned by experience that it was better not even to parley with such people.

"I have nothing for you," said he, loosing the latch by an inch. "Go away!"

He closed the door, but the bell clanged once more. "Get away! Get away!" he cried impatiently, and walked back into his consulting-room. He had hardly seated himself when the bell went for the third time. In a towering passion he rushed back, flung open the door.

"What the——?"

"If you please, sir, we need a doctor."

In an instant he was rubbing his hands again with his blandest professional smile. These were patients, then, whom he had tried to hunt from his doorstep—the very first patients, whom he had waited for so impatiently. They did not look very promising. The man, a tall, lank-haired gypsy, had gone back to the horse's head. There remained a small, hard-faced woman with a great bruise all round her eye. She wore a yellow silk handkerchief round her head, and a baby, tucked in a red shawl, was pressed to her bosom.

"Pray step in, madam," said Dr. Horace Wilkinson, with his very best sympathetic manner. In this case, at least, there could be no mistake as to diagnosis. "If you will sit on this sofa, I shall very soon make you feel much more comfortable."

He poured a little water from his carafe into a saucer, made a compress of lint, fastened it over the injured eye, and secured the whole with a spica bandage, secundum artem.

"Thank ye kindly, sir," said the woman, when his work was finished; "that's nice and warm, and may God bless your honour. But it wasn't about my eye at all that I came to see a doctor."

"Not your eye?" Dr. Horace Wilkinson was beginning to be a little doubtful as to the advantages of quick diagnosis. It is an excellent thing to be able to surprise a patient, but hitherto it was always the patient who had surprised him.

"The baby's got the measles."

The mother parted the red shawl, and exhibited a little dark, black-eyed gypsy baby, whose swarthy face was all flushed and mottled with a dark-red rash. The child breathed with a rattling sound, and it looked up at the doctor with eyes which were heavy with want of sleep and crusted together at the lids.

"Hum! Yes. Measles, sure enough—and a smart attack."

"I just wanted you to see her, sir, so that you could signify."

"Could what?"

"Signify, if anything happened."

"Oh, I see—certify."

"And now that you've seen it, sir, I'll go on, for Reuben— that's my man—is in a hurry."

"But don't you want any medicine?"

"Oh, now you've seen it, it's all right. I'll let you know if anything happens."

"But you must have some medicine. The child is very ill." He descended into the little room which he had fitted as a surgery, and he made up a two-ounce bottle of cooling medicine. In such cities as Sutton there are few patients who can afford to pay a fee to both doctor and chemist, so that unless the physician is prepared to play the part of both he will have little chance of making a living at either.

"There is your medicine, madam. You will find the directions upon the bottle. Keep the child warm and give it a light diet."

"Thank you kindly, sir." She shouldered her baby and marched for the door.

"Excuse me, madam," said the doctor nervously. "Don't you think it too small a matter to make a bill of? Perhaps it would be better if we had a settlement at once."

The gypsy woman looked at him reproachfully out of her one uncovered eye.

"Are you going to charge me for that?" she asked. "How much, then?"

"Well, say half-a-crown." He mentioned the sum in a half-jesting way, as though it were too small to take serious notice of, but the gypsy woman raised quite a scream at the mention of it.

"'Arf-a-crown! for that?"

"Well, my good woman, why not go to the poor doctor if you cannot afford a fee?"

She fumbled in her pocket, craning awkwardly to keep her grip upon the baby.

"Here's sevenpence," she said at last, holding out a little pile of copper coins. "I'll give you that and a wicker footstool."

"But my fee is half-a-crown." The doctor's views of the glory of his profession cried out against this wretched haggling, and yet what was he to do? "Where am I to get 'arf-a-crown? It is well for gentlefolk like you who sit in your grand houses, and can eat and drink what you like, an' charge 'arf-a-crown for just saying as much as, ''Ow d'ye do?' We can't pick up' arf-crowns like that. What we gets we earns 'ard. This sevenpence is just all I've got. You told me to feed the child light. She must feed light, for what she's to have is more than I know."

Whilst the woman had been speaking, Dr. Horace Wilkinson's eyes had wandered to the tiny heap of money upon the table, which represented all that separated him from absolute starvation, and he chuckled to himself at the grim joke that he should appear to this poor woman to be a being living in the lap of luxury. Then he picked up the odd coppers, leaving only the two half-crowns upon the table.

"Here you are," he said brusquely. "Never mind the fee, and take these coppers. They may be of some use to you. Good-bye!" He bowed her out, and closed the door behind her. After all she was the thin edge of the wedge. These wandering people have great powers of recommendation. All large practices have been built up from such foundations. The hangers-on to the kitchen recommend to the kitchen, they to the drawing-room, and so it spreads. At least he could say now that he had had a patient.

He went into the back room and lit the spirit-kettle to boil the water for his tea, laughing the while at the recollection of his recent interview. If all patients were like this one it could easily be reckoned how many it would take to ruin him completely. Putting aside the dirt upon his carpet and the loss of time, there were twopence gone upon the bandage, fourpence or more upon the medicine, to say nothing of phial, cork, label, and paper. Then he had given her fivepence, so that his first patient had absorbed altogether not less than one sixth of his available capital. If five more were to come he would be a broken man. He sat down upon the portmanteau and shook with laughter at the thought, while he measured out his one spoonful and a half of tea at one shilling eightpence into the brown earthenware teapot. Suddenly, however, the laugh faded from his face, and he cocked his ear towards the door, standing listening with a slanting head and a sidelong eye. There had been a rasping of wheels against the curb, the sound of steps outside, and then a loud peal at the bell. With his teaspoon in his hand he peeped round the corner and saw with amazement that a carriage and pair were waiting outside, and that a powdered footman was standing at the door. The spoon tinkled down upon the floor, and he stood gazing in bewilderment. Then, pulling himself together, he threw open the door.

"Young man," said the flunky, "tell your master, Dr. Wilkinson, that he is wanted just as quick as ever he can come to Lady Millbank, at the Towers. He is to come this very instant. We'd take him with us, but we have to go back to see if Dr. Mason is home yet. Just you stir your stumps and give him the message."

The footman nodded and was off in an instant, while the coachman lashed his horses and the carriage flew down the street.

Here was a new development. Dr. Horace Wilkinson stood at his door and tried to think it all out. Lady Millbank, of the Towers! People of wealth and position, no doubt. And a serious case, or why this haste and summoning of two doctors? But, then, why in the name of all that is wonderful should he be sent for?

He was obscure, unknown, without influence. There must be some mistake. Yes, that must be the true explanation; or was it possible that some one was attempting a cruel hoax upon him? At any rate, it was too positive a message to be disregarded. He must set off at once and settle the matter one way or the other.

But he had one source of information. At the corner of the street was a small shop where one of the oldest inhabitants dispensed newspapers and gossip. He could get information there if anywhere. He put on his well-brushed top hat, secreted instruments and bandages in all his pockets, and without waiting for his tea closed up his establishment and started off upon his adventure.

The stationer at the corner was a human directory to every one and everything in Sutton, so that he soon had all the information which he wanted. Sir John Millbank was very well known in the town, it seemed. He was a merchant prince, an exporter of pens, three times mayor, and reported to be fully worth two millions sterling.

The Towers was his palatial seat, just outside the city. His wife had been an invalid for some years, and was growing worse. So far the whole thing seemed to be genuine enough. By some amazing chance these people really had sent for him.

And then another doubt assailed him, and he turned back into the shop.

"I am your neighbour, Dr. Horace Wilkinson," said he. "Is there any other medical man of that name in the town?"

No, the stationer was quite positive that there was not.

That was final, then. A great good fortune had come in his way, and he must take prompt advantage of it. He called a cab and drove furiously to the Towers, with his brain in a whirl, giddy with hope and delight at one moment, and sickened with fears and doubts at the next lest the case should in some way be beyond his powers, or lest he should find at some critical moment that he was without the instrument or appliance that was needed. Every strange and outre case of which he had ever heard or read came back into his mind, and long before he reached the Towers he had worked himself into a positive conviction that he would be instantly required to do a trephining at the least.

The Towers was a very large house, standing back amid trees, at the head of a winding drive. As he drove up the doctor sprang out, paid away half his worldly assets as a fare, and followed a stately footman who, having taken his name, led him through the oak-panelled, stained-glass hall, gorgeous with deers' heads and ancient armour, and ushered him into a large sitting-room beyond. A very irritable-looking, acid-faced man was seated in an armchair by the fireplace, while two young ladies in white were standing together in the bow window at the further end.

"Hullo! hullo! hullo! What's this—heh?" cried the irritable man. "Are you Dr. Wilkinson? Eh?"

"Yes, sir, I am Dr. Wilkinson."

"Really, now. You seem very young—much younger than I expected. Well, well, well, Mason's old, and yet he don't seem to know much about it. I suppose we must try the other end now. You're the Wilkinson who wrote something about the lungs? Heh?"

Here was a light! The only two letters which the doctor had ever written to The Lancet—modest little letters thrust away in a back column among the wrangles about medical ethics and the inquiries as to how much it took to keep a horse in the country— had been upon pulmonary disease. They had not been wasted, then. Some eye had picked them out and marked the name of the writer. Who could say that work was ever wasted, or that merit did not promptly meet with its reward?

"Yes, I have written on the subject."

"Ha! Well, then, where's Mason?"

"I have not the pleasure of his acquaintance."

"No?—that's queer too. He knows you and thinks a lot of your opinion. You're a stranger in the town, are you not?"

"Yes, I have only been here a very short time."

"That was what Mason said. He didn't give me the address. Said he would call on you and bring you, but when the wife got worse of course I inquired for you and sent for you direct. I sent for Mason, too, but he was out. However, we can't wait for him, so just run away upstairs and do what you can."

"Well, I am placed in a rather delicate position," said Dr. Horace Wilkinson, with some hesitation. "I am here, as I under-stand, to meet my colleague, Dr. Mason, in consultation. It would, perhaps, hardly be correct for me to see the patient in his absence. I think that I would rather wait."

"Would you, by Jove! Do you think I'll let my wife get worse while the doctor is coolly kicking his heels in the room below? No, sir, I am a plain man, and I tell you that you will either go up or go out."

The style of speech jarred upon the doctor's sense of the fitness of things, but still when a man's wife is ill much may be overlooked. He contented himself by bowing somewhat stiffly. "I shall go up, if you insist upon it," said he.

"I do insist upon it. And another thing, I won't have her thumped about all over the chest, or any hocus-pocus of the sort. She has bronchitis and asthma, and that's all. If you can cure it well and good. But it only weakens her to have you tapping and listening, and it does no good either."

Personal disrespect was a thing that the doctor could stand; but the profession was to him a holy thing, and a flippant word about it cut him to the quick.

"Thank you," said he, picking up his hat. "I have the honour to wish you a very good day. I do not care to undertake the responsibility of this case."

"Hullo! what's the matter now?"

"It is not my habit to give opinions without examining my patient. I wonder that you should suggest such a course to a medical man. I wish you good day."

But Sir John Millbank was a commercial man, and believed in the commercial principle that the more difficult a thing is to attain the more valuable it is. A doctor's opinion had been to him a mere matter of guineas. But here was a young man who seemed to care nothing either for his wealth or title. His respect for his judgment increased amazingly.

"Tut! tut!" said he; "Mason is not so thin-skinned. There! there! Have your way! Do what you like and I won't say another word. I'll just run upstairs and tell Lady Millbank that you are coming."

The door had hardly closed behind him when the two demure young ladies darted out of their corner, and fluttered with joy in front of the astonished doctor.

"Oh, well done! well done!" cried the taller, clapping her hands.

"Don't let him bully you, doctor," said the other. "Oh, it was so nice to hear you stand up to him. That's the way he does with poor Dr. Mason. Dr. Mason has never examined mamma yet. He always takes papa's word for everything. Hush, Maude; here he comes again." They subsided in an instant into their corner as silent and demure as ever.

Dr. Horace Wilkinson followed Sir John up the broad, thick-carpeted staircase, and into the darkened sick room. In a quarter of an hour he had sounded and sifted the case to the uttermost, and descended with the husband once more to the drawing-room. In front of the fireplace were standing two gentlemen, the one a very typical, clean-shaven, general practitioner, the other a strik-ing-looking man of middle age, with pale blue eyes and a long red beard.

"Hullo, Mason, you've come at last!"

"Yes, Sir John, and I have brought, as I promised, Dr. Wilkin-son with me."

"Dr. Wilkinson! Why, this is he."

Dr. Mason stared in astonishment. "I have never seen the gen-tleman before!" he cried.

"Nevertheless I am Dr. Wilkinson—Dr. Horace Wilkinson, of 114 Canal View."

"Good gracious, Sir John!" cried Dr. Mason.

"Did you think that in a case of such importance I should call in a junior local practitioner! This is Dr. Adam Wilkinson, lecturer on pulmonary diseases at Regent's College, London, physician upon the staff of the St. Swithin's Hospital, and author of a dozen works upon the subject. He happened to be in Sutton upon a visit, and I thought I would utilise his presence to have a first-rate opin-ion upon Lady Millbank."

"Thank you," said Sir John, dryly. "But I fear my wife is rather tired now, for she has just been very thoroughly examined by this young gentleman. I think we will let it stop at that for the present; though, of course, as you have had the trouble of coming here, I should be glad to have a note of your fees."

When Dr. Mason had departed, looking very disgusted, and his friend, the specialist, very amused, Sir John listened to all the young physician had to say about the case.

"Now, I'll tell you what," said he, when he had finished. "I'm a man of my word, d'ye see? When I like a man I freeze to him. I'm a good friend and a bad enemy. I believe in you, and I don't believe in Mason. From now on you are my doctor, and that of my family. Come and see my wife every day. How does that suit your book?"

"I am extremely grateful to you for your kind intentions toward me, but I am afraid there is no possible way in which I can avail myself of them."

"Heh! what d'ye mean?"

"I could not possibly take Dr. Mason's place in the middle of a case like this. It would be a most unprofessional act."

"Oh, well, go your own way!" cried Sir John, in despair. "Never was such a man for making difficulties. You've had a fair offer and you've refused it, and now you can just go your own way."

The millionaire stumped out of the room in a huff, and Dr. Horace Wilkinson made his way homeward to his spirit-lamp and his one-and-eightpenny tea, with his first guinea in his pocket, and with a feeling that he had upheld the best traditions of his profession.

And yet this false start of his was a true start also, for it soon came to Dr. Mason's ears that his junior had had it in his power to carry off his best patient and had forborne to do so. To the honour of the profession be it said that such forbearance is the rule rather than the exception, and yet in this case, with so very junior a practitioner and so very wealthy a patient, the temptation was greater than is usual. There was a grateful note, a visit, a friendship, and now the well-known firm of Mason and Wilkinson is doing the largest family practice in Sutton.

The Curse of Eve

Robert Johnson was an essentially commonplace man, with no feature to distinguish him from a million others. He was pale of face, ordinary in looks, neutral in opinions, thirty years of age, and a married man. By trade he was a gentleman's outfitter in the New North Road, and the competition of business squeezed out of him the little character that was left. In his hope of conciliating customers he had become cringing and pliable, until working ever in the same routine from day to day he seemed to have sunk into a soulless machine rather than a man. No great question had ever stirred him. At the end of this snug century, self-contained in his own narrow circle, it seemed impossible that any of the mighty, primitive passions of mankind could ever reach him. Yet birth, and lust, and illness, and death are changeless things, and when one of these harsh facts springs out upon a man at some sudden turn of the path of life, it dashes off for the moment his mask of civilisation and gives a glimpse of the stranger and stronger face below.

Johnson's wife was a quiet little woman, with brown hair and gentle ways. His affection for her was the one positive trait in his character. Together they would lay out the shop window every Monday morning, the spotless shirts in their green cardboard boxes below, the neckties above hung in rows over the brass rails, the cheap studs glistening from the white cards at either side, while in the background were the rows of cloth caps and the bank of boxes in which the more valuable hats were screened from the sunlight. She kept the books and sent out the bills. No one but she knew the joys and sorrows which crept into his small life. She had shared his exultations when the gentleman who was going to India had bought ten dozen shirts and an incredible number of collars, and she had been as stricken as he when, after the goods had gone, the bill was returned from the hotel address with the intimation that no such person had lodged there. For five years they had worked, building up the business, thrown together all the more closely because their marriage had been a childless one. Now, however, there were signs that a change was at hand, and that speedily. She was unable to come downstairs, and her mother, Mrs. Peyton, came over from Camberwell to nurse her and to welcome her grandchild.

Little qualms of anxiety came over Johnson as his wife's time approached. However, after all, it was a natural process. Other men's wives went through it unharmed, and why should not his? He was himself one of a family of fourteen, and yet his mother was alive and hearty. It was quite the exception for anything to go wrong. And yet in spite of his reasonings the remembrance of his wife's condition was always like a sombre background to all his other thoughts.

Dr. Miles of Bridport Place, the best man in the neighbour-
hood, was retained five months in advance, and, as time stole on,
many little packets of absurdly small white garments with frill
work and ribbons began to arrive among the big consignments of
male necessities. And then one evening, as Johnson was ticketing
the scarfs in the shop, he heard a bustle upstairs, and Mrs. Peyton
came running down to say that Lucy was bad and that she thought
the doctor ought to be there without delay.

It was not Robert Johnson's nature to hurry. He was prim and
staid and liked to do things in an orderly fashion. It was a quarter
of a mile from the corner of the New North Road where his shop
stood to the doctor's house in Bridport Place. There were no cabs
in sight so he set off upon foot, leaving the lad to mind the shop. At
Bridport Place he was told that the doctor had just gone to Harman Street to attend a man in a fit. Johnson started off for Harman
Street, losing a little of his primness as he became more anxious.
Two full cabs but no empty ones passed him on the way. At Harman Street he learned that the doctor had gone on to a case of
measles, fortunately he had left the address—69 Dunstan Road, at
the other side of the Regent's Canal. Robert's primness had vanished now as he thought of the women waiting at home, and he
began to run as hard as he could down the Kingsland Road. Some
way along he sprang into a cab which stood by the curb and drove
to Dunstan Road. The doctor had just left, and Robert Johnson felt
inclined to sit down upon the steps in despair.

Fortunately he had not sent the cab away, and he was soon
back at Bridport Place. Dr. Miles had not returned yet, but they
were expecting him every instant. Johnson waited, drumming his
fingers on his knees, in a high, dim lit room, the air of which was
charged with a faint, sickly smell of ether. The furniture was massive, and the books in the shelves were sombre, and a squat black
clock ticked mournfully on the mantelpiece. It told him that it was
half-past seven, and that he had been gone an hour and a quarter.
Whatever would the women think of him! Every time that a distant door slammed he sprang from his chair in a quiver of eagerness. His ears strained to catch the deep notes of the doctor's
voice. And then, suddenly, with a gush of joy he heard a quick step

outside, and the sharp click of the key in the lock. In an instant he was out in the hall, before the doctor's foot was over the threshold.

"If you please, doctor, I've come for you," he cried; "the wife was taken bad at six o'clock."

He hardly knew what he expected the doctor to do. Something very energetic, certainly—to seize some drugs, perhaps, and rush excitedly with him through the gaslit streets. Instead of that Dr. Miles threw his umbrella into the rack, jerked off his hat with a somewhat peevish gesture, and pushed Johnson back into the room.

"Let's see! You DID engage me, didn't you?" he asked in no very cordial voice.

"Oh, yes, doctor, last November. Johnson the outfitter, you know, in the New North Road."

"Yes, yes. It's a bit overdue," said the doctor, glancing at a list of names in a note-book with a very shiny cover. "Well, how is she?"

"I don't——"

"Ah, of course, it's your first. You'll know more about it next time."

"Mrs. Peyton said it was time you were there, sir."

"My dear sir, there can be no very pressing hurry in a first case. We shall have an all-night affair, I fancy. You can't get an engine to go without coals, Mr. Johnson, and I have had nothing but a light lunch."

"We could have something cooked for you—something hot and a cup of tea."

"Thank you, but I fancy my dinner is actually on the table. I can do no good in the earlier stages. Go home and say that I am coming, and I will be round immediately afterwards."

A sort of horror filled Robert Johnson as he gazed at this man who could think about his dinner at such a moment. He had not imagination enough to realise that the experience which seemed so appallingly important to him, was the merest everyday matter of business to the medical man who could not have lived for a year had he not, amid the rush of work, remembered what was due to his own health. To Johnson he seemed little better than a monster. His thoughts were bitter as he sped back to his shop.

"You've taken your time," said his mother-in-law reproachfully, looking down the stairs as he entered.

"I couldn't help it!" he gasped. "Is it over?"

"Over! She's got to be worse, poor dear, before she can be better. Where's Dr. Miles!"

"He's coming after he's had dinner." The old woman was about to make some reply, when, from the half-opened door behind a high whinnying voice cried out for her. She ran back and closed the door, while Johnson, sick at heart, turned into the shop. There he sent the lad home and busied himself frantically in putting up shutters and turning out boxes. When all was closed and finished he seated himself in the parlour behind the shop. But he could not sit still. He rose incessantly to walk a few paces and then fell back into a chair once more. Suddenly the clatter of china fell upon his ear, and he saw the maid pass the door with a cup on a tray and a smoking teapot.

"Who is that for, Jane?" he asked.

"For the mistress, Mr. Johnson. She says she would fancy it."

There was immeasurable consolation to him in that homely cup of tea. It wasn't so very bad after all if his wife could think of such things. So light-hearted was he that he asked for a cup also. He had just finished it when the doctor arrived, with a small black leather bag in his hand.

"Well, how is she?" he asked genially.

"Oh, she's very much better," said Johnson, with enthusiasm.

"Dear me, that's bad!" said the doctor. "Perhaps it will do if I look in on my morning round?"

"No, no," cried Johnson, clutching at his thick frieze overcoat. "We are so glad that you have come. And, doctor, please come down soon and let me know what you think about it."

The doctor passed upstairs, his firm, heavy steps resounding through the house. Johnson could hear his boots creaking as he walked about the floor above him, and the sound was a consolation to him. It was crisp and decided, the tread of a man who had plenty of self-confidence. Presently, still straining his ears to catch what was going on, he heard the scraping of a chair as it was drawn along the floor, and a moment later he heard the door fly open and someone come rushing downstairs. Johnson sprang up with his hair bristling, thinking that some dreadful thing had occurred, but it was only his mother-in-law, incoherent with excitement and searching for scissors and some tape. She vanished again and Jane passed up the stairs with a pile of newly aired linen. Then, after an interval of silence, Johnson heard the heavy, creaking tread and the doctor came down into the parlour.

"That's better," said he, pausing with his hand upon the door. "You look pale, Mr. Johnson."

"Oh no, sir, not at all," he answered deprecatingly, mopping his brow with his handkerchief.

"There is no immediate cause for alarm," said Dr. Miles. "The case is not all that we could wish it. Still we will hope for the best."

"Is there danger, sir?" gasped Johnson.

"Well, there is always danger, of course. It is not altogether a favourable case, but still it might be much worse. I have given her a draught. I saw as I passed that they have been doing a little building opposite to you. It's an improving quarter. The rents go higher and higher. You have a lease of your own little place, eh?"

"Yes, sir, yes!" cried Johnson, whose ears were straining for every sound from above, and who felt none the less that it was very soothing that the doctor should be able to chat so easily at such a time. "That's to say no, sir, I am a yearly tenant."

"Ah, I should get a lease if I were you. There's Marshall, the watchmaker, down the street. I attended his wife twice and saw him through the typhoid when they took up the drains in Prince Street. I assure you his landlord sprung his rent nearly forty a year and he had to pay or clear out."

"Did his wife get through it, doctor?"

"Oh yes, she did very well. Hullo! hullo!"

He slanted his ear to the ceiling with a questioning face, and then darted swiftly from the room.

It was March and the evenings were chill, so Jane had lit the fire, but the wind drove the smoke downwards and the air was full of its acrid taint. Johnson felt chilled to the bone, though rather by his apprehensions than by the weather. He crouched over the fire with his thin white hands held out to the blaze. At ten o'clock Jane brought in the joint of cold meat and laid his place for supper, but he could not bring himself to touch it. He drank a glass of the beer, however, and felt the better for it. The tension of his nerves seemed to have reacted upon his hearing, and he was able to follow the most trivial things in the room above. Once, when the beer was still heartening him, he nerved himself to creep on tiptoe up the stair and to listen to what was going on. The bedroom door was half an inch open, and through the slit he could catch a glimpse of the clean-shaven face of the doctor, looking wearier and more anxious than before. Then he rushed downstairs like a lunatic, and running to the door he tried to distract his thoughts by watching what; was going on in the street. The shops were all shut, and some rollicking boon companions came shouting along from the public-house. He stayed at the door until the stragglers had thinned down, and then came back to his seat by the fire. In his dim brain he was asking himself questions which had never intruded themselves before. Where was the justice of it? What had his sweet, innocent little wife done that she should be used so? Why was nature so cruel? He was frightened at his own thoughts, and yet wondered that they had never occurred to him before.

As the early morning drew in, Johnson, sick at heart and shivering in every limb, sat with his great coat huddled round him, staring at the grey ashes and waiting hopelessly for some relief. His face was white and clammy, and his nerves had been numbed into a half conscious state by the long monotony of misery. But suddenly all his feelings leapt into keen life again as he heard the bedroom door open and the doctor's steps upon the stair. Robert Johnson was precise and unemotional in everyday life, but he almost shrieked now as he rushed forward to know if it were over.

One glance at the stern, drawn face which met him showed that it was no pleasant news which had sent the doctor downstairs. His appearance had altered as much as Johnson's during the last few hours. His hair was on end, his face flushed, his forehead dotted with beads of perspiration. There was a peculiar fierceness in his eye, and about the lines of his mouth, a fighting look as befitted a man who for hours on end had been striving with the hungriest of foes for the most precious of prizes. But there was a sadness too, as though his grim opponent had been overmastering him. He sat down and leaned his head upon his hand like a man who is fagged out.

"I thought it my duty to see you, Mr. Johnson, and to tell you that it is a very nasty case. Your wife's heart is not strong, and she has some symptoms which I do not like. What I wanted to say is that if you would like to have a second opinion I shall be very glad to meet anyone whom you might suggest."

Johnson was so dazed by his want of sleep and the evil news that he could hardly grasp the doctor's meaning. The other, seeing him hesitate, thought that he was considering the expense.

"Smith or Hawley would come for two guineas," said he. "But I think Pritchard of the City Road is the best man."

"Oh, yes, bring the best man," cried Johnson.

"Pritchard would want three guineas. He is a senior man, you see."

"I'd give him all I have if he would pull her through. Shall I run for him?"

"Yes. Go to my house first and ask for the green baize bag. The assistant will give it to you. Tell him I want the A. C. E. mixture. Her heart is too weak for chloroform. Then go for Pritchard and bring him back with you."

It was heavenly for Johnson to have something to do and to feel that he was of some use to his wife. He ran swiftly to Bridport Place, his footfalls clattering through the silent streets and the big dark policemen turning their yellow funnels of light on him as he passed. Two tugs at the night-bell brought down a sleepy, half-clad assistant, who handed him a stoppered glass bottle and a cloth bag which contained something which clinked when you moved it. Johnson thrust the bottle into his pocket, seized the green bag, and pressing his hat firmly down ran as hard as he could set foot to ground until he was in the City Road and saw the name of Pritchard engraved in white upon a red ground. He bounded in triumph up the three steps which led to the door, and as he did so there was a crash behind him. His precious bottle was in fragments upon the pavement.

For a moment he felt as if it were his wife's body that was lying there. But the run had freshened his wits and he saw that the mischief might be repaired. He pulled vigorously at the night-bell.

"Well, what's the matter?" asked a gruff voice at his elbow. He started back and looked up at the windows, but there was no sign of life. He was approaching the bell again with the intention of pulling it, when a perfect roar burst from the wall.

"I can't stand shivering here all night," cried the voice. "Say who you are and what you want or I shut the tube."

Then for the first time Johnson saw that the end of a speaking-tube hung out of the wall just above the bell. He shouted up it,—

"I want you to come with me to meet Dr. Miles at a confinement at once."

"How far?" shrieked the irascible voice.

"The New North Road, Hoxton."

"My consultation fee is three guineas, payable at the time."

"All right," shouted Johnson. "You are to bring a bottle of A. C. E. mixture with you."

"All right! Wait a bit!"

Five minutes later an elderly, hard-faced man, with grizzled hair, flung open the door. As he emerged a voice from somewhere in the shadows cried,—

"Mind you take your cravat, John," and he impatiently growled something over his shoulder in reply.

The consultant was a man who had been hardened by a life of ceaseless labour, and who had been driven, as so many others have been, by the needs of his own increasing family to set the commercial before the philanthropic side of his profession. Yet beneath his rough crust he was a man with a kindly heart.

"We don't want to break a record," said he, pulling up and panting after attempting to keep up with Johnson for five minutes. "I would go quicker if I could, my dear sir, and I quite sympathise with your anxiety, but really I can't manage it."

So Johnson, on fire with impatience, had to slow down until they reached the New North Road, when he ran ahead and had the door open for the doctor when he came. He heard the two meet outside the bed-room, and caught scraps of their conversation. "Sorry to knock you up—nasty case—decent people." Then it sank into a mumble and the door closed behind them.

Johnson sat up in his chair now, listening keenly, for he knew that a crisis must be at hand. He heard the two doctors moving about, and was able to distinguish the step of Pritchard, which had a drag in it, from the clean, crisp sound of the other's footfall. There was silence for a few minutes and then a curious drunken, mumbling sing-song voice came quavering up, very unlike anything which be had heard hitherto. At the same time a sweetish, insidious scent, imperceptible perhaps to any nerves less strained than his, crept down the stairs and penetrated into the room. The voice dwindled into a mere drone and finally sank away into silence, and Johnson gave a long sigh of relief, for he knew that the drug had done its work and that, come what might, there should be no more pain for the sufferer.

But soon the silence became even more trying to him than the cries had been. He had no clue now as to what was going on, and his mind swarmed with horrible possibilities. He rose and went to the bottom of the stairs again. He heard the clink of metal against metal, and the subdued murmur of the doctors' voices. Then he heard Mrs. Peyton say something, in a tone as of fear or expostulation, and again the doctors murmured together. For twenty minutes he stood there leaning against the wall, listening to the occasional rumbles of talk without being able to catch a word of it. And then of a sudden there rose out of the silence the strangest little piping cry, and Mrs. Peyton screamed out in her delight and the man ran into the parlour and flung himself down upon the horse-hair sofa, drumming his heels on it in his ecstasy.

But often the great cat Fate lets us go only to clutch us again in a fiercer grip. As minute after minute passed and still no sound came from above save those thin, glutinous cries, Johnson cooled from his frenzy of joy, and lay breathless with his ears straining. They were moving slowly about. They were talking in subdued tones. Still minute after minute passing, and no word from the voice for which he listened. His nerves were dulled by his night of trouble, and he waited in limp wretchedness upon his sofa. There he still sat when the doctors came down to him—a bedraggled, miserable figure with his face grimy and his hair unkempt from his long vigil. He rose as they entered, bracing himself against the mantelpiece.

"Is she dead?" he asked.

"Doing well," answered the doctor.

And at the words that little conventional spirit which had never known until that night the capacity for fierce agony which lay within it, learned for the second time that there were springs of joy also which it had never tapped before. His impulse was to fall upon his knees, but he was shy before the doctors.

"Can I go up?"

"In a few minutes."

"I'm sure, doctor, I'm very—I'm very——" he grew inarticulate. "Here are your three guineas, Dr. Pritchard. I wish they were three hundred."

"So do I," said the senior man, and they laughed as they shook hands.

Johnson opened the shop door for them and heard their talk as they stood for an instant outside.

"Looked nasty at one time."

"Very glad to have your help."

"Delighted, I'm sure. Won't you step round and have a cup of coffee?"

"No, thanks. I'm expecting another case."

The firm step and the dragging one passed away to the right and the left. Johnson turned from the door still with that turmoil of joy in his heart. He seemed to be making a new start in life. He felt that he was a stronger and a deeper man. Perhaps all this suffering had an object then. It might prove to be a blessing both to his wife and to him. The very thought was one which he would have been incapable of conceiving twelve hours before. He was full of new emotions. If there had been a harrowing there had been a planting too.

"Can I come up?" he cried, and then, without waiting for an answer, he took the steps three at a time.

Mrs. Peyton was standing by a soapy bath with a bundle in her hands. From under the curve of a brown shawl there looked out at him the strangest little red face with crumpled features, moist, loose lips, and eyelids which quivered like a rabbit's nostrils. The weak neck had let the head topple over, and it rested upon the shoulder.

"Kiss it, Robert!" cried the grandmother. "Kiss your son!"

But he felt a resentment to the little, red, blinking creature. He could not forgive it yet for that long night of misery. He caught sight of a white face in the bed and he ran towards it with such love and pity as his speech could find no words for.

"Thank God it is over! Lucy, dear, it was dreadful!"

"But I'm so happy now. I never was so happy in my life."

Her eyes were fixed upon the brown bundle.

"You mustn't talk," said Mrs. Peyton.

"But don't leave me," whispered his wife.

So he sat in silence with his hand in hers. The lamp was burning dim and the first cold light of dawn was breaking through the window. The night had been long and dark but the day was the sweeter and the purer in consequence. London was waking up. The roar began to rise from the street. Lives had come and lives had gone, but the great machine was still working out its dim and tragic destiny.

Sweethearts

It is hard for the general practitioner who sits among his patients both morning and evening, and sees them in their homes between, to steal time for one little daily breath of cleanly air. To win it he must slip early from his bed and walk out between shuttered shops when it is chill but very clear, and all things are sharply outlined, as in a frost. It is an hour that has a charm of its own, when, but for a postman or a milkman, one has the pavement to oneself, and even the most common thing takes an ever-recurring freshness, as though causeway, and lamp, and signboard had all wakened to the new day. Then even an inland city may seem beautiful, and bear virtue in its smoke-tainted air.

But it was by the sea that I lived, in a town that was unlovely enough were it not for its glorious neighbour. And who cares for the town when one can sit on the bench at the headland, and look out over the huge, blue bay, and the yellow scimitar that curves before it. I loved it when its great face was freckled with the fishing boats, and I loved it when the big ships went past, far out, a little hillock of white and no hull, with topsails curved like a bodice, so stately and demure. But most of all I loved it when no trace of man marred the majesty of Nature, and when the sun-bursts slanted down on it from between the drifting rainclouds. Then I have seen the further edge draped in the gauze of the driving rain, with its thin grey shading under the slow clouds, while my headland was golden, and the sun gleamed upon the breakers and struck deep through the green waves beyond, showing up the purple patches where the beds of seaweed are lying. Such a morning as that, with the wind in his hair, and the spray on his lips, and the cry of the eddying gulls in his ear, may send a man back braced afresh to the reek of a sick-room, and the dead, drab weariness of practice.

It was on such another day that I first saw my old man. He came to my bench just as I was leaving it. My eye must have picked him out even in a crowded street, for he was a man of large frame and fine presence, with something of distinction in the set of his lip and the poise of his head. He limped up the winding path leaning heavily upon his stick, as though those great shoulders had become too much at last for the failing limbs that bore them. As he approached, my eyes caught Nature's danger signal, that faint bluish tinge in nose and lip which tells of a labouring heart.

"The brae is a little trying, sir," said I. "Speaking as a physician, I should say that you would do well to rest here before you go further."

He inclined his head in a stately, old-world fashion, and seated himself upon the bench. Seeing that he had no wish to speak I was silent also, but I could not help watching him out of the corners of my eyes, for he was such a wonderful survival of the early half of the century, with his low-crowned, curly-brimmed hat, his black satin tie which fastened with a buckle at the back, and, above all, his large, fleshy, clean-shaven face shot with its mesh of wrinkles. Those eyes, ere they had grown dim, had looked out from the box-seat of mail coaches, and had seen the knots of navvies as they toiled on the brown embankments. Those lips had smiled over the first numbers of "Pickwick," and had gossiped of the promising young man who wrote them. The face itself was a seventy-year almanack, and every seam an entry upon it where public as well as private sorrow left its trace. That pucker on the forehead stood for the Mutiny, perhaps; that line of care for the

Crimean winter, it may be; and that last little sheaf of wrinkles, as my fancy hoped, for the death of Gordon. And so, as I dreamed in my foolish way, the old gentleman with the shining stock was gone, and it was seventy years of a great nation's life that took shape before me on the headland in the morning.

But he soon brought me back to earth again. As he recovered his breath he took a letter out of his pocket, and, putting on a pair of horn-rimmed eye-glasses, he read it through very carefully. Without any design of playing the spy I could not help observing that it was in a woman's hand. When he had finished it he read it again, and then sat with the corners of his mouth drawn down and his eyes staring vacantly out over the bay, the most forlorn-looking old gentleman that ever I have seen. All that is kindly within me was set stirring by that wistful face, but I knew that he was in no humour for talk, and so, at last, with my breakfast and my patients calling me, I left him on the bench and started for home.

I never gave him another thought until the next morning, when, at the same hour, he turned up upon the headland, and shared the bench which I had been accustomed to look upon as my own. He bowed again before sitting down, but was no more inclined than formerly to enter into conversation. There had been a change in him during the last twenty-four hours, and all for the worse. The face seemed more heavy and more wrinkled, while that ominous venous tinge was more pronounced as he panted up the hill. The clean lines of his cheek and chin were marred by a day's growth of grey stubble, and his large, shapely head had lost something of the brave carriage which had struck me when first I glanced at him. He had a letter there, the same, or another, but still in a woman's hand, and over this he was moping and mumbling in his senile fashion, with his brow puckered, and the corners of his mouth drawn down like those of a fretting child. So I left him, with a vague wonder as to who he might be, and why a single spring day should have wrought such a change upon him.

So interested was I that next morning I was on the look out for him. Sure enough, at the same hour, I saw him coming up the hill; but very slowly, with a bent back and a heavy head. It was shocking to me to see the change in him as he approached.

"I am afraid that our air does not agree with you, sir," I ventured to remark.

But it was as though he had no heart for talk. He tried, as I thought, to make some fitting reply, but it slurred off into a mumble and silence. How bent and weak and old he seemed—ten years older at the least than when first I had seen him! It went to my heart to see this fine old fellow wasting away before my eyes. There was the eternal letter which he unfolded with his shaking fingers. Who was this woman whose words moved him so? Some daughter, perhaps, or granddaughter, who should have been the light of his home instead of——I smiled to find how bitter I was growing, and how swiftly I was weaving a romance round an unshaven old man and his correspondence. Yet all day he lingered in my mind, and I had fitful glimpses of those two trembling, blue-veined, knuckly hands with the paper rustling between them.

I had hardly hoped to see him again. Another day's decline must, I thought, hold him to his room, if not to his bed. Great, then, was my surprise when, as I approached my bench, I saw that he was already there. But as I came up to him I could scarce be sure that it was indeed the same man. There were the curly-brimmed hat, and the shining stock, and the horn glasses, but where were the stoop and the grey-stubbled, pitiable face? He was clean-shaven and firm lipped, with a bright eye and a head that poised itself upon his great shoulders like an eagle on a rock. His back was as straight and square as a grenadier's, and he switched at the pebbles with his stick in his exuberant vitality. In the buttonhole of his well-brushed black coat there glinted a golden blossom, and the corner of a dainty red silk handkerchief lapped over from his breast pocket. He might have been the eldest son of the weary creature who had sat there the morning before.

"Good morning, Sir, good morning!" he cried with a merry waggle of his cane.

"Good morning!" I answered how beautiful the bay is looking."

"Yes, Sir, but you should have seen it just before the sun rose."

"What, have you been here since then?"

"I was here when there was scarce light to see the path."

"You are a very early riser."

"On occasion, sir; on occasion!" He cocked his eye at me as if to gauge whether I were worthy of his confidence. "The fact is, sir, that my wife is coming back to me to day."

I suppose that my face showed that I did not quite see the force of the explanation. My eyes, too, may have given him assurance of sympathy, for he moved quite close to me and began speaking in a low, confidential voice, as if the matter were of such weight that even the sea-gulls must be kept out of our councils.

"Are you a married man, Sir?"

"No, I am not."

"Ah, then you cannot quite understand it. My wife and I have been married for nearly fifty years, and we have never been parted, never at all, until now."

"Was it for long?" I asked.

"Yes, sir. This is the fourth day. She had to go to Scotland. A matter of duty, you understand, and the doctors would not let me go. Not that I would have allowed them to stop me, but she was on their side. Now, thank God! it is over, and she may be here at any moment."

"Here!"

"Yes, here. This headland and bench were old friends of ours thirty years ago. The people with whom we stay are not, to tell the truth, very congenial, and we have, little privacy among them. That is why we prefer to meet here. I could not be sure which train would bring her, but if she had come by the very earliest she would have found me waiting."

"In that case——" said I, rising.

"No, sir, no," he entreated, "I beg that you will stay. It does not weary you, this domestic talk of mine?"

"On the contrary."

"I have been so driven inwards during these few last days! Ah, what a nightmare it has been! Perhaps it may seem strange to you that an old fellow like me should feel like this."

"It is charming."

"No credit to me, sir! There's not a man on this planet but would feel the same if he had the good fortune to be married to such a woman. Perhaps, because you see me like this, and hear me speak of our long life together, you conceive that she is old, too."

He laughed heartily, and his eyes twinkled at the humour of the idea.

"She's one of those women, you know, who have youth in their hearts, and so it can never be very far from their faces. To me she's just as she was when she first took my hand in hers in '45. A wee little bit stouter, perhaps, but then, if she had a fault as a girl, it was that she was a shade too slender. She was above me in station, you know—I a clerk, and she the daughter of my employer. Oh! it was quite a romance, I give you my word, and I won her; and, somehow, I have never got over the freshness and the wonder of it. To think that that sweet, lovely girl has walked by my side all through life, and that I have been able——"

He stopped suddenly, and I glanced round at him in surprise. He was shaking all over, in every fibre of his great body. His hands were clawing at the woodwork, and his feet shuffling on the gravel. I saw what it was. He was trying to rise, but was so excited that he could not. I half extended my hand, but a higher courtesy constrained me to draw it back again and turn my face to the sea. An instant afterwards he was up and hurrying down the path.

A woman was coming towards us. She was quite close before he had seen her—thirty yards at the utmost. I know not if she had ever been as he described her, or whether it was but some ideal which he carried in his brain. The person upon whom I looked was tall, it is true, but she was thick and shapeless, with a ruddy, full-blown face, and a skirt grotesquely gathered up. There was a green ribbon in her hat, which jarred upon my eyes, and her blouse-like bodice was full and clumsy. And this was the lovely girl, the ever youthful! My heart sank as I thought how little such a woman might appreciate him, how unworthy she might be of his love.

She came up the path in her solid way, while he staggered along to meet her. Then, as they came together, looking discreetly out of the furthest corner of my eye, I saw that he put out both his hands, while she, shrinking from a public caress, took one of them in hers and shook it. As she did so I saw her face, and I was easy in my mind for my old man. God grant that when this hand is shaking, and when this back is bowed, a woman's eyes may look so into mine.

A Physiologist's Wife

Professor Ainslie Grey had not come down to breakfast at the usual hour. The presentation chiming-clock which stood between the terra-cotta busts of Claude Bernard and of John Hunter upon the dining-room mantelpiece had rung out the half-hour and the three-quarters. Now its golden hand was verging upon the nine, and yet there were no signs of the master of the house.

It was an unprecedented occurrence. During the twelve years that she had kept house for him, his youngest sister had never known him a second behind his time. She sat now in front of the high silver coffee-pot, uncertain whether to order the gong to be resounded or to wait on in silence. Either course might be a mistake. Her brother was not a man who permitted mistakes.

Miss Ainslie Grey was rather above the middle height, thin, with peering, puckered eyes, and the rounded shoulders which mark the bookish woman. Her face was long and spare, flecked with colour above the cheek-bones, with a reasonable, thoughtful forehead, and a dash of absolute obstinacy in her thin lips and prominent chin. Snow white cuffs and collar, with a plain dark dress, cut with almost Quaker-like simplicity, bespoke the primness of her taste. An ebony cross hung over her flattened chest. She sat very upright in her chair, listening with raised eyebrows, and swinging her eye-glasses backwards and forwards with a nervous gesture which was peculiar to her.

Suddenly she gave a sharp, satisfied jerk of the head, and began to pour out the coffee. From outside there came the dull thudding sound of heavy feet upon thick carpet. The door swung open, and the Professor entered with a quick, nervous step. He nodded to his sister, and seating himself at the other side of the table, began to open the small pile of letters which lay beside his plate.

Professor Ainslie Grey was at that time forty-three years of age—nearly twelve years older than his sister. His career had been a brilliant one. At Edinburgh, at Cambridge, and at Vienna he had laid the foundations of his great reputation, both in physiology and in zoology.

His pamphlet, On the Mesoblastic Origin of Excitomotor Nerve Roots, had won him his fellowship of the Royal Society; and his researches, Upon the Nature of Bathybius, with some Remarks upon Lithococci, had been translated into at least three European languages. He had been referred to by one of the greatest living authorities as being the very type and embodiment of all that was best in modern science. No wonder, then, that when the commercial city of Birchespool decided to create a medical school, they were only too glad to confer the chair of physiology upon Mr. Ainslie Grey. They valued him the more from the conviction that their class was only one step in his upward journey, and that the first vacancy would remove him to some more illustrious seat of learning.

In person he was not unlike his sister. The same eyes, the same contour, the same intellectual forehead. His lips, however, were firmer, and his long, thin, lower jaw was sharper and more decided. He ran his finger and thumb down it from time to time, as he glanced over his letters.

"Those maids are very noisy," he remarked, as a clack of tongues sounded in the distance.

"It is Sarah," said his sister; "I shall speak about it."

She had handed over his coffee-cup, and was sipping at her own, glancing furtively through her narrowed lids at the austere face of her brother.

"The first great advance of the human race," said the Professor, "was when, by the development of their left frontal convolutions, they attained the power of speech. Their second advance was when they learned to control that power. Woman has not yet attained the second stage."

He half closed his eyes as he spoke, and thrust his chin forward, but as he ceased he had a trick of suddenly opening both eyes very wide and staring sternly at his interlocutor.

"I am not garrulous, John," said his sister.

"No, Ada; in many respects you approach the superior or male type."

The Professor bowed over his egg with the manner of one who utters a courtly compliment; but the lady pouted, and gave an impatient little shrug of her shoulders.

"You were late this morning, John," she remarked, after a pause.

"Yes, Ada; I slept badly. Some little cerebral congestion, no doubt due to over-stimulation of the centers of thought. I have been a little disturbed in my mind."

His sister stared across at him in astonishment. The Professor's mental processes had hitherto been as regular as his habits. Twelve years' continual intercourse had taught her that he lived in a serene and rarefied atmosphere of scientific calm, high above the petty emotions which affect humbler minds.

"You are surprised, Ada," he remarked. "Well, I cannot wonder at it. I should have been surprised myself if I had been told that I was so sensitive to vascular influences. For, after all, all disturbances are vascular if you probe them deep enough. I am thinking of getting married."

"Not Mrs. O'James" cried Ada Grey, laying down her egg-spoon.

"My dear, you have the feminine quality of receptivity very remarkably developed. Mrs. O'James is the lady in question."

"But you know so little of her. The Esdailes themselves know so little. She is really only an acquaintance, although she is staying at The Lindens. Would it not be wise to speak to Mrs. Esdaile first, John?"

"I do not think, Ada, that Mrs. Esdaile is at all likely to say anything which would materially affect my course of action. I have given the matter due consideration. The scientific mind is slow at arriving at conclusions, but having once formed them, it is not prone to change. Matrimony is the natural condition of the human race. I have, as you know, been so engaged in academical and other work, that I have had no time to devote to merely personal questions. It is different now, and I see no valid reason why I should forego this opportunity of seeking a suitable helpmate."

"And you are engaged?"

"Hardly that, Ada. I ventured yesterday to indicate to the lady that I was prepared to submit to the common lot of humanity. I shall wait upon her after my morning lecture, and learn how far my proposals meet with her acquiescence. But you frown, Ada!"

His sister started, and made an effort to conceal her expression of annoyance. She even stammered out some few words of congratulation, but a vacant look had come into her brother's eyes, and he was evidently not listening to her.

"I am sure, John, that I wish you the happiness which you deserve. If I hesitated at all, it is because I know how much is at stake, and because the thing is so sudden, so unexpected." Her thin white hand stole up to the black cross upon her bosom. "These are moments when we need guidance, John. If I could persuade you to turn to spiritual——"

The Professor waved the suggestion away with a deprecating hand.

"It is useless to reopen that question," he said. "We cannot argue upon it. You assume more than I can grant. I am forced to dispute your premises. We have no common basis."

His sister sighed.

"You have no faith," she said.

"I have faith in those great evolutionary forces which are leading the human race to some unknown but elevated goal."

"You believe in nothing."

"On the contrary, my dear Ada, I believe in the differentiation of protoplasm."

She shook her head sadly. It was the one subject upon which she ventured to dispute her brother's infallibility.

"This is rather beside the question," remarked the Professor, folding up his napkin. "If I am not mistaken, there is some possibility of another matrimonial event occurring in the family. Eh, Ada? What!"

His small eyes glittered with sly facetiousness as he shot a twinkle at his sister. She sat very stiff, and traced patterns upon the cloth with the sugar-tongs.

"Dr. James M'Murdo O'Brien——" said the Professor, sonorously.

"Don't, John, don't!" cried Miss Ainslie Grey.

"Dr. James M'Murdo O'Brien," continued her brother inexorably, "is a man who has already made his mark upon the science of the day. He is my first and my most distinguished pupil. I assure you, Ada, that his 'Remarks upon the Bile-Pigments, with special reference to Urobilin,' is likely to live as a classic. It is not too much to say that he has revolutionised our views about urobilin."

He paused, but his sister sat silent, with bent head and flushed cheeks. The little ebony cross rose and fell with her hurried breathings.

"Dr. James M'Murdo O'Brien has, as you know, the offer of the physiological chair at Melbourne. He has been in Australia five years, and has a brilliant future before him. To-day he leaves us for Edinburgh, and in two months' time, he goes out to take over his new duties. You know his feeling towards you. It, rests with you as to whether he goes out alone. Speaking for myself, I cannot imagine any higher mission for a woman of culture than to go through life in the company of a man who is capable of such a research as that which Dr. James M'Murdo O'Brien has brought to a successful conclusion."

"He has not spoken to me," murmured the lady.

"Ah, there are signs which are more subtle than speech," said her brother, wagging his head. "But you are pale. Your vasomotor system is excited. Your arterioles have contracted. Let me entreat you to compose yourself. I think I hear the carriage. I fancy that you may have a visitor this morning, Ada. You will excuse me now."

With a quick glance at the clock he strode off into the hall, and within a few minutes he was rattling in his quiet, well-appointed brougham through the brick-lined streets of Birchespool.

His lecture over, Professor Ainslie Grey paid a visit to his laboratory, where he adjusted several scientific instruments, made a note as to the progress of three separate infusions of bacteria, cut half-a-dozen sections with a microtome, and finally resolved the difficulties of seven different gentlemen, who were pursuing researches in as many separate lines of inquiry. Having thus conscientiously and methodically completed the routine of his duties, he returned to his carriage and ordered the coachman to drive him to The Lindens. His face as he drove was cold and impassive, but he drew his fingers from time to time down his prominent chin with a jerky, twitchy movement.

The Lindens was an old-fashioned, ivy-clad house which had once been in the country, but was now caught in the long, red-brick feelers of the growing city. It still stood back from the road in the privacy of its own grounds. A winding path, lined with laurel bushes, led to the arched and porticoed entrance. To the right was a lawn, and at the far side, under the shadow of a hawthorn, a lady sat in a garden-chair with a book in her hands. At the click of the gate she started, and the Professor, catching sight of her, turned away from the door, and strode in her direction.

"What! won't you go in and see Mrs. Esdaile?" she asked, sweeping out from under the shadow of the hawthorn.

She was a small woman, strongly feminine, from the rich coils of her light-coloured hair to the dainty garden slipper which peeped from under her cream-tinted dress. One tiny well-gloved hand was outstretched in greeting, while the other pressed a thick, green-covered volume against her side. Her decision and quick, tactful manner bespoke the mature woman of the world; but her upraised face had preserved a girlish and even infantile expression of innocence in its large, fearless, grey eyes, and sensitive, humorous mouth. Mrs. O'James was a widow, and she was two-and-thirty years of age; but neither fact could have been deduced from her appearance.

"You will surely go in and see Mrs. Esdaile," she repeated, glancing up at him with eyes which had in them something between a challenge and a caress.

"I did not come to see Mrs. Esdaile," he answered, with no relaxation of his cold and grave manner; "I came to see you."

"I am sure I should be highly honoured," she said, with just the slightest little touch of brogue in her accent. "What are the students to do without their Professor?"

"I have already completed my academic duties. Take my arm, and we shall walk in the sunshine. Surely we cannot wonder that Eastern people should have made a deity of the sun. It is the great beneficent force of Nature—man's ally against cold, sterility, and all that is abhorrent to him. What were you reading?"

"Hale's Matter and Life."

The Professor raised his thick eyebrows.

"Hale!" he said, and then again in a kind of whisper, "Hale!"

"You differ from him?" she asked.

"It is not I who differ from him. I am only a monad—a thing of no moment. The whole tendency of the highest plane of modern thought differs from him. He defends the indefensible. He is an excellent observer, but a feeble reasoner. I should not recommend you to found your conclusions upon Hale."

"I must read Nature's Chronicle to counteract his pernicious influence," said Mrs. O'James, with a soft, cooing laugh.

Nature's Chronicle was one of the many books in which Professor Ainslie Grey had enforced the negative doctrines of scientific agnosticism.

"It is a faulty work," said he; "I cannot recommend it. I would rather refer you to the standard writings of some of my older and more eloquent colleagues."

There was a pause in their talk as they paced up and down on the green, velvet-like lawn in the genial sunshine.

"Have you thought at all," he asked at last, "of the matter upon which I spoke to you last night?"

She said nothing, but walked by his side with her eyes averted and her face aslant.

"I would not hurry you unduly," he continued. "I know that it is a matter which can scarcely be decided off-hand. In my own case, it cost me some thought before I ventured to make the suggestion. I am not an emotional man, but I am conscious in your presence of the great evolutionary instinct which makes either sex the complement of the other."

"You believe in love, then?" she asked, with a twinkling, upward glance.

"I am forced to."

"And yet you can deny the soul?"

"How far these questions are psychic and how far material is still sub judice," said the Professor, with an air of toleration. "Protoplasm may prove to be the physical basis of love as well as of life."

"How inflexible you are!" she exclaimed; "you would draw love down to the level of physics."

"Or draw physics up to the level of love."

"Come, that is much better," she cried, with her sympathetic laugh. "That is really very pretty, and puts science in quite a delightful light."

Her eyes sparkled, and she tossed her chin with the pretty, wilful air of a woman who is mistress of the situation.

"I have reason to believe," said the Professor, "that my position here will prove to be only a stepping-stone to some wider scene of scientific activity. Yet, even here, my chair brings me in some fifteen hundred pounds a year, which is supplemented by a few hundreds from my books. I should therefore be in a position to provide you with those comforts to which you are accustomed. So much for my pecuniary position. As to my constitution, it has always been sound. I have never suffered from any illness in my life, save fleeting attacks of cephalalgia, the result of too prolonged a stimulation of the centres of cerebration. My father and mother had no sign of any morbid diathesis, but I will not conceal from you that my grandfather was afflicted with podagra."

Mrs. O'James looked startled.

"Is that very serious?" she asked.

"It is gout," said the Professor.

"Oh, is that all? It sounded much worse than that."

"It is a grave taint, but I trust that I shall not be a victim to atavism. I have laid these facts before you because they are factors which cannot be overlooked in forming your decision. May I ask now whether you see your way to accepting my proposal?"

He paused in his walk, and looked earnestly and expectantly down at her.

A struggle was evidently going on in her mind. Her eyes were cast down, her little slipper tapped the lawn, and her fingers played nervously with her chatelain. Suddenly, with a sharp, quick gesture which had in it something of ABANDON and recklessness, she held out her hand to her companion.

"I accept," she said.

They were standing under the shadow of the hawthorn. He stooped gravely down, and kissed her glove-covered fingers.

"I trust that you may never have cause to regret your decision," he said.

"I trust that you never may," she cried, with a heaving breast.

There were tears in her eyes, and her lips twitched with some strong emotion.

"Come into the sunshine again," said he. "It is the great restorative. Your nerves are shaken. Some little congestion of the medulla and pons. It is always instructive to reduce psychic or emotional conditions to their physical equivalents. You feel that your anchor is still firm in a bottom of ascertained fact."

"But it is so dreadfully unromantic," said Mrs. O'James, with her old twinkle.

"Romance is the offspring of imagination and of ignorance. Where science throws her calm, clear light there is happily no room for romance."

"But is not love romance?" she asked.

"Not at all. Love has been taken away from the poets, and has been brought within the domain of true science. It may prove to be one of the great cosmic elementary forces. When the atom of hydrogen draws the atom of chlorine towards it to form the perfected molecule of hydrochloric acid, the force which it exerts may be intrinsically similar to that which draws me to you. Attraction and repulsion appear to be the primary forces. This is attraction."

"And here is repulsion," said Mrs. O'James, as a stout, florid lady came sweeping across the lawn in their direction. "So glad you have come out, Mrs. Esdaile! Here is Professor Grey."

"How do you do, Professor?" said the lady, with some little pomposity of manner. "You were very wise to stay out here on so lovely a day. Is it not heavenly?"

"It is certainly very fine weather," the Professor answered.

"Listen to the wind sighing in the trees!" cried Mrs. Esdaile, holding up one finger. "it is Nature's lullaby. Could you not imagine it, Professor Grey, to be the whisperings of angels?"

"The idea had not occurred to me, madam."

"Ah, Professor, I have always the same complaint against you. A want of rapport with the deeper meanings of nature. Shall I say a want of imagination. You do not feel an emotional thrill at the singing of that thrush?"

"I confess that I am not conscious of one, Mrs. Esdaile."

"Or at the delicate tint of that background of leaves? See the rich greens!"

"Chlorophyll," murmured the Professor.

"Science is so hopelessly prosaic. It dissects and labels, and loses sight of the great things in its attention to the little ones. You have a poor opinion of woman's intellect, Professor Grey. I think that I have heard you say so."

"It is a question of avoirdupois," said the Professor, closing his eyes and shrugging his shoulders. "The female cerebrum averages two ounces less in weight than the male. No doubt there are exceptions. Nature is always elastic."

"But the heaviest thing is not always the strongest," said Mrs. O'James, laughing. "Isn't there a law of compensation in science? May we not hope to make up in quality for what we lack in quantity?"

"I think not," remarked the Professor, gravely. "But there is your luncheon-gong. No, thank you, Mrs. Esdaile, I cannot stay. My carriage is waiting. Good-bye. Good-bye, Mrs. O'James."

He raised his hat and stalked slowly away among the laurel bushes.

"He has no taste," said Mrs. Esdaile—" no eye for beauty."

"On the contrary," Mrs. O'James answered, with a saucy little jerk of the chin. "He has just asked me to be his wife."

As Professor Ainslie Grey ascended the steps of his house, the hall-door opened and a dapper gentleman stepped briskly out. He was somewhat sallow in the face, with dark, beady eyes, and a short, black beard with an aggressive bristle. Thought and work had left their traces upon his face, but he moved with the brisk activity of a man who had not yet bade good-bye to his youth.

"I'm in luck's way," he cried. "I wanted to see you."

"Then come back into the library," said the Professor; "you must stay and have lunch with us."

The two men entered the hall, and the Professor led the way into his private sanctum. He motioned his companion into an arm-chair.

"I trust that you have been successful, O'Brien," said he. "I should be loath to exercise any undue pressure upon my sister Ada; but I have given her to understand that there is no one whom I should prefer for a brother-in-law to my most brilliant scholar, the author of Some Remarks upon the Bile-Pigments, with special reference to Urobilin."

"You are very kind, Professor Grey—you have always been very kind," said the other. "I approached Miss Grey upon the subject; she did not say No."

"She said Yes, then?"

"No; she proposed to leave the matter open until my return from Edinburgh. I go to-day, as you know, and I hope to commence my research to-morrow."

"On the comparative anatomy of the vermiform appendix, by James M'Murdo O'Brien," said the Professor, sonorously. "It is a glorious subject—a subject which lies at the very root of evolutionary philosophy."

"Ah! she is the dearest girl," cried O'Brien, with a sudden little spurt of Celtic enthusiasm—"she is the soul of truth and of honour."

"The vermiform appendix——" began the Professor.

"She is an angel from heaven," interrupted the other. "I fear that it is my advocacy of scientific freedom in religious thought which stands in my way with her."

"You must not truckle upon that point. You must be true to your convictions; let there be no compromise there."

"My reason is true to agnosticism, and yet I am conscious of a void—a vacuum. I had feelings at the old church at home between the scent of the incense and the roll of the organ, such as I have never experienced in the laboratory or the lecture-room."

"Sensuous-purely sensuous," said the Professor, rubbing his chin. "Vague hereditary tendencies stirred into life by the stimulation of the nasal and auditory nerves."

"Maybe so, maybe so," the younger man answered thoughtfully. "But this was not what I wished to speak to you about. Before I enter your family, your sister and you have a claim to know all that I can tell you about my career. Of my worldly prospects I have already spoken to you. There is only one point which I have omitted to mention. I am a widower."

The Professor raised his eyebrows.

"This is news indeed," said he.

"I married shortly after my arrival in Australia. Miss Thurston was her name. I met her in society. It was a most unhappy match."

Some painful emotion possessed him. His quick, expressive features quivered, and his white hands tightened upon the arms of the chair. The Professor turned away towards the window.

"You are the best judge," he remarked "but I should not think that it was necessary to go into details."

"You have a right to know everything—you and Miss Grey. It is not a matter on which I can well speak to her direct. Poor Jinny was the best of women, but she was open to flattery, and liable to be misled by designing persons. She was untrue to me, Grey. It is a hard thing to say of the dead, but she was untrue to me. She fled to Auckland with a man whom she had known before her marriage. The brig which carried them foundered, and not a soul was saved."

"This is very painful, O'Brien," said the Professor, with a deprecatory motion of his hand. "I cannot see, however, how it affects your relation to my sister."

"I have eased my conscience," said O'Brien, rising from his chair; "I have told you all that there is to tell. I should not like the story to reach you through any lips but my own."

"You are right, O'Brien. Your action has been most honourable and considerate. But you are not to blame in the matter, save that perhaps you showed a little precipitancy in choosing a life-partner without due care and inquiry."

O'Brien drew his hand across his eyes.

"Poor girl!" he cried. "God help me, I love her still! But I must go."

"You will lunch with us?"

"No, Professor; I have my packing still to do. I have already bade Miss Grey adieu. In two months I shall see you again."

"You will probably find me a married man."

"Married!"

"Yes, I have been thinking of it."

"My dear Professor, let me congratulate you with all my heart. I had no idea. Who is the lady?"

"Mrs. O'James is her name—a widow of the same nationality as yourself. But to return to matters of importance, I should be very happy to see the proofs of your paper upon the vermiform appendix. I may be able to furnish you with material for a foot-note or two."

"Your assistance will be invaluable to me," said O'Brien, with enthusiasm, and the two men parted in the hall. The Professor walked back into the dining-room, where his sister was already seated at the luncheon-table.

"I shall be married at the registrar's," he remarked; "I should strongly recommend you to do the same."

Professor Ainslie Grey was as good as his word. A fortnight's cessation of his classes gave him an opportunity which was too good to let pass. Mrs. O'James was an orphan, without relations and almost without friends in the country. There was no obstacle in the way of a speedy wedding. They were married, accordingly, in the quietest manner possible, and went off to Cambridge together, where the Professor and his charming wife were present at several academic observances, and varied the routine of their honeymoon by incursions into biological laboratories and medical libraries. Scientific friends were loud in their congratulations, not only upon Mrs. Grey's beauty, but upon the unusual quickness and intelligence which she displayed in discussing physiological questions. The Professor was himself astonished at the accuracy of her information. "You have a remarkable range of knowledge for a woman, Jeannette," he remarked upon more than one occasion. He was even prepared to admit that her cerebrum might be of the normal weight.

One foggy, drizzling morning they returned to Birchespool, for the next day would re-open the session, and Professor Ainslie Grey prided himself upon having never once in his life failed to appear in his lecture-room at the very stroke of the hour. Miss Ada Grey welcomed them with a constrained cordiality, and handed over the keys of office to the new mistress. Mrs. Grey pressed her warmly to remain, but she explained that she had already accepted an invitation which would engage her for some months. The same evening she departed for the south of England.

A couple of days later the maid carried a card just after breakfast into the library where the Professor sat revising his morning lecture. It announced the re-arrival of Dr. James M'Murdo O'Brien. Their meeting was effusively genial on the part of the younger man, and coldly precise on that of his former teacher.

"You see there have been changes," said the Professor.

"So I heard. Miss Grey told me in her letters, and I read the notice in the British Medical Journal. So it's really married you are. How quickly and quietly you have managed it all!"

"I am constitutionally averse to anything in the nature of show or ceremony. My wife is a sensible woman—I may even go the length of saying that, for a woman, she is abnormally sensible. She quite agreed with me in the course which I have adopted."

"And your research on Vallisneria?"

"This matrimonial incident has interrupted it, but I have resumed my classes, and we shall soon be quite in harness again."

"I must see Miss Grey before I leave England. We have corresponded, and I think that all will be well. She must come out with me. I don't think I could go without her."

The Professor shook his head.

"Your nature is not so weak as you pretend," he said. "Questions of this sort are, after all, quite subordinate to the great duties of life."

O'Brien smiled.

"You would have me take out my Celtic soul and put in a Saxon one," he said. "Either my brain is too small or my heart is too big. But when may I call and pay my respects to Mrs. Grey? Will she be at home this afternoon?"

"She is at home now. Come into the morning-room. She will be glad to make your acquaintance."

They walked across the linoleum-paved hall. The Professor opened the door of the room, and walked in, followed by his friend. Mrs. Grey was sitting in a basket-chair by the window, light and fairy-like in a loose-flowing, pink morning-gown. Seeing a visitor, she rose and swept towards them. The Professor heard a dull thud behind him. O'Brien had fallen back into a chair, with his hand pressed tight to his side.

"Jinny!" he gasped—"Jinny!"

Mrs. Grey stopped dead in her advance, and stared at him with a face from which every expression had been struck out, save one of astonishment and horror. Then with a sharp intaking of the breath she reeled, and would have fallen had the Professor not thrown his long, nervous arm round her.

"Try this sofa," said he.

She sank back among the cushions with the same white, cold, dead look upon her face. The Professor stood with his back to the empty fireplace and glanced from the one to the other.

"So, O'Brien," he said at last, "you have already made the acquaintance of my wife!"

"Your wife, " cried his friend hoarsely. "She is no wife of yours. God help me, she is MY wife."

The Professor stood rigidly upon the hearthrug. His long, thin fingers were intertwined, and his head sunk a little forward. His two companions had eyes only for each other.

"Jinny!" said he.

"James!"

"How could you leave me so, Jinny? How could you have the heart to do it? I thought you were dead. I mourned for your death—ay, and you have made me mourn for you living. You have withered my life."

She made no answer, but lay back among her cushions with her eyes still fixed upon him.

"Why do you not speak?"

"Because you are right, James. I HAVE treated you cruelly—shamefully. But it is not as bad as you think."

"You fled with De Horta."

"No, I did not. At the last moment my better nature prevailed. He went alone. But I was ashamed to come back after what I had written to you. I could not face you. I took passage alone to England under a new name, and here I have lived ever since. It seemed to me that I was beginning life again. I knew that you thought I was drowned. Who could have dreamed that fate would throw us together again! When the Professor asked me——"

She stopped and gave a gasp for breath.

"You are faint," said the Professor—"keep the head low; it aids the cerebral circulation." He flattened down the cushion. "I am sorry to leave you, O'Brien; but I have my class duties to look to. Possibly I may find you here when I return."

With a grim and rigid face he strode out of the room. Not one of the three hundred students who listened to his lecture saw any change in his manner and appearance, or could have guessed that the austere gentleman in front of them had found out at last how hard it is to rise above one's humanity. The lecture over, he performed his routine duties in the laboratory, and then drove back to his own house. He did not enter by the front door, but passed through the garden to the folding glass casement which led out of the morning-room. As he approached he heard his wife's voice and O'Brien's in loud and animated talk. He paused among the rose-bushes, uncertain whether to interrupt them or no. Nothing was further from his nature than play the eavesdropper; but as he stood, still hesitating, words fell upon his ear which struck him rigid and motionless.

"You are still my wife, Jinny," said O'Brien; "I forgive you from the bottom of my heart. I love you, and I have never ceased to love you, though you had forgotten me."

"No, James, my heart was always in Melbourne. I have always been yours. I thought that it was better for you that I should seem to be dead."

"You must choose between us now, Jinny. If you determine to remain here, I shall not open my lips. There shall be no scandal. If, on the other hand, you come with me, it's little I care about the world's opinion. Perhaps I am as much to blame as you. I thought too much of my work and too little of my wife."

The Professor heard the cooing, caressing laugh which he knew so well.

"I shall go with you, James," she said.

"And the Professor——?"

"The poor Professor! But he will not mind much, James; he has no heart."

"We must tell him our resolution."

"There is no need," said Professor Ainslie Grey, stepping in through the open casement. "I have overheard the latter part of your conversation. I hesitated to interrupt you before you came to a conclusion."

O'Brien stretched out his hand and took that of the woman. They stood together with the sunshine on their faces. The Professor paused at the casement with his hands behind his back, and his long black shadow fell between them.

"You have come to a wise decision," said he. "Go back to Australia together, and let what has passed be blotted out of your lives."

"But you—you——" stammered O'Brien.

The Professor waved his hand.

"Never trouble about me," he said.

The woman gave a gasping cry.

"What can I do or say?" she wailed. "How could I have foreseen this? I thought my old life was dead. But it has come back again, with all its hopes and its desires. What can I say to you, Ainslie? I have brought shame and disgrace upon a worthy man. I have blasted your life. How you must hate and loathe me! I wish to God that I had never been born!"

"I neither hate nor loathe you, Jeannette," said the Professor, quietly. "You are wrong in regretting your birth, for you have a worthy mission before you in aiding the life-work of a man who has shown himself capable of the highest order of scientific research. I cannot with justice blame you personally for what has occurred. How far the individual monad is to be held responsible for hereditary and engrained tendencies, is a question upon which science has not yet said her last word."

He stood with his finger-tips touching, and his body inclined as one who is gravely expounding a difficult and impersonal subject. O'Brien had stepped forward to say something, but the other's attitude and manner froze the words upon his lips. Condolence or sympathy would be an impertinence to one who could so easily merge his private griefs in broad questions of abstract philosophy.

"It is needless to prolong the situation," the Professor continued, in the same measured tones. "My brougham stands at the door. I beg that you will use it as your own. Perhaps it would be as well that you should leave the town without unnecessary delay. Your things, Jeannette, shall be forwarded."

O'Brien hesitated with a hanging head.

"I hardly dare offer you my hand," he said.

"On the contrary. I think that of the three of us you come best out of the affair. You have nothing to be ashamed of."

"Your sister——"

"I shall see that the matter is put to her in its true light. Good-bye! Let me have a copy of your recent research. Good-bye, Jeannette!"

"Good-bye!"

Their hands met, and for one short moment their eyes also. It was only a glance, but for the first and last time the woman's intuition cast a light for itself into the dark places of a strong man's soul. She gave a little gasp, and her other hand rested for an instant, as white and as light as thistle-down, upon his shoulder.

"James, James!" she cried. "Don't you see that he is stricken to the heart?"

He turned her quietly away from him.

"I am not an emotional man," he said. "I have my duties—my research on Vallisneria. The brougham is there. Your cloak is in the hall. Tell John where you wish to be driven. He will bring you anything you need. Now go."

His last two words were so sudden, so volcanic, in such contrast to his measured voice and mask-like face, that they swept the two away from him. He closed the door behind them and paced slowly up and down the room. Then he passed into the library and looked out over the wire blind. The carriage was rolling away. He caught a last glimpse of the woman who had been his wife. He saw the feminine droop of her head, and the curve of her beautiful throat.

Under some foolish, aimless impulse, he took a few quick steps towards the door. Then he turned, and throwing himself into his study-chair he plunged back into his work.

There was little scandal about this singular domestic incident. The Professor had few personal friends, and seldom went into society. His marriage had been so quiet that most of his colleagues had never ceased to regard him as a bachelor. Mrs. Esdaile and a few others might talk, but their field for gossip was limited, for they could only guess vaguely at the cause of this sudden separation.

The Professor was as punctual as ever at his classes, and as zealous in directing the laboratory work of those who studied under him. His own private researches were pushed on with feverish energy. It was no uncommon thing for his servants, when they came down of a morning, to hear the shrill scratchings of his tireless pen, or to meet him on the staircase as he ascended, grey and silent, to his room. In vain his friends assured him that such a life must undermine his health. He lengthened his hours until day and night were one long, ceaseless task.

Gradually under this discipline a change came over his appearance. His features, always inclined to gauntness, became even sharper and more pronounced. There were deep lines about his temples and across his brow. His cheek was sunken and his complexion bloodless. His knees gave under him when he walked; and once when passing out of his lecture-room he fell and had to be assisted to his carriage.

This was just before the end of the session and soon after the holidays commenced the professors who still remained in Birchespool were shocked to hear that their brother of the chair of physiology had sunk so low that no hopes could be entertained of his recovery. Two eminent physicians had consulted over his case without being able to give a name to the affection from which he suffered. A steadily decreasing vitality appeared to be the only symptom—a bodily weakness which left the mind unclouded. He was much interested himself in his own case, and made notes of his subjective sensations as an aid to diagnosis. Of his approaching end he spoke in his usual unemotional and somewhat pedantic fashion. "It is the assertion," he said, "of the liberty of the individual cell as opposed to the cell-commune. It is the dissolution of a co-operative society. The process is one of great interest."

And so one grey morning his co-operative society dissolved. Very quietly and softly he sank into his eternal sleep. His two physicians felt some slight embarrassment when called upon to fill in his certificate.

"It is difficult to give it a name," said one.

"Very," said the other.

"If he were not such an unemotional man, I should have said that he had died from some sudden nervous shock—from, in fact, what the vulgar would call a broken heart."

"I don't think poor Grey was that sort of a man at all."

"Let us call it cardiac, anyhow," said the older physician.

So they did so.

The Case of Lady Sannox

The relations between Douglas Stone and the notorious Lady Sannox were very well known both among the fashionable circles of which she was a brilliant member, and the scientific bodies which numbered him among their most illustrious confreres. There was naturally, therefore, a very widespread interest when it was announced one morning that the lady had absolutely and for ever taken the veil, and that the world would see her no more. When, at the very tail of this rumour, there came the assurance that the celebrated operating surgeon, the man of steel nerves, had been found in the morning by his valet, seated on one side of his bed, smiling pleasantly upon the universe, with both legs jammed into one side of his breeches and his great brain about as valuable as a cap full of porridge, the matter was strong enough to give quite a little thrill of interest to folk who had never hoped that their jaded nerves were capable of such a sensation.

Douglas Stone in his prime was one of the most remarkable men in England. Indeed, he could hardly be said to have ever reached his prime, for he was but nine-and-thirty at the time of this little incident. Those who knew him best were aware that, famous as he was as a surgeon, he might have succeeded with even greater rapidity in any of a dozen lines of life. He could have cut his way to fame as a soldier, struggled to it as an explorer, bullied for it in the courts, or built it out of stone and iron as an engineer. He was born to be great, for he could plan what another man dare not do, and he could do what another man dare not plan. In surgery none could follow him. His nerve, his judgment, his intuition, were things apart. Again and again his knife cut away death, but grazed the very springs of life in doing it, until his assistants were as white as the patient. His energy, his audacity, his full-blooded self-confidence—does not the memory of them still linger to the south of Marylebone Road and the north of Oxford Street?

His vices were as magnificent as his virtues, and infinitely more picturesque. Large as was his income, and it was the third largest of all professional men in London, it was far beneath the luxury of his living. Deep in his complex nature lay a rich vein of sensualism, at the sport of which he placed all the prizes of his life. The eye, the ear, the touch, the palate—all were his masters. The bouquet of old vintages, the scent of rare exotics, the curves and tints of the daintiest potteries of Europe—it was to these that the quick-running stream of gold was transformed. And then there came his sudden mad passion for Lady Sannox, when a single interview with two challenging glances and a whispered word set him ablaze. She was the loveliest woman in London, and the only one to him. He was one of the handsomest men in London, but not the only one to her. She had a liking for new experiences, and was gracious to most men who wooed her. It may have been cause or it may have been effect that Lord Sannox looked fifty, though he was but six-and-thirty.

He was a quiet, silent, neutral-tinted man, this lord, with thin lips and heavy eyelids, much given to gardening, and full of home-like habits. He had at one time been fond of acting, had even rented a theatre in London, and on its boards had first seen Miss Marion Dawson, to whom he had offered his hand, his title, and the third of a county. Since his marriage this early hobby had become distasteful to him. Even in private theatricals it was no longer possible to persuade him to exercise the talent which he had often shown that he possessed. He was happier with a spud and a watering-can among his orchids and chrysanthemums.

It was quite an interesting problem whether he was absolutely devoid of sense, or miserably wanting in spirit. Did he know his lady's ways and condone them, or was he a mere blind, doting fool? It was a point to be discussed over the teacups in snug little drawing-rooms, or with the aid of a cigar in the bow windows of clubs. Bitter and plain were the comments among men upon his conduct. There was but one who had a good word to say for him, and he was the most silent member in the smoking-room. He had seen him break in a horse at the university, and it seemed to have left an impression upon his mind.

But when Douglas Stone became the favourite, all doubts as to Lord Sannox's knowledge or ignorance were set for ever at rest. There, was no subterfuge about Stone. In his high-handed, impetuous fashion, he set all caution and discretion at defiance. The scandal became notorious. A learned body intimated that his name had been struck from the list of its vice-presidents. Two friends implored him to consider his professional credit. He cursed them all three, and spent forty guineas on a bangle to take with him to the lady. He was at her house every evening, and she drove in his carriage in the afternoons. There was not an attempt on either side to conceal their relations; but there came at last a little incident to interrupt them.

It was a dismal winter's night, very cold and gusty, with the wind whooping in the chimneys and blustering against the window-panes. A thin spatter of rain tinkled on the glass with each fresh sough of the gale, drowning for the instant the dull gurgle and drip from the eves. Douglas Stone had finished his dinner, and sat by his fire in the study, a glass of rich port upon the malachite table at his elbow. As he raised it to his lips, he held it up against the lamplight, and watched with the eye of a connoisseur the tiny scales of beeswing which floated in its rich ruby depths. The fire, as it spurted up, threw fitful lights upon his bold, clear-cut face, with its widely-opened grey eyes, its thick and yet firm lips, and the deep, square jaw, which had something Roman in its strength and its animalism. He smiled from time to time as he nestled back in his luxurious chair. Indeed, he had a right to feel well pleased, for, against the advice of six colleagues, he had performed an operation that day of which only two cases were on record, and the result had been brilliant beyond all expectation. No other man in London would have had the daring to plan, or the skill to execute, such a heroic measure.

But he had promised Lady Sannox to see her that evening and it was already half-past eight. His hand was outstretched to the bell to order the carriage when he heard the dull thud of the knocker. An instant later there was the shuffling of feet in the hall, and the sharp closing of a door.

"A patient to see you, sir, in the consulting-room, said the butler.

"About himself?"

"No, sir; I think he wants you to go out."

"It is too late, cried Douglas Stone peevishly. "I won't go."

"This is his card, sir."

The butler presented it upon the gold salver which had been given to his master by the wife of a Prime Minister.

"'Hamil Ali, Smyrna.' Hum! The fellow is a Turk, I suppose."

"Yes, sir. He seems as if he came from abroad, sir. And he's in a terrible way."

"Tut, tut! I have an engagement. I must go somewhere else. But I'll see him. Show him in here, Pim."

A few moments later the butler swung open the door and ushered in a small and decrepit man, who walked with a bent back and with the forward push of the face and blink of the eyes which goes with extreme short sight. His face was swarthy, and his hair and beard of the deepest black. In one hand he held a turban of white muslin striped with red, in the other a small chamois leather bag.

"Good-evening," said Douglas Stone, when the butler had closed the door. "You speak English, I presume?"

"Yes, sir. I am from Asia Minor, but I speak English when I speak slow."

"You wanted me to go out, I understand?"

"Yes, sir. I wanted very much that you should see my wife."

"I could come in the morning, but I have an engagement which prevents me from seeing your wife to-night."

The Turk's answer was a singular one. He pulled the string which closed the mouth of the chamois leather bag, and poured a flood of gold on to the table.

"There are one hundred pounds there," said he, "and I promise you that it will not take you an hour. I have a cab ready at the door."

Douglas Stone glanced at his watch. An hour would not make it too late to visit Lady Sannox. He had been there later. And the fee was an extraordinarily high one. He had been pressed by his creditors lately, and he could not afford to let such a chance pass. He would go.

"What is the case?" he asked.

"Oh, it is so sad a one! So sad a one! You have not, perhaps, heard of the daggers of the Almohades?"

"Never."

"Ah, they are Eastern daggers of a great age and of a singular shape, with the hilt like what you call a stirrup. I am a curiosity dealer, you understand, and that is why I have come to England from Smyrna, but next week I go back once more. Many things I brought with me, and I have a few things left, but among them, to my sorrow, is one of these daggers."

"You will remember that I have an appointment, sir," said the surgeon, with some irritation. "Pray confine yourself to the necessary details."

"You will see that it is necessary. To-day my wife fell down in a faint in the room in which I keep my wares, and she cut her lower lip upon this cursed dagger of Almohades."

"I see," said Douglas Stone, rising. "And you wish me to dress the wound? "

"No, no, it is worse than that."

"What then?"

"These daggers are poisoned."

"Poisoned!"

"Yes, and there is no man, East or West, who can tell now what is the poison or what the cure. But all that is known I know, for my father was in this trade before me, and we have had much to do with these poisoned weapons."

"What are the symptoms?"

"Deep sleep, and death in thirty hours."

"And you say there is no cure. Why then should you pay me this considerable fee?"

"No drug can cure, but the knife may."

"And how?"

"The poison is slow of absorption. It remains for hours in the wound."

"Washing, then, might cleanse it?"

"No more than in a snake-bite. It is too subtle and too deadly."

"Excision of the wound, then?"

"That is it. If it be on the finger, take the finger off. So said my father always. But think of where this wound is, and that it is my wife. It is dreadful!"

But familiarity with such grim matters may take the finer edge from a man's sympathy. To Douglas Stone this was already an interesting case, and he brushed aside as irrelevant the feeble objections of the husband.

"It appears to be that or nothing," said he brusquely. It is better to lose a lip than a life."

"Ah, yes, I know that you are right. Well, well, it is kismet, and must be faced. I have the cab, and you will come with me and do this thing."

Douglas Stone took his case of bistouries from a drawer, and placed it with a roll of bandage and a compress of lint in his pocket. He must waste no more time if he were to see Lady Sannox.

"I am ready," said he, pulling on his overcoat. Will you take a glass of wine before you go out into this cold air?"

His visitor shrank away, with a protesting hand upraised.

"You forget that I am a Mussulman, and a true follower of the Prophet," said he. "But tell me what is the bottle of green glass which you have placed in your pocket?"

"It is chloroform."

"Ah, that also is forbidden to us. It is a spirit, and we make no use of such things."

"What! You would allow your wife to go through an operation without an anaesthetic?"

"Ah! she will feel nothing, poor soul. The deep sleep has already come on, which is the first working of the poison. And then I have given her of our Smyrna opium. Come, sir, for already an hour has passed."

As they stepped out into the darkness, a sheet of rain was driven in upon their faces, and the hall lamp, which dangled from the arm of a marble caryatid, went out with a fluff. Pim, the butler, pushed the heavy door to, straining hard with his shoulder against the wind, while the two men groped their way towards the yellow glare which showed where the cab was waiting. An instant later they were rattling upon their journey.

"Is it far?" asked Douglas Stone.

"Oh, no. We have a very little quiet place off the Euston Road."

The surgeon pressed the spring of his repeater and listened to the little tings which told him the hour. It was a quarter past nine. He calculated the distances, and the short time which it would take him to perform so trivial an operation. He ought to reach Lady Sannox by ten o'clock. Through the fogged windows he saw the blurred gas-lamps dancing past, with occasionally the broader glare of a shop front. The rain was pelting and rattling upon the leathern top of the carriage and the wheels swashed as they rolled through puddle and mud. Opposite to him the white headgear of his companion gleamed faintly through the obscurity. The surgeon felt in his pockets and arranged his needles, his ligatures and his safety-pins, that no time might be wasted when they arrived. He chafed with impatience and drummed his foot upon the floor.

But the cab slowed down at last and pulled up. In an instant Douglas Stone was out, and the Smyrna merchant's toe was at his very heel.

"You can wait," said he to the driver.

It was a mean-looking house in a narrow and sordid street. The surgeon, who knew his London well, cast a swift glance into the shadows, but there was nothing distinctive—no shop, no movement, nothing but a double line of dull, flat-faced houses, a double stretch of wet flagstones which gleamed in the lamplight, and a double rush of water in the gutters which swirled and gurgled towards the sewer gratings. The door which faced them was blotched and discoloured, and a faint light in the fan pane above it served to show the dust and the grime which covered it. Above, in one of the bedroom windows, there was a dull yellow glimmer. The merchant knocked loudly, and, as he turned his dark face towards the light, Douglas Stone could see that it was contracted with anxiety. A bolt was drawn, and an elderly woman with a taper stood in the doorway, shielding the thin flame with her gnarled hand.

"Is all well?" gasped the merchant.

"She is as you left her, sir."

"She has not spoken?"

"No; she is in a deep sleep."

The merchant closed the door, and Douglas Stone walked down the narrow passage, glancing about him in some surprise as he did so. There was no oilcloth, no mat, no hat-rack. Deep grey dust and heavy festoons of cobwebs met his eyes everywhere. Following the old woman up the winding stair, his firm footfall echoed harshly through the silent house. There was no carpet.

The bedroom was on the second landing. Douglas Stone followed the old nurse into it, with the merchant at his heels. Here, at least, there was furniture and to spare. The floor was littered and the corners piled with Turkish cabinets, inlaid tables, coats of chain mail, strange pipes, and grotesque weapons. A single small lamp stood upon a bracket on the wall. Douglas Stone took it down, and picking his way among the lumber, walked over to a couch in the corner, on which lay a woman dressed in the Turkish fashion, with yashmak and veil. The lower part of the face was exposed, and the surgeon saw a jagged cut which zigzagged along the border of the under lip.

"You will forgive the yashmak," said the Turk. "You know our views about woman in the East."

But the surgeon was not thinking about the yashmak. This was no longer a woman to him. It was a case. He stooped and examined the wound carefully.

"There are no signs of irritation," said he. "We might delay the operation until local symptoms develop."

The husband wrung his hands in incontrollable agitation.

"Oh! sir, sir!" he cried. "Do not trifle. You do not know. It is deadly. I know, and I give you my assurance that an operation is absolutely necessary. Only the knife can save her."

"And yet I am inclined to wait," said Douglas Stone.

"That is enough!" the Turk cried, angrily. "Every minute is of importance, and I cannot stand here and see my wife allowed to sink. It only remains for me to give you my thanks for having come, and to call in some other surgeon before it is too late."

Douglas Stone hesitated. To refund that hundred pounds was no pleasant matter. But of course if he left the case he must return the money. And if the Turk were right and the woman died, his position before a coroner might be an embarrassing one.

"You have had personal experience of this poison?" he asked.

"I have."

"And you assure me that an operation is needful."

"I swear it by all that I hold sacred."

"The disfigurement will be frightful."

"I can understand that the mouth will not be a pretty one to kiss."

Douglas Stone turned fiercely upon the man. The speech was a brutal one. But the Turk has his own fashion of talk and of thought, and there was no time for wrangling. Douglas Stone drew a bistoury from his case, opened it and felt the keen straight edge with his forefinger. Then he held the lamp closer to the bed. Two dark eyes were gazing up at him through the slit in the yashmak. They were all iris, and the pupil was hardly to be seen.

"You have given her a very heavy dose of opium."

"Yes, she has had a good dose."

He glanced again at the dark eyes which looked straight at his own. They were dull and lustreless, but, even as he gazed, a little shifting sparkle came into them, and the lips quivered.

"She is not absolutely unconscious," said he.

"Would it not be well to use the knife while it would be painless?"

The same thought had crossed the surgeon's mind. He grasped the wounded lip with his forceps, and with two swift cuts he took out a broad V-shaped piece. The woman sprang up on the couch with a dreadful gurgling scream. Her covering was torn from her face. It was a face that he knew. In spite of that protruding upper lip and that slobber of blood, it was a face that he knew. She kept on putting her hand up to the gap and screaming. Douglas Stone sat down at the foot of the couch with his knife and his forceps. The room was whirling round, and he had felt something go like a ripping seam behind his ear. A bystander would have said that his face was the more ghastly of the two. As in a dream, or as if he had been looking at something at the play, he was conscious that the Turk's hair and beard lay upon the table, and that Lord Sannox was leaning against the wall with his hand to his side, laughing silently. The screams had died away now, and the dreadful head had dropped back again upon the pillow, but Douglas Stone still sat motionless, and Lord Sannox still chuckled quietly to himself.

"It was really very necessary for Marion, this operation," said he, "not physically, but morally, you know, morally."

Douglas Stone stooped forwards and began to play with the fringe of the coverlet. His knife tinkled down upon the ground, but he still held the forceps and something more.

"I had long intended to make a little example," said Lord Sannox, suavely. "Your note of Wednesday miscarried, and I have it here in my pocket-book. I took some pains in carrying out my idea. The wound, by the way, was from nothing more dangerous than my signet ring."

He glanced keenly at his silent companion, and cocked the small revolver which he held in his coat pocket. But Douglas Stone was still picking at the coverlet.

"You see you have kept your appointment after all," said Lord Sannox.

And at that Douglas Stone began to laugh. He laughed long and loudly. But Lord Sannox did not laugh now. Something like fear sharpened and hardened his features. He walked from the room, and he walked on tiptoe. The old woman was waiting outside.

"Attend to your mistress when she awakes," said Lord Sannox.

Then he went down to the street. The cab was at the door, and the driver raised his hand to his hat.

"John," said Lord Sannox, "you will take the doctor home first. He will want leading downstairs, I think. Tell his butler that he has been taken ill at a case."

"Very good, sir."

"Then you can take Lady Sannox home."

"And how about yourself, sir?"

"Oh, my address for the next few months will be Hotel di Roma, Venice. Just see that the letters are sent on. And tell Stevens to exhibit all the purple chrysanthemums next Monday and to wire me the result."

A Question of Diplomacy

The Foreign Minister was down with the gout. For a week he had been confined to the house, and he had missed two Cabinet Councils at a time when the pressure upon his department was severe. It is true that he had an excellent undersecretary and an admirable staff, but the Minister was a man of such ripe experience and of such proven sagacity that things halted in his absence. When his firm hand was at the wheel the great ship of State rode easily and smoothly upon her way; when it was removed she yawed and staggered until twelve British editors rose up in their omniscience and traced out twelve several courses, each of which was the sole and only path to safety. Then it was that the Opposition said vain things, and that the harassed Prime Minister prayed for his absent colleague.

The Foreign Minister sat in his dressing-room in the great house in Cavendish Square. It was May, and the square garden shot up like a veil of green in front of his window, but, in spite of the sunshine, a fire crackled and sputtered in the grate of the sick-room. In a deep-red plush armchair sat the great statesman, his head leaning back upon a silken pillow, one foot stretched forward and supported upon a padded rest. His deeply-lined, finely-chiselled face and slow-moving, heavily-pouched eyes were turned upwards towards the carved and painted ceiling, with that inscrutable expression which had been the despair and the admiration of his Continental colleagues upon the occasion of the famous Congress when he had made his first appearance in the arena of European diplomacy. Yet at the present moment his capacity for hiding his emotions had for the instant failed him, for about the lines of his strong, straight mouth and the puckers of his broad, overhanging forehead, there were sufficient indications of the restlessness and impatience which consumed him.

And indeed there was enough to make a man chafe, for he had much to think of and yet was bereft of the power of thought. There was, for example, that question of the Dobrutscha and the navigation of the mouths of the Danube which was ripe for settlement. The Russian Chancellor had sent a masterly statement upon the subject, and it was the pet ambition of our Minister to answer it in a worthy fashion. Then there was the blockade of Crete, and the British fleet lying off Cape Matapan, waiting for instructions which might change the course of European history. And there were those three unfortunate Macedonian tourists, whose friends were momentarily expecting to receive their ears or their fingers in default of the exorbitant ransom which had been demanded. They must be plucked out of those mountains, by force or by diplomacy, or an outraged public would vent its wrath upon Downing Street. All these questions pressed for a solution, and yet here was the Foreign Minister of England, planted in an arm-chair, with his whole thoughts and attention riveted upon the ball of his right toe! It was humiliating—horribly humiliating! His reason revolted at it. He had been a respecter of himself, a respecter of his own will; but what sort of a machine was it which could be utterly thrown out of gear by a little piece of inflamed gristle? He groaned and writhed among his cushions.

But, after all, was it quite impossible that he should go down to the House? Perhaps the doctor was exaggerating the situation. There was a Cabinet Council that day. He glanced at his watch. It must be nearly over by now. But at least he might perhaps venture to drive down as far as Westminster. He pushed back the little round table with its bristle of medicine-bottles, and levering himself up with a hand upon either arm of the chair, he clutched a thick oak stick and hobbled slowly across the room. For a moment as he moved, his energy of mind and body seemed to return to him. The British fleet should sail from Matapan. Pressure should be brought to bear upon the Turks. The Greeks should be shown—Ow! In an instant the Mediterranean was blotted out, and nothing remained but that huge, undeniable, intrusive, red-hot toe! He staggered to the window and rested his left hand upon the ledge, while he propped himself upon his stick with his right. Outside lay the bright, cool, square garden, a few well-dressed passers-by, and a single, neatly-appointed carriage, which was driving away from his own door. His quick eye caught the coat-of-arms on the panel, and his lips set for a moment and his bushy eyebrows gathered ominously with a deep furrow between them. He hobbled back to his seat and struck the gong which stood upon the table.

"Your mistress!" said he as the serving-man entered.

It was clear that it was impossible to think of going to the House. The shooting up his leg warned him that his doctor had not overestimated the situation. But he had a little mental worry now which had for the moment eclipsed his physical ailments. He tapped the ground impatiently with his stick until the door of the dressing-room swung open, and a tall, elegant lady of rather more than middle age swept into the chamber. Her hair was touched with grey, but her calm, sweet face had all the freshness of youth, and her gown of green shot plush, with a sparkle of gold passementerie at her bosom and shoulders, showed off the lines of her fine figure to their best advantage.

"You sent for me, Charles?"

"Whose carriage was that which drove away just now?"

"Oh, you've been up!" she cried, shaking an admonitory forefinger. "What an old dear it is! How can you be so rash? What am I to say to Sir William when he comes? You know that he gives up his cases when they are insubordinate."

"In this instance the case may give him up," said the Minister, peevishly; "but I must beg, Clara, that you will answer my question."

"Oh! the carriage! It must have been Lord Arthur Sibthorpe's."

"I saw the three chevrons upon the panel," muttered the invalid.

His lady had pulled herself a little straighter and opened her large blue eyes.

"Then why ask?" she said. "One might almost think, Charles, that you were laying a trap! Did you expect that I should deceive you? You have not had your lithia powder."

"For Heaven's sake, leave it alone! I asked because I was surprised that Lord Arthur should call here. I should have fancied, Clara, that I had made myself sufficiently clear on that point. Who received him?"

"I did. That is, I and Ida."

"I will not have him brought into contact with Ida. I do not approve of it. The matter has gone too far already."

Lady Clara seated herself on a velvet-topped footstool, and bent her stately figure over the Minister's hand, which she patted softly between her own.

"Now you have said it, Charles," said she. "It has gone too far—I give you my word, dear, that I never suspected it until it was past all mending. I may be to blame—no doubt I am; but it was all so sudden. The tail end of the season and a week at Lord Donnythorne's. That was all. But oh! Charlie, she loves him so, and she is our only one! How can we make her miserable?"

"Tut, tut!" cried the Minister impatiently, slapping on the plush arm of his chair. "This is too much. I tell you, Clara, I give you my word, that all my official duties, all the affairs of this great empire, do not give me the trouble that Ida does."

"But she is our only one, Charles."

"The more reason that she should not make a mesalliance."

"Mesalliance, Charles! Lord Arthur Sibthorpe, son of the Duke of Tavistock, with a pedigree from the Heptarchy. Debrett takes them right back to Morcar, Earl of Northumberland."

The Minister shrugged his shoulders.

"Lord Arthur is the fourth son of the poorest duke in England," said he. "He has neither prospects nor profession."

"But, oh! Charlie, you could find him both."

"I do not like him. I do not care for the connection."

"But consider Ida! You know how frail her health is. Her whole soul is set upon him. You would not have the heart, Charles, to separate them?"

There was a tap at the door. Lady Clara swept towards it and threw it open.

"Yes, Thomas?"

"If you please, my lady, the Prime Minister is below."

"Show him up, Thomas."

"Now, Charlie, you must not excite yourself over public matters. Be very good and cool and reasonable, like a darling. I am sure that I may trust you."

She threw her light shawl round the invalid's shoulders, and slipped away into the bed-room as the great man was ushered in at the door of the dressing-room.

"My dear Charles," said he cordially, stepping into the room with all the boyish briskness for which he was famous, "I trust that you find yourself a little better. Almost ready for harness, eh? We miss you sadly, both in the House and in the Council. Quite a storm brewing over this Grecian business. The Times took a nasty line this morning."

"So I saw," said the invalid, smiling up at his chief. "Well, well, we must let them see that the country is not entirely ruled from Printing House Square yet. We must keep our own course without faltering."

"Certainly, Charles, most undoubtedly," assented the Prime Minister, with his hands in his pockets.

"It was so kind of you to call. I am all impatience to know what was done in the Council."

"Pure formalities, nothing more. By-the-way, the Macedonian prisoners are all right."

"Thank Goodness for that! "

"We adjourned all other business until we should have you
with us next week. The question of a dissolution begins to press.
The reports from the provinces are excellent."

The Foreign Minister moved impatiently and groaned.

"We must really straighten up our foreign business a little,"
said he. "I must get Novikoff's Note answered. It is clever, but the
fallacies are obvious. I wish, too, we could clear up the Afghan
frontier. This illness is most exasperating. There is so much to be
done, but my brain is clouded. Sometimes I think it is the gout,
and sometimes I put it down to the colchicum."

"What will our medical autocrat say?" laughed the Prime
Minister. "You are so irreverent, Charles. With a bishop one may
feel at one's ease. They are not beyond the reach of argument. But
a doctor with his stethoscope and thermometer is a thing apart.
Your reading does not impinge upon him. He is serenely above
you. And then, of course, he takes you at a disadvantage. With
health and strength one might cope with him. Have you read Hahnemann? What are your views upon Hahnemann?"

The invalid knew his illustrious colleague too well to follow
him down any of those by-paths of knowledge in which he
delighted to wander. To his intensely shrewd and practical mind
there was something repellent in the waste of energy involved in a
discussion upon the Early Church or the twenty-seven principles
of Mesmer. It was his custom to slip past such conversational
openings with a quick step and an averted face.

"I have hardly glanced at his writings," said he. "By-the-way, I
suppose that there was no special departmental news?"

"Ah! I had almost forgotten. Yes, it was one of the things
which I had called to tell you. Sir Algernon Jones has resigned at
Tangier. There is a vacancy there."

"It had better be filled at once. The longer delay the more
applicants."

"Ah, patronage, patronage!" sighed the Prime Minister.
"Every vacancy makes one doubtful friend and a dozen very positive enemies. Who so bitter as the disappointed place-seeker? But

you are right, Charles. Better fill it at once, especially as there is some little trouble in Morocco. I understand that the Duke of Tavistock would like the place for his fourth son, Lord Arthur Sibthorpe. We are under some obligation to the Duke."

The Foreign Minister sat up eagerly.

"My dear friend," he said, "it is the very appointment which I should have suggested. Lord Arthur would be very much better in Tangier at present than in—in——"

"Cavendish Square?" hazarded his chief, with a little arch query of his eyebrows.

"Well, let us say London. He has manner and tact. He was at Constantinople in Norton's time."

"Then he talks Arabic?"

"A smattering. But his French is good."

"Speaking of Arabic, Charles, have you dipped into Averroes?"

"No, I have not. But the appointment would be an excellent one in every way. Would you have the great goodness to arrange the matter in my absence?"

"Certainly, Charles, certainly. Is there anything else that I can do?"

"No. I hope to be in the House by Monday."

"I trust so. We miss you at every turn. The Times will try to make mischief over that Grecian business. A leader-writer is a terribly irresponsible thing, Charles. There is no method by which he may be confuted, however preposterous his assertions. Good-bye! Read Porson! Goodbye!"

He shook the invalid's hand, gave a jaunty wave of his broad-brimmed hat, and darted out of the room with the same elasticity and energy with which he had entered it.

The footman had already opened the great folding door to usher the illustrious visitor to his carriage, when a lady stepped from the drawing-room and touched him on the sleeve. From behind the half-closed portière of stamped velvet a little pale face peeped out, half-curious, half-frightened.

"May I have one word?"

"Surely, Lady Clara."

"I hope it is not intrusive. I would not for the world overstep the limits——"

"My dear Lady Clara!" interrupted the Prime Minister, with a youthful bow and wave.

"Pray do not answer me if I go too far. But I know that Lord Arthur Sibthorpe has applied for Tangier. Would it be a liberty if I asked you what chance he has?"

"The post is filled up."

"Oh!"

In the foreground and background there was a disappointed face.

"And Lord Arthur has it."

The Prime Minister chuckled over his little piece of roguery.

"We have just decided it," he continued.

"Lord Arthur must go in a week. I am delighted to perceive, Lady Clara, that the appointment has your approval. Tangier is a place of extraordinary interest. Catherine of Braganza and Colonel Kirke will occur to your memory. Burton has written well upon Northern Africa. I dine at Windsor, so I am sure that you will excuse my leaving you. I trust that Lord Charles will be better. He can hardly fail to be so with such a nurse."

He bowed, waved, and was off down the steps to his brougham. As he drove away, Lady Clara could see that he was already deeply absorbed in a paper-covered novel.

She pushed back the velvet curtains, and returned into the drawing-room. Her daughter stood in the sunlight by the window, tall, fragile, and exquisite, her features and outline not unlike her mother's, but frailer, softer, more delicate. The golden light struck one half of her high-bred, sensitive face, and glimmered upon her thickly-coiled flaxen hair, striking a pinkish tint from her closely-cut costume of fawn-coloured cloth with its dainty cinnamon ruchings. One little soft frill of chiffon nestled round her throat, from which the white, graceful neck and well-poised head shot up like a lily amid moss. Her thin white hands were pressed together, and her blue eyes turned beseechingly upon her mother.

"Silly girl! Silly girl!" said the matron, answering that imploring look. She put her hands upon her daughter's sloping shoulders and drew her towards her. "It is a very nice place for a short time. It will be a stepping stone."

"But oh! mamma, in a week! Poor Arthur!"

"He will be happy."

"What! happy to part?"

"He need not part. You shall go with him."

"Oh! mamma!"

"Yes, I say it."

"Oh! mamma, in a week?"

"Yes indeed. A great deal may be done in a week. I shall order your trousseau to-day."

"Oh! you dear, sweet angel! But I am so frightened! And papa? Oh! dear, I am so frightened!"

"Your papa is a diplomatist, dear."

"Yes, ma."

"But, between ourselves, he married a diplomatist too. If he can manage the British Empire, I think that I can manage him, Ida. How long have you been engaged, child?"

"Ten weeks, mamma."

"Then it is quite time it came to a head. Lord Arthur cannot leave England without you. You must go to Tangier as the Minister's wife. Now, you will sit there on the settee, dear, and let me manage entirely. There is Sir William's carriage! I do think that I know how to manage Sir William. James, just ask the doctor to step in this way!"

A heavy, two-horsed carriage had drawn up at the door, and there came a single stately thud upon the knocker. An instant afterwards the drawing-room door flew open and the footman ushered in the famous physician. He was a small man, clean-shaven, with the old-fashioned black dress and white cravat with high-standing collar. He swung his golden pince-nez in his right hand as he walked, and bent forward with a peering, blinking expression, which was somehow suggestive of the dark and complex cases through which he had seen.

"Ah" said he, as he entered. "My young patient! I am glad of the opportunity."

"Yes, I wish to speak to you about her, Sir William. Pray take this arm-chair."

"Thank you, I will sit beside her," said he, taking his place upon the settee. "She is looking better, less anaemic unquestionably, and a fuller pulse. Quite a little tinge of colour, and yet not hectic."

"I feel stronger, Sir William."

"But she still has the pain in the side."

"Ah, that pain!" He tapped lightly under the collar-bones, and then bent forward with his biaural stethoscope in either ear. "Still a trace of dulness—still a slight crepitation," he murmured.

"You spoke of a change, doctor."

"Yes, certainly a judicious change might be advisable."

"You said a dry climate. I wish to do to the letter what you recommend."

"You have always been model patients."

"We wish to be. You said a dry climate."

"Did I? I rather forget the particulars of our conversation. But a dry climate is certainly indicated."

"Which one?"

"Well, I think really that a patient should be allowed some latitude. I must not exact too rigid discipline. There is room for individual choice—the Engadine, Central Europe, Egypt, Algiers, which you like."

"I hear that Tangier is also recommended."

"Oh, yes, certainly; it is very dry."

"You hear, Ida? Sir William says that you are to go to Tangier."

"Or any——"

"No, no, Sir William! We feel safest when we are most obedient. You have said Tangier, and we shall certainly try Tangier."

"Really, Lady Clara, your implicit faith is most flattering. It is not everyone who would sacrifice their own plans and inclinations so readily."

"We know your skill and your experience, Sir William. Ida shall try Tangier. I am convinced that she will be benefited."

"I have no doubt of it."

"But you know Lord Charles. He is just a little inclined to decide medical matters as he would an affair of State. I hope that you will be firm with him."

"As long as Lord Charles honours me so far as to ask my advice I am sure that he would not place me in the false position of having that advice disregarded."

The medical baronet whirled round the cord of his pince-nez and pushed out a protesting hand.

"No, no, but you must be firm on the point of Tangier."

"Having deliberately formed the opinion that Tangier is the best place for our young patient, I do not think that I shall readily change my conviction."

"Of course not."

"I shall speak to Lord Charles upon the subject now when I go upstairs."

"Pray do."

"And meanwhile she will continue her present course of treatment. I trust that the warm African air may send her back in a few months with all her energy restored."

He bowed in the courteous, sweeping, old-world fashion which had done so much to build up his ten thousand a year, and, with the stealthy gait of a man whose life is spent in sick-rooms, he followed the footman upstairs.

As the red velvet curtains swept back into position, the Lady Ida threw her arms round her mother's neck and sank her face on to her bosom.

"Oh! mamma, you ARE a diplomatist!" she cried.

But her mother's expression was rather that of the general who looked upon the first smoke of the guns than of one who had won the victory.

"All will be right, dear," said she, glancing down at the fluffy yellow curls and tiny ear. "There is still much to be done, but I think we may venture to order the trousseau."

"Oh I how brave you are!"

"Of course, it will in any case be a very quiet affair. Arthur must get the license. I do not approve of hole-and-corner marriages, but where the gentleman has to take up an official position some allowance must be made. We can have Lady Hilda Edgecombe, and the Trevors, and the Grevilles, and I am sure that the Prime Minister would run down if he could."

"And papa?"

"Oh, yes; he will come too, if he is well enough. We must wait until Sir William goes, and, meanwhile, I shall write to Lord Arthur."

Half an hour had passed, and quite a number of notes had been dashed off in the fine, bold, park-paling handwriting of the

Lady Clara, when the door clashed, and the wheels of the doctor's carriage were heard grating outside against the kerb. The Lady Clara laid down her pen, kissed her daughter, and started off for the sick-room. The Foreign Minister was lying back in his chair, with a red silk handkerchief over his forehead, and his bulbous, cotton-wadded foot still protruding upon its rest.

"I think it is almost liniment time," said Lady Clara, shaking a blue crinkled bottle. "Shall I put on a little?"

"Oh! this pestilent toe!" groaned the sufferer. "Sir William won't hear of my moving yet. I do think he is the most completely obstinate and pig-headed man that I have ever met. I tell him that he has mistaken his profession, and that I could find him a post at Constantinople. We need a mule out there."

"Poor Sir William!" laughed Lady Clara. But how has he roused your wrath?"

"He is so persistent-so dogmatic."

"Upon what point? "

"Well, he has been laying down the law about Ida. He has decreed, it seems, that she is to go to Tangier."

"He said something to that effect before he went up to you."

"Oh, he did, did he?"

The slow-moving, inscrutable eye came sliding round to her. Lady Clara's face had assumed an expression of transparent obvious innocence, an intrusive candour which is never seen in nature save when a woman is bent upon deception.

"He examined her lungs, Charles. He did not say much, but his expression was very grave."

"Not to say owlish," interrupted the Minister.

"No, no, Charles; it is no laughing matter. He said that she must have a change. I am sure that he thought more than he said. He spoke of dulness and crepitation. and the effects of the African air. Then the talk turned upon dry, bracing health resorts, and he agreed that Tangier was the place. He said that even a few months there would work a change."

"And that was all?"

"Yes, that was all."

Lord Charles shrugged his shoulders with the air of a man who is but half convinced.

"But of course," said Lady Clara, serenely, if you think it better that Ida should not go she shall not. The only thing is that if she should get worse we might feel a little uncomfortable afterwards. In a weakness of that sort a very short time may make a difference. Sir William evidently thought the matter critical. Still, there is no reason why he should influence you. It is a little responsibility, however. If you take it all upon yourself and free me from any of it, so that afterwards——"

"My dear Clara, how you do croak!"

"Oh! I don't wish to do that, Charles. But you remember what happened to Lord Bellamy's child. She was just Ida's age. That was another case in which Sir William's advice was disregarded."

Lord Charles groaned impatiently.

"I have not disregarded it," said he.

"No, no, of course not. I know your strong sense, and your good heart too well, dear. You were very wisely looking at both sides of the question. That is what we poor women cannot do. It is emotion against reason, as I have often heard you say. We are swayed this way and that, but you men are persistent, and so you gain your way with us. But I am so pleased that you have decided for Tangier."

"Have I?"

"Well, dear, you said that you would not disregard Sir William."

"Well, Clara, admitting that Ida is to go to Tangier, you will allow that it is impossible for me to escort her?

"Utterly."

"And for you?

"While you are ill my place is by your side."

"There is your sister?"

"She is going to Florida."

"Lady Dumbarton, then?"

"She is nursing her father. It is out of the question."

"Well, then, whom can we possibly ask? Especially just as the season is commencing. You see, Clara, the fates fight against Sir William."

His wife rested her elbows against the back of the great red chair, and passed her fingers through the statesman's grizzled curls, stooping down as she did so until her lips were close to his ear.

"There is Lord Arthur Sibthorpe," said she softly.

Lord Charles bounded in his chair, and muttered a word or two such as were more frequently heard from Cabinet Ministers in Lord Melbourne's time than now.

"Are you mad, Clara!" he cried. "What can have put such a thought into your head?"

"The Prime Minister."

"Who? The Prime Minister?"

"Yes, dear. Now do, do be good! Or perhaps I had better not speak to you about it any more."

"Well, I really think that you have gone rather too far to retreat."

"It was the Prime Minister, then, who told me that Lord Arthur was going to Tangier."

"It is a fact, though it had escaped my memory for the instant."

"And then came Sir William with his advice about Ida. Oh! Charlie, it is surely more than a coincidence!"

"I am convinced," said Lord Charles, with his shrewd, questioning gaze, "that it is very much more than a coincidence, Lady Clara. You are a very clever woman, my dear. A born manager and organiser."

Lady Clara brushed past the compliment.

"Think of our own young days, Charlie," she whispered, with her fingers still toying with his hair. "What were you then? A poor man, not even Ambassador at Tangier. But I loved you, and believed in you, and have I ever regretted it? Ida loves and believes in Lord Arthur, and why should she ever regret it either?"

Lord Charles was silent. His eyes were fixed upon the green branches which waved outside the window; but his mind had flashed back to a Devonshire country-house of thirty years ago, and to the one fateful evening when, between old yew hedges, he paced along beside a slender girl, and poured out to her his hopes, his fears, and his ambitious. He took the white, thin hand and pressed it to his lips.

"You, have been a good wife to me, Clara," said he.

She said nothing. She did not attempt to improve upon her advantage. A less consummate general might have tried to do so, and ruined all. She stood silent and submissive, noting the quick play of thought which peeped from his eyes and lip. There was a sparkle in the one and a twitch of amusement in the other, as he at last glanced up at her.

"Clara," said he, "deny it if you can! You have ordered the trousseau."

She gave his ear a little pinch.

"Subject to your approval," said she.

"You have written to the Archbishop."

"It is not posted yet."

"You have sent a note to Lord Arthur."

"How could you tell that?"

"He is downstairs now."

"No; but I think that is his brougham."

Lord Charles sank back with a look of half-comical despair.

"Who is to fight against such a woman?" he cried. "Oh! if I could send you to Novikoff! He is too much for any of my men. But, Clara, I cannot have them up here."

"Not for your blessing?"

"No, no!"

"It would make them so happy."

"I cannot stand scenes."

"Then I shall convey it to them."

"And pray say no more about it—to-day, at any rate. I have been weak over the matter."

"Oh! Charlie, you who are so strong!"

"You have outflanked me, Clara. It was very well done. I must congratulate you."

"Well," she murmured, as she kissed him, "you know I have been studying a very clever diplomatist for thirty years."

A Medical Document

Medical men are, as a class, very much too busy to take stock of singular situations or dramatic events. Thus it happens that the ablest chronicler of their experiences in our literature was a lawyer. A life spent in watching over death-beds—or over birth-beds which are infinitely more trying—takes something from a man's sense of proportion, as constant strong waters might corrupt his palate. The overstimulated nerve ceases to respond. Ask the surgeon for his best experiences and he may reply that he has seen little that is remarkable, or break away into the technical. But catch him some night when the fire has spurted up and his pipe is reeking, with a few of his brother practitioners for company and an artful question or allusion to set him going. Then you will get some raw, green facts new plucked from the tree of life.

It is after one of the quarterly dinners of the Midland Branch of the British Medical Association. Twenty coffee cups, a dozen liqueur glasses, and a solid bank of blue smoke which swirls slowly along the high, gilded ceiling gives a hint of a successful gathering. But the members have shredded off to their homes. The line of heavy, bulge-pocketed overcoats and of stethoscope-bearing top hats is gone from the hotel corridor. Round the fire in the sitting-room three medicos are still lingering, however, all smoking and arguing, while a fourth, who is a mere layman and young at that, sits back at the table. Under cover of an open journal he is writing furiously with a stylographic pen, asking a question in an innocent voice from time to time and so flickering up the conversation whenever it shows a tendency to wane.

The three men are all of that staid middle age which begins early and lasts late in the profession. They are none of them famous, yet each is of good repute, and a fair type of his particular branch. The portly man with the authoritative manner and the white, vitriol splash upon his cheek is Charley Manson, chief of the Wormley Asylum, and author of the brilliant monograph—Obscure Nervous Lesions in the Unmarried. He always wears his collar high like that, since the half-successful attempt of a student of Revelations to cut his throat with a splinter of glass. The second, with the ruddy face and the merry brown eyes, is a general practitioner, a man of vast experience, who, with his three assistants and his five horses, takes twenty-five hundred a year in half-crown visits and shilling consultations out of the poorest quarter of a great city. That cheery face of Theodore Foster is seen at the side of a hundred sick-beds a day, and if he has one-third more names on his visiting list than in his cash book he always promises himself that he will get level some day when a millionaire with a

chronic complaint—the ideal combination—shall seek his services. The third, sitting on the right with his dress shoes shining
on the top of the fender, is Hargrave, the rising surgeon. His face
has none of the broad humanity of Theodore Foster's, the eye is
stern and critical, the mouth straight and severe, but there is
strength and decision in every line of it, and it is nerve rather than
sympathy which the patient demands when he is bad enough to
come to Hargrave's door. He calls himself a jawman "a mere jawman" as he modestly puts it, but in point of fact he is too young
and too poor to confine himself to a specialty, and there is nothing
surgical which Hargrave has not the skill and the audacity to do.

"Before, after, and during," murmurs the general practitioner
in answer to some interpolation of the outsider's. "I assure you,
Manson, one sees all sorts of evanescent forms of madness."

"Ah, puerperal!" throws in the other, knocking the curved grey
ash from his cigar. "But you had some case in your mind, Foster."

"Well, there was only one last week which was new to me. I
had been engaged by some people of the name of Silcoe. When the
trouble came round I went myself, for they would not hear of an
assistant. The husband who was a policeman, was sitting at the
head of the bed on the further side. 'This won't do,' said I. 'Oh yes,
doctor, it must do,' said she. 'It's quite irregular and he must go,'
said I. 'It's that or nothing,' said she. 'I won't open my mouth or
stir a finger the whole night,' said he. So it ended by my allowing
him to remain, and there he sat for eight hours on end. She was
very good over the matter, but every now and again HE would
fetch a hollow groan, and I noticed that he held his right hand just
under the sheet all the time, where I had no doubt that it was
clasped by her left. When it was all happily over, I looked at him
and his face was the colour of this cigar ash, and his head had
dropped on to the edge of the pillow. Of course I thought he had
fainted with emotion, and I was just telling myself what I thought
of myself for having been such a fool as to let him stay there, when
suddenly I saw that the sheet over his hand was all soaked with
blood; I whisked it down, and there was the fellow's wrist half cut
through. The woman had one bracelet of a policeman's handcuff
over her left wrist and the other round his right one. When she
had been in pain she had twisted with all her strength and the iron

had fairly eaten into the bone of the man's arm. 'Aye, doctor,' said she, when she saw I had noticed it. 'He's got to take his share as well as me. Turn and turn,' said she."

"Don't you find it a very wearing branch of the profession?" asks Foster after a pause.

"My dear fellow, it was the fear of it that drove me into lunacy work."

"Aye, and it has driven men into asylums who never found their way on to the medical staff. I was a very shy fellow myself as a student, and I know what it means."

"No joke that in general practice," says the alienist.

"Well, you hear men talk about it as though it were, but I tell you it's much nearer tragedy. Take some poor, raw, young fellow who has just put up his plate in a strange town. He has found it a trial all his life, perhaps, to talk to a woman about lawn tennis and church services. When a young man IS shy he is shyer than any girl. Then down comes an anxious mother and consults him upon the most intimate family matters. 'I shall never go to that doctor again,' says she afterwards. 'His manner is so stiff and unsympathetic.' Unsympathetic! Why, the poor lad was struck dumb and paralysed. I have known general practitioners who were so shy that they could not bring themselves to ask the way in the street. Fancy what sensitive men like that must endure before they get broken in to medical practice. And then they know that nothing is so catching as shyness, and that if they do not keep a face of stone, their patient will be covered with confusion. And so they keep their face of stone, and earn the reputation perhaps of having a heart to correspond. I suppose nothing would shake YOUR nerve, Manson."

"Well, when a man lives year in year out among a thousand lunatics, with a fair sprinkling of homicidals among them, one's nerves either get set or shattered. Mine are all right so far."

"I was frightened once," says the surgeon. "It was when I was doing dispensary work. One night I had a call from some very poor people, and gathered from the few words they said that their child was ill. When I entered the room I saw a small cradle in the corner. Raising the lamp I walked over and putting back the curtains I looked down at the baby. I tell you it was sheer Providence that I didn't drop that lamp and set the whole place alight. The head on the pillow turned and I saw a face looking up at me which seemed to me to have more malignancy and wickedness than ever I had dreamed of in a nightmare. It was the flush of red over the cheekbones, and the brooding eyes full of loathing of me, and of everything else, that impressed me. I'll never forget my start as, instead of the chubby face of an infant, my eyes fell upon this creature. I took the mother into the next room. 'What is it?' I asked. 'A girl of sixteen,' said she, and then throwing up her arms, 'Oh, pray God she may be taken!' The poor thing, though she spent her life in this little cradle, had great, long, thin limbs which she curled up under her. I lost sight of the case and don't know what became of it, but I'll never forget the look in her eyes."

"That's creepy," says Dr. Foster. "But I think one of my experiences would run it close. Shortly after I put up my plate I had a visit from a little hunch-backed woman who wished me to come and attend to her sister in her trouble. When I reached the house, which was a very poor one, I found two other little hunched-backed women, exactly like the first, waiting for me in the sitting-room. Not one of them said a word, but my companion took the lamp and walked upstairs with her two sisters behind her, and me bringing up the rear. I can see those three queer shadows cast by the lamp upon the wall as clearly as I can see that tobacco pouch. In the room above was the fourth sister, a remarkably beautiful girl in evident need of my assistance. There was no wedding ring upon her finger. The three deformed sisters seated themselves round the room, like so many graven images, and all night not one of them opened her mouth. I'm not romancing, Hargrave; this is absolute fact. In the early morning a fearful thunderstorm broke out, one of the most violent I have ever known. The little garret burned blue with the lightning, and thunder roared and rattled as if it were on the very roof of the house. It wasn't much of a lamp I had, and it was a queer thing when a spurt of lightning came to see those three twisted figures sitting round the walls, or to have the voice of my patient drowned by the booming of the thunder. By Jove! I don't mind telling you that there was a time when I nearly bolted from the room. All came right in the end, but I never heard the true story of the unfortunate beauty and her three crippled sisters."

"That's the worst of these medical stories," sighs the outsider. "They never seem to have an end."

"When a man is up to his neck in practice, my boy, he has no time to gratify his private curiosity. Things shoot across him and he gets a glimpse of them, only to recall them, perhaps, at some quiet moment like this. But I've always felt, Manson, that your line had as much of the terrible in it as any other."

"More," groans the alienist. "A disease of the body is bad enough, but this seems to be a disease of the soul. Is it not a shocking thing—a thing to drive a reasoning man into absolute Materialism—to think that you may have a fine, noble fellow with every divine instinct and that some little vascular change, the dropping, we will say, of a minute spicule of bone from the inner table of his skull on to the surface of his brain may have the effect of changing him to a filthy and pitiable creature with every low and debasing tendency? What a satire an asylum is upon the majesty of man, and no less upon the ethereal nature of the soul."

"Faith and hope," murmurs the general practitioner.

"I have no faith, not much hope, and all the charity I can afford," says the surgeon. "When theology squares itself with the facts of life I'll read it up."

"You were talking about cases," says the outsider, jerking the ink down into his stylographic pen.

"Well, take a common complaint which kills many thousands every year, like G. P. for instance."

"What's G. P.?"

"General practitioner," suggests the surgeon with a grin.

"The British public will have to know what G. P. is," says the alienist gravely. "It's increasing by leaps and bounds, and it has the distinction of being absolutely incurable. General paralysis is its full title, and I tell you it promises to be a perfect scourge. Here's a fairly typical case now which I saw last Monday week. A young farmer, a splendid fellow, surprised his fellows by taking a very rosy view of things at a time when the whole country-side was grumbling. He was going to give up wheat, give up arable land, too, if it didn't pay, plant two thousand acres of rhododendrons and get a monopoly of the supply for Covent Garden—there was no end to his schemes, all sane enough but just a bit inflated. I called at the farm, not to see him, but on an altogether different matter. Something about the man's way of talking struck me and I watched him narrowly. His lip had a trick of quivering, his words slurred themselves together, and so did his handwriting when he had occasion to draw up a small agreement. A closer inspection showed me that one of his pupils was ever so little larger than the other. As I left the house his wife came after me. 'Isn't it splendid to see Job looking so well, doctor,' said she; 'he's that full of energy he can hardly keep himself quiet.' I did not say anything, for I had not the heart, but I knew that the fellow was as much condemned to death as though he were lying in the cell at Newgate. It was a characteristic case of incipient G. P."

"Good heavens!" cries the outsider. "My own lips tremble. I often slur my words. I believe I've got it myself."

Three little chuckles come from the front of the fire.

"There's the danger of a little medical knowledge to the layman."

"A great authority has said that every first year's student is suffering in silent agony from four diseases," remarks the surgeon. " One is heart disease, of course; another is cancer of the parotid. I forget the two other."

"Where does the parotid come in?"

"Oh, it's the last wisdom tooth coming through!"

"And what would be the end of that young farmer?" asks the outsider.

"Paresis of all the muscles, ending in fits, coma, and death. It may be a few months, it may be a year or two. He was a very strong young man and would take some killing."

"By-the-way," says the alienist, "did I ever tell you about the first certificate I signed? I came as near ruin then as a man could go."

"What was it, then?"

"I was in practice at the time. One morning a Mrs. Cooper called upon me and informed me that her husband had shown signs of delusions lately. They took the form of imagining that he had been in the army and had distinguished himself very much. As a matter of fact he was a lawyer and had never been out of England. Mrs. Cooper was of opinion that if I were to call it might alarm him, so it was agreed between us that she should send him up in the evening on some pretext to my consulting-room, which would give me the opportunity of having a chat with him and, if I were convinced of his insanity, of signing his certificate. Another doctor had already signed, so that it only needed my concurrence to have him placed under treatment. Well, Mr. Cooper arrived in the evening about half an hour before I had expected him, and consulted me as to some malarious symptoms from which he said that he suffered. According to his account he had just returned from the Abyssinian Campaign, and had been one of the first of the British forces to enter Magdala. No delusion could possibly be more marked, for he would talk of little else, so I filled in the papers without the slightest hesitation. When his wife arrived, after he had left, I put some questions to her to complete the form. 'What is his age?' I asked. 'Fifty,' said she. 'Fifty!' I cried. 'Why, the man I examined could not have been more than thirty! And so it came out that the real Mr. Cooper had never called upon me at all, but that by one of those coincidences which take a man's breath away another Cooper, who really was a very distinguished young officer of artillery, had come in to consult me. My pen was wet to sign the paper when I discovered it," says Dr. Manson, mopping his forehead.

"We were talking about nerve just now," observes the surgeon. "Just after my qualifying I served in the Navy for a time, as I think you know. I was on the flag-ship on the West African Station, and I remember a singular example of nerve which came to my notice at that time. One of our small gunboats had gone up the Calabar river, and while there the surgeon died of coast fever. On the same day a man's leg was broken by a spar falling upon it, and it became quite obvious that it must be taken off above the knee if his life was to be saved. The young lieutenant who was in charge of the craft searched among the dead doctor's effects and laid his hands upon some chloroform, a hip-joint knife, and a volume of Grey's Anatomy. He had the man laid by the steward upon the cabin table, and with a picture of a cross section of the thigh in front of him he began to take off the limb. Every now and then, referring to the diagram, he would say: 'Stand by with the lashings, steward. There's blood on the chart about here.' Then he would jab with his knife until he cut the artery, and he and his assistant would tie it up before they went any further. In this way they gradually whittled the leg off, and upon my word they made a very excellent job of it. The man is hopping about the Portsmouth Hard at this day.

"It's no joke when the doctor of one of these isolated gunboats himself falls ill," continues the surgeon after a pause. "You might think it easy for him to prescribe for himself, but this fever knocks you down like a club, and you haven't strength left to brush a mosquito off your face. I had a touch of it at Lagos, and I know what I am telling you. But there was a chum of mine who really had a curious experience. The whole crew gave him up, and, as they had never had a funeral aboard the ship, they began rehearsing the forms so as to be ready. They thought that he was unconscious, but he swears he could hear every word that passed. 'Corpse comin' up the latchway!' cried the Cockney sergeant of Marines. 'Present harms!' He was so amused, and so indignant too, that he just made up his mind that he wouldn't be carried through that hatchway, and he wasn't, either."

"There's no need for fiction in medicine," remarks Foster, "for the facts will always beat anything you can fancy. But it has seemed to me sometimes that a curious paper might be read at some of these meetings about the uses of medicine in popular fiction."

"How?"

"Well, of what the folk die of, and what diseases are made most use of in novels. Some are worn to pieces, and others, which are equally common in real life, are never mentioned. Typhoid is fairly frequent, but scarlet fever is unknown. Heart disease is common, but then heart disease, as we know it, is usually the sequel of some foregoing disease, of which we never hear anything in the romance. Then there is the mysterious malady called brain fever, which always attacks the heroine after a crisis, but which is unknown under that name to the text books. People when they are over-excited in novels fall down in a fit. In a fairly large experience I have never known anyone do so in real life. The small complaints simply don't exist. Nobody ever gets shingles or quinsy, or mumps in a novel. All the diseases, too, belong to the upper part of the body. The novelist never strikes below the belt."

"I'll tell you what, Foster," says the alienist, there is a side of life which is too medical for the general public and too romantic for the professional journals, but which contains some of the richest human materials that a man could study. It's not a pleasant side, I am afraid, but if it is good enough for Providence to create, it is good enough for us to try and understand. It would deal with strange outbursts of savagery and vice in the lives of the best men, curious momentary weaknesses in the record of the sweetest women, known but to one or two, and inconceivable to the world around. It would deal, too, with the singular phenomena of waxing and of waning manhood, and would throw a light upon those actions which have cut short many an honoured career and sent a man to a prison when he should have been hurried to a consulting-room. Of all evils that may come upon the sons of men, God shield us principally from that one!"

"I had a case some little time ago which was out of the ordinary," says the surgeon. "There's a famous beauty in London society—I mention no names—who used to be remarkable a few seasons ago for the very low dresses which she would wear. She had the whitest of skins and most beautiful of shoulders, so it was no wonder. Then gradually the frilling at her neck lapped upwards and upwards, until last year she astonished everyone by wearing quite a high collar at a time when it was completely out of fashion. Well, one day this very woman was shown into my consulting-room. When the footman was gone she suddenly tore off the upper part of her dress. 'For Gods sake do something for me!' she cried. Then I saw what the trouble was. A rodent ulcer was eating its way upwards, coiling on in its serpiginous fashion until the end of it was flush with her collar. The red streak of its trail was lost below the line of her bust. Year by year it had ascended and she had heightened her dress to hide it, until now it was about to invade her face. She had been too proud to confess her trouble, even to a medical man."

"And did you stop it?"

"Well, with zinc chloride I did what I could. But it may break out again. She was one of those beautiful white-and-pink creatures who are rotten with struma. You may patch but you can't mend."

"Dear! dear! dear!" cries the general practitioner, with that kindly softening of the eyes which had endeared him to so many thousands. "I suppose we mustn't think ourselves wiser than Providence, but there are times when one feels that something is wrong in the scheme of things. I've seen some sad things in my life. Did I ever tell you that case where Nature divorced a most loving couple? He was a fine young fellow, an athlete and a gentleman, but he overdid athletics. You know how the force that controls us gives us a little tweak to remind us when we get off the beaten track. It may be a pinch on the great toe if we drink too much and work too little. Or it may be a tug on our nerves if we dissipate energy too much. With the athlete, of course, it's the heart or the lungs. He had bad phthisis and was sent to Davos. Well, as luck would have it, she developed rheumatic fever, which left her heart very much affected. Now, do you see the dreadful dilemma in which those poor people found themselves? When he came below four thousand feet or so, his symptoms became terrible. She could come up about twenty-five hundred and then her heart reached its limit. They had several interviews half way down the valley, which left them nearly dead, and at last, the doctors had to absolutely forbid it. And so for four years they lived within three miles of each other and never met. Every morning he would go to a place which overlooked the chalet in which she lived and would wave a great white cloth and she answer from below. They could see each other quite plainly with their field glasses, and they might have been in different planets for all their chance of meeting."

"And one at last died," says the outsider.

"No, sir. I'm sorry not to be able to clinch the story, but the man recovered and is now a successful stockbroker in Drapers Gardens. The woman, too, is the mother of a considerable family. But what are you doing there?"

"Only taking a note or two of your talk."

The three medical men laugh as they walk towards their overcoats.

"Why, we've done nothing but talk shop," says the general practitioner. "What possible interest can the public take in that?"

Lot No. 249

Of the dealings of Edward Bellingham with William Monkhouse Lee, and of the cause of the great terror of Abercrombie Smith, it may be that no absolute and final judgment will ever be delivered. It is true that we have the full and clear narrative of Smith himself, and such corroboration as he could look for from Thomas Styles the servant, from the Reverend Plumptree Peterson, Fellow of Old's, and from such other people as chanced to gain some passing glance at this or that incident in a singular chain of events. Yet, in the main, the story must rest upon Smith alone, and the most will think that it is more likely that one brain, however outwardly sane, has some subtle warp in its texture, some strange flaw in its workings, than that the path of Nature has been overstepped in open day in so famed a centre of learning and light as the University of Oxford. Yet when we think how narrow and how devious this path of Nature is, how dimly we can trace it, for all our lamps of science, and how from the darkness which girds it round great and terrible possibilities loom ever shadowly upwards, it is a bold and confident man who will put a limit to the strange by-paths into which the human spirit may wander.

In a certain wing of what we will call Old College in Oxford there is a corner turret of an exceeding great age. The heavy arch which spans the open door has bent downwards in the centre under the weight of its years, and the grey, lichen-blotched blocks of stone are, bound and knitted together with withes and strands of ivy, as though the old mother had set herself to brace them up against wind and weather. From the door a stone stair curves upward spirally, passing two landings, and terminating in a third one, its steps all shapeless and hollowed by the tread of so many generations of the seekers after knowledge. Life has flowed like water down this winding stair, and, waterlike, has left these smooth-worn grooves behind it. From the long-gowned, pedantic scholars of Plantagenet days down to the young bloods of a later age, how full and strong had been that tide of young English life. And what was left now of all those hopes, those strivings, those fiery energies, save here and there in some old-world churchyard a few scratches upon a stone, and perchance a handful of dust in a mouldering coffin? Yet here were the silent stair and the grey old wall, with bend and saltire and many another heraldic device still to be read upon its surface, like grotesque shadows thrown back from the days that had passed.

In the month of May, in the year 1884, three young men occupied the sets of rooms which opened on to the separate landings of the old stair. Each set consisted simply of a sitting-room and of a bedroom, while the two corresponding rooms upon the ground-floor were used, the one as a coal-cellar, and the other as the living-room of the servant, or gyp, Thomas Styles, whose duty it was to wait upon the three men above him. To right and to left was a line of lecture-rooms and of offices, so that the dwellers in the old turret enjoyed a certain seclusion, which made the chambers popular among the more studious undergraduates. Such were the three who occupied them now—Abercrombie Smith above, Edward Bellingham beneath him, and William Monkhouse Lee upon the lowest storey.

It was ten o'clock on a bright spring night, and Abercrombie Smith lay back in his arm-chair, his feet upon the fender, and his briar-root pipe between his lips. In a similar chair, and equally at his ease, there lounged on the other side of the fireplace his old school friend Jephro Hastie. Both men were in flannels, for they had spent their evening upon the river, but apart from their dress no one could look at their hard-cut, alert faces without seeing that they were open-air men—men whose minds and tastes turned naturally to all that was manly and robust. Hastie, indeed, was stroke of his college boat, and Smith was an even better oar, but a coming examination had already cast its shadow over him and held him to his work, save for the few hours a week which health demanded. A litter of medical books upon the table, with scattered bones, models and anatomical plates, pointed to the extent as well as the nature of his studies, while a couple of single-sticks and a set of boxing-gloves above the mantelpiece hinted at the means by which, with Hastie's help, he might take his exercise in its most compressed and least distant form. They knew each other very well—so well that they could sit now in that soothing silence which is the very highest development of companionship.

"Have some whisky," said Abercrombie Smith at last between two cloudbursts. "Scotch in the jug and Irish in the bottle."

"No, thanks. I'm in for the sculls. I don't liquor when I'm training. How about you?"

"I'm reading hard. I think it best to leave it alone."

Hastie nodded, and they relapsed into a contented silence.

"By-the-way, Smith," asked Hastie, presently, have you made the acquaintance of either of the fellows on your stair yet?"

"Just a nod when we pass. Nothing more."

"Hum! I should be inclined to let it stand at that. I know something of them both. Not much, but as much as I want. I don't think I should take them to my bosom if I were you. Not that there's much amiss with Monkhouse Lee."

"Meaning the thin one?"

"Precisely. He is a gentlemanly little fellow. I don't think there is any vice in him. But then you can't know him without knowing Bellingham."

"Meaning the fat one?"

"Yes, the fat one. And he's a man whom I, for one, would rather not know."

Abercrombie Smith raised his eyebrows and glanced across at his companion.

"What's up, then?" he asked. "Drink? Cards? Cad? You used not to be censorious."

"Ah! you evidently don't know the man, or you wouldn't ask. There's something damnable about him—something reptilian. My gorge always rises at him. I should put him down as a man with secret vices—an evil liver. He's no fool, though. They say that he is one of the best men in his line that they have ever had in the college."

"Medicine or classics?"

"Eastern languages. He's a demon at them. Chillingworth met him somewhere above the second cataract last long, and he told me that he just prattled to the Arabs as if he had been born and nursed and weaned among them. He talked Coptic to the Copts, and Hebrew to the Jews, and Arabic to the Bedouins, and they were all ready to kiss the hem of his frock-coat. There are some old hermit Johnnies up in those parts who sit on rocks and scowl and spit at the casual stranger. Well, when they saw this chap Bellingham, before he had said five words they just lay down on their bellies and wriggled. Chillingworth said that he never saw anything like it. Bellingham seemed to take it as his right, too, and strutted about among them and talked down to them like a Dutch uncle. Pretty good for an undergrad. of Old's, wasn't it?"

"Why do you say you can't know Lee without knowing Bellingham? "

"Because Bellingham is engaged to his sister Eveline. Such a bright little girl, Smith! I know the whole family well. It's disgusting to see that brute with her. A toad and a dove, that's what they always remind me of."

Abercrombie Smith grinned and knocked his ashes out against the side of the grate.

"You show every card in your hand, old chap," said he. "What a prejudiced, green-eyed, evil-thinking old man it is! You have really nothing against the fellow except that."

"Well, I've known her ever since she was as long as that cherry-wood pipe, and I don't like to see her taking risks. And it is a risk. He looks beastly. And he has a beastly temper, a venomous temper. You remember his row with Long Norton?"

"No; you always forget that I am a freshman."

"Ah, it was last winter. Of course. Well, you know the towpath along by the river. There were several fellows going along it, Bellingham in front, when they came on an old market-woman coming the other way. It had been raining—you know what those fields are like when it has rained—and the path ran between the river and a great puddle that was nearly as broad. Well, what does this swine do but keep the path, and push the old girl into the mud, where she and her marketings came to terrible grief. It was a blackguard thing to do, and Long Norton, who is as gentle a fellow as ever stepped, told him what he thought of it. One word led to another, and it ended in Norton laying his stick across the fellow's shoulders. There was the deuce of a fuss about it, and it's a treat to see the way in which Bellingham looks at Norton when they meet now. By Jove, Smith, it's nearly eleven o'clock!"

"No hurry. Light your pipe again."

"Not I. I'm supposed to be in training. Here I've been sitting gossiping when I ought to have been safely tucked up. I'll borrow your skull, if you can share it. Williams has had mine for a month.

I'll take the little bones of your ear, too, if you are sure you won't need them. Thanks very much. Never mind a bag, I can carry them very well under my arm. Good-night, my son, and take my tip as to your neighbour."

When Hastie, bearing his anatomical plunder, had clattered off down the winding stair, Abercrombie Smith hurled his pipe into the wastepaper basket, and drawing his chair nearer to the lamp, plunged into a formidable green-covered volume, adorned with great colored maps of that strange internal kingdom of which we are the hapless and helpless monarchs. Though a freshman at Oxford, the student was not so in medicine, for he had worked for four years at Glasgow and at Berlin, and this coming examination would place him finally as a member of his profession. With his firm mouth, broad forehead, and clear-cut, somewhat hard-featured face, he was a man who, if he had no brilliant talent, was yet so dogged, so patient, and so strong that he might in the end overtop a more showy genius. A man who can hold his own among Scotchmen and North Germans is not a man to be easily set back. Smith had left a name at Glasgow and at Berlin, and he was bent now upon doing as much at Oxford, if hard work and devotion could accomplish it.

He had sat reading for about an hour, and the hands of the noisy carriage clock upon the side table were rapidly closing together upon the twelve, when a sudden sound fell upon the student's ear—a sharp, rather shrill sound, like the hissing intake of a man's breath who gasps under some strong emotion. Smith laid down his book and slanted his ear to listen. There was no one on either side or above him, so that the interruption came certainly from the neighbour beneath—the same neighbour of whom Hastie had given so unsavoury an account. Smith knew him only as a flabby, pale-faced man of silent and studious habits, a man, whose lamp threw a golden bar from the old turret even after he had extinguished his own. This community in lateness had formed a certain silent bond between them. It was soothing to Smith when the hours stole on towards dawning to feel that there was another so close who set as small a value upon his sleep as he did. Even now, as his thoughts turned towards him, Smith's feelings were kindly. Hastie was a good fellow, but he was rough, strong-fibred, with no imagination or sympathy. He could not tolerate departures from what he looked upon as the model type of manliness. If a man could not be measured by a public-school standard, then he was beyond the pale with Hastie. Like so many who are themselves robust, he was apt to confuse the constitution with the character, to ascribe to want of principle what was really a want of circulation. Smith, with his stronger mind, knew his friend's habit, and made allowance for it now as his thoughts turned towards the man beneath him.

There was no return of the singular sound, and Smith was about to turn to his work once more, when suddenly there broke out in the silence of the night a hoarse cry, a positive scream—the call of a man who is moved and shaken beyond all control. Smith sprang out of his chair and dropped his book. He was a man of fairly firm fibre, but there was something in this sudden, uncontrollable shriek of horror which chilled his blood and pringled in his skin. Coming in such a place and at such an hour, it brought a thousand fantastic possibilities into his head. Should he rush down, or was it better to wait? He had all the national hatred of making a scene, and he knew so little of his neighbour that he would not lightly intrude upon his affairs. For a moment he stood in doubt and even as he balanced the matter there was a quick rattle of footsteps upon the stairs, and young Monkhouse Lee, half dressed and as white as ashes, burst into his room.

"Come down!" he gasped. "Bellingham's ill."

Abercrombie Smith followed him closely down stairs into the sitting-room which was beneath his own, and intent as he was upon the matter in hand, he could not but take an amazed glance around him as he crossed the threshold. It was such a chamber as he had never seen before—a museum rather than a study. Walls and ceiling were thickly covered with a thousand strange relics from Egypt and the East. Tall, angular figures bearing burdens or weapons stalked in an uncouth frieze round the apartments. Above were bull-headed, stork-headed, cat-headed, owl-headed statues, with viper-crowned, almond-eyed monarchs, and strange, beetle-like deities cut out of the blue Egyptian lapis lazuli. Horus and Isis and Osiris peeped down from every niche and shelf, while across the ceiling a true son of Old Nile, a great, hanging-jawed crocodile, was slung in a double noose.

In the centre of this singular chamber was a large, square table, littered with papers, bottles, and the dried leaves of some graceful, palm-like plant. These varied objects had all been heaped together in order to make room for a mummy case, which had been conveyed from the wall, as was evident from the gap there, and laid across the front of the table. The mummy itself, a horrid, black, withered thing, like a charred head on a gnarled bush, was lying half out of the case, with its clawlike hand and bony forearm resting upon the table. Propped up against the sarcophagus was an old yellow scroll of papyrus, and in front of it, in a wooden arm-chair, sat the owner of the room, his head thrown back, his widely-opened eyes directed in a horrified stare to the crocodile above him, and his blue, thick lips puffing loudly with every expiration.

"My God! he's dying!" cried Monkhouse Lee distractedly.

He was a slim, handsome young fellow, olive-skinned and dark-eyed, of a Spanish rather than of an English type, with a Celtic intensity of manner which contrasted with the Saxon phlegm of Abercombie Smith.

"Only a faint, I think," said the medical student. "Just give me a hand with him. You take his feet. Now on to the sofa. Can you kick all those little wooden devils off? What a litter it is! Now he will be all right if we undo his collar and give him some water. What has he been up to at all?"

"I don't know. I heard him cry out. I ran up. I know him pretty well, you know. It is very good of you to come down."

"His heart is going like a pair of castanets," said Smith, laying his hand on the breast of the unconscious man. "He seems to me to be frightened all to pieces. Chuck the water over him! What a face he has got on him!"

It was indeed a strange and most repellent face, for colour and outline were equally unnatural. It was white, not with the ordinary pallor of fear but with an absolutely bloodless white, like the under side of a sole. He was very fat, but gave the impression of having at some time been considerably fatter, for his skin hung loosely in creases and folds, and was shot with a meshwork of wrinkles. Short, stubbly brown hair bristled up from his scalp, with a pair of thick, wrinkled ears protruding on either side. His light grey eyes were still open, the pupils dilated and the balls projecting in a fixed and horrid stare. It seemed to Smith as he looked down upon him that he had never seen nature's danger signals flying so plainly upon a man's countenance, and his thoughts turned more seriously to the warning which Hastie had given him an hour before.

"What the deuce can have frightened him so?" he asked.

"It's the mummy."

"The mummy? How, then?"

"I don't know. It's beastly and morbid. I wish he would drop it. It's the second fright he has given me. It was the same last winter. I found him just like this, with that horrid thing in front of him."

"What does he want with the mummy, then?"

"Oh, he's a crank, you know. It's his hobby. He knows more about these things than any man in England. But I wish he wouldn't! Ah, he's beginning to come to."

A faint tinge of colour had begun to steal back into Bellingham's ghastly cheeks, and his eyelids shivered like a sail after a calm. He clasped and unclasped his hands, drew a long, thin breath between his teeth, and suddenly jerking up his head, threw a glance of recognition around him. As his eyes fell upon the mummy, he sprang off the sofa, seized the roll of papyrus, thrust it into a drawer, turned the key, and then staggered back on to the sofa.

"What's up?" he asked. "What do you chaps want?"

"You've been shrieking out and making no end of a fuss," said Monkhouse Lee. "If our neighbour here from above hadn't come down, I'm sure I don't know what I should have done with you."

"Ah, it's Abercrombie Smith," said Bellingham, glancing up at him. "How very good of you to come in! What a fool I am! Oh, my God, what a fool I am!"

He sunk his head on to his hands, and burst into peal after peal of hysterical laughter.

"Look here! Drop it!" cried Smith, shaking him roughly by the shoulder.

"Your nerves are all in a jangle. You must drop these little midnight games with mummies, or you'll be going off your chump. You're all on wires now."

"I wonder," said Bellingham, "whether you would be as cool as I am if you had seen——"

"What then?"

"Oh, nothing. I meant that I wonder if you could sit up at night with a mummy without trying your nerves. I have no doubt that you are quite right. I dare say that I have been taking it out of myself too much lately. But I am all right now. Please don't go, though. Just wait for a few minutes until I am quite myself."

"The room is very close," remarked Lee, throwing open the window and letting in the cool night air.

"It's balsamic resin," said Bellingham. He lifted up one of the dried palmate leaves from the table and frizzled it over the chimney of the lamp. It broke away into heavy smoke wreaths, and a pungent, biting odour filled the chamber. "It's the sacred plant— the plant of the priests," he remarked. "Do you know anything of Eastern languages, Smith?"

"Nothing at all. Not a word."

The answer seemed to lift a weight from the Egyptologist's mind.

"By-the-way," he continued, "how long was it from the time that you ran down, until I came to my senses?"

"Not long. Some four or five minutes."

"I thought it could not be very long," said he, drawing a long breath. "But what a strange thing unconsciousness is! There is no measurement to it. I could not tell from my own sensations if it were seconds or weeks. Now that gentleman on the table was packed up in the days of the eleventh dynasty, some forty centuries ago, and yet if he could find his tongue he would tell us that this lapse of time has been but a closing of the eyes and a reopening of them. He is a singularly fine mummy, Smith."

Smith stepped over to the table and looked down with a professional eye at the black and twisted form in front of him. The features, though horribly discoloured, were perfect, and two little nut-like eyes still lurked in the depths of the black, hollow sockets. The blotched skin was drawn tightly from bone to bone, and a tangled wrap of black coarse hair fell over the ears. Two thin teeth, like those of a rat, overlay the shrivelled lower lip. In its crouching position, with bent joints and craned head, there was a suggestion of energy about the horrid thing which made Smith's gorge rise. The gaunt ribs, with their parchment-like covering, were exposed, and the sunken, leaden-hued abdomen, with the long slit where the embalmer had left his mark; but the lower limbs were wrapt round with coarse yellow bandages. A number of little clove-like pieces of myrrh and of cassia were sprinkled over the body, and lay scattered on the inside of the case.

"I don't know his name," said Bellingham, passing his hand over the shrivelled head. "You see the outer sarcophagus with the inscriptions is missing. Lot 249 is all the title he has now. You see it printed on his case. That was his number in the auction at which I picked him up."

"He has been a very pretty sort of fellow in his day," remarked Abercrombie Smith.

"He has been a giant. His mummy is six feet seven in length, and that would be a giant over there, for they were never a very robust race. Feel these great knotted bones, too. He would be a nasty fellow to tackle."

"Perhaps these very hands helped to build the stones into the pyramids," suggested Monkhouse Lee, looking down with disgust in his eyes at the crooked, unclean talons.

"No fear. This fellow has been pickled in natron, and looked after in the most approved style. They did not serve hodsmen in that fashion. Salt or bitumen was enough for them. It has been calculated that this sort of thing cost about seven hundred and thirty pounds in our money. Our friend was a noble at the least. What do you make of that small inscription near his feet, Smith?"

"I told you that I know no Eastern tongue."

"Ah, so you did. It is the name of the embalmer, I take it. A very conscientious worker he must have been. I wonder how many modern works will survive four thousand years?"

He kept on speaking lightly and rapidly, but it was evident to Abercrombie Smith that he was still palpitating with fear. His hands shook, his lower lip trembled, and look where he would, his eye always came sliding round to his gruesome companion. Through all his fear, however, there was a suspicion of triumph in his tone and manner. His eye shone, and his footstep, as he paced the room, was brisk and jaunty. He gave the impression of a man who has gone through an ordeal, the marks of which he still bears upon him, but which has helped him to his end.

"You're not going yet?" he cried, as Smith rose from the sofa.

At the prospect of solitude, his fears seemed to crowd back upon him, and he stretched out a hand to detain him.

"Yes, I must go. I have my work to do. You are all right now. I think that with your nervous system you should take up some less morbid study."

"Oh, I am not nervous as a rule; and I have unwrapped mummies before."

"You fainted last time," observed Monkhouse Lee.

"Ah, yes, so I did. Well, I must have a nerve tonic or a course of electricity. You are not going, Lee?"

"I'll do whatever you wish, Ned."

"Then I'll come down with you and have a shake-down on your sofa. Good-night, Smith. I am so sorry to have disturbed you with my foolishness."

They shook hands, and as the medical student stumbled up the spiral and irregular stair he heard a key turn in a door, and the steps of his two new acquaintances as they descended to the lower floor.

In this strange way began the acquaintance between Edward Bellingham and Abercrombie Smith, an acquaintance which the latter, at least, had no desire to push further. Bellingham, however, appeared to have taken a fancy to his rough-spoken neighbour, and made his advances in such a way that he could hardly be repulsed without absolute brutality. Twice he called to thank Smith for his assistance, and many times afterwards he looked in with books, papers, and such other civilities as two bachelor neighbours can offer each other. He was, as Smith soon found, a man of wide reading, with catholic tastes and an extraordinary memory. His manner, too, was so pleasing and suave that one came, after a time, to overlook his repellent appearance. For a jaded and wearied man he was no unpleasant companion, and Smith found himself, after a time, looking forward to his visits, and even returning them.

Clever as he undoubtedly was, however, the medical student seemed to detect a dash of insanity in the man. He broke out at times into a high, inflated style of talk which was in contrast with the simplicity of his life.

"It is a wonderful thing," he cried, "to feel that one can command powers of good and of evil—a ministering angel or a demon of vengeance." And again, of Monkhouse Lee, he said,— "Lee is a good fellow, an honest fellow, but he is without strength or ambition. He would not make a fit partner for a man with a great enterprise. He would not make a fit partner for me."

At such hints and innuendoes stolid Smith, puffing solemnly at his pipe, would simply raise his eyebrows and shake his head, with little interjections of medical wisdom as to earlier hours and fresher air.

One habit Bellingham had developed of late which Smith knew to be a frequent herald of a weakening mind. He appeared to be forever talking to himself. At late hours of the night, when there could be no visitor with him, Smith could still hear his voice beneath him in a low, muffled monologue, sunk almost to a whisper, and yet very audible in the silence. This solitary babbling annoyed and distracted the student, so that he spoke more than once to his neighbour about it. Bellingham, however, flushed up at the charge, and denied curtly that he had uttered a sound; indeed, he showed more annoyance over the matter than the occasion seemed to demand.

Had Abercrombie Smith had any doubt as to his own ears he had not to go far to find corroboration. Tom Styles, the little wrinkled man-servant who had attended to the wants of the lodgers in the turret for a longer time than any man's memory could carry him, was sorely put to it over the same matter.

"If you please, sir," said he, as he tidied down the top chamber one morning, "do you think Mr. Bellingham is all right, sir?"

"All right, Styles?"

"Yes sir. Right in his head, sir."

"Why should he not be, then?"

"Well, I don't know, sir. His habits has changed of late. He's not the same man he used to be, though I make free to say that he was never quite one of my gentlemen, like Mr. Hastie or yourself, sir. He's took to talkin' to himself something awful. I wonder it don't disturb you. I don't know what to make of him, sir."

"I don't know what business it is of yours, Styles."

"Well, I takes an interest, Mr. Smith. It may be forward of me, but I can't help it. I feel sometimes as if I was mother and father to my young gentlemen. It all falls on me when things go wrong and the relations come. But Mr. Bellingham, sir. I want to know what it is that walks about his room sometimes when he's out and when the door's locked on the outside."

"Eh! you're talking nonsense, Styles."

"Maybe so, sir; but I heard it more'n once with my own ears."

"Rubbish, Styles."

"Very good, sir. You'll ring the bell if you want me."

Abercrombie Smith gave little heed to the gossip of the old man-servant, but a small incident occurred a few days later which left an unpleasant effect upon his mind, and brought the words of Styles forcibly to his memory.

Bellingham had come up to see him late one night, and was entertaining him with an interesting account of the rock tombs of Beni Hassan in Upper Egypt, when Smith, whose hearing was remarkably acute, distinctly heard the sound of a door opening on the landing below.

"There's some fellow gone in or out of your room," he remarked.

Bellingham sprang up and stood helpless for a moment, with the expression of a man who is half incredulous and half afraid.

"I surely locked it. I am almost positive that I locked it," he stammered. "No one could have opened it."

"Why, I hear someone coming up the steps now," said Smith.

Bellingham rushed out through the door, slammed it loudly behind him, and hurried down the stairs. About half-way down Smith heard him stop, and thought he caught the sound of whispering. A moment later the door beneath him shut, a key creaked in a lock, and Bellingham, with beads of moisture upon his pale face, ascended the stairs once more, and re-entered the room.

"It's all right," he said, throwing himself down in a chair. "It was that fool of a dog. He had pushed the door open. I don't know how I came to forget to lock it."

"I didn't know you kept a dog," said Smith, looking very thoughtfully at the disturbed face of his companion.

"Yes, I haven't had him long. I must get rid of him. He's a great nuisance."

"He must be, if you find it so hard to shut him up. I should have thought that shutting the door would have been enough, without locking it."

"I want to prevent old Styles from letting him out. He's of some value, you know, and it would be awkward to lose him."

"I am a bit of a dog-fancier myself," said Smith, still gazing hard at his companion from the corner of his eyes. "Perhaps you'll let me have a look at it."

"Certainly. But I am afraid it cannot be to-night; I have an appointment. Is that clock right? Then I am a quarter of an hour late already. You'll excuse me, I am sure."

He picked up his cap and hurried from the room. In spite of his appointment, Smith heard him re-enter his own chamber and lock his door upon the inside.

This interview left a disagreeable impression upon the medical student's mind. Bellingham had lied to him, and lied so clumsily that it looked as if he had desperate reasons for concealing the truth. Smith knew that his neighbour had no dog. He knew, also, that the step which he had heard upon the stairs was not the step of an animal. But if it were not, then what could it be? There was old Styles's statement about the something which used to pace the room at times when the owner was absent. Could it be a woman? Smith rather inclined to the view. If so, it would mean disgrace and expulsion to Bellingham if it were discovered by the authorities, so that his anxiety and falsehoods might be accounted for. And yet it was inconceivable that an undergraduate could keep a woman in his rooms without being instantly detected. Be the explanation what it might, there was something ugly about it, and Smith determined, as he turned to his books, to discourage all further attempts at intimacy on the part of his soft-spoken and ill-favoured neighbour.

But his work was destined to interruption that night. He had hardly caught tip the broken threads when a firm, heavy footfall came three steps at a time from below, and Hastie, in blazer and flannels, burst into the room.

"Still at it!" said he, plumping down into his wonted armchair. "What a chap you are to stew! I believe an earthquake might come and knock Oxford into a cocked hat, and you would sit perfectly placid with your books among the ruins. However, I won't bore you long. Three whiffs of baccy, and I am off."

"What's the news, then?" asked Smith, cramming a plug of bird's-eye into his briar with his forefinger.

"Nothing very much. Wilson made 70 for the freshmen against the eleven. They say that they will play him instead of Buddicomb, for Buddicomb is clean off colour. He used to be able to bowl a little, but it's nothing but half-vollies and long hops now."

"Medium right," suggested Smith, with the intense gravity which comes upon a 'varsity man when he speaks of athletics.

"Inclining to fast, with a work from leg. Comes with the arm about three inches or so. He used to be nasty on a wet wicket. Oh, by-the-way, have you heard about Long Norton?"

"What's that?"

"He's been attacked."

"Attacked?"

"Yes, just as he was turning out of the High Street, and within a hundred yards of the gate of Old's."

"But who——"

"Ah, that's the rub! If you said 'what,' you would be more grammatical. Norton swears that it was not human, and, indeed, from the scratches on his throat, I should be inclined to agree with him."

"What, then? Have we come down to spooks?"

Abercrombie Smith puffed his scientific contempt.

"Well, no; I don't think that is quite the idea, either. I am inclined to think that if any showman has lost a great ape lately, and the brute is in these parts, a jury would find a true bill against it. Norton passes that way every night, you know, about the same hour. There's a tree that hangs low over the path—the big elm from Rainy's garden. Norton thinks the thing dropped on him out of the tree. Anyhow, he was nearly strangled by two arms, which, he says, were as strong and as thin as steel bands. He saw nothing; only those beastly arms that tightened and tightened on him. He yelled his head nearly off, and a couple of chaps came running, and the thing went over the wall like a cat. He never got a fair sight of it the whole time. It gave Norton a shake up, I can tell you. I tell him it has been as good as a change at the sea-side for him."

"A garrotter, most likely," said Smith.

"Very possibly. Norton says not; but we don't mind what he says. The garrotter had long nails, and was pretty smart at swinging himself over walls. By-the-way, your beautiful neighbour would be pleased if he heard about it. He had a grudge against Norton, and he's not a man, from what I know of him, to forget his little debts. But hallo, old chap, what have you got in your noddle?"

"Nothing," Smith answered curtly.

He had started in his chair, and the look had flashed over his face which comes upon a man who is struck suddenly by some unpleasant idea.

"You looked as if something I had said had taken you on the raw. By-the-way, you have made the acquaintance of Master B. since I looked in last, have you not? Young Monkhouse Lee told me something to that effect."

"Yes; I know him slightly. He has been up here once or twice."

"Well, you're big enough and ugly enough to take care of yourself. He's not what I should call exactly a healthy sort of Johnny, though, no doubt, he's very clever, and all that. But you'll soon find out for yourself. Lee is all right; he's a very decent little fellow. Well, so long, old chap! I row Mullins for the Vice-Chancellor's pot on Wednesday week, so mind you come down, in case I don't see you before."

Bovine Smith laid down his pipe and turned stolidly to his books once more. But with all the will in the world, he found it very hard to keep his mind upon his work. It would slip away to brood upon the man beneath him, and upon the little mystery which hung round his chambers. Then his thoughts turned to this singular attack of which Hastie had spoken, and to the grudge which Bellingham was said to owe the object of it. The two ideas would persist in rising together in his mind, as though there were some close and intimate connection between them. And yet the suspicion was so dim and vague that it could not be put down in words.

"Confound the chap!" cried Smith, as he shied his book on pathology across the room. "He has spoiled my night's reading, and that's reason enough, if there were no other, why I should steer clear of him in the future."

For ten days the medical student confined himself so closely to his studies that he neither saw nor heard anything of either of the men beneath him. At the hours when Bellingham had been accustomed to visit him, he took care to sport his oak, and though he more than once heard a knocking at his outer door, he resolutely refused to answer it. One afternoon, however, he was descending the stairs when, just as he was passing it, Bellingham's door flew open, and young Monkhouse Lee came out with his eyes sparkling and a dark flush of anger upon his olive cheeks. Close at his heels followed Bellingham, his fat, unhealthy face all quivering with malignant passion.

"You fool!" he hissed. "You'll be sorry."

"Very likely," cried the other. "Mind what I say. It's off! I won't hear of it!"

"You've promised, anyhow."

"Oh, I'll keep that! I won't speak. But I'd rather little Eva was in her grave. Once for all, it's off. She'll do what I say. We don't want to see you again."

So much Smith could not avoid hearing, but he hurried on, for he had no wish to be involved in their dispute. There had been a serious breach between them, that was clear enough, and Lee was going to cause the engagement with his sister to be broken off. Smith thought of Hastie's comparison of the toad and the dove, and was glad to think that the matter was at an end. Bellingham's face when he was in a passion was not pleasant to look upon. He was not a man to whom an innocent girl could be trusted for life. As he walked, Smith wondered languidly what could have caused the quarrel, and what the promise might be which Bellingham had been so anxious that Monkhouse Lee should keep.

It was the day of the sculling match between Hastie and Mullins, and a stream of men were making their way down to the banks of the Isis. A May sun was shining brightly, and the yellow path was barred with the black shadows of the tall elm-trees. On either side the grey colleges lay back from the road, the hoary old mothers of minds looking out from their high, mullioned windows at the tide of young life which swept so merrily past them. Black-clad tutors, prim officials, pale reading men, brown-faced, straw-hatted young athletes in white sweaters or many-coloured blazers, all were hurrying towards the blue winding river which curves through the Oxford meadows.

Abercrombie Smith, with the intuition of an old oarsman, chose his position at the point where he knew that the struggle, if there were a struggle, would come. Far off he heard the hum which announced the start, the gathering roar of the approach, the thunder of running feet, and the shouts of the men in the boats beneath him. A spray of half-clad, deep-breathing runners shot past him, and craning over their shoulders, he saw Hastie pulling a steady thirty-six, while his opponent, with a jerky forty, was a good boat's length behind him. Smith gave a cheer for his friend, and pulling out his watch, was starting off again for his chambers, when he felt a touch upon his shoulder, and found that young Monkhouse Lee was beside him.

"I saw you there," he said, in a timid, deprecating way. "I wanted to speak to you, if you could spare me a half-hour. This cottage is mine. I share it with Harrington of King's. Come in and have a cup of tea."

"I must be back presently," said Smith. "I am hard on the grind at present. But I'll come in for a few minutes with pleasure. I wouldn't have come out only Hastie is a friend of mine."

"So he is of mine. Hasn't he a beautiful style? Mullins wasn't in it. But come into the cottage. It's a little den of a place, but it is pleasant to work in during the summer months."

It was a small, square, white building, with green doors and shutters, and a rustic trellis-work porch, standing back some fifty yards from the river's bank. Inside, the main room was roughly fitted up as a study—deal table, unpainted shelves with books, and a few cheap oleographs upon the wall. A kettle sang upon a spirit-stove, and there were tea things upon a tray on the table.

"Try that chair and have a cigarette," said Lee. "Let me pour you out a cup of tea. It's so good of you to come in, for I know that your time is a good deal taken up. I wanted to say to you that, if I were you, I should change my rooms at once."

"Eh?"

Smith sat staring with a lighted match in one hand and his unlit cigarette in the other.

"Yes; it must seem very extraordinary, and the worst of it is that I cannot give my reasons, for I am under a solemn promise—a very solemn promise. But I may go so far as to say that I don't think Bellingham is a very safe man to live near. I intend to camp out here as much as I can for a time."

"Not safe! What do you mean?"

"Ah, that's what I mustn't say. But do take my advice, and move your rooms. We had a grand row to-day. You must have heard us, for you came down the stairs."

"I saw that you had fallen out."

"He's a horrible chap, Smith. That is the only word for him. I have had doubts about him ever since that night when he fainted—you remember, when you came down. I taxed him to-day, and he told me things that made my hair rise, and wanted me to stand in with him. I'm not strait-laced, but I am a clergyman's son, you know, and I think there are some things which are quite beyond the pale. I only thank God that I found him out before it was too late, for he was to have married into my family."

"This is all very fine, Lee," said Abercrombie Smith curtly. "But either you are saying a great deal too much or a great deal too little."

"I give you a warning."

"If there is real reason for warning, no promise can bind you. If I see a rascal about to blow a place up with dynamite no pledge will stand in my way of preventing him."

"Ah, but I cannot prevent him, and I can do nothing but warn you."

"Without saying what you warn me against."

"Against Bellingham."

"But that is childish. Why should I fear him, or any man?"

"I can't tell you. I can only entreat you to change your rooms. You are in danger where you are. I don't even say that Bellingham would wish to injure you. But it might happen, for he is a dangerous neighbour just now."

"Perhaps I know more than you think," said Smith, looking keenly at the young man's boyish, earnest face. "Suppose I tell you that some one else shares Bellingham's rooms."

Monkhouse Lee sprang from his chair in uncontrollable excitement.

"You know, then?" he gasped.

"A woman."

Lee dropped back again with a groan.

"My lips are sealed," he said. "I must not speak."

"Well, anyhow," said Smith, rising, "it is not likely that I should allow myself to be frightened out of rooms which suit me very nicely. It would be a little too feeble for me to move out all my goods and chattels because you say that Bellingham might in some unexplained way do me an injury. I think that I'll just take my chance, and stay where I am, and as I see that it's nearly five o'clock, I must ask you to excuse me."

He bade the young student adieu in a few curt words, and made his way homeward through the sweet spring evening feeling half-ruffled, half-amused, as any other strong, unimaginative man might who has been menaced by a vague and shadowy danger.

There was one little indulgence which Abercrombie Smith always allowed himself, however closely his work might press upon him. Twice a week, on the Tuesday and the Friday, it was his invariable custom to walk over to Farlingford, the residence of Dr. Plumptree Peterson, situated about a mile and a half out of Oxford. Peterson had been a close friend of Smith's elder brother Francis, and as he was a bachelor, fairly well-to-do, with a good cellar and a better library, his house was a pleasant goal for a man who was in need of a brisk walk. Twice a week, then, the medical student would swing out there along the dark country roads, and spend a pleasant hour in Peterson's comfortable study, discussing, over a glass of old port, the gossip of the 'varsity or the latest developments of medicine or of surgery.

On the day which followed his interview with Monkhouse Lee, Smith shut up his books at a quarter past eight, the hour when he usually started for his friend's house. As he was leaving his room, however, his eyes chanced to fall upon one of the books which Bellingham had lent him, and his conscience pricked him for not having returned it. However repellent the man might be, he should not be treated with discourtesy. Taking the book, he walked downstairs and knocked at his neighbour's door. There was no answer; but on turning the handle he found that it was unlocked. Pleased at the thought of avoiding an interview, he stepped inside, and placed the book with his card upon the table.

The lamp was turned half down, but Smith could see the details of the room plainly enough. It was all much as he had seen it before—the frieze, the animal-headed gods, the banging crocodile, and the table littered over with papers and dried leaves. The mummy case stood upright against the wall, but the mummy itself was missing. There was no sign of any second occupant of the room, and he felt as he withdrew that he had probably done Bellingham an injustice. Had he a guilty secret to preserve, he would hardly leave his door open so that all the world might enter.

The spiral stair was as black as pitch, and Smith was slowly making his way down its irregular steps, when he was suddenly conscious that something had passed him in the darkness. There was a faint sound, a whiff of air, a light brushing past his elbow, but so slight that he could scarcely be certain of it. He stopped and listened, but the wind was rustling among the ivy outside, and he could hear nothing else.

"Is that you, Styles?" he shouted.

There was no answer, and all was still behind him. It must have been a sudden gust of air, for there were crannies and cracks in the old turret. And yet he could almost have sworn that be heard a footfall by his very side. He had emerged into the quadrangle, still turning the matter over in his head, when a man came running swiftly across the smooth-cropped lawn.

"Is that you, Smith?"

"Hullo, Hastie!"

"For God's sake come at once! Young Lee is drowned! Here's Harrington of King's with the news. The doctor is out. You'll do, but come along at once. There may be life in him."

"Have you brandy?"

"No. "

"I'll bring some. There's a flask on my table."

Smith bounded up the stairs, taking three at a time, seized the flask, and was rushing down with it, when, as he passed Bellingham's room, his eyes fell upon something which left him gasping and staring upon the landing.

The door, which he had closed behind him, was now open, and right in front of him, with the lamp-light shining upon it, was the mummy case. Three minutes ago it had been empty. He could swear to that. Now it framed the lank body of its horrible occupant, who stood, grim and stark, with his black shrivelled face towards the door. The form was lifeless and inert, but it seemed to Smith as he gazed that there still lingered a lurid spark of vitality, some faint sign of consciousness in the little eyes which lurked in the depths of the hollow sockets. So astounded and shaken was he that he had forgotten his errand, and was still staring at the lean, sunken figure when the voice of his friend below recalled him to himself.

"Come on, Smith!" he shouted. "It's life and death, you know. Hurry up! Now, then," he added, as the medical student reappeared, "let us do a sprint. It is well under a mile, and we should do it in five minutes. A human life is better worth running for than a pot."

Neck and neck they dashed through the darkness, and did not pull up until, panting and spent, they had reached the little cottage by the river. Young Lee, limp and dripping like a broken water-plant, was stretched upon the sofa, the green scum of the river upon his black hair, and a fringe of white foam upon his leaden-hued lips. Beside him knelt his fellow-student Harrington, endeavouring to chafe some warmth back into his rigid limbs.

"I think there's life in him," said Smith, with his hand to the lad's side. "Put your watch glass to his lips. Yes, there's dimming on it. You take one arm, Hastie. Now work it as I do, and we'll soon pull him round."

For ten minutes they worked in silence, inflating and depressing the chest of the unconscious man. At the end of that time a shiver ran through his body, his lips trembled, and he opened his eyes. The three students burst out into an irrepressible cheer.

"Wake up, old chap. You've frightened us quite enough."

"Have some brandy. Take a sip from the flask."

"He's all right now," said his companion Harrington. "Heavens, what a fright I got! I was reading here, and he had gone for a stroll as far as the river, when I heard a scream and a splash. Out I ran, and by the time that I could find him and fish him out, all life seemed to have gone. Then Simpson couldn't get a doctor, for he has a game-leg, and I had to run, and I don't know what I'd have done without you fellows. That's right, old chap. Sit up."

Monkhouse Lee had raised himself on his hands, and looked wildly about him.

"What's up?" he asked. "I've been in the water. Ah, yes; I remember."

A look of fear came into his eyes, and he sank his face into his hands.

"How did you fall in?"

"I didn't fall in."

"How, then?"

"I was thrown in. I was standing by the bank, and something from behind picked me up like a feather and hurled me in. I heard nothing, and I saw nothing. But I know what it was, for all that."

"And so do I, " whispered Smith.

Lee looked up with a quick glance of surprise. "You've learned, then!" he said. "You remember the advice I gave you?"

"Yes, and I begin to think that I shall take it."

"I don't know what the deuce you fellows are talking about," said Hastie, "but I think, if I were you, Harrington, I should get Lee to bed at once. It will be time enough to discuss the why and the wherefore when he is a little stronger. I think, Smith, you and I can leave him alone now. I am walking back to college; if you are coming in that direction, we can have a chat."

But it was little chat that they had upon their homeward path. Smith's mind was too full of the incidents of the evening, the absence of the mummy from his neighbour's rooms, the step that passed him on the stair, the reappearance—the extraordinary, inexplicable reappearance of the grisly thing—and then this attack upon Lee, corresponding so closely to the previous outrage upon another man against whom Bellingham bore a grudge. All this settled in his thoughts, together with the many little incidents which had previously turned him against his neighbour, and the singular circumstances under which he was first called in to him. What had been a dim suspicion, a vague, fantastic conjecture, had suddenly taken form, and stood out in his mind as a grim fact, a thing not to be denied. And yet, how monstrous it was! how unheard of! how entirely beyond all bounds of human experience. An impartial judge, or even the friend who walked by his side, would simply tell him that his eyes had deceived him, that the mummy had been there all the time, that young Lee had tumbled into the river as any other man tumbles into a river, and that a blue pill was the best thing for a disordered liver. He felt that he would have said as much if the positions had been reversed. And yet he could swear that Bellingham was a murderer at heart, and that he wielded a weapon such as no man had ever used in all the grim history of crime.

Hastie had branched off to his rooms with a few crisp and emphatic comments upon his friend's unsociability, and Abercrombie Smith crossed the quadrangle to his corner turret with a strong feeling of repulsion for his chambers and their associations. He would take Lee's advice, and move his quarters as soon as possible, for how could a man study when his ear was ever straining for every murmur or footstep in the room below? He observed, as he crossed over the lawn, that the light was still shining in Bellingham's window, and as he passed up the staircase the door opened, and the man himself looked out at him. With his fat, evil face he was like some bloated spider fresh from the weaving of his poisonous web.

"Good-evening," said he. "Won't you come in?"

"No," cried Smith, fiercely.

"No? You are busy as ever? I wanted to ask you about Lee. I was sorry to hear that there was a rumour that something was amiss with him."

His features were grave, but there was the gleam of a hidden laugh in his eyes as he spoke. Smith saw it, and he could have knocked him down for it.

"You'll be sorrier still to hear that Monkhouse Lee is doing very well, and is out of all danger," he answered. "Your hellish tricks have not come off this time. Oh, you needn't try to brazen it out. I know all about it."

Bellingham took a step back from the angry student, and half-closed the door as if to protect himself.

"You are mad," he said. "What do you mean? Do you assert that I had anything to do with Lee's accident?"

"Yes," thundered Smith. "You and that bag of bones behind you; you worked it between you. I tell you what it is, Master B., they have given up burning folk like you, but we still keep a hangman, and, by George! if any man in this college meets his death while you are here, I'll have you up, and if you don't swing for it, it won't be my fault. You'll find that your filthy Egyptian tricks won't answer in England."

"You're a raving lunatic," said Bellingham.

"All right. You just remember what I say, for you'll find that I'll be better than my word."

The door slammed, and Smith went fuming up to his chamber, where he locked the door upon the inside, and spent half the night in smoking his old briar and brooding over the strange events of the evening.

Next morning Abercrombie Smith heard nothing of his neighbour, but Harrington called upon him in the afternoon to say that Lee was almost himself again. All day Smith stuck fast to his work, but in the evening he determined to pay the visit to his friend Dr. Peterson upon which he had started upon the night before. A good walk and a friendly chat would be welcome to his jangled nerves.

Bellingham's door was shut as he passed, but glancing back when he was some distance from the turret, he saw his neighbour's head at the window outlined against the lamp-light, his face pressed apparently against the glass as he gazed out into the darkness. It was a blessing to be away from all contact with him, but if for a few hours, and Smith stepped out briskly, and breathed the soft spring air into his lungs. The half-moon lay in the west between two Gothic pinnacles, and threw upon the silvered street a dark tracery from the stone-work above. There was a brisk breeze, and light, fleecy clouds drifted swiftly across the sky. Old's was on the very border of the town, and in five minutes Smith found himself beyond the houses and between the hedges of a May-scented Oxfordshire lane.

It was a lonely and little frequented road which led to his friend's house. Early as it was, Smith did not meet a single soul upon his way. He walked briskly along until he came to the avenue gate, which opened into the long gravel drive leading up to Farlingford. In front of him he could see the cosy red light of the windows glimmering through the foliage. He stood with his hand upon the iron latch of the swinging gate, and he glanced back at the road along which he had come. Something was coming swiftly down it.

It moved in the shadow of the hedge, silently and furtively, a dark, crouching figure, dimly visible against the black background. Even as he gazed back at it, it had lessened its distance by twenty paces, and was fast closing upon him. Out of the darkness he had a glimpse of a scraggy neck, and of two eyes that will ever haunt him in his dreams. He turned, and with a cry of terror he ran for his life up the avenue. There were the red lights, the signals of safety, almost within a stone's throw of him. He was a famous runner, but never had he run as he ran that night.

The heavy gate had swung into place behind him, but he heard it dash open again before his pursuer. As he rushed madly and wildly through the night, he could hear a swift, dry patter behind him, and could see, as he threw back a glance, that this horror was bounding like a tiger at his heels, with blazing eyes and one stringy arm outthrown. Thank God, the door was ajar. He could see the thin bar of light which shot from the lamp in the hall. Nearer yet sounded the clatter from behind. He heard a hoarse gurgling at his very shoulder. With a shriek he flung himself against the door, slammed and bolted it behind him, and sank half-fainting on to the hall chair.

"My goodness, Smith, what's the matter?" asked Peterson, appearing at the door of his study.

"Give me some brandy!"

Peterson disappeared, and came rushing out again with a glass and a decanter.

"You need it," he said, as his visitor drank off what he poured out for him. "Why, man, you are as white as a cheese."

Smith laid down his glass, rose up, and took a deep breath.

"I am my own man again now," said he. "I was never so unmanned before. But, with your leave, Peterson, I will sleep here to-night, for I don't think I could face that road again except by daylight. It's weak, I know, but I can't help it."

Peterson looked at his visitor with a very questioning eye.

"Of course you shall sleep here if you wish. I'll tell Mrs. Burney to make up the spare bed. Where are you off to now?"

"Come up with me to the window that overlooks the door. I want you to see what I have seen."

They went up to the window of the upper hall whence they could look down upon the approach to the house. The drive and the fields on either side lay quiet and still, bathed in the peaceful moonlight.

"Well, really, Smith," remarked Peterson, "it is well that I know you to be an abstemious man. What in the world can have frightened you?"

"I'll tell you presently. But where can it have gone? Ah, now look, look! See the curve of the road just beyond your gate."

"Yes, I see; you needn't pinch my arm off. I saw someone pass. I should say a man, rather thin, apparently, and tall, very tall. But what of him? And what of yourself? You are still shaking like an aspen leaf."

"I have been within hand-grip of the devil, that's all. But come down to your study, and I shall tell you the whole story."

He did so. Under the cheery lamplight, with a glass of wine on the table beside him, and the portly form and florid face of his friend in front, he narrated, in their order, all the events, great and small, which had formed so singular a chain, from the night on which he had found Bellingham fainting in front of the mummy case until his horrid experience of an hour ago.

"There now," he said as he concluded, "that's the whole black business. It is monstrous and incredible, but it is true."

Dr. Plumptree Peterson sat for some time in silence with a very puzzled expression upon his face.

"I never heard of such a thing in my life, never!" he said at last. "You have told me the facts. Now tell me your inferences."

"You can draw your own."

"But I should like to hear yours. You have thought over the matter, and I have not."

"Well, it must be a little vague in detail, but the main points seem to me to be clear enough. This fellow Bellingham, in his Eastern studies, has got hold of some infernal secret by which a mummy—or possibly only this particular mummy—can be temporarily brought to life. He was trying this disgusting business on the night when he fainted. No doubt the sight of the creature moving had shaken his nerve, even though he had expected it. You remember that almost the first words he said were to call out upon himself as a fool. Well, he got more hardened afterwards, and carried the matter through without fainting. The vitality which he could put into it was evidently only a passing thing, for I have seen it continually in its case as dead as this table. He has some elaborate process, I fancy, by which he brings the thing to pass. Having done it, he naturally bethought him that he might use the creature as an agent. It has intelligence and it has strength. For some purpose he took Lee into his confidence; but Lee, like a decent Christian, would have nothing to do with such a business. Then they had a row, and Lee vowed that he would tell his sister of Bellingham's true character. Bellingham's game was to prevent him, and he nearly managed it, by setting this creature of his on his track. He had already tried its powers upon another man—Norton—towards whom he had a grudge. It is the merest chance that he has not two murders upon his soul. Then, when I taxed him with the matter, he had the strongest reasons for wishing to get me out of the way before I could convey my knowledge to anyone else. He got his chance when I went out, for he knew my habits, and where I was bound for. I have had a narrow shave, Peterson, and it is mere luck you didn't find me on your doorstep in the morning. I'm not a nervous man as a rule, and I never thought to have the fear of death put upon me as it was to-night."

"My dear boy, you take the matter too seriously," said his companion. "Your nerves are out of order with your work, and you make too much of it. How could such a thing as this stride about the streets of Oxford, even at night, without being seen?"

"It has been seen. There is quite a scare in the town about an escaped ape, as they imagine the creature to be. It is the talk of the place."

"Well, it's a striking chain of events. And yet, my dear fellow, you must allow that each incident in itself is capable of a more natural explanation."

"What! even my adventure of to-night?"

"Certainly. You come out with your nerves all unstrung, and your head full of this theory of yours. Some gaunt, half-famished tramp steals after you, and seeing you run, is emboldened to pursue you. Your fears and imagination do the rest."

"It won't do, Peterson; it won't do."

"And again, in the instance of your finding the mummy case empty, and then a few moments later with an occupant, you know that it was lamplight, that the lamp was half turned down, and that you had no special reason to look hard at the case. It is quite possible that you may have overlooked the creature in the first instance."

"No, no; it is out of the question."

"And then Lee may have fallen into the river, and Norton been garrotted. It is certainly a formidable indictment that you have against Bellingham; but if you were to place it before a police magistrate, he would simply laugh in your face."

"I know he would. That is why I mean to take the matter into my own hands."

"Eh?"

"Yes; I feel that a public duty rests upon me, and, besides, I must do it for my own safety, unless I choose to allow myself to be hunted by this beast out of the college, and that would be a little too feeble. I have quite made up my mind what I shall do. And first of all, may I use your paper and pens for an hour?"

"Most certainly. You will find all that you want upon that side table."

Abercrombie Smith sat down before a sheet of foolscap, and for an hour, and then for a second hour his pen travelled swiftly over it. Page after page was finished and tossed aside while his friend leaned back in his arm-chair, looking across at him with patient curiosity. At last, with an exclamation of satisfaction, Smith sprang to his feet, gathered his papers up into order, and laid the last one upon Peterson's desk.

"Kindly sign this as a witness," he said.

"A witness? Of what?"

"Of my signature, and of the date. The date is the most important. Why, Peterson, my life might hang upon it."

"My dear Smith, you are talking wildly. Let me beg you to go to bed."

"On the contrary, I never spoke so deliberately in my life. And I will promise to go to bed the moment you have signed it."

"But what is it?"

"It is a statement of all that I have been telling you to-night. I wish you to witness it."

"Certainly," said Peterson, signing his name under that of his companion. "There you are! But what is the idea?"

"You will kindly retain it, and produce it in case I am arrested."

"Arrested? For what?"

"For murder. It is quite on the cards. I wish to be ready for every event. There is only one course open to me, and I am determined to take it."

"For Heaven's sake, don't do anything rash!"

"Believe me, it would be far more rash to adopt any other course. I hope that we won't need to bother you, but it will ease my mind to know that you have this statement of my motives. And now I am ready to take your advice and to go to roost, for I want to be at my best in the morning."

Abercrombie Smith was not an entirely pleasant man to have as an enemy. Slow and easytempered, he was formidable when driven to action. He brought to every purpose in life the same deliberate resoluteness which had distinguished him as a scientific student. He had laid his studies aside for a day, but he intended that the day should not be wasted. Not a word did he say to his host as to his plans, but by nine o'clock he was well on his way to Oxford.

In the High Street he stopped at Clifford's, the gun-maker's, and bought a heavy revolver, with a box of central-fire cartridges. Six of them he slipped into the chambers, and half-cocking the weapon, placed it in the pocket of his coat. He then made his way to Hastie's rooms, where the big oarsman was lounging over his breakfast, with the Sporting Times propped up against the coffeepot.

"Hullo! What's up?" he asked. "Have some coffee?"

"No, thank you. I want you to come with me, Hastie, and do what I ask you."

"Certainly, my boy."

"And bring a heavy stick with you."

"Hullo!" Hastie stared. "Here's a hunting-crop that would fell an ox."

"One other thing. You have a box of amputating knives. Give me the longest of them."

"There you are. You seem to be fairly on the war trail. Anything else?"

"No; that will do." Smith placed the knife inside his coat, and led the way to the quadrangle. "We are neither of us chickens, Hastie," said he. "I think I can do this job alone, but I take you as a precaution. I am going to have a little talk with Bellingham. If I have only him to deal with, I won't, of course, need you. If I shout, however, up you come, and lam out with your whip as hard as you can lick. Do you understand?"

"All right. I'll come if I hear you bellow."

"Stay here, then. It may be a little time, but don't budge until I come down."

"I'm a fixture."

Smith ascended the stairs, opened Bellingham's door and stepped in. Bellingham was seated behind his table, writing. Beside him, among his litter of strange possessions, towered the mummy case, with its sale number 249 still stuck upon its front, and its hideous occupant stiff and stark within it. Smith looked very deliberately round him, closed the door, locked it, took the key from the inside, and then stepping across to the fireplace, struck a match and set the fire alight. Bellingham sat staring, with amazement and rage upon his bloated face.

"Well, really now, you make yourself at home," he gasped.

Smith sat himself deliberately down, placing his watch upon the table, drew out his pistol, cocked it, and laid it in his lap. Then he took the long amputating knife from his bosom, and threw it down in front of Bellingham.

"Now, then," said he, "just get to work and cut up that mummy."

"Oh, is that it?" said Bellingham with a sneer.

"Yes, that is it. They tell me that the law can't touch you. But I have a law that will set matters straight. If in five minutes you have not set to work, I swear by the God who made me that I will put a bullet through your brain!"

"You would murder me?"

Bellingham had half risen, and his face was the colour of putty.

"Yes."

"And for what?"

"To stop your mischief. One minute has gone."

"But what have I done?"

"I know and you know."

"This is mere bullying."

"Two minutes are gone."

"But you must give reasons. You are a madman—a dangerous madman. Why should I destroy my own property? It is a valuable mummy."

"You must cut it up, and you must burn it."

"I will do no such thing."

"Four minutes are gone."

Smith took up the pistol and he looked towards Bellingham with an inexorable face. As the second-hand stole round, he raised his hand, and the finger twitched upon the trigger.

"There! there! I'll do it!" screamed Bellingham.

In frantic haste he caught up the knife and hacked at the figure of the mummy, ever glancing round to see the eye and the weapon of his terrible visitor bent upon him. The creature crackled and snapped under every stab of the keen blade. A thick yellow dust rose up from it. Spices and dried essences rained down upon the floor. Suddenly, with a rending crack, its backbone snapped asunder, and it fell, a brown heap of sprawling limbs, upon the floor.

"Now into the fire!" said Smith.

The flames leaped and roared as the dried and tinderlike debris was piled upon it. The little room was like the stoke-hole of a steamer and the sweat ran down the faces of the two men; but still the one stooped and worked, while the other sat watching him with a set face. A thick, fat smoke oozed out from the fire, and a heavy smell of burned rosin and singed hair filled the air. In a quarter of an hour a few charred and brittle sticks were all that was left of Lot No. 249.

"Perhaps that will satisfy you," snarled Bellingham, with hate and fear in his little grey eyes as he glanced back at his tormenter.

"No; I must make a clean sweep of all your materials. We must have no more devil's tricks. In with all these leaves! They may have something to do with it."

"And what now?" asked Bellingham, when the leaves also had been added to the blaze.

"Now the roll of papyrus which you had on the table that night. It is in that drawer, I think."

"No, no," shouted Bellingham. "Don't burn that! Why, man, you don't know what you do. It is unique; it contains wisdom which is nowhere else to be found."

"Out with it!"

"But look here, Smith, you can't really mean it. I'll share the knowledge with you. I'll teach you all that is in it. Or, stay, let me only copy it before you burn it!"

Smith stepped forward and turned the key in the drawer. Taking out the yellow, curled roll of paper, he threw it into the fire, and pressed it down with his heel. Bellingham screamed, and grabbed at it; but Smith pushed him back, and stood over it until it was reduced to a formless grey ash.

"Now, Master B.," said he, "I think I have pretty well drawn your teeth. You'll hear from me again, if you return to your old tricks. And now good-morning, for I must go back to my studies."

And such is the narrative of Abercrombie Smith as to the singular events which occurred in Old College, Oxford, in the spring of '84. As Bellingham left the university immediately afterwards, and was last heard of in the Soudan, there is no one who can contradict his statement. But the wisdom of men is small, and the ways of nature are strange, and who shall put a bound to the dark things which may be found by those who seek for them?

The Los Amigos Fiasco

I used to be the leading practitioner of Los Amigos. Of course, everyone has heard of the great electrical generating gear there. The town is wide spread, and there are dozens of little townlets and villages all round, which receive their supply from the same centre, so that the works are on a very large scale. The Los Amigos folk say that they are the largest upon earth, but then we claim that for everything in Los Amigos except the gaol and the death-rate. Those are said to be the smallest.

Now, with so fine an electrical supply, it seemed to be a sinful waste of hemp that the Los Amigos criminals should perish in the old-fashioned manner. And then came the news of the eleotrocutions in the East, and how the results had not after all been so instantaneous as had been hoped. The Western Engineers raised their eyebrows when they read of the puny shocks by which these men had perished, and they vowed in Los Amigos that when an irreclaimable came their way he should be dealt handsomely by, and have the run of all the big dynamos. There should be no reserve, said the engineers, but he should have all that they had got. And what the result of that would be none could predict, save that it must be absolutely blasting and deadly. Never before had a man been so charged with electricity as they would charge him. He was to be smitten by the essence of ten thunderbolts. Some prophesied combustion, and some disintegration and disappearance. They were waiting eagerly to settle the question by actual demonstration, and it was just at that moment that Duncan Warner came that way.

Warner had been wanted by the law, and by nobody else, for many years. Desperado, murderer, train robber and road agent, he was a man beyond the pale of human pity. He had deserved a dozen deaths, and the Los Amigos folk grudged him so gaudy a one as that. He seemed to feel himself to be unworthy of it, for he made two frenzied attempts at escape. He was a powerful, muscular man, with a lion head, tangled black locks, and a sweeping beard which covered his broad chest. When he was tried, there was no finer head in all the crowded court. It's no new thing to find the best face looking from the dock. But his good looks could not balance his bad deeds. His advocate did all he knew, but the cards lay against him, and Duncan Warner was handed over to the mercy of the big Los Amigos dynamos.

I was there at the committee meeting when the matter was discussed. The town council had chosen four experts to look after the arrangements. Three of them were admirable. There was Joseph M'Conner, the very man who had designed the dynamos, and there was Joshua Westmacott, the chairman of the Los Amigos Electrical Supply Company, Limited. Then there was myself as the chief medical man, and lastly an old German of the name of Peter Stulpnagel. The Germans were a strong body at Los Amigos, and they all voted for their man. That was how he got on the committee. It was said that he had been a wonderful electrician at home, and he was eternally working with wires and insulators and Leyden jars; but, as he never seemed to get any further, or to have any results worth publishing he came at last to be regarded as a harmless crank, who had made science his hobby. We three practical men smiled when we heard that he had been elected as our colleague, and at the meeting we fixed it all up very nicely among ourselves without much thought of the old fellow who sat with his ears scooped forward in his hands, for he was a trifle hard of hearing, taking no more part in the proceedings than the gentlemen of the press who scribbled their notes on the back benches.

We did not take long to settle it all. In New York a strength of some two thousand volts had been used, and death had not been instantaneous. Evidently their shock had been too weak. Los Amigos should not fall into that error. The charge should be six times greater, and therefore, of course, it would be six times more effective. Nothing could possibly be more logical. The whole concentrated force of the great dynamos should be employed on Duncan Warner.

So we three settled it, and had already risen to break up the meeting, when our silent companion opened his month for the first time.

"Gentlemen," said he, "you appear to me to show an extraordinary ignorance upon the subject of electricity. You have not mastered the first principles of its actions upon a human being."

The committee was about to break into an angry reply to this brusque comment, but the chairman of the Electrical Company tapped his forehead to claim its indulgence for the crankiness of the speaker.

"Pray tell us, sir," said he, with an ironical smile, "what is there in our conclusions with which you find fault?"

"With your assumption that a large dose of electricity will merely increase the effect of a small dose. Do you not think it possible that it might have an entirely different result? Do you know anything, by actual experiment, of the effect of such powerful shocks?"

"We know it by analogy," said the chairman, pompously. "All drugs increase their effect when they increase their dose; for example—for example——"

"Whisky," said Joseph M'Connor.

"Quite so. Whisky. You see it there."

Peter Stulpnagel smiled and shook his head.

"Your argument is not very good," said he. "When I used to take whisky, I used to find that one glass would excite me, but that six would send me to sleep, which is just the opposite. Now, suppose that electricity were to act in just the opposite way also, what then?"

We three practical men burst out laughing. We had known that our colleague was queer, but we never had thought that he would be as queer as this.

"What then?" repeated Philip Stulpnagel.

"We'll take our chances," said the chairman.

"Pray consider," said Peter, "that workmen who have touched the wires, and who have received shocks of only a few hundred volts, have died instantly. The fact is well known. And yet when a much greater force was used upon a criminal at New York, the man struggled for some little time. Do you not clearly see that the smaller dose is the more deadly?"

"I think, gentlemen, that this discussion has been carried on quite long enough," said the chairman, rising again. "The point, I take it, has already been decided by the majority of the committee, and Duncan Warner shall be electrocuted on Tuesday by the full strength of the Los Amigos dynamos. Is it not so?"

"I agree," said Joseph M'Connor.

"I agree," said I.

"And I protest," said Peter Stulpnagel.

"Then the motion is carried, and your protest will be duly entered in the minutes," said the chairman, and so the sitting was dissolved.

The attendance at the electrocution was a very small one. We four members of the committee were, of course, present with the executioner, who was to act under their orders. The others were the United States Marshal, the governor of the gaol, the chaplain, and three members of the press. The room was a small brick chamber, forming an outhouse to the Central Electrical station. It had been used as a laundry, and had an oven and copper at one side, but no other furniture save a single chair for the condemned man. A metal plate for his feet was placed in front of it, to which ran a thick, insulated wire. Above, another wire depended from the ceiling, which could be connected with a small metallic rod projecting from a cap which was to be placed upon his head. When this connection was established Duncan Warner's hour was come.

There was a solemn hush as we waited for the coming of the prisoner. The practical engineers looked a little pale, and fidgeted nervously with the wires. Even the hardened Marshal was ill at ease, for a mere hanging was one thing, and this blasting of flesh and blood a very different one. As to the pressmen, their faces were whiter than the sheets which lay before them. The only man who appeared to feel none of the influence of these preparations was the little German crank, who strolled from one to the other with a smile on his lips and mischief in his eyes. More than once he even went so far as to burst into a shout of laughter, until the chaplain sternly rebuked him for his ill-timed levity.

"How can you so far forget yourself, Mr. Stulpnagel," said he, "as to jest in the presence of death?"

But the German was quite unabashed.

"If I were in the presence of death I should not jest," said he, "but since I am not I may do what I choose."

This flippant reply was about to draw another and a sterner reproof from the chaplain, when the door was swung open and two warders entered leading Duncan Warner between them. He glanced round him with a set face, stepped resolutely forward, and seated himself upon the chair.

"Touch her off!" said he.

It was barbarous to keep him in suspense. The chaplain murmured a few words in his ear, the attendant placed the cap upon his head, and then, while we all held our breath, the wire and the metal were brought in contact.

"Great Scott!" shouted Duncan Warner.

He had bounded in his chair as the frightful shock crashed through his system. But he was not dead. On the contrary, his eyes gleamed far more brightly than they had done before. There was only one change, but it was a singular one. The black had passed from his hair and beard as the shadow passes from a landscape. They were both as white as snow. And yet there was no other sign of decay. His skin was smooth and plump and lustrous as a child's.

The Marshal looked at the committee with a reproachful eye.

"There seems to be some hitch here, gentle-men," said he.

We three practical men looked at each other.

Peter Stulpnagel smiled pensively.

"I think that another one should do it," said I.

Again the connection was made, and again Duncan Warner sprang in his chair and shouted, but, indeed, were it not that he still remained in the chair none of us would have recognised him. His hair and his beard had shredded off in an instant, and the room looked like a barber's shop on a Saturday night. There he sat, his eyes still shining, his skin radiant with the glow of perfect health, but with a scalp as bald as a Dutch cheese, and a chin without so much as a trace of down. He began to revolve one of his arms, slowly and doubtfully at first, but with more confidence as he went on.

"That jint," said he, "has puzzled half the doctors on the Pacific Slope. It's as good as new, and as limber as a hickory twig."

"You are feeling pretty well?" asked the old German.

"Never better in my life," said Duncan Warner cheerily.

The situation was a painful one. The Marshal glared at the committee. Peter Stulpnagel grinned and rubbed his hands. The engineers scratched their heads. The bald-headed prisoner revolved his arm and looked pleased.

"I think that one more shock——" began the chairman.

"No, sir," said the Marshal "we've had foolery enough for one morning. We are here for an execution, and a execution we'll have."

"What do you propose?"

"There's a hook handy upon the ceiling. Fetch in a rope, and we'll soon set this matter straight."

There was another awkward delay while the warders departed for the cord. Peter Stulpnagel bent over Duncan Warner, and whispered something in his ear. The desperado started in surprise.

"You don't say?" he asked.

The German nodded.

"What! Noways?"

Peter shook his head, and the two began to laugh as though they shared some huge joke between them.

The rope was brought, and the Marshal himself slipped the noose over the criminal's neck. Then the two warders, the assistant and he swung their victim into the air. For half an hour he hung— a dreadful sight—from the ceiling. Then in solemn silence they lowered him down, and one of the warders went out to order the shell to be brought round. But as he touched ground again what was our amazement when Duncan Warner put his hands up to his neck, loosened the noose, and took a long, deep breath.

"Paul Jefferson's sale is goin' well," he remarked, "I could see the crowd from up yonder," and he nodded at the hook in the ceiling.

"Up with him again!" shouted the Marshal, "we'll get the life out of him somehow."

In an instant the victim was up at the hook once more.

They kept him there for an hour, but when he came down he was perfectly garrulous.

"Old man Plunket goes too much to the Arcady Saloon," said he. "Three times he's been there in an hour; and him with a family. Old man Plunket would do well to swear off."

It was monstrous and incredible, but there it was. There was no getting round it. The man was there talking when he ought to have been dead. We all sat staring in amazement, but United States Marshal Carpenter was not a man to be euchred so easily. He motioned the others to one side, so that the prisoner was left standing alone.

"Duncan Warner," said he, slowly, "you are here to play your part, and I am here to play mine. Your game is to live if you can, and my game is to carry out the sentence of the law. You've beat us on electricity. I'll give you one there. And you've beat us on hanging, for you seem to thrive on it. But it's my turn to beat you now, for my duty has to be done."

He pulled a six-shooter from his coat as he spoke, and fired all the shots through the body of the prisoner. The room was so filled with smoke that we could see nothing, but when it cleared the prisoner was still standing there, looking down in disgust at the front of his coat.

"Coats must be cheap where you come from," said he. "Thirty dollars it cost me, and look at it now. The six holes in front are bad enough, but four of the balls have passed out, and a pretty state the back must be in."

The Marshal's revolver fell from his hand, and he dropped his arms to his sides, a beaten man.

"Maybe some of you gentlemen can tell me what this means," said he, looking helplessly at the committee.

Peter Stulpnagel took a step forward.

"I'll tell you all about it," said he.

"You seem to be the only person who knows anything."

"I AM the only person who knows anything. I should have warned these gentlemen; but, as they would not listen to me, I have allowed them to learn by experience. What you have done with your electricity is that you have increased this man's vitality until he can defy death for centuries."

"Centuries!"

"Yes, it will take the wear of hundreds of years to exhaust the enormous nervous energy with which you have drenched him. Electricity is life, and you have charged him with it to the utmost. Perhaps in fifty years you might execute him, but I am not sanguine about it."

"Great Scott! What shall I do with him?" cried the unhappy Marshal.

Peter Stulpnagel shrugged his shoulders.

"It seems to me that it does not much matter what you do with him now," said he.

"Maybe we could drain the electricity out of him again. Suppose we hang him up by the heels?"

"No, no, it's out of the question."

"Well, well, he shall do no more mischief in Los Amigos, anyhow," said the Marshal, with decision. "He shall go into the new gaol. The prison will wear him out."

"On the contrary," said Peter Stulpnagel, "I think that it is much more probable that he will wear out the prison."

It was rather a fiasco and for years we didn't talk more about it than we could help, but it's no secret now and I thought you might like to jot down the facts in your case-book.

The Doctors of Hoyland

Dr. James Ripley was always looked upon as an exceedingly lucky dog by all of the profession who knew him. His father had preceded him in a practice in the village of Hoyland, in the north of Hampshire, and all was ready for him on the very first day that the law allowed him to put his name at the foot of a prescription. In a few years the old gentleman retired, and settled on the South Coast, leaving his son in undisputed possession of the whole country side. Save for Dr. Horton, near Basingstoke, the young surgeon had a clear run of six miles in every direction, and took his fifteen hundred pounds a year, though, as is usual in country practices, the stable swallowed up most of what the consulting-room earned.

Dr. James Ripley was two-and-thirty years of age, reserved, learned, unmarried, with set, rather stern features, and a thinning of the dark hair upon the top of his head, which was worth quite a hundred a year to him. He was particularly happy in his management of ladies. He had caught the tone of bland sternness and decisive suavity which dominates without offending. Ladies, however, were not equally happy in their management of him. Professionally, he was always at their service. Socially, he was a drop of quicksilver. In vain the country mammas spread out their simple lures in front of him. Dances and picnics were not to his taste, and he preferred during his scanty leisure to shut himself up in his study, and to bury himself in Virchow's Archives and the professional journals.

Study was a passion with him, and he would have none of the rust which often gathers round a country practitioner. It was his ambition to keep his knowledge as fresh and bright as at the moment when he had stepped out of the examination hall. He prided himself on being able at a moment's notice to rattle off the seven ramifications of some obscure artery, or to give the exact percentage of any physiological compound. After a long day's work he would sit up half the night performing iridectomies and extractions upon the sheep's eyes sent in by the village butcher, to the horror of his housekeeper, who had to remove the debris next morning. His love for his work was the one fanaticism which found a place in his dry, precise nature.

It was the more to his credit that he should keep up to date in his knowledge, since he had no competition to force him to exertion. In the seven years during which he had practised in Hoyland three rivals had pitted themselves against him, two in the village itself and one in the neighbouring hamlet of Lower Hoyland. Of these one had sickened and wasted, being, as it was said, himself the only patient whom he had treated during his eighteen months of ruralising. A second had bought a fourth share of a Basingstoke practice, and had departed honourably, while a third had vanished one September night, leaving a gutted house and an unpaid drug bill behind him. Since then the district had become a monopoly, and no one had dared to measure himself against the established fame of the Hoyland doctor.

It was, then, with a feeling of some surprise and considerable curiosity that on driving through Lower Hoyland one morning he perceived that the new house at the end of the village was occupied, and that a virgin brass plate glistened upon the swinging gate

which faced the high road. He pulled up his fifty guinea chestnut
mare and took a good look at it. "Verrinder Smith, M. D.," was
printed across it in very neat, small lettering. The last man had had
letters half a foot long, with a lamp like a fire-station. Dr. James
Ripley noted the difference, and deduced from it that the newcomer might possibly prove a more formidable opponent. He was
convinced of it that evening when he came to consult the current
medical directory. By it he learned that Dr. Verrinder Smith was
the holder of superb degrees, that he had studied with distinction
at Edinburgh, Paris, Berlin, and Vienna, and finally that he had
been awarded a gold medal and the Lee Hopkins scholarship for
original research, in recognition of an exhaustive inquiry into the
functions of the anterior spinal nerve roots. Dr. Ripley passed his
fingers through his thin hair in bewilderment as he read his rival's
record. What on earth could so brilliant a man mean by putting
up his plate in a little Hampshire hamlet.

But Dr. Ripley furnished himself with an explanation to the
riddle. No doubt Dr. Verrinder Smith had simply come down
there in order to pursue some scientific research in peace and
quiet. The plate was up as an address rather than as an invitation
to patients. Of course, that must be the true explanation. In that
case the presence of this brilliant neighbour would be a splendid
thing for his own studies. He had often longed for some kindred
mind, some steel on which he might strike his flint. Chance had
brought it to him, and he rejoiced exceedingly.

And this joy it was which led him to take a step which was
quite at variance with his usual habits. It is the custom for a newcomer among medical men to call first upon the older, and the etiquette upon the subject is strict. Dr. Ripley was pedantically exact
on such points, and yet he deliberately drove over next day and
called upon Dr. Verrinder Smith. Such a waiving of ceremony was,
he felt, a gracious act upon his part, and a fit prelude to the intimate relations which he hoped to establish with his neighbour.

The house was neat and well appointed, and Dr. Ripley was
shown by a smart maid into a dapper little consulting room. As he
passed in he noticed two or three parasols and a lady's sun bonnet
hanging in the hall. It was a pity that his colleague should be a mar-

ried man. It would put them upon a different footing, and interfere with those long evenings of high scientific talk which he had pictured to himself. On the other hand, there was much in the consulting room to please him. Elaborate instruments, seen more often in hospitals than in the houses of private practitioners, were scattered about. A sphygmograph stood upon the table and a gasometer-like engine, which was new to Dr. Ripley, in the corner. A book-case full of ponderous volumes in French and German, paper-covered for the most part, and varying in tint from the shell to the yoke of a duck's egg, caught his wandering eyes, and he was deeply absorbed in their titles when the door opened suddenly behind him. Turning round, he found himself facing a little woman, whose plain, palish face was remarkable only for a pair of shrewd, humorous eyes of a blue which had two shades too much green in it. She held a pince-nez in her left hand, and the doctor's card in her right.

"How do you do, Dr. Ripley? " said she.

"How do you do, madam?" returned the visitor. "Your husband is perhaps out?"

"I am not married," said she simply.

"Oh, I beg your pardon! I meant the doctor—Dr. Verrinder Smith."

"I am Dr. Verrinder Smith."

Dr. Ripley was so surprised that he dropped his hat and forgot to pick it up again.

"What!" he grasped, "the Lee Hopkins prizeman! You!"

He had never seen a woman doctor before, and his whole conservative soul rose up in revolt at the idea. He could not recall any Biblical injunction that the man should remain ever the doctor and the woman the nurse, and yet he felt as if a blasphemy had been committed. His face betrayed his feelings only too clearly.

"I am sorry to disappoint you," said the lady drily.

"You certainly have surprised me," he answered, picking up his hat.

"You are not among our champions, then?"

"I cannot say that the movement has my approval."

"And why?"

"I should much prefer not to discuss it."

"But I am sure you will answer a lady's question."

"Ladies are in danger of losing their privileges when they usurp the place of the other sex. They cannot claim both."

"Why should a woman not earn her bread by her brains?"

Dr. Ripley felt irritated by the quiet manner in which the lady cross-questioned him.

"I should much prefer not to be led into a discussion, Miss Smith."

"Dr. Smith," she interrupted.

"Well, Dr. Smith! But if you insist upon an answer, I must say that I do not think medicine a suitable profession for women and that I have a personal objection to masculine ladies."

It was an exceedingly rude speech, and he was ashamed of it the instant after he had made it. The lady, however, simply raised her eyebrows and smiled.

"It seems to me that you are begging the question," said she. "Of course, if it makes women masculine that WOULD be a considerable deterioration."

It was a neat little counter, and Dr. Ripley, like a pinked fencer, bowed his acknowledgment.

"I must go," said he.

"I am sorry that we cannot come to some more friendly conclusion since we are to be neighbours," she remarked.

He bowed again, and took a step towards the door.

"It was a singular coincidence," she continued, "that at the instant that you called I was reading your paper on 'Locomotor Ataxia,' in the Lancet."

"Indeed," said he drily.

"I thought it was a very able monograph."

"You are very good."

"But the views which you attribute to Professor Pitres, of Bordeaux, have been repudiated by him."

"I have his pamphlet of 1890," said Dr. Ripley angrily.

"Here is his pamphlet of 1891." She picked it from among a litter of periodicals. "If you have time to glance your eye down this passage——"

Dr. Ripley took it from her and shot rapidly through the paragraph which she indicated. There was no denying that it completely knocked the bottom out of his own article. He threw it down, and with another frigid bow he made for the door. As he took the reins from the groom he glanced round and saw that the lady was standing at her window, and it seemed to him that she was laughing heartily.

All day the memory of this interview haunted him. He felt that he had come very badly out of it. She had showed herself to be his superior on his own pet subject. She had been courteous while he had been rude, self-possessed when he had been angry. And then, above all, there was her presence, her monstrous intrusion to rankle in his mind. A woman doctor had been an abstract thing before, repugnant but distant. Now she was there in actual practice, with a brass plate up just like his own, competing for the same patients. Not that he feared competition, but he objected to this lowering of his ideal of womanhood. She could not be more than thirty, and had a bright, mobile face, too. He thought of her humorous eyes, and of her strong, well-turned chin. It revolted him the more to recall the details of her education. A man, of course. could come through such an ordeal with all his purity, but it was nothing short of shameless in a woman.

But it was not long before he learned that even her competition was a thing to be feared. The novelty of her presence had brought a few curious invalids into her consulting rooms, and, once there, they had been so impressed by the firmness of her manner and by the singular, new-fashioned instruments with which she tapped, and peered, and sounded, that it formed the core of their conversation for weeks afterwards. And soon there were tangible proofs of her powers upon the country side. Farmer Eyton, whose callous ulcer had been quietly spreading over his shin for years back under a gentle regime of zinc ointment, was painted round with blistering fluid, and found, after three blasphemous nights, that his sore was stimulated into healing. Mrs. Crowder, who had always regarded the birthmark upon her second daughter Eliza as a sign of the indignation of the Creator at a third helping of raspberry tart which she had partaken of during a critical period, learned that, with the help of two galvanic needles, the mischief was not irreparable. In a month Dr. Verrinder Smith was known, and in two she was famous.

Occasionally, Dr. Ripley met her as he drove upon his rounds. She had started a high dogcart, taking the reins herself, with a little tiger behind. When they met he invariably raised his hat with punctilious politeness, but the grim severity of his face showed how formal was the courtesy. In fact, his dislike was rapidly deepening into absolute detestation. "The unsexed woman," was the description of her which he permitted himself to give to those of his patients who still remained staunch. But, indeed, they were a rapidly-decreasing body, and every day his pride was galled by the news of some fresh defection. The lady had somehow impressed the country folk with almost superstitious belief in her power, and from far and near they flocked to her consulting room.

But what galled him most of all was, when she did something which he had pronounced to be impracticable. For all his knowledge he lacked nerve as an operator, and usually sent his worst cases up to London. The lady, however, had no weakness of the sort, and took everything that came in her way. It was agony to him to hear that she was about to straighten little Alec Turner's club foot, and right at the fringe of the rumour came a note from his mother, the rector's wife, asking him if he would be so good as to act as chloroformist. It would be inhumanity to refuse, as there was no other who could take the place, but it was gall and wormwood to his sensitive nature. Yet, in spite of his vexation, he could not but admire the dexterity with which the thing was done. She handled the little wax-like foot so gently, and held the tiny tenotomy knife as an artist holds his pencil. One straight insertion, one snick of a tendon, and it was all over without a stain upon the white towel which lay beneath. He had never seen anything more masterly, and he had the honesty to say so, though her skill increased his dislike of her. The operation spread her fame still further at his expense, and self-preservation was added to his other grounds for detesting her. And this very detestation it was which brought matters to a curious climax.

One winter's night, just as he was rising from his lonely dinner, a groom came riding down from Squire Faircastle's, the richest man in the district, to say that his daughter had scalded her hand, and that medical help was needed on the instant. The coachman had ridden for the lady doctor, for it mattered nothing to the Squire who came as long as it were speedily. Dr. Ripley rushed from his surgery with the determination that she should not effect an entrance into this stronghold of his if hard driving on his part could prevent it. He did not even wait to light his lamps, but sprang into his gig and flew off as fast as hoof could rattle. He lived rather nearer to the Squire's than she did, and was convinced that he could get there well before her.

And so he would but for that whimsical element of chance, which will for ever muddle up the affairs of this world and dumbfound the prophets. Whether it came from the want of his lights, or from his mind being full of the thoughts of his rival, he allowed too little by half a foot in taking the sharp turn upon the Basingstoke road. The empty trap and the frightened horse clattered away into the darkness, while the Squire's groom crawled out of the ditch into which he had been shot. He struck a match, looked down at his groaning companion, and then, after the fashion of rough, strong men when they see what they have not seen before, he was very sick.

The doctor raised himself a little on his elbow in the glint of the match. He caught a glimpse of something white and sharp bristling through his trouser leg half way down the shin.

"Compound!" he groaned. "A three months' job," and fainted.

When he came to himself the groom was gone, for he had scudded off to the Squire's house for help, but a small page was holding a gig-lamp in front of his injured leg, and a woman, with an open case of polished instruments gleaming in the yellow light, was deftly slitting up his trouser with a crooked pair of scissors.

"It's all right, doctor," said she soothingly. "I am so sorry about it. You can have Dr. Horton to-morrow, but I am sure you will allow me to help you to-night. I could hardly believe my eyes when I saw you by the roadside."

"The groom has gone for help," groaned the sufferer.

"When it comes we can move you into the gig. A little more light, John! So! Ah, dear, dear, we shall have laceration unless we reduce this before we move you. Allow me to give you a whiff of chloroform, and I have no doubt that I can secure it sufficiently to——"

Dr. Ripley never heard the end of that sentence. He tried to raise a hand and to murmur something in protest, but a sweet smell was in his nostrils, and a sense of rich peace and lethargy stole over his jangled nerves. Down he sank, through clear, cool water, ever down and down into the green shadows beneath, gently, without effort, while the pleasant chiming of a great belfry rose and fell in his ears. Then he rose again, up and up, and ever up, with a terrible tightness about his temples, until at last he shot out of those green shadows and was in the light once more. Two bright, shining, golden spots gleamed before his dazed eyes. He blinked and blinked before he could give a name to them. They were only the two brass balls at the end posts of his bed, and he was lying in his own little room, with a head like a cannon ball, and a leg like an iron bar. Turning his eyes, he saw the calm face of Dr. Verrinder Smith looking down at him.

"Ah, at last!" said she. "I kept you under all the way home, for I knew how painful the jolting would be. It is in good position now with a strong side splint. I have ordered a morphia draught for you. Shall I tell your groom to ride for Dr. Horton in the morning?"

"I should prefer that you should continue the case," said Dr. Ripley feebly, and then, with a half hysterical laugh,—"You have all the rest of the parish as patients, you know, so you may as well make the thing complete by having me also."

It was not a very gracious speech, but it was a look of pity and not of anger which shone in her eyes as she turned away from his bedside.

Dr. Ripley had a brother, William, who was assistant surgeon at a London hospital, and who was down in Hampshire within a few hours of his hearing of the accident. He raised his brows when he heard the details.

"What! You are pestered with one of those!" he cried.

"I don't know what I should have done without her."

I've no doubt she's an excellent nurse."

"She knows her work as well as you or I."

"Speak for yourself, James," said the London man with a sniff. "But apart from that, you know that the principle of the thing is all wrong."

"You think there is nothing to be said on the other side?"

"Good heavens! do you?"

"Well, I don't know. It struck me during the night that we may have been a little narrow in our views."

"Nonsense, James. It's all very fine for women to win prizes in the lecture room, but you know as well as I do that they are no use in an emergency. Now I warrant that this woman was all nerves when she was setting your leg. That reminds me that I had better just take a look at it and see that it is all right."

"I would rather that you did not undo it," said the patient. "I have her assurance that it is all right."

Brother William was deeply shocked.

"Of course, if a woman's assurance is of more value than the opinion of the assistant surgeon of a London hospital, there is nothing more to be said," he remarked.

"I should prefer that you did not touch it," said the patient firmly, and Dr. William went back to London that evening in a huff.

The lady, who had heard of his coming, was much surprised on learning his departure.

"We had a difference upon a point of professional etiquette," said Dr. James, and it was all the explanation he would vouchsafe.

For two long months Dr. Ripley was brought in contact with his rival every day, and he learned many things which he had not known before. She was a charming companion, as well as a most assiduous doctor. Her short presence during the long, weary day was like a flower in a sand waste. What interested him was precisely what interested her, and she could meet him at every point upon equal terms. And yet under all her learning and her firmness ran a sweet, womanly nature, peeping out in her talk, shining in her greenish eyes, showing itself in a thousand subtle ways which the dullest of men could read. And he, though a bit of a prig and a pedant, was by no means dull, and had honesty enough to confess when he was in the wrong.

"I don't know how to apologise to you," he said in his shame-faced fashion one day, when he had progressed so far as to be able to sit in an arm-chair with his leg upon another one; "I feel that I have been quite in the wrong."

"Why, then?"

"Over this woman question. I used to think that a woman must inevitably lose something of her charm if she took up such studies."

"Oh, you don't think they are necessarily unsexed, then?" she cried, with a mischievous smile.

"Please don't recall my idiotic expression."

"I feel so pleased that I should have helped in changing your views. I think that it is the most sincere compliment that I have ever had paid me."

"At any rate, it is the truth," said he, and was happy all night at the remembrance of the flush of pleasure which made her pale face look quite comely for the instant.

For, indeed, he was already far past the stage when he would acknowledge her as the equal of any other woman. Already he could not disguise from himself that she had become the one woman. Her dainty skill, her gentle touch, her sweet presence, the community of their tastes, had all united to hopelessly upset his previous opinions. It was a dark day for him now when his convalescence allowed her to miss a visit, and darker still that other one which he saw approaching when all occasion for her visits would be at an end. It came round at last, however, and he felt that his whole life's fortune would hang upon the issue of that final inter-view. He was a direct man by nature, so he laid his hand upon hers as it felt for his pulse, and he asked her if she would be his wife.

"What, and unite the practices?" said she.

He started in pain and anger.

"Surely you do not attribute any such base motive to me!" he cried. "I love you as unselfishly as ever a woman was loved."

"No, I was wrong. It was a foolish speech," said she, moving her chair a little back, and tapping her stethoscope upon her knee.

"Forget that I ever said it. I am so sorry to cause you any disappointment, and I appreciate most highly the honour which you do me, but what you ask is quite impossible."

With another woman he might have urged the point, but his instincts told him that it was quite useless with this one. Her tone of voice was conclusive. He said nothing, but leaned back in his chair a stricken man.

"I am so sorry," she said again. "If I had known what was passing in your mind I should have told you earlier that I intended to devote my life entirely to science. There are many women with a capacity for marriage, but few with a taste for biology. I will remain true to my own line, then. I came down here while waiting for an opening in the Paris Physiological Laboratory. I have just heard that there is a vacancy for me there, and so you will be troubled no more by my intrusion upon your practice. I have done you an injustice just as you did me one. I thought you narrow and pedantic, with no good quality. I have learned during your illness to appreciate you better, and the recollection of our friendship will always be a very pleasant one to me."

And so it came about that in a very few weeks there was only one doctor in Hoyland. But folks noticed that the one had aged many years in a few months, that a weary sadness lurked always in the depths of his blue eyes, and that he was less concerned than ever with the eligible young ladies whom chance, or their careful country mammas, placed in his way.

The Surgeon Talks

"Men die of the diseases which they have studied most," remarked the surgeon, snipping off the end of a cigar with all his professional neatness and finish. "It's as if the morbid condition was an evil creature which, when it found itself closely hunted, flew at the throat of its pursuer. If you worry the microbes too much they may worry you. I've seen cases of it, and not necessarily in microbic diseases either. There was, of course, the well-known instance of Liston and the aneurism; and a dozen others that I could mention. You couldn't have a clearer case than that of poor old Walker of St. Christopher's. Not heard of it? Well, of course, it was a little before your time, but I wonder that it should have been forgotten. You youngsters are so busy in keeping up to the day that you lose a good deal that is interesting of yesterday.

"Walker was one of the best men in Europe on nervous disease. You must have read his little book on sclerosis of the posterior columns. It's as interesting as a novel, and epoch-making in its way. He worked like a horse, did Walker—huge consulting practice—hours a day in the clinical wards—constant original investigations. And then he enjoyed himself also. 'De mortuis,' of course, but still it's an open secret among all who knew him. If he died at forty-five, he crammed eighty years into it. The marvel was that he could have held on so long at the pace at which he was going. But he took it beautifully when it came.

"I was his clinical assistant at the time. Walker was lecturing on locomotor ataxia to a wardful of youngsters. He was explaining that one of the early signs of the complaint was that the patient could not put his heels together with his eyes shut without staggering. As he spoke, he suited the action to the word. I don't suppose the boys noticed anything. I did, and so did he, though he finished his lecture without a sign.

"When it was over he came into my room and lit a cigarette.

"'Just run over my reflexes, Smith,' said he.

"There was hardly a trace of them left. I tapped away at his knee-tendon and might as well have tried to get a jerk out of that sofa-cushion. He stood with his eyes shut again, and he swayed like a bush in the wind.

"'So,' said he, 'it was not intercostal neuralgia after all.'

"Then I knew that he had had the lightning pains, and that the case was complete. There was nothing to say, so I sat looking at him while he puffed and puffed at his cigarette. Here he was, a man in the prime of life, one of the handsomest men in London, with money, fame, social success, everything at his feet, and now, without a moment's warning, he was told that inevitable death lay before him, a death accompanied by more refined and lingering tortures than if he were bound upon a Red Indian stake. He sat in the middle of the blue cigarette cloud with his eyes cast down, and the slightest little tightening of his lips. Then he rose with a motion of his arms, as one who throws off old thoughts and enters upon a new course.

"'Better put this thing straight at once,' said he. 'I must make some fresh arrangements. May I use your paper and envelopes?'

"He settled himself at my desk and he wrote half a dozen letters. It is not a breach of confidence to say that they were not addressed to his professional brothers. Walker was a single man, which means that he was not restricted to a single woman. When he had finished, he walked out of that little room of mine, leaving every hope and ambition of his life behind him. And he might have had another year of ignorance and peace if it had not been for the chance illustration in his lecture.

"It took five years to kill him, and he stood it well. If he had ever been a little irregular he atoned for it in that long martyrdom. He kept an admirable record of his own symptoms, and worked out the eye changes more fully than has ever been done. When the ptosis got very bad he would hold his eyelid up with one hand while he wrote. Then, when he could not co-ordinate his muscles to write, he dictated to his nurse. So died, in the odour of science, James Walker, aet. 45.

"Poor old Walker was very fond of experimental surgery, and he broke ground in several directions. Between ourselves, there may have been some more ground-breaking afterwards, but he did his best for his cases. You know M'Namara, don't you? He always wears his hair long. He lets it be understood that it comes from his artistic strain, but it is really to conceal the loss of one of his ears. Walker cut the other one off, but you must not tell Mac I said so.

"It was like this. Walker had a fad about the portio dura—the motor to the face, you know—and he thought paralysis of it came from a disturbance of the blood supply. Something else which counterbalanced that disturbance might, he thought, set it right again. We had a very obstinate case of Bell's paralysis in the wards, and had tried it with every conceivable thing, blistering, tonics, nerve-stretching, galvanism, needles, but all without result.

Walker got it into his head that removal of the ear would increase the blood supply to the part, and he very soon gained the consent of the patient to the operation.

"Well, we did it at night. Walker, of course, felt that it was something of an experiment, and did not wish too much talk about it unless it proved successful. There were half-a-dozen of us there, M'Namara and I among the rest. The room was a small one, and in the centre was in the narrow table, with a macintosh over the pillow, and a blanket which extended almost to the floor on either side. Two candles, on a side-table near the pillow, supplied all the light. In came the patient, with one side of his face as smooth as a baby's, and the other all in a quiver with fright. He lay down, and the chloroform towel was placed over his face, while Walker threaded his needles in the candle light. The chloroformist stood at the head of the table, and M'Namara was stationed at the side to control the patient. The rest of us stood by to assist.

"Well, the man was about half over when he fell into one of those convulsive flurries which come with the semi-unconscious stage. He kicked and plunged and struck out with both hands. Over with a crash went the little table which held the candles, and in an instant we were left in total darkness. You can think what a rush and a scurry there was, one to pick up the table, one to find the matches, and some to restrain the patient who was still dashing himself about. He was held down by two dressers, the chloroform was pushed, and by the time the candles were relit, his incoherent, half-smothered shoutings had changed to a stertorous snore. His head was turned on the pillow and the towel was still kept over his face while the operation was carried through. Then the towel was withdrawn, and you can conceive our amazement when we looked upon the face of M'Namara.

"How did it happen? Why, simply enough. As the candles went over, the chloroformist had stopped for an instant and had tried to catch them. The patient, just as the light went out, had rolled off and under the table. Poor M'Namara, clinging frantically to him, had been dragged across it, and the chloroformist, feeling him there, had naturally claped the towel across his mouth and nose. The others had secured him, and the more he roared and kicked the more they drenched him with chloroform. Walker was very nice about it, and made the most handsome apologies. He offered to do a plastic on the spot, and make as good an ear as he could, but M'Namara had had enough of it. As to the patient, we found him sleeping placidly under the table, with the ends of the blanket screening him on both sides. Walker sent M'Namara round his ear next day in a jar of methylated spirit, but Mac's wife was very angry about it, and it led to a good deal of ill-feeling.

"Some people say that the more one has to do with human nature, and the closer one is brought in contact with it, the less one thinks of it. I don't believe that those who know most would uphold that view. My own experience is dead against it. I was brought up in the miserable-mortal-clay school of theology, and yet here I am, after thirty years of intimate acquaintance with humanity, filled with respect for it. The, evil lies commonly upon the surface. The deeper strata are good. A hundred times I have seen folk condemned to death as suddenly as poor Walker was. Sometimes it was to blindness or to mutilations which are worse than death. Men and women, they almost all took it beautifully, and some with such lovely unselfishness, and with such complete absorption in the thought of how their fate would affect others, that the man about town, or the frivolously-dressed woman has seemed to change into an angel before my eyes. I have seen death-beds, too, of all ages and of all creeds and want of creeds. I never saw any of them shrink, save only one poor, imaginative young fellow, who had spent his blameless life in the strictest of sects. Of course, an exhausted frame is incapable of fear, as anyone can vouch who is told, in the midst of his sea-sickness, that the ship is going to the bottom. That is why I rate courage in the face of mutilation to be higher than courage when a wasting illness is fining away into death.

"Now, I'll take a case which I had in my own practice last Wednesday. A lady came in to consult me—the wife of a well-known sporting baronet. The husband had come with her, but remained, at her request, in the waiting-room. I need not go into details, but it proved to be a peculiarly malignant case of cancer. 'I knew it,' said she. 'How long have I to live?' 'I fear that it may exhaust your strength in a few months,' I answered. 'Poor old Jack!' said she. 'I'll tell him that it is not dangerous.' 'Why should you deceive him?' I asked. 'Well, he's very uneasy about it, and he is quaking now in the waiting-room. He has two old friends to dinner to-night, and I haven't the heart to spoil his evening. To-morrow will be time enough for him to learn the truth.' Out she walked, the brave little woman, and a moment later her husband, with his big, red face shining with joy came plunging into my room to shake me by the hand. No, I respected her wish and I did not undeceive him. I dare bet that evening was one of the brightest, and the next morning the darkest, of his life.

"It's wonderful how bravely and cheerily a woman can face a crushing blow. It is different with men. A man can stand it without complaining, but it knocks him dazed and silly all the same. But the woman does not lose her wits any more than she does her courage. Now, I had a case only a few weeks ago which would show you what I mean. A gentleman consulted me about his wife, a very beautiful woman. She had a small tubercular nodule upon her upper arm, according to him. He was sure that it was of no importance, but he wanted to know whether Devonshire or the Riviera would be the better for her. I examined her and found a frightful sarcoma of the bone, hardly showing upon the surface, but involving the shoulder-blade and clavicle as well as the humerus. A more malignant case I have never seen. I sent her out of the room and I told him the truth. What did he do? Why, he walked slowly round that room with his hands behind his back, looking with the greatest interest at the pictures. I can see him now, putting up his gold pince-nez and staring at them with perfectly vacant eyes, which told me that he saw neither them nor the wall behind them. 'Amputation of the arm?' he asked at last. 'And of the collar-bone and shoulder-blade,' said I. 'Quite so. The collar-bone and shoulder-blade,' he repeated, still staring about him with those lifeless eyes. It settled him. I don't believe he'll ever be the same man again. But the woman took it as bravely and brightly as could be, and she has done very well since. The mischief was so great that the arm snapped as we drew it from the night-dress. No, I don't think that there will be any return, and I have every hope of her recovery.

"The first patient is a thing which one remembers all one's life. Mine was commonplace, and the details are of no interest. I had a curious visitor, however, during the first few months after my plate went up. It was an elderly woman, richly dressed, with a wickerwork picnic basket in her hand. This she opened with the tears streaming down her face, and out there waddled the fattest, ugliest, and mangiest little pug dog that I have ever seen. 'I wish you to put him painlessly out of the world, doctor,' she cried. 'Quick, quick, or my resolution may give way.' She flung herself down, with hysterical sobs, upon the sofa. The less experienced a doctor is, the higher are his notions of professional dignity, as I need not remind you, my young friend, so I was about to refuse the commission with indignation, when I bethought me that, quite apart from medicine, we were gentleman and lady, and that she had asked me to do something for her which was evidently of the greatest possible importance in her eyes. I led off the poor little doggie, therefore, and with the help of a saucerful of milk and a few drops of prussic acid his exit was as speedy and painless as could be desired. 'Is it over?' she cried as I entered. It was really tragic to see how all the love which should have gone to husband and children had, in default of them, been centred upon this uncouth little animal. She left, quite broken down, in her carriage, and it was only after her departure that I saw an envelope sealed with a large red seal, and lying upon the blotting pad of my desk. Outside, in pencil, was written: 'I have no doubt that you would willingly have done this without a fee, but I insist upon your acceptance of the enclosed.' I opened it with some vague notions of an eccentric millionaire and a fifty-pound note, but all I found was a postal order for four and sixpence. The whole incident struck me as so whimsical that I laughed until I was tired. You'll find there's so much tragedy in a doctor's life, my boy, that he would not be able to stand it if it were not for the strain of comedy which comes every now and then to leaven it.

"And a doctor has very much to be thankful for also. Don't you ever forget it. It is such a pleasure to do a little good that a man should pay for the privilege instead of being paid for it. Still, of course, he has his home to keep up and his wife and children to support. But his patients are his friends—or they should be so. He goes from house to house, and his step and his voice are loved and welcomed in each. What could a man ask for more than that? And besides, he is forced to be a good man. It is impossible for him to be anything else. How can a man spend his whole life in seeing suffering bravely borne and yet remain a hard or a vicious man? It is a noble, generous, kindly profession, and you youngsters have got to see that it remains so."